The
Smithy
Stories

'Smithy,' 'Smithy Abroad,' 'Smithy and the Hun,' 'Nobby, or Smithy's Friend Nobby' and 'Army Reform,'

Edgar Wallace

LEONAUR

The Smithy Stories
'Smithy,' 'Smithy Abroad,' 'Smithy and the Hun,' 'Nobby, or Smithy's Friend Nobby'
and 'Army Reform,'

by Edgar Wallace

FIRST EDITION

First published under the titles
Smithy, Army Reform, Smithy Abroad, Smithy and the Hun and
Nobby, or Smithy's Friend Nobby

Leonaur is an imprint
of Oakpast Ltd

ISBN: 978-1-78282-313-1 (hardcover)
ISBN: 978-1-78282-314-8 (softcover)

http://www.leonaur.com

Publisher's Notes
The views expressed in this book are not necessarily
those of the publisher.

Contents

Smithy 7

Army Reform Opinions of Private Smith 93

Smithy Abroad 97

Smithy and the Hun 263

Nobby or Smithy's Friend Nobby 341

Smithy

Military "crime" is not crime at all, as we law-abiding citizens recognise it.

The outbreak in the Anchester Regiment was not a very serious affair; from what I can gather, it mostly took the form of breaking out of barracks after "lights out."

But, explained Smithy, it got a bit too thick, and one of the consequences was that the guard was doubled, pickets were strengthened, and the ranks of the regimental military police were, as a temporary measure, considerably augmented. I explain this for the benefit of my military readers, who may wonder how it was that both Smithy and Nobby Clark happened to be together on Number One post on the night of The Adjutant's Madness.

"I was tellin' the troops only the other night," said Smithy, "what would 'appen if they didn't give over actin' the billy goat.

"'Some of you bloomin' recruits,' I sez, 'think you're doin' somethin' very wonderful, climbin' over the wall, an' goin' into town when you ought to be in bed asleep; but it's the likes of me, an' Nobby, and 'Appy Johnson, chaps with twelve years' service, who's got to suffer. I'll bet you old Uncle Bill will start doublin' the guard tomorrer.'

"'Don't be down'arted; Nobby sez; 'take a brighter view of life, Smithy.'

"Sure enough, next day it came out in orders that the guard was to be doubled, an' me an' Nobby was for it.

"When we mounted guard, the adjutant, old Umferville, came over an' inspected us.

"'Who's first relief on Number One post?' 'e sez.

"'Clark an' Smith, sir,' sez the sergeant.

"'I don't want you chaps to make too much noise walkin' about,

7

or shoutin',' sez the adjutant, an' I'm blowed if 'is face wasn't as red as a piller-box.

"'What's the matter with Uncle Bill?' sez Nobby, as we was marchin' off.

"'I believe 'e's frightened about somethin',' I sez, puzzled.

"Number One post is between the back of the adjutant's 'ouse and the wall where the chaps nip over. It used to be the colonel's 'ouse; but when Uncle Bill got married a couple of years ago, the colonel generously 'anded it over, an' took an 'ouse in town that wasn't so damp.

"It was the most excitin' guard me an' Nobby ever did, an' it was all through Uncle Bill. You never saw such goin's on in your life. 'E dodged in an' out of 'is 'ouse all day long. 'E'd start to walk across the square, then stop, as if 'e'd forgot something, then walk back to the 'ouse, then walk out again, then stop an' bite 'is nails an' stare more ghastly at nothin'.

"Once as 'e was passin', me an' Nobby shouldered arms to 'im, an' 'e stopped dead an' looked at us. 'E didn't move, but stood stock still for about five minutes starin' at me an' Nobby, sayin' nothin', an' me and Nobby felt quite uncomfortable.

"'Everything all right, sentry?' 'e sez at last.

"'Yes, sir,' sez me an' Nobby.

"'Sentry—' 'e sez, then stopped.

"'Which one, sir?' sez Nobby, an' the officer stared.

"'Are there two of you?' 'e sez.

"'Yes, sir,' sez me an' Nobby, an' 'e got very red an' muttered somethin' an' walked off.

"We was talkin' about it in the guardroom that night when we was drinkin' our guard allowance—one pint a man, accordin' to regulations. All the other chaps 'ad noticed Uncle Bill's strangeness, too.

"'It's drink,' sez Nobby, shakin' 'is 'ead. 'Wot a pity to see a pore young chap go wrong, all for the sake of the cursed liquor—after you with that pot, Smithy.'

"'You've 'ad your whack, Nobby,' I sez; 'don't come it on a pal.'

"'Did I?' sez Nobby. 'I must 'ave been thinkin' of the adjutant.'

"'I think 'es 'aunted,' sez a chap from 'D'—a young chap.

"''Aunted!' sez Nobby, scornful. 'Why, there ain't no ghosts after Christmas, fat'ead!'

"'Never mind about Christmas,' sez the young chap; 'it's my belief 'es 'aunted, there's a spirit or somethin' follerin' 'im about.'

"'Dry up,' sez Nobby, shudderin', for me an' 'im was on the worst relief, ten to midnight, an' four to six.

"When we mounted at 'last post' Nobby sez to me:—

"'Do you think there's anythin' in that ghost idea, Smith?'

"'No,' I sez. 'Still,' I sez, 'you never know.'

"'What's that?' sez Nobby, pointin' to a shadder movin' along the wall.

"So I shouts ''Alt!—who goes there?'

"It turned out to be little Bobby Burns tryin' to break out of barracks, an' me an' Nobby captured 'im an' shoved 'im in the clink.

"Just before twelve me an' Nobby was standin' at ease, when we 'eard a most 'orrid groan. We jumps round with our 'arts in our mouths, an' there was the adjutant in 'is overcoat an' slippers.

"'What the dickens are you starin' at?' 'e sez.

"'Beg pardon, sir,' stammers Nobby, 'I thought you was a ghost!'

"But the adjutant didn't seem to 'ear what we said. 'E just walks up an' down mutterin' to hisself. Bimeby 'e sez, 'Keep a sharp look-out, an' don't make too much noise—d'ye hear, you Clark ; d'ye 'ear, you Smith?' 'e sez fiercely.

"'Yes, sir,' sez me an' Nobby; an' then the adjutant went indoors.

"'Drink,' sez Nobby solemnly. 'Let this be a warnin' to you, Smithy.'

"When we come on duty again at four in the mornin', the two chaps we relieved looked scared out of their lives. 'I shall be bloomin' glad when its daylight,' sez one of 'em; 'we've 'ad an 'orrid time.'

"'Ow so?' sez Nobby.

"'The adjutant's gone orf 'is napper: mad, that's wot 'e is,' sez the chap. ''E's bin walkin' up an' down talkin' to 'isself an' moanin' an' chuckin' 'is arms about.'

"'Nice thing, ain't it?' sez Nobby, after we was posted; 'if you ask me—why, 'ere the beggar comes again.'

"'What shall we do?' I sez.

"'Wait till 'e gets violent, then bang 'im with the butt of your rifle.'

"'You do it,' I sez.

"'No, you'd better do it, Smithy; you're the oldest soldier!'

"Up comes Umferville, and I'll take my oath there was tears in 'is eyes.

"'Sentry' 'e sez in a chokin' voice, 'challenge all persons approachin' your post.'

"'Yes, sir,' sez me an' Nobby.

9

"'Don't allow nobody to pass without challengin', 'e sez wildly, an' then run back to 'is 'ouse like mad.

"'Balmy,' sez Nobby; 'let's go an' tell the sergeant.'

"'Better wait,' I sez. So we waited.

"'The beggar 'ain't bin to bed,' sez Nobby after a bit, 'there's lights in all the rooms.'

"'I wonder what 'is missus thinks,' I sez, an' I felt sorry for Mrs. Umferville, who's a lady bred an' born.

"It wanted about an hour to daybreak when out rushes the adjutant again an' makes straight for us.

"''Ere 'e comes,' I sez, liftin' up the butt of my rifle. 'Nobby, you're evidence that I only 'it 'im to save your life,' I sez.

"'Your life!' sez Nobby hastily.

"Up comes Umferville, sort of laughin' an' cryin'.

"'Sentry,' 'e sez, 'wot about your orders?'

"'Wot orders, sir?' I sez.

"'Someone's come into barracks,' 'e sez excitedly, an' you 'aven't challenged 'im.'

"''E ain't passed 'ere,' sez me an' Nobby together.

"'Yes, 'e 'as,' sez the adjutant. 'Listen'

"We listens.

"''Ear anythin'?' sez the adjutant.

Suddenly Nobby lets out a yell.

"'Guard, turn out,' 'e shouts, an' out come the guard with a run.

"'Wot's up?' sez the sergeant of the guard.

"'Present arms!' sez Nobby, 'to the adjutant's new baby,' 'e sez."

2.—Military Motoring

"What'll be the badge for that?" asked Smithy

We were talking of the new course of military motoring that is contemplated.

"Cross guns for marksman, cross flags for signaller, cross swords for instructor, cross choppers for pioneer." mused Smithy.

"Cross pedestrians for military chauffeur," said I humorously.

"Cross corpses, if I know anything about it," said Smithy pessimistically. "Some of the chaps I know who are goin' in for motorin' I wouldn't trust with a clockwork p'rambulator."

"As you say," I began. "There—"

"Let alone motorcars," interrupted Smithy gloomily.

"Of course there are—"

"Let alone bloomin' motorcars," repeated Smithy, with a knowing nod of his head.

"I suppose," he went on, "you don't happen to know Spud Murphy, of 'B'—he's doin' duty now, but he used to be groom-of-the-chambers to Major What's-his-name?"

I know hundreds of Spud Murphys; but I could not recall this particular one.

"You wouldn't think," said Smithy, impressively, that a tin-eyed rooster with four years' service, a low down cellar-flapper from Islington that joined the army to get away from the police, would 'ave the neck to apply for a job as shover to a choof-choof?"

"I should imagine," I remarked gently, "that the position of chauffeur requires—"

"Well," went on the indignant Smithy, "this unmentionable person did. You know Uncle Bill?"

I owned up to an acquaintance with that very kindly young officer, Captain Umfreville, of Smithy's battalion.

"Uncle Bill," said the irreverent soldier, "is one of the widest chaps in the regiment. There was a man in town who was agent for all kinds of motorcars, but the one he was most fond of was a little thing he invented hisself. A four-'orse-power machine with bicycle wheels. He called it the 'Ravin' Jupiter,' and it was one of them run-away-and-play-whilst-papa-mends-the-carburator sort of machines.

"Well, Uncle Bill turns up in barrack one day as large as life, sittin' in a sort of bassinette and steamroller combined. He'd bought a 'Ravin' Jupiter,' and, what's more, he'd got it cheap.

"People used to larf, especially when it hurt somebody; but Uncle Bill knew a thing or two.

"A week afterwards he turned up with a ninety-'orse-power Little Nipper, or Nipper Minor, or something of the sort.

"His 'Ravin' Jupiter' had gone wrong, and while it was bein' righted the maker had lent him this car.

"I can tell you," said Smithy, with a reminiscent grin, "that old Uncle Bill didn't use that 'Ravin' Jupiter' three times a year; mostly he was cuttin' round the country in the Nipper, or a Damyer, or a Poosher, wot was lent him while the 'Ravin' 'car was gettin' a new inside.

The artfulness of Captain Umfreville caused Smithy a few minutes' amusement.

Then he returned with a scowl to the enormities of the miserable Spud Murphy.

"Spud comes to me one day an' sez, 'I'm goin' to be Bill's shover.'

"'Bill's how much?' I sez.

"'Bill's choofer,' he sez.

"'Wot do you know about motorcars?' I sez.

"'E larfs. 'Never you mind,' 'e sez; 'I've driv' an ingin before now,' 'e sez.

"'Beer ingin?' I sez.

"'No,' 'e sez, 'a real ingin at a sawmills.'

"So Spud got his job," Smithy went on, "an' for a week he was messin' about the parade ground doin' fancy work, with Uncle Bill sittin' by his side givin' instructions.

"We used to sit outside the canteen and watch him and the officer.

"'E used to play on the thing with his 'ands and feet, and the tunes 'e got out of it was extr'ord'nary. Bill was a wonderful instructor.

"'Mark time on that blanky clutch,' he'd yell, and Spud would put his foot on the brake-pedal.

"'The other foot, you soor,' Bill'd shout, he 'avin' been in India with the other battalion.

"''Arf right!' And Spud would give the steerin'-wheel a yank to the left, an' the language of the captain was a disgrace to his company.

"I tell you Spud perspired, but he persevered, too, and used to work in little bits he learnt at the sawmill, and one day he comes up to me as pleased as Punch, an' waves a bit o' blue paper.

"'I've got me licence,' he sez.

"'O,' sez Nobby Clark—a caution, he is—'I suppose they'll let you out without a chain now,' 'e sez.

"'Don't you be funny,' sez Spud; 'I'm a licensed shover.'

"'What's that?' I sez. 'French for beer-can boy at a sawmills?'

"Well, right enough, about a week after, me and a couple of chaps was walkin' out in the country—it was a Sunday—when we 'eard a motorcar comin' up behind.

"'*Hoomp! Hoomp! Hoomp!*'

"Then, like a flash of dirty lightnin', somethin' dashed past in a cloud of dust, and there was me and the other chaps covered all over with muck, and a smell in the air like a paraffin stove.

"Bimeby," resumed Smithy, "we comes up with a motorcar pulled up at the side of a road with somebody crawlin' underneath.

"'There's only one man in the world that takes fourteen boots,' sez Nobby, 'and that's Spud Murphy;' so we pulls 'im out.

"'Now, then, you men,' sez Spud, doin' the haughty act, 'just leave me alone, will yer?'

"What's up, Spud?' I sez.

"'The off 'ind cylinder 'as come into contact with the sparkin' plug,' sez Spud, as bold as brass.

"'Sawmills,' sez Nobby Clark softly.

"'Wot are you goin' to do?' I sez, and the other chaps started lookin' underneath too.

"'I shall petrolise the trembler, and throw back the clutch into the ignition coil,' sez Spud, shuttin' 'is eyes and thinkin'.

"'Sawmills,' sez Nobby Clark quite plainly.

"Spud give him a look, then dives underneath the car with a spanner, while me an' Nobby tried to see what made the fog'orn work.

"'*Oomph!*'

"'Ere,' sez Spud Murphy, underneath the car, 'just you leave that 'orn alone.'

"'*Oomph!*'

"Spud wriggled out from under the car with a spanner in one 'and and a oilcan in the other.

"''E was red in the face, an' as wild as anything.

"'Didn't I tell you to leave it alone?' 'e sez to Nobby.

"'Sawmills!' sez Nobby; and that's why Spud 'it 'im."

Smithy heaved a sigh.

"Take my tip, don't you ever try to separate two chaps when one chap has a spanner in his 'and," he said, and continued:—

"Well, Spud lost 'is job, for a couple of red-caps, (military police), came up an' pinched 'im, an' the car 'ad to be dragged home by a fatigue party, and Uncle Bill drives his own car now; he's fed up with military shovers, and won't 'ave another."

"How do you know?" I asked curiously.

"I offered to drive for 'im," said Smithy modestly.

3.—Advertising the Army

"It's a great thing, getting a staff billet," remarked Private Smithy, resplendent in mufti of the hand-me-down pepper-and-salt variety. Smithy wore mufti consequent upon his recent appointment as groom to Major Somebody-or-Other, Deputy-Assistant-Adjutant-General (a) to Goodness- Knows-What-District.

"It's a relief to get out of regimentals," he sighed, self-consciously thrusting fingers into unaccustomed pockets. I ventured to murmur that he looked ever so much better in a scarlet coat and white belt, but Smithy demurred.

"Red tunics is all right in a way," he remarked philosophically, "but give me a smart civilian suit, turn-down collar, and a pair of brown boots for a change." At Smithy's request I "waited a bit" whilst he explored a small tobacconist's in the High Street.

He returned after a short absence, red in the face, but triumphant.

"Seven for a shilling—and an imitation crocodile leather case thrown in," he explained. "Have one?" Smithy added, with the air of a connoisseur, that it was "almost impossible to buy a good cigar under tuppence."

Two draws convinced me that it was quite as impossible to get the genuine article at the rate of a shilling for seven.

"The red coat attracts a few, I'll admit," resumed Smithy. "I've known two silly jossers in my time who've joined the army for the sake of the scarlet. One got his ticket three months after."

"Ticket," I may say in parenthesis, is the terse barrack-room formula for certificate of discharge.

"Colour blind, 'e was," Smithy went on, with an amused smile. "No, red coats don't bring recruits, nor," added Smithy emphatically, "nothing that the War Office ever did brings recruits." We were passing a hoarding as he spoke, and suddenly clutching my arm, he stopped dead and pointed to a placard. It was neatly printed in red and blue, and was about the size of a newspaper contents bill. It ran:

Recruits Wanted
For Every Branch of
The Army
God Save the King!

I nodded, and we resumed our walk.

"God save the King!" repeated Smithy flippantly. "God save the King if he don't get no more recruits than that there notice will bring him!" and Smithy laughed sarcastically.

He was silent for a while, and so occupied with his thoughts that I was able to drop my cigar down a friendly drain without observation.

"They can't get recruits nowadays," he resumed at length, and then, striking off at a tangent, "Why do fellers enlist?"

I thought it might be for the glory of a noble profession, and ventured to express this thought.

Smithy's reply was conveyed in one coarse, contemptuous word.

"Do you know why I enlisted?" he asked.

I did not hazard an opinion, and he continued: "Broke," he said tersely. "Broke to the wide, wide world; out of a job and had a row with the girl—but mostly I was out of a job.

"Show me a soldier," said Smithy, with a sort of gloomy enthusiasm, "and I'll show you a man who at some time or other has got down to his last tanner.

"Mind you," he added cautiously, "there are thousands of chaps in the army—sergeants on the strength and all that, who've got on well and 'ave educated theirselves—they'll tell you, if you ask 'em, why they 'listed; it's because they struck pa with a roll of music and ran away from home."

Smithy ended this speech in a hoarse falsetto, presumably in imitation of some person or persons unknown.

"Why!" I know a man—quartermaster-sergeant, who's got two houses of his own, and can vamp the accompaniment to any song you like. When he 'listed he walked into barracks on his uppers.

"And now he's got two houses—being a quartermaster-sergeant," added Smithy darkly, and not a little vaguely.

"And so long as the War Office is the War Office," he went on, "you'll always have an army of hard-ups. Because why?"

"Because," I submitted rather sadly, "the greater bulk of the population—"

"Not a bit," said the optimist, demolishing the results of systematic observation with a fine disregard for statistics. "Not a bit. It's because the War Office don't know what attracts soldiers.

"Why! may I be (three expurgated words) if I didn't see a bill the other day outside St. George's Barracks—it was called 'The Advantages of the Army'—and what do you think the pictures on it were about?

"One showed what a happy life a fine young feller could lead in the Royal Engineers. Picture of two pore Tommies in their shirt-sleeves carrying about a ton of wood, whilst three others was diggin' a big hole in the ground. 'Bridge-buildin' and Trenchin',' said the picture.

"Didn't you buy one of them books they was advertising so much last year?" Smithy asked abruptly.

I confessed.

"Did they send you a book showing you the advantages of buying a—what-do-you-call-it Britannia?"

I owned up to three pamphlets, eight letters, and a telegram.

"Ah !" said Smithy craftily, "and did they send you a picture showing you how you might get the brokers in if you didn't pay your instalment? No, of course they didn't. Well, this 'ere bill had six pictures. A pore slave of a lancer cleanin' his saddlery—advantages of the cavalry; a Tommy got up in marchin' order, with fifty pounds of equipment on his back—advantages of the Line ; and so on. What made 'em stop short of havin' one showin' Tommy being frogmarched to the clink," added Smithy, with gentle irony, "an' labellin' it. 'Advantages of the Canteen,' I can't imagine."

"What would attract a desirable class of recruits to the army?" I made bold to ask.

"You'll laugh when I tell you," said Smithy very seriously. "A neat uniform for walkin' out; neat regulation boots instead of beetle crushers; a cap that ain't a pastrycook's cap.

"Make your bloomin' soldier advertise the army make him look so as every counter-jumpin', quill-pushin' board-schoolboy who thinks 'es a cut above Tommy will be proud to change clothes with him. Dress him as ugly as you like for fightin'; but when he's at home, where he'll meet his pals and, likely as not, the girl he left his happy home for, give him a uniform that a civilian might envy." Smithy grew warm.

"If you want to show the advantages of the army in pictures, give a picture of a soldier as he fancies himself best. Show his institutes; show him playin' billiards; show him in India lyin' on 'is charpoy with a bloomin' nigger servant taking orf his boots and another one pullin' a *punkah*. Show him in China ridin' like a lord in a *ricksha*; show him in his white helmet smokin' a cigar—ten for four *annas*—or in Gibraltar seein' a bullfight; but don't show him in his shirtsleeves carryin' coal!"

★★★★★★

I was saying goodbye to Smithy when Nobby Clark of "B" Company met us.

Rude criticism of Smithy's civilian clothes was followed by a proposal that Smithy should accompany Nobby for a stroll round the town.

Smithy drew himself up.

"I hope, Private Clark," he said haughtily, " that I respect myself too highly to be seen walking about the streets with a common soldier!"

4.—ARMY MANNERS

Officers commanding regiments are instructed to note among their subordinates such defects as shortness of temper or weakness of character likely to harm them in their career. —*vide* Army Order.

I stepped back quickly on to the kerb; the cab wheel that brushed against the sleeve of my coat spattered me with black mud.

The cabman threw over his shoulder the rudest expression he could summon at the moment, and I, who am a terrific linguist where the bad language of foreign countries is concerned, fired off three choice morsels of Tamil, which, had they been translated, would have brought that cabman back thirsting for my blood.

Smithy, from a place of safety on the pavement, chuckled.

"Don't lose your temper," advised my military friend—on furlough, by the way, and spending the Christmas holidays with a married sister off Portobello Road. "Puttin' down bad temper's a new army reform." We had crossed the road in safety and were walking up Queen Victoria Street.

"Wot we want in the army nowadays is politeness; bad language we can't abide; if we can't be good soldiers, let's be little gentlemen. The Anchester Regiment is the politest regiment goin'; they call us the 'After you's'; our motto is, '*Quo fus et gloria ducunt*,' which means, '*It's far better to be decent than glorious*'; in fact—"

"In fact you're talking a lot of rot," I said irritably. Smithy smiled in a superior way.

"The other day," he went on, without taking further notice of my interruption, "we 'ad a lecture; Uncle Bill it was, the chap that 'ad the motorcar. 'Company will parade at 11 a.m. in "B" Company's barrackroom for a lecture on military manners, by Captain Umfreville.'

"We all like lectures," explained Smithy; "you can sit down to 'em, an' there's generally a fire in the room. Well, Uncle Bill starts off with a long yarn about a new Army Order, sayin' that chaps must not lose their tempers with other chaps; they ought to be polite an' kind an' courteous, an' he finishes up by sayin' he hoped he'd see an improvement in the company, that before we let our angry passions rise we ought to count twenty.

"After lecture we all goes over to the canteen; me an' Nobby Clark an' Spud Murphy an' Ugly Johnson.

All the chaps was talkin' about Uncle Bill's lecture, an' a chap of the 'G' Company says they's bin havin' a lecture too, about losin' your temper, in fact, the whole bloomin' regiment was lectured on it.

"We take it in turns to buy beer," explained Smithy; "this day it happened to be Spud's turn, but he seemed to forget it.

"'Pardon me, Spud,' sez Nobby, as polite as you please, 'talkin' about beer—'

"'I wasn't talkin' about beer, dear friend,' sez Spud, liftin' his cap.

"'Well,' sez Nobby, tryin' to smile in a friendly manner, 'suppose you talk about it—comrade?'

"Nobby nearly choked sayin 'Comrade,' owin' to his hatin' Spud Murphy worse than poison.

"So Spud shuts his eyes an' makes a noise like a chap thinkin'. 'Um—m—ah—oh, yus,' *et cet'ra,* whilst me an' the other chaps stood gaspin' for a drink.

"'When you've done makin' faces,' sez Nobby, gettin' red in the face, 'p'raps, gallant comrade, you'll buy some beer.'

"'It ain't my turn, dear Nobby,' sez Spud, as bold as brass.

"Nobby sort of went blue.

"'Not your turn!' 'e sez in an 'usky voice, 'not your turn—gallant soldier; not your bloomin' turn—brother?'

"'No,' sez Spud shortly; 'I bought it yesterday—comrade.'

"Nobby looks round at all the chaps who was watchin' 'im be polite to Spud, an' sez:—

"'Bought it yesterday—comrade? Why, you funny-faced perisher, it was Me wot bought it yesterday!'

"'Be polite,' sez Spud; 'don't lose your temper,' 'e sez 'or you'll be gettin' what you're askin' for,' 'e sez.

"'Wot's that?' sez Nobby, 'beer, you daylight robber, you thievin' recruit!'

"'Wot you're askin' for—comrade,' sez Spud, still tryin' to be polite, 'is a thick ear.'"

Smithy went on to a faithful recital of what Private Clark had said in response to this threat of personal violence.

For reasons purely private I suppress the lurid details.

"So at last Nobby paid for his own pint," Smithy resumed, "and sat in a corner by hisself, countin' twenty. For about a week after the barracks was like a Sunday school.

"The orderly sergeant comin' round to warn chaps for duty was like a parson givin' out notices just before the collection.

"'Is Private Jordan here?' sez the sergeant.

"'Yes, Sergeant,' sez Jerry Jordan.

"'I regret that I must warn you for picket duty tomorrow evenin'.'

"'Thank you kindly, Sergeant,' sez Jerry, who'd made arrangements to take his girl out that night.

"'Is Private Purser here?'

"'Yes, Sergeant, at your service,' sez Long Purser.

"'It's my painful duty to inform you that you must appear at company office tomorrow morning to answer the charge of not complying with an order.'

"'Don't mention it, Sergeant,' said Purser.

"One night Nobby comes to me an' sez, 'Look 'ere, Smithy, I'm about fed up with this countin' business.'

"'Are you, comrade?' I sez.

"'Not so much of the "comrade,"' sez Nobby nastily; 'I'm gettin' tired of hearin' Spud Murphy call me "ole friend" an' "chummy" an' "comrade," an' the very next time he comes snackin' me, I'll put him through the mill.'

"'Will you, dear friend?' sez I.

"'Yes, I will, fat 'ead,' sez Nobby.

"Next day, me an' Nobby bein' orderly men, we went down to the cookhouse about four o'clock to draw the tea.

"Spud's our cook; so Nobby sez to 'im:—

"'Ullo, greasy, wot's the price of drippin'?' Spud's got a second-class certificate, so rather fancies hisself.

"'Be a little more polite, Private Clark,' 'e sez in a loud voice so's the sergeant-cook could hear.

"So Nobby sez something to him.

"'Did you 'ear that!' sez Spud in an 'orrified voice.

"So Nobby sez something else to 'im.

"'Don't use that language in this clean cook'ouse.' sez Spud loudly, but the sergeant didn't take no notice. 'I'm surprised at you, Private Clark, losin' your temper like that.'

"So Nobby sez something else to 'im.

"'Say that again,' sez Spud, takin' off his coat.

"'Count twenty,' sez Nobby, with a sneer, 'like I do.'

"'Say that again,' sez Spud, so Nobby did."

Smithy paused to ruminate on that joyous memory.

"We got 'em apart at last, an' the sergeant-cook fell-in four of us to put 'em both in the guard-room.

"Next morning they was both up at company office. an' Uncle Bill sez, 'Did you count twenty, Clark?'

19

"'Yes, sir,' sez Nobby, 'five at a time,' 'e sez.

"'I ought to send you before the colonel,' sez Uncle Bill, but I won't; you'll be both let orf with a caution.'"

"That was very sporting on the part of Umfreville," I remarked in some surprise.

"Yes," said Smithy, with a ghost of a smile. "Uncle Bill doesn't like takin' men before the colonel."

"Why?" I asked.

"Him an' the colonel ain't on speaking terms," explained Smithy naïvely.

5.—The Umpire

Smithy sprawled lazily on the grassy cliff. A gentle breeze blew in from the south, and the glassy, sunlit sea was dotted with laden transport boats.

Grazing within a radius afforded by the loose rein that Smithy held was the major's horse. In the soiled mustard-coloured garb that the soldier affects on manoeuvres, Smithy had followed both Red and Blue forces, for Major Somebody-or-other, whose serf he was, had been umpiring.

"If," said Smithy reflectively, "if we'd fought with umpires in South Africa, who do you think would have won?

"I can tell you," he went on, without waiting for an answer. "Take Ladysmith. Why, if that job had been part of manoeuvres, you'd have seen twenty little umpires come streaking up in their Panniers and Napiers and Baby Peugeots, blinding the Boers with dust, and they'd have had a conference on Wagon Hill and then they'd've sent for George White.

"'Good mornin', Sir George,' they'd say. 'Fine weather we're havin'. 'Ow are the birds in this part of the world? My fifty-horse-power Damyer put up a dozen brace between here and Colenso,' they'd say. Then Sir George would talk about the shootin'.

"'Oh, by the way,' sez the umpire, 'wot about Ladysmith?'

"'Wot about it?' sez Sir George.

"'Well,' sez one of the umpires, polishin' his motor-goggles, 'I think you're out of action, don't you?'

"Sir George gets huffy.

"'Nothin' of the sort,' he sez; 'I can hold Ladysmith for months and months,' he sez.

"Then all the umpires larf, except one with spectacles.

"'Pardon me,' sez this one, 'you don't seem to understand that the strategic defensive calls for the preponderance of the tactical defensive—'

"'You dry up,' sez Sir George quick; 'I'm goin' to hold Ladysmith as long as we've got boots to eat.'

"But he'd have had to give way before the umpires, and Ladysmith would have gone in.

"Then," went on the great man, "take Colenso. The umpires would 'ave gone up to Botha—no, I don't know how they'd have got to him unless they went up in a balloon—and there would be me bold Botha directin' the fire of the First Loyal Sjamboks.

"'Cease fire,' shout the umpires, and Botha stares. 'Wot for?' he sez.

"'You're defeated,' sez the umpire, and then goes on affably: 'What sort of a season are you havin' in this part of the world? Nice weather for the crops, By the bye, as I was comin' along in my ninety-four horse-power Wolseley, I put up twenty brace—'

"Then Botha gets mad.

"'What the howling *raadzaal* do you mean by sayin' that I'm defeated, when I've got a position here that I could hold for a month of Sundays?' he sez as wild as anything.

"The umpire gets very stiff.

"'I'd have you know, general, that you're not allowed to hold this position.'

"'Why?' sez Botha, very astonished.

"'Because it's out of bounds,' sez the umpire and so we'd have got Colenso."

Smithy stopped to watch a bare-footed sailor, with two little yellow and red hand-flags, wave erratic arms seaward.

He spelt out the message, having some knowledge of the semaphore.

"Make—your—own—arrangements," spelt Smithy, and added, with a dry laugh, "That's just the bloomin' thing the umpires don't allow for.

"I remember once," he continued, with unaccustomed animation, "when we were messing about after De Wet. You know the sort of thing—twenty miles a day in every direction. Every night we used to come up to the place where De Wet was the night before. There was half a battalion of Ours, one squadron of scallywags, two squadron of bushrangers, and a couple of pom-poms.

"Well, one day, when we wasn't exactly lookin' for De Wet, De Wet was lookin' for us, and you can bet he found us!

"Before we knew where he was he'd got our horses, and we was all lyin' flat on our chests envyin' the little ants that had as much cover as they wanted.

"We'd been shootin' away for about an hour, and it was easy to see we were pretty well surrounded.

"There was a sort of general in charge of our three columns, and he was twenty miles away with the other two.

"Bimeby we got a helio message from him—'Make the best arrangements you can; I can't get to you under six hours.' So our old man, and the scallywag captain—Somebody's Horse it was—an' the Australian major, had a sort of council of war underneath a water-barrel.

"'Well, gentlemen,' sez our old man, 'I'm afraid we're pipped,' he sez; 'rightly speakin',' he sez, 'we ought to shove up the white flag,' he sez; but I give everybody fair warnin',' he sez, 'that I'll shoot the man who as much as blows his nose with a white handkerchief,' he sez, with a wicked laugh.

"And the scallywag and the bushranger and the little gunner who had just crawled up, said, 'Hear, hear!'

"Then our old man goes on: 'The main body of the enemy is in a *donga* three hundred yards to our left,' he sez, 'and we've got to get that *donga*,' sez our old man."

Smithy's eyes were far away.

"Bimeby," he went on, "I heard the old man shouting, 'Concentrate your fire on that *donga*,' he sez ; then after a bit, when the dust begins to go up, he yells, 'Fix bayonets!'"

Smithy turned and looked me squarely in the face. "What would the umpire have said?" he asked. Why, we'd have been bloomin' well decimated—but we wasn't. The Boers didn't wait for the bayonet—they pushed off, and we got away with the guns.

"There's only one kind of war," said Smithy sagely, "and that's the kind that hurts. When the chap that's playin' the real game makes a misdeal or revokes, there's no reshuffle. If he puts up a big bluff and it comes off, he's a great man, and gets his picture in the papers. If it don't come off, why—"

Smithy's silence was eloquent.

"Umpires in war," he went on, "are food and feet and fingers—fingers for holdin' on to positions where, rightly, you should 'a' been kicked off.

"I know regiments that could never be put out action unless every man was killed—what's an umpire goin' to do with a lot like that?" he demanded. Somewhere down on the shingly beach below to a stentorian voice roared:

"Smith!"

Smith rose with alacrity.

"Comin', sir," he shouted. Then, as he led his officer's charger seaward, he turned.

"He's an umpire," he said, with a jerk of his thumb toward the beach, "but he's a very decent chap otherwise."

6.—ERUDITION

"It was read out in reg'mental orders," said Smithy, "on the 9.30 parade, that a new lot of books 'ad arrived for the lib'ry. 'Suitable books for the Soldier,' it said, so that afternoon me an' Nobby goes over to the coffee-shop where the lib'ry is to 'ave a look. There was lots of other chaps there, an' we 'ad to take our turn.

"All the chaps was shoutin', 'Come on, Mac, give me that red one,' an' poor old Macmanus got 'isself all tied up in a knot tryin' to put dawn the names of the chaps that took out the new books. When it come to me an' Nobby's turn there was only two books left. Nobby got a blue one an' I got a red one.

"'Wot's yours, Smithy?' sez Nobby, an' I read it out: '*Temp'rance Statistics of the Army in India.*'

"'Who Stat What's-'is-name?' sez Nobby.

"'Some bloomin' teetotaller,' I sez. 'Wot's yours?'

"''*Ydraulics for Garrison Artillery,*' 'e sez. 'Whose she, I wonder?'

"Spud Murphy got a book about *Tactics in the Crimea*, George Botter (of 'G') got a yaller book about *Afghanistan in Relation to the Frontier Question*, Mouldy Thompson got a big book about *The 'Istory of the Army Service Corps*, whilst old 'Appy Johnson got the best of the lot, *Records an' Nicknames of the British Army.*'

"We all takes our books to the barrack-room, an' there was me an' Nobby an' all the rest of the chaps sittin' down 'oldin' our 'eads tryin' to understand what the books was about.

"When we gets over to the canteen that night everybody was tryin' to show off.

"Spud comes strollin' up to where me an' Nobby was sittin'.

"''Ullo, Nob,' 'e sez.

"'Ullo!' sez Nobby; 'what do you want, funny face?'

"Spud sits down alongside of me an' Nobby.

"'Talkin' about the Crimea—' 'e sez, like a chap sayin' a piece.

"'I wasn't talkin' about the Crimea,' sez Nobby.

"'Ave" you ever noticed that a great strategic opportunity was lost—'

"Nobby puts down the can 'e was drinkin' out of.

"''Old 'ard,' 'e sez. I think I grasp your meanin', Spud. You're referrin', unless I am mistaken, to the time when the garrison artillery didn't start workin' their 'ydraulics in a proper manner.'

"'No, I ain't,' snaps Spud. I'm talkin' about the tactics in the Crimea.'

"'An' I'm talkin' about 'ydraulics,' sez Nobby, as calm as a cucumber, 'becos that's the book that I'm a-readin'.'

"It was pretty sickenin'," explained Smithy, "wot with George Botter tryin' to pretend 'e knew all about Afghanistan, an' 'Appy Johnson wantin' to make bets about who was the first colonel of the Anchesters. Mouldy Thompson got to 'igh words with a driver of the A.S.C. about the Army Service Corps.

"'I suppose you don't know, Cocky,' sez Mouldy to this chap, 'that the old A.S.C. used to be called the Muck Train?'

"'No, I don't,' sez the A.S.C. chap nastily, 'an' wot's more, I don't see no call to go makin' personal remarks.'

"'Where no offence is meant, it is 'oped that no offence will be took,' sez Mouldy. 'Well, as I was sayin', the Muck Train—'

"'Shut up,' sez the A.S.C. chap, 'or 'I'll shut you up.'

"Just before 'fust post' me an' Nobby was sittin' in the corner talkin' about 'ydraulics and drink, when in come Gus Ward of the R.A.M.C.

"Up goes Mouldy to 'im as pleased as anything.

"'D'you know what they call the Medical Staff?' sez Mouldy.

"The medical bloke looks over 'is pot an' sez nothin'."

"They call 'em the "Linseed Lancers,"' sez Mouldy, laughin'.

"The medical finished 'is beer, puts down 'is pot, and sez to Mouldy:

"'Do you know what I call you?' 'e sez.

"'Don't be naaty,' sez Mouldy; 'this is in a book.'

"'In a book, is it?' sez the medical. 'Well, you homoeopathic, subcutaneous mnemonic, what I'm going to call you won't be found in any book.'

"So then the medical chap started callin' Mouldy all the things 'e could remember at the minute, an' finished up with a few words out of the sick report.

"You must understand," explained Smithy, "that all the bloomin' battalion was on the same lay. There they was the next afternoon lyin' in their cots a readin' an' a mutterin' an' gettin' ready to show off.

"Wastin' their time"—Smithy was indignan—"an' well knowin' that we 'aven't got a decent bowler in the regiment. I didn't see anything of Nobby till I went over to the canteen that night. Everybody was talkin' about everything—all talkin' together. Suddenly I 'eard Nobby's voice:

"'No, you're wrong, Mouldy,' 'e sez; 'you're wrong about the artillery.'

"'Wrong!' sez Mouldy, very indignant; ''ow do you know?'

"'Because I do,' sez Nobby, 'an' what's more, Spud Murphy's wrong about the army in the Crimea, an' George Botter's talkin' through 'is 'at about Afghanistan, an' Dusty Miller's silly when 'e sez that Athens is in Germany (Dusty got a book on the decay of the classy or somethin' of the sort), an' when Billy Mason gits up an' talks about Africa—I've got a word to say.'

"An' with that old Nobby starts to criticise everybody, not confinin' hisself to 'ydraulics, you understand, but goin' all over the shop.

"Bimeby, old Spud Murphy, who'd been dazed by Nobby tellin' 'im a lot about the battle of Alma, strikes 'is for'ead an' shouts:

"'Old 'ard, Nobby—I see your little game—it's A's what your talkin' about.'

"'What d'ye mean?' sez Nobby, goin' red.

"'Why,' sez Spud, excited, 'you're talkin' about Abukir an' Abyssinia an' adjutants an' ants—they're all A's,' roars Spud.

"'Well,' sez Nobby, 'wot about it?'

"'Ask 'im a C question, somebody,' shouts Spud, gleeful.

"'Wot about crocodiles?' sez Dusty.

"'Crocodiles an' alligators are all the same,' sez Nobby. 'Everybody knows that.'

"''Ear, 'ear,' I sez; an' the other chaps said the same.

"'Well,' sez Spud, thinkin', 'I'll give you a "M"—wot about monkeys?'

"Nobby thought a bit.

"'Apes,' 'e begins, 'was first invented—'

'Monkeys!' sez Spud.

"'Apes an' monkeys are all the same,' sez Nobby.

"'Well, tell us somethin' about colonels—that's a C,' sez Spud, who was gettin' wild.

"It took Nobby a long time to think this out, then 'e starts:

"'Adjutants was first invented—'

"'I thought so,' sez Spud, joyful. 'P'raps you'll tell me when 'Cyclopaedias' was invented—fortnightly 'cyclopedias, wot you buy for sevenpence,' sez Spud.

"An' Nobby looked quite uncomfortable."

7.—BERTIE

"You don't 'appen to know our Bertie, do you?" asked Private Smith; "'E's a new chap only just joined from the depot: 'ighly educated an' all that: one of the struck-pa-with-a-roll-of-music-and-enlisted sort of fellows."

Smithy paused to ruminate upon the accomplished Bertie.

"I've 'eard 'im use words that wasn't in any dictionary," Smithy continued with enthusiasm, "an' 'e's settled arguments we've 'ad in the canteen without so much as lookin' in a book.

"There was a bit of a friendly discussion the other night about 'ow much alch'ol there was in beer, an' 'ow many pints it'd take to poison a chap. Gus Ward, the medical staff chap, worked it all out on a bit of paper, but some of the other chaps said 'e was talkin' through 'is 'at.

"To settle it—none of the other chaps would come outside when Gussie invited 'em—we sent over for Bertie.

"Over comes Bertie with a wot-can-I-do-for-you-my-poor-child sort of smile, an' we puts the question to 'im.

"'Twenty-two gallons an' a pint,' sez Bertie prompt.

"'You're a liar!' sez Nobby, an' the medical chap asked Bertie to come outside an' settle the question.

"'Don't be absurd,' sez Bertie. 'Nobody can tell me anything about alch'ol: it was discovered by a monk in 1320, when 'e was searchin' for the philosopher's stone. It is known at Lloyd's as a deadly sporadic an—'

"'Shut up,' sez Nobby; 'we don't want to know the geography an' 'istory of it, we want to know 'ow many pints of beer it takes to kill a chap.'

"'Thirty-one gallons an' two pints, as said before,' sez Bertie, huffily; 'an' in future, Private Clark, I don't want you to send for me to settle canteen controversialities.'

"'Wot's that last word?' sez Nobby, after Bertie had gone. 'Somethin' insultin', I'll lay.'

★★★★★★

"Me an' Nobby 'appened to be over at the coffee shop next night—it was the night before payday, or we wouldn't 'ave been wastin' our time—when in comes Bertie.

"'E's got an 'orrid languid way of lookin' round, an' it was a minute or two before 'e spots me an' Nob.

"''Ullo, Clark,' 'e sez, with a nod just the same as if 'e was an officer. ''Ullo, Smithy.'

"''Ullo, face,' sez Nobby, who's always got a kind word for everyone.

"'I'm gettin' tired of this sort of life,' sez Bertie, in a weary voice. 'I've got too much wot the French call *savoir faire*.'

"'See a doctor,' sez Nobby, 'or take plenty of exercise, like I do.'

"'You misunderstand me, Clark,' sez Bertie, with a sad smile. 'But, there, 'ow should you know, my poor feller?'

"'Bertie,' sez Nobby.

"'What?' sez Bertie.

"'Don't call me a "pore feller,"' sez Nobby, 'or I'll give you a dig in the eye.'

"'Don't lose your temper, Clark,' sez Bertie, hasty. 'What I meant to say was, you can't be expected to comprehend 'ow it feels for a chap who's drove 'is own brougham to be ordered about by cads of officers, cads an' bounders that my *alma mater* wouldn't 'ave in 'er set.'

"'Who's she?' sez. Nobby.

"'My rich aunt,' sez Bertie.

"'Livin' in the Marylebone Road?' sez Nobby.

"'No,' sez Bertie, carelessly. 'Porchester Gate.'

"'Ah,' sez Nobby, thoughtful, 'that's a work'ouse that must 'ave been built quite lately—'ow London grows, to be sure.'

"Bertie smiled an' shook 'is 'ead.

"'Ah, Clark!' 'e sez with a pityin' look, 'there's a good old French sayin' that goes, "*Ontry noo sivvoo play*," which means, "*Don't argue with a fool*."'

"'There's another good ole French proverb, sez Nobby, 'that sez, "*Chuprao soor*."'

"'What does that mean?' sez Bertie surprised, so Nobby told 'im.

★★★★★★

"Bertie wasn't what you might call popular with the troops. For one thing 'e used long words that nobody even 'eard before, an' for the other, 'e was a bun-wallah of the worst kind."

(It is, I might say, one of the wilful fallacies of the army that teetotallers live entirely on lemonade and buns.)

"We don't mind so much a chap bein' a teetotaller; every man to 'is taste, an' I've known some very good chaps in that line, but Bertie used to carry 'is fads a bit too far.

"For instance, 'e got me an' Nobby one night down to an A.T.A. (Army Temperance Association) meetin', an' so worked on Nobby's feelin's, by promisin' to lend him 'arf a crown till payday, that Nobby ups an' signs the pledge.

"'I feel a diff'rent man already,' sez Nobby, after Bertie 'ad parted with the money, 'I do, indeed.'

"'Ah,' sez Bertie, proudly, 'you'll feel better when you've 'ad a week of it. Don't let your boon companions lure you back to the old 'abit,' 'e sez.

"'No fear,' sez Nobby, putting the 'arf-crown in 'is pocket.

"'Not so much of the boon companions, Bertie,' I sez, knowin' what 'e was eayin' was a smack for me.

"'When: they offer you the pot—refuse it like a man,' sez Bertie, working hisself up to a great state.

"'I will,' sez Nobby.

"'Look 'ere,' sez Bertie, excitedly, 'come up to the canteen now, an' put yourself to the test.'

"'Right you are,' sez Nobby, quick; 'let's 'urry up before it's shut.'

"So we all went up to the canteen, an' the first thing that 'appened when we got inside was Dusty Miller offerin' Nobby 'arf a gallon can.

"'Drink 'arty, Nobby,' sez Dusty.

"Nobby looks at the can, then looks at Bertie, an' Bertie was smilin' 'appily all over 'is face."

"'No,' sez Nobby, chokin', 'no, Dusty, you mean well, but I'm on the tack—on the lemonade tack,' 'e sez.

"'Good Nobby,' sez Bertie.

"'Let me take one last look at the cursed stuff,' sez Nobby, takin' the pot in 'is 'and; 'one last sniff,' 'e sez, 'one last taste o' the poison,' 'e sez, an' before we knew what 'ad 'appened 'e'd 'arf emptied the can.

"'It's no good, Bertie,' 'e sez sadly, 'the temptation is too strong, it's in me blood,' 'e sez. 'You can 'ave your 'arf-crown back on payday."

★★★★★★

"What chaps didn't like about Bertie most was the way 'e was always goin' on about 'is come-down in the world, 'ow 'e might have been livin' up in the West End, goin' to theatres every night of 'is life, an' drinkin' port wine with 'is meals, if 'e 'adn't been such a fool as to enlist.

"One night when 'e was' playin' billiards in the library Nobby got Bertie to settle a point whether an earl was an 'igher rank than a countess,

"'A countess, of course,' sez Bertie.

"'For why?' sez Nobby.

"Bertie gave a pityin' sort of laugh.

"'A countess is a lady count, an' a count is next to a marquis,' 'e sez.

"'Ow do you know?' sez Nobby.

"Bertie gave a sort of a tired sigh, an' looked at the ceilin'.

"'My dear Clark,' 'e sez, 'it ain't for me to boast of the people I met before I come down in the world, but I might say I've met certain parties—no names mentioned—that our officers ain't even on speakin' terms with.'

"'In shops?' sez Nobby.

"'No, in country 'ouses,' sez Bertie stiffly.

"'Leave off pullin' Bertie's leg,' sez Spud Murphy, who always likes to get a rise out of Nobby. 'Anybody can see Bertie's mixed with 'igh-class people.'

"We was all silent for a bit, watchin' Dusty Miller, who was playin' Mouldy Turner a hundred up, tackle an' ''ard-lines cannon.

"We was very interested in it, especially Bertie, who, couldn't take 'is eyes from the cloth.

"Dusty fluked 'is cannon an' missed the next shot, an' then Nobby got a sort of inspiration, an' calls out to Bertie:

"'Call the game, marker!'

"'Seventy-six plays forty-two: spot to play, sir,' sez Bertie, absent-mindedly.

8.—Nobby's Part

"I didn't see you at our piece," remarked Smithy.

"I mean," he explained, "the Grand Amateur Performance of *The Soldier's Revenge*, played by the Regimental Dramatic Club, on behalf of the new wing of the Anchester Lunatic Asylum." Smithy stopped to clear the stem of his pipe with a hairpin. I regarded him suspiciously—and the hairpin with inward misgivings.

"There was about two dozen of our chaps in the piece," he resumed, "and the band was goin' to play durin' the intervals. Some of 'em—our chaps, I mean, not the band—was goin' to be soldiers, some of 'em was servants, some of 'em was villagers, but half of 'em was 'rioters' in the last act. 'B' Company and 'F' tossed up to see who'd be rioters and 'B' won, so 'F' had to be policemen. Nobby Clark comes to me the day before the performance an' sez, 'Look here, Smithy, come an' act.'

"'The goat?' I sez.

"'No,' he sez, 'come an' be Mike Dolan, the Escaped Convict, in Act 4,' he sez; 'Fatty can't get into the clothes,' he sez.

"'No, thanks,' I sez. 'If you want Escaped Convicts, apply to "C" Company—there's lots of chaps there that would do it natural,' I sez.

"'Don't you be gay,' sez Nobby, 'or else you'll strain your funny bone. I'm goin' to be a gentleman visitor in Act 2—one of the 'ouse party.'

"'One of the gentlemen that washes up the plates?' I sez.

"'Loud larfter,' sez Nobby, sarcastically. 'I'm goin' to be a good shepherd in the last act,' he sez, 'an' when the rioters are goin' to bash the police I say, "'Old! what would you do, rash men?" an' then I tell 'em to think about their wives an' children,' he sez.

"It was pretty sickenin' them last two days in barracks before the performance. There was Jimmy Spender walkin' about holdin' his head an' mutterin'; 'My lord, my lord, the enemy is on us; fly for your life!' an' Smiler Williams walkin' up an' down the square after 'lights out' talkin' to hisself, 'Come, comrades, let us drink to the 'ealth of our noble commander,' till Smiler's company officer, Captain Darby, gave him seven days for creatin' a disturbance in barracks after lights out. Ugly Johnson broke his collar-bone when he was rehearsin' his rescue from a burnin' buildin'.

"A lot of chaps was supposed to catch him in a blanket as he jumped out of a winder, sayin', 'A British soldier fears nothin'; but the chaps who was holdin' the blanket larfed so much at Ugly's mug, that they hadn't the strength to catch him."

Smithy laughed, too, at the recollection.

"Well, the night come, an', havin' bought two seats in the gallery, I goes round to the house where Nobby's girl lives an' asked her to come an' see the play.

"'Nobby won't like my goin' out with you,' sez Nobby's girl.

"'Don't worry about that,' I sez; 'he'd have sent you a ticket hisself, only he's so shy,' I sez.

"So she put on her things," said Smithy, vaguely, "and went."

"We got two front seats where we could see everything, an' after the band gave a selection and the officers an' their ladies, an' the bishop, an' the mayor had come in, the curtain went up, an' there was Nobby strollin' about with a gun under his arm, pretendin' to be an actor. "Bimeby the old squire come in with his lovely daughter. 'Ah, Captain Beecher,' she sez to Nobby—she was a real actress, too—'why, it seems like old times to see you at "Silverton Grange."

"'Bai Jove!' sez Nobby, twistin' his moustache like he'd seen his superiors do. 'Bai Jove,' he sez, an' then he forgot what to say.

"'The pleasure is mutual,' sez a holler voice from behind the, scenes.

"'The pleasure is beautiful,' sez poor Nobby, still twistin' his moustache.

"After a bit the old squire was murdered by Monty Warne, of 'H,' dressed up like a burglar, an' he did it well, too," commended Smithy, "stranglin' him so much that they had to send out for three-pennorth of brandy to bring him round.

"In the second act Nobby was supposed to be a visitor in evenin' dress.

"'Don't he look fine?' sez Nobby's girl.

"Nobby didn't have much so say in that act, except when young Fisher, who's got a baker's shop in the Highstreet, was falsely accused of murder, an' then Nobby seized his hand, an' said, 'I believe you to be an innocent man,' an' we all said, 'Hear, hear.'

"It was really Smiler Williams who ought've said that line, as Nobby was really supposed to be a villain, an' Smiler an' Nobby had words about it afterwards, till Nobby explained that young Fisher had promised him a job when he left the army, an' he wanted to keep in with him.

"But the last scene was best," continued Smithy, "when the hungry rioters of 'B' come face to face with the policemen of 'F,' an' Nobby comes down to the footlights dressed up as a parson, and says, 'Hold!'

"Just as he started to say his little piece one of the policemen, tryin' to be funny, hit him in the chest with a truncheon.

"'Hold hard,' sez Nobby, forgettin' all about the piece; 'wot are you tryin' to do, Corky?'—speakin' to Corky Speddings, who hit him.

"'Go on with the piece,' sez Corky, who was wild because had had nothin' to say in the play.

"Nobby took orf his parson's hat an' raised it an' said, 'Hold! What would you do, rash—' then another policeman threw a bit of bread at him.

"Before anybody know what was happenin', Nobby dropped his hat an' landed the nearest policeman on the nose, an' then there was the most realistic riot that has ever been on a stage.

"Next mornin' Nobby asked me what I thought of his performance.

"'Fine,' I sez.

"'Do you think so?' he sez, very pleased, 'Don't you wish you could act, Smithy, an' take the part of a young lord or something?'

"'I can act,' I sez. 'I was actin' last night—*The Absent Soldier*.'

"'Talk sense,' sez Nobby, puzzled; 'you hadn't got a part.'

"'Oh yes I had,' I sez.

"'What part?' sez Nobby.

"'Your part,' I sez.

"But Nobby didn't understand."

9.—THE CLAIRVOYANT

"Do you believe in ghosts?" asked Private Smithy.

"What kind of ghosts?" I asked cautiously.

"There's a chap in H Company," explained Smithy—"his name's Turner, Mouldy Turner, we call him, owin' to his havin' been a moulder by trade. You never saw such a chap in your life," said Smithy enthusiastically. "Give him a pack o' cards an' a table an' he'll tell you things about your past life wot you've never heard before.

"He charges tuppence a time, an' it's worth it. I had twopenn'orth myself the other day.

"'Smithy,' he sez, dealin' out the cards all over the table, you're expectin' a letter from a dark man.'

"'No, I ain't,' I sez.

"'Well, you'll get it, he sez. 'It will bring good news.'

"An' sure enough," said Smithy, impassively, "that very afternoon Spud Murphy paid me two shillin's he borrered on the manoeuvres."

"But," I expostulated, "that wasn't a letter."

"It was better than a letter," said the satisfied Smithy.

"Well, old Mouldy counts the cards, seven to the left an' seven to the right.

"'There's a fair woman wot loves you,' sez Mouldy.

"'How fair?,' I sez, thinkin' of all the red-haired gals I know.

"'Pretty fair,' sez Mouldy, 'you're goin' on a long journey acrorse the sea.'

"'Battersea?' sez Nobby, who was lookin on.

"'You shut up, Nobby,' I sez, 'go on, Mouldy.'

"'Tho nine o' spades,' sez Mouldy, scowlin' like anything at Nobby, 'is a sign of death. You'll hear of a friend dyin'. Not much of a friend, either, but a ignorant chap with big feet,' he sez.

"'You leave my feet alone,' sez Nobby.

"All the chaps used to come to Mouldy, an' he was doin' well. I could see Nobby didn't like the way Mouldy was rakin' in the iron, an' one night, when me an' a few chaps was in the canteen torkin' about how teetotallers die when they get into a hot climate, Pug Williams came dashin' in, lookin' as white as a ghost.

"'Nobby Clark's took ill!' he sez, an' we rushes over to the barrack-room to find old Nobby sittin' on his bed with a horrible stare in his eye.

"'Wot's up, Nobby?' I sez, and just then Mouldy Turner comes in.

"'I see,' sez Nobby, in a moany sort of voice, 'I see a public house.'

"'You've seen too many public houses,' sez Mouldy, hastily.

"'The inside of a public house, sez Nobby.

"'That's the part I mean,' sez Mouldy.

"'I see a man with side whiskers an' a big watch-chain,' sez Nobby moanily; 'he's servin' be'ind the counter, an' there's a red-faced gel with yeller hair a-countin' money. Her name's Gertie,' sez Nobby, holding his for'ead. "Old Mouldy's jaw dropped an' he went white.

"'Where's my George? Where's my soldier boy?' moans Nobby, 'that's what she's a-sayin' of.'

"Mouldy's face got red.

"'Boys,' sez Mouldy, in a scared voice, 'old Nobby's got second-sight; he's a seein' the pub I go to up in London an' my young lady.'

"'Where's my brave soldier?' sez Nobby, groanin'; 'that's what she's a-sayin' of; where is my brave soldier wot rescued the colonel at Paardeberg?'

"'He's a wunderin' now,' sez Mouldy, blushin'.

"'Let's take him to the, hospital,' sez Pug Williams, but just at that minute Nobby sort of woke up.

"'Where am I?' he sez faintly.

"We told him what he'd been sayin', an' tried to persuade him to go to bed an' sleep it off.

"The next day the news got about that Nobby was second-sighted, an' when me and Nobby went to get our dinner pint all the chaps crowded round an' asked him to give a performance.

"It appeared from what Nobby told 'em that he'd always been second-sighted, an' when he was a kid he had to wear spectacles.

"'Can you tell fortunes, Nobby?' sez Oatsey.

"'I can with hands, sez Nobby, lookin' at Mouldy; 'not with cards. Cards,' he sez, 'is swindlin'.'

"'Can you tell mine, Nobby?' sez Pug Williams, holdin' out his hand.

"'Certainly,' sez Nobby, who'd known Pug all his life, an' went to school with him.

"'You was born under an unlucky star,' sez Nobby, lookin' at the hand.

"'That's quite right,' sez Pug, quite proud.

"'At school you was always gettin' into trouble,' sez Nobby, who happened to know that Pug did six months at a truant school.

"'That's right!' sez Pug, highly delighted.

"'You've had a lot a trouble through a dark man,' sez Nobby, knowin' that Pug got forty-two days for knockin' a nigger about, when the reg'ment was in India.

"'Marvellous!' sez Pug.

"From that day Nobby made money. Chaps used to come from every company to get their fortune told. Mouldy an' his cards did no bus'ness at all.

"Nobby charged thruppence a hand, cash on the nail; fourpence if he 'ad to wait till payday.

"For sixpence Nobby used to have a fit an' see things. Sometimes two chaps would club together, an' then Nobby would have two fits for ninepence.

"One day up comes Ugly Johnson, of 'D.'

"'I want you to tell my fortune, Nobby,' he sez.

"'Cross me hand with silver, pretty lady,' sez Nobby.

"'Don't snack a chap about his face,' sez Ugly, very fierce.

"'No offence, Ugly,' sez Nobby.

"'And I ain't go'in' to cross your bloomin' hand with silver,' sez Ugly, "cos I've only got three'apence.'

"'That'll do, sez Nobby, who never let a customer go.

"'You've got a long life in front of you,' sez Nobby, lookin' at the hands.

"'Ah,' sez Ugly.

"'You've 'ad a stormy career in the past,' sez Nobby, 'but all will

34

come right!'

"'Ah,' sez Ugly.

"'You've been crorsed in love,' sez Nobby.

"'That's a lie,' sez Ugly.

"'So it is,' sez Nobby, lookin' close at Ugly's paw, 'wot I thought was the crorsed-in-love line is only dirt. You've got a sensitive 'art, you think everybody's passin' remarks about your face,' sez Nobby.

"'Never mind about my face,' snarls Ugly.

"'I don't mind it,' sez Nobby, 'even if other people do,' he sez.

"Well, old Ugly got mad an' went round puttin' it about that Nobby couldn't tell fortunes for nuts, and Mouldy sez that Nobby was tellin' a lot of lies an' makin' fun of the chaps, an' business began to fall orf.

"One afternoon Nobby sez to me, 'Smithy, trade's bad.'

"'Is it?' I sez.

"'Yes,' he sez, 'it's about time I had another fit.'

"'Have it now,' I sez, 'don't mind me.'

"That night, when we was all cleanin' up for commondin' officer's parade, an' the barrack-room was full, Nobby suddenly stood up, moanin' like anything.

"'I see!' he sez starin' about him, 'a man with a ugly mug. 'E's a-standing' on the blink—I mean brink of destruction.'

"We all walks over an' looks at Nobby. He was a ghastly sight, rollin' his eyes an' moanin'.

"'I see a chap,' sez Nobby, twistin' about as if he'd swollered a corkscrew, 'wot pretends to tell fortunes by cards. 'E's standin' on the brink of destruction too.'

"'Wake up, Nobby,' I sez, soothin' him; 'it's all right.'

"'I see,' began Nobby again, an' just at that minute in walks the colour-sergeant.

"He looks at Nobby rollin' an' squirmin' about, an' then sez to me:

"'Are you the oldest soldier here, Smith?'

"'Yes, colour-sergeant,' I sez.

"'Well,' sez the colour bloke, 'take a couple of men an' put Private Clark in the guardroom.'

"'Wot for?' sez Nobby, wakin' up sudden from his trance.

"'Drunk,' sez the colour-sergeant.

"'I ain't drunk,' roars Nobby, very indignant.

"'Pretendin' to be drunk, then,' sez the colour-sergeant; 'that's worse.'

"'I'm seein' spirits,' sez Nobby.

"'You've, been drinkin' 'em,' sez the colour bloke, an' Nobby was so wild that it took six of us to get him to the guardroom.

"You might say seven," added Smithy, "for Old Mouldy did the work of two men."

10.—Boots

Young and growing soldiers are prone to wear boots that are too small and too narrow mainly because of their smart appearance.—*Army Council Memorandum to Officers.*

"I shouldn't like to be on the Army Council," said Smithy, with all seriousness.

I looked at my young military friend with feigned surprise.

"No, I ain't coddin'," he said earnestly. "I s'pose it's a good job; but never 'avin' been an officer, I can't say what it's like. But stands to reason it's a wearin' sort of life.

"Suppose the Army Council's meetin' today, the orderly on duty lights a fire, gets out new pens and blottin' paper, an' Army Form B47, just the same as if it was a court-martial—and," said Smithy, as a brilliant idea came to him— "it is a court-martial, and the army's the prisoner.

"Well, in comes the Court, all in civilian clothes, Lyttelton in a soft felt 'at, an' Plumer in a red necktie, and Douglas got up to the nines.

"'Wot's on today?' sez Lyttelton.

"Reformin' the army,' sez all the others together.

"'Rot,' sez Lyttelton. 'I don't believe the army wants reformin'—except reformin' back to the place it was when civilians started holdin' *post-mortems* on it.'

"''Ear, 'ear,' sez all the Army Council, except Lord Don't-Know-Who, who looked embarrassed, 'e bein' a civilian.

"Wot about tight boots?' sez someone after a long pause, durin' which the financial secretary was doin' sums on the blottin' paper an' crossin' 'em out when 'e found they was wrong.

"'Ah,' sez Some One Else, 'wot about tight boots?' So they all sits round givin' their opinions why soldiers should be Ugly and Comfortable.

"Well, after a bit they make up an order:—

No lady-killin' boots allowed. Soldiers in possession of boots weighin' eight ounces will immediately exchange them for boots of the Regulation (or Policeman) Pattern, weighin' four pound. '*Fiat experimentum in corpore vili*,' or '*If necessary make the experiment on a villainous corporal.*'

Yours truly,

The Army Council.

"Then they all get up an' stretch their legs.

"'What's on tomorrer?' sez one.

"'Army Reform,' sez the president; 'an' let's see you all 'ere at nine, sharp.'

"Then they all go home to their little flats, an' read the newspapers, an' wish they was Japanese sittin' tight in front of Kuropatkin instead of bein' soldiers tryin' to reform the army so as to suit civilians' ideas.

"Sometimes it's boots, sometimes it's swearin', sometimes it's 'air—an' the 'smart, soldier-like appearance' order: this new order about boots, though, rather takes it."

Smithy's "It" is fairly obvious.

"They was talkin' about it in the canteen yesterday, when me an' Nobby went over to get our dinner beer.

"Wilkie—that red-lookin' chap with the shavin'-brush moustache—was puttin' it about that the order was only meant for 'B' Company.

"'Don't none of you chaps get worried about it,' sez Wilkie, who's an 'H' chap. 'This 'ere order's only meant for chaps with big feet tryin' to pretend they're Cinderellas.'

"'Meanin' me, Wilkie?' sez Nobby.

"'No names, no pack drill,' sez Wilkie.

"'Meanin' me, you red-'aired Bloomsbury scavenger?' sez Nobby.

"'If the cap—meanin' to say the boot—fits you, Private Clark, lace it up,' sez Wilkie; 'an', what's more.' 'e sez, 'don't forget the last army order about swearin' an' losing your temper.'

"Next day," continued Smithy, "was commandin' officers' parade, an' when the company officers walked round the ranks there was trouble.

"'Where's your boots?' sez the captain to young Skipper Mainland.

"'Under my trousers,' sez Skipper.

"'Too small,' sez the officer; 'put this man down for a new pair, colour-sergeant.'

"'What's these, Clark?' sez the officer.

"'My feet, sir,' sez Nobby, gettin' red in the face.

"'Beg pardon,' sez the officer, I thought they was a pontoon section,' 'e sez and we all laughed.

"I tell you," said Smithy enthusiastically, "our officer's a comic chap.

"That night you couldn't get into the 'Igh Street for feet. All the chaps was wearin' their biggest boots, an' one chap standin' on the kerb got 'is toes run over by a tramcar the other side of the street—in a manner of speaking," corrected Smithy hastily.

"''Oo should we meet when me an' Nobby was strollin' down Church Lane but Wilkie. Nice toonic, smart tight trousers with officers' stripes in 'em, saucy little boots, an' a cane with a silver knob on the end of it—that's Wilkie.

"'Hullo, Wilkie,' sez Nobby, 'wot Christmas-tree did you blow orf of?'

"Wilkie looked a bit pleased with hisself, an' was goin' to say somethin', when up comes the provost sergeant with 'is badge on 'is sleeve.

"'Evenin', Sergeant,' sez Wilkie very pleasant.

"But the provost sergeant didn't say nothin', only looked at Wilkie's feet

"'Nice weather for this time of the year,' sez Wilkie. 'It is indeed,' 'e sez.

"But provost sergeant only stared at Wilkie's feet.

"So Wilkie got red in the face.

"'Beg pardon, sergeant,' 'e sez; 'nothing wrong, I 'ope?'

"The provost just kept on lookin'. Then 'e said, speakin' slowly, like a chap recitin':

"'The proper fittin' of boots on which the marchin' of an army depends is a matter of the first importance,' 'e sez.

"Wilkie looks at 'im; so did me an' Nobby.

"'I don't do no marchin' in these boots,' sez Wilkie, an' my boots an' Nobby's sort of shuffled into the gutter out of sight.

"'Young soldiers,' sez the provost sergeant, takin' no notice of what Wilkie said, are prone—'

"'Are what?' sez Wilkie.

"'Are prone to take a boot too short—in fact,' sez the provost sergeant, 'where did you get them ridiculous lady's shoes from, Mr. Bloomin' Wilkie?'

"' I got 'em,' sez Wilkie, from—.

"'No man who wasn't a lunatic would wear such fal-lal; they was meant for women, not soldiers.'

"'I got 'em—' sez Wilkie.

"'Makin' yourself a laughin'-stock,' sez the Provost, gettin' wild, 'wearin' boots that nobody but a fat-headed, dandified, ijiotic recruit would think of disgracin' 'is foot by puttin' inside.'

"'I got 'em off the colonel's groom,' sez Wilkie, short.

"'Where'd 'e get 'em?' sez the provost.

"'They're a pair of the colonel's old 'uns,' sez Wilkie, what 'e got rid of—they was too big,' 'e sez."

11.—JU-JITSU

Politics form no part of the barrack-room debating society. Mr. Atkins lives in a world of his own, and is not interested in the subjects that agitate his civilian brother.

He is interested in personalities, certainly, and Mr. Chamberlain and Lord Rosebery are very real persons to him; but talk about the respective merits of Free Trade and Protection and he will yawn. Very high politics, politics that make for war; parliamentary proceedings that have direct bearing upon pay, promotion, and uniform, are of the first importance; and does an hon. member ask the Secretary of State for War whether his attention has been called to the refusal of the proprietor of the "Green Man" to supply two soldiers in uniform with liquid refreshment, that hon. member may be certain that he will achieve a popularity out of all proportion to the service he has rendered the army.

High politics include, of course, the Russo-Japanese War. As to the cause of that unhappy conflict no opinion is offered, since that is a matter which does not greatly concern the soldier; but the conduct of the campaign has won unstinted admiration for the plucky little Easterners.

I learnt this much from Smithy (we were watching an Army Cup match), and I learnt also that the popularity of a foreign Power may easily be exploited with profit.

"We 'ad a long talk about it the other night down in our room. Dusty Miller—him with the crooked nose—said that the Japs was winnin' because they'd got a better rifle than the Russians. Jimmy Walters said it was because the officers was more friendly with the men than what ours was.

"'All you chaps are talkin' through your 'eads,' sez Nobby; 'it ain't rifles, it ain't guns, and it ain't officers.'

"'You know a fat lot,' Spud Murphy stuck in, 'If it ain't none of them, what is it?'

"'*Jue Jitsoo*,' sez Nobby, with a cough.

"'Who's she, Nobby?' I sez, an' all the other chaps said the same.

"'*Jue Jitsoo*,' sez Nobby slowly, 'is a sort of thing that you hit a chap without touchin' him, in a manner of speakin'.'

"'Talk sense, Nobby,' sez Spud, 'an',' he sez, 'don't try to talk about things you don't know nothin' about.'

"'I'll show you what I mean,' sez Nobby, gettin' up from 'is cot. 'I read about it in a book I bought—come 'ere, Dusty.'

"'What for?' sez Dusty, shrinkin' back.

"'I want to show you 'ow it's done,' sez Nobby, takin' orf 'is coat an' rolling up 'is sleeves.

"'Show Smithy,' sez Dusty.

"'Show Spud,' I sez, very hasty.

"Spud didn't like the idea, but Nobby said it was all right.

"'If you 'urt me,' sez Spud, threatenin', 'it's me an' you for it, Nobby.'

"'Don't cry,' sez Nobby, takin' 'old of Spud's arm an' then started to explain.

"'Suppose you're a thief,' 'e sez.

"'No snacks,' sez Spud.

"'Suppose you come up to me on pay-night an' try to pick my pocket.'

"'You ain't ever got anything on a pay-night,' sez Spud, with a larf.

"'Well,' went on Nobby, not takin' any notice of Spud, 'I just ketch 'old of you like this—an' that—an' there you are.'

"An' before Spud knew what was happenin' there he was, on the floor—*whack!*

"'Don't you do that again,' sez Spud, gettin' up.

"'Now,' sez Nobby, gettin' Spud by the throat, 'suppose you're a dangerous criminal an' I'm a policeman—'

"'Leggo,' sez Spud, strugglin'.

"'I just push you in the face, kick your leg, butt you with my 'ead—and there you are!' An' down went Spud on 'is back—*bang!*

"'Look 'ere,' sez Spud—he never could take a joke—'look 'ere,' he sez, 'don't you try your funny tricks on me, Nobby, or—'

"'What's the good of gettin' out of temper,' sez Nobby, an' we all said the same, so did a lot of chaps who'd come up from the room downstairs when they 'eard Spud fall. So we told him it was for the good of the reg'ment, an' we was all learnin' Ju-What's-its-name, an' we said no one else was strong enough to be, experimented on, an' so we calmed him down, an' he said he'd go on bein' an experiment.

"'Suppose I'm a robber,' sez Nobby, 'an' try to pinch your watch. Now what you've got to do is to catch 'old of my throat an' 'arf strangle me.'

"'I can do that,' sez Spud, brightenin' up.

"'An' what I've got to do is to prevent you,' sez Nobby. 'Now here I come, pretendin' to lift your watch.'

"It was as good as a pantomime to watch Spud waitin' to land one on Nobby when 'e got close enough; but somehow when Spud jumped forward to choke Nobby, Nobby wasn't there, an' down went Spud all in a 'eap.

"'E got up, feelin' 'is legs to see if they was broke, an' Shiner Williams, who happened only to arrive at that minute, asked Nobby to do it again, because he wasn't lookin' at the time.

"'That's what you call *Ju-jitsoo,* is it?' sez Spud.

"'Yes,' sez Nobby, puttin' on 'is coat, 'that's why the Japs always win, an' the Russians always lose.'

"'That's *Ju-jitsoo,* is it!' sez Spud, takin' orf 'is coat.

"'That's it, Spud,' sez Nobby. 'I 'ope it'll be a lesson to you—I don't charge you anything for learnin' you—but I'm willin' to give lessons at fourpence a time to any young military gentleman present. Who'll 'ave four-penn'oth?'

"'That's *Ju-jitsoo,* is it' sez Spud, in a sort of dream; an' that 'e makes a rush, an' knocks poor old Nobby over an' sits on him.

"'What's the *Ju-jitsoo* for this, Nobby?' sez Spud, givin' him a punch.

"'Lemme get up,' sez Nobby.

"'Suppose you're a big-footed liar of a soldier what gets flattened out an' sat on for bein' too comic—what do you do next?' sez Spud, givin' Nobby a smack on the 'ead.

"'I haven't read that part yet,' gasps Nobby 'Let me get up an' 'ave a dekko at the book.'

"'Let 'im get up, Spud,' I sez.

"'Hullo, Smithy,' sez Spud, 'what are you stickin' your ugly nose in for?'

"'Never mind my nose,' I sez ;'let Nobby get up, or I'll give you a wipe in the eye,' I sez.

"'I see,' sez Spud. '*Ju-jitsoo* means always havin' a fat-'eaded pal handy to take your part,' he sez"

12.—The New Officer

"The officer," said Private Smithy, of the 1st Anchesters, "is a new officer. It isn't the new kind of uniform, or the new Salvation Army cap, or the new silly way of wearing his shoulder sash. He's a changed officer, if you understand. He don't look no different, and in many ways he's not altered a bit. He still plays polo an' bridge—what's bridge?"

I explained.

"Well, he still does all these things just about as much as ever he did, but I tell you 'e's an astounding blighter in many ways."

"It ain't so long ago," reflected this monument of the First Army Corps, "when officers used to come on parade at 10 a.m.—commanding officers' parade drill order—and we used to look at 'em hard to discover whether we'd seen 'em before. They used to troop down from the officers' mess buttoning up their brown gloves and hooking on their swords under their patrol jackets. They'd stand about for a minute or two yawnin' their blankey 'eads orf an' then the bugled sound 'Officers come and be blowed,' an' they'd fall in.

"Well, the colour-sergeant was always waitin' for 'em.

"'What's on this mornin',' says me fine captain.

"'Battalion drill, sir,' says the flag.

"'Oh, dash battalion drill,' sez the captain, walkin' round an' inspectin' the company. Take this man's name, colour-sergeant, for wearing his pouch on the right side.'

"'Beg pardon, sir,' sez the flag, 'they're wore on the right side.'

"'So they are,' sez the intelligent captain, givin' a casual glance along the line. 'Well, take his name for 'aving a dirty belt.'

"'Right, sir,' sez the colour-sergeant.

★★★★★★

"When the inspection was over the officer would draw his sword and read the writin' on it, and draw noughts and crosses with it on the ground; then fall in six paces ahead of the centre of his company. Bimeby he'd see something 'appening to the company ahead of his.

"'What's goin' on there, colour-sergeant?' he'd ask.

"'Formin' fours, sir,' sez the colour-sergeant.

"'Oh, I forgot all about,' that, sez his nibs. 'Company! Form fours!'

an' not a man moves.

"'You 'aven't numbered 'em, sir,' sez the colour-sergeant.

"'Hey?' sez the captain, gettin' red. 'Then why the dickens ain't they numbered when they fall in? Number off from the right, an' be quick about it.'

"Then comes the battalion drill," continued Smithy, with a sad, reminiscent smile. "The colonel shouts something.

"'What's that he said, colour-sergeant,' sez the officer.

"'Into line, right form, sir,' sez the flag.

"'What do I do?' sez the captain.

"'Turn half-right, sir, and wait for the word "march,"'" whispers the flag.

"And right through the drill it was the same. Sometimes the captain was right, sometimes he was wrong. Sometimes he had the whole company jumbled up in horrid confusion, and the colonel would come prancing along and say things he was probably sorry for afterwards.

"Well, an hour of this sort of thing went on, and then it was 'Right turn—Dismiss,' and the officer would run away and change his sword an' uniform for a Sunday suit an' a panamar hat, and we didn't see him again till tomorrow."

★★★★★★

Smithy raised himself on his elbow and addressed the orderly man staggering tentward with a big kettle of steaming tea.

Would the orderly man be so kind as to give Smithy a basin of tea and save him the trouble of coming to the tent for it. Without checking his career, the orderly man remarked, "Oh, yes, why not, not 'arf. Would Smithy like him (the orderly man) to drink it for him (Smithy)? Did he want waiting on? Should he fetch it in a feeding bottle?" and sundry other ejaculations of a bitterly satirical character.

Whereupon Smithy, realising that the enemy was rapidly getting out of range, delivered a rapid *feu de joie* of personalities, calculated to annoy and distress a young and ambitious orderly man.

"'Pon my word," said Smithy gloomily, "these blanked Brodericks are gettin' worse an' worse; the men 'ave changed as much as the officers."

"How have the officers changed?" I asked.

"I was going to tell you,' said Smithy. "As I said before, it's only' an inward change. You know soldiers, don't you?"

"I do."

"Well, you've seen Tommy get converted—get religion, haven't you? He drops the wet canteen, and spends his time in the library playin' bagatelle with other bun-wallahs. The cloth is always torn, and the cues 'ave no tips," added Smithy inconsequently. "He goes to chapel on week nights and shows up the regiment by prayin' in public; joins the Templars with fancy grips and passwords and sashes. Well, beyond giving up booze and saying 'confound' instead of '——' or '——' or '——', there ain't much difference, outwardly at least. He still parts his hair; he still mashes the girls; he still does all things 'uman—except swear and drink.

"So it is with the officer—'e's changed inwardly. He plays polo and golf—which is a, rotten game in my opinion—and motors.

"But somehow we seem to see more of him than we used. He comes nosing around at all hours of the day. He does colour-sergeants' work and corporal's work—in fact, he knows as much about soldiering now as we do. He doesn't make mistakes on parade; he turns up at the rifle range even when it ain't his turn for duty; he'll take a dozen chaps out into the country and teach them how to sketch; he spends a lot of his spare time learning flag-wagging—in fact, in fact," said Smith, struggling for a climax, "he's a more astoundin' person than ever."

★★★★★★

Smithy refilled and relit his pipe and ruminated for some moments.

"Yesterday," said he, "the little man French had us out attackin' or defendin'—I don't know which—a bit of a village, over there." Smithy pointed vaguely. "I was with a half company under Mr. Brick-Taylor—he gets his company next month. We've got a new colour-sergeant from the second battalion who's been used to giving officers tips all his life.

"We were scoutin' ahead, and we sighted the enemy outside a pub near Frinham. We could see them, they couldu't see us.

"'Git into that *donga*,' sez the officer, pointin' to a big, deep ditch.

"'Beg pardon, sir,' says the flag, 'I think you ought to extend the men and retire, sir.'

"'Oh, you do, do you?' sez the officer, 'well, I don't; get into the *donga* as quick as you can.'

"'Beg pardon, sir,' sez the flag, 'but the book sez—'

"'What book?' sez the officer.

"'Drill book, sir,' sez the colour-bloke.

"'Never read it,' sez the little man as calm as you please.

"'I'm takin' cover and hidin', because I once got plugged in the neck by a Mauser bullet for not doin' so. I am not retiring in open order accordin' to the book because I tried something like it at Magersfontein and appeared in all the London papers the next mornin' as 'dangerously.'

A bugle call rang out sharp and clear, a, dozen tents disgorged one or two men, who buttoned their coats as they hurried to the guard tent.

"Defaulters," said Smithy, shifting his position to one of greater comfort; "all young soldiers, an' punishment's good for 'em—it's surprisin' how a few kicks help a man in the army."

13.—THE AGITATOR

"Heard about our secret society?" asked Smithy.

I assured him that I had not heard the faintest whisper of anything so alarming.

Smithy laughed, as though he had suddenly remembered something amusing.

"Chap named Oats—Shaker Oats we call him—got nine months' service, an' to hear him talk you'd a-thought he was born in Buckin'ham Palace, the side he put on.

"He blew into the army when no one was lookin', and he was so surprised to find hisself in airproof clothes an' boots that didn't let in the showery weather that he began to swell; and when he'd got used to not feelin' hungry he began to let on about the way the pore soldier was treated, an' how civilians thought soldiers was dogs, an' how we was defendin' the Empire for a shillin' a day whilst bits of putty-faced boys earnin' a pound a week was walkin' out our girls.

"One day Nobby comes to me an' sez, 'Where's Oatsey?'

"'Defendin' the Empire,' I sez, 'by learnin' which end of the rifle the bang comes from'—for Oatsey about that time was doin' his recruit's course of musketry.

"'Heard about the secret society?' sez Nobby.

"'Good Templars?' I sez.

"'No, Oatsey's,' sez Nobby.

"It appears that Oatsey got a lot of chaps together in the wet canteen an' told 'em he was goin' to form to secret society called 'The Pore Soldiers' Anti-Slavery League.' The chaps wouldn't listen to him at first, but he paid for a pint all round an' told 'em all about it.

"The news that Oatsey was havin' a meetin' an' standin' free beer got out, an' Nobby Clark was nearly trampled to death tryin' to get into the canteen to second old Oatsey's motion.

"Well, they got a lot of rules out, an' a new kind of grip invented by Nobby, an' a password, an' a sign, so that everybody should know a brother.'

"It didn't want no password or sign, or grip either.

"You couldn't miss the brothers. They used to sit round Oatsey, sayin' 'Hear, hear,' while Oatsey was payin' for the beer, an' when Oatsey had spent all his money, one of the brothers would rise an' move that the meetin' should adjourn till next payday.

"'Our motter is,' Oatsey would say, 'a fair day's work for a fair day's pay, an' one man's as good as another'; an' the general idea was that the secret society should be a trade union of soldiers.

"There was lots of special ideas, but most of 'em wasn't worth mentionin'.

"One was that every brother should pay for his own beer. Oatsey put that in hisself, an' it nearly broke up the society.

"Me and Nobby didn't go to any of the meetin's after that rule was made. Oatsey said that all the army would join if we once got it fairly started.

"S'pose we was at war.

"The 1st Anchesters (the Anchester branch of the Pore Soldiers' Anti-Slavery League, as it'd be then) would be waitin' to attack.

"Up gallops one of the glitterin' staff.

"'Take your battalion forward, Colonel Gollingham,' he sez.

"'Very good, sir,' sez the colonel, an' orders the bugler to sound the advance.

"Not a chap moves.

"'What the somethin' bad does this mean?' yells the colonel. 'Advance! you unmentionable horrors!'

"Then Oatsey steps out of the ranks—him bein' the perpetual President of the League—with all his sashes an' decorations on.

"'Beg pardon, sir,' he sez, 'we can't go on. A fair day's work for a fair day's pay,' he sez, 'is a motter we all adore, an' we've done our eight hours already.'

"'But,' sez the colonel, 'think of the regiment—think of yourselves—think of the country.'

"'There ain't no joy in workin' unless you're workin' for yourself,' Oatsey sez gloomily; 'the country can look after itself, an' as to the trade—I mean the reg'ment —we only do what we do because we're paid for it.'

"By this time the colonel's half orf his head.

"'But the enemy—you blitherin' flat-footed ass—they'll defeat us—they'll—'

"'We're indifferent to the enemy,' sez Oatsey proudly, 'an' the sooner they know it the better.'

"Or p'raps," Smithy went on, letting his fancy run free, "p'raps we're advancin' in workin' hours, an' suddenly Oatsey shouts out, 'Halt!'

"Along comes the colonel, sayin' 'Rotterdam' as fast as he can.

"'What's the meanin' of this?' he sez.

"'Very sorry,' sez Oatsey, as cool as you please, 'but we can't charge alongside of the North Wessex Regiment.'

"'Why?' sez the colonel, among other things.

"'Because,' sez Oatsey, 'the North Wessex is a non-union regiment,' he sez, an' wot's more, the Colonel of the Wessex has got shares in a tied-house brewery, wot's a monopoly.'

"'Think of the honour of the country,' sez the pore old colonel.

"'I can't,' sez Oatsey, as bold as brass, 'an' wot's more, I can't let the members—I mean the men— think either; it would overstrain their physical capacity,' sez Oatsey.

"So we get defeated again," said Smithy, with some relish. "Sometimes the army would stand out for extra overtime, just when the enemy was gettin' guns into position; sometimes we'd want to knock off on Saturdays at two o'clock. Sometimes, at the minute the enemy was goin' to strike, we'd strike too.

"That was Oatsey's idea.

"He said one man was as good as another, an' every man that worked for hisself was workin' for the country, an' it didn't much matter about the country, anyway.

"One night I met Nobby Clark down town.

"'Smithy,' he sez 'do you want to join another secret society?'

"' Who's payin' for the beer this time?' I sez.

"'Nobody,' sez Nobby, larfin'.

"'Wot's it called?' I sez.

"'The Society for Givin' Old Oatsey a Barrack-Room Court-Martial,' sez Nobby.

"'Put me down as a honor'y member,' I sez quick.

"That night when Oatsey was defendin' the Empire by sleepin' in his cot, me an' Nobby an' Bill Tasker an' Pug Williams an' a few more chaps pulled him out of bed by the leg.

"'Wot's up?' sez Oatsey, nubbin' his eyes.

"'The Empire's in danger,' sez Nobby.

"'No larks!' sez Oatsey, tryin' to get up.

"So we sat him on a form an' read the funeral service out of his own Prayer Book. Then Nobby, bein' the President of the Court, sez:—

"'Private Oatsey, you are charged, accordin' to King's Regulations an' the manual of Military Law, with conspirin' with others not yet in custody—'

"'You drunk my beer, anyway,' sez Oatsey.

"'Don't make your crime worse, young feller.' sez Nobby—'With mutiny an' other crimes too numerous to mention. With tryin' to form a silly fool of a league *an' cetrer, an' cetrer.*'

"So they sentenced him," said Smithy cheerfully.

"To what?" I asked.

"To punishment," answered Smithy evasively.

"Anyway, that broke up our secret society, for old Oatsey paraded at the orderly-room the next mornin' an' asked to be transferred to another reg'ment. He said the Anchesters was so noisy they made his head ache."

14.—MISSING WORDS

Many years ago a popular periodical offered a pound a week for life as a prize for the solution of a problem.

It is one of the glorious traditions of the British Army that this prize went to a soldier.

Since when, as Smithy pointed out, newspaper competitions have enjoyed considerable popularity in the junior service.

I am inclined to agree with my military friend that sufficient attention has not been paid to the soldier in the matter of competitions, and although, as I am willing to admit, there were points about Private Clark's venture which border perilously close upon the illegal, not to say criminal, I share Smithy's admiration for the genius of the inventor.

"A chap named Macpherson—the chap that said 'e was as good as the colonel if 'e'd bin born in diff'rent circumstances—won a prize from the *Anchester Guardian*," said Smithy. "We all went in for it, me an' Nobby Clark, Spud Murphy, 'Appy Johnson, Dusty Miller—oh, an' a lot of us.

"The competition was to fill in a word at the end of a line. It went some'ow like this:—

The British soldier is renowned all the world over for his pluck.
On the march nothin' is so remarkable as his tremendous—

"You 'ad to fill in a bit of paper with the last word that wasn't there, and send it in.

"I put 'weariness,' Spud put 'grousin,' Dusty Miller put 'stiffness,' 'Appy Johnson got a word out of the dictionary, 'acumen,' another chap in 'H' put 'thirst,' an' Nobby sent two papers—they cost a penny each too—one with 'feet,' an' the other with 'corns.'

"It appears that old Mac sent in 'endurance,' an' got the prize, an' Nobby was very wild, an' said it wasn't fair to use words that wasn't in the dictionary.

"'E got more friendly towards night, though, an' when old Mac come into the canteen for 'is supper beer, Nobby walks up to 'im an' shakes 'ands.

"'Good luck to you, Mac,' sez Nobby, 'I'm very glad it's you that's got it,' 'e sez; if it'd been anybody else they wouldn't 'ave offered to share all round, share an' share alike.'

"'No more don't I,' sez Mac, short an' sweet.

"'Don't say that, Mac,' sez Nobby, very hurt; don't say that, an' you a Socialist, too.'

"'I ain't a Socialist when I've got any money,' sez Mac 'it's only poverty that makes men Socialists.'

"'Ain't you goin' to share, you long-'aired anarchist?' sez Nobby.

"'No,' sez Mac, 'I ain't.'

"Old Nobby thought a bit. 'Well, don't, 'e sez, an' something else.

"'Go there yourself,' sez Mac.

"Next mornin' after the eleven o'clock parade Nobby comes to me an' sez:—

"'Comin' in my competition, Smithy?'

"'Wot competition?' I sez.

"'A new one I've got up for the troops,' 'e sez, an', sure enough, 'e wasn't jokin', for it was all over barracks that Nobby was offerin' two quid to anybody who answered a question what he writ on a bit of paper in the canteen.

"This was the competition. Nobby put down this on a paper.

Notice

I have writ down two words, an' the first chap who comes up to me and gives me sixpence an' says them will have two pounds.

"Of course, nobody believed old Nobby, but 'e showed 'em the two sovereigns an' the paper with the words on, all sealed up with sealin'-wax, an' by and by Weary Walker, of 'G,' sez, 'Well, I'll 'ave sixpennorth. 'Ere's your tanner, Nobby—is it "Good mornin'?"'

"'No,' sez Nobby, prompt.

"So then Tiny White spent sixpence, an' said: 'Wot, Nobby!' But Nobby shook 'is 'ead an' bought a pint of beer with the money.

"Chaps come from every company to try then luck. Some said, 'Nice day'; some said, 'How's things?' some said 'Buck up,' but Nobby only shook 'is 'ead an' took the money.

"Our corporal got fed up with people always rushin' into our barrack-room just as we were going to 'ave dinner.

"'I've got it, Nobby,' they'd say, tremblin' with excitement.

"'Give us your money first,' sez Nobby; an' they'd part like birds.

"'It's "Shoulder arms"' they'd say, or 'Mark time,' or 'Form fours,' an' 'old out their mits for the two pounds.

"'Wrong,' sez Nobby sadly, an' they'd go away quite disappointed.

"One day our corporal, Pidgin' Partridge, the chap with the funny face, said, 'Look here, Clark, if any more of them corner boys of 'H' come running in at dinner-time, I'll say two words. "Guard room," they'll be, an' don't you forget it.'

"Well, it got about somehow that the two words Nobby put down was what you'd call a chap who dropped a rifle on your toe, or breathed on your buttons, or put an oil rag on your white belt, an' for three days the troops used to come up to Nobby, pay 'im sixpence, an' swear at him.

"One night when Nobby was out in town, old Tom Coke of 'G' comes runnin' into my barrack-room.

"'Where's Nobby?' 'e sez.

"'Down town,' I sez.

"'I've thought of the two words,' 'e sez, all in a twitter. 'Where can I find 'im?'

"'Down at the theatre seein' *The Gallant Soldier Lad.'*

"'In the gallery or in the pit?' 'e sez.

"'In the private boxes, fat'ed,' I sez, and 'e runs out.

"It appears Nobby was sittin' in the front row of the gallery, when old Cokey came in and spotted 'im.

"The villain was smokin' a cigarette an' tellin' the 'ero that 'e was only a common soldier, an' all the girls in the audience was snivellin', and all the chaps was blowin' their noses, when Cokey shouts:

"'Nobby!'

"Nobby looks round, an' so did the audience.

"'Catch this tanner, Nobby,' an' Cokey threw a sixpence.

"Nobby 'adn't got the face to catch it, so it fell on the 'ead of a young militia officer in the stalls.

"'Turn 'im out!' shouts everybody, an' the villain on the stage lit another cigarette.

"'It's blank, blank!' shouts Cokey, strugglin' with a chucker-out.

"Well, the end of it was that old Cokey got seven days for usin' horrible language in a public theatre and creatin' a disturbance.

"Then it got about that the two words was what you'd say to a chap if you wanted to stand treat, an' 'arf a dozen fellers paid sixpence to say, 'Drink up,' ''Ave another,' an' 'What's yours?' but Nobby always said 'Beer,' an' took their sixpences.

"They got fed up after a bit: Nobby 'ad collected thirty-seven an' six, an' nobody managed to guess the words.

"'Let's see that paper, Nobby,' sez Spud Murphy one night; 'we're tired of payin' you tanners, and we're goin' to give the riddle up. What's the words?'

"Nobby looked at me an' sort of considered.

"'I'll give you all another chance,' 'e sez, at 'arf price.'

"But there was no takers.

"'Let's see the paper, Nobby,' sez Mac, who'd spent two an' six on five guesses.

"'What paper?' sez Nobby.

"'The paper them words are on,' sez Spud.

"Nobby thought a bit, then took the paper from 'is pocket an' broke the sealin'-wax.

"All the chaps crowded round when Nobby opened the paper, an' looked over 'is shoulder.

"'Why, there's nothin' written on it at all!' sez Spud Murphy, very indignant.

"Nobby looked surprised.

"'I must 'ave forgotten to put 'em down,' 'e sez. ''Ere, Smithy, lend us a bit of pencil, an' I'll put 'em down now,' 'e sez."

15.—The New Rules

"You mustn't think," warned Smithy, "that soldiers are soft or silly, or easily got over, just because Nobby Clark's got a way of takin' 'em in."

"Nobby's got what I call an artful way, an' there's no doubt at all," added Private Smith, impressively, "that what Nobby don't know ain't worth knowin'.

"We was havin' a talk the other night about cricket. Well, everybody knows that 'B' Company is the worst cricket company in the regiment, an' the other chaps was chaffin' me an' Nobby about it.

"'Look 'ere, Spud,' sez Nobby, solemnly, 'when you talk about us not knowin' how to play cricket you're only showin' up your ignorance. It's you that don't know how to play cricket—real cricket.'

"'How so, Nobby?' sez Spud.

"'Why, sez Nobby, 'you chaps don't play accordin' to the new military rules.'

"'What new rules?' sez Spud.

"So Nobby explained a few of the new rules for military players, an' everybody was very surprised' to hear 'em.

"'Where did you pick 'em up?' sez Spud, suspiciously.

"'When I was a referee,' 'e sez.

"'You mean umpire,' sez Spud.

"'It's called referee under the new rules,' sez Nobby, calmly.

"'It's my belief,' sez Spud Murphy, 'you don't know anything about the new rules.'

"Still," explained Smithy, with an admiring wag of his head, "it was easy to see that a lot of chaps believed old Nobby—especially chaps of our company—when Nobby told 'em that if the game'd been played under proper rules they wouldn't 'ave lost a match last year, an' the end of it was our company agreed to play 'G'—the best cricket company in the regiment—an' Nobby offered to be referee.

"Spud Murphy wanted two referees, but Nobby said that wasn't allowed under the new rules. So Spud. 'ad to be content—although 'e groused! like anything an refused to play for us.

"'Let 'im play for "G",' sez Nobby, and Spud was allowed to play for the other side.

"There was lots of bets on the game, an' Spud made a bit of row because he 'eard that Nobby was backin' 'B' company very heavy.

"'Umpires ain't allowed to bet,' sez Spud, an' Nobby referred 'im to the new rules. Spud went all over the town tryin' to buy a book of the new rules, but couldn't.

"Everybody went over to the cricket ground to see the match, an' Nobby was there with a book under his arm.

"The other side won the toss, an' Crawley an' Spud Murphy was the first men in, an' I could see Spud didn't 'arf like it.

"'None of your larks, Nobby,' sez Spud.

"'Go on, my man,' sez Nobby, very haughtily, 'attend to your business, an' don't talk to the referee.'

"'If you give me out,' sez Spud, wettin' 'is hand, an' catchin' hold of the bat, 'you just look out for yourself.'

"'Out!' sez Nobby.

"'What for?' roars Spud, an' all the chaps come runnin' up.

"'I warn you off the field,' sez Nobby, firmly, 'for threatenin' the referee.'

"There was an 'orrible row, an' one of the chaps went over an' brought Corporal Mason, who's a football referee, to decide it. 'E come over an' said 'e didn't know anything about cricket, but if Spud insulted the referee, 'e'd have to leave the field, which Spud did amid loud cheers from 'B' Company.

"In one way an' another," said Smithy, "Nobby got all the 'G' chaps out for eleven.

"Spiky Brown was put out for hittin' a ball outside the boundary, old 'Ampshire Giles got run out naturally, Billy Pain was out for makin' remarks to the referee, two other chaps was out for hittin' the ball with the wrong side of the bat, an' the rest was out under one of Nobby's new rules.

"Me an' 'Appy Johnson was the first to bat for our side, an' Billy Pain was the bowler.

"The first ball I got I just managed to touch, an' it" sort of glanced off my bat into Spud Murphy's hands.

"How's that?' yells Spud.

"'Not out!' sez Nobby.

"'It is out!' roars Spud, indignantly.

"'What did you want to ask me for?' sez Nobby, 'if you knew all about it? Go on with the game.'

"But they wouldn't go on until Nobby explained the rule. It appears, by Nobby's rule, a chap that's been warned off the field by the referee ain't allowed to get a man out, either by catchin' or bowlin'.

"'It's part of the punishment, Spud,' sez Nobby, sadly. 'I can't help you, my poor feller; I didn't make the rules,'

"'I don't know so much about that,' sez Spud, fiercely.

"We went on with the game, an' bimeby a ball come along an' sent my middie stump flyin'.

"'How's that?' sez the bowler.

"Nobby hesitated for a bit an' looks at the stumps, an' then looks at me.

"'How's that!' shouts 'G' Company, very wild.

"'Out,' sez Nobby, 'quite out, by the rules of the game.'

"After this 'G' Company began to brighten up a bit; they could see there was something in Nobby's rules after all.

"There was a bit of sensation in court, in a manner of speakin', a few minutes after, when 'Appy Johnson gave 'is bat a swing backward an' knocked the bails off.

"'How's that?' shouts the wicket-keeper.

"'Not out,' sez Nobby, very prompt.

"'Why not?' shouts Spud Murphy, gettin' red in the face.

Nobby turns on 'im sternly. 'I've 'ad to speak to you once before, young feller, an' if I 'ave any more cheek from you, I'll deal severely with you.'

"'But why ain't 'Appy out?' sez Spud, very persistent.

"Nobby thought an' thought, while everybody stood waitin', an' then, when 'e couldn't think of anything to say, 'e sez: 'I refuse to discuss the matter; go on with the game.'

"''Appy got out after a bit by bein' clean bowled, an' although Nobby said it was a 'no ball,' 'e allowed 'Appy to go out, becos' the other side was doin' so badly.

"The game stood eleven all when our last man, Dusty Miller, went in, an' the excitement was intense.

"Before the play started, Nobby goes up to Dusty an' starts givin' him tips.

"'What you want to do, Dusty,' sez Nobby,, 'is to keep well in front of the wicket, an' if you see the ball comin' straight for the stumps, put your bat down so as it can't get past. Get a bye if possible, because that's easiest, an—'

"'Ere!' interrupts Spud Murphy, who was gettin' quite vexed, ''ere, Nobby, you're the bloomin' umpire; you ain't allowed to give tips.'

"'Ho! ain't I?' sez Nobby, indignant. 'Ain't allowed to give tips, when I've got four shillin's on the game?'

"'No,' roars Spud.

"'Proceed with the game,' sez Nobby politely, 'an' keep your face closed, Mr. Murphy, if you please.'

"Dusty did very well," commended Smithy. "All the balls that come straight for the wicket 'e stopped, either with his bat or with his leg, an' Nobby patted him on the back once and said 'Bravo.'

"'Then a nice slow ball come along, an' Dusty, bein' encouraged by what Nobby said, went 'arf way down the pitch to meet it.

"'E gave it such a sort of swingin' round-about cut an' drove it be'ind 'im.

"It would 'ave got a boundary, only Nobby appeared to be standin' in the way.

"The ball caught 'im in the middle of the chest, an' down dropped Nobby, blue in the face an' gaspin'.

"We all gathered round, an' Gus Ward, who was lookin' on, gave Nobby some artificial—what-do-you-call-it?—sort of dumb-bell exercise for drownded people.

"Bimeby Nobby came round, an' 'e glares at Dusty.

"'Are you 'urt, Nobby?' sez Dusty, anxious.

"'Urt!' gasps Nobby, faintly; 'yes, I am,' 'e sez, 'but you!—you're "out" an' warned orf the field by the new rules,' 'e sez."

16.—THE CHEF

"The thing about the army, that's the most curious," said the informing Smithy, "is that you never know what a chap's been before he enlisted.

"You see a smart-lookin' chap, smart tunic, white belt, little boots, an' a nice curl down over 'is for-'ead, an' you say to yourself, 'That chap was a gentleman before 'e enlisted, I'll bet;' but the chances are he was only a costermonger.

"Similarly you see a chap untidy, a chap who don't like shavin', an' generally keeps hisself to hisself, an' you put 'im down as a corner boy, when the chances are he's 'ad a good education, an' as likely as not 'e's been a chap like you—made 'is livin' by puttin' bits in the paper.

"There's quite a lot of respectable young fellers in the army supposed to be single who dursen't go near a work'ouse for fear 'arf a dozen little 'eads will pop over the wall an' start shoutin' 'Father!' an' *visa versa*.

"I don't trouble my 'ead very much about what a chap's been, although I've often wondered what Nobby was before 'e enlisted.

"We 'ad a bit of an argument about it the other day when Nobby was out, an' Spud Murphy said he thought Nobby must 'ave been somethin' that gets money without work.

"'I'll bet,' sez Spuds, 'if you look on Nobby's attestation paper you'll see 'im described as a "labourer," like all chaps are that don't like work.'

"Dusty Miller thought Nobby must 'ave been a railway porter, because 'e never gets pally with a chap unless 'e's got some money.

"At any rate," said Smithy, with a faint grin, "the question was, in a manner of speaking settled, for a few days after Nobby was sent for to the orderly-room an' paraded before the adjutant.

"'I see,' sez the adjutant, who was looking over Nobby's papers, 'that you describe yourself as a "cook"—is that right?'

"'Yes, sir,' sez Nobby, without battin' an eye.

"'What sort of a cook are you?' says the adjutant, lookin' 'ard at Nobby.

"'Very good, sir,' sez Nobby modestly.

"'Well,' sez the adjutant, 'we're tryin' a new system of messin', so you can report yourself to the master cook for duty—you're "B" Company's cook.'

"There was tremendous excitement in 'B' when it got out that Nobby was the new cook. Spud Murphy went up an' saw the adjutant, an' asked to be transferred to another company.

"'I don't want to say anything about Private Clark, sir,' 'e sez, 'but I'm a very delikit eater, an' Clark an' me ain't good friends.'

"All the chaps got round Nobby in the barrack room, an' started firin' questions at him.

"'What are you going to make us, Nobby?' they sez.

"'Wait an' see,' sez Nobby, cautious.

"'Are you a French cook, Nobby?' sez Weary Thompson.

"'A bit French,' sez Nobby, 'an' a bit Spanish. I'm what you call a chef.'

"'What's that, Nobby?'

"'That's the bit of French I was tellin' you about,' sez 'e.

"Nobby went into the town an' bought a cookery book that tells you 'ow to take stains out of silk dresses an' 'ow to clean old pictures, an' started studyin' this for all 'e was worth.

"Nobby took over the duty on Monday, and after havin' a few words with the master cook about some kit the sergeant missed as soon as Nobby come on duty, he sort of calmed him by tellin' him about a few French dishes e'd learnt about.

"'We'll 'ave some "*Poulett de Anchester*" today,' sez Nobby.

"'What's that?' sez the master cook—Sergeant Brown, the fat sergeant, you know.

"'Roast chicken an' caper sauce,' sez Nobby, proudly.

"'Don't be a fool, Clark,' sez the sergeant, nastily. 'We 'aven't got any chicken, you know that.'

"'Then we'll have *pot pourri*,' sez Nobby very quick.

"'What's that?' sez the sergeant, bewildered.

"'Anything we got,' sez Nobby.

"Everybody was talkin' about the dinner, an' we was all wonderin' what we'd got in the way of food.

"Spud Murphy got his name took on the ten o'clock parade for speakin' in the ranks.

"'This afternoon,' 'e sez, very gloomy, 'the pioneers'll be wheelin' a barrer round the square, ringin' a bell an' shoutin' "Bring out your dead," the same as it was at the great fire or London.'

"When the cook-house bugle went there wasn't a man of 'B' left in the canteen—they was all sittin' tight in the barrack-room waitin' for the orderly man to bring in the dinner.

"It come up all 'ot and steamin'.

"There was potatoes an' cabbage an' a curious-lookin' lot of meat an' stuff. Spud Murphy looks over it, sniffs, an' sez: 'I'll have some potato and cabbage.'

"As a matter of fact," explained Smithy, "the dinner was very nice indeed, an' Spud began to feel small when we told 'im how we was enjoyin' it.

"When we'd nearly finished it, there was a bit of a commotion outside, an' in rushes a chap from 'C' Company. He dashes up to the table an' takes a long look at the tin the dinner come up in, an' then shouts:

"''Ere! you bloomin' thieves, you're got our dinner, an' we've got yours.'

"'Well.' sez the corporal, very kindly, 'you're welcome to it.'

"'Ho are we!' sez the 'C' man, shakin' his 'ead fiercely. 'Well, just come an' 'ave a look at the stuff we've got.'

"So we all finished up our dinner quick, with the 'C' chap lookin' on with tears in his eyes, an' walks over to 'C' Company room. The dinner was steamin' on the table, an' everybody was standin' a long way off lookin' wild an' hungry.

"'What's up?' sez our corporal.

"'That,' sez the corporal of the other room, very agitated, 'that's what's up,' sez 'e, pointin' to the dinner.

"We all looked at it; it looked all right. We smelt it; it smelt all right.

"'Taste it,' sez the other corporal.

"Our corporal 'esitated a bit, then sampled the gravy.

"Just then the orderly officer arrived to ask if there was any complaints. 'E was just goin' to ask when 'e saw our corporal.

"'What's the matter with Corporal White?' 'e sez; 'is 'e took ill?'

"'No sir,' sez the other corporal, an' then explains about the dinner, whilst me and another chap assisted our corporal into the fresh air.

"When we got back the officer was talkin'.

"'Send for Private Clark,' he sez. So they did, an' in a minute in walks Nobby lookin' very pleased with hisself —one of our chaps had told him what a success our dinner was, an' he thought the orderly officer had sent for 'im to show the 'C' cook 'ow to make a dinner.

"I will say," said Smithy, enthusiastically, "old Nobby looked every inch a chef! White coat, white 'at, an' very nearly white apron.

"'Clark,' sez the orderly sternly. 'did you prepare this?'

"Nobby was surprised to see 'B's dinner in 'C's room, but 'e looked at it, an' sez, 'Yes.'

"'What do you call it?' sez the officer.

"'*Pot pourri*,' sez Nobby, boldly.

"'Why *pot pourri?*' sez the officer.

"Nobby thought a bit.

"'Because it's poured out of a pot,' 'e sez.

"The officer looks very 'ard at Nobby.

"'What's this?' 'e sez, stirrin' a curious lookin' thing round with 'is cane.

"Nobby looks at it an' gasps, an' just then the master cook, who'd been sent for, come in.

"'Sergeant!' Nobby sez, quite excited, 'look at this!' The sergeant looked, an' he gasped.

"'P'raps,' sez , Nobby, sternly. 'you'll apologise now for accusin' me or stealin' your blackin' brush.'

17.—The Journalist

I met Smithy in the High Street, and I will not attempt to deny that Smithy did not seem the least bit pleased to see me. He was in uniform, hence I conjectured that he had lost his job as groom to Major-Somebody-or-Other on the Staff.

"Fact is," confessed Smithy, in answer to my reproaches, "I'm a bit down on newspaper chaps just now."

This was indeed mournful news.

From the day I had first met Private Smithy of the 1st Anchester Regiment, at Orange River Station, when he gave a memorable reproof to the haughty C.I.V., down, so to speak, to yesterday, Smithy's regard and esteem for the members of my profession had been most flattering.

"It's hard enough," complained Smithy bitterly, "when they won't put your bits in the paper; but when they do, and, what's more," he added, with rising wrath, "they put your blue-light name to it, why— why, it's emphatically, unprintably hard!"

And Smithy relapsed into a moody silence.

"Nobby Clark sez to me," he resumed, plunging into the thick of his grievance, "'e sez, 'Smithy, how much money've you got?'

"'Four dee,' I sez—and it was three days off payday," added Smithy, in vindication of his penury.

"'Go and borrer a couple of bob from the flag,' 'e sez.

"'You go,' I sez.

"'I've been,' 'e sez sadly.

"'So 'ave I,' I sez.

"'What did 'e say?' sez Nobby, an' I told him.

"You wouldn't think a man with a colour-sergeant's rank would use such language, would you?" asked Smithy, who gave me *verbatim* the "flag's" insulting reply to Smithy's modest demands.

"'Well,' sez Nobby, 'we must git some money somewhere; what about puttin' a bit in the papers?'

"'What shall we put?' I sez, catchin' on to the idea, for a chap I know—Fatty James, of 'B' Company—got ten shillings once for writin' to a paper that a picture of a sheep and a fence meant 'Ramsgate.'

"'Make something up,' sez Nobby; so me an' 'im went over to the library an' thought an' thought an' thought." Smithy lowered his voice to a reverential huskiness at the recollection of that evening of tremendous mental exertion.

"After about two hours," he resumed thoughtfully, "we made up a piece." He stopped beneath a street lamp, and produced a soiled half-sheet of notepaper, bearing the regimental crest.

"I copied it," he said simply, and I read:

We are give to understand upon the highest unimpechible authority that a severe muttiny broke out in the barracks of the Anchester Regiment on Friday last at 10 o'clock oweing to the uppish conduct of a certain colour-sargent of B Company trying to come the old soldier over the gallant heros of that famous regiment. We think this should be put a stop to at once as much bloodshed would not take place if certain parties knew where to draw the line.

I handed the paper back to Smithy.

"What do you think of that?" he asked anxiously. I gave it my unqualified approval.

"Well," resumed the sensationalist, "we sent it to the *Anchester Gazette*, an' they put a bit of it in, an' sends me half a james."

Which, to be exact, is ten shillings, a handsome reward, considering the *Gazette* had evidently omitted the more startling portion of the news.

"So me and Nobby writes another bit," Smithy went on—"'ere it is." A second soiled fragment of history was produced:

We hear from two who knows that another horrible muttiny came off at the barracks of the Anchester Regiment yesterday at 1.35, oweing to a certain party being a bit too clever and talking big in the canteen about his rich relations.

"That," explained Smithy hastily, "was a party named Briggs, who's got an uncle in the linen-drapin' line."

"Did they print that?" I asked.

"No," said Smithy, with a cough. "I got a letter from the head man:

Dear sir, we're tired of mutinies try us with something else.'

Smithy had the sarcastic message by heart.

"So we did," he went on gloomily; "so we did. Nobby an' me, we thought an' thought for two days."

"'Let's say there was a horrible fire in barracks,' he sez.

"'No,' I sez, 'let's say there was a horrible suicide in "B" Company,' I sez.

"'No,' sez Nobby, who's got a down on 'D' owin' to the company cook an' him being bad friends, 'let's say "D" Company has been horribly poisoned to death owin' to the way the meat's cooked!'

"Well," said Smithy, with a sigh, "we thought of everything, from a horrible discovery in the officers' quarters to the quartermaster-sergeant doin' a horrible bunk with the pay, till at last old Nobby says. 'I've got it!'

"I've got it," repeated Smithy, with a groan.

"'Is it a horrible?' I sez,

"'No,' sez Nobby, 'it ain't; it's Fanny,' he sez.

"'Oh!' I sez. 'Is it a horrible murder of the colonel's daughter?' I sez.

"'We call her Fanny," Smithy explained.

"'She's a nice girl,' sez Nobby, sort of musin'.

"'I've never noticed it,' I sez.

"'She ought to be married,' sez Nobby. 'Let's marry 'er to some-one.'

"So me an' Nobby sat up half the night tryin' to think who we could marry her to. He started with the doctor, who got Nobby seven days for shammin' toothache, and then we thought of the adjutant, who's always on my collar; but bimeby we said let bygorns be bygorns, an' we married her to the general."

I gasped, for General Stucker, blank old Stucker as be is nicknamed, because of the choice and variety of his expletives, is the most peppery old warrior in the British Army.

"We married her to the general," and Smithy's native sense of humour was responsible for the faint chuckle he gave. "Here—read this."

Another friendly lamp-post obliged.

We beg to announce with much pleasure that Miss Fanny Gollingham our colonel's daughter is walking out with General Stucker whose heroic conduct is greatly admired and the happy couple will soon leave on their honeymoon, We hope kind friends will rally round they being the first to help others.

"Did they print that?" I asked in an awestruck whisper.

"They did," said Smithy in a pained undertone.

"Well?" I asked.

"It was Nobby Clark who done it " said Smithy explosively; "he sez, 'Let's sign it "Captain Clark of 'B'" and "Major Smith of 'H,'" for a lark.'

"'Where's the lark?' I sez.

"'Why, fathead,' he sez, 'they won't put it in unless they think we know all about it,' he sez; so we signed it."

Smithy drew a crumpled newspaper cutting from his pocket:

We are happy, on the authority of Major Smith, of H Company, and Captain Clark, of B, to announce the engagement of Major-General Sir George Stucker, K.C.B., to the eldest daughter of Lieut.-Colonel Gollingham. The wedding will he celebrated at an early date, and Major Smith is to be best man.

I handed the cutting back.

"Major Smith best man!" I murmured in amazement. "So that's why you lost your job?"

"Yes" said Smithy bitterly; "Nobby put that bit in when I wasn't lookin'!"

18.—THE PHOTOGRAPHER

The War Office requests Officers Commanding Units to submit photographs and films suitable for conversion into lantern slides.   —*War Office Memorandum.*

The Officer Commanding wishes to notify N.C.O.'s and men in possession of cameras that all reasonable facilities will be given them for the purpose of securing photographs portraying Army life.   —"A" Company's orders.

★★★★★★

"It appears," explained Private Smith, "that they want to advertise the army with a magic lantern. They've got a bit tired of showin' a picture of a soldier in marchin' order, an' callin' it 'the advantages of the army.'

"We was talkin' about it the other night down in the 'Ole in the Wall, me an' Nobby Clark an' a new chap of 'A'—I forget his right name for the minute, but we call 'im Smiley—an' Spud Murphy, an' 'Appy Johnson.

"'Wot's the idea, Nobby?' sez Spud, who's been gettin' on friendly terms with me an' Nobby lately; 'wot do they want our photos for?'

"'I don't know,' sez Nobby, 'but me an' Smithy are goin' in for it—ain't we, Smithy?'

"'No,' I sez.

"'Me an' Smithy's got a camera,' sez Nobby, takin' no notice of wot I said, 'an' tomorrer we are goin' round barracks to see what we can do in the photo line.'

"I thought old Nobby was coddin', but 'e wasn't, for up 'e comes next mornin' with one of them concertina machines that pull in an' out, an at ten o'clock up goes Nobby to the Orderly Room an' asks to see the old man.

"'Well, Clark,' sez the colonel, 'what do you want?'

"'Beg pardon, sir,' sez Nobby, 'but me an' Smithy's got a camera, an' we'd like to take a few photos for the War Office,'

"The old man was as pleased as Punch. 'Very good; very good, indeed,' sez 'e. Sergeant—Major, see that Smith an' Clark are excused all parades for a week,' 'e sez. 'Is that what you want?'

"'Yes, sir,' sez Nobby.

"So me an' Nobby walked about for the rest of the week doin' nothin, an' the other chaps was very wild.

"We used to go an' watch 'em on parade an' pretend to take snapshots of 'em.

"Nobby caused a bit of unpleasantness by sayin' to the adjutant that 'e'd like to take a photograph of the regiment on parade in full marchin' order.

"'You ought to know better,' sez Spud Murphy, very fierce. 'I'm surprised at you, Nobby. There ain't another marchin' order parade for a month, an' 'ere you've been an' got orders put in for one tomorrer.'

"All the chaps in the room who was busy cleanin' their straps an' packin their valises said "'Ear, 'ear,' but me an' Nobby sat on a bed cot doin' nothin'.

"'You wait till you see yourselves in a magic lantern,' sez Nobby. 'An', besides,' 'e sez, 'I'm goin' to take a lot of you chaps by yourselves tomorrow.'

"'Free?' sez Spud, eagerly.

"'Don't be a miser,' sez Nobby, sternly; 'don't be, a miser, Spud, A tanner won't break you, will it? It costs me that.'

"''Ow do you do it, Nobby?' sez Smiler.'

"'It's as simple as drinkin', sez Nobby, gettin' down 'is camera. I point it at you, push this button, an' you're took in a minute.'

"Well, Nobby kept the regiment standing half an hour on parade next morning waitin' for the sun to come out.

"Me an' 'im was in the corner of the parade ground, 'im 'olding 'is camera, me waggin' my 'ead backward an forward, tryin' to look as if I knew all about it, an' the battalion standin' stiff to attention."

"Bimeby the adjutant sings out:

"''Ave you taken it?'

"'No, sir,' sings out Nobby.

"'Well, 'urry up,' sez he; an' Nobby obeys orders an' pushes the button.

"'I want to see that picture tomorrer,' sez the adjutant.

"'Yessir,' sez Nobby.

"Some'ow old Nobby was a bit depressed all that day. After tea 'e sez to me:

"'Smithy, come for a walk in town; I want to 'ave a bit of a chin wag.'

"'Smithy,' 'e sez when we got out that night, 'do you know anything about photos?'

"'No,' I sez.

"'No more don't I,' 'e sez, with a sort of sigh.

"'What!' I sez.

"'No,' 'e sez, 'I don't know a bloomin' thing about it. I bought this camera from a chap down the 'Igh Street. 'E sold it cheap, bein' sligh'ly damaged. It 'adn't got one of its parts. I forget which. Any'ow, the chap said it didn't matter.'

"'Look 'ere, Nobby,' I sez, stoppin' in the street, 'ave you got the monkey box with you?'

"'Yes,' 'e sez, 'I never let it out of my sight,' an' 'e pulls it out of his overcoat pocket.

"'We'll take in to that chap that takes photos, an' see what's wrong with it.'

"So we took it into the photo shop; an' Nobby tells the chap all about it. The chap looks at the camera for a bit, an' me an' Nobby looks at 'im very anxious.'

"'What do you want me to do?'

"'Take out the photos we've took,' sez Nobby.

"'*You've* took, Nobby; not me,' I sez.

"'We're both in, Smithy,' sez Nobby.''

"'There ain't no photos,' sez the photo chap.

"'No photos!' sez me an' Nobby together, an' Nobby went pale.

"'No,' sez the photo chap, 'their ain't no films.'

"'Hey?' sez Nobby.

"'Nor no lens neither,' sez the photo chap.

"'Does that make any difference?' sez Nobby.

"'You've done it!' I sez, an' I told the photo chap all about 'ow Nobby took the picture of the regiment on parade, an' 'ow the adjutant sez 'e wanted a copy of the photo tomorrow.

"'Where was it took?' sez the photo chap.

"'On parade,' I sez.

"'I've got a photo of a regiment at' 'ome took on that very parade,'

64

sez the photo chap. 'I'll tell you what I'll do when I get 'ome tonight; I'll send it on to you. You can say you took it, an' it'll be all right.'

"Old Nobby brightens up wonderful.

"'Is it our regiment?' 'e sez.

"'No,' sez the photo chap; 'but it's so small, you can't tell what regiment it is.'

"'That'll do,' sez Nobby. 'Send it straight to the adjutant.' An' we both went back to barracks 'ighly satisfied.

"Next mornin' we was sent for to the orderly room.

"'Good mornin' Clark; good mornin', Smith,' sez the adjutant, when 'e saw us. 'Nice photograph that you sent us.'

"'Yes, sir,' sez Nobby; but I said nothin'.

"'Took it yourself?' sez the adjutant.

"'Yes, sir,' sez Nobby.

"'Ah,' sez the adjutant, very affable, 'the colonel is very interested in it.'

"'Very glad to 'ear that, sir,' sez Nobby.

"The adjutant took the photo from 'is pocket an' 'anded it to Nobby.

"Nobby looks at it: so did. Then we saluted an' went back to the barrack room.

"Nobby didn't speak for a long time. When 'e did, 'e said something about the photo chap, an' then——

"'Was there anything I said to the photo chap last night that'd make 'im think we was 'Ighlanders, Smithy?'"

19.—THE BOOKMAKER

"There's lots of chaps," said Smithy, "who are walkin' about the streets without keepers who ought by rights to be down at the master tailor's bein' measured for strait weskets."

It was Smithy's Saturday to Monday vacation, which he had agreed to spend at my house. Smithy takes a delight in the discussion of all kinds of gloomy subjects. He revels in the positively dreadful and is keenly interested in the indescribably ghastly.

We had spent a pleasant Saturday evening. Starting with how it feels to be hung, we had moved by easy stages to murder as a fine art; thence to the vexed question, Should executions be public? which I think we threshed out very thoroughly. We drifted to criminal lunacy, taking a short cut by way of suicide, and it was at this point that Smithy expressed his doubt regarding the sanity of the majority of his fellow-creatures.

"With some chaps it's gels," philosophized Smithy; they get quite balmy about 'em. I know one chap—a very good character, too, with a couple of badges—' who writes poetry to his gel.

"There's a chap!" said Smithy hopelessly, "plays the concertena like—like Paddyrisky," he illustrated daringly, "an' you see him sittin' down night after night chewin' his pen like anything.

"There he sits—Cole's his name—thinkin' an' frownin' and writin' an' scratchin' out again.

"'Wot rhymes with "dear"?' he sez to Nobby Clark.

"'Beer,' sez Nobby as quick as lightnin'.

"'That won't do,' sez poor Cole. 'Wot rhymes with "waken"?'

"'Eggs an' bacon,' sez Nobby.

"'That won't do, either,' sez poor old Cole, and goes on scribblin' an' scratchin' out. Bimeby he sez:

"'What rhymes with "bell"?'

"So Nobby tells him, an' old Cole gets offended. 'I'm writin' to my gel,' he sez, 'an' I can't use that sort of language.'

"So he goes on writin' an' arskin' advice an' not takin' it. He spends nights an' nights writin' a poem about love, an' when his gel gets it, she thinks old Cole's been drinkin', an' she don't notice the words come in rhyme at the end of the lines till she's read it twice—an' then she thinks it's an accident."

Private Cole was evidently one of Smithy's eligible, for an Institute of Restraint.

"Then there's Yatesey—Yatesey of 'C'—he's another of 'em," resumed Smithy indignantly; "no, Yatesey don't write poetry, far from it. Yatesey is wot I call a dangerous lunatic. I don't so much mind a chap wot writes poetry, or even a chap wot collects stamps an' is always tryin' to swap a blue Cape of Good Hope for a pink Channel Island, but Yatesey is worse."

"Yatesey" is Smithyesque for "Yates," I may remark in passing.

"Yatesey's got a bit of money wot his father sends him from time to time. Some weeks it's a dollar, some weeks it's a couple of shillin's, just how the coke business happens to be.

"Yatesey wouldn't be a bad chap if it wasn't for his system.

"When Nobby Clark is short of money, he lures old Yatesey into the wet canteen and gets him to talk about it.

"'I think I'd like you to talk about that system of yourn, Yatesey,' sez Nobby—I tell you Nobby's one of the artfullest chaps goin'—'I've got an idea I'd like to have it explained, I've got a little bit of money left me by an uncle wot went abroad.'

"Yatesey's system is a sort of mixture. You back a first favourite for a shillin' an' if it don't come orf you back a second favourite next day for two shillin's, if that don't come orf you back the third favourite the next day for four shillin's, and by that time you've got no money left, so you can't lose much money at it," explained Smithy lucidly.

"Nobby comes to me one day an' sez:

"'I'm gettin' fed up with this chap an' his bloomin' system. It's no joke, Smithy, listenin' for an hour about how Nazzems could beat Pretty Bertie if the distance wasn't so far an' the weights was differ-ent.'

"Yatesey," explained Smithy, "used to sit down with a book of form an' a ready reckoner, an' work out how much money he'd make if he only had a startin' capital of a hundred pounds, but he never used to do no bettin' hisself till Nobby persuaded him. Some days he'd sit down with his little books an' his pint of beer an' buy a pub, an' a dogcart, an' marry a young lady in the High Street. Another day he'd go round the world on a motorcar, smokin' shillin' cigars; another day he'd buy his discharge an' then go an' give a bit of his mind to the sergeant-major, an' drive out of barracks in his own carriage, throwin' five-pound notes away out of the winder.

"I must say," confessed Smithy, "his system looked all right on pa-per, but I found out afterwards that when it didn't exactly work out he used to pretend to hisself that the horse he ought've backed accordin' to his system was another one altogether.

"Well, to get back to Nobby

"'Smithy,' sez he, lookin' round to see if nobody was listenin', 'Smithy, you've come into a tidy bit of money.'

"'Have I?' I sez.

"'Yes' he sez, 'your grandmother's left you a small fortune,' he sez, with a wink.

"'Go to!' I sez.

"'Wot's more,' sez Nobby, 'you're goin' to make a book.'

"'Wot sort of a book?' I sez, puzzled, an' then Nobby tells me, an' next mornin' when Yatesey comes along an' slips a bit of paper into my hand with a couple of bob I thanked him kindly.

"'Nonsuch, 2s. to win,' sez the paper, so I gave a shillin' to Nobby an' kept one for myself an' tore the paper up.

"Nobby comes up to me that night—

"'It's all right,' he sez, 'Nonsuch was a bad ninth,' so we spent the two shillin's.

"Next day Yatesey gives me another paper an' our shillin's.

"'Sooner, 4s. to win,' sez the paper, so me and Nobby divided the money.

"'Sooner didn't win,' sez Nobby that night. 'He stopped to scratch his ear an' dead-heated with the starter.' So we had a very pleasant evenin'.

"Old Yatesey looked a bit tired next mornin', but he turned up with a bit of paper an' eight shillin's, an' I shook hands with him, an' Nobby called him a true sportsman.

"'Pride of Devonshire, 8s. to win,' sez the paper. So me an' Nobby had four shillin's each."

Smithy helped himself to a fill of Craven.

"That night Nobby comes up lookin' ill. 'Pride of Devonshire won,' he sez, 'at ten to one,' he sez.

"An', sure enough, along comes old Yatesey, lookin' as pleased as Punch.

"'I'll trouble you for four pound eight,' he sez.

"'Wait a bit, young feller,' I sez sternly. 'Saturday's my settlin' day,' I sez, an' Nobby chips in:

"'I'm surprised at you, Yatesey, a true sportsman like you, come worryin' Smithy for a paltry four quid,' he sez, 'it'd serve you right if Smithy wouldn't bet with you again,' he sez, and Yatesey begged pardon an' hoped no offence was taken where none was meant.

"Me an' Nobby went down town to think it out," continued Smithy.

"'Let's give him back his eight shillin's an' owe him the rest,' I sez; 'tell him it was a joke.'

"Nobby was readin' the sportin' in the *Evening News*, an' bimeby he gave a yell.

"'Pride of Devonshire's disqualified,' he sez, 'for borin' an' crossin',' he sez.

"So we spent the eight shillin's and went back to barracks to break the news to Yatesey.

"Next mornin' Yatesey didn't turn up with his paper so me an' Nobby went down to see him.

"'No,' sez Yatesey, 'that system wasn't much good—it don't make no allowances for a horse bein' disqualified,' he sez. 'I'm workin' out a new system altogether.'

"'When you've got it worked out,' I sez, 'let's hear from you.'"

20.—BACK TO CIVIL LIFE

(A.k.a. Employing the Soldier)

"It's only nacheral," said Smithy, "that a feller that's been doin' nothin' for a livin' for seven years gits the idea into his 'ead that as soon as 'es out of the army 'e can go on doin' nothin' an' live comfortable.

"A chap generally enlists because 'e's very 'ard up, or there ain't no work to be got. If you understand me rightly, a chap's pushed into the army by the crowd of out-of-works behind him, an' by the time 'e's got his breath, 'an' is full up with army rations, an' finds 'e's got plenty of elbow room, 'e begins to forget all about the crowd outside, an' when his seven years' service is nearly in 'e begins to fancy that 'e really enlisted for the love of the thing, an' not because 'e was feelin' peckish.

"Then the colonel sends for 'im.

"'Ah, Thompson,' sez the colonel, 'eartily, 'I understand you're goin' away on the reserve?'

"'Yes, sir,' sez Thompson.

"'Do you think that's wise?' sez the colonel.

"'Ho, yes,' sez the clever chap, cockily.

"'It's very 'ard in civilian life just now,' sez the colonel. 'What are you goin' to do for a livin'?'

"'Anything,' sez the clever chap, prompt.

"'Humph!' sez the colonel; 'that means "nothing"—are you sure you won't sign on for another five years?'

"'I'll watch it,' sez the clever chap.

"So he goes away in a pair of loud check trousis an' a Trilby 'at, an' a tuppenny cigar, to show 'is independence.

"'E gits up to London, goes 'ome to see his people, 'as a couple of drinks, goes to a music-'all, an' spends a sovereign as free as you please. For a week 'e's as 'appy as a king. Gets up what time 'e likes, an' don't shave unless 'e wants to.

"'E's got no sergeants an' corporals to bully 'im, no officers to salute, no fatigues an' no drills, an' when 'e goes out in town 'e needn't look clean unless 'e feels inclined.

"After a week of riotous livin', most of 'is money bein' spent, 'e pops off to look for work in 'is loud check trousis with the beer stains, an' 'is Trilby 'at a bit out of shape.

"'Want a job, do you?' sez the chap where 'e goes to. 'What can you do?'

"'Anything,' sez the clever chap.

"'Outside!' sez the chap at the works. 'We don't want "anything" fellers here.'

"'What's your last job?' sez another feller 'e applies to.

"'Army,' sez the clever chap, producin' 'is discharge.

"'What can you do?' sez the foreman.

"The clever chap's learnt a lesson, so 'e's a bit cautious.

"'Messenger,' 'e sez.

"'We've got boys for messengers, sez the foreman.

"'Timekeeper,' sez the clever chap.

"'We've got a clock for that.'

"'Caretaker,' sez the clever chap.

"'We don't want no sleepin' partners,' sez the foreman.

"'Well,' sez the clever chap, desperate, 'hall porter.'

"'We ain't got a hall,' sez the foreman.

"What some of these clever jossers want," said Smithy, scornfully, "is a job where there ain't any work to do—jobs you can lay down an' watch; old men's jobs, boys' jobs, jobs that don't blister a chap's 'ands, an' that's why all the bloomin' Soldiers' 'Elp Associations in the world won't do any good, because there ain't enough of them jobs to go round.

★★★★★★

"The other day Spud Murphy gave it out that as soon as his seven years was in he was going to leave. He was" talkin' to me an' Nobby about it.

"'No more bloomin' soldierin' for me, thank you,' sez Spud.

"'Don't thank me,' sez Nobby.

"'I'm goin' to be a free man.' sez Spud, 'like I was before I enlisted.'

"'Ah!' sez Nobby, lookin' up to the sky with a smile.

"'When you chaps are bein' turned out of bed at six in the mornin' I shall be gettin' my eye down, nice an' snug.'

"'Ah!' sez Nobby.

"'No more church parades, no more kit inspections, no more bloomin' guards,' sez Spud.

"'No,' sez Nobby, getting up—we was sittin' oh the grass in the cricket field—'No,' sez Nobby, sadly. 'You'll be a free man, free to get your livin' or starve. There won't be no kit inspection, 'cos you'll 'ave no kit to show, nor no guards either, becos' nobody would trust you to guard a threepenny-bit. Pore feller,' sez Nobby, shaking his 'ead an' lookin' at Spud, 'pore old Spud.'

"Spud ain't goin' away," Smithy went on to explain, "because Nobby put it about in barracks that 'e was only leavin' the army because the doctor wouldn't pass him for an extension of service, an' just to show Nobby was a liar Spud went an' took on for another five years.

"If you understand," said Smithy earnestly, "it ain't the chap's fault that 'e can't get a job when 'e leaves the service, it's the army's. A chap that 'as to leave civil life because 'e ain't got a trade in his 'ands can't expect to go back to civil life an' find a job sittin' up on its 'ind-legs an' beggin'"

"The army don't teach 'im nothin'," continued Smithy, seriously, "except to turn about by numbers, an' not to talk back to his superiors, an that's not much use for civil life.

★★★★★★

"When 'is time's up 'e goes out an' asks Civil Life to find him work.

"'What can you do?' sez Civil Life.

"'Stand erect, with me feet at an angle of forty-five degrees, 'ead up, shoulders back, an' me 'ands 'ung loosely by me side, thumbs in rear of the seams of me trousis,' sez the Army.

"'Very sorry,' sez Civil Life, but we 'aven't got a job like that. Can you do anything else?'

"'Yes,' sez the Army, 'I can challenge all persons approachin' my post between tattoo an' reveille, turn out the guard to generals an' all armed parties, an' take charge of all government property in view of me post,' sez the Army.

"' Can you fix a 'lectric bell?' sez Civil Life.

"'No,' sez the Army.

"'Can you drive a traction engine?' sez Civil Life.

"'No,' sez the Army.

"'Can you make a box, or set a line of type, or draw a plan, or make out a specification, or do anything that the crowd round the docks can't do?'

"'No.' sez the Army.

"'Well,' sez Civil Life, regretful, 'you'd better join the mob at the docks—an' you'll find the Salvation Army shelter down the second turnin' on the right.'

"Seven years!" said; Smithy, reflectively, "an' about two years of that spare time. A chap could learn anything in seven years—if there was anybody to teach 'im.

"'Teach me a trade,' sez the Army.

"'Good gracious!' sez the Country, 'orrified. 'I couldn't think of such a thing— don't I clothe you, an' feed you, an' pay you?'

"'Yes,' sez the Army; but teach me something—if it's only makin' mats, like you do in prison, or carpentering, like you do in work'ouses an' reformat'ry schools.'

"'But,' sez the Country, very agitated, 'if I teach you this you'll be competin' with the taxpayer.'

"'That's all right,' sez the Army, 'I want to be a taxpayer myself.'"

21.—Brothers

I myself would be the last man in the world to suspect Nobby Clark of justifying or attempting to justify the questionable conduct of his father. He had a clear appreciation both of his parent's genius and shortcomings, and valued both at their worth. That is how I read his attitude of mind. I think Private Clark is possessed of a large charity of mind. I imagine that he is generous and lenient in some degrees when he finds himself reviewing his father's acts, but if, in his filial respect, he cannot condemn, there is a certain irony in his tone when he tells these stories which makes it quite apparent that he does not condone.

"Me father was highly respected by his family," explained Nobby once. "Uncle Jim, Uncle George, an' Uncle Alf couldn't say enough about father an' the way he was looked up to by all his relations.

"Uncle Alf wouldn't have anybody but father to bail him out, an' the way Uncle Jim's family used to come and live with us when Uncle Jim was doin' four months for jumpin' on a policeman, was very touchin'.

"Then in the summer-time, when there was no unemployed work going on, Uncle George used to come an' pay us a visit, an' once I remember all three uncles with their families came at once.

"'You're a true brother,' sez Uncle George; 'an' if you can ever make a bit out of me or Alf or Jim you're free to do so.'

"'Hear, hear,' sez me other uncles.

"Father kept the advice in his mind, an' the first time there was a reward offered for Uncle Jim ('believed to be concerned with others in breakin' an' enterin') father stepped in an' took the prize.

"'It ain't much that I can do to get back the money they've cost me,' sez me father; 'but what I can do I will do with a cheerful heart.'

"Father went to see Uncle Jim in Wormwood Scrubs.

"'I didn't think you'd put me away for six months.' sez Uncle Jim.

"'I didn't think I would myself,' sez father. I thought you'd get two years.'

"Relations are best apart, especially poor relations, if you don't happen to be so poor as them, an' I've never known, so far as the army goes, any brothers who lived together in harmony longer than four months.

"It stands to reason, in a way, that brothers get on badly. They know each other too well, an' half the secret of keepin' friends with another feller is not to know anythin' about him, except the side he cares to show.

"Brothers are fairly common in the army, because soldierin' runs in some families like measles, an' crooked noses, but the two strangest brothers I ever know'd was the Joneses—B. Jones an' H. Jones. It was a long time before we knew they was brothers, because one of 'em was in 'B' Company an' the other in 'H'—that's how they got their initials.

"The first time I ever thought they was brothers was when H. Jones came into B. Jones's room an' borrowed his blackin' brushes without askin'. That was a pretty sure sign they was related. They never walked out in town together, never drank together, an' one took as much notice of the other as if he'd been a fly on the wall.

"I sez to one of 'em—to 'B.'—

"'You're a funny sort of feller,' sez I, 'not to have anythin' to do with your own brother—it don't seem natural.'

"'What don't seem natural to me,' he sez politely. 'is for you to see anybody else's business goin' on without wantin' to stick your long ugly nose in!'

"'B. Jones,' I sez sternly. 'I'm actin' for the best; as man to man, for the sake of peace an' harmony, an' for two pins I'd swipe the head off you.'

"I left 'em alone after that, but me an' the other chaps used to wonder what it was that'd, so to speak, come between two brotherly hearts.

"'I shouldn't be surprised,' sez Spud Murphy, 'if one of 'em hasn't done the other out of the family property; I've read cases like it in books.'

"Spud always was a bit romantic, an' that was the sort of book he read.

"'Perhaps B.'s the real heir to the property, an' H. is a changeling,' he sez, 'perhaps the wicked earl done 'em both out—'

"'To be continued in our next,' sez Smithy, very nasty, 'perhaps they're only ordinary brothers who are fed up with one another, just as me an' Nobby are fed up with you.'

"It wasn't long after this that Mr. Kroojer began pilin' his *burjers* on the border, an' the Anchester Regiment, bein'—though I say it as shouldn't—one of the best regiments in the army, was sent out.

"It was tough work in South Africa, the toughest work that most soldiers have done, an' somehow the Anchesters always got in the hot an' hungry places.

"We hadn't been in the country three months before we had a casualty list as long as the Rowley Mile, an' what with the closin' up of the ranks, an' the reconstruction of companies, B. Jones an' H. Jones got into the same company.

"Considerin' we was fightin' every day, an' livin' on half rations most of the time, you'd have thought that these two chaps would have shown a more companionable spirit, but not they. Somehow war, an' the dangers of war, made no difference. They was on noddin' terms, borrered little things from one another, but each went his own way.

"If they'd been people in books they'd been fallin' on one another's necks after every fight, but they was just ordinary folks an' did nothin.'

"This went on all through the war, an' toward the end our battalion was ordered out to march with a convoy through the Western Transvaal.

"Our job was to guard it, an' it needed a bit of guardin'.

"We'd hardly got ten miles out of Klerksdorp when Dela Rey come down on us, an' it took us four hours to fight his commando off. Next day De Wet, who was in that neighbourhood, saw us an' came along to pick us up. But it was our early closin' day, an' De Wet went away sick an' sorry. Then when we was halfway on our journey, three commandoes combined to settle us for good, an' at dawn one mornin' began a fight which lasted till sunset. We held a little hill to the right of the convoy, an' this position bore the whole of the attack.

"It was the only time durin' the war that I ever saw the Boers charge a position, an' twice that day we had to give way before their attacks. When night came, one out of every four men had been hit.

"We posted strong guards that night expectin' an attack, an' we got all we expected.

"Firin' began before sun-up. Some of the Boers took up a position on a ridge where they could shoot from good cover, an' two companies were ordered to clear the ridge. A an' B companies went an' did it. We took the position with the bayonet, an' then found that it wasn't worth holdin'.

"We got the order to retire on our main post, an' started to march away. Halfway down the slope lay a wounded Boer. He wasn't a real Boer, bein' a half-breed nigger, but as we passed he raised himself up an' shouted 'Water!'

"'Fall out Jones,' sez the officer, an' give that man a drink.'

"What happened exactly I don't know. We went marchin' on, leavin' Jones behind, an' suddenly I heard the crack of a rifle, an' looked round. The half-breed was runnin' like mad toward the Boer lines, a rifle in his hand, an' poor B. Jones lay very quiet on the hillside.

"'Shoot that man!' shouts the officer, an' a dozen men dropped on their knees an' fired at the flyin' murderer, but he dropped over the crest of the rise as quick as a flash.

"We doubled back an' carried the poor chap into camp, but it was all up with him, we could see that much. He was shot through the chest, an' we carried him carefully to the rear.

"Soon after this, the Boers returned to the attack, an' we was so busily engaged wonderin' when we'd be wounded ourselves that we had no time to think of B. Jones.

"At one o'clock that afternoon the Boer firin' went suddenly quiet, an' half an hour later we heard a faraway pom-pom come into action, an' knew a relief force was on its way.

"Methuen it was, with his column, an' most of us were very glad to see him. We had time now to count heads, an' see who was up an' who was down.

"That," said Nobby sadly, "is always the worse part of war. It's the part where a corporal an' twelve men go off with spades, an' another party sews men up in blankets—men you've spoke to that mornin'; men you've larked with, an' drank with.

"I was fixin' up me kit an' givin' me rifle a clean, when H. Jones strolled up.

"He nodded to me an' Smithy.

"'I hear me young brother's down,' he sez, quiet.

"Yes, H.,' I sez.

"'How did it happen?' sez H. Jones. So I told him.

75

"'What like was this nigger?' he asked after I finished.

"As well as I could I described him. He was easy to describe, because he had a big yeller face an a crop of woolly hair.

"'Come along,' he sez, after a bit, 'an' see me brother—he's a pal of yours, ain't he?'

"We found poor B. lyin' on the ground, on the shady side of an ox-wagon. The doctor was there, an' when he saw H. he took him aside.

"'I suppose you know your brother is dyin'?' he sez, an' H. nodded, then turned to his brother.

"'How goes it, Jack?' he sez gentle, an' poor B. grinned.

"'So so,' he sez weakly, 'me number's up.'

"'So they was tellin' me,' sez H. 'Well, we've all got to go through it sooner or later.'

"The dyin' man nodded, an' for a little while neither of 'em spoke.

"'Got any message to mother?' sez H., an' the poor chap on the ground nodded again.

"'Give her my kind regards,' he sez. 'Take care of yourself, Fred.'

"It seemed strange to me," said Nobby, thoughtfully, "that these two brothers, one of them dyin', should talk so calm one with the other, an' I never realised till then how little a feller like me knows about the big things of life, an' death.

"Poor old B. died an hour later, an' his brother was with him to the last. After it was all over he came to me.

"'Nobby,' he sez, 'which way did the Boers go?'

"As it happened I'd heard one of Methuen's staff officers describin' the line of march the Boers were takin', to I was able to tell him.

"'Thanks,' he sez. That night he deserted.

"What happened afterwards I heard from a Boer prisoner who told one of our sergeants.

"H. Jones left the camp soon after midnight, an' dodgin' the sentries, an' the outposts, he made his way in the direction of the Boers. For two days he tramped, sleepin' at night on the open *veldt* an' with nothin' to eat but a biscuit he took away with him.

"He was found by a Boer patrol, an' as luck would have it, was taken to the very commando that held the ridge.

"By all accounts, the chap in charge was a young lawyer who'd been educated in England an' spoke English better than H. Jones ever could hope to speak it.

"'Hullo!' he sez, when H. was marched before him, 'an' that the devil do you want?'

"'I'm lookin' for the feller that killed me young brother,' says H.

"The young commandant shook his 'head with a little smile.

"'I'm afraid,' he sez very gently, 'there are many people in this unfortunate country who are lookin' for the man who killed their brothers.'

"'My brother was murdered,' says H. doggedly, an' told the tale.

"'I don't believe any of me men would have done such a thing,' he sez. 'What sort of a man was it?'

"So H. described him, an' the young lawyer frowned.

"'Bring Van Huis here,' he sez to a Boer, an' by an' by the man he sent for came—a half-bred Dutchman with a dash of Hottentot in him.

"'Oh, Van Huis,' sez the commandant careless, 'they tell me you killed an English soldier at Valtspruit the other day?'

"The man grinned.

"'*Ja*,' he sez 'I shot him dead.'

"'Tell me how you did it,' sez the commandant, pickin' his teeth with a splinter of wood.

"'Hear,' sez the half-breed, 'I called him to bring me water, then I shot him.'

"The commandant nodded.

"'That was very clever,' he sez, 'so clever that I am goin' to hang you to that tree, an' this soldier shall be your executioner.'

"H. Jones came back with an escort of Boers, an' was placed under arrest, until the C.O. read the letter that the Boer commandant sent, then he was released.

"'What I can't understand,' sez Smithy to me afterwards, is, how is it that these two chaps, who never took any notice of one another—'

"But I stopped old Smithy because I knew what he was going to say.

"'Friends are friends,' I sez, 'an' brothers are brothers—,' then I stopped too, for what more can you say than that?"

22.—The Ghost of Heilbron Kopje

Nobby Clark, by all showing, is a man of great humanity. I have known him to do things that would make him very angry did be know I knew.

I have seen him, on a certain march—which lasted some six weeks, and was the most fatuous, futile, and wicked operation of the whole war—share his scanty rations with a man he hated. I have seen him by sickbeds as tender as a woman. It is said that in a certain fight on the Vaal River, where the grass caught fire, and the wounded lay helplessly sizzling in the flames, he and Private Smith went again and again into this perfect hell of torment to carry their wounded fellows to safety.

It is said, too, and, I do not doubt, with truth, that they lied their way out of a Victoria Cross, stoutly affirming that they took no part in the rescue, and persisting in the statement that those who thought they saw them were suffering from hallucinations, or, as Nobby put it coarsely, were drunk.

Knowing that deep down in the bottom of his heart Nobby Clark is a sentimentalist, and that away back in the base of his brain he is a shrewd, common-sense individual, the story of the ghost of the Hussar officer leaves me in an unsatisfactory condition of doubt. Is it Nobby's heart or Nobby's head that directs the recital? The facts, such as he gives me, I offer to the world in general, and the Psychical Research Society in particular.

"Me father," said Private Clark, by way of introduction, "was a feller who believed in ghosts. We used to have a family ghost when we lived at Clark's Hall, Bermondsey, but it was seized for rent, along with our other valuables.

"It used to walk the picture-gallery in the east wing," said Nobby, with a far-away look in his eye, an' father was very proud of it. Some said it was the ghost of Sir Guy de Clark, who was executed at Tower Hill; some said it was the ghost of Bill Clark, who was executed at Newgate; some said it was rats, an' I expect one of the three ideas was right.

"Nobody ever saw it but father, because it was one of them snobbish ghosts that never appeared to common people.

"Father used to see it on Christmas night, an' that was always a sign for mother to send for the doctor.

"Hullo, Clark,' sez the doctor, 'been seein' that ghost of yours?'

"'Yes, sir,' sez father.

"'Hum!' sez the doctor, feelin' his pulse, 'did you see anythin' else?'

"'Yes, sir,' sez father. 'I saw a lot of pink beetles an' a mouse with an elephant's head.'

"Then the doctor would write his prescription, an' father would be a teetotaller for months an' months.

"If I said our family ghost was pinched for rent, I'm bein' what you might call exaggeracious. What happened was that father got an execution in for rent, an' him an' the broker's man got into a friendly argument as to how much whisky a man can drink without dyin'. Father went down to the grocer's an' swapped two coal tickets for two bottles, an' the broker's man obligingly sat down to prove his words. . . It seems that he saw our ghost, an' the ghost must have took a likin' to him, for the broker's man wouldn't talk about anything but that ghost an' the other animals he saw for days an' days after. It was bad business for the broker's man, because whilst he was in his trance father an' mother got all the furniture out of the house an' disappeared.

"I never took much stock of ghosts meself, an' didn't believe in 'em till the South African War." Nobby was silent for a little while, and his face grew suddenly serious and old looking.

"If you think what I'm goin' to tell you is a lie, you needn't be frightened to tell me," he said. "I don't understand the rights of it me-self, an' don't expect I ever shall.

"When we was in South Africa, durin' the second half of the war, we went down to a place called Heilbron in the O.R.C. (Orange River Colony.)

"There *had* been fightin' there, but the only fight we saw was be-tween Darkie Williams an' Tom Sparrer of 'G' for the championship of the Anchesters, Darkie winnin' in two rounds owin' to his havin' filled his boxin' glove with sand.

"But De Wet was in the neighbourhood, browsin' round, an' though we never got a shot at him, there was enough excitement in the possibility of his getting' a shot at *us* that we were kept fairly busy. There was another regiment at Heilbron at the time—the Warwicks I think it was, or the '8th of Kings'—an' they'd been there long before we were.

"In a station like Heilbron all sorts an' kinds of duty had to be done; there were guards, pickets an' outlyin' pickets, flyin' sentries an' patrols, an' if a chap wasn't on one, he was on another, but I did every one of 'em before it came to me duty to do flyin' sentry. Me beat was two miles long, from the base guard to 'Hussars Kopje.'

"It was called 'Hussars Kopje' because in one of the early fights of the war the Hussars took this little hill after a fight in which they lost an officer.

"Flyin' sentry isn't such a bad job, partly because a feller was on his own. He could have a smoke, an' so long as he covered the ground, an' kept his eyes open, he was doin' all that was expected of him.

"It was a lonely walk over a deserted bit of country, but the night I went on flyin' sentry duty there was a full moon.

"Three men an' a corporal, that was the flyin' guard, an' we took over duty from the other regiment.

"Just before the old guard marched off, one of the fellows sez:—

"'Don't any of you fellers go up "Hussars Kopje."'

"'For why?' I sez.

"'Because of the ghost,' sez the feller, it'll probably scare you chaps, bein' new to the game.'

"'If it don't scare a woolly-headed Warwickshire cow-chaser,' I sez politely, it won't scare a feller of the Dashin' Anchesters.'

"'You'll dash all right,' sez the Warwick, when that ghost comes after you.'

"Soon after this the Warwicks marched off.

"'Don't go up that *kopje*—keep to the road,' sings out the Warwick as he left, an' havin' shouted a few insultin' remarks after him, we settled down to the guard.

"I was first relief, an' went straight out on me two-mile walk. I had me rifle loaded an' slung, with the safety catch down, an' with me hands in me overcoat pockets, the night bein' rather cold, I loafed along.

"Halfway to the *kopje*, I came up to a mounted patrol of the Imperial Yeomanry, an' after I'd given him me opinion of yeomen in general, an' he'd been very candid about foot-sloggers, we parted bad friends.

"'Look out for the ghost,' he sez.

"'Mind you don't fall off that horse,' I sez.

"'I'd gone a little way when I heard him come canterin' after me.

"'Hi, Tommy,' he called, an' I turned round.

"'Not so much of the Tommy,' I sez, 'or I'll stick a pin in your gallant charger!'

"'No offence,' sez the yeoman, an' then went on to tell me about the ghost. I hadn't took much notice of the yarn till then, an' I got a bit interested.

"'I've never seen it,' sez the yeoman, 'but one of our sergeants did. Let's go up the *kopje* together an' see what it's like.'

"'Catch me climbin' a hill,' I sez, 'when I can walk on the nice level road.'

"'You're afraid,' he sez.

"'I am,' I sez. 'I'm afraid of tirin' me feet.'

"We continued discussin' the matter till we came up to the hill, an' all the time I was gettin' more an' more curious. When he put his horse at the *kopje*, I sez:—

"'All right, I'll come up with you—I ain't seen a ghost for years.'

"It was a *kopje* as like as two pins any other *kopje* I've seen.

"There were thousands similar to it in South Africa. A gentle rise covered with boulders an' stunted bush, with big stones underfoot to make the goin' worse.

"It was, as I've told you, a bright, moonlight night, a clear sky an' not a breath of wind stirrin', an' as we got farther an' farther up the side of the hill, the country sort of unrolled itself beneath. Over to the north, an' seemin'ly under our feet, was the lights of Heilbron. You could hear sentries challengin' in the town, an' even the tramp of their feet as they marched up an' down.

"I was warm enough by the time I reached the top, an' me an' the yeoman stopped an' looked round.

"'Where's your ghost?' I sez.

"I'd hardly got the words out of me mouth when I had a queer sensation. I didn't hear anythin', or see anythin', but I *knew* that there was somebody behind me, an' I spun round, slippin' me rifle from me shoulder.

"An' then I saw.

"Comin' up the hill, the same way we had come, was an officer. He was in full kit, with his helmet tilted over his eyes, an' he was walkin' slowly.

"Me heart was in me mouth at first, but when I saw it was an officer I recovered.

"'Visitin' rounds,' I sez to the yeoman; but the yeoman said nothin', an' his horse started snortin' an' rearin'.

"The officer was comin' very slowly, with his head bent down as though he was lookin' for somethin' on the ground. Now an' again he'd stop, an' look left an' right, but always on the ground.

"'What's he lost? ' I sez in a low voice.

"He didn't seem to notice us, though we stood out clear enough in the moonlight, an' I brought my rifle to the port.

"'Halt! Who comes there?' I sez, but he took no notice.

"Nearer an' nearer he came, his eyes bent on the ground, an' I challenged again

"'Halt! Who comes there?'

"Then he looked up, an' I saw that I was talkin' to a dead man!

"It was the face of a man who was dead: a grey face with a little red mark just above his right eye.

"I staggered back; then, as the yeoman put spurs to his horse, an' went clatterin' an' blunderin' down the other side of the hill, I caught hold of his stirrup-leather an' run with him. . . .

"The other fellers of the guard said I'd been moonstruck, an' the corporal of the guard smelt me breath, but none of 'em took the trouble to go up the *kopje* and investigate.

"Next mornin', when the guard was relieved, I was sent for to orderly room.

"'I understand you saw a ghost, Clark?' sez the colonel.

"'Yes, sir,' I sez, an' told 'im all about it.

"Now the rum thing was that the colonel didn't laugh. He listened very quietly, noddin' his head, an' sayin' nothin. When I finished he sez:—

"'This is all true, you have been tellin' me?'

"'Yes, sir,' I sez, 'I'm willin' to take me oath.'

"He said no more, an' I went back to me tent.

"The fellers didn't half roast me. Even Smithy called me a liar, an' 'Nobby's ghost' was the talk of the camp for weeks.

"After the war was over, we was ordered home.

"I forget the name of the ship we came home on, but I think it was the 'Drayton Grange.' We brought home a lot of 'details,' Engineers, Army Service Corps, an' two squadrons of the 22nd Hussars.

"After we'd all settled down an' got to know one another, we used to have little bow-wows on the fo'c'sle head, an' spent a lot of time tellin' one another what gallant fellers we'd been.

"There was a hussar chap named Paul.

"'The most curious thing I've ever seen,' he sez one afternoon, when we were all gassin', 'was the taking of Hussar Kop—any of you chaps know it, it's near Heilbron?'

"There was a bit of a laugh when he said this, an' the chaps all looked at me.

"'We had a young officer,' sez the hussar, 'Lieutenant Enden, his name was—a regular boy. He was engaged to a young lady in Canterbury, an' I've never seen a feller so much in love in me life. Used to carry her picture in a little gold locket round his neck. I've seen him, when he thought nobody was lookin', take it out, an' have a dekko.

"'Well, about this fight I was speakin' of. The Boers held the *kopje*, an' two squadrons of ours was sent to dislodge 'em. There wasn't such a number of the enemy on the kop that we couldn't tackle 'em.

"'We galloped up to the foot of the hill an' dismounted under the cover of a little ridge, an' then we began to go up, takin' cover as best we could.

"'Lieutenant Enden was leadin' us, crouchin' behind such rocks as he could find, an' dodgin' from boulder to boulder.

"'Suddenly I see him stand up an' clasp his hand to his breast. I thought at first he was shot, but as he began lookin' around, left an' right searchin' the ground, I knew he'd lost somethin'—an' guessed it was the locket.

"'He stood up with the bullets whistlin' round him, his eyes travellin' over the ground—an' then he collapsed!

"'Shot stone dead, he was. . . .

"'We buried him at the foot of the hill. . . an' we never found the locket.'"

Nobby stopped here and blew his nose vigorously.

"There are times," he said, "when I think of Heilbron, an' the *kopje* outside the town, an' a grey-faced young officer, searchin', searchin', searchin' forever an' ever for that locket he lost. An' when I think of him I want to cry."

23.—SACRIFICE

According to a man's environments so his life is, so his tragedies are, and his end will be.

To be mauled by a lion is an extraordinary and painful experience that comes to very few of us. Yet it is the common lot of the menagerie attendant. So with the soldier, whether living here in peaceful England or going about his duty in Bombay, Karachi, or some like place, his life, shaped by environment, is full of that incident which makes for tragedy.

There are conditions of life so colourless, so even, that the slightest deviation from the smooth and normal flow of existence stands out as a landmark to be looked back upon and discussed for a score of years.

The sedate government office, with its days made up of returns, dockets, references and cross-references, remembers vividly that remarkable day in '83 when young Swink upset the red ink over the Public Works ledger—Swink himself, now a stout veteran of forty-four, will reconstruct the scene for you. At the vicarage at Bascombe-cum-Marsh, how often do they talk of that memorable Sunday when the dear bishop drank a wine-glassful of vinegar under the impression that it was *Château Lafayette?*

In a thousand peaceful homes, the extraordinary happening that is retailed through the ages is very small potatoes, indeed, and well may their worthy occupants shake their heads doubtingly when I talk of the abnormalities of army life. For death in terrible guise is on calling terms with the regiment. He comes, not in conscious majesty, as one who knows that panic will grip the heart of all who observe him, but apologetically, rather like a man slighted.

When we, in the army, with stately march and bowed head, follow the laden gun-carriage to the little military cemetery, and come back merrily, with the band playing unseemly tunes, you call us "callous," and are a little shocked, but the explanation is this: we are teaching the young recruits that this grisly monster is not so terrible a fellow; not one to be shivered over or shuddered at, but one to be treated with a certain amount of good-natured contempt.

"When we was stationed in England," said Smithy, *apropos*, "an' when we was on manoeuvres, we pitched a camp one Saturday near a little village, an' the colonel got the local parson to come along an' chew the mop on Sunday. He was a nice young feller, but he'd never seen real solders before, an' it worried him. By all accounts he sat up half the night makin' up his sermon, an' then he come along an' preached about what fine soldiers the ancient Israelites was, an' how we ought to be like 'em. An' he sez that when we was killed, an' if we happened to have time to think the matter over, we should realize that it was all for a good cause, an' take it in good part.

"When the sermon was over, an' we was dismissed, he walked round the camp talkin' to the men. Of course, everybody was polite. It was 'yessir,' an' 'no, sir,' an' Nobby, who's one of the best, even went so far as to promise to call round at the church that night. But what was surprisin' about this parson was he would talk about dyin', an' accordin' to him, a chap ought to use all his spare time to sit down quietly by hisself an' say, 'Well, here's another day nearer the grave.' It was a comic idea, but it didn't catch on.

"Now, there's lots of fellers in the world who think like him, that to be good you've got to have a dial as long as a wet week, an' that the surest sign of badness is gladness.

"It's a wrong idea, an' the proof is this that the best man that ever wore a uniform was the happiest—and that man was Father John Stronard, C.F. (Chaplain to the Forces.)

"The first time I ever saw Father John was in Aldershot in '94. He ran a soldiers' home in North Camp, an' was one of those fellers with a thin, refined face, that had 'Priest' written all over him. He wasn't an R.C., for all that. He was Church, very High Church, so some of the chaps said, an' wore little medals on his watch chain. But high or low, he was the whitest kind of white man that ever lived. He was friends with all the other chaplains—that's the best sign. Friends with 'em all, from Father O'Leary to Mr. Stemm, the Baptist lay preacher. He'd got no fads, he smoked a big fat pipe all day, an' was ready to put on the gloves with any feller that thought he had the beatin' of him. He never threw religion at you, but when a man acted the goat, you'd see that man go miles out of his way to avoid Father John.

"Fellers trusted him an' told him things. There was a wild devil in ours called Cross. Cross by name and crook by nature. There wasn't a decent-minded man of ours who would have anything to do with him. It wasn't that his language was bad—it was worse than that. After he started swearin' you felt that the room ought to be disinfected.

"One day on the ranges, firin' our annual course, we was usin' a new cartridge, 'Mark 10.'

"Nobby was lyin' alongside of me, an' was passin' sarcastic remarks about the markers.

"He fired a round, an' got an 'outer'; then he tried to pull back the breech block.

"'Hullo,' sez Nobby, she's jammed.'

"It took him nigh on five minutes to get the exploded cartridge out, then he whistled, got up, an' walked to the officer in charge.

"'Beg pardon, sir,' sez Nobby, 'see this?'

"He held up the cartridge.

"The officer-boy, who hadn't been from Sandhurst a week or so, frowned most terrible, an' sez, 'What's wrong with it?'

"'It's split all up the side, sir,' Nobby sez, 'an' this is the second time it's happened—the cartridges are defective!'

"If the officer-boy had known cow-heel from tripe he'd have called up the officer in charge, who was at another part of the range, but bein' only a kid at the game, an' not wishin' to take advice from a private, he sez, very stern:—

"'Go back to your place, me man, an' don't talk nonsense.'

"So Nobby came back an' lay down.

"By an' by, the colour-sergeant come up. 'Why aren't you firing, Clark?' he sez, an' Nobby told him.

"The 'flag' took the cartridge, an' looked at it, an' shouted, 'Cease fire!'

"Up dashed the officer-boy.

"'What the dickens is wrong, colour-sergeant' he sez angrily.

"'Defective cartridges, sir,' sez the 'flag.'

"'Who said so?' sez the officer. 'Go on firin' till I tell you to stop.'

"So we went on firin' for two minutes, an' then the breech block of Sam Cross's rifle blew out, an' Sam went down screamin', with half his face shot off.

"I'm not going to tell you how the officer was tried an' cashiered, or how the ammunition was called in, an' the fuss the papers made about it.

"When Cross got back to his senses, the first man he asked for was Father John, an' Father John was at the hospital before you could say knife. Practically he didn't leave him for two days an' nights. He was with him when the doctors operated on poor old Sam, an' with him through the night when it was a toss-up whether the patient would live or die, an' with him for a couple of hours every day till Sam was turned out of hospital cured.

"Now the rum thing about it was this, that although he'd sent for the Father, an' although they was together so long, not one word of religion passed between them.

"At first Father John used to only sit an' read in his soft voice—bits out of books—an' then, when young Sam got better an' could talk, they'd discuss the coal business what Sam's brother was in, an' county cricket, an' things like that, but for all this, Sam came back to the battalion a new man.

"The only thing that was ever said, was said before witnesses, an' that was the day before Sam came out.

He walked with the Father to the door of the ward, an' stood a bit awkward tryin' to put the words together.

"'Father,' he sez, sudden, 'how could a chap like me get to be a chap like you?'

"'How d'ye mean, Sam?' sez Father John.

"'I mean,' sez Sam, 'you're a man same as me, barrin' education; how did you get to be patient, an' gentle, an' all?

"'By sacrifice,' sez Father John sadly.

"That was Sam's motto when he came back to barracks. He'd got the idea in a dim sort of way into his thick head, that sacrifice meant not doin' somethin' you wanted to do, an' doin' things you didn't want to do.

"Sometimes the devil in him got up; an' I've seen him standin' by his bed-cot, with the veins in his forehead swollen an' his eyes glarin' at somebody who had annoyed him, but he wouldn't speak, an' his hands would be clenched till the knuckles were white—then you'd see his lips move, an' you could almost read the word 'sacrifice' on his lips.

"Then the regiment was ordered to India, an' we left the *padre* behind. He marched down to the station by Sam's side, an' he shook hands with him on the platform. I believe that poor Sam never felt anything so much as he did that partin', but he 'stuck it'—he was learnin' his lesson.

"We hadn't been in India a year, movin' from station to station, before a feller by the name of Dah Yussef, who was a sort of head thief in the hills, came down an' burned a village, killed a lot of people, an' carried off some women an' cattle. He was a *pukka badmash*, (real rogue), was old Joseph, an' this was about the ninth *dacoity* he'd committed in the year, the government lookin' on an' sendin' polite messages to him, askin' him to kindly return the goods an' no questions would be asked. We was stationed on the border, an' naturally we was very bitter about the government not doin' anything.

"'It's a scandal,' sez Nobby, very indignant. 'I've a good mind to write home to the *Islington Gazette* about it. It's this Liberal Government,' sez Nobby, gloomily.

"'It's a Conservative Government in now,' I sez, but Nobby sez it didn't affect the argument.

"Old Joseph, or Yussef, or whatever his name was, naturally got bolder an' bolder, an' not satisfied with raiding the villages near his hills, he came farther into the open, an' started ructions almost on the plains.

"That's what the Government of India was waitin' for. The Guides an' a battalion of Ghoorkas was waitin' *doggo*, an' came by forced march, an' the Anchesters, the Wessex, the Punjab Lancers, an' two batteries of Artillery was sent off at a minutes' notice to call on Uncle Joseph.

"We got the order at midnight, an' by daybreak we was twelve miles on the road.

"It was supposed to be one of them cut an' come again campaigns, all over in ten minutes, but the government had left it a little bit too late, an' the Afridis were up in arms. We fought two sharp battles, an' then the enemy retired an' took up a strong position on the foothills.

We shelled 'em, but we couldn't shift 'em then the Guides, the Ghoorkas, an' the Anchesters tried to take the position by assault—but we failed.

"The general in command drew us off, an' we waited for reinforcements. They came in twenty-four hours the Kents, Lancasters, an' a battery of howitzers—an' with 'em came Father John. He was in India for duty, an' although we hadn't known it, he'd been there for some time.

"Nobby, watchin' the reinforcements march in, was the first to spot him, in his khaki uniform, an' with the black Maltese cross on his collar. Nobby dashed back to our lines lookin' for Sam Cross, an' found him sittin' down quietly, drinkin' cold tea.

"'Sam,' sez Nobby, very excited, 'who do you think's turned up?'

"'Father John,' sez Sam, calmly, an' Nobby was rather disappointed, because he wanted to create a little sensation.

"'I had a feelin' he was comin',' sez Sam, gettin' up, but I didn't durst go down to see 'em marchin' in, for fear I'd be disappointed. No,' he sez, shakin' his head at Nobby's question, 'I didn't know he was in India.'

"Nobby told me afterwards it made his flesh creep to hear him—it was like listenin' to a man that's in the habit of seein' ghosts. Nobody saw 'em meet, but when I met Sam comin' from the Kent's lines—where the *padre's* tent was—his eyes were red, like a man who'd been cryin'.

"Next mornin' we formed up for the grand assault. Soon after daybreak the guns got into action, the howitzers goin' close up under the escort of the Guides' Cavalry, an' shellin' the *sangar*, where the enemy was lyin' as thick as bees in a hive. At eleven o'clock the infantry moved, the Guides an' the Anchesters on the enemy's front, the Ghoorkas an' the Wessex on the left, the Kents an' Punjabis on the right, and the Lancasters in reserve. I've only got a dim idea of what the fight was like. We went ahead by short rushes from cover to cover. The air seemed to be filled with flyin' bullets, an' the enemy had got an old gun into position, an' was dealin' out bits of scrap-iron at regular intervals.

"It was terrible hard, when we began the ascent of the hill, for the ground was broken up, an' big boulders 'an stones came flyin' down to meet us. These were worse than the bullets. We'd got into a tight place, with a big, deep *nullah* in front of us, an' between us an' the enemy, an' we lay down firin' steady. The *nullah* had to be crossed, an' we had to rest before we could do it, in the face of the fire. We could hear the chaps on the right come into action, an' from where we was we could see the Ghoorkas an' Wessex comin' up on the left, an' I was just wonderin' why it was that the Wessex, which is a rotten regiment in peace time, should be such a decent corps in war time, when I heard Sam Cross shout, 'Go back—go back, for God's sake, Father John!'

"I looked round.

"Father John was comin' up the hill behind us—not foolhardy, but takin' cover.

"Sam's face was white, but the *padre* was smilin' when he reached us. His big pipe was in his mouth, an' he crouched down behind the little rampart of stones that protected us, with a pleasant nod.

"Personally, I thought it was a bit silly of him to come into danger like this, but I found out afterwards that he'd heard the general say that the success of the fight would depend upon the Guides an' the Anchesters. You see, the intelligence staff knew nothing about the big *nullah* on the hill, an' even we who was lyin' along the side of it, didn't know what a terrible business it would be crossin' it, for it ran so that it was fully exposed to the enemy's fire, an' every man who scrambled out on the other side could be picked off by the enemy's marksmen.

"When Father John knew what we were in for he came up. Lyin' down there, with his pipe goin' he was full of spirits, an' made some of our youngsters, who'd got a bit fidgety, cheerful, too.

"'Sing,' he sez, as the fire got heavier an' heavier.

"'What shall we sing, Father?' sez Nobby.

"'Anything,' sez Father John, an' he started us goin' with 'Where are the boys of the Old Brigade?' an' from one end of the line to the other we roared the chorus :—

Steadily, shoulder to shoulder,
Steadily, blade by blade;
Steady an' strong,
Marchin' along—
Like the boys of the Old Brigade.

"In the middle of it the helio from headquarters began to wink, an' by an' by the order was passed down the lines, 'Get ready!'

"Then, when there came a slackenin' of fire from the enemy, our bugle went, 'Come along! come along! come along, Anchesters!'—that's our regimental call—an' the 'Advance!'

"We were in the *nullah* an' over the edge of it before the execution began. The minute I reached the other side I could see the danger. Up the hill, as far as the *nullah*, the ground had been steep an' covered with big stones—it was from this *nullah* that they'd rolled the boulders down on us. Now, we were on a gentle slope, as bare of cover as a soup-plate, an' there was no protection from the fire from the ridge above.

"The Guides on our right got the first blast of the storm, an' they went down in little patches, as if some blight had struck 'em, passin' a man here, an' takin' a man there.

"'Steady, the Anchesters!' yelled the adjutant; 'fix bayonets!'

"We was a hundred an' fifty yards from the position, an' I braced myself for the run.

"'Charge!'

"With a yell that was almost like a scream, we dashed forward. I never ran so fast, or with any less effort, in my life.

"The bullets made a noise like a gramophone before the tune starts, an' I've got an idea that I saw a feller fallin', but I hadn't time to notice properly before I'd followed Nobby over the breastworks.

"Nobby is the finest bayonet fighter in the regiment, an' the second man he met was dead before the first one had fallen.

"I got home with the bayonet on a big Afridi, who made a slice at me with his big knife, an' then someone fell against me with a cough. In a fraction of a second, as I half turned to see who it was, I saw an Afridi pass his knife through Sam Crow.

"Then two fellers came at me—I got the first, easy. I parried a blow, an' gave him a short-arm thrust that brought him down—an' the other feller was shot dead by Captain Marsham, an' then the 'cease fire' sounded.

"I looked round. Nobby, who never loses an opportunity for business, was pickin' up all the valuable-lookin' articles, such as gold-mounted swords, within reach. I was thinkin', regretful, of poor Sam, when, to my astonishment, he came up. He was bleedin' from a cut head, where some Afridi had got home on him, but there was no other sign of injury.

"'Smithy,' he sez, quietly, come an' help me with Father John—I—I mustn't lift him.'

"'Good God,' whispers Nobby, droppin' his swords, 'not—not—?'

"Sam nodded.

"'Father John was killed as we came over there.' He pointed to the ramparts.

"He made no sign of grief, not even that evenin', when we laid the Father in a deep grave at the foot of the hills—an' he was the only man who didn't cry as we buried the greatest an' kindest of Christians an' friends.

"Sam only stood, with his bandaged head an' his white face; sway-in' a little from side to side. Me an' Nobby, in our rough way, tried to cheer him when we got back to the camp—although we wasn't feel-ing any too cheerful ourselves, for some good men went out that day. But he was as calm as possible.

"'It's only proper that Father John should die that way,' he said. 'It's the right end—sacrifice. He risked his life because he wanted to help us.'

"He put his hand to his side as though he was in pain, an' he was, too, though we didn't guess it.

"'I thought,' he went on, 'that Father John would like we to see him put away nice an' comfortable—that's why I kept alive!'

"He said this all so calm that I didn't understand what he meant.

"'Let me down gently,' he sez, an' Nobby saw the blood on his lips, an' put his arms round him.

"We lowered him carefully down, an' two doctors came. Sam lay very still an' quiet.

"They stripped off his coat. His shirt was caked with blood, an' one of the doctors whistled as he saw the wound.

"'Is he dead, sir?' whispered Nobby.

"The doctor nodded.

"'How he has lived for six hours with a knife wound in his heart,' he said, 'God knows. Why, by every law of science, he ought to have been dead this morning!'

"The adjutant came up.

"'How do you account for it, doctor?' he asked.

"The doctor shook his head an' couldn't say, but me an' Nobby could have explained. It was love, an' will, an' sacrifice that kept poor Sam alive—but mostly sacrifice."

Army Reform
Opinions of Private Smith
(*Daily Mail*, September, 1906)

Private Smith—his comrades, I am informed, call him "Smithy" for short—entertained me yesterday with many stories of army reform.

There was a time, explained Smithy, when all the chaps used to get very excited if it came out that there was going to be a brand new army. You see a lot in the papers, you hear a lot about what's going to happen, but reveille still goes at 6 a.m., 'B' Company still has jam for breakfast three days a week, and you step off with the left foot, just about the same as usual. The only feller I ever knew, he said, who made anything out of army reform was Nobby Clark—Private Clark, of B. He continued:—

A Business Head.

Nobby is a chap with a business head, as you may say; I mean that he is always thinking out new ways of making money without working for it. One day—oh, years an' years ago it was—one of the young fellers at the War Office got out a new idea. I don't exactly know what it was, and it afterwards came out that he didn't either. But what he did know was that the army before he came to the War Office was in a very bad state, and it was a good job for everybody he'd happened to be driving down Pall Mall and noticed it. We all got a bit excited when we heard we were going to be reformed, and lots of fellers joined the Army Temperance Association, because Nobby put it about that all teetotallers were going to get a penny a day extra. They gave Nobby their money to mind, so that the temptation of the cursed drink should not overcome 'em, and later, when It was found out that there was nothing about being teetotal in the now army reform, they

93

had quite a lot of trouble in getting their money back.

"It's no good your comin' to me," sez Nobby to one of 'em, a young teller named Spud Murphy. "I'm goin' to keep you out of the accursed canteen so that you can get the extra penny a day for bein' a temp'rance soldier."

"There ain't any penny a day," sez Spud, wrathful.

"Wait and see," sez Nobby, very calm.

So they waited for a week, then went to Nobby again. They couldn't find him, because he'd got a telegram from London saying:

Come at once, your sister is horribly ill. Bring Prlvate Smith, as she wants to see him.

So me and Nobby got five days' leave and went up to town, and had the time of our lives.

When we got back all the young fellers who'd given Nobby money to mind said that if Nobby didn't hand it over there was going to be trouble. So Nobby gave 'em all that he had, an' said he kept the rest for interest.

A Reform That Did Not Come Off.

Then Nobby put it about that the new army reform was going to make all soldiers wear collars and ties, but somehow, the fellers wouldn't believe it; an' the stock collars and pink ties that Nobby bought cheap at Hills', the drapers in the High street, was a dead loss.

But we thought something must be going to happen, because the newspapers were filled with army reform, and old chaps, writing from the Army and Navy Club, saying what a disgraceful thing it was. "Colonel, Retired," they signed theirselves.

There was all sorts of rumours in the regiment. Once we heard that soldiers was to have eggs for breakfast every day of their lives; once it was put about that there was going to be no more church parades; but things went on as usual, and as far as I could see the only change we got was in the weather, for it rained for three weeks on end, an' we didn't have a single parade, which was very good.

That was the first army reform I remember. Then there was another one. It came out in orders that a lot of Army Corps was to be formed, an' the Anchester Regiment was ordered down to Salisbury to join the 45th Army Corps. When we got there we was the only soldiers in sight.

"Where's the Army Corps?" sez the colonel, an' nobody knew. The adjutant asked a chap who happened to be on Salisbury Plain, and the chap said he didn't know, but just before we arrived he'd seen a dog eating something, so the colonel told him he was a fool. And the adjutant asked another man—a man from Salisbury—and the man began turning out his pockets to prove that he hadn't got it. We never saw the 45th Army Corps, an' we never found it, though I think (here Smithy paid a delicate compliment to the power of the Press) that if they'd put an advertisement in the papers:

LOST.—A small Army Corps; lame in one leg, bob-tailed, does tricks, wears a sailor hat, and answers to the name of "Broddie,"

—they might have got it.

Then we had another army reform, but I don't think that one came off.

"Value For Cash."

The other day Nobby came into the canteen in a great state of mind.

"There's a new army reform," he sez.

"Is it something you want to sell?" sez Spud Murphy.

"No, its——"

"Do you want to mind our money?" sez Spud.

"Don't be silly," sez Nobby; 'It's about every man being worth his money——"

"Ah!" sez Spud, noddin' his head, "I knew it was something about money."

Well, from what Nobby said, it appears that there's a new army reform made up by a new chap at the War Office, and it's pretty serious this time.

"Every soldier must be worth his money," sez Nobby, and he read a bit out of the paper.

"What does that mean?" sez Spud; so Nobby explained.

Nobby is a very plausible chap, an' by the time he'd finished explaining how the army was going to be run on piecework lines he'd got all the chaps feeling very uneasy.

"I'm sorry for you, Spud, because I know, you don't like work—I don't suppose you'll draw more than half a crown a week."

"But how are they going to work it out?" sez Spud, trying to do sums in his head.

So Nobby went on explaining.

"Penny for drill parade, tuppence for commanding officers's parade, threepence for kit inspection, fourpence for guard, fourpence-ha'penny for gymnasium, an' so on," sez Nobby, very glib.

Spud, who's a pal of the colour-sergeant's, and is excused all parades, looked very miserable, and said you can't believe all that you read in the papers.

Real, and Parliamentary

"I don't know what this new army reform is going to do," Smithy went on, philosophically, "but I don't suppose it will do much. You see there are two armies. The army that you and me know—fellers who wear uniforms an' go walking out on Sundays with their best girls—the army that marches an' cleans its rifles an' gets run in for making an improper reply to a non-commissioned officer. Then there's another army that nobody understands except civilians, and that's all about money and Acts of Parliament and politics. The Act of Parliament army is the army they're always reforming without our noticing it."

A feller of ours, a chap named Bertie, who was a billiard marker before he enlisted and sounds all his aitches, started giving me and Nobby his opinion about the army the other day.

"The fact is, my dear Clark," he sez in his haw-haw voice, 'economics and efficiency are not necessarily incom-somethlng-or-other."

Nobby pulls him up sharp.

"Talking about eco-what-d'ye-call-it, Bertie, I think it's your turn to pay for the beer," he sez.

"I'm talking about army reform," sez Bertie.

"And I'm talking about beer," sez Nobby, "so don't change the subject."

Smithy Abroad

DEDICATION

Only an hour to halt and to bury the dead.
The cloud of dust that floats in the face of the sun
Is the mark of an enemy broken: the wrack of his run
Strewing the face of the plain, is a trail to be read.
Only an hour to halt and bury the dead.

Shallow, indeed, is the grave that the bayonets have made;
Stony and hard is the soil with its alien heart.
Haste, for the hour is short and the column must start,
And These are but pawns put aside in a game that is played.
Shallow, indeed, is the grave that our bayonets made.

Here, on the brink of the pit, where the silent ones lie—
Here, with an eye to the book that he holds in his hand.
Chanting God's pitiful promise, the man in command
Reads. . . with an eye to the dust in the westerly sky.

We are lending a spell to sit by the black pit's head.
We have builded a cairn on the place of their lonely sleep,
And a cross, rough-hewn, and a crude-cut name, to keep
A title of fame for a week, for the blessed dead.
We are lending a spell to sit by the black pit's head.

From the mists of a crumbling world came the spell at their call—
The world slipping fast from their ken . . and the sun going out . .
And the blue of the sky bloody red . . and the terror and doubt . .
And the crash . . . and the blackness of night ending all.
From the mists of a crumbling world came the spell at their call . .

The spell that we leave as we trek for the reddening west—
A pillar of dust on earth seeking an aerial cloud—

97

Is the faith of the silent men, in their hasty shroud,
That Living or Dead, whatever Was, was Best.
This is the spell we left as we trekked to the west.

1.—The Arms Store

Smithy sat on the edge of his cot and sorted his belongings. The solid black trunk that a paternal government provided for the reception of the soldiers' worldly possessions was wide open, and the inside of the lid was a picture gallery of cigarette pictures. "When Nobby became my bed chum," reflected Smithy, "I had three pairs of socks—I had two new blacking brushes and a bit of scented soap—likewise a brand new shavin' brush."

Private Clark, stretched full length on the adjoining cot, immersed in the mysteries of an elementary French grammar (Nobby is studying for a first-class certificate) treated the insinuation with silent contempt.

"A man who wastes his time tryin' to learn a language wot nobody speaks except French people," complained Smithy, bitterly, "ought to have time to go through his kit, an' sort out stolen property: a man who can afford to buy——"

"I have not the socks of my friend," interrupted Nobby, dreamily. "I have not seen the socks of my comrade. *Ah, nong, jammy.*"

"I lent you——" disputed Smithy hotly.

"Have you the pen of my sister, no but I have the paper of my aunt. Be'old! I have the chalk of my cousin," murmured Nobby.

"Have you got my socks?" demanded the wrathful Smithy.

"*Nong, mais j'avvy——*"

"Talk English, you big-footed barman."

"I haven't got your socks, an' I'd be very sorry to be seen wearin' 'em," said the exasperated Nobby. "If that ain't English enough, I'll talk Lal Sahib to you."

Smithy grinned.

"Never heard about Lal Sahib, have you?"—he smiled grimly— "he was the chap to talk English." Smithy waited for his audience to collect and prefaced his narrative with a homily on soldiering.

"There's three kinds of soldiers." said Smithy. "There's old soldiers, recruits, an' soldiers—just soldiers. You can always tell the 'roosters' by their silliness: you don't often see 'em in the streets because they're mostly in hospital with heart disease, an' lunacy, an' any old disease that'll get 'em a ticket, (discharge certificate). The old soldiers you can generally spot: they're the chaps who come round for the washin' on Monday mornin's. They also get charge of fatigue parties that do work that a lance-corporal wouldn't bemean hisself to do. The soldier—well, anybody can tell a *pukka* soldier. A fine-lookin', healthy upstandin'—well, take me for example.

"Young soldiers spend their time wantin' things that ain't good for 'em, and the thing they mostly want is foreign service an' a war.

"Any hour of the day you can hear 'em sayin' 'Roll on the big ship an' the white helmet,' an' they're no sooner abroad than they're singin', with tears in their eyes—

Motherland. Motherland!
See thy exiled children stand,

or words to that effect.

"When we was stationed in Peshawar, which is halfway between India an' hell, our second battalion was at Gib. an' we got a draft of young chaps sent to us. They was the haughtiest draft you could ever imagine. Half a dozen of 'em was sent to 'B' Company. One of the chaps, whose name was Sigee, fairly made your head ache to listen to him.

"We always try to be nice an' polite to new chaps, so, just by way of makin' him feel at home, Nobby told him all the news, how there was a lot of cholera about, an' how Fatty Pink was down with sunstroke.

"'Heat don't worry me,' sez Sigee, very cocky. 'I'm used to foreign service—been on the Rock a year.'

"'But this heat,' sez Nobby.

"'Nothin' to the Rock,' sez the young feller.

"'An' the cholera,' sez Nobby.

"'Nothin' to the enteric you get on the Rock,' sez Sigee.

"'There's a lot of gun-runnin'' sez Nobby.

"'You ought to see the smugglers nippin' over to La Linea from the Rock,' sez Sigee, an' that made Nobby wild.

"'What Rock?' he sez.

"'Gibraltar,' sez the other.

"'Where's that?' sez Nobby, innocent. 'In the Isle of Wight?'

"You see," explained Smithy, "it's very hard to convince a chap who's never been further out of England than Douglas, Isle of Man, that Gibraltar ain't abroad.

"We had a long argument about it the night the draft arrived, an' Nobby said that 'abroad' didn't begin till the nacheral colour of the inhabitants of the place was black, an' that brought up the question of Black and White.

"Sigee was one of them chaps that's prepared to argue always on the other side. He waited till he saw we was all in agreement about the question, then he hopped in to prove that the native was twenty times a better man than the white.

"'He's our black brother, too,' he sez.

"'He ain't no brother of mine,' sez Nobby.

"What made me an' Nobby so cross was the way Sigee took up with Lal Ra—'Lal Sahib' the natives called him.

"He was a *pukka* Pathan, that some silly old general had found when he was a kid. I forget what expedition it was on, but it was one of them shoot-quick-an'-get-away fights that we're always havin' in the hills. The general found this little Pathan an' took him home. Got to like him, an' havin' more money than sense had him educated like a proper sahib. Went to Oxford, this kid did, an' learnt Greek an' algebra and mathematics, an' when the old feller died he come back to Peshawar an' started a native school in the city. To hear him talk, you would think you was listenin' to a real gentleman. Somehow our officers didn't cotton on to him, so he tried the men, an' we wasn't takin' him either. But Sigee stuck on to him like a fly on treacle, and it made us sick to see 'em walkin' through the bazaar together as thick as thieves.

"'He's a gentleman, born and bred,' says Sigee, 'I've seldom met a better.'

"'That I can quite understand,' sez Nobby, politely.

"What put the tall hat on Sigee was the order that came out that the native town was out of bounds, and that soldiers were practically confined to barracks.

"'It's a bit of spite,' sez Sigee, 'to prevent me meetin' my friend.' As a matter of fact, our colonel, who gave the order, didn't know anything about Sigee, but what he did know was, that there was going to be a bit of trouble down in that part of the world.

"We chaps didn't know what the game was fully till one afternoon, the order came out that there was to be double guards on all the out-lying posts. Then we smelt bloodshed.

"An' it came all right.

"That night, when me an' Nobby was sittin' outside the canteen with a lot of chaps, an' watchin' the twinklin' lights of the native town down below the hill, we hears a shot, then another, an' in a minute we heard the sentry on the main guard shout, 'Guard, turn out!'

"Then the sdjutant came pelting across the square, an' we could see in the moonlight he had a revolver in his hand. 'Assembly!' I heard him shout, then he went off like a streak in the direction of the Arms Store, which is just on the edge of the cantonment.

"We didn't wait for the assembly to sound. Me an' Nobby jumped for our bungalow. The colour-sergeant, as white as a sheet, was opening the ammunition locker.

"He chucked half a dozen packets at me an' Nobby.

"'Take your rifles and double as hard as you can to the Arms Store,' he shouted, and in a minute there was half a dozen of us runnin' like mad in the direction the Adjutant had taken.

"He was there with a file of the guard when we reached him, bending over something on the ground.

"It was poor little Jayson, of 'H.'. . . . a horrible sight. . . . They had smashed in the door of the store and got away with a dozen rifles.

"There was a double guard on after that night, but the worst was to come.

"The Arms Store is a fairly lonely post. Ammunition is stored there, an' naturally it's got to be a certain distance away from the barracks. There was a lot of bad Pathans in the Town, who wanted to get rifles. When I say 'bad Pathans' I mean extra bad, because I've never met a Pathan that was good for anything but murder.

"It appears that there was trouble brewin' on the frontier somebody was preachin' a Holy war, and rifles was selling at 200 *rupees* in the town.

"'I've known about this for weeks,' sez Sigee, very proud—he was just goin' on guard— 'my friend, Lal Sahib, told me that owin' to the foolish and short-sighted policy of the government———'

"'Dry up,' sez Nobby, 'we ain't interested in your nigger pal, nor what he says.'

"Nobby has never forgiven hisself for snappin' pore old Sigee's head orf, for next mornin', when the corporal of the guard went to relieve Sigee an' his chum, they found 'im stark and dead, with an Afghan knife laying carelessly round to show how it was done.

"We buried poor old Sigee that night, and his black pal, Lal Sahib, sent a wreath with some Greek poetry on it. After that, Arms guard got a bit too jumpy.

"Sigee was killed on the Tuesday night. On the Friday night Harry Bayle, of 'C,' and young Turner were laid out on the same post, practically in sight of the camp, an' nobody was any the wiser. At neither time did the Pathans manage to get away with rifles except the guns of the poor chaps they slaughtered.

"And the curious thing about it was that although there was a strict battalion order that the sentries were never to separate, but to stick together throughout their guard, they were always found one on one side of the Arms building, and the other poor chap on the other.

"On the Sunday night, me and Nobby was sent for to the officers' quarters.

"The adjutant took us to his room.

"'Smith,' he sez, 'I am putting you and Clark on Arms guard to-morrow—and you'll be first relief. I've sent for you two, because, being old soldiers, I can depend on you.'

"'Yessir,' sez me an' Nobby.

"'You can be depended upon to carry out orders,' he sez, slowly, 'an' these are your orders: if anyone approaches your post challenge them once—then fire or use your bayonet.'

"As this was the ordinary regulation, we was puzzled at the adjutant sendin' specially for us.

"'Understand,' he sez more slowly, 'if you challenge an' the person you challenge can't give you the countersign straight off—you're to kill him.'

"We nodded.

"'Even,' sez the adjutant, '*even if it's me!*'

"Nobby was very troubled as we walked back to our barrack-room.

"'These murders have got a bit on Uncle Bill's mind,' he sez, 'surely he ain't goin' dotty?'

"I thought it was rum, too.

"We fell in for guard at Retreat next night, an' the adjutant inspected us.

"'You remember what I told you?' he sez, 'an' don't forget you are not to separate, *even if I order it!*'

"'That's done it,' sez Nobby, as we was marchin' off. 'Uncle Bill's been in the sun.'

"But I had my own views about Uncle Bill, an' I said nothin' at all.

"The first relief was from six to eight, an' nothin' happened. It's not nice to do a guard on a place where four chaps have been murdered—four chaps you knew quite well an' have laughed an' joked with. The

Arms Store is a little square buildin' on a risin' bit of ground, and durin' the day time there's two sentry boxes, one each side of the door. When the store's locked up, the sentry boxes are pushed in front of the door—or had been since the Pathans made their first attack.

"'What I can't understand,' sez Nobby, ' is why them chaps left each other, an' I don't mind tellin' you, Smithy, that if I catch you tryin' to leave me, I'll beat your head off with the butt end of me rifle.'

"We was relieved at eight, an' nothin' further happened till just as I was dreamin' somebody had left me a million pounds an' a feather bed, the corporal of the guard shook me up.

"'Come on, Smithy,' he sez, 'it's your turn.'

"It was black dark when me an' Nobby took over the post, and there was only just enough light from the stars to see how dark it was. We walked round the buildin' twice, and then took up our position in the boxes.

"We stood for a long time sayin' nothin', for somehow the silence of the night didn't invite conversation.

"By an' bye Nobby whispered:

"'Smithy, what's the word again?'

"So I whispers 'Bristol,' which was the countersign of the night.

"I don't know how long we stood there, but after a while Nobby sez:

"'Let's walk round again.'

"I'd just slung my rifle to the slope, when I heard somebody coming along the path. Not stealthily or quietly, but just steppin' out briskly an' whistlin'.

"We dropped our rifles to the charge and saw a man coming towards us.

"We could hear the 'slap slap' of his sword as it hit against his leggings.

"'Halt! Who comes there?' I shouted.

"'It's all right,' he sez, an' I recognised the adjutant's voice. Then like a flash I remembered his warnin'.

"'Stand, sir!' I sez, quick, 'and give the countersign!'

"He laughed.

"'Oh, all right, my man, I'm just looking round—one of you men go to the other side of the building and see if all's clear.'

"Nobby was startin' when I grabbed his arm.

"'It's against, orders, sir,' I sez. I could see he was comin' to test us.

"Then suddenly at my side I could hear Nobby breathing hard, an' he started a little forward.

"'Don't come nearer,' he sez, harshly, 'give me the countersign!'

"'Oh, rot!' sez the officer, an' came walkin' casually toward us.

"Before I could stop him, Nobby had shortened his rifle and as the officer came nearer, I saw the flash of Nobby's bayonet leap out toward him.

"It struck him with a soft thud, and I heard him sob as he slid down on his knees.

"'My God!' I whispered, 'what have you done?'

"'Killed him,' sez Nobby, 'accordin' to orders,' then 'Look out!' he shouted and I saw three crouching figures coming up the rise.

"I shot the first and got the bayonet home on the second, and the third Nobby settled.

"Then we heard the guard runnin'.

"'Smithy,' sez Nobby, very solemn, 'I'd give ten million pounds to hear the adjutant's voice damning somebody's eyes.' He got it for nothin' in a minute, for well ahead of the guard came the adjutant in his pyjamas with a little electric lamp in his hand.

"'Halt!' shouts Nobby, an' the adjutant stopped.

"'Thank God,' I heard the officer mutter; then he gave the word.

"'Are you all right?' he sez.

"'We're all right,' sez Nobby, anxious. 'Are you all right?—because, sir, hopin' there's no offence, I put eight inches of bayonet through your chest a few seconds ago.'

"The adjutant flashed his lamp over the dead man at Nobby's feet.

"He was dressed in a proper officer's uniform, but his face was as black as the ace of spades.

"'Lal Sahib!' sez the adjutant.

★★★★★★

"'I always suspected him,' sez the officer a little while later to the colonel, 'especially after I'd heard that his voice was so like mine that you couldn't distinguish the difference in the dark. It was easy enough for him to deceive the men on guard; sending one to the other side of the building where his friends were, whilst he knifed the other. He was the Lord High Gun Runner in this part of the world—you can't educate a Pathan out of his Pathanism.'"

2.—THE BAPTISM OF STEVENS

Those who make a close study of the human mind, and the devious processes of its working, inform me that years of research and study do not return such satisfactory results as a week's acquaintance with the average regiment of the line.

When, as I sometimes do, deliver a lecture on the adventures of war-corresponding, I am invariably asked by somebody at the end of the lecture what, in the course of my wild and questionable career, I might regard as being my most exciting adventure, I invariably reply my introduction to semaphore signalling. For in the early days, when men switched off the wagging flag, and took to waving their arms like windmills to give expression to their thoughts, it chanced that I was practising the new method unconscious of the fact that there was passing on the road below the hill on which I stood, a wild Irish regiment. I thought nothing of the incident save that the men regarded me with scowls and mutterings.

That night a picket of the Royal Artillery rescued me from a gang of infuriated Irishers, who had risen to slay "the black-hearted Orangeman who mocked them by crossing himself as good Catholics passed." Those who understand the gyrations that semaphore signalling calls into play, will appreciate the incident. Discussing this matter with Smithy, passed by easy stages to theology—theology in words of one syllable.

Now it is a very serious fact that there are two subjects taboo in a barrack room; the king and religion. There may be regulations, and probably are, which prohibit such discussions, but regulations are nothing where two or three soldiers are gathered together. Rather is it from an innate sense of delicacy that these matters are avoided. As Kipling will tell you, there are other dangerous matters, such as casting doubt upon your comrade being "legitimate issue," as the lawyers have it. This is an indiscretion invariably settled with bloodshed, great uproar, a hurrying of armed men, and sometimes a frog-marching procession to the guard room. Harking back to religion:

"When we was at the Cape," said Smithy, "we was stationed at Wynberg. 'B' Company was detached for duty at Simonstown, which, as everybody knows, is one of the cushiest stations abroad. There's a couple of guards, one on the artillery barracks an' one on the magazine *kloof*, an' as in them days there was only room enough outside the barracks to fall in one company, it follered there wasn't much drill. There's a few engineer chaps, a lot of Garrison Artillery, an' whips of sailors.

"There was a couple of the medical staff, a corporal of the Army

Service Corps, an' an army pay chap. It was what Nobby called an ideal army corps, where nobody did any work, an' the food was good.

"As a matter of fact there wasn't enough work, an' the consequence was that one half the detachment took to drink an' the other half got serious mainly because of Stevens—Jimmy Stevens. Stevens is a chap who's a big thinker, an' most of his thinkin' is about what's goin' to happen to him when he dies. I never knew a chap to change his religion as often as Jimmy has.

"He started Church an' turned Wesleyan; then he become a Baptist, an' then went back to the Church. Then he became a Plymouth Brother, an' a Congregationalist, an' a Christian Sciencer, an' a Unitarian. He's only had two checks, once when he tried to be a suffragette under the impression it was a new religion, an' once when he tried to turn R.C.

"He went up an' saw Father O'Leary, an' pulled a long face, an' said he'd seen the errer of his ways, but the Father cut him short.

"'Phwat are ye wantin'?' sez Father O'Leary. 'Is it religion ye want, ye ecclesiastical chandler's shop? or is it the flat of me boot ye're askin' for?'

"You see, Father O'Leary knew everything about everybody, an' all he knew about Jimmy wasn't worth worryin' about. Soon after that the regiment went to Burma, an' Jimmy took up Buddhist outfit. Used to sit on his bed cot for hours fixin' his eye on the ceilin' an' saying nothin'.

"'What are you doin'?' sez Nobby.

"'Searchin' me soul,' sez Jimmy, very solemn.

"'You search it very careful,' sez Nobby, fiercely, 'an' if you find a blackin' brush marked No. 7,143, it belongs to Private Clark.'

"Nobby had been losin' things.

"Well, I was tellin' you about Simonstown. Three weeks after we arrived Jimmy got mighty serious on the question of his soul. What always worried him was he could never find any kind of sec', Christian, Mahommedan, or Buddhist, that gave him all the peace of mind he wanted without his havin' to do somethin' he didn't want.

"'I've tried 'em all,' he sez, very melancholy, 'it's no good bein' a Christian because you've got to give up drinkin'; no good bein' a Buddhist, cos you've got to give up eatin'; no good bein' a Jew unless you're born that way, or made so, and Mahommedism the same.

"I don't know where he got the idea from unless it was from one of them encyclo-who-is-its that used to come out in monthly parts, but he got struck with the idea of bein' a 'cynic.'

"It's a foreign word as far as I can understand that means grouser. The way to be a cynic is to keep on sayin' 'Ah, yes! I dessay!' in a pityin' kind of voice when anybody makes a pleasant observation. Or suppose you're writin' home to your girl an' Jimmy knew it, he'd talk about absence making the heart grow fonder—fonder of the other feller. He quite enjoyed this sort of thing for a month, an' used to go cynicin' round, till one day Nobby an' him fell out over this question of a bit of cynicisation concernin' Nobby's feet. Nobby's very sensitive about his feet, an' I must say he's got a lot to be sensitive about.

"Jimmy wasn't very much hurt, but the wall where his head hit was a bit dented. But it changed Jimmy's religion. I felt sorry for him in a way. You see, he'd gone through the whole lot, an' there was nothin' for him to be except a Socialist—an' that's politics.

"For a fortnight or more he used to mooch about barracks an' go wanderin' about the hills by hisself, an' then one night, when me an' Nobby was takin' a friendly pint in the Artillery canteen Jimmy stuck his head in the door very mysterious, an' beckoned us out. We went. He was waitin' for us on the little slopin' square that leads down to the hospital.

"'Smithy,' he sez, 'an' Clark—I don't bear no ill-will.'

"'Quite right,' sez Nobby.

"'But,' sez Jimmy, 'feelin' you take a bit of an interest in me I want you chaps to do me a favour.'

"'Owin',' sez Nobby, 'to me bein' put under stoppages for a new shirt——'

"'It ain't money,' sez Jimmy, bitterly, 'it's a sympathisin' an' friendly act.'

"'Certainly,' sez Nobby, very relieved.

"'You see before you,' sez Jimmy, mournful, 'a man that's misunderstood, a man that's suspected——'

"'I found them socks,' sez Nobby, generously, 'an' I beg your pardon for thinkin'——'

"'A man that's suspected of tryin' new religions for what he can get out of 'em,' sez Jimmy, 'so I've decided to commit suicide.'

"'Go on?' sez Nobby, 'you're jokin'?'

"'No,' sez Jimmy sadly, 'I've seen enough of this life—I've had my whack of joys an' sorrows. I've sipped the—the, you know what I mean. I've seen the wonders of India, an' a dam rotten hole it is, too. I've been to Burma, I've been to Africa, I've got me second class certificate—there's nothin' worth livin' for.'

"He went on like this walkin' back to barracks, an' kept it up for half an hour, an' at last he told us his plans. He was goin' to chuck hisself into the sea, an' he wanted me an' Nobby to come along an' see fair play.

"The next mornin' it was goin' to be—at four o'clock, before anyone was about.

"Nobby was fairly excited, an' started askin' questions, an' makin' suggestions.

"'How are you goin' to do it?' he sez, very anxious. 'Walk straight in an' get it over—or go out in a boat an' drop overboard! A very good way,' sez Nobby, musin', 'is to get two big stones, or pinch a couple of weights from the meat store——'

"'We'll see,' sez Jimmy, rather coldly, I thought; 'you wait till tomorrer—you don't mind gettin' up at four?'

"'Not a bit,' sez Nobby, eager, 'make it three if you like.'

"'I'll wake you,' sez Jimmy, very gloomy.

"'Don't worry,' sez Nobby. 'I'll stay awake all night so as not to miss this treat—I mean so as not to miss helpin' a friend.'

"I don't know whether Nobby did stay awake, but at any rate he was the first one up. We had to move quiet for fear of wakin' the other chaps. I forgot to tell you that Jimmy was actin' company storeman, so he had a little room to himself. It took Nobby quite a time to wake him up, an' when he did, Jimmy sat up rubbin' his eyes an' askin' what was the matter.

"'Come on, old feller,' whispers Nobby, 'it's time for the job.'

"Jimmy didn't look too pleased, but he struggled into his clothes. He was an awful long time dressin', but we got him out at last. It wasn't two minutes walk to the beach, but Jimmy said he thought we'd best go a mile or so along the road where nobody could see us.

"'That's right,' sez Nobby, admiringly; 'we'll go up by the fort; there's a rare current there for pullin' a chap under—can you swim he sez, anxious.

"'Yes, a bit,' sez he, a bit sulky.

"'Then,' sez Nobby, 'we'd better tie your hands.'

"'You'll do nothin' of the sort!' snarled Jimmy.

"He was mighty hard to please was Jimmy. First one place wouldn't suit because there was no rocks, an' another place wouldn't do because it was too near the sewer. Then he wanted a bit of beach near where there was some grass an' flowers.

"'So,' he sez, 'when they find me body it will be reclinin' just as though I was asleep amidst the simple flowers.'

"'You get on with the suicide,' sez Nobby, very short, 'leave me an' Smithy to make you ornamental.'

"He was a terrible time before he decided, then he chose a place, an' started takin' his coat off.

"'What's that for?' sez Nobby.

"'I don't want to get my clothes wet, do I?' snaps Jimmy.

"'Of course not,' sez Nobby, brightenin' up. 'That's very thoughtful of you, Jimmy—I suppose me an' Smithy can have our pick, can't we? I'd like your jacket, if you don't mind.'

"But Jimmy was slowly peelin'.

"'It's a far, far better thing that I do—or am goin' to do—perhaps, than I have ever done before,' he sez.

"'Hurry up,' sez Nobby.

"'Here lies one who fought an' failed,' sez Jimmy, takin' off his weskit. 'One cut off in the prime of his strength, so to speak. A bit of wreckage—human wreckage—driven by a coldhearted world——'

"'Get your trousis off,' sez Nobby.

"'I say this,' sez Jimmy, standin' on the beach in his shirt an' shiverin'. 'I say this, that it would be a brighter, happier universe if love and kindness was shown to the unfortunate——'

"'Goodbye, old feller,' sez Nobby. 'It's all for the best.'

"Jimmy walked towards the water, an' a little wave struck his feet an' he nipped back.

"'My word! it's cold,' he sez, with his teeth chatterin'. 'An' they call this sunny Africa!'

"'Go on—don't lose heart,' urged Nobby. 'Them trousis are mine, Smithy,' he hissed; 'an' keep your hand out of the pockets.'

"'Farewell, life,' sez Jimmy, 'farewell, army; farewell, "B" Company: farewell——'

"'Say *etcetra*,' sez Nobby.

"'Farewell, Captain Umfreville; farewell, Sergeant-Major Towns; farewell, Colour-Sergeant——'

"'Look here, Jimmy,' sez Nobby, very angry, 'you don't expect me an' Smithy to sit here whilst you call the roll, do you?'

"'It's a far, far better thing that I no now,' sez Jimmy.

"'Do it!' sez Nobby. 'Don't talk about it. Be a man.'

"Jimmy looked at him an' looked at the water.

"'I will,' he sez. 'I will be a man. Give me them trousis.'

"'What for?' sez Nobby.

"'Is it manly?' sez Jimmy. 'Is it manly to seek a watery grave? Is it manly to slink out of the world an' me for duty tomorrer? Is it manly to give everybody a lot of trouble? No! Give me them trousis.'

"Nobby was struck all of a heap.

"'What!' he sez, very fierce. 'Do you mean to say that you ain't goin' to do it?'

"'No,' sez Jimmy, very firm. 'It's cowardly. It come over me like a flash when I was lookin' at the water. Somethin' seemed to say to me——'

"'Look here,' sez Nobby, very earnest. 'Me an' Smithy specially got up to give you a hand, didn't we?'

"'You did,' sez Jimmy, 'for which I'm much obliged.'

"'Never mind about that,' sez Nobby. 'You thought it all over, and considered this was the best thing you could do, didn't you?'

"'Yes,' sez Jimmy, 'In me excitement I thought——'

"'Never mind about your excitement,' sez Nobby; 'but you lured us down here to see fair play an' assist, didn't you?'

"'I did,' sez Jimmy, shiverin' in his shirt.

"'Very well,' sez Nobby, grabbin' him by the scruff of his neck. 'Very well, then, me an' Smithy are goin' to assist you.'

"'Leggo,' sez Jimmy.

"'Not so,' sez Nobby, holdin' him tight. 'I'm not goin' to see a chap spoil a good mind. Catch hold of his legs, Smithy.'

"'Help! Murder!' yells Jimmy, strugglin' hard.

"'It's a far, far better thing,' sez Nobby, 'that me an' Smithy are doin' now than we have ever done before. In with him!'

"It's a very easy beach. You can wade out for a dozen yards without wettin' your knees. But Jimmy got wet because he fell on his back. You might have heard his yell ten miles away as he jumped up an' made for the beach.

"'No, you don't,' sez Nobby. 'Think of yourself lyin' as if asleep amongst,' he sez 'the buttercups an' daisies an' pig lilies.'

"So we chucked him in again.

"He yelled blue murder this time, but he might have saved himself the trouble.

"'Nobody can hear you,' sez Nobby. 'Farewell, Jimmy; Farewell, Stevens; farewell, Buddhist; farewell, Wesleyan ; farewell, follow-the-band; farewell, passive resister——'

"Jimmy made a dart, an' Nobby jumped to catch him, an' missed

110

him, an' Jimmy scuttled along the beach in his shirt as hard as he could lick.

"'Stop!' shouts Nobby. Then 'Pick up them clothes, Smithy,' he sez. An' we grabbed Jimmy's kit an' pelted after him.

"He got on to the main road an' run like mad me an' Nobby follerin'.

"Through the little bit of town an' up the hill to the main guard he run, an' bimeby we could see the sentry an' the sergeant of the guard comin' out.

"'Stop that man!' shouts Nobby. '*He's an escaped suicide!*'

★★★★★★

"No," reflected Smithy, "solderin' wouldn't be very comfortable if chaps was allowed to go in for all kinds of fancy religions every time their livers got a bit out of order. Fellers that think too much about their souls generally don't think enough about their bodies ; an' I've known a No. 9 pill turn a rank Atheist into a Presbyterian —I've known a good kicking to have the same effect. Jimmy Stevens has forgiven Nobby now.

"'Nobby,' he sez, one day, 'havin' a charitable 'art, I believe you when you say that my kit dropped into the sea and was lost. I believe it, although every time I see Smithy wearing my braces, an' you with my trousis on, it makes me homesick. But you pointed out the right way. A Baptist I am, an' a Baptist I'll remain, he sez."

3.—THE ROTTEN AFFAIR

My knowledge of India being limited to all that can be acquired in a brief visit to Bombay, I must perforce take my description of Nurpore from Smithy. According to that veracious chronicler, Nurpore is as picturesque as the floor of a baker's oven—and as hot.

Many years ago, when the regiment was stationed in this out-of-the-way corner of India, strange rumours filtered through to the Pall Mall clubs regarding the "unsatisfactory condition" of the battalion—a vague enough stricture, but one which suggested the gravest possibilities. If a good churchman learnt that the Archbishop of Brighton kept a "separate establishment," or a bank director was informed that his head cashier had lost £20,000 on the St. Leger, the combined agony of their feelings is as nothing to the shame and sorrow that come to men who love their army, when the news is abroad that such and such a regiment is "unsatisfactory." For it may imply anything from slackness to mutiny, from uncleanliness to cowardice.

The "unsatisfactory condition" of the Anchesters had filled me with dismay, and I had sought far and wide for the inner truth of the rumour, going so far as to beard in his den at the War Office, the suave, handsome gentleman, who administers the internal affairs of the army. From him I received soothing and comforting assurances. Outside, in Pall Mall, a thought struck me—had not the Anchesters a new colonel?

I crossed to my club, and, looking up the back files of the *Gazette*, I discovered the entry:

Anchester Regiment. To be second in command, Major Fallock-Ruttin, from the 33rd (Duke of Straburg's Own) Dragoon Guards, April 14th.

Pursuing my investigations to a later date I learnt that "Lieut.-Col. Samson, C.B., of the 1st Anchester Regiment, had been granted leave of absence for six months," and putting the two notices together, I drew my own conclusions. I knew the 33rd Dragoon Guards. So does everybody else in the army. Frankly and briefly, it is a rabble. An undisciplined, uncleanly, untrustworthy, and altogether an undesirable collection of larrikins. It is a tradition that the regiment has always been so; and most ignobly does it live up to its tradition. So that its rank and file are the scourings of the streets, and its officers the groundlings of Sandhurst.

Now as to Major Fallock-Ruttin. "When he came to us," said Smithy, who only recently gave me the full story, "we didn't grouse because we thought he must be such a decent feller that he couldn't stick the 33rd any longer. I think, now, that he must have been a bit too thick, even for them!

"We was at Nurpore when he came. It wasn't much of a station for a soldier an' there was little or nothin' to do except a guard or so, an' a day-break parade every mornin'.

"His comin' didn't make much difference for a bit. You see he wasn't used to a foot-sloggin' crush like ours an' he was a bit astray, an' then, of course, our colonel is one of them chaps that don't stand any interference from seconds-in-command. So we got along all right till the colonel went on leave. The old man's train was hardly out of the station before his nibs started in to reorganise the regiment.

"He had us on parade the next mornin' and gave us an hour's battalion drill, and when it was all over, he formed us into a hollow square, an' addressed a few unfriendly remarks to us.

"I can see him sittin' on his horse now. He was a strong-built chap with one of them sulky faces that gets into the illustrated papers occasionally. He had a heavy, black moustache an' straight, black eyebrows that ran from one side of his face to the other without stoppin' at his nose, an' when he spoke it was like a peacock singin' the 'dead march.'

"'What I have to tell you, men, is this,' he sez, 'your drill is as bad as it can be; you've no more idea of smartness than my horse has of playing draughts; the regiment wants waking up—there will be another parade at sunset.'

"We was flabbergasted at him.

"'I like that feller's nerve,' sez Nobby, as we was goin' back to the bungalow, 'why, he ain't got the smell of the 33rd stables out of him before he comes bargin' about the decentest regiment he's ever been in. I wonder what our officers think about it?'

"Accordin' to Fatty Wilkes, who's Umfreville's servant, what the officers said couldn't be repeated in respectable society. But this here Major Rotten wasn't upset by what anybody thought. He was out to make trouble an' he made it. Two parades a day, all kinds of foolish fatigues, lectures in the hot afternoons, an' kit inspection as often as was disagreeable. And that wasn't the worst of it. He took it into his head that the non-commissioned officers was screenin' the men, and he prowled about lookin' for crime. Dozens of chaps was run in for little things that ain't worth talkin' about. He broke two sergeants an' a corporal by forcin' 'em to answer back to him an' then tryin' 'em by court martial. He gave us a lecture—'B' Company—one day on tactics. He asked questions, an' was particularly down on poor old Spud Murphy. After he'd fairly mixed up Spud with questions about field strategy, he sez:

"'What is the function of dragoons?'

"'Beg pardon, sir?' sez poor Spud.

"'Don't you understand English!' he roars. 'What are dragoons for?' he sez.

"'God knows,' sez Spud, very earnest. He got ten days for that.

"He ran in Nobby for not salutin' properly.

"'The slovenly way you men behave would disgrace a militia regiment,' he sez. 'You want smartenin' up. I'd like to transfer you to the 33rd for a month.'

"'If it's all the same to you I'd rather go to prison, sir,' sez Nobby.

"'You're an impertinent scoundrel,' shouts Major Rotten, 'an' you'll go to cells for seven days!'

"'Thank you, sir,' sez Nobby.

"'An' another three days for your damned cheek,' sez the major.

"When Nobby came out of cells he didn't say much about Rotten.

"'His ways ain't our ways,' he sez, quite philosophic, which wasn't like Nobby at all.

"The colonel hadn't been on leave three months before the regiment was as nice a little hell upon earth as you could wish. Full of chaps wishin' they was dead, an' you couldn't talk to a corporal or a sergeant without gettin' your head snapped off.

"There was a sergeant by the name of Biron, a good-natured, soft kind of chap, who had only recently joined us from the 2nd Battalion. He'd been married about a year an' brought his wife out with him. When Major Rotten inspected the married quarters, Sergeant Biron was the only N.C.O. that didn't get nasty remarks thrown at him. In fact, the major was quite polite to Mrs. Biron.

"She wasn't what you'd call popular in the regiment. Too fond of complainin' about the life, an' talkin' about the good home she left, an' how she wished she hadn't. She was pretty in a slim, white kind of way. I only spoke to her once, before Major Rotten came. Me an' Nobby was on duty at a gymkhana. To be exact, we was servin' drinks in the sergeants' tent, an' she complained about the claret cup.

"'It tastes like vinegar,' she sez.

"'Very likely,' sez Nobby, 'that's what claret's supposed to taste like.'

"'Not the claret I'm used to,' she sez, 'but I suppose you don't know the difference between good an' bad?'

"'No, m'am,' sez Nobby, 'I always make my claret cup out of beer.'

"I didn't see her again till the sergeant was ordered down to Poona for a course of signallin', an' then I was sent up to the married quarters to get his kit. We had a bit of a talk. 'I suppose you're sorry to be left behind,' I sez.

"She laughed a bit careless.

"'I can't say that I am,' she sez, 'I shall be rid of Biron for a bit.'

"It's not nice to hear a woman talk like that, so I changed the subject.

"'I wish I had a chance of gettin' away from this hole,' I sez, 'an' that kind, Christian Major of ours.'

"She flushed up in a minute.

"'It seems to me,' she sez, hotly, 'you don't know a good officer when you see him. Major Ruttin has a very good heart.'

"'Perhaps he has,' I sez, 'an' I only hope I'm present at his post-mortem to see for meself.'

"Well, Sergeant Biron went, an' his wife got haughtier an' haughtier.

"Nobby was the only chap who took any interest in her, an' I had to speak to him about it.

"'You keep away from the married quarters,' I sez, 'or you'll find someone there who'll give you a bit of trouble.'

"'That's all right,' he sez, 'I saw someone there last night who's given me all the trouble I want.'

"We hadn't much time to notice Mrs. Biron, however, for we was too much took up with our own troubles. The C.O. went from bad to worse, and things came to a head one mornin' on parade. He used to march us out on to the plain so as we should have to march back in the sun, an' he'd kept us there that mornin' marchin' an' doublin' till the sun was well up an' then he fell us into a hollow square to have his usual palaver. Somethin' had happened to put him out. One of the officers had answered him short, so he was all for takin' it out of us.

"He slanged us for ten minutes by the clock an' finished up with tellin' us we was street-corner loafers who had joined the army because it was easier than goin' into the workhouse.

"'You're lazy,' he shouts, 'you've been havin' too easy a time, no one has ever got the better of me yet, and I'll teach you to be soldiers if I have to break every one of you.'

"He stopped short an' you could have heard a pin drop—when a voice from the rear files of 'B' Company said quite distinct, 'What about Mrs. Biron?'

"'Who was it?' he gasped, mad with temper, 'who was the black-guard?'

"But nobody answered.

"'If I find the man—' screamed the major, when the adjutant came trottin' over.

"He rode straight to where Nobby stood.

"'Fall out, Private Clark,' he sez, quietly, 'it was you who spoke.'

"Nobby stepped forward and a couple of chaps fell in on each side.

"'Was it you, you dog?' sez Rotten.

"'Yes,' sez Nobby.

"Quick as a flash the officer's hand came up, but it was Umfreville who got the blow for he sprang between them.

"'You must not do that, sir,' he said, breath in' hard, 'this man has no right to speak in the ranks— he has already lodged a complaint.'

"Complaint,' roared the major, 'what the devil do you mean?'

"'He has reported certain occurrences to me—I needn't go into the matter here. He considered it was his duty to a comrade—to Sergeant Biron.'

"I saw the major stagger. He pulled himself together with an effort.

"'March the men back to barracks,' he sez.

"As we turned into the gates of the cantonment I saw three strange officers standin' by the guard-room. One was very tall, with a face burnt brick red an' curious light blue eyes.

"'That's Kitchener,' whispered somebody. 'Look at him scowlin'!'

"We swung into column on the parade an' 'K' walked round the ranks as silent as the grave, the major explainin' things in a flustered way.

"Bimeby, 'K' spoke, an' we chaps in the front company could hear every word.

"'How long have you had this command, major?' he sez.

"'Three months, sir,' sez Rotten.

"'K' nods his head thoughtful.

"'An' a damned fine mess you've made of it,' he sez.

"They didn't try Nobby by court martial an' they didn't try Rotten by court martial. Nobby got seven days' C.B. for talkin' in the ranks, an' a sort of inquiry was held over the major.

"One mornin' the major didn't turn up at parade, an' in general orders that night it read:

Retirement

Anchester Regiment: Major Fallock-Ruttin, from June 17th; the king having no further use for his services.

4.—THE BACHELORS' CLUB

Smithy's foreign service covers India, South Africa, and the Far East. It also embraces the Western circuit. You must know that there is a sort of Military-Cook's-Tour, that begins pleasantly at Bermuda, continues luxuriously to Halifax, N.S., goes on to Jamaica and the islands about, and ends unsatisfactorily in South Africa. Unsatisfactory because in South Africa it sometimes takes a new lease of life, and wanders from the Cape to Natal, then to Mauritius, and from there to Colombo, Singapore, Hong Kong, and so home. In the days of which Smithy speaks there used to be a regular itinerary for the corps that missed India. Smithy does not count Gibraltar as foreign service; he has his doubts about Malta, and Egypt is only "foreign" in the hot months.

"Crete's a rum place, an' so is Aden, Suez is—well, everybody knows what Suez is; Singapore ain't so bad. One of our chaps, under the influence of drink, drowned a Chinaman in a water-butt an' got fourteen days' cells for pollutin' the water supply. Hong Kong's foggy, and Barbadoes is too full of land-crabs to be pleasant. Bermuda's too much like home an' Colombo's too much like abroad. South Africa ain't so bad, but Natal's hot. There isn't what you'd call an ideal foreign station, because where beer's cheap there ain't other things, and where other things can be picked up for next to nothin' beer's a tanner a pint. It's what Wattsey calls 'the infernal lore of contemplation.'

"When you hear a chap ravin' about a station, what a splendid place it is; what magnificent walks you can get, an' how the climate makes you skip like a goat, you can bet a pair of socks to a tin hat he's got a girl somewhere round the corner. It's wonderful what effect a girl has on the climate. There was a chap of ours—Burkey his name was—wot got married to a *chee-chee* girl in Mauritius. As white as you an' me, she was, an' whiter, but her grandpa's dial must have been in mournin'. He married her an' left the regiment an' went to live in some out-of-the-way corner of the island, near Curepipe it was. Three weeks before the regiment left they brought him into Port Louis on a stretcher. He was dosed with fever an' as thin as a cigarette paper. I went to see him in hospital. He was nearly gone an' was ravin', but he recognised me.

"'Splendid climate, Smithy,' he sez, very weak. Then he added, 'Grow any kind of vegetables. The sunsets are simply wonderful, an' she's been a good wife to me.'

"I went to his funeral.

"Nobby Clark was very sarcastic comin' back.

"'Bein' in love,' he sez bitterly, 'blinds a chap so that he can't tell a pertater-barrer from the Cafe Royal. An' it upsets his taste an' his smell an' his sense generally. Drink's bad enough, but not so bad as love. Love don't make a chap want to fight, it only makes him want to lie down in a quiet place an' snivel. It's worse than that pipe-shop orf the Queen's Road, where you lay down an' smoke dope till you see the

New Cut fried fish shops an' other lovely visions. It's worse——'

"'Close your face, Private Clark,' sez the sergeant, who was marchin' alongside, an' Nobby took the hint.

"Soon after this we went to Wynberg, an' that's where Nobby started his Bachelors' Club.

"We were in the canteen one night, a lot of us chaps—Spud Murphy, Little Green, Tiny White, Pug Wilson, and the rest of 'em, an' Spud was talkin' about the standoffishness of girls at the Cape.

"'There's a girl,' sez Spud, 'that lives on the main road. Her father's a carpenter. Him an' me got friendly owin' to our havin' both come from the same part of England—no, it ain't Whitechapel, Nobby—and asked me down to his house to tea.'

"Nobby sniffed.

"'Asked me down to his house to tea,' sez Spud, with relish, 'an' there was the girl.'

"'She didn't see you comin', perhaps?' sez Nobby.

"'There was the girl,' sez Spud, very impassive, 'a-sittin' down at the table with a nice white dress on, an' a gold belt, an' one of them wide, feathery hats, an' kid gloves all up to the nines.'

"'What about her boots?' sez Nobby.

"'I sez to her,' sez Spud, takin' no notice. 'I sez, 'Good evenin', miss; hope you're quite well.''

"'As it leaves us all at present,' sez Nobby.

"'I hope you're quite well, miss,' I sez.

"'Very well, thank you, how are you?' she sez.

"'Oh,' I sez, 'I'm so-so——'

"'She could see *that*,' sez Nobby.

"'So I sez, ''What a lovely evenin' for a walk!''

"'Yes,' she sez, 'but it looks a bit threatenin'.'

"'She was referrin' to you,' sez Nobby, impatient.

"Don't keep us all night, Spud, monopolisin' the conversation about what 'she sez' an' what 'I sez'—other people want to talk. Did she go out with you?'

"'No, she didn't!' sez Spud, sulky, 'she don't walk out with soldiers.'

"'There's soldiers an' there's soldiers,' sez Nobby, 'but you can be sure of one thing, Spud. She ain't in love with you. If she was she'd walk out with you.'

"'Any fool knows that,' sez Spud.

"'Because,' sez Nobby, 'love is as blind as a bat under chloroform, an' she'd have to be very blind, in addition to being naturally silly, before she took on a lop-sided woman-hater like you.'

"'I ain't a woman-hater!' sez Spud, very indignant.

"'Yes, you are,' sez Nobby, calmly. 'All chaps that girls won't walk out with are woman-haters.'

"There was something about this girl, Laura Haste was her name, that sort of fascinated our battalion. Her father got to be the most popular civilian in the camp owin' to chaps wantin' to be pleasant an' friendly an' be asked home to tea. She was as nice as nice could be, too, used to listen an' say "Ah, yes!" an' "Oh, no!" to all they had to say, an' laugh an' joke, but when the feller sez, 'What a beautiful evenin' for a walk,' she used to get up an' say, 'Well, I won't detain you, Mr. So-and-So,' an' that's where *his* little plan came unglued.

"Me an' Nobby kept a list of the chaps who went to the house to tea. Sergeant Mandy of 'H' went, Corporal Toms of 'G,' Yatesy went, an' so did 'Click' Morris, an' dozens of other chaps I could name. Me and Nobby used to sit on a gate near the house every Sunday night an' watch 'em comin' away. When they came up to us, Nobby used to say quite innocent, 'Fine evenin' for a walk, sergeant,' or 'corporal,' as the case might be, and the chap would scowl and say somethin' about goin' to rain.

"An' the rum thing about it was, as Nobby pointed out, that it didn't matter what the weather was, wet or fine, blowin' a south-easter, or so bloomin' hot that walkin' was a horrible an' upsettin' business, these chaps who went to tea all thought the same thing—that it was just the weather for a little walk, which proves that Nobby wasn't a man of umgumption.

"It was after there were a dozen or so fellers wanderin' about barracks lookin' as if they didn't care whether it snowed, that Nobby got his idea for a Bachelors' Club. Everybody who wanted to remain a bachelor was invited to join an' pay a penny a week.

"'Wot's that for?' sez Spud, highly suspicious.

"'Well, it's like this,' sez Nobby, slowly. 'I've noticed that a lot of young chaps have been hangin' round Miss Haste, tryin' to kid her to go for a walk——'

"'Not me,' sez Spud, very loud. 'I went there to oblige her father.'

"'I went down to see the old man, too,' sez Fatty Wilkes, an' all the others took their oath that *they'd* never asked the girl to go out with 'em.

"'As a matter of fact,' sez Spud, carelessly, 'I hardly noticed the girl—what's she like?'

"'It ain't so much a question of what she's like,' sez Nobby, very careful, 'as what she likes; an' I'm thinkin',' sez Nobby, 'that maybe one of these days she'll take a sudden fancy for one of you chaps, an' then the pennies we put by will make a sort of sweepstake for the lucky feller.'

"Nobby's got a terrible oily tongue, an' the way he persuaded them chaps to part with their pennies was worth goin' a long way to see. Nobby called it a Bachelors' Club, but, as a matter of fact, it was a sort of lucky dip, an' the chap that got the girl got the prize.

"I wouldn't come into it at first, because I didn't think it was playin' the game with the girl, an' I told Nobby so, but he said it was a sort of tournament where a lot of gallant knights in armour chopped each other's heads off just to show they loved some young lady sittin' in the pit stalls.

"'It's chivalry, that's what it is!' sez Nobby, enthusiastic; 'an' it simply makes me thrill to see Sir Fatty de Green an' Sir Tiny de White go ridin' forth to capture the lovely Laura de Haste.'

"'What about you?' I sez.

"'Me?' sez Nobby, sadly. 'I'm too old for that sort of thing, Smithy; I'm a hermit in a manner of speakin'. It cheers my old heart to collect——'

"'You're collectin' their money, ain't you?' I sez.

"'That's what I was goin' to say,' sez Nobby. So I joined the club for Nobby's benefit.

"The Bachelors' Club was a big success from the start. Fellers who hadn't tried their luck joined it because they thought there wasn't a girl on earth that could say 'no' when they said 'Let's go for a walk.' An' chaps who had tried and didn't get any further forward, they came in to try their luck again.

"Miss Laura Haste got to hear all about it. Some girls would have taken offence even after Nobby had explained she was doin' the Queen of Beauty act; but Miss Laura Haste wasn't that sort of a girl. It took a lot of worship to upset her.

"'I'm very much obliged to you, Mr. Clark,' she sez, 'for tellin' me, an' I think your friends are very silly—don't you?' an' she gave him the goo-goo eye.

"'I do,' sez Nobby, very serious, an' that seemed to annoy her. (We was down one Thursday afternoon lookin' at the old man's pigeons.)

"'I'm glad you think so, Mr. Clark,' she sez, sweetly. 'I can't imagine you being so silly,' she sez.

"'I can,' sez Nobby, an' she brightened up.

"'I got sunstroke in India,' sez Nobby, very solemn, 'an' sometimes I'm not quite all there.'

"She tossed up her head an' said, hadn't we better be goin' into the garden to see the Blue Rocks an' Dead Homers.

"She had another cut at Nobby before we left.

"'Father,' she sez, 'why don't you ask Mr. Smith an' Mr. Clark to come to tea next Sunday?' So the old man did.

"'Thanks,' sez Nobby, 'I don't mind if I do—so long as I can get away at six o'clock.'

"'You're always in such a hurry to get away, Mr. Clark,' she sez, very tart.

"Nobby didn't speak for a minute; he was standin' thinkin'. Bime-by, he sez, 'It's a nice evenin' for—'

"She jumped in eagerly.

"'I'm sorry——' she started.

"'For this time of the year,' sez Nobby, very solemn.

"From the look she gave Nobby, I gathered she was vexed.

"Some of the fellers saw us comin' out of the house an' one of them started chippin' us.

"'Hullo, Nobby,' sez one, 'this ain't Sunday.'

"'No,' sez Nobby, 'we've been havin' a sort of matinay,' he sez.

"I had a talk with old man Haste in the week.

"'Ain't you gettin' tired of the military display in your house?' I sez.

"He shook his head.

"'It'd be the same thing if I was,' he sez, very gloomy; 'she's her mother all over again—you didn't know her mother, did you?'

"He shook his head again, an' started sighin'.

"'My daughter's a very nice girl,' he sez, in a melancholy tone of voice, 'and I shall miss her when she's married; but,' he sez, 'if I miss her too much I'll move up near the barracks, where I can hear people shoutin' words of command from mornin' till night.'

"Nobby got hisself up very spruce for Sunday; borrered a tunic from one chap an' nice *squarpushir,* (captivating), boots from another, white gloves from Bill Mason, who borrered 'em from a young lady friend; an' we started off.

"She said she was very glad to see us, an' pretended she'd forgotten we was comin', an' we had a pleasant afternoon.

121

"When she was pourin' out the tea, she sez to Nobby, 'I've been hearing all sorts of things about you, Mr. Clark.'

"'Oh!' sez Nobby, very polite.

"'I've heard you're a great lady's man,' she sez, with a knowin' smile.

"'First time I've heard about it,' sez Nobby, very interested. 'Tell us some more.'

"'They say you've been engaged twice,' she sez.

"'That's right,' sez Nobby, 'once by a doctor, an' once on a Pickford's van: I used to take round the medicine for the doctor, an' got chucked out for leavin' the corn plaster at the house of a lady with the toothache.'

"'I mean engaged to girls,' she sez, huffily.

"Nobby shook his head.

"'The only girl I was ever engaged to,' he sez, 'was a girl in a piece called 'The Soldier's Vengeance,' that we played at Aldershot on behalf of the Soldiers' Home. Little Tyke Allison was the girl, an' looked it, but got a little too much to drink on the night of the play, an' when I was a-rescuin' her from a watery grave (the ship havin' been wrecked), she stood upon one of the waves an' wanted to fight me for the price of two drinks. It took six chaps to get her off the stage, an' then we had to clout her with the moon (which happened to be lyin' about),' he sez.

"Up went her head.

"'I've been misinformed,' she sez, very cold.

"'You have,' sez Nobby. 'Anybody who knows me will tell you that I can't stand girls at any price. I'd sooner walk from here to Simonstown on my lonely than I'd step across to the other side of the street with a feminine.'

"'I think you're very rude,' she sez.

"'I know I am,' sez Nobby; 'it's me only protection.'

"All through tea time she was lookin' at him curiously. When the meal was over, she sez, musin'ly:

"'What a lovely evenin'.'

"'Is it, miss?' sez Nobby, lookin' out of the winder.

"'Just the evenin' for——' she sez, an' stopped.

"'For what, miss?' sez Nobby, innocently.

"'Nothin'!' she snaps.

"Goin' home that night Nobby was as pleased with hisself as a cat with two tails.

"'That prize money's as good as mine, Smithy,' he sez. 'We'll call down at the house on Wednesday an' I'll walk her up to hear the band.'

"On Monday night he came round to see me—'B' Company were in two separate bungalows at Wynberg.

"'Smithy,' he sez, 'I've been countin' up the subscriptions, an' the fellers think I ought to hand it over to somebody who's quite impartial,' he sez.

"'Is that what they said?'

"'They ain't the exact words,' sez Nobby, carelessly 'They said somethin' about wantin' to be sure they got the money when it was due—anyhow, I don't mind.'

"He told me he'd handed the funds—seven and twopence—over to old Drum-Corporal Browne. 'It don't matter much who has 'em for the present,' he sez. 'It's as good as in my pocket. Let this be a lesson to you. Smithy,' he sez, 'never run after gels. Treat 'em proper an' they'll run after you.' I didn't see him the next night because I was busy, but on Wednesday he called for me, an' we made our way down town. He was in a light-hearted mood an' kept givin' me good advice, which is the only thing Nobby ever gives away—except hisself occasionally.

"'Haughtiness pays in the long run,' he sez. 'So does standoffishness; nobody never wants anythin' till it's impossible to get. That's why dead people are always such good chaps, an' everybody wishes they were alive again.'

"When we got to the house, there was the girl waitin' as if she expected us; an' I could see Nobby simply swellin' with pride at hisself.

"We talked about the weather for a bit, and then Nobby asked after the pigeons, an' when we'd been speakin' for half an hour without saying anything particular she turns suddenly on Nobby.

"'Doesn't the band play tonight?' she sez.

"'I believe it does,' sez Nobby.

"'I should like to hear the band play,' she sez, thoughtfully.

"'Would you?' sez Nobby.

"'I should,' she sez, 'if there was anybody to take me.'

"'What a pity there ain't,' sez Nobby.

"She sighed.

"'Of course,' she sez, 'if I asked somebody to take me they couldn't very well refuse, could they?'

"'Not very well,' sez Nobby—an' I could see that inside of him he was dancing for joy—'could they, Smithy?'

123

"'No,' I sez.

"She thought a bit.

"'Isn't there a ridiculous prize for the first soldier who is seen walkin' with me?' she sez, with that saucy toss of her head.

"'There is,' sez Nobby, quite overjoyed.

"She thought a bit more.

"'Well,' she sez, slowly, 'will you take me up to hear the band?'

"'Certainly, Miss!' sez Nobby, smilin' all over his face.

"There was a pause.

"'I wasn't talking to you,' she sez, icily; 'I was talking to Mr. Smith—will you, Mr. Smith?'

"'Yes,' I sez, like a shot.

"'I like you,' she sez, dreamily. 'You don't talk so much as your friend Nosey.'

"'Nobby!' sez Nobby, very fierce.

"'An' you're so much smarter,' she sez, nicely.

"'Will you wait till I get my hat on?'"

5.—Why "Featherweight Jackson" Enlisted

If you complain that I serve for your amusement no other army fare than the extremes of tragedy and broad farce, and if you demand, pathetically, querulously, curiously, or idly: Is there no humdrum *via media* between laughter and tears in everyday barrack life? I answer: Very possibly there is. For there are washing days and spring-cleaning days, when the appalling odour of military soap-suds and regimental fresh paint permeates the social atmosphere, and life becomes a tedious and insupportable burden. Days of pipe-claying and scrubbing, coal-carrying and whitewashing; preparations for G.O.C.'s inspection, when men grow crotchety and short of speech, when the canteen is a wilderness smelling of sawdust, and the "library" a desert redolent with the aroma of last night's coffee. Days of dreadful busyness, when the soldier complains bitterly that he is earning his shilling.

Yet (if you will forgive the platitude) there is a silver lining to every cloud, and I have known a gloomy battalion all spick and span, belted, strapped, immaculately blancoed and polished, geometrically trussed in its Slade-Wallace equipment, ready for the bugle to sound the "fall in" for C.O.'s inspection, to be suddenly transformed into an ecstatically joyful, almost hysterical band of happy schoolboys.

Picture the scene. The helmeted men putting the last touches on their *toilette*—a dab of pipe-clay here, a rub of the rag there; then:

"It's rainin'!" says a voice. A hush falls on the room. Men crowd to the windows. Down comes the rain, a steady, persistent drizzle.

No man dares to voice his hope, the gloom continues that the gods may be propitiated, for a too premature demonstration of joy might arrest the downpour.

Three minutes to parade time—two minutes—a minute, then, from the barrack square, a *staccato* bugle call, to which some imaginative soul has put suitable words:

There's no parade today! There's no parade today!
The colonel has the stomach-ache—the adjutant's away.

A cheerful yell from every room—you can hear the faint cheering from the furthermost barrack quarters.

What though they have spent days and, perhaps, weeks preparing for this particular function? What though all their labours, their whitening, their blackening, their brushing, polishing, boning, rolling, and strapping, have been to no purpose? What though their efforts have gone for naught? This is their compensation: that somebody has been fooled. Somebody in a cocked hat, with a cross-hilted sword, who expected to see them on parade, in marching order, has been foiled, and last, but by no means least, *Mr. Atkins has got out of doing something that he ought to have done!*

"You understand as well as I do," said Smithy, "that soldiers hate workin' at their job, they hate soldierin', they hate goin' on guard an' lookin' nice an' pretty. There was a feller once—was it you?—who wrote a lot of stuff about the ideal uniform for a soldier, but he went wide of the mark, because the ideal uniform would be a green an' blue-striped jersey, an' ole pair of kharki trousis, a pair of pink carpet slippers, an' a golf cap. An' if that was the uniform, he'd probably think the green an' blue jersey was a bit too quiet an' go in for something more tasty. If you ask me, the kit some fellers get into when they're slack prevents the army ever gettin' humdrum. There's a chap by the name of Miggs, in 'H,' who brought down a girl's motor-cap, bein' under the impression that it was the newest thing in civilian hats, an' another chap in the same company, who wore suspenders to keep his socks up till his colour sergeant found him out and ran him before the old man for bein' in possession of civilian clothin'. The greatest dandy we ever had in ours, an' the biggest surprise packet was a chap who joined us at 'Gib.' His name was Jackson—Walter Jackson, which is a rotten name because there's no possibilities in it, except Wally.

"From his roof to his basement he was the neatest, dapperest, *squar-pushi* you could hope to meet. All his clothes was specially altered to fit him like a glove. Used to wear socks with little fir-trees runnin' up each side, silk shirts, ball-bearin' braces, an'——(Smithy's details as to underwear need not be enumerated).

"Nobby used to sit on his cot quite fascinated whilst Wally was gettin' hisself up.

"'You oughter been a girl, Wally,' he sez.

"'Think so?' sez Wally, partin' his hair with a little silver-mounted brush.

"'I do,' sez Nobby, 'except,' he sez, thoughtful, 'that your dial ain't all it might be.'

"'It's the best I've got,' sez Wally, cheerful.

"'Have you tried pummice stone?' sez Nobby.

"Wally laughed. He was a good-natured sort of chap.

"'Or parin' bits off,' sez Nobby.

"Wally looked at Nobby.

"'Judgin' by results,' he sez, lookin' at Nobby's face very critical, 'I ain't encouraged to try the experiment.'

"'I want none of your insultin' remarks,' sez Nobby, very severe.

"Wally was sprayin' some scent over hisself—he was a perfect gentleman in his way, was Wally.

"'If any of you chaps would like a pint,' he sez, in his lordly style, 'I'll be down on the Waterport, at —.'

"'Don't trouble to tell us where,' sez Nobby, 'we'll be able to smell you.' If a feller keeps hisself nice an' clean an' tries to make hisself look smart, he's bound to make more enemies than if he stole other chaps' kits. It's human nature. Therefore you can bet there were dozens of men layin' for Wally. They used to call him Hikey, and the Duke of Westminster, an' all sorts of insultin' names, but he took it all good-natured.

"One night, in the canteen, Spud Murphy started gassin' about Wally.

"'He's a disgrace to the regiment, that's what he is.'

"He spoke so mysterious that we knew he'd got some yarn to spin.

"'I could tell you somethin' about him that'd make your bloomin' hair stand up an' beg,' he sez.

"We waited patiently for Spud to go on, but he kept winkin' and noddin'.

"'Switch yourself off,' sez Nobby, 'If you're waitin' for us to give you free drinks for information received you've gone past the house—try back.'

"After a lot of hummin' an' hawin' Spud told us.

"Some friend of his—a chap in the Marines—had seen Wally with a girl in a nice lonely part of the Europa-road.

"'She's a lady, too,' sez Spud, very triumphant, a *pukka* Spanish lady, *mantilla*, fan an' everythin', an' the way they was lookin' at each other was too terrible for words.'

"'Like how?' sez Nobby.

"'Like this,' sez Spud, lookin' languishin'.

"'Ah, I see,' sez Nobby, 'drunk.'

"'No, not drunk,' sez Spud, 'but just like this,' an' he gave another imitation.

"'If they looked like that,' sez Nobby, 'you can bet pore old Wally had been eatin' crab-apples—what's the scandal part?'

"This was what Spud had been waitin' for.

"'She's married,' he sez.

"'How do you know?' asks Nobby.

"Then it came out that Spud had seen her one day when he was on guard at Government House an' she was the Senora Maria Castiano de Piaz.

"'Her husband's a little chap, in the shipping line', sez Spud.

"Afterwards me and Nobby had a talk about it.

"'It's no business of mine or yours,' he sez, 'the only real hard part about it is, that Wally ain't you or me.'

"Nobby's very broad-minded as I've always said, 'it's easy enough to shut up Spud—but if these scorpions, ("Rock Scorpion" nickname of the civilian citizens of Gibraltar), get talkin' there'll be trouble for Wally.'

"It's curious how things happen," moralised Smithy, "I once met a chap named Oggley. I'd never met anybody by the name of Oggley before, but before the day was over I'd met two other chaps named Oggley, an' neither of 'em was related. It's what they call the 'odd chance.' The next day was Sunday, an' me an' Nobby went for a walk to Europa Point. When we was crossin' the Alameda, Spud Murphy came up.

"'Hullo,' he sez, 'walkin'?'

"'No,' sez Nobby, 'we're ridin' on the top of an omnibus.'

"'I asked a civil question,' sez Spud, 'are you walkin'?'

"'To be exact,' sez Nobby, very polite, 'at the present moment, we're lyin' down in bed—tell the slavey to call us in time for tea.'

"'Well, I'll walk along with you,' sez Spud.

"'I don't mind,' sez Nobby, 'if we meet anybody we know, we'll pretend you're sellin' matches.'

"'Don't you want me?' sez Spud.

"'I'd sooner take the dog for a run,' sez Nobby, 'but if you're anxious to be seen in respectable society, you can come along.'

"Spud started straight away to talk about Wally, an' 'his carryin' on.'

"'I can't think,' he sez, 'what a lady can see in that feller.'

"'You wouldn't,' sez Nobby.

"'He ain't good lookin',' sez Spud.

"'Except about the face,' sez Nobby.

"'He does things that I wouldn't do,' sez Spud.

"'Washes hisself twice a day, for one thing,' sez Nobby, 'changes his shirt, an' never gets drunk—yes, you're right.'

"Spud was goin' to say something rude but we suddenly turned a corner of the road, an' he stopped dead, an' grabbed my arm.

"'There they are!' he gasps.

"And sure enough there they was strollin' ahead of us, arm in arm, my bold Wally an' a girl.

"They heard our footsteps an' Wally dropped her arm quick, and they both looked round.

"There was no doubt about it—she was pretty, with a fair complexion, like you see in lots of the Southern Spaniards, an' eyes that laughed all the time.

"They stood still to let us pass an' Wally just nodded. There's something about Nobby that's very fine at times. He didn't stare at her, but just as he was passin' he lifted up his hand to the salute, an sez, '*Buenos días, señora.*'

"She smiled, not a bit put out, and said, '*Buenos días, señor.*' Then, with a twinkle in her eyes, she sez, '*Habla usted español, senor?*'

"'*Una poquito,*' sez Nobby, very modest.

"We only checked our walk, because Nobby was afraid she'd find out he didn't know much about the language.

"'*Adiós,*' he sez, an' we went on.

"You see Nobby, like all the other chaps at 'Gib.' knew enough Spanish to say 'Good day,' and when anybody asked him, 'Do you speak Spanish?' to answer, 'A little.'

"'If she'd gone any further I'd have been stumped,' he sez. We'd forgotten all about Spud, but he was absolutely twitterin' with excitement.

"'Did you see that?' he sez, jumpin' with joy. 'What did I tell you? Did you catch what she sez when we went away?'

"'Walter, *mio*,' she sez, 'why——'

"'Spud,' sez Nobby, very stern, 'my advice to you is never interfere between man an' wife.'

"'She ain't married to him!' sez Spud.

"'I didn't say she was,' sez Nobby. 'I said *man an' wife*—an' he's the man!'

"If Spud had took that bit of advice it might have saved trouble. I've never understood why it was that he disliked Wally so much. Perhaps it was because—but it's no use guessing. It's pretty certain that Spud was one of the people who was down on Wally. It came to a head one night in the barrack room, when Wally happened to come in just as we was gettin' ready for next day's parade. Everybody was busy and messy with pipe-clay an' cleanin' rags, an' Wally, who looked as if he'd just come out of a glass case that had previously been used for holdin' otter of roses, was a bit out of place.

"It was unfortunate that the subject we was discussin' just as Wally came in was a bit Mike Hogan had seen in a Sunday newspaper how strict Spanish women are looked after by their husbands.

"'Ho!' sez Spud, very loud, as Wally came in, 'a fat lot that chap on the newspaper knows.'

"'What about?' sez Wally, quite innocent.

"'About Spanish women,' sez Spud. 'I know a thing or two,' he sez. Nobby was polishin' his buttons. He put his coat down an' walked over to Spud.

"'Dry up,' he sez, quiet.

"'What for?' sez Spud.

"'To save that funny face of yourn,' sez Nobby.

"'What's the game?' sez Wally, lookin' very puzzled.

"'Nothin',' sez Nobby, 'hop it—you.'

"As Wally was walkin' out the temptation was too strong for Spud.

"'How's Maria?' he sez, an' Wally whipped round.

"He came straight back to Spud.

"'What did you say?' he asks.

"'How's Maria?' sez Spud, bold as brass.

129

"'Meanin',' sez Wally, very careful, 'the Donna Maria de Piaz?'

"'That's her,' sez Spud.

"'She's very well,' sez Wally, calmly. 'How are you?'

"Spud grinned.

"'I'm all right,' he sez.

"'That's a lie!' sez Wally.

"Smack!

"Nobody saw Wally's arm move, but Spud was on the floor. It was a treat to see Wally strip. Took off his white gloves an' folded 'em. Unbuckled his belt, an' laid it on Nobby's bed, undid his tunic, took it off, folded it inside out, an' put that on the table—blowin' the dust off the table. Slipped off his ball-bearin' braces an' rolled back his silk sleeves.

"Spud got up by this time, lookin' dazed.

"'If you'll take of your boots, Spud,' sez Wally, very anxious, 'I'd be obliged, because I don't want mine scratched.'

"'What do you think you're goin' to do?' sez Spud.

"'I think I'm goin' to give you a lot of trouble,' sez Wally.

"'You're not big enough for me,' sez Spud. 'I can't fight a little chap like you.'

"'Don't worry,' sez Wally, 'you'll be feelin' small enough this time ten minutes.'

"It's no use my tryin' to describe the scrap," said Smithy. "You might say that Spud got up an' was knocked down about twenty times, an' at last he decided that the best thing to do was to stay down.

"'Had enough?' sez Wally.

"'Thank you,' sez Spud, who ain't a bad feller at heart, 'I've had two or three helpin's too much.'

"Wally nodded an' started dressin' again just as careful as possible. When he'd finished he said:

"'Make yourself as free as you like with me—I like it. Only keep other people's names out of your mouth, Mister Spud.'

"Spud was still dreamin' when Wally left. He sat on the edge of his bed sayin' nothing, but thinkin' hard. 'Bimeby,' he said in a wonderin' sort of way:

"'He belted me an' down I went; I got up, an' he belted me again. I tried to get home on his jaw, an' got about half-way when the floor came up an' hit me. The question is,' sez Spud, musin', 'Have I lost my dash?'

"He got up slowly and went out of the room. He was gone ten minutes, an' when he came back his other eye was black, but he was very cheerful.

"'I've been to see Bill Hackett,' he sez. 'I whipped Bill with one hand, in a manner of speakin'; pushed him all over the room, an' nearly knocked his head orf, so I can't have lost me dash.' He thought a bit an' shook his head. 'And Wally's only about nine stone.' He shook his head again. 'It's supernatural, that's what it is.'

"A fortnight after that we had our cricket match against the R.A., an' everybody turned up to see it.

" Nobby an' me was discussin' the fieldin' of Fatty Green, and was saying what a pity Jessop couldn't see him, or George Robey, or some other chap who likes to see comic things, when Nobby stopped short an' sez:

"'Well, I'm blowed!'

"An' well he might be, for who should come into the field but Wally, an' walkin' with him was the Spanish lady.

"They strode along as though they didn't know that everybody was lookin' at 'em, an' sayin' the same as Nobby.

"Wally spotted me, an' walked the girl toward us.

"'Hullo, Smithy,' he sez, as cool as a meat store; 'how's things?' Before I could get my voice he beckoned to someone, an' I looked round to find it was Spud Murphy.

"'This is Spud Murphy, a pal of mine,' he sez to the girl in English, an' she gave Spud a smile that'd make a bloomin' aloe flower all the year round.

"'I have been talking to Walter,' she sez, an' she spoke English as well as I could. 'I've been telling him he ought to let you know.'

"'I'm sure, ma'am,' sez poor Spud, lookin' very uncomfortable, 'that I'm very sorry I've made any remarks that's given offence——'

"She laughed.

"'You're the only sufferer, Mr. Murphy,' she sez,, 'and I'm very angry with Walter, but I want to tell you a story.'

"'I'm sure, ma'am, we all believe——' sez Spud.

"'Years ago,' she sez, 'I was left an orphan—oh, yes, I'm English—with only a brother a few years older to look after me. He was a good boy and a brave boy, for he worked hard when he was only a little chap to feed and clothe me. When he was seventeen he began to earn a lot of money, because a gentleman had seen him boxing at a gymnasium and "took him up." It wasn't very long before his name was in all the papers as a champion light-weight. When I was eighteen I met Senor de Piaz, my husband. He proposed to me, and I accepted him, for he is a charming gentleman—isn't he, Walter?'

"Wally nodded.

"'When I told Walter, he said, "You're going to be a lady now, Ria, and I'm not going to disgrace you by remaining a professional boxer. I'll go into a business where fighting means glory." So he enlisted—didn't you, Walter?'

"Wally nodded.

"'I tried to persuade him, but he was determined, and so to keep his sister——'

"Spud started forward an' looked very earnest at Wally.

"'You ain't "Featherweight Jackson," are you?' he sez.

"'That's me,' sez Wally, with a grin.

"Spud drew a long breath.

"'It appears,' he sez, thoughtfully, 'that when I took you on I was entertainin' an angel unawares, in a manner of speakin'.'"

6.—NOBBY'S LOVE STORY

Some there are who collect china and faded prints and grow ridiculously enthusiastic over aged soup tureens and improper pictures. Some collect postage stamps—an ignoble pursuit. One man I know has an unrivalled collection of writs and judgment summonses in one room, and a rainbow variety of bookmakers' tickets in another. He calls one room Cause and the other Effect. From the material standpoint my own collection of curios is insignificant: a war drum from Bolengi, spears from the Upper Congo, an execution knife from the N'Gombi country, a Spanish sword or two, a dozen *Kaffir* sticks, and an ornamental dressing-gown *jellab* from Fez; these comprise what Smithy would call my "parcel."

But, in the secret places of my heart, I have a collection which I am jealous of sharing, a collection of army memories, of marches, of canteen conversations, of sun-scorched battlefields, where bullets pattered like hail, and good men went out into the dark Beyond, knowing little of what had struck them, and caring less. In this hidden store-place there are pictures more precious than Titian ever drew or Rubens painted; gorgeous colourings than Paul Veronese lifted from palette to canvas for the joy of the eye. Rosy flushes of sunlight on virgin snows, evening skies of primrose and claret red, plains of purple darkness cut across by twisting silver ribbons of water.

Smithy set the train of thought running by his reference to South Africa, and more especially to Johannesburg. I had met the regiment in the golden city, but a war correspondent, harassed by a thousand and one Press regulations, and with the responsibility of "covering" the whole of the Transvaal, had little time to interest himself in the domestic problems of the 1st Anchesters. Least of all did I know the circumstances attending Nobby Clark's love affair. That a man on active service should have either sufficient leisure or opportunity for love-making is, on the face of it, extraordinary enough; but the South African War was a peculiar one.

"You'd be marchin' in the wilderness one day, in a manner of speakin'," said Smithy, "with Boers snipin' at you from every *randlje*, an' cowguns comin' into action every half-hour. The next day you'd be in Johannesburg takin' afternoon tea at a cafe an' wonderin' whether you was dreamin' or not."

"The day after we fought De Wet outside Bloemfontein me an' Nobby went to the theatre an' saw 'Sweet Lavender.' But being stationed at Johannesburg was the queerest, because there was fightin' goin' on all round the town up to the very last, an' it was always a toss up when you woke up in the mornin' whether you was goin' to the races or sudden death.

"Two companies of ours was up at the Fort; an' 'B' was one of 'em, so we were practically in the heart of the town, an' anythin' that was goin' in the way of amusement used to come our way.

"There wasn't much at first, because the theatrical companies couldn't get passes to come up, an' local talent wasn't the earth, but there was quite enough English people in the town to make things lively. We was one of the first regiments to reach the city. The streets were practically deserted, all the shops were barricaded, an' most of the houses empty.

"'A,' 'B,' 'D,' an' 'H' companies were told off for police duty. So many chaps were quartered in each district, an' our section was sent to a place called Parktown, which is on the outskirts of the city.

"The adjutant paraded us.

"'You've got your orders,' he sez. 'You are to stop lootin' an' any kind of violence, an' you mustn't hesitate to shoot any man dead, Briton or Boer, who breaks the law.' There was a sort of country lane, with a dozen or so houses at intervals, an' that's where me an' Nobby was sent. It was a quiet sort of a job, for the houses was empty as far as we could see, an' after we'd walked up an' down three or four times, me an' Nobby sat down underneath a tree to yarn.

"'I've often wanted to be a policeman,' sez Nobby; 'it's a nice, lazy kind of life. What a pity,' he sez, regretful, 'that Spud Murphy or some bad character don't come along and give us a chance of pinchin' him.'

"He was silent for a bit, then he sez:

"'Did I ever tell you about my cousin wot's in the Manchester Police?'

"I'd heard about most of Nobby's relations, but not about any of 'em who was in the police. In fact, most of his family seemed to be quite the contrary.

"'Well,' sez Nobby, settin' hisself down comfortable, "my cousin was——'

"'Soldier.'

"It was such a nice, quiet, soft voice that I don't think Nobby heard.

"'. . . he was what I'd call a. . .'

"'Soldier.'

"I looked up.

"We were sittin' under an hedge, an' behind that was the garden of one of these deserted houses.

"'Who's that?' I sez, an' jumped up.

"I saw the greenery of the bushes move as if they was bein' pulled aside, an' then I saw a girl's face.

"I don't go out of my way very often to gas about pretty girls, but this one was beautiful. She was pale, an' had big, sorreful eyes like you sees in pictures—especially the pictures in the churches of Malta. That's what mostly struck me—her eyes, grey an' big an' solemn.

"'I'm afraid! Oh, I'm afraid'! she sez, an' there was no doubt about it—she spoke ther truth.

"'What's the matter, miss?' sez Nobby. He was starin' at her as if she was a ghost.

"The girl looked over her shoulder an' shuddered.

"'My mother is ill in the house,' she said, falterin' like, 'an' there's a man—he's—he's the doctor,' an' she shuddered again.

"Then we heard a voice callin', a nice, smooth, fat voice: 'Miss Vanhys—where are you?'

"Nobby was always a chap for an emergency.

"'Look here, miss,' he sez, quick, 'don't you be afraid of any bloom—I mean blessed feller; we shall be here, off an' on, for a week, an' when we ain't here a pal of mine—well, not exactly a pal, but a chap named Spud Murphy'll be hereabouts. Have you got a whistle?'

"She nodded.

"'Well, you blow it if you want military assistance. See?'

"'Wherever have you got to, Miss Vanhys,' sez the voice on the other side of the hedge, an' the girl disappeared.

"We stood listenin'.

"'Why do you run away from me, eh, child?' it sez. 'I was distract-ed——' an' then we couldn't hear any more. That night, when Tubby Wilkinson an' Spud Murphy came to relieve us, Nobby took Spud aside an' told him.

"'All right,' sez Spud.

"'I know,' sez Nobby, kindly, 'that you ain't to be trusted with money, an' all that, an' you're a flat-footed rooster generally, but you'll keep your eye on that house.'

"'I might,' sez Spud, careless.

"'You will, dear comrade,' sez Nobby. 'If you don't I'll come along in the mornin' an' beat your thick head orf.'

"'Able's a good word,' sez Spud, quite calm.

"Next mornin' he said nothin' had happened. We prowled about for half a day tryin' to get a glimpse of the girl, but it was no go.

"We'd found out something about her from an old chap who was left in charge of one of the houses higher up. Her mother was an Eng-lishwoman, who had married a Hollander gentleman. He'd lorst most of his money in a gold mine—well, it wasn't exactly a gold mine, but he thought it was. Then he went an' died. We was talkin' about it, or, at least, I was. Nobby seemed to get silent all of a sudden.

"I was tellin' him what a bad sign it was when a feller with his nacheral gift of conversation dried up, when I heard a faint sound; Nobby heard it too.

"'It's the whistle,' he sez, between his teeth, an' was over the edge in one jump. I followed him.

"There was a broad lawn an' flower beds an' a narrer path that led to the house.

"We raced up to the door. It was shut. As we were tryin' it the whistle went again, an' Nobby put his shoulder to the door an' I put mine.

"'Heave!' sez Nobby, an' in went the door with a crash. Upstairs we flew. We could hear her cryin' out.

"'It's the room at the end of the passage!' shouts Nobby, an' we made for it. As we reached it, it was flung open an' a man came out.

"He was a tall chap, with a thick, black moustache an' heavy eyebrows.

"'What d'ye want?' he snarls, an' the girl darted under his arm an' came flyin' out of the room.

"'Save me!' she gasps, an' fell all of a heap at Nobby's feet.

"The man made a leap, but Nobby's fist caught him under the jaw an' he went down like a log. It took us some time to pacify her. She was all broken up with terror. . . .

"It wasn't a nice tale, an' him a doctor an' all, even though he was only a Polish chap who got his American degree for tuppence-ha'penny. He was the only doctor they could get at the time who'd come out an' stay with the mother. . . .

"We had to guess half the story, an' it didn't want much guessin'. .

"The curious thing was she sort of clung to Nobby as though she'd known him for years, an' he was as gentle an' sweet with her as if she was a little child, pattin' her hand an' talkin' softly. I can see her now, she was only a little thing, with her white face against his soiled old khaki jacket, an' his big, raw hands smoothin' her hair.

"The doctor feller had got up, but he didn't try to escape. In his agitation he sort of dropped into broken English.

"'This voomans she's a spy,' he sez, 'her brother he fights wit' De-larey's commando.'

"I didn't say anything.

"'She von Boer—yes,' he sez, 'a dam Boer, vat you tink?'

"'It don't matter to me,' I sez, steady, 'if she was the wors' kind of spy, an' if her brother was De Wet—you've got to come outside.'

"I pointed the way, an' he walked ahead.

As I turned to go down the stairs, I looked back for a second. Nobby had one of the girl's little hands in his an' was kissin' it as if it had been the hand of a queen.

"The relief piquet came at six o'clock, an' I reported:

"This man attempted to commit a crime at the house with the sunblinds. I arrested him an' he tried to escape, so I shot him.'

"You see I was the oldest soldier, an' in a manner of speakin' re-sponsible, so I didn't say anything about the duel with rifles him an' Nobby had fought—me standin' by to see fair play, an' the girl cryin' at the bedside of her dead mother.

******

"The next day when we went on duty there was a little Dutch boy waitin' with a note for Nobby.

136

Dearest friend,—I have left to join my brother, now that my dear mother has gone, there is no one in the world to care for me. Some day I shall meet you again. God bless you.

"Nobby was cut up in his silent way. He said nothin,' starin' at the house, an' hardly spoke the whole of the day. He cut a little twig off the bush where he had seen her first, an' put it inside his coat.

"Two days afterwards we was relieved by the Derby's an' went down the line to Krugersdorf. There wasn't much time for sentimental worry because old man Delarey was bein' as lively as a flea, an' if you ask me my opinion, I'd say that De Wet was a cabhorse compared with Delarey, for the old man had a knack of hittin' at two places at once without seemin'ly bein' at either.

"We took a convoy down towards Klerksdorp, an' got cut up, lost half of 'H' Company an' more than we could spare of ' B.' Then we joined Methuen an' had two months' fightin' on end. All the time we—me and Nobby—was trying to get news of the girl. When we got prisoners we used to ask 'em if she had come to their commando, but they all said, 'No.' Delarey didn't allow women with him like the other generals, an' if they came he sent 'em back. Which proves that the old man was a better soldier than most of 'em.

"Then we struck a bad streak, fightin' an' snipin' from mornin' till night, and from night till mornin'.

"There was a little commando under a chap called Joubert that hung on to us, an' punished us. We could never get at him. He caught the Wigshire Yeomanry an' wiped 'em out, he came down on to the railway an' smashed up the Taunboro' Militia, an' we spent all our time nippin' round tryin' to catch him.

"We'd nearly given it up when he gave himself away. I suppose he'd been a bit too successful and got careless. We found him on a *kopje*, an' he had plenty of time to get away, but he must have gone a bit daft, for he sat down tight an' waited for us.

"We did nothin' for half a day, but our heliographs was winkin,' an' the telegraph wires a-hummin,' an' down came Morant's Column, guns, horses, an' men by special train an' forced march, an' before Mr. Joubert knew what was happenin', we was round him. Then the fun began.

"The guns opened at 3,000 yards an' under cover of a horse battery the Anchesters went up the *kopje* at a run. They fought game, but we was sick of marchin,' an' in ten minutes it was white-flag-an'-hands-up. It was dusk when we started in to collect the dead an' wounded. Nobby an' me went round with a lantern. 'Here's one,' sez Nobby, an' we pulled out an old Boer with a long white beard, who was shot through the mouth. There we found a boy, quite a young chap, lyin' in his face.

"'Poor kid,' sez Nobby, an' felt his hand. It was warm. Nobby turned him over gently.

"'He ain't dead,' he sez, 'show a light, Smithy.'

"I showed the light. . . . then I took it away for decency sake, for Nobby was lyin' flat on the ground sobbin' like a child. . . .

"We got her down to the field hospital—she looked so tiny in her boy's clothes—an' the doctor made an inspection.

"'She'll live,' he sez, cheerful, an' she opened her eyes an' seein' Nobby smiled.

"He had his arms round her all the time, holdin' her so that the doctor could make his examination, an' she turned her face an' laid her cheek against his for a minute. . . .

"Her brother got her away to the coast. It appears she'd joined the commando on the day before we surrounded Joubert.

"After the doctor had said she would live me an' Nobby went back to our work. Nobby was all shook up, but he stuck to his job.

"Toward midnight, when a light rain was fallin', we heard a groan, an' found Spud Murphy between two rocks with a bullet through his leg.

"We put down our lanterns an' got him out. When we'd laid him on the stretcher he sez to Nobby in a wonderin' way:

"'Nobby, you blighter, how did you manage to get me out without hurtin' me?'

"Nobby shook his head.

"'It takes a lot to hurt a chump like you,' he sez, gruffly.

"'It ain't that,' sez Spud, 'someone's been teachin' you to be gentle,'" he sez.

"And that's the truth.

"Someday or other she an' Nobby will meet again, please God."

7.—THE CHUCAJEE PLATE

There was once a man, wiser, saner, and more erudite than myself (said Edgar Wallace, modestly), who remarked that the morality of an action depended upon the motive of the actor. I put forward this dogma to all and sundry who take exception to the lapses of Private Clark and to the indecorous, reprehensible, and altogether undisguised admiration and approval of his friend, Private Smith. The justification of both lies in the morality of intention. The good St. Augustine asks: Why do you blush to confess what you did not at all blush to commit? Smithy blushes neither at the confession nor at the commission. The exact measure of his sin raises, therefore, a nice ethical point.

Speaking as a man of the world, and one, moreover, who has for many years been supporting a number of eminent bookmakers, it seems to me that the affair of the Chucajee Plate was as flagrant a "ramp" as ever I have read about or seen, and I know what a "ramp" is, for I was at Hurst Park when—but no matter.

"It was when we were up in the Punjab," said Smithy, in telling the story, "We'd been havin' a nice, easy time, with nothin' to do but count the days when we'd be goin' home. One day there came an order to move—an' we moved, d——quick. We weren't bein' attacked by hillsmen, an' there wasn't any wars, nor any riots. But at a camp twenty miles away, where the Wigshires lay, there was a colour-sergeant named Button who was late for parade. To be exact, he didn't turn up at the daybreak parade at all, so the sergeant-major sent for him, an' found him just before he died. Before night two other fellers was buried, an' as cholera moves faster than sound—when so inclined—our old man shifted us. We marched to a place called Chucajee, a little village on the plains. We got there in two days, an' sat down waitin' for the cholera to pass.

"As camps go, it wasn't a bad place; plenty of sweet water an' enough greenery to keep you from thinkin' you was the Children of Israel wanderin' in the wilderness.

"The officers got together an' arranged a programme of amusements to keep the young recruits from thinkin' about death, an' lots of chaps you'd never have suspected found out they could sing.

"'Cholera-dodgin's bad enough,' sez Nobby, very despairin', 'but the concert "A" Company is goin' to give nex' Saturday, in a manner o' speakin', makes you realise there's worse things than cholera.'

"We had gymkhanas an' cricket matches, an' bun fights an' sports till every bloomin' day was like a holiday on Blackheath.

"Then Tubby Mainland gave out that he was the catch-as-you-like-but-no-biting champion of Chucajee, an' issued a challenge to Hackenschmidt, Madrali, or Pybosco to wrestle 'em for the championship of the world an' ten *rupees* aside.

"In the unavoidable absence of Hackenschmidt, Nobby Clark took him on, an' shook the *rupees* out of him in three minutes. Tubby said it was only a lark, but Nobby said that there's no lark when money's mentioned, an' if he didn't weigh out the ten he'd put a Bobby Bums rib hook on him. Nobby took four *rupees*, three *annas*, an' a pair of old trousis, an' settled with him for that.

"At that time me an' Nobby an' a lot of other celebrated people in 'B' Company was goin' through our M.I, (Mounted Infantry), course, so we had more to occupy our time than the other chaps. My horse was called '63' in the books, but me an' Nobby named him 'Alfred' after a cousin of Nobby's, who had the same kind of long, solemn nose.

"Nobby's horse was the pick of the squadron. I think he'd been in a circus, because he used to sit up on 'is hind legs an' beg like a bloomin' dog. Nobby called him a new name every day, except one day when this here horse bit him playfully in the leg, an' then Nobby found a new name for him every minute. But the name that Nobby mostly stuck to was 'Pie Dog,' an' the way that horse understood Nobby was simply wonderful.

"Used to foller Nobby about like a child—an' would have caught him too, only Nobby was a bit nippy on his feet.

"I remember one morning, after Nobby had hit 'Pie Dog' on the nose with a broom handle to show him who was master, that affectionate horse followed Nobby for half a mile; in fact, from the stables to the nearest fence, wot Nobby climbed up. There wasn't any stables in Chucajee, an' Nobby used to tie up 'Pie Dog' to the biggest tree; he said you never know when a tree's likely to be struck by lightnin', an' he'd like 'Pie Dog' to have the first chance.

"It was when the sports was gettin' a bit tame that Nobby had his great idea, an' went an' saw the sergeant-major. The S.M. took him up to the colonel, an' after the officers had had a bit of a powwow it was settled.

"There was goin' to be a race—a real horse race, with M.I. horses and jockeys, proper an' regular.

"Any feller could enter his horse for a *rupee*, an' the officers made up the stake to fifty *rupees*.

"'It's the "Chucajee Plate,"' sez Nobby when he explained it, 'for horses that ought never to have been born, with fifty *rupees* added. I'm enterin' "Fiery Dragon"——'

"'Who's she?' I sez.

"'"Fiery Dragon's" the Sunday name for "Pie Dog,"' sez Nobby, calmly; 'he gets a breedin' allowance, because he ought to have been born a pig, an' I expect to win in me famous light blue, purple sleeves, primrose an' green cap.'

"It was one of the most successful ideas Nobby has ever had, because it wasn't goin' to be run for a week, an' what with the excitement of trainin' an' the excitement of handicappin', the sports an' concerts went away right into the background.

"Nobby wanted to do the handicappin', because the idea of the race was his, but the sergeant-major only looked very hard at him an' said: He thought *not*.

"When the handicap came out there wasn't much difference in the weights, although Nobby said 'Pie Dog,' bein' the worst horse in the lines, oughtn't to have more than about six ounces to carry.

"As I was sayin', the excitement was extr'ordinary. There was forty horses in the squadron, an' there was forty-one entries, owing to Billy Mason enterin' his horse 'Julep' under two names to see wot got the least weight.

"The adjutant struck out a lot of the horses. He struck out Teddy Doyle's because he was in hospital, an' Tubby's, because Tubby tried to pass off a bad *rupee* for his entrance. What with duty horses an' horses too fat to run, we got the entry down to twelve.

"We ran a little printin' press in those days, for printin' battalion orders an' such like, an' the printer got out a full list of probable starters. I've still got the list:—

'Nobby' Clark's 'Noble Roman.'
'Spud' Murphy's 'Beautiful Dewdrop.'
'Tiny' White's 'Has Been.'
Private Smith's 'Alfred.'
Gus Ward's 'Sneezing Fairy.'
'Ginger' Brown's 'Chilblain.'
'Dusty' Miller's 'Gadjet.'
Yatesey's 'Walworth Road.'
'Jiggy' Jones's 'Promtheus.'
Alf. Williams's 'Wormwood Scrubbs.'
'Cadger' Cox's 'Mad Horse.'
Sid Taylor's 'Spavins.'

"I said there was a week to train in, an' we started next mornin'. I didn't take any trouble with 'Alfred,' because I knew exac'ly where he'd be in the race; but Nobby was very much took up with the chance of 'Pie Dog.'

"'That horse,' sez Nobby, 'has got points about him; points you could hang your hat on. I'm goin' to train him.'

"'What you've got to do when you first start trainin' a horse,' sez Nobby, 'is to feed him properly—Smithy, run down to the canteen tent an' get a bob's worth of Quaker Oats.'

"Nobody could have looked after a racehorse better than Nobby did 'Pie Dog.' Nothing was too good for him. Oatmeal for breakfast and a pint of milk at dinnertime, an' any little scraps of meat that was lyin' about. I've often seen Nobby walkin' down to the horse lines with a mutton bone wrapped up in the *Times of India*. Not that 'Pie Dog' was a delicate feeder: anything that happened to come his way was good enough for him. After finishin' his government ration he used to start eatin' the manger; he once ate a pair of Nobby's braces when Nobby wasn't lookin'.

"'Pie Dog's' as fresh an' as frisky as a two-year-old,' sez Nobby, the second day of the trainin'. 'We'll take him out tomorrer mornin' an' give him a spin.'

"So next mornin' we took him out. Spud Murphy met us on the way. He was ridin' 'Beautiful Dewdrop,' an' he pulled up when he saw us.

"'Where are you goin'?' he sez.

"'We're goin' to have a secret trial,' sez Nobby. "'I'll come along an' see it,' sez Spud. 'Where's the horse?'

"'I'm sittin' on it,' sez Nobby, shortly, an' Spud begged his pardon. 'We don't want no race-course touts hangin' round us,' sez Nobby, 'so the best thing you can do is to hop it whilst you're safe.'

"Spud was very indignant.

"'I'm a Nownor!' he sez, 'an' a trainer,' he sez, 'an' I'm entitled to see all the trials.'

"We couldn't shake him off, so we pretended he wasn't there.

"Bye an' bye:

"'This seems a nice bit of country,' sez Nobby. 'Smithy, you be the starter.'

"So I got an handkerchief an' tied it on to a stick.

"'Are you ready?" I sez, wavin' the flag in front of 'Pie Dog's' nose. 'One, two——'

"By this time 'Pie Dog' was tryin' to stand on his head.

"Stop wavin' that flag!' shouts Nobby, with his arms round 'Pie Dog's' neck. 'What are you tryin' to do?'

"'I'm tryin' to start you,' I sez.

"'You've started us all right!' sez Nobby. 'Whoa! you one-eyed basket—stop jumpin', you walkin' bit of cats' meat!'

"There was two or three chaps present, an' they managed to get 'Pie Dog' quiet, by holdin' on to him.

"'Now,' sez Nobby, when he was peaceful again, 'don't wave the flag—the flag's been done away with—say "Go"—now.'

"So I sez 'Go!' very loud.

"Nobby gave 'Pie Dog' a whack, but 'Pie Dog' looked round, admirin' the scenery.

"'Go!' I sez again, an' Nobby fetched him a clip on the ribs, but 'Pie Dog' just sniffed an' tried to scratch his ear with his hind leg like a real human dog.

"'What you want,' sez Spud Murphy, 'is a 'bus bell an' a policeman to say "Higherup"!'

"'What I don't want,' sez Nobby, very red in the face, 'is any advice from a low down private soldier. You be careful, young feller, or I'll have you warned off.'

"Just about then 'Pie Dog' warned off Nobby. He sort of doubled hisself up an' jumped twenty feet in the air, an' come down again on his hind legs.

"Nobby came down later.

"That night, when we was in the canteen tent, Nobby told me he had another trial in the afternoon when nobody was about.

"'Are you much hurt?' sez Spud, very anxious, but Nobby took no notice.

"'I always said "Pie Dog" was fast,' he sez, very enthusiastic, 'an' the way he galloped was wonderful. He simply flew, that "Pie Dog" did! I've never seen anythin' like it.'

"'I don't suppose you have,' sez Spud, 'if the truth was told.'

"Nobby's second secret trial got all over camp, an' when Yatesey scratched 'Walworth Road' an' started makin' a book, 'Pie Dog' was favourite. There wasn't another horse backed. Everybody backed 'Pie Dog' or 'Noble Roman,' to give him his fancy name.

"'Have you backed him?' I sez to Nobby.

"'No,' sez Nobby, 'I'm goin' halves with Yatesey.'

"That set me thinkin'.

"'If pore old "Pie Dog" don't happen to win,' sez Nobby, in a thoughtful voice, 'if he can't run as fast as I think he can; if "Sneezing Fairy," or "Wormwood Scrubbs," or any of them thoroughbreds win, Yatesey will have a sharin' out that'll make a co-op. dividend look sick.'

"'You're not goin' to lose on purpose,' I sez, sternly, 'don't tell me, Nobby Clark, that you're goin' to chuck the race away!'

"Nobby looked around to see if anybody was listenin'.

"'Smithy!' he sez, very solemn, 'I give you me word that I'm not goin' to try to lose—"Pie Dog" will do all the tryin' necessary, and,' he sez, 'as a friend, let me advise you to have a few *rupees* on "Pie Dog," because even if you don't win, you can be pretty sure that the money will do somebody a bit of good.'

"I didn't back 'Pie Dog.' But I was one of the few that didn't—why, even the officers had a bit on!

"If you think it's strange that officers should act the goat, you don't know what officers will do when it comes to a question of keepin' a cholera-scared battalion amused.

"The night before the race Nobby nearly got into clink owin' to his havin' forgotten to bring in a bucket of sand for cleanin' purposes, but the colour-sergeant overlooked it. Me an' Nobby an' a tailor chap named Sinks was sittin' in a tent. We was makin' up Nobby's racin' colours out of an old signallin' flag an' a shirt.

"'Smithy,' sez Nobby, all of a sudden, 'do you know that the whole bloomin' regiment's backed my horse?'

"'Nearly everyone,' I sez.

"'Everyone,' sez Nobby, 'including the other chaps who are ridin' in the race: we've got over two hundred *rupees* comin' to us if we lose.'

"'What about if you win?' I sez.

"'Don't trouble your fat head about that,' he sez, politely.

"The day of the race was a hot 'un, an' the sports started with a tug of war between 'H' an' 'G' companies. Then there was a sack race, an' an egg an' spoon race. Then came the Chucajee Plate.

"Eight runners weighed out, an' the adjutant was clerk of the scales—borrered from the meat store.

"The colours the chaps wore was fine. Spud's was 'white with black spots,' an' although the ink never washed out of the shirt afterwards he was very proud of hisself. Ginger Brown was yaller, with black sleeves, made out of an old khaki jacket, an' Alf. Williams was yaller, with broad arrers.

"The course had been marked out over the plain with little flags, an' Lieutenant Forster, of 'G,' was the starter.

"Me an' Nobby rode down together.

"'I like your colours, Smithy,' he sez, admiringly, an I must confess

I was rather took with 'em miself. They was made out of an old chair cover that I'd got from the steward of the officers' mess, an' was Faded Blue, with Faded Red flowers, with Grease Stains.

"'Who's goin' to win?' I sez, but Nobby shook his head.

"'I don't know,' he sez, '*but I can tell you who ain't.*' We was the last to ride down to the post, an' all the boys cheered us.

"'Good ole "Pie Dog!"' 'Bravo, Nobby!' An' you could hear Yatesey's voice shoutin' 'Here! Two to one "Pie Dog!"'

"The other horses was waitin' for us at the post.

"'Come along, you two,' sez the starter, 'get in line. Clark, you go in the middle, where we can see you.' An' he put Nobby between Spud Murphy an' Tiny White.

"There was a bit of delay, owin' to 'Pie Dog' tryin' to eat 'Sneezin' Fairy's' tail.

"'Now then, you fellers,' sez the starter.

"'It's Clark, sir,' sez Gus Ward, indignant; 'his horse is bitin' my horse's brush.'

"After a while we got into line.

"'Now, then! ' shouts the starter, 'Go!'

"And off we went.

"For some mysterious reason 'Pie Dog' started with the rest of 'em.

"'Here, Spud!' sez Nobby, turnin' in his saddle, very fiercely, 'What cher mean by stickin' a pin in my horse?'

"'I've backed him,' sez Spud, very gently.

"We kept together for the first furlong, an' then Nobby started to pull 'Pie Dog' back.

"'What are you doin'?' sez Spud, indignant.

"'I'm judgin' the pace,' sez Nobby.

"'So am I,' sez Spud, an' he gave 'Pie Dog' a whack over the head that sent him nearly six lengths ahead.

"'Don't do it!' sez Nobby, reinin' in, but as soon as he'd got back to the others, Tiny White leant over an' gave 'Pie Dog' a belt on the other side.

"Then suddenly.

"'Stop him!' yells Spud, 'he's tryin' to run out of the course!'

"So Gus Ward headed him off, an' with Gus whackin' 'Pie Dog' on one side, an' Spud stickin' a pin that he'd got fastened to a stick in the other side, an' Alf Williams an' Ginger Brown layin' into 'Pie Dog' with long sticks from behind, Nobby passed the winnin' post first, to the cheers of the excited fellers that backed him.

"I felt very sorry for Nobby and Yatesey. 'Pie Dog' was so warmed up to his work that Nobby couldn't pull him up till he had gone another half mile, an' round a sand hill.

"When Nobby came back the cheers was deafenin'. Everybody was dancin' with joy, except old Yatesey, who looked like a chap who'd been arrested at a funeral. Nobby got off 'Pie Dog' very slowly and careful.

"'Well, Clark,' sez the adjutant, 'you've won.'

"'Yes, sir,' sez Nobby, followin' the officer to the scales.

"There was a big crowd round the tent door to see Nobby weigh in.

"'Let me see,' sez the adjutant, "your weight is ten stone, isn't it?"

"'Yes, sir,' sez Nobby.

"He sat on the scales an' the adjutant looked at the dial.

"'Hullo!' he sez, "what the devil's happened?'

"Nobby's weight was 13 stone 8 pounds!

"'Why, you're over three stone overweight,' sez the adjutant.

"'Yes, sir!' sez Nobby, calmly, 'ridin' always makes me put on flesh.'

"The adjutant shook his head.

"'I don't know what monkey tricks you've been up to,' he sez, 'but you've lost the prize.'

"'Don't say that, sir,' sez Nobby, with tears in his eyes.

"'But I do say it,' sez the adjutant, an' he went to the door of the tent an' shouted, 'Clark's horse is disqualified for carryin' overweight— the prize goes to Private Murphy's "Beautiful Dewdrop"!'

"When Nobby came out of the tent you could have heard a pin drop. The fellers looked at him with their mouths open, too upset to speak.

"We got back to our tent. There was nobody there, an' he stooped down an' unfastened two strings that was tied round his trousers' legs.

"An' then about half a hundredweight of sand came pourin' out into two little heaps.

"'There's a lot of sand behind that sand hill,' he sez, 'an' I remembered the colour-sergeant wanted some,' he sez."

8.—THE WANDERER

The influence of trades upon features, of professions upon physiognomy, have from time to time inspired learned articles in the expensive, but incomprehensible reviews. A well-known writer of fiction has based a notable creation upon the esoteric indications of servitude. Thus:—

That man is a policeman; large feet, heavy tread, sleepy eyes— you know my methods, Watson?" You may not tell the soldier in mufti by any malformation of thumb, stoop of shoulder, or from the fact that he carries a stethoscope in his top hat and has Baker-street mud on his patent shoes. None the less he is unmistakable. I can distinguish a soldier by the parting in his hair; whether he be cavalry or infantry by the shape of his moustache; whether a non-commissioned officer or a private by the carriage of his arm. The ex-non-commissioned carries his right arm a little forward in walking, being conscious of his chevrons.

Mostly you may tell the old soldier by his cleanliness, his gait, and the fact that he is out of work.

The army stamps a man with an indefinable "something," it implants in him in a surprisingly short space of time a new sense of patriotism, a curious dignity, and unimagined moral qualities.

It takes a weedy youth from the street corners. He is not a pleasant looking youth. He is thin, pale, anaemic, smokes cheap cigarettes, wears a choker and has a large sized "boy on his back." He has a smattering of education. For seven years a despairing board schoolmaster has been engaged in implanting a medley of the multiplication table and a knowledge of Shakespeare's plays into his unreceptive mind. He can read well enough to study the probable starters and jockeys, and write sufficiently legibly to convey to an opulent bookmaker that he desires to back "Santo Strato 1s. each way, any to come Canonite 1s. to win, all on Yentoi."

Then comes the recruiting sergeant, jocose and sarcastic: What, join the army? "He'd watch it!" says our pallid youth. Perhaps, hints the wily recruiter, he hasn't the chest or height or weight? Thus challenged, the boy shuffles one fine morning before an army doctor, who strips him, taps him, measures him, and makes him hop on one leg, all of which being satisfactorily accomplished, the weed becomes a soldier.

Six months are supposed to elapse, as the play bills say, and our youth reappears one day in his old haunts. But what a change! Such a swaggering, chest-throwing, straight-backed youth! Such a quick stepping, head erect, arm swinging warrior, full of such mysterious phrases as "chance my arm," "chewing the mop," "fed up" and surprisingly conversant with foreign languages, calling bread "*rutee*" and water "*pawney*," and telling younger brothers to "*chuberow*" when he desires silence.

In ninety-nine cases out of a hundred the recruit falls into the new life as though his childhood had been spent in making preparation for the event; he becomes amenable to discipline, conforms to military custom, and in course of time goes forth to war or foreign service with the *blasé* air of a man whose whole life has been engaged in warfare and travel.

But one man in a hundred is a misfit. He doesn't suit the army or the army him. His career is marked by a succession of errors, his defaulter's sheet runs into three editions: punishments and good advice are alike thrown away on him. If by chance he escapes being discharged with ignominy, he pursues his military career serenely superior to all misfortune, a constant worry to his colour-sergeant, a nuisance to his comrades, and a source of anxiety to his commanding officer. He may be a bad character out of sheer devilry or from sheer indifference. Such a man was "Wandering" Monks.

"Old Wanderer wasn't a bad sort," explained Smithy. "He seldom drank, never fought, never did a mean, rotten thing like I've known other chaps to do. He'd lend his last bob to a pal at a push. But he was what you might call unresponsible for his actions. I don't know whether that quite hits off Wanderer, because if he wanted to do a thing, there was nothin' on earth or in the king's regulations that stopped him.

"I shall never forget the first time I ever heard him buckin' up against the army. It was down Aldershot, just about a year before the war. Corporal Smith—Tom Smith, him that's got a government billet in Malta—was orderly corporal, an' came into the barrack room to 'warn' the duty men.

"'You're for guard on Thursday, Clark,' he sez. 'Smith, you'll be orderly room orderly on Thursday; Monks, you're for town piquet.'

"'I'm sorry,' sez Wanderer, quite calm, 'but I've got another engagement on Thursday.'

"'You'll have to postpone it,' sez Tom, smilin'—he was the best chap in the world was Corporal Smith, a strong built feller, with hair goin' a little grey, an' a little moustache.

"'I can't,' sez Wanderer. 'You'll have to get somebody else for piquet on Thursday.'

"Any other corporal would have put Wanderer straight into clink, but Tom just talked to him like a father; showed him what a silly ass he was in quite a nice way. It was the only time I've ever known Wanderer to be influenced, an' perhaps it was because Tom happened to say that if Wanderer didn't turn up, he might get into trouble.

"Anyhow, Wanderer turned up at the piquet parade all right.

"I want to say about Wanderer that he was a good, clean soldier, an' I've seen him spend hours sittin' on his bed cot burnishin' his bayonet, an' doin' his straps, but somehow he'd got an idea that one man was as good as another, an' perhaps better, an' that nobody in the army or out of the army had any right to order anybody else about.

"'It stands to reason,' he sez, 'whether a chap's a colonel or a colour-sergeant or a bloomin' drummer boy, he's only a human bein' like you an' me with two legs an' two eyes.'

"'You're talkin' out of the back of your head,' sez Nobby. 'One man's bound to be better than another. I'm better than you.'

"'For why?' sez Wanderer.

"'Because I could take you by the scruff of your neck, an' chuck you from here to the married quarters,' sez Nobby.

"'That don't prove anything,' sez Wanderer, very calm, 'except that you're a liar,' he sez, thoughtfully.

"He got his name of 'Wanderer' from his habits. He used to go for long solitary walks. He never knew where he was goin', but as soon as he got out of barracks he used to turn to the right or left, an' keep goin' until he was tired. He was never worried about not getting home. Once he walked from Aldershot to Winchester, an' slept at Winchester. Next day he walked on towards Bournemouth, but changed his mind—if he ever had a mind—an' went round to Salisbury. Four days later the military police arrested him outside a pub in Andover, an' he got ten days for bein' absent without leave. A month after he went out of barracks an' the brilliant idea came to him to walk to London. He got as far as Surbiton an' was collared by the civil police for not bein' in possession of a pass. He got ten days for that, too.

"One afternoon Corporal Juggy Jones warned him for guard.

"'When?' sez Wanderer.

149

"'Tomorrow,' sez Juggy, who was a bit of a rotter. 'Make it Sunday,' sez Wanderer, 'I'm goin' to Frimley tomorrow.'

"'If you give me any of your lip,' sez Juggy, 'I'll put you in the guardroom.'

"'All right,' sez Wanderer, 'put me there.'

"'I'll give you one more chance,' sez Juggy.

"'I'd sooner go to the guardroom than take favours from a feller with a face like yours,' sez Wanderer.

"He got seven days for that.

"He had plenty of luck, because he didn't often come to grips with chaps like Juggy, but that didn't save him from trouble.

"'I'm a born Wanderer,' he sez to me one day; 'it's in me blood. I like to go walkin' through country, an' see the flowers, the hedge roses an' blue bells, an' I'd sooner walk on the grass than walk on velvet— it's nature.'

"'It's insanity,' sez Nobby. 'Fancy walkin' anywhere when you can take a 'bus.'

"'I like to hear the little birds a-singin',' sez Wanderer, 'an' smell the 'ay in the fields.'

"'Then take my tip,' sez Nobby, 'buy yourself a canary an' a truss of green meat, it'll come cheaper in the long run.'

"But Wanderer kept wandering.

"I don't know what would have happened, only the Boer War broke out an' we went off to the front, an' as there's no chance of a chap strollin' off for a ten-mile ramble on a troopship, he kept fairly free from crime. But he still managed to wander.

"He wandered down into the stoke hole one day, an' wandered up to the mast head one dark night; there wasn't a part of the bloomin' ship from the captain's cabin to the refrigerator where he didn't wander into.

"'I'll put you in irons,' sez the adjutant, very wild, 'if you don't stop your infernal wanderin'.'

"Next mornin' Wanderer was missin' from parade. We hunted the ship from bow to stern an' we couldn't find him. We looked into lockers, an' under doormats, but still couldn't find him, an' a report went round that poor old Wanderer had been walkin' in his sleep an' had gone for a short stroll over the side.

"We found him at last. He'd gone for a wander into the engine-room an' had fallen down a hole amongst some machinery. It's a wonder he wasn't smashed to little bits. They had to stop the ship an' scotch-up the engines before they could get him out.

"'After this,' sez the adjutant, 'there's only one thing to be done.'

"So they put leg-irons on old Wanderer, an' a special sentry was told off to keep him from straying. When we got to Cape Town, we were entrained.

"'Have you got a prison van or a dog box?' sez the adjutant to the railway chap, 'because I've got a man with unreliable legs.'

"We managed to get him up to the front, an' as we was marchin' an' fightin' every day, the life suited old Wanderer to a T.

"He had all the walkin' he wanted, an' all the variety, too, an' it wasn't till we began sittin' down tight on station duty that he got restive.

"We was stationed at Krugersdorp for two months, holding a line of blockhouses, an' the life got a bit too monotonous for Wanderer.

"'I'm gettin' fed up with this,' he sez to Nobby. 'Doin' nothin' day after day—why, we might as well be Grenadier Guards,' he sez.

"'It suits me,' sez Nobby.

"'It don't suit me,' sez Wanderer. 'Look at them Boers,' he sez, wistful. 'That's the sort of life! Free an' easy; no parades, goin' about all over the country. They don't have to shave an' they don't have to wash—it's a gentleman's life.'

"When a chap like Wanderer begins to brood he does it quick. Other fellers I know would brood an' brood an' brood for days on end. Wanderer never brooded longer than two seconds, because, by the end of that time, he's either made up his mind or else something comes along to distract his attention.

"There is a little hotel in Krugersdorp near the kirk an' there's a sort of livery stable attached.

"One day the hotel keeper came to see the colonel to collect an account.

"'What account?' sez the colonel in surprise.

"'For that Cape cart an' two horses you had yesterday an' haven't returned,' sez the hotel chap.

"'What!' sez the colonel.

"'For a case of whisky, two tins of biscuits, twenty-tins of potted tongue an' a jar of jam,' sez the hotel chap, readin' from a list, 'also for six pounds of tobacco an' two dozen matches.'

"'But I've never ordered 'em,' sez the colonel, 'an' never had 'em.'

"'Oh, yes, you have,' sez the hotel feller, 'you had 'em yesterday. Your servant came to the hotel an' took 'em—he drove the cart away himself.'

"'My servant,' sez the old man. 'Why, my servant's in hospital—what was he like?'

"The hotel man thought a bit.

"'A chap with an habit of yawnin',' he sez, 'rather tall an' thin, an' stoops a little.'

"'Monks!' sez the adjutant, who was standin' by—for Wanderer had been missin' since the previous night.

"That afternoon a little Boer boy brought a note to the adjutant. Chummy Briggs, who's the adjutant's batman, copied it out when the adjutant was on parade.

Dere Sir,
This comes hopping to find you quiet well, I have left the army owing to me going to be a Bore. Trusting you are the same, with love to all,
> Your sincere private,
>> W. Monks.

"This was one of the most astonishin' things that has ever happened in the Anchester Regiment. There wasn't a man, from the colonel down to Spud Murphy, who wasn't knocked out of time by what Wanderer had done.

"I heard the adjutant speakin' to Major Groves.

"'It's not treason or treachery—it's just downright mad folly,' he sez. 'I'd give a month's pay to have met him on the road—I'd have given him the biggest thrashing he ever had and sent him back.'

"When I told some of our chaps this, they didn't agree.

"'It's High Treason an' desertin' to the enemy,' sez Spud Murphy, 'an' from what I know of Courts——'

"'What you know of courts,' sez Nobby, 'especially courts where you're fined seven-an'-six or seven days for bein' drunk an' disorderly, ain't worth discussin'; the question is what made old Wanderer go an' do a silly ass trick like this?'

"We tried all sorts of ways to get him back. The colonel sent four signallers in various directions, knowin' that Wanderer was a first-class signaller, an' they spent hours with the helio an' lamp, tryin' to get into communication with him, but it was useless.

"We heard nothing of him for about six weeks. Boer prisoners knew nothing either, an' it seemed as though Wanderer was just loafin' through the wilderness with the cart he borrered an' the whisky an' jam he'd pinched, enjoyin' hisself to his heart's content. Then came one of the big 'drives,' when we, with ten other regiments, started clearin' the country around Krugersdorp. It was hard work. Trekkin' an' fightin', day an' night. The Boers just spread an' let us through, then closed up again behind us. It was like fishin' for whitebait with a torpedo net. The only good it did was to keep the Boers movin', but as it also kept us movin' it had, what I might call, disadvantages. And all the time never a word did we get of Wanderer.

"One night the regiment was camped at a place called Brakpan. It was right in the middle of the *veldt*, with a long range of hills three miles away to our right front, and another two miles off on our left front. Our job was to prevent the enemy doublin' back through the valley.

"The hills on the left were held by the Kents, an' the hills on the right was supposed to be too difficult for the Boers to try. On the other side of the left hills was Morant and the Australians, so, generally speakin', we had the Boers coopered. We stood to arms most of the night. I was on duty with 'B,' who held a trench in advance of the camp.

"Toward midnight a storm broke on the other side of the left hill. You could see the lightning zigzagging, an' the thunder, practically speakin', never ceased.

"The adjutant an' two of our officers were up by me. They were lying on the rough trench lookin' ahead through their glasses.

"Nobby was by my side an' suddenly he said:

"'Beg pardon, sir—that was a gun!'

"The adjutant looked round.

"'Thunder, I think,' he sez.

"'It was guns,' sez Nobby; 'there it goes again on the other side of the hill.'

"The adjutant was undecided—an' so was I, for it's hard to tell which is a gun an' which is thunder at a distance. Then:

"*omp—oomp—oomp*!

"'Guns, by jove!' sez the adjutant, jumpin' up; 'that was a pom-pom.'

"He turned to the signaller.

"'Send a message to the camp,' he sez. 'Morant is in action.'

"But the signaller was starin' into the darkness ahead.

"'What is the matter?' sez the adjutant, sharply.

"'Someone's signallin' ahead, sir,' sez the chap.

"Sure enough, miles away on the hills to the right, a little light was winkin'.

"'What, in the name of fate, is this?' I heard the officer mutter.

"'Callin' Anchester Regiment, sir,' sez the signaler.

"'Answer O.K.,' sez the adjutant, an' then the lamp in front began talkin', an' as it talked the signaller read it:

Anchester Regiment.—Kind regards from Wanderer. How's this for a penny lamp and a biscuit tin? Boers are moving back on your right, not on your left. There's a road halfway up the mountain. Give my love to Nobby. I am having a fine holiday. I have not joined the Boers—there are too many bosses. Don't forget the Boers are on your right with two guns. One lot just passed. Give my regards——

"Then the light went out, an' the adjutant whistled. Have you ever seen a regiment move out of camp at midnight, leavin' its equipment behind? Have you ever seen companies of men hurryin' through darkness without a word?

"Have you ever seen guns dragged by hand over two miles of rough country, so as the horses shouldn't neigh an' give the show away, or harness jingle? Well, if you have, you know what it was like when we took up our new position on the right. Now the curious thing was that nobody thought of doubtin' Wanderer's word. He was a deserter, he'd gone over to the enemy, an' if he'd have been caught he would have been shot,—but we believed him, the colonel believed him, an' changed his whole scheme, on Wanderer's word.

"At last we was fixed up.

"The storm had passed away. The guns were goin' on our left quite distinct, an' the thunder was only a rumble. Then the moon came out an' we could see the side of the hill quite plainly.

"'Two thousand yards,' sez the gunner captain, an' at two thousand yards our guns opened with common shell. But the Boers were nearer than we thought. A party of horsemen came swervin' down the hill right on to the guns.

"'Steady, Anchesters! Fire steadily—don't get flurried!' You could hear the colonel's voice clear above the yellin' and chatterin'.

"An' steady we was.

"Three hundred surrendered, an' we buried twenty-seven. The Boer commandant was a gentlemanly feller. When it was all over he sat on a box smokin' a cigar an' chattin' with the officers.

"'Oh, by the way,' he sez, after a bit, 'I'm afraid we rather messed up a poor chap of yours.'

"'Yes?' sez the adjutant, quietly.

"'We found him signallin', an' when we tried to capture him he turned his rifle on to the commando—killed two men before we could stop him—we shot him down, of course.'

"'Of course,' sez the adjutant.

"He turned to the colonel.

"'That would be Private Monks, sir,' he sez; 'Shall I send a party out to bury him?'

"'Yes,' sez the colonel.

"The adjutant thought a bit.

"'With military honours, sir?' he sez.

"'With military honours, of course,' sez the colonel, gravely."

9.—The Fight

The learned Erasmus, if we accept Udall's translation literally, created an apothegm to the effect *"That same man that runnith awaie, mai again fight an other daie."* I state the truth when I affirm that the Anchester Regiment wots little of Erasmus the Beloved, that great scholar, though with this particular apothegm they are familiar enough, and even Smithy, who is no whale at the science of Inductive Logic, pulverised the philosopher's argument in a few well-chosen words.

"It's not worth two penn'oth of gin," he said, "because what's the sense of runnin' away from a fight, if there's another fight waitin' round the corner for you? Might as well get it over at once."

"I've never been in a fight yet, though," confessed Smithy, thoughtfully, "where I didn't want to run—but I've never had the pluck. It takes more courage to bolt than lots of people think. It's much easier to lie down flat on your chest an' imagine what a horrid mess a jagged bit of iron would make, if it hit you fair in the stomach, than it is to get up an' start runnin'. It's easier to go forward than go backward, because it's a slower job an' ever so much more satisfactory. You've got cover, for one thing, which is what you wouldn't have if you was tryin' to beat Walker's record in the direction of Home an' Mother. An' then it's six to four you'll get in amongst the enemy, sooner or later, with the bayonet, an' have a chance of puttin' in some fancy fightin'.

"To most chaps fightin' is easier than runnin'. If it's even money against a feller bein' a John L. Sullivan in warfare, it's a hundred to one against him bein' a champion sprinter, an' Pretty Polly at six stone can't beat a bullet for speed.

"I've only known the runaway game pay once, an' then it didn't really pay, an' that was when Chatty Wilson was challenged by Private Augustus Toms. Gustus was one of those fellers who disgraced hisself by joinin' the army. In case you didn't know it, or forget it, he used to tell you so every day. Since he left his country-seat in the Brixton-road an' took the shillin', his family disowned him. His Pa was a city merchant, an' his sisters was young ladies at the same shop, an' naturally when Gustus said he wasn't goin' to foller in his father's footsteps an' say, 'What can we do for you today, miss—underwear?—Mr. Riggs, forward!' the old man got the needle an' cut Gustus out of his will.

"As Gustus said, it meant a clear loss of twenty pound to him, but he up an' joined the army.

"If you've got any broodin' to do, Gibraltar's the place to do it. With the exception that it keeps perfectly still an' steady, in the worst kind of weather, it's a ship an' a prison an' the private ground of a lunatic asylum all combined. There's nothing to do, an' no walks to go. Once you've been out to Europa Point an' climbed up to the Moorish Castle an' loafed round the Alameda Gardens listenin' to the band, you've done Gibraltar, an' there's nothin' else to do but to sit down an' wonder why you wanted to go abroad.

"I'm not sayin' that Gustus was a brooder; as a matter of fact, he had his mind, in a manner of speakin' fully occupied. For he was a smart young feller, an' very soon saw that the only way to get out of doin' hard work in the army is to go in for promotion, an' he was workin' day an' night for the dog's leg, (lance-corporal's chevron). But he used to find time to tell us of his adventures, an' from what he said he was a bit of a dog in his civilian days.

"'I've been chucked out of the Empire,' he sez, 'three times; the last time it took four men an' a policeman to get me out.'

"'What a terror you must have been,' sez Nobby, very awestruck.

"'I was one of the finest boxers in Brixton—at eight stone,' sez Gustus. 'I once had a fight with a cabman, an' he was in hospital for nine weeks.'

"'*Delirium tremens?*' asks Nobby.

★★★★★★

"My experience is," Smithy reflected, "that in the army, just like anywhere else, people take you at your own value, an' if you give out that you're a fightin' man, an' say it often enough, chaps won't interfere with you, because although you're probably pullin' their legs, it might cost a black eye to find out you're speakin' the truth—an' nobody wants to buy information.

"So in his spare time Gustus worked up quite a reputation, what with his tales of what he used to do an' his fightin', an' he might have been one of the popular heroes of the regiment, if Chatty Wilson hadn't come to us from the 1st Battalion.

"I say 'might' because it's two chances to one that Nobby would have run foul of him sooner or later, an' Nobby's got no respect for reputations.

"Chatty was one of them fattish chaps you sometimes see. If he was in civilian clothes you wouldn't be able to tell whether he was the Terrible Greek or a retired publican. I got the first news about him from Nobby.

"'Have you seen this feller Wilson?' he sez. 'He's down in the canteen tellin' the chaps how he saved the life of Lord Dewberry's beautiful daughter when she was attacked by wild Indians in something—*boco*. I can see Gustus takin' a back seat.'

"Chatty was one of them men who've done everything. He was one of the most remarkable chaps in the world—an' wasn't above ownin' up to it. He used to stand in the canteen with all the other chaps sittin' round with their mouths wide open drinkin' down all the lies he told 'em, an' askin' for more, an' Gustus's face was a picture.

"'I remember,' sez Chatty, very solemn, 'when I was second mate of the *Inky Belle*—bound from Liverpool to Australia. We was goin' through the Suez Canal an' a storm was ragin'. All the stairs of the ship was battered down, an' the sailors was a-rollin' about the floor something awful. I was standin' on the bridge by the wheel, when suddenly the chap at the masthead shouts out, "Rocks ahead!" We had forty thousan' bags of dynamite stowed away in the hold, an' I knew if we ran against a rock there would be an explosion. What did I do?'

"'Woke up?' suggested Nobby.

"'What did I do?' sez Chatty. 'The waves was runnin' mountains high, an' I waited till I saw a big one comin' up behind. Then I went ahead full speed. The wave caught us an' lifted us about as high as Mount Misery. *We went clean over the rock without touching it!* I remember another time when I was lying at——'

"'*That* don't take much recollecting,' sez Nobby, 'for I don't suppose there's a place in the world where you haven't lied at or lied about.'

"Gustus, who'd stood as much as was humanly possible, pulled

Chatty up short.

"'Where was this?' he sez.

"'In the Suez Canal,' sez Chatty.

"'There ain't no rocks an' there ain't no storms in the Suez Canal,' sez Gustus.

"'Have you ever been there?' sez Chatty.

"'No—but I've got a geography——'

"'Here's a feller,' sez Chatty, fiercely, 'who as good as calls me a liar on the strength of a geography book.'

"That was only the beginnin' of the feud. After this Gustus turned up regularly at the canteen when Chatty was talkin'. It was always a question of geography. First of all, Gustus contradicted Chatty about Bon-us-Airs. Chatty said it was in South Africa, an' told a yarn how he was nearly ate by cannibals there.

"'They're a savage, blood-thirsty tribe called the Walloo-Walloos,' sez Chatty. 'I 'appened to be strollin' through the island——'

"'You said it was in South Africa just now,' sneered Gustus.

"'It's a little island near South Africa,' sez Chatty.

"'You're a liar,' sez Gustus.

"'Have you been there?' sez Chatty.

"'No,' sez Gustus, 'but I've got a map.'

"'A map!' sez Chatty, with a bitter larf. 'Why, I helped to draw that map!'

"'That settles the bloomin' map,' sez Nobby.

"The feud got fiercer and fiercer. Whenever Chatty stood up to tell a yarn, Gustus was there to contradict him. It was like an Atheist meetin' in Hyde Park. There wasn't a part of the world Chatty hadn't been to, an' Nobby, who kept count of the three years Chatty had served before the mast, an' the two years he had been prospectin' gold in Siberia, an' the twelve months he had been huntin' bears in the Rocky Mountains, reckoned up Chatty's age to be 107.

"But Chatty's best stories was about his fights. He told 'em so seriously that I believed 'em, an' the other chaps believed 'em—all except Nobby, who never believed anything unless he read it in the newspapers. Gustus took the scrappin' stories very much to heart—you see, Chatty was, in a manner of speakin', poachin' on his preserves.

"'The best fight I ever had was with a chap named Fitzsimmons,' sez Chatty, modestly, "Bob, his name was, an' in America he was a bit of a champion. I 'appened to be stayin' in Monty Vidy-oh——'

"'Where's that?' sez Gustus.

"'When you leave Noo York, you turn to the left an' it's the first town on the right,' sez Chatty, quite calm, an' that staggered Gustus.

"'I was havin' a glass of beer in one of the public-houses in the High-street, when a chap came out of the bar-parlour and sez, "Hello, Chatty——"'

"'Yah,' sez Gustus, very wild; 'there ain't any High-street in Monte Video—it stands to reason. It's a Spanish town. What's Spanish for High-street?'

"'*Uptopo Streetarato*,' sez Chatty quick, an' was goin' on when Gustus stopped him.

"'Chatty,' he sez, 'you never was in Monte Video; you never was the captain of a ship; you never shot lions in Kentucky, or was ate by cannibals in Bone-us-Airs. You never fought Bob Fitzsimmons or Corbett—you're a liar first an' last, an' if I wasn't goin' to be a corporal I'd bite your ear off.'

"Chatty began to take his coat off slowly.

"'You've brought this on yourself,' he sez, ' an' all because you've got a cheap little geography book an' think you know better than people of experience—like me an' Nobby——'

"'Don't ask me to father your adventures,' sez Nobby.

"'I'm not goin' to hurt you very much,' sez Chatty rollin' up his sleeves. 'I'll give you a punch like I gave to Gunner Moir when we was stationed together at Aldershot—an' one of the taps I dropped on to young Josephs when we fought ten roun's at Wonderland. You won't feel it,' he sez, takin' off his braces; 'you'll be unconscious.'

"Gustus was very pale, an' so was Chatty—in fact, Chatty was the palest.

"'Don't mind me,' he sez to Nobby; 'my teeth always chatter when I start fightin.' I once killed a navvy in Somerstown, an' I'm always afraid of what's goin' to happen. I remember when I knocked out Bill Anderson, of Walworth——'

"'Get on with it,' sez Nobby, impatient; 'we'll listen to the history of your bloomin' life another time.'

"Gustus was takin' off his coat, an' his knees was tremblin', too.

"'This reminds me,' he sez, in a shaky voice, 'of when I put Harry Bagg to sleep in fourteen rounds at the Polytechnic—pore old Harry, he never got over it.'

"'Hurry up,' sez Nobby, helpin' him off with his coat; 'you'll have the canteen sergeant here in five minutes.'

"'Ain't he here?' sez Chatty, very pale.

"'No,' sez Nobby.

"'Then,' sez Chatty, determined, 'I'm not goin' to get him into trouble—I'll fight out of barracks tomorrer.'

"We tried our best to persuade him to get it over, but he wouldn't hear of it an' Gustus sort of backed him up.

"'The sergeant's got a wife an' family,' he sez firmly, 'suppose I kill this putty-faced blighter? What's the first question they'll ask at orderly room? "Where was the canteen sergeant?"'

"An' he put on his coat.

"'Quite right,' sez Chatty, 'one of the first questions the doctor will ask when he sees this linen draper will be: "Where did this pore feller meet with his shockin' injuries."'

"It was arranged that the fight should come off the next day in a quiet place up the Mount, behind South Barracks—but it didn't. At the last minute Chatty wouldn't fight unless a purse or a stake was put up.

"'I'm a professional fighter,' he sez, 'an' if it got about I was scrappin' for love, I should lose me license.'

"A lot of us chaps got together and put up a purse of ten *pesetas*, but then Gustus jibbed.

"'I'm not goin' to lose my amateur standin',' he sez, 'by fightin' for a purse—if it leaked out at the Polytechnic that I was fightin' for money, I'd lose my amateur certificate—what I've got at home in a gold frame.'

"Then we arranged that the purse was only for Chatty, but they both said that wasn't fair.

"For one reason an' another the fight hung fire for a fortnight, an' just as we'd got it fixed up Chatty said he wouldn't fight without four ounce gloves an' Gustus wanted ten ounce gloves.

"'I always wear four ounce gloves,' sez Chatty, 'that time when I killed a chap I was wearin' ten ounce gloves an' I've never——'

"'Look here!' sez Nobby, very exasperated, 'me an' Smithy, an' a few other sportsmen have done our dabdest to bring you two champions together—are you goin' to fight or ain't you?'

"'There's plenty of time,' sez Chatty, 'I ought to go into trainin' for a month: When I fought young Jennings, of Oldham——'

"'Half-a-mo,' sez Nobby, 'don't let's go into your bloomin' dreamfights: Are you an' Gustus goin' to scrap?'

"'As soon as the articles are signed,' sez Chatty.

"'I see what you mean,' sez Nobby, with one of those nasty glitters

160

in his eye. 'I take your meanin' exactly.'

"That night, when we was standing in the canteen talkin' about the fight, an' sayin' what a national calamity it would be if it didn't come off, Spud Murphy came rush in' in excitedly.

"'They've had their fight!' he sez.

"We couldn't believe our ears.

"'They've just brought Chatty in,' sez Spud agitatedly, 'two artillery chaps leadin' him—he can only see out of one eye.'

"'What about Gustus?' I sez.

"'He's stayin' behind to find two of his teeth wot he's lost,' sez Spud.

"'Run an' tell Nobby,' sez somebody, an' at that minute in come Gustus lookin' as if he'd been run over.

"He walked up to the counter without a word an' ordered a pint of beer.

"Everybody held their breaths. By-em-by he turns round.

"'Had my fight,' he sez, an' his voice was a bit thick, 'Met Chatty an' Nobby in a quiet place. Chatty didn't want to fight, no more did I. Nobby said we was afraid, an' we called him a liar.'

"He drank up his beer.

"'We didn't fight, me an' Chatty,' he sez, after a bit.

"'But what about your face?' I sez.

"He looked at me.

"'Nobby did that,' he sez."

10.—THE MISER

Once I walked the mountainous streets of Toledo in quest of a house. From the great public square, a little hill fell steeply, and a short distance down, a small unlovely *casa* held a precarious foothold on its uneven foundations. I made my pilgrimage because in that house Cervantes discovered the truth about the army—which has undergone no change since. For what is true of the Pedros and Bombitta Chicos of the sixteenth century, is equally true of the Smithys and Nobbys and Spuds of this.

"The army," said the wise Cervantes, "is a school in which the niggardly become generous, and the generous prodigal; and if there are some soldiers misers, they are a kind of monster, but very rarely seen."

I had half-written the story of Nobby Clark's Patriotism when a chance-used phrase brought to my mental vision the picture of Grimmer—"Miser" Grimmer of "H" Company. Therefore, I put aside the tale of Nobby's International Outrage for another day—and relate Private Smith's story of the Miser.

"Old Grimmer came to the battalion when we was in Gib.," said Smithy, "an' one of the first things that struck me an' Nobby about him was his standoffishness. Not one of the 'haw-haw' sort, mind you: no grumblin' about the food or the work, or havin' to obey orders. That wasn't Grimmer's line. My own experience is that when a feller comes into the army, an' starts cursin' his grub, an' sayin' what a rotten life soldierin' is, he's a feller who's spent his valuable life at servants' entrances an' sayin', 'Here's-the-plate-an'-thank-you-mum.'

"Grim's game was altogether different. He was standoffish in the worst sense of the word. He never went out with people, he never entered the canteen, wet or dry, and he never spent money.

"If they was to feed you up like they do at the Ritz Hotel, soldiers would always buy extras for breakfast an' tea. I've known Nobby Clark to get as much as four separate penn'oths of butter in one week. Nobby is a very managing sort of chap, an' that's how we first found out that Grim was a miser.

"Nobby had a pal in town, who was in the provision line of business—a short, fat, little chap. We was takin' a 'bock' down at the 'Glass Barrel' when this feller, whose name was Nathan—one of the Scotch Nathans—sez:

"'Look here, Mr. Clark, don't your friends eat eggs?'

"'Rather,' sez Nobby.

"'Well,' says Nathan, 'We've got a line of eggs that have just arrived, new laid 'uns, that we can do cheap; why don't you buy 'em up an' get your pals to buy 'em from you?'

"That was the sort of idea that, in a manner of speakin', appealed to Nobby, an' he was all over it in twice. Nathan let him have the eggs on credit, an' they was to be sent up to barracks after Nobby had prepared the troops for the treat that was comin'.

"It was pay-day next day, an' Nobby started at breakfast time to get the ground ready, so to speak.

"'What's for breakfast?' he sez to the orderly man.

"'Kippers,' sez Spud.

"'Kippers!' sez Nobby in a horrowfied tone of voice. 'Why, I thought that kippers had been barred.'

"'What for?' sez Spud.

"'Oh, nothin',' sez Nobby, careless, 'only a feller in "E" Company was poisoned last week with kippers—one of the deadliest fishes known, kippers is.'

"By this time Spud had served out two kippers a man, but the chaps didn't start to eat 'em; they just looked at 'em very suspicious.

"'Many a chap,' sez Nobby, speakin' loud so that the fellers of the new draft that had just come out from England could hear, 'many a chap has found a soldier's grave in a far off foreign land, far from his relations an' girl, owin' to kippers.'

"Spud looked at his an' turned 'em over with the point of his fork.

"'What's wrong with 'em?' he sez.

"But Nobby shook his head. "'I'm not well up in these medical words,' he sez, 'but from what I heard the doctor sayin' to the colonel the other day, the heat of the sun brings out a sort of microbe, called the *microbinks kipperino*, that makes you come out in yaller spots.'

"'I don't believe it,' sez Spud.

"'Of course, you don't,' sez Nobby, gently, an' carefully picked up his own kipper with a bit of paper. 'Smithy,' he sez, 'run an' borrer a spade from the pioneer sergeant; we'll give this pore kipper a decent buryin'.'

"The rest of the fellers said they didn't believe it neither; but somehow they didn't eat their kippers.

"'You ain't gettin' on with yours, old friend,' sez Nobby, an' Spud turned on him.

"'I ain't no friend of yours,' he snarls.

"Nobby smiled sadly.

"'I want to be friends,' he sez. 'I don't want people to say I made your last hours unhappy,' he sez.

"'The fact is,' sez Spud, 'I don't fancy kippers this mornin',' I was out late last night. I'll go down to the dry-canteen an' get some potted beef.'

"'Potted beef!' sez Nobby, 'don't do it!'

"Then he went on to give a full description of how potted beef was made: that settled potted beef.

"'In fact,' sez Nobby, thoughtfully, 'there's only one thing that a feller can eat with safety—an' that's eggs.'

"'Eggs!' sez Spud, wrathful, 'who can afford tuppence apiece for eggs?'

"Nobby got very indignant.

"'Tuppence!' he sez, 'why, that's robbery. You can get the best eggs in the market for a penny apiece. Smithy, why don't you write to your friend Mr. Nathan, an' ask him to send us some up?'

"I didn't write, but the eggs turned up all the same—two big baskets of 'em, an' Nobby sold 'em out in half-an-hour.

"It was a bargain day in eggs.

"'I could have sold another basketful,' sez Nobby, regretfully. 'Every chap in the company bought some—except that blighter Grimmer.'

"Nobby couldn't persuade Grimmer to take 'em, anyhow. He offered him seven for sixpence. He offered him three cracked ones for a penny—but Grim just shook his head. That's what first drew Nobby's attention to Grim.

"'He's a feller you can't get a cent, out of,' sez Nobby, very bitter; 'a chap like that oughtn't to be in the army.'

"Nobby didn't say much more about Grim just then, for his mind was occupied by complaints about the eggs.

"It made Nobby's life a perfect misery. We'd be sittin' down to tea when in would come one chap after the other. You didn't need to ask what they'd come about. You could, in a manner of speakin' hear 'em comin'. Harry Gray, who'd been a pretty liberal buyer, came in with six at one meal.

"'What d'ye call these, Nobby?' he sez.

"'Eggs,' sez Nobby, calmly.

"'Look at 'em!' sez Harry, indignantly.

"'I can see 'em,' sez Nobby, very hasty, 'from where I am—don't bring 'em any closer.'

"'Do you call these eggs?'

"'Certainly,' sez Nobby, as bold as brass. 'What did you think I called 'em—Welsh rabbits?'

"Once the orderly officer was makin' his meal-time inspection. He came into our room.

"'Any complaints?' he sez; then he stopped an' sniffed.

"'What's the matter with the drains?' he sez, an' the room-corporal explained that it was Nobby's eggs.

"After that an order came out that every egg in barracks was to be collected, an' Nobby was told off to dig a hole an' bury 'em.

"Then, as the newspapers say, it subsequently transpired that Grimmer had bought two from a feller named Cohen for a penny. Cohen had paid a penny each for these eggs, but when he got them into his room, an' tried to look through 'em before the gas, he saw somethin' movin' inside, so, bein' a very careful chap, he cut his loss an' offered

Grimmer the bargain.

"'I want my money back,' sez Grimmer.

"'I'm very sorry,' sez Nobby, 'but not bein' a client of mine I can't oblige you; we don't change second-hand goods.'

"The way Grimmer carried on was something frightful. You'd have thought it was the last penny he had in the world—in fact, he got so excited that Nobby did what I've never known him to do before—parted with money.

"'It's perfectly sickenin' to see what a hold the accursed money has on Grim,' sez Nobby, solemnly, an' Nobby knew a thing or two about holdin' cash.

"Grimmer continued to keep hisself to hisself, an' hoardin' every penny he could get.

"I've got an idea that he used to work in his spare time for a little bootmaker on the Romps.

"One thing he never did was to read a newspaper, not even when it was lent to him, an' when Nobby read out the police-court cases, an' the inquests an' murder trials, an' other fashionable intelligence, Grimmer used to skip out of the room.

"Another thing was, he couldn't sleep for more than a couple or three hours at a time. We found that out on guard, an' the chap that slept in the next cot to him in his barrack-room said the same.

"'Grimmer's got somethin' on his conscience,' sez Nobby one day. 'I'll bet that years an' years ago he gave away half a sovereign in mistake for a sixpence.'

"The rummiest thing of all about Grimmer was this: he was quite a decent feller, except where money was concerned; pleasant to talk to, quiet an' retirin', an' as handy with his fists as the next man.

"Now, I've always said that the army is the queerest place in the world, because you never know exactly who you're goin' to meet. Grimmer was a curious bird, but a more curiouser bird was Simmy. (I presume the gentleman's name was "Sims."—E.W.)

"Simmy came out with a draft from England. He was one of them fox-faced chaps that nobody cares much about. Had a shufflin' way of walkin,' an' used to look at you sideways. He perduced a bad effect on Nobby by trying to borrer a bob till payday, but he perduced the worst effect of all on Grimmer.

"Grimmer happened to come into our room by accident, an' came face to face with Simmy. Miser's face went white, an' he staggered back as if he was shot.

165

"Simmy just grinned.

"'Hullo, Jack, so this is where you've got to!' he sez, 'fancy meetin' you!'

"Grimmer sez nothin'. He just turned on his heels an' walked out of the room.

"'He don't seemed pleased to meet an ole pal,' sez Simmy, still smilin'. 'What's he call hisself here?'

"Somebody told him.

"'Grimmer, eh?' sez Simmy, 'an' a very nice name, too.' He was remarkably curious about Miser Grimmer, wanted to know what he did with hisself an' all that. When we told him—it was Spud who told him, as a matter of fact—what a miser his pal was, he larfed an' larfed, in a chucklin' kind of way.

"As far as I know these two chaps didn't meet again, till they came together in the canteen a week later. It was unusual to see Miser Grimmer in the canteen spendin' his own money, but we'd had a bit of excitement that day, an' everybody was doin' unusual things.

"Somebody had broken into the orderly room an' forced the safe. There was only a few pounds in it, so it didn't seem quite worth the trouble.

"Simmy was givin' his opinion about the robbery when Grimmer came in.

"'It's a fair show-up for the regiment,' sez Simmy, very indignant. 'Fancy only a couple of quid in the regimental safe—why, it makes us look like paupers.'

"'It's a funny thing,' sez Nobby, 'but that side of the question never struck me.'

"Just then Grimmer walked up.

"'I want a word with you, Simmy,' he sez, but Simmy just stared at him.

"'Got anything to say, say it here,' he sez.

"'Oh, I'm not afraid to say it,' sez Grimmer, 'it's this: Don't come that game again.'

"'What game?'

"'You know,' sez Grimmer, and his face was white with passion, 'don't do it again, that's all.'

"'I don't know what you are talking about,' sez Simmy, very cool. 'Me an' Nobby was talkin' about the burglary when you stuck your nose in. I was tellin' him that it reminded me of a job down in Essex, done by two brothers by the name of Clancy. One got caught an' got seven years, the other sneaked away an' ain't been seen since.'

"I could see Grimmer's hands closin' an' unclosin' like a man in a fit.

"'That's a lie,' he sez in a low voice. 'There was only one brother in it—the other burglar was a low thief—a dirty little Whitechapel hound, who led the boy away. The other brother was straight—he was a fool, but he was straight.'

"Simmy larfed.

"'You seem to know a lot about it,' he sez, with a sneer, an' turned his back on Grimmer.

"Miser stood for a bit, then he caught my eye an' walked out. I went out after him.

"'Smithy,' he sez, 'where will I find the colonel?'

"'He's at mess,' I sez, wonderin'.

"'I'm goin' to see him,' he sez.

"'But you must get a N.C.O. to take you,' I told him.

"We walked across the square to the mess. We met a chap who had just seen the old man go into his quarters, an' we followed that direction, me tryin' to persuade him to see a sergeant. As luck would have it, we found the colonel an' Major Morris sittin' in front of the quarters smokin'.

"'Who's that?' sez the old man, for it was dark.

"'Private Grimmer, sir,' sez Miser.

"'Who is with you?'

"'Private Smith, sir,' I sez.

"'What do you want, Smith?' sez the colonel.

"'Private Grimmer wants to speak to you, sir,' I sez, feelin' a bit blue.

"'Why, what's the meaning of this?' sez the colonel, 'you know this is against regulations—you should have seen the sergeant-major.'

"Before I could say anything Miser spoke.

"What he said I don't know to this day, but I think it was in French, because he talked through his nose, but when he'd finished the colonel sez:

"'You needn't wait, Smith,' an' I left Grimmer talkin'.

"When I got back to the canteen Simmy was still on the subject of the burglary down in Essex.

"'Seven years that young bloke got,' he sez, 'an' the stuff he pinched wasn't worth seven pence. A green young chap, quite the gentleman that burglar was: his first 'click' an' he made enough row to wake the

167

dead. That's why he was caught. His brother was awful upset about it: he didn't know——'

"'Thought you said he was the other burglar?' sez Spud.

"'That was only my kid,' sez Simmy. 'Well this—'

"The canteen door opened an' in walked Sergeant Jackson.

"He walks up to Simmy.

"'I want you,' he sez.

"'What for?' sez Simmy, without battin' an eyelid.

"'About twenty things,' sez the sergeant. 'Makin' a false statement on attestation for one thing; callin' yourself Sims when your name is Pilker for another; bein' concerned in burglary for another.'

"Miser had walked in after the sergeant.

"'Oh, it's you, is it?' sez Simmy, calmly, 'you've give me away—why, his brother's doin' seven years!' he said, pointin' to Miser.

"'We know all about that,' sez the sergeant, 'an' we know who put 'im there.'

"'All right,' sez Simmy, careless. 'It's a cop an' I'll go quiet.'

"Two men fell in, one on each side of him.

"'Saw your brother before I came out, Jack,' he sez to Grimmer. 'Went to have *dekko* at him in Wormwood Scrubbs.'

"Miser said nothin'.

"'I gave him away all right,' sez Simmy, as cool as a cucumber, 'it was a case of givin' him away or givin' myself away—but he didn't know that when I saw him.'

"Grimmer stood with his head bowed.

"'He told me,' Simmy went on, 'that you'd got a government job somewhere, an' was savin' up money to make a start in a new country when he came out of prison. Have you saved much, Miser?'

"He grinned as they marched him away, an' when he'd left nobody said a word.

"Then Nobby came up to Grimmer.

"'Grim,' he sez, 'you an' me had a little dispute over eggs—I'm willin' to admit that I was in the wrong—I owe you tuppence.'

"It was the only time that Nobby was ever known to offer to pay back money he'd got from a chap.

"'Thanks, Nobby,' sez Grimmer with a smile, 'but there's no need any longer: the colonel is going to help us when I leave the army.'

"Walkin' back to barracks Nobby was very thoughtful.

"'Smithy,' he sez, 'it's rum that I've never thought of touchin' the colonel for money—it opens up what I might call *vistas*.'"

11.—NOBBY, LIMITED

"I have every reason to believe," stated Captain Umfreville, of the Anchester Regiment, in his evidence before the Court of Enquiry, "that Private Clark was animated by a most sincere, however mistaken, sense of duty and patriotism."

I am referring to the Court that was held in Aldershot in 1902 to enquire into an act of sacrilege preferred against certain men of the Anchester Regiment.

This sounds very serious, but it is not quite so serious as it sounds. I do not intend making a long story of Private Clark's deed—it may be told in a few words.

When the Anchester Regiment returned to England at the close of the South African War, the transport was six hours out of Gibraltar, to which port she had called to land the Kent Regiment, when something happened.

Whether it was her propeller that went *konk*, or her water tubes that went *phutt*, I have never been able to discover, and I am prepared to brain the man who would enlighten me. Certain it is that the ship put into Cadiz, that in Cadiz is the Church of Emanuel of Saragossa, that in this church are certain tattered standards captured from an old enemy, and that one of these standards is the King's colours of the 109th, which today is known as the Anchester Regiment.

It is not difficult for me to appreciate the state of mind in which Nobby Clark smuggled himself ashore with the object and intention of pinching the lost colours. I know that to relieve the tedium of the wait Major Morris had lectured to the men on the history of Cadiz, and that he had been sufficiently ill-advised to mention the fact that the old-time colours of the regiment graced the walls of the Inglesia de S. Emanuelo de Saragossa.

Nobby went ashore, and came back. Round his waist and beneath his coat was wound a faded rag inscribed with mystic words. He had had a difficulty in getting away with his booty, for the church is popular with sightseers.

But he had succeeded. Later came the news to the ship that an act of sacrilege had been committed, some felonious and unknown person had stolen a banner specially designed so that it might harmonise with the solemn interior of the church—a banner with this strange device (in Spanish):—"Visitors are cautioned to beware of pickpockets." As to the captured standard of the Anchesters, it had long since been removed to Seville.

Somehow, poor Nobby's "errow," as he described it bitterly, became "public property" in the regiment, hence the Court of Enquiry held behind closed doors, before five prejudiced officers, all anxious to find excuses for the unhappy soldier who stood before them.

In view of the evidence which is known to have been given, the finding of the court is a curious one:—

1. We find that Private Clark, of the Anchester Regiment, carried away from the Iglesia de S. Emanuelo a banner, the property of the church.

2. We find that he did this in error, and that he had no intention of stealing this banner.

3. We censure him for going ashore without leave at Cadiz, but exonerate him from all knowledge of the character of the banner he inadvertently brought away with him."

Now, I hold this finding to be equivocal, but in the best of taste. Furthermore, it is devilishly ingenious.

I tell you this story for a reason.

If at any future time I refer carelessly to Nobby Clark's three mistakes, you will understand that this was one of them. There was another, about which I will some day write, and yet another, the particulars of which are hereunder set forth.

"Did ever I tell you about a chap called Nathan?" asked Smithy. "His real name was Higgins, but he knew enough about the army to call hisself a Jew when he enlisted. When other fellers was gettin' ready for kit inspection on Saturdays, Mr. Bloomin' Nathan would be strollin' down town lookin' for religious instruction, an' on Sundays, when we'd be toilin' to church in our best Sunday clothes, he'd be loafin' in the High-street waitin' for the Gentiles synagogue to open at 1 p.m. It was Nobby who found out this chap was a Christian—never mind how he found it out—an' Nobby had a very great respect for Higgins ever after. In fact, Nobby would have changed his religion quick but for certain reasons I needn't go into.

"'It's the artfullest idea I've ever heard of,' sez Nobby, admiringly; 'he has two Sundays a week, an' all sorts of fancy holidays chucked in—it's hard on two Christians like you an' me, Smithy.'

"It was Nobby who found out his name was Higgins—or said he'd found it out, which comes to much the same thing, for what Nobby sez, he believes.

"Now, about that affair at Cadiz, Nobby made two mistakes, one of 'em you know all about, an' the other was over this chap Higgins, or Nathan.

"Nathan was a terrible financial chap—knew all about how to make money out of nothin', how fire assurances was run, an' things like that, an' when we got up the indignation meetin' over our flag, it was Nathan's idea that we should run a sort of limited company.

"As a rule, Nobby can do all the money gatherin' that has to be done, but he was sort o' hypnotised by Nathan, an' before we knew where we was the company was formed, Nathan got a lot of shares for nothin', and voted hisself a salary on the top of it.

"'What sort of business do you call that?' sez Nobby.

"'High finance,' sez Nat.

"'Thanks for the tip,' sez Nobby.

"Long after the affair at Cadiz had been done with, I could see there was somethin' on Nobby's mind. I thought it was the row he got into, but that wouldn't depress Nobby.

"An' he was depressed.

"All the time we was in England before the order came for the regiment to go back to Gibraltar, whatever it was, it sort of made him downhearted.

"One night down at the 'Glass Barrel' I asked him what was bitin' him, an' he up an' told me.

"'It's that turn-up in Cadiz,' he sez, an' when I started to comfort him, he sez: 'Oh, it ain't not gettin' the flag, or any fool nonsense like that—it's the money part of it.'

"He paused a bit.

"'Look here,' he sez, 'I didn't get the flag, did I?'

"'No,' I sez, 'You got a winder blind with "Beware of——"'

"'Never mind about that,' sez Nobby, very lofty. 'I did me best. I spent money, didn't I?'

"'You did,' I sez. 'Some of my money.'

"'An' none of the shareholders didn't get anything back?'

"'No,' I sez; 'Spud Murphy sez it was a swindle.'

"'Forget Spud Murphy,' sez Nobby, who's a bit touchy at times.

"'Well, nobody got anything out of it—except Nathan.'

"'Did he?' I sez.

"'He did,' sez Nobby, very emphatic. 'He got half-a-quid out of it, an' made out I owed him another—now how do you account for that?'

"Not knowin', I couldn't give my opinion.

"'It's high finance,' sez Nobby, very impressive. 'It's puzzled me, but that's what it is. I've just got a book on it; it's a new lay, an' I'm goin' to try it meself.'

"Now Nobby's got a reputation throughout the regiment for makin' money, an' fellers'll sit for hours listening to him when he spins a tale. Them two are Nobby's great gifts, an' if there's another chap in the army who can make tuppence go farther than Nobby I'd like to meet him.

"I think it must have been Nobby who brought the conversation round to hisself that night at the canteen, for after he'd been talkin' for half-an-hour, Billy Mason sez:

"'I'll bet you've got a fine old stockin', Nobby.'

"'I have,' sez Nobby, which was rather surprisin', for I've never known him to give his private affairs away before.

"'How much have you got pouched?' sez Billy.

"'Hundreds of pounds,' sez Nobby, prompt.

"'How much do you reckon to make a week?' sez Billy.

"'Two or three pounds,' sez Nobby; an' I gasped. "'You're a wonder,' sez Billy, shakin' his head, 'an' you've never been found out?'

"'It ain't a question of bein' found out,' sez Nobby, rather huffily; 'all my business is square an' above board. It's high finance.'

"'Is that another name for stealin'?' sez Spud Murphy.

"'You can all do the same,' sez Nobby. 'You can all have a share in the profits if you want it.'

"An' then he explained what high finance was, an' how they could take shares in him. Nathan was the first to jump at it.

"'Turn yourself into a company, Nobby,' he sez, quick. 'I'll float you.'

"'Thanks,' sez Nobby, very cold, 'but if there's anything to be made out of *this* job, I'd rather make it meself.'

"But Nathan was very nice about it. He said he didn't want to make a cent, but was willin' to give Nobby all the advice for nothin', an' the end of it was Nobby turned himself into a company, an' me an' a lot of other fellers took shares in him. Nathan wrote down the arrangements. We handed our money over to Nobby, an' he was to use it to the best advantage.

"Business went on splendid. The first night Nobby made twenty-eight shillin's at nap; the second day he sold a lot of eggs (what I've told you about), the third day he backed two winners at the pony races, an' the company was in a flourishin' condition.

"'It's the greatest idea that ever was,' sez Nathan, very enthusiastic, 'an' I'm glad I'm a preferential shareholder.'

"'What's that?' sez Nobby, suspicious.

"'Why, what I told you when we formed the company,' sez Nat.

"'I remember,' sez Nobby, slowly, 'you told me there was two kinds of shareholders, them that get money, an' them that get a balance-sheet.'

"'That's right,' sez Nathan. 'I'm one of them that get money.'

"'What am I?' sez Nobby, 'an' what do I get?'

"'You'll get a vote of thanks from the shareholders.'

"I don't think Nathan quite understood Nobby's fine temperament. Come the end of the week, Nobby Limited was the successfullest business in Gibraltar.

"We turned up in the canteen for our dividends, an', to everybody's surprise, we got paid out. It was one of the curiousest things that had ever happened. Everybody was satisfied except Nathan.

"'I think you've made a bit of a mistake, Nobby,' he sez.

"'No, I haven't,' sez Nobby.

"'My share's twice this,' sez Nathan, 'I'm a preferential shareholder.'

"'Oh, no, you're not,' sez Nobby, as bold as brass, 'you're one of the ordinary ones. *I've reconstructed meself!*'

"You see Nobby had learned a thing or two from the book. Nathan swallered something in his throat.

"'What about them Articles of Association?' he sez.

"'I've lost 'em,' sez Nobby, very calm.

"Nathan pulled hisself together, an' talked quite pleasantly. Asked what was the prospects for next week, an' how much money he had in hand.

"Nobby had nearly six pounds.

"'We ought to have a good week next week,' sez Nobby. 'I know a horse that's a certainty for the Gibraltar Hunt Cup, an' I'm thinkin' of startin' a new secret society that ought to be good for a pound.'

"On the Monday night, just as Nobby an' me was gettin' ready to go down town to see a chap about buyin' a job lot of cards—"What is home without a bulldog," an' things of that sort—Nathan strolled into the room. There was nobody there but us three, an' Nathan sat down at the table.

"'I've got an idea, Nobby,' he sez, 'that might help the funds of the company.'

"'What's that?' sez Nobby.

"'Why don't you play "spot the lady" on the troops,' sez Nathan, an' pulls out three cards; 'it's the easiest way of makin' money.'

"'It's too easy,' sez Nobby.

"'It's not so easy,' sez Nathan, shufflin' the cards awkwardly. 'Now, I'm no expert, but I'll bet you couldn't pick out the Queen of Diamonds.'

"'What'll you bet?' sez Nobby, quick. He saw a way of getting money, an' he never lost an opportunity.

"'Ten *pesetas*,' sez Nathan, an' Nobby whacked down the money, an' picked a card.

"It was the deuce of spades.

"'It's not so easy, is it?' sez Nat, pocketin' the money.

"'Let's see you do it again,' sez Nobby, an' Nat placed the cards an' shuffled them like lightnin'.

"'That's it,' sez Nobby, pointin'.

"'What'll you bet?' sez Nat.

"'Four dollars,' sez Nobby, an' picked up the card.

"It was the three of clubs.

"Nobby had five pounds in his pocket, an' had lost another.

"'Try me again,' he sez.

"So Nat shuffled the cards, an' Nobby chose one.

"'For how much?' sez Nat.

"'For a quid,' sez Nobby, an' picked the deuce of spades again.

"Things were pretty serious for Nobby. Two pounds of the 'stock money' was gone, an' I could see the perspiration standin' out on his forehead.

"'I'll have another go,' he sez, an' lost another two quid in the twinklin' of an eye.

"Nat was smilin' as sweet as an angel.

"'Try again,' he sez.

"'Yes,' sez Nobby, very slow, 'but you've got to give me odds.'

"'I'll bet you two to one,' sez Nat, an' shuffled the cards.

"'Wait a bit,' sez Nobby, an' went to his box, an' fished out three more quids. 'It's six pounds or nothin',' he sez.

"Nat shuffled the cards again.

"'Now,' he sez.

"Nobby looks at the cards.

"'If I'm to believe me own eyes,' he sez, 'it's the one in the middle, but it can't be that one, or you wouldn't let me see it. So it must be one of the other two, an' I'll toss for it: heads right, tails left,' an' he flicked up a *peseta*.

"'Left,' he sez.

"I saw Nat frown, but Nobby's hand was on the card an' turned it over; it was the Queen of Diamonds. Nat sort of staggered.

"Nobby wiped the perspiration from his forehead.

"'Nat,' he sez, as he picked up his six pounds, 'I've made another mistake in regard to you,' he picked up the cards from the table an' put 'em in his pocket, 'I thought you was a gentleman.'

"He walked sorrerfully from the room an' me with him."

"When we got down to the waterport he brightened up.

"'That was nearly a fatal errow,' he sez; 'did you see Nathan palm the Queen of Diamonds off the table into his pocket?'

"'No,' I sez, in surprise.

"'He did,' sez Nobby.

"'But,' I sez, a bit bewildered, 'the Queen of Diamonds was on the table, you turned it up yourself.'

"Nobby was silent for a bit.

"'Nathan ain't the only chap who can palm,' he said, very mysteriously, 'I found a Queen of Diamonds in my box when I was gettin' out the money. It's a good job Nathan didn't want to see the back of the card.'

"He was silent again, then he said with a sigh:

"'High finance is a bit tryin', Smithy—but I think we'll pay a dividend this week.'"

12.—AN ACT OF WAR

You are very much mistaken if you imagine that the British soldier is a person whose foreign relations have to do with coloured ladies and gentlemen exclusively. Generally speaking, his business is with people who have not yet arrived at a point where clothing is regarded as a necessity, who worship strange images, occasionally cannibalize, and from time to time slay a missionary. A simple, pastoral, light-hearted people with primitive amusements.

We also know that Mr. Atkins is brought into the closest touch with the fellaheen, being on familiar terms with descendants of Pharoah, and as well acquainted with the masterpieces of Cheops as you or I are with St. Paul's Cathedral or the Memorial Hall. His way lies through historic Eastern cities, to rub elbow with the Ayrian races. He knows the Taj Mahal by sight, but not to speak to, and if there is one shop in Calcutta where good beer is sold you may be sure that he knows all about it, and can take you by the hand and lead you to it. He has an encyclopædic knowledge of strange things that do not appear in any respectable guide book—mostly I grant, about countries and peoples in the vicinity of the equator. He has not interfered in European politics since 1857, so it may be that he is a little rusty so far as the Continent is concerned.

When I say "has not interfered" I mean, of course, publicly interfered. Interfered in such a manner as would attract the attention of the public press, or effect in any way the insurance risks at Lloyds.

But there are curious stories in vogue in the army concerning unofficial happenings, in which it would seem that the little British Army has really committed most outrageous and unlawful acts, calculated not only to disharmonise the concert of Europe, but to render totally incapable the big drum of Germany, the double bass of St. Petersburg, and the little tin whistle of a certain southern state which shall be nameless.

I liken the concert of Europe to an itinerant brass band that performs at street corners. Once, when that band was playing a soulstirring triumphal march, there came before it a small boy sucking a visible lemon—and the band went out of business, temporarily.

It is betraying no confidence when I say that the small boy was none other than Private Smith, of the Anchester Regiment, and that he was aided and abetted by Nobby Clark, of B Company.

The principal instrumentalist in the band for the time being was a certain M.Vladyskisch, Minister Plenipotentiary of the Southern state which shall be nameless.

Smithy told me the story, and I have no reason to disbelieve it.

"Do you know Croto?" he asked. "It's where the castor oil comes from. It's a bit of an island about so far from Cyprus an' so far from Malta—direct sailin'. It don't belong to nobody, this island don't, so everybody claimed it. Italy claimed it, an' Russia, an' France said that now you come to mention it, she lost an island somewhere about there in B.C. 45; an' Germany said 'No, there was some mistake, because she'd left an island in exactly the same spot hundreds of years ago, an' she recognised it by some green spots an' blue mountains.' So all the Powers called a conference, and whilst they was arguin' the point England nipped in an' pinched it.

"We didn't say we pinched it. We said we occupied it as a temp'ry measure, but everybody knew what that meant, an' the conference broke up in a hurry an' bolted for the island to pick up the scraps that England left.

"After that there was another conference, an' it was decided that it belonged to all the countries, an' so there was an international force sent to occupy it. All this time nobody thought of the people of Croto themselves, an' when they asked if the country didn't belong to them as they happened to be livin' there, all the Powers said, 'Certainly not,' an' cussed 'em for bein' ungrateful.

"There was a sort of movement amongst the Croto people for independence, but the Powers sat on the head of that, an' after a while, the trouble sort of died down, an' troops was withdrawn from the island, bit by bit, till there was only a skeleton force of British, French, German, Russian, Greek, Turkish, Italian, Austrian, an' Spanish troops left.

"We were stationed at Malta at the time, an' H Company was on duty at the Island. They was very cocky about it, an' said they'd been chosen to represent the British Army because they was the smartest company in the battalion, but, as a matter of fact, when H went to Croto, there was a danger of a massacre, an' the colonel sent the company that he could spare the best.

"The night before the company sailed we had a farewell 'barney' at the canteen, an' Nobby made a speech to the H chaps who were there—an' they were all there, owin' to the drinks bein' free.

"'Friends an' comrades,' sez Nobby; 'You are about to sail for a foreign land, from which very few of you will ever come back alive. We shall miss you sadly. There'll be nothin' left for the adjutant to grumble at. When you are gone the honour of being the dirtiest crowd on parade will be taken up by C Company.'

"Nobby bein' a verv agile feller, escaped from the canteen before they got at him, but poor little Tubby Wilson—they fairly danced on him.

"We saw 'em away from the harbour next day, the band playin' 'Will you no' come back again?'—a very sarcastic tune that was—an' H Company cheerin' themselves like one o'clock.

"In two days we'd forgotten all about H, an' all about Croto.

"What brought 'em up again was a discussion we was havin' in barracks one night about politics.

"Spud Murphy was sayin' what a good thing it would be if there was a big war.

"'Fat lot of good that would do,' said Nobby, who always waits to hear what Spud sez an' then takes the opposite side of the question. 'What's the sense of shootin' white people?'

"'Loot,' sez Spud, very emphatic. 'That's where the sense is. Suppose you're fightin' in Europe. You go into a town after the scrap's all over, walk into the bank, an' come out with pockets full of five pound notes.'

"That was an argument which entirely shut up Nobby. Anything with money in it appealed to him.

"Next day I found him in the library with a bit of pencil an' a paper workin' out how much gold a chap could carry.

"'Four sov'reigns weigh an ounce,' he sez, thoughtful; 'sixteen ounces one pound—that makes £64 a pound. Now, I think I could carry about a couple of hundredweight, which is about £7,000. Smithy, there's somethin' in what Spud sez.

"Then he worked out that a chap could carry half a million in £5 notes, an' a million in tenners, an' ten million in hundred pound notes.

"That night, when we was lyin' in bed after lights out—Nobby always sleeps in the next cot to mine—he was makin' up what he would do with the money; how he would put it in envelopes addressed, N. Clark, Esq.—to be called for—an' post it to the Penny Bank in the Old Kent-road, an' how he would buy a pub in Walworth, an' drive about in a motor-car.

"He rambled on till the corporal asked him if he was talkin' in his sleep.

"'No,' sez Nobby; 'I'm goin' over me financial affairs.'

"'Then close your port,' sez the corporal, 'or you'll be goin' over to the guard room.'

"Just before I went to sleep I heard Nobby's voice mutterin', 'Six fours is twenty-six—six an' carry two; two hundred times twenty-six is——'

"I must have been asleep two hours when something woke me.

"It was the noise of feet on the barrack square, an' the voice of the adjutant.

"A little while later in came the colour-sergeant, half-dressed, an' carryin' a lantern.

"'Rouse up you fellers,' he sez, 'as quietly as you can; fall in in an hour's time, full marchin' order.'

"Just then we heard a faint bugle call from the Wigshires lines.

"'There's the noisy Wigshire blighters,' sez the colour-sergeant, bitterly. 'Can't go out to war without advertisin' it.'

"'War?' sez Nobby, jumpin' out of bed an' blinkin' at the light. 'War, colour-sergeant? Six fours is thirty-two, four thirty-twos is a hundred an' sixty, ten——'

"'Wake up, *you*!' said the colour chap, an' Nobby started hurryin' into his clothes.

"'Smithy,' he sez;' I've been dreamin' about this. It's come, Smithy. I'm goin' to put the notes in me haversack, an' the gold in me valise. No silver or coppers to be taken away, cheques——'

"'You've got your trousis on inside out,' I sez, for I was not in any Dolly Daydream mood, not at one o'clock in the mornin'!

"A torpedo boat had come in from Croto with the news that the Croto people was out of hand, an' was attackin' the international force, an' two battalions, ours an' the Wigshires, were ordered to embark on a couple of battleships for the scene of action.

"It was just before daybreak when the Anchesters got aboard the old *Caliope*, an' the sun was just comin' up when we moved out of the harbour.

"We got to Croto on the second day.

"The town we landed at was called Ampea, an' it was lively landin', for all the time we was bein' rowed ashore some patriotic Croto gentleman was snipin' us from the hills. It was no good the battleship shellin' 'em, because they was in ones an' twos.

"There was no sign of the allied forces. They'd retired hurt into the interior of the island, an' was very busy settlin' the question amongst theirselves as to who was in command. The French officer sez he was, an' the Italian sez he was, an' the German asked where he came in, an' the Austrian refused to take orders from the Turk, an' the Englishman wouldn't take orders from anybody. The streets of the city was deserted. Some of the shops were burnt, an' others had been looted, an' bits of cloth an' boots an' things was strewed all over the town. The general, who had come with us from Malta, formed three strong piquets to patrol the town, an' B was one of 'em.

"With fixed bayonets an' our magazines charged we marched to the east end of the town, keepin' to the broad streets an' avoidin' the narrow ones.

"It was as quiet as death, just a few wanderin' dogs, an' an ole woman, that's all we saw until we came to a big square.

"It was a public square with a garden an' a statue an' a fountain in it, an' at one of the big houses standin' out by itself a flag was flyin'.

179

"'That is an Embassy,' I heard our officer say, an' just then a little man came runnin' out an' stopped dead at the sight of us. He had a big leather wallet in his hand, an' he stood by a bit, hesitating as though he wasn't decided whether he should come on or run back.

"Then he slowly walked over to us.

"'I'm M'sieur Pollysnitch,' he sez; 'I'm the Minister for Blamong-ia.'

"Our officer saluted.

"'I desire to see the general,' sez the little man, very eager. 'My government has a bank here, an' we are most anxious to get a guard——'

"'You'll find the general on the quay,' sez the officer. "Where is your bank?'

"'I will lead you to it,' sez the little chap, an' starts hoppin' off ahead. We followed him till we came to a stone buildin'. Most of the winders was smashed, but there was shutters up on the inside.

"The little chap opened the door with a key, an' I noticed his hand shook.

"'I'll put up a couple of men inside,' sez the officer. 'They can hold it till the town is quietened down—where are all the people, by the way?'

"The little chap waved his hand to the hills.

"'There,' he sez, an' then he hesitated again, 'couldn't your men hold this buildin' from the outside?'

"'No,' sez the officer sharply, 'I can't leave two men in the open street to be shot down by your friends.'

"'Not my friends,' sez the little man, quick; 'they are wicked rebels.'

"The officer nodded—it was Major Morris.

"'I understood things were very quiet in Croto,' he sez, 'that the population was disarmed; that no rifles was comin' to the island, an' the sale of ammunition was stopped by law—where did they get their guns from?'

"The little chap shrugged an' shrugged, till I thought he'd break his collar-bone.

"'Who knows?' he sez.

"The officer was lookin' over the company.

"'Fall out, Smith an' Clark,' he sez, 'you two men will go inside this building, an' will hold it. You will shoot down any person attemptin' to enter——'

"'Except me,' sez the ambassador, quick.

"'Except his Excellency,' sez the officer, 'an' if you are attacked you will defend yourself as well as you can until you are relieved.'

"Again the little feller tried to persuade the officer to leave us outside, but Nobby, who was all a-twitter with excitement, put his spoke in.

"'Beg pardon, sir.' he sez, 'it would take a couple of hundred chaps to hold this buildin' from the outside.'

"'I think it would,' sez the officer.

"The upshot of it was that we went in, an' the door was shut on us.

"Nobby almost collapsed when we was safe inside.

"'Smithy,' he gasps, 'it's come!'

"I looked round the big room we was in. There was a lot of desks an' stools an' scales, but I didn't see no bank-notes. I told Nobby so.

"'Besides,' I sez, 'you can't pinch things you're set to guard.'

"'I know that,' sez Nobby, who's a great feller for reasonin' things out, 'but you must understand, Smithy, that this is a government bank, an',' he sez, as the brilliant idea struck him, 'perhaps it's the enemy's bank. Pr'aps this is where the enemy puts its money by.'

"I tried to show him what a silly ass notion it was, but he was very enthusiastic about it.

"'At any rate,' he sez, after a bit, 'we can look round an' find out where the money is in case it turns out that what I say is right.'

"So we loafed about, lookin' under tables an' tryin' the drawers of the desks.

"Then we tried the doors leadin' out of the office, but they was locked.

"All except one.

"That was locked, too, as a matter of fact, but the chap that locked it must have been in a hurry, for he had turned the key before the door was shut close, an' when we pushed it, it swung open, an' showed us a flight of steps leadin' down to the cellar.

"Nobby struck a match, an' led the way down, an' then he made his discovery.

"We found ourselves in a big cellar. There wasn't any need for matches, because a dim kind of light came from a gratin'—which was a sort of ventilator.

"Piled up round the walls was long boxes—there must have been two hundred.

"Somethin' was stencilled on 'em, an' they were all sealed with red sealin' wax.

"'Gelt,' read Nobby, 'what does that mean, Smithy?'

"'Gilt,' I sez.

"'Gilt!' sez Nobby, very excited, 'why, that's slang for gold!'

He tried to lift one of the boxes, an' it was as much as he could do.

"We looks at each other.

"'Smithy,' sez Nobby, very solemn, 'there's a million pounds here— what a pity old Pollysnitch ain't the enemy.'

"He reached up to one of the top layers of boxes, an' lifted it up.

"'Gilt,' he sez, mournful, 'enough bloomin' gilt to gild the dome of St. Paul's.'

"I don't know how it happened, but he must have pushed it out of its place.

"'Look out!' I sez, an' he jumped back as the box toppled over, an' crashed to the ground.

"Smashed it was, an' there was somethin' wrapped in oiled paper inside.

"As soon as he saw what he'd done, all the loot business went out of Nobby.

"I don't suppose he'd ever thought serious of lootin', for Nobby's too good a soldier.

"'Here's a mess!' he sez, 'help me lift it up.'

"He stooped down, then jumped up quick.

"'Gilt!' he sez, 'why, Smithy, these are rifles!'

"An' so they were—boxes of 'em, an' ammunition stored in most of 'em.

"Nobby whistled, an' just then there came a bang at the bank door.

"'Up you get, Smithy,' he sez, an' we raced up together.

"There was a little trap hole in the door—a sort of place like a pay box at a theatre, an' Nobby looked out.

"'It's Pollysnitch.' he whispers, an' Spud Murphy's with him.'

"Then he yelled out:

"'Don't come any nearer or I'll fire,' an' Pollysnitch skipped back.

"'What's the game?' sez Spud, comin' up to the hole.

"'Spud,' sez Nobby in a low voice, 'what's happened?'

"'You're relieved,' sez Spud, 'this here ambassor has decided there's no need for a guard, so the adjutant sent me along with him to tell you.'

"'I mean,' sez Nobby, 'what's happenin' in the town?'

"Spud shook his head.

"'Blowed if I know,' he sez, 'these blokes are goin' in for their independence, there's thousands of 'em outside the town, an' I heard the colonel say to the adjutant that if we can't stop 'em from armin' before tonight they're goin' to have "coody tar" (*coup d'état*)—what's that?'

"'Some horrible foreign drink,' sez Nobby—but I think he got the idea, for he opened the door, an' saluted the little ambassador.

"'Won't you come in, sir?' he sez, an' Pollysnitch walked in.

"Then Nobby suddenly slammed the door, an' grabbed him by the neck.

"'Pollysnitch,' he sez, 'you're for the high jump.'

"Polly struggled like mad, but Nobby had got him well fixed.

"By an' bye we tied him down to a chair. He was white with rage.

"'My man,' he sez—he spoke English as well as me or you. 'My man, you will get into serious trouble—do you know that this is an act of war?'

"'I do,' sez Nobby, calmly. 'Spud,' he sez, 'nip back to the piquet, an' tell the major I've located the enemy, an' captured his bloomin' ammunition train.'"

13.—The Football Match

I do not deny that the Wigshires give themselves airs They refer to themselves modestly as the "Old and bold, ever fighting, never-failing 175th." This, to the intense indignation of the rest of the army, and more especially to the 5th Northumberland Fusiliers, from whom they have stolen the nickname.

The Wigshires have a very bad reputation in the army. They are called "The Cuckoos," partly because they calmly appropriate the treasured traditions of others, and partly because—but we need not discuss the other reason, which is probably untrue. From what I know of the Wigshire Regiment, it is a very sound, hard-marching, straight-fighting corps, and its amiable weakness may well be overlooked in the light of its manifest qualities, but the rest of the army would not share my views.

As you know, the "honours" of a regiment are the names of the battles in which it has fought, and which are inscribed on its colours. Some regiments have thirty or so, and are vastly puffed up in consequence. The Rifle Brigade has forty (I speak from memory), but has no colours to put them on. The Anchesters have twenty-three—but the Wigshires have only four, and this is a very sore point with the regiment.

When they marched into North Camp in '94, some wag of the Anchesters displayed a sheet from the barrack-room window on which was inscribed,

Though Shalt Not Kill

and the subtle, if irreverent, jibe is remembered to this day.

Therefore, I do not blame the childless Wigshires if they insist upon adopting the children of more favoured corps.

I remember that when they were stationed in Malta, they called themselves "The Holy Boys," and the Norfolk Regiment in far-off Belgaum was blissfully unconscious of the blatant plagiarism. Then at Wynberg, taking a mean advantage of the absence of the 17th Lancers, they took the style of the "Death or Glory Boys."

One very bad mistake they made, and that was at Dover, four years ago, when they blossomed forth as 'The Die-Hards." Now the regiment entitled to that distinction is the Middlesex Regiment, and it happened that the Middlesex were stationed at Chatham; and it was the worst of bad luck that the Middlesex and the Wigshires should have been brigaded together for the autumn manoeuvres.

For it came to pass that, learning of the outrageous liberty taken by the Wigshires, the Middlesex descended upon them one night, and beat, belted, and kicked them into a realisation of their sinfulness.

None the less the Wigshires turned up nothing daunted next day, and instantly and unblushingly converted to their own use the style and title of "The Old Guard."

"What always annoyed us about the Wigshires," explained Private Smithy, "was the fact that they got an idea that they was the most sportin' regiment in the army. They once got in the final for the Army Cup. Nobody knows how it happened, unless they got in when nobody was lookin'.

"They were beat by 19 goals to nothin', but that didn't upset 'em. They gave out that they was the undefeated champion footballers of the army. Whilst they was stationed at home this didn't matter very much, because everybody knew the Wigshire class an' only larfed, but when they got abroad, it became serious, especially when they came to Wynberg an' used to stand round our football field, passin' sarcastic remarks about our play.

"One afternoon we had a company match, 'H' against 'B.' It was a walk-over for 'B,' because Nobby was playin' in hobnailed boots.

"I was standin' by, watchin' the match. There was a bit of an interval whilst the doctor was givin' artificial restitution to Toby Martin, wot Nobby happened to tread on, an' one of the Wigshires, who was standin' by, sez to me:

"'What are your chaps playin'?'

"'Football!' I sez.

"'Oh!' he sez, very polite, 'I thought you was preparin' for the military tournament.'

"When Nobby came off the field, this chap goes up to him an' sez:

"'Are you the captain of this team?'

"'I am,' sez Nobby.

"'Well,' sez the chap (whose name was Mudley), 'any time you'd like to see how football's played, you can come over to our field an' watch our regimental team!'

"'Thanks,' sez Nobby, very politely, 'I'll put on an old suit that won't get soiled by walkin' through your lines, an' look you up.'

"'Our lines are as clean as yours,' sez the chap, firin' up.

"'Not so clean as they was before you came,' sez Nobby, nicely.

"'We can teach you somethin' about football, anyway,' sez the Wigshire feller.

"'I shouldn't wonder,' Nobby sez, 'regiments that never do any fightin' have plenty of time to learn football.'

"'We was in the final for the Army Cup,' sez the Wigshire man, swellin' with pride.

"'So I'm told,' sez Nobby, 'though I've never believed it.'

"'Why, it was in all the papers!' sez young Wigshire, very indignant.

"Nobby shook his head.

"'Don't you believe everythin' you read in the papers,' he sez.

"The upshot of this was that we got a challenge from the Wigshires that same night.

"It was brought into the canteen, an' posted up.

"The Wigshires offered to play the best team we could get together for anything we liked, an' Nobby accepted the challenge.

"There was a bit of a row afterwards because Nobby wasn't the captain of the regimental team by any manner of means, but he managed to smooth down Sergeant Pike, who's the real captain, an' started to get the team together.

"The Anchesters have got a lot of chaps who can play good football, an' Nobby persuaded most of 'em to come into the team; an' there were some artillery fellers....

"'It's a walk-over for us,' sez Nobby. 'Smithy, stroll over to the Wigshire's canteen an' see if you can find anybody who bets.' So me an' Yatesey turned up at the Wigshire's bar an' took all the bets that was goin'.

"The match was to be played on a Saturday, an' on the Friday night Nobby came to see me in a state of agitation.

"'Smithy,' he sez, 'd'ye know when I asked the Wigshire feller if they minded us playin' an outsider? '

"'Yes,' I sez.

"'They sez they didn't; so I got two chaps of the R.A., an' the Wigshires sez they'd get in a chap or two, as well.'

"'Yes,' I sez.

"'Well,' sez Nobby, 'they've got Baggs, the civilian goalkeeper of the Capetown club, an' Hiker, the centre- forward of the Caledonians, an' they've borrered the half-back chap from the Rondebosch team—in fact, the whole bloomin' team's made up of African league players!'

"It didn't want much explainin' after that why the Wigshires come over in their thousands that night tryin' to get bets about the match. Nobby met the captain from the other side.

"'What about a referee?' sez Nobby.

"'How would our sergeant-major do?' sez the Wigshire feller.

"'Not at all,' sez Nobby, 'how about *our* sergeant-major?'

"'Let's keep the game as honest as we can,' sez the Wigshire man, earnestly. 'I've been thinkin' about the referee: now we don't want a chap who will favour us, an' you don't want a chap who will favour you——'

"'Speak for yourself,' sez Nobby, 'never mind about what we want.'

"'I've been talkin' to our team——'

"Nobby larfed sarcastic.

"'Our team,' sez the Wigshire captain, 'thinks that for the honour of the old corps, the Ever Fightin', Never Failin'——'

"'Don't try that game on with me,' sez Nobby, 'your team! Why, they're bloomin' civilians! Fat lot they care about the honour of the Wigs—an' anyway, there ain't enough honour to go round. Let's settle the referee—how would I do?'

"This staggered the Wigshire chap so that he couldn't speak for a minute or two.

"'You?' he gasps.

"'Me,' sez Nobby, 'I can't play, I've sprained me knee.'

"After the Wigshire chap had said where he'd see hisself before he let Nobby referee, an' where he'd see Nobby, an' the 'ole of the Anchester Regiment, Nobby struck in:

"'When you've finished arskin' someone to take away your eyesight,' he sez, very severe, 'perhaps you'll listen to reason. Suppose I'm referee. I can't favour our side, can I? Wouldn't everybody say "Nobby Clark's workin' it for the Anchesters?" It stands to reason that if I'm referee the Wigshires'll have a better show than if you got a chap from another regiment.'

"This seemed to strike the Wigshire man as bein' very sensible. It took him a long time to convince the other Wigshire chaps, because he couldn't talk as glib as Nobby.

"At first they wouldn't hear of it, then they wanted to appoint one of their own men, on the same lines—but Nobby said he wouldn't put temptation in any man's way.

"Our own fellows was beside theirselves with joy when Nobby was appointed referee.

"'It's a pinch for us,' sez Spud Murphy, 'with you refereein' an' '

"'Why?' sez Nobby.

"'Because,' sez Spud, 'we'll be able to——'

"'You won't be able to do anythin',' sez Nobby, shortly.

"'When I'm a referee I'm a referee—don't let that silly idea of yours get about.'

"The mornin' of the match came: it was Saturday, an' Nobby had got permission for the team to be excused parade. Umfreville, the adjutant, sent for Nobby.

"'What is this match you're playing?' he sez, so Nobby explained.

"The adjutant looks straight in Nobby's eye.

"'Some of the officers were talking about going down to the field to see it,' he sez.

"Nobby looked uncomfortable.

"'I'd rather they didn't, sir,' he sez.

"'Why?' sez the adjutant.

"'Well, sir,' sez Nobby slowly, 'there'll be a lot of rough play, an' pop'lar feelin' may run high.'

"'Um,' sez the adjutant, suspicious, 'who's the referee?'

"'Me, sir,' sez Nobby, modestly.

"'Thank you,' sez the adjutant, prompt.

"There were no officers present that afternoon, an' very few non-coms.

"Nobby turned up in a beautiful pair of knickers that he borrered from a chap, an' he had one of the loudest whistles he could buy.

"When he went on to the field, blowin' his whistle to let everybody know he was there, he got one of the biggest receptions I've ever seen a referee get. The Wigshire fellers cheered him because he was goin' to do the fair thing to them, an' our fellers cheered him because they thought he was goin' to do the fair thing to us, an' as little Jerry Jordan said, 'bar a miracle we couldn't be beat.' I don't know too much about football. I've watched it, an' played it, an' read about it, but I don't know the delicate touches like Nobby does.

"First thing Nobby did was to make the Wigshire chaps change their goalkeeper.

"The Wigshires was a bit surprised, an' especially the professional fellers who were playin', but Nobby pointed out that by order of the Army Council no chap over five foot four was allowed to keep goal, and the civilian professionals took it all in good part.

"Then the game commenced.

"The Wigshires took the ball straight up to our goal, an' my heart went up into my mouth.

Suddenly, Nobby's whistle blew.

"'What's up?' sez the Wigshire captain, very wrathful.

"'Foul,' sez Nobby; 'foul against the Wigshires.'

"'Why?' sez the Wigshire feller.

"'Never mind why,' sez Nobby, an' the foul had to be allowed. To show how impartial Nobby was, soon after that he gave a foul against the Anchesters.

"It's true, the ball was right up the other end of the field, an' there was not any danger to us from a penalty, but Nobby gave it, an' this made the Wigshire people more easy in their minds.

"They got hold of the ball again, an' carried it like lightnin' into our country. Then there was a wild an' desperate mix-up with Nobby in the middle of it, blowin' his whistle.

"'What's the matter now?' shouts the Wigshire chap.

"'Offside!' sez Nobby.

"'It's not offside,' yells the Wig.

"'Then it's hands,' sez Nobby, calmly; 'it's the same thing.'

"Somehow our chaps couldn't keep the ball away from our goal try as hard as they could, an' the Wigshires would have scored only Nobby happened to get in the way of the ball once or twice.

"Just before half-time the Wigshire captain got a beautiful shot, an' took it. He missed the ball an' went sprawlin'.

"To this day," asserted Smithy, solemnly, "nobody knows the truth about that accident. Some say Nobby tripped him up, an' others say he fell against him by accident. Anyway the Wigshires yelled like blazes, an' one of the professionals sez Nobby was a disgrace to the umpirin' business.

"At half-time the game stood at 'love-all,' an' Nobby was loudly cheered by our chaps in consequence.

"The Wigshire captain had a few words to say to Nobby.

"'I thought you was a gentleman,' he sez, bitterly.

"'Whatever made you think that?' sez Nobby, an' that floored the Wig.

"The finest player on the other side was a chap called Shaw, but Nobby soon settled him in the second half. Just as the Wigs was pushin' the ball towards our goal—they did this all the afternoon—Nobby's whistle blew.

"'Shaw,' he sez, very stern, 'that's the second time I've had to warn you. If it occurs again I shall order you off this field.'

"'What have I done?' sez poor Shaw.

"'Never mind,' sez Nobby, an' blew his whistle.

"By some accident our chaps got hold of the ball, an' rushed it down to the Wigs' goal, an' kept it at that end for five minutes. All this time Nobby's whistle didn't blow once, not even when the Wigshires asked for 'offside.'

"A good many of our fellers think Nobby lost a big chance by not givin' a penalty kick or so, but Nobby said he did think of it, but couldn't trust any of our fellers to kick straight enough.

"When Spud Murphy took a runnin' kick at the Wigshire captain an' the Wigshires yelled 'foul!' somebody shouted from their side, 'Have you lost your whistle?' but Nobby took no notice, an' when the ball came down to the Anchester end again he jolly soon showed 'em that the whistle was in good order.

"That's where he warned Shaw off the field an' cautioned Hackitt, an' gave three fouls against the Wigs, all in about three minutes.

"I don't know any other regiment that Nobby would have dared take such liberties with.

"What I might call the climax of the game came just before the close of play. Nobby had given a penalty kick against the Wigs, an' all the fellers were clusterin' as thick as bees round the Wigs' goal.

"Nobby's whistle blew, an' the ball fell amongst 'em. You couldn't see the ball, only a lot of strugglin' an fightin' chaps in football jerseys, and Nobby dived right in amongst 'em.

"He disappeared, but by an' bye, the crowd fell apart, an' the ball came flyin' out, smack! right into the Wigs' goal!

"Our fellers nearly went mad with delight. You couldn't hear anything for the cheerin' an' shoutin': you couldn't have heard Nobby's whistle if he'd been blowin' it. As a matter of fact, he was havin' a terrible argument with the Wigs' captain.

"'Who shot that goal?' sez the Wig, fiercely.

"'Spud Murphy,' sez Nobby.

"'You're a liar,' sez the Wig, as wild as wild. 'You shot that goal, you big-footed thief.'

"'As a referee,' sez Nobby——

"'Never mind about referee,' sez the Wig captain, almost tearin' his hair. 'As man to man I tell you you're a liar. I see you do it, you robber. I see you push aside "Corfy" Jackson an' kick it.'

"'If, in the excitement of the moment,' sez Nobby, 'I happened to touch the ball—an' I don't believe I did—I apologise. I see somethin' on the ground that looked big an' round an' empty an' I kicked it. But I was under the impression at the time that it was your head.'

"The Wigs got even, because they sent an account of the match to the 'Cape Times.' I've got the bit about it to this day. Here it is:—

"'An interesting match was played yesterday between a thirteen of the Royal East Wigshires (the Fighting Pompadours) and fourteen picked men of the Anchesters. The novices of the Anchesters played as well as possible, but stood little chance against the veterans of Wigshire. Private Clark scored the only goal of the afternoon. The game was played without a referee.'"

14.—THATCHER'S BROTHER

Superior young non-commissioned officers, possessing first-class certificates, are wont to take me to task from time to time for misrepresenting the army.

Now by *Allah* and The Prophet, and by Ali, his unfortunate but most worthy son, I swear I do not heed the strictures of any N.C.O., for I secretly dislike young N.C.O.'s, and am a private at heart.

I regard the private soldier as the backbone of the British Army, the commissioned soldier as the brains, and, to pursue the anatomical simile, I look upon the superior young non-commissioned officer as the nerves of the junior service.

In my life I have seen truly great soldiers of non-commissioned rank, who could never secure the coveted "first," fine corporals and soldierlike sergeants, born leaders of men, to whom this education test is an insuperable barrier.

In my soldiering days, I took my "first" without batting a lid. Had I borne an exemplary military character, instead of having behind me the record of two terms of imprisonment for military offences, I might well have been made corporal, sergeant, or the like, although I was no more fitted to command men than the proverbial tom-cat. But a "first" was dead easy for me, because I was one of those lazy beggars who would sooner read than work, and naturally I had a pull over the men who loved soldiering for soldiering's sake, and had no time to fool round after the sensational details of Wat Tyler's rebellion.

The story of Thatcher proves nothing. It was an extraordinary incident. Thatcher may, or may not, have had a "first"—he probably had. Smithy has lately supplied me with particulars regarding the affair at Pretoria.

You may not have heard it. I, previously, knew little more of the affair than was half revealed in a two-line paragraph in the *Times* newspaper. Later I saw a more detailed account in the "Johannesburg Star," but Smithy has filled in the gaps of that story, which is now fully set forth for the first time.

"War," said Smithy, philosophically, "is wilful murder on a large scale. You can look at it any way you like, an' it works out the same. It's just as though it came out in orders like this.

Battalion Orders
Nov. 1, 19——.

1. Owin' to a slight disagreement between us an' Blanmongia, the followin' structural alterations to the Ten Commandments will be carried out:

For 'Thou shalt not kill' the following words will be substituted:

Soldiers in action are reminded that the most vital spot in the enemy's body is his stomach; soldiers firin' high will be tried by Court Martial on a charge of wasting ammunition.

By Order.

"It stands to reason that war upsets a feller. All his life he's been brought up with the idea that beyond hittin' his young brother, or jumpin' on his wife, there's very little violent exercise that the law allows. He's taught that murder is a horrid thing, only to be read about in the Sunday papers, an' that nobody uses firearms except American policemen an' Instructors of Musketry.

"In the army they give him a rifle, but if they find him in possession of ammunition they run him into the 'clink.' They teach him to shoot the wild bull's-eye, an' the fierce magpie, but more often than not he hits a wanderin' outer. It's when he don't hit nothin' that they get upset: it's when you can hear his bullet '*whow-w-w-in*' in the air that the musketry officer gets sick.

"'Good heavens!' he sez, as pale as death, 'where did your bullet go, you careless feller?—perhaps you've hit somebody on the other side of the hill!'

"An' he's taught that he mustn't point his rifle at anyone, an' mustn't fix his bayonet in the barrack-room, an' mustn't do anything that's likely to hurt anybody.

"Now, this is all right in a way, because you get chaps into the army who ain't fit to trust with a catapult, never mind about rifles.

"Nobody in their senses could complain because the army was cautious, but it only goes to prove what I say—that all the trainin' the young soldier gets is in one direction—that the wickedest thing in the world to do is to hurt anybody else.

"Then comes the war an'—whack! goes the trainin' of a lifetime.

"'Do you see that Afridi?' sez the officer; 'that one in the white shirt on the little hill? Him that's wavin' his arms?'

"'Yes, sir,' sez the young soldier.

"'Well, put him out of mess,' sez the officer; 'aim at his belt—range 850 yards—allow a foot for windage—now.'

"'*Bang!*'

"'Very good,' sez the officer, 'I rather think you hit him in the head, there's another one. Don't aim so high—now!'

"'*Bang!*'

"'That's better,' sez the officer, very pleased. 'That got him fairly; try that old chap with the whiskers.'

"An' so it goes on.

"A war might last a week, an' it might last three years. When it lasts a week it's called a 'punitive expedition,' an' it means that you come on the enemy unawares, catch him a swipe in the jaw, an' run away like blazes before he recovers hisself.

"When the war lasts longer, like the South African war did, it upsets a chap more than a short war, because a short war's a sort of horrible dream, an' it's all over before you've time to change your habits.

"But three years of war does no good for the young soldier, because it comes at the time when he's, so to speak, formin' his character.

"He's got the habit of takin' his rifle an' shootin' quick; he's got the habit of countin' his success by the number of chaps he's killed, an' that's not healthy.

"When the South African war broke out there was a corporal of ours, named Thatcher, a big feller with a loose lip an' a scowl that never seemed to leave him. He wasn't exactly popular. He'd been a colour-sergeant in the Wigshires, an' had been reduced to corporal for some affair with a woman. They transferred him to us in India, because he said he couldn't soldier as a corporal in a regiment where he'd been colour-sergeant, and from the very first day he came to us he was hated.

"You'd think you could get even with a chap like that, who was unpopular all round, but as a matter of fact, it was impossible unless you did somethin' particularly low-down, an' none of our chaps would do that. For Corporal Thatcher was a good soldier, an' knew his work from A to Z, an' there wasn't any change to be got out of him.

"He'd a bitter tongue, an' had the instinct for findin' out a feller's tender spots.

"He fell foul of Nobby the first day he was in the regiment. 'You talk too much,' he sez to Nobby, 'you're like an old woman.'

"'Do I, corporal?' sez Nobby, innocent.

"'Yes, you do,' sez the corporal; 'perhaps you don't know it.'

"'I don't,' sez Nobby. 'I don't know how an old woman talks, or young woman either; I never go to the married quarters.'

"Nobby's got a nasty tongue of his own, I might say, an' I saw Thatcher go white with rage at Nobby's hint.

"After that, Thatcher got Nobby 'set'—always givin' him dirty little jobs to do.

"One day when there was only Thatcher, Nobby an' me in the bungalow—we was in Bombay at the time—Nobby walks up to the corporal an' sez:

"'Corporal, can I have a word with you?'

"Thatcher looks at him as though he was a new kind of insec'.

"'You get on with your work,' he sez.

"'Never mind about the work,' sez Nobby, 'what I want to know is, are you a man?'

"'What!' roars Thatcher.

"'Because, if you are,' sez Nobby, 'an' will drop your rank for ten minutes, I'll push your face round to the back of your head'—or words to that effect.

"'You heard that!' sez Thatcher to me, an' ran to the bungalow door yellin' for the guard.

"They came across at the double, an' Nobby' was taken to the guard room in quick time. Next day, at orderly room, I was called as evidence.

"'Did you hear this, Smith?' sez the adjutant.

"'Hear what, sir?' I sez.

"'Hear Private Clark threaten the corporal?'

"'No, sir,' I sez.

"'What!' sez Thatcher, 'didn't you hear him threaten to strike me?'

"'No,' I sez; 'from what I gathered he was addressin' his remarks to me.'

"The adjutant looks at me.

"'But I thought you an' Clark were such good friends,' he sez, suspicious.

"'We used to be,' I sez, regretful, 'but we had misunderstandin's lately.'

"That got Nobby off, and Thatcher never forgave me.

"Soon after this we went home, then came the war, an' we was ordered to hold ourselves in readiness for South Africa. There was some delay' about our leavin' Aldershot, because we were expectin' a draft from the other battalion in Egypt, an' the news went round that amongst the draft was Thatcher's brother.

"'Bloomin' fine regiment this will be,' sez Nobby, gloomily, 'bad enough with Thatcher—what'll it be with a deuce of 'em?'

"The strange thing about it was, that most of us had a likin' for young Thatcher before he arrived, an' the reason was that somebody had heard the corporal talkin' about him one night in the corporal's room.

"'He's a mealy cub,' sez Thatch, 'been tied up to his mother's apron strings too long. The old woman's dead now, an' he's come into the army. I'll make him sit up.'

"The draft arrived three days before we sailed for Africa, an' young Thatcher was the sickliest lookin' of the lot. How the doctor came to pass him for Egyptian service is one mystery, an' how our doctor marked him fit for active service is another. He was more like a girl than a man, a timid, pale-faced boy, shy an' awkward.

"I was in the room when he came in to see his brother.

"'Hullo, Bill,' he sez.

"'Not so much of the Bill,' sez Thatch; 'I'm Corporal Thatcher to you my boy, an' don't you forget it.'

"This enthusiastic reception so staggered the kid that he didn't say another word.

"I don't know any of Thatch's private business, but there must have been bad blood between the two, jealousy, or somethin' of the sort, for the corporal started makin' the boy's life a hell.

"All the rotten things he used to give Nobby to do he gave to the boy.

"He wasn't a good sailor, an' that made it worse, for it was on the voyage out that Thatcher started his pranks.

"'I'll make a man of you,' he sez, an' started to put work on to him that a low-caste sweeper wouldn't have stood. Half the time the kid was seasick, an' the other half he was gettin' over it, an' somehow Thatcher always chose the most disagreeable jobs for his brother. It got so bad that Nobby went to Thatch.

"'Corporal,' he sez, quietly, 'I want you to take me before the commanding officer.'

"'What for?' sez Thatch.

" 'I'm goin' to make a complaint about the way you treat your brother,' sez Nobby.

"'Look here,' sez Thatch, through his teeth, 'you keep your nose out of my business or it'll be the worse for you.'

"'Never mind about that,' sez Nobby, 'I want to see the commanding officer.'

"'Suppose you see him?' sez Thatch with a sneer, 'where's your evidence?'

"'Your brother's evidence's enough,' sez Nobby.

"Thatch laughed.

"'You fool, do you think he's goin' to give evidence against me—did Smithy give evidence against you?'

195

"That upset Nobby's plan—he knew he couldn't depend on the brother, because he'd already sounded him, an' found him shy of chargin' Thatch.

"Toward the end of the voyage, the youngster had a better time because the corporal nearly met with an accident.

"One night, when he was leanin' over the ship's side, Billy Mason fell against him an' nearly knocked him overboard.

"'You did that for the purpose,' gasps Thatch, with a face like a taller candle.

"But Billy swore he tripped over a bucket an' couldn't help it, an' there was the bucket on the deck to prove it. I know it was there, because I saw Nobby an' Billy put it there.

"Nobby said the idea was to frighten Thatch, an' that was probably true.

"Anyhow, the youngster had a more peaceful life till the ship reached port, an' we entrained for up country. Then the dog's life began all over again.

"The boy was a weaklin', but he'd got plenty of grit. He'd march on one leg sooner than chuck it up. But whatever he did, nothin' satisfied his brother. It was nag, nag, nag from day to day, an' things worse than naggin'. He'd post him on the lonesomest post he could find, send him out scoutin' whenever he happened to be in his sections.

"The kid was plucky under fire, an' so long as a fight was goin' on, but when it was all over, an' it came to collectin' the dead an' wounded, I've seen him beg, with tears in his eyes, to be excused the duty of bringin' in the casualties.

"'I can't stand it, Bill,' he sez, once. 'I can't bear to see people in pain.'

"'I've told you about Bill-ing me,' sez the corporal. 'Now, do as you're told—go out with No. 3 party, you miserable little worm.'

"This sort of thing went on for the best part of three years, an' somehow the kid got quieter an' quieter, an' he used to sit broodin' for hours at a time.

"One day he turned on his brother.

"'You're tryin' to make me as big a brute as yourself,' he sez, 'an' it'll be a bad day's work for you when you succeed.'

"The corporal 'run' him for that; charged him usin' threatening language to a superior. I believe our colonel was a bit shocked at one brother chargin' the other, because although that sort of thing is all right in story-books, it don't look so nice when it actually happens.

But the charge was proved, an' young Thatcher awarded 'field punishment,' which meant that he had to be tied up to the wheel of an ammunition waggon for two hours.

"Till the war was all over, the youngster said nothin' an' did nothin.' We went into barracks at Pretoria, an' settled down for a bit to a quiet, peaceful life. One day the whole secret about Thatcher an' the boy came out.

"It was over a letter—we was all sat round the table peelin' 'em for dinner, when in walked Thatcher with the letter in his hand. He walked straight up to the youngster who was sittin' at one end of the table, an' the boy didn't lift his eyes.

"'Here—you,' sez Thatcher, roughly. 'I've got some news for you—father's dead.'

"'My father?' sez the youngster, jumpin' up.

"'No—*my* father,' sez Thatcher, with a sneer; 'don't try to kid us you don't know who your father was.'

"The youngster looked dazed.

"'You don't suppose you was kicked round at home for nothin', do you? You don't suppose my father had a down on you because you was *his* son, do you?' sez Thatcher. 'Why you——'

"He used a word that ain't allowed in a barrack-room, an' Nobby reached out an' caught him by the collar.

"'Hands off,' shouted Thatcher, an' sprang back.

"I don't know why it was but nobody moved as the boy staggered to his bed cot an' fumbled like a blind man at the arm-rack. Before we could get near him he had his rifle in his hand and the breach open. I heard the cold tinkle of the cartridge fallin' into its place.

"'Bill,' he sez, and the corporal seemed paralysed with fear. 'Bill,' he sez, 'father's in Hell, go to him an' tell him why I sent you.'

"Thatcher was dead before he touched the ground."

15.—The Invention Craze

In compiling military text books, it frequently happens that mistakes occur, but your military text book being an unimaginative and wholly utilitarian production, such mistakes are inartistically but effectively corrected by a slip pasted at the beginning of the book. It is as well that this should be done. For in a little manual on regimental routine, I once read the following astounding instruction:—

The burglar on duty should be wakened half-an-hour before reveille by the sergeant of the guard, so that he should more effectively and punctually perform his duty.

But for the amending slip that prefaced the volume I should have gone through life under the impression that the Anchester Regiment, so far from discouraging, actually fostered crime. But the slip reassured me. It ran:—

Para 24. line 6. For 'burglar' read 'bugler.'

In the days when the *Anchester Journal* appeared, such printer's errors were a source of considerable annoyance. The *Anchester Journal* was the regimental magazine. It was published monthly at 2d., and was worth the money. Especially was it precious in the days when Private Clark undertook its composition. For one learnt of such interesting happenings as:

the reGMentall sportS went of WITH graet suCesS.
And
a New Draft Has arriven froM anchEsters."

Nobby, I must explain, took on the duty of compositor at a time when Jinky—very properly and naturally called "Inky"—Taylor went into hospital with a broken rib, acquired at great expense one pay night at the "Glass Barrel."

Nobby had never set a line of type before, but he was very willing, and the result was creditable. Though Captain Umfreville objected, somewhat captiously, I think, to the abbreviation of his name to "Cap. Umf.," Nobby's explanation that he couldn't find the box with the "I's" in was accepted.

"The thing that everybody's got to remember about Nobby," defended Smithy, "is that he's willin'. It don't matter what sort of job's offered to Nobby he'd take it on, if he'd never seen it done before. When we got to Belfast, in the Transvaal, durin' the war, we found a lot of railway engines, an' the general called for volunteers who knew somethin' about engine-drivin' to come forward.

"Nobby was one of the first chaps to stand out.

"'What do you know about engines, Clark?' sez the adjutant.

"'Everythin' that's known,' sez Nobby, prompt.

"'Can you drive one?'

"'Drive 'em, sir?' sez Nobby, very much amused at the idea of his *not* bein' able to drive 'em. 'Why, the man that drives the "Flyin' Scotsman" used to live next door to us at home!'

"'But can *you* drive 'em?' sez the officer.

"'I'm willin' to try,' sez Nobby. 'I can't say no fairer than that, sir.'

"'But,' sez the officer, very persistent, 'have you ever worked an engine?'

"'Yes, sir,' sez Nobby; 'a beer engine,' he sez.

"I can't understand why Nobby didn't get the job, an' it only goes to prove that there's no encouragement given in the army to chaps who want to learn a trade.

"There was never a job goin' in barracks, with extra pay attached, that Nobby didn't apply for: cook, armourer, shoemaker, tailor, or odd paintin' work. Nobby put in for 'em all at some time or another. He got one or two, but somehow he never stuck to 'em. You see, Nobby's got ideas of his own, an' the army, bein' what I might call conservative, don't encourage a chap to go off the beaten track.

"For instance, when Nobby was tailorin', he thought out a plan for a new regimental weskit, an' a plan for a pocket in your cap, so as a chap could carry his shavin' kit when he went on leave. When he was at the armourer's he thought out a new bullet with a bit of string fastened to it, so that when you'd shot a feller you could extract the bullet without callin' in the doctor. Nobby worked it out, that it would save the government hundreds of pounds a year in bullets alone.

"But Nobby's greatest invention was his latest. It was when Sanitas Domount, the balloon bloke, was creatin' such a stir that Nobby got the idea for a flyin' machine.

"I don't say that he ever carried it out, because, as a matter of fact, he couldn't raise the money; but the idea was a fine one.

"Nobby had been studyin' birds, sparrers an' canaries an' things, an' he saw the idea in a flash.

"His invention was to make a lot of bla-monges—them white puddin's—an' put 'em round the edge of a balloon basket. Then you had to stick thousan's of feathers all over 'em. Then you had to shake the bla-monges to make 'em tremble, an' as soon as they started tremblin' an' the feathers wavin', up the bloomin' car would go.

"That was Nobby's best invention, but the money didn't come in, even though Nobby pointed out to the chaps that even if the experiment didn't come to anything it would be simple to pick the feathers out, an' eat the bla-monges.

"This was just about the time when the regiment was invention-mad. A feller of ours named Hawkey had invented a new cut-off for the rifle. A silly simple thing it was, that anybody could have thought of, if they'd happened to be thinkin' of it. Yet Mr. Bloomin' Hawkey got twenty pounds from the War Office an' might have had promotion if it hadn't been for a slight argument he had with a civil policeman in town (we was at Gib. at the time).

"The moment it got about that Hawkey had made twenty pounds the regiment reclined in various thoughtful attitudes, an' put together inventions. That's when Nobby produced the pull-out bullet an' the razor-case cap an' the reversible shirt that didn't require washin'. Spud Murphy invented a holler bayonet with holes in it that you could play like a flute, an' Yatesey invented a patent boot that laced itself up, an' Bill Mason, who was a first-class armourer, invented a new kind of handcuff. He tried 'em on Spud, an' when he went to take 'em off they wouldn't work, an' it took the armourer-sergeant a whole day to file 'em off.

"Then Nobby invented a penny-in-the-slot machine out of a biscuit-box an' an old alarum clock. You put your penny in one end an' got a packet of Woodbines out of the other.

"Lots of chaps tried that. The pennies went in all right, but nothin' seemed to come out at the other end.

"'It's very funny,' sez Nobby. 'It worked all right this mornin'—try it again.'

"So the chap who was makin' the experiment—a recruit named Bowen—put another penny in, but nothin' happened.

"Nobby kept shakin' the box to make it work, but it was no go.

"'Try it again,' sez Nobby.

"'No, thanks,' sez the young feller, 'it's cost me threepence already.'

"'The chances are,' sez Nobby, thoughtfully, 'that the next penny that's put in will bring out four packets—who'll have a penn'orth?'

"Tiny White tried on the off chance of gettin' the four, an' Harry Dyke had two tries because Nobby said that as likely as not the whole bloomin' stock of cigarettes would come out at one pop.

"Spud said it was a swindle, an' most of the other fellers who had lost money said the same.

"But, as Nobby pointed out, you can't expect a new invention to work smooth at first, an' it showed the invention was genuine because one part of it was workin' splendidly.

"'Which part?' sez Spud.

"'The part where the money goes in,' sez Nobby.

"After that Nobby invented a burglar alarm an' Spud sez it wasn't before it was wanted.

"It was soon after that Nobby took on the *Anchester Journal*. I think

I told you about Inky Taylor goin' sick. Nobby wasn't the greatest compositor in the world. He's the sort of modest chap who'd admit it. But he did his dabdest an' angels can do no more. When Inky came out of hospital an' started sortin' out the type that Nobby had mixed up, he said that Nobby was the most experimental chap he'd ever worked with. There wasn't a single kind of type in the office that Nobby hadn't messed about, an' it took Inky the best part of three months to put 'em straight. You'd find little 'X's' in the boxes where the 'B's' live, an' 'G's' an' 'C's' all piggin' together in one happy family.

"Nobby wanted Inky to take him on an' learn him the trade.

"I forget exactly where Inky said he'd see Nobby to before he allowed him within a hundred miles of his office, but it was somewhere unpleasant.

"But Nobby was terribly taken up with the printin' business an' went off to see the sergeant-major, who was the editor of the regimental journal. It so happened that the feller who used to do the general work on the paper, had just gone away on the reserve an' when Nobby asked for the job, an' said his brother was the editor of the *Times*, an' his uncle George was the head man on the *Telegraph*, and his cousin Peter drew the pictures in the *Sunday Chronicle* the sergeant-major gave him the job.

"News is pretty scarce in a regiment, beyond cricket an' football an' a concert or two at the sergeants' mess, an' the shootin', there's nothin' to write about except 'We hear with regret of the death of Mr. Thomas Samson, who served as a private in the Anchester Regiment durin' the Peninsular War,' an' similar excitin' items of news.

"When the battalion got to India, it was even worse, because the regiment had to depend upon the officers for news. We'd have a '*Short Account of my Pig-Stickin' Expedition to the Chootee Hills*,' an' a '*Brief Note of a Tiger Hunt in Bengal*.' All these was very interestin' to the chaps who wrote 'em, but for the fellers who bought the paper they wasn't worth two penn'orth of snuff.

"It was when we was in Chucajee waitin' for the cholera to pass that Nobby got charge of the paper owin' to the sergeant-major goin' sick.

"That's when it began to get bright.

"Nobby started a new column called 'Tittle Tattle' that caused more excitement in one day than the *Journal* had caused all its life.

"There were little paragraphs like this:—

Spud took another bath last Tuesday. How time flies!

Ugly J. has entered for the Chucajee Beauty Competition.

Diary of the Week.

Tuesday.—Money market tight.

Wednesday (Pay Day).— Bill Mason *ditto*.

"An' such light-hearted chatter. An' he had a leader about recruits payin' respect to old soldiers.

"But the finest thing in the whole magazine was the Foreign News—an' of all the things that Nobby ever invented in his life this was the most wonderful an' astonishin' for more reasons than one.

"I think I told you about Chucajee an' the sort of place it was. It was miles from everywhere, an' there wasn't no wire, an' no telephone, or anything. We got all the news we got from mounted messengers an' from a helio station twenty miles away on the hills.

"Bein' in a cholera camp the officers was quite willin' to do anythin' to prevent the young soldiers dyin' of funk, an' when Nobby asked the adjutant if he could make up news the adjutant sez, Yes.

"'In fact,' sez the adjutant, 'I never expected anything like the truth from a paper you have to do with, Clark, an' I shall be very much disappointed if I 'eard a single line in the *Journal* that I can believe.'

"'Thank you, sir,' sez Nobby, gratefully.

"So me an' Nobby sat down to write the foreign news.

"We started by sayin' that the wife of a Wolverhampton labourer had had triplets, an' got the king's bounty.

"'We're pretty safe in sayin' that,' sez Nobby, who reads the newspapers; 'they're always havin' triplets in Wolverhampton.'

"'What about a fire in the City?' I sez.

"'That's a good idea,' sez Nobby, an' wrote:

A terrible fire occurred in the City of London. Damage was done to the extent of hundreds of pounds. The place was insured.

"And then we put in a bit about a Liverpool gentleman who committed suicide owin' to the loss of his high hat, a bit about a scene in Parliament, an' a bit about the German emperor.

"'We can't go wrong in sayin' this,' sez Nobby, very confident, 'because this is the sort of news that's in the papers all the year round.'

"Just then we was all full of the Chucajee Plate, what Nobby lost owin' to his bein' overweight, an' it was only natural that Nobby should want to do the sportin' news very well. So he went to a young officer in the sportin' line of business, young Lieutenant Tollemache, an' asked him if he could tell him what races was on just about then.

"'Well, Clark,' sez the officer, smilin, 'there's all kinds of races—there's the Manchester November Handicap next week.'

"'What's goin' to run. sir?' sez Nobby.

"'Not bein' gifted as you are, Clark,' sez the officer, 'with the divine gift of secon' sight, I can't tell you—but I've got the entries,' an' he dug 'em out.

'There was forty-three entries, an' me an' Nobby sat down to write about the race.

"'We'll make The Brewer win,' sez Nobby, 'an' Otuka second.'

"An' he sat down and wrote the description just like, you read about in the papers.

The Manchester November Handicap was run yesterday amidst great excitement. Epsom Downs was crowded with people and so were the trains. It was a glorious sight. "The Brewer" was the first at the post and spent some time chatting with the starter. The noble animal leant idly against the starting gate watching the animated scene with his beautiful eyes. Suddenly the whistle blew and "The Brewer" roaring with excitement, leapt into the air. "They're off!" was the cry, and in a few minutes the horses were tearing round the cinder track as though they meant business. They disappeared behind the Bushes. Three minutes passed, five minutes passed, and the excitement became phenomenal. Suddenly the horses came into sight. "The Brewer" was leading. The other horses were behind. "'The Brewer' wins!" they cried, as the field came round Tattenham Comer, and bets were freely made. The bell rang joyously. "The Brewer" had won; Otuka second; Hammond Lady third. Betting: 50 to 1 agst "The Brewer," 1,000 to 1 agst Otuka, 5,000 to 1 agst Hammond Lady. The favourite won by six lengths.

"That was the finest bit of writin' that Nobby ever done in his life, an' when the *Journal* came out everybody was delighted with it. In fact, there never was a *Journal* that had a bigger sale than Nobby's number.

"Billy Mason said he'd have Nobby into court for deflamation of character, an' Spud Murphy liked the paragraph about his bath so much that he said that for two pins he'd break Nobby's jaw, but the officers was very pleased an' the colonel sent for Nobby.

"'Very well done, Clark,' he sez, 'very excellent spoof. What a liar you are; you're a born journalist,' an' similar compliments.

"Young Tollemache sent for Nobby, too.

"'Clark,' he sez. 'what the devil made you hit upon The Brewer—I've never heard of the horse. Is it a runner?'

"'I don't know, sir,' sez Nobby: 'it ought to be,' he sez.

"The young officer looks at Nobby.

"'H'm,' he sez, 'the race is run in two days' time.' He shook his head an' said nothin' else.

"Soon after that we got orders to move to Poona, an' we weren't particularly sorry to get there. The night we arrived, Nobby an' me was discussin' things.

"'I've got a feelin',' sez Nobby, 'that old Tolly has sent a cable home an' backed The Brewer, an' that it'll win, an' old Tolly will come in to me an' say, with tears in his eyes, "Nobby, you've saved me family from ruin—here's a hundred for you, don't make a beast of yourself with it, an'——"'

"Then a most surprisin' thing happened, for the very thing that Nobby was speakin' about come to pass. In walked Tolly an' another officer, an' they was lookin' so pleased with theirselves that I could almost hear the money clinkin' into Nobby's pockets.

"'Ah, Clark,' sez the officer, 'I thought you'd like to know that I took your spoof tip an' cabled home to back The Brewer.'

"'Yes, sir,' sez Nobby, quite fluttered.

"'It didn't win,' said the officer, an' Nobby's face fell to six o'clock.

"'Beg pardon, sir?' he sez.

"'It didn't win, because there isn't such a horse.'

"Nobby gasped.

"'But it was in that paper you gave me, sir,' he sez.

"'Brewer's not the name of a horse—it's the name of a trainer,' he sez."

16.—Marshy, Detective

It is a fact which my military friends do not dispute, that the average officer does not know the average soldier. If he knows him, it is the result of furtive study; round about deductions; secret overlookings.

A distinguished scientist told me the other day that nothing struck him so much when he was engaged in research work in a London hospital, as the fact that there is an hour in the day when the patients go on duty. For twenty-three hours they have been cheerful souls, exchanging badinage with their fellow sufferers, ripe for amusement, ready and willing to give or take a joke. Then comes the hour of the doctor's visit—and they become "officially ill," depressed, saddened, altogether melancholy. So it is in the army.

Brought face to face with his officer, the soldier becomes "officially military." He plays the part he thinks he is called upon to play, becomes inhumanly automatic. His very expression alters. His face is a mask, betraying no emotion. His speech is monosyllabic, it would need a most penetrating observer to pierce the mystery of the outward shell and reach the soul of this silent man, who stands to attention and says, "Yes, sir," or "No, sir," monotonously.

Thus it is that young officers say, in speaking of their men, that they are "very good chaps, but——," and thus it is also that these very officers return from active service bubbling over with joy at a discovery. That discovery is that there is no "but" in the case, but the British soldier is a splendidly, tip-topping, top-notching, ripping good fellow.

In war time the soldier is his human self without disguise. A man is brought before his company officer.

"You wish to see me, Jones?" says the officer.

"Yes, sir; I want three days' leave."

"For what purpose?"

"My sister is very ill."

Perhaps the officer may know that the man has no sister, and may wax indignant at the unnecessary lie.

But the soldier is acting up to the settled traditions of the army—not in lying, but in offering a conventional excuse for a conventional privilege.

"Sister ill," "mother ill," "a funeral," "a wedding," these events are regarded as sufficient excuse for three days' leave. Did the man "know'" his officer, or the officer his man, did mutual confidence exist between them, the soldier would say out plump and plain, "I want three days' leave because my girl has got a short holiday and I wish to spend the time profitably."

But it is his "duty face" that he turns to his officer, a machine made, artificial manner, with which he greets him. Beneath its surface very few officers are privileged to reach.

"Nobody likes an officer to be too friendly," said Smithy, "an' at the same time nobody cares for an officer that treats a soldier as if he was a new kind of dangerous animal.

"I knew an officer once who was a whale on collectin' butterflies an' similar reptiles. After parade he used to go wanderin' all over the fields lookin' for a patent new moth that was very rare.

"One mornin', just before the cold weather started, he told his servant to give his new forty-guinea fur coat an airin'. When the servant shook the coat out he shook out half a bushel of loose fur, an' the officer nearly went daft.

"'What the devil's the meanin' of this?' he sez, an' just then a feeble little moth sort of staggered into the air. The officer caught it, an' lo! it was his new patent moth!

"Between gettin' the moth an' losin' his coat he was in a horrible state of mind, an' that's about the condition of an officer who tries to get too friendly with the men, He gains a little an' loses a lot.

"Did I ever tell you about Marshy? He was the chap who took up with detectiving, an' was always goin' about solvin' mysteries that nobody wanted solvin'. He could tell by the colour of your eyes how many entries you had on your defaulter sheet, an' by the colour of your hands, how often you washed yourself. Perfectly marvellous he was. I told you a long time ago about what he did with Captain Brinky—found out how he was selling the plans of the barracks to Germany.

"As Nobby said at the time, it was very serious. Suppose them plans fell into the hands of Germany, the Germans had only to train their guns on our canteens an' the whole bloomin' regiment would be decimated. It turned out afterwards that the plans which old Marshy had seen Brinky workin' at was only the plans of the new meat store, an' that rather discouraged him for a bit. But bless you, he turned up smilin' some time after that.

We were stationed at Wynberg at the time, an' one of the guards was stationed on the outskirts of the town near an orchard. A beautiful orchard full of peaches an' grapes an' quinces very nearly ripe. It was in the spring time.

"Now, there was a very mysterious thing about this guard. Chaps who came off it was taken suddenly ill with pains that doubled 'em up. Every day the same thing happened, fellers bein' carried off to hospital tied in knots, cussin' the day they ever wandered into other people's orchards.

"Marshy had a theory about this mysterious illness.

"They've been poisoned,' he sez to Nobby, very solemn: 'they've got secret enemies who carry little glass phials full of deadly poison.'

"'The poison *they* get,' sez Nobby, 'has got pips in it.'

"But Marshy was very confident, an' went up to the hospital to see Bill Clare, who was one of the last chaps to suffer.

"'Hullo, Bill,' he sez, 'I've just come to cheer you up—you're lookin' bad?'

"'I *am* bad,' sez Bill.

"'Bill,' sez Marshy, very earnest, 'have you got any enemies?'

"'Hundreds,' sez Bill, who was one of those chaps bred an' born with a grievance.

"'That's it!' sez Marshy, 'that just proves what I've said—you've been poisoned.'

"'I know I have,' groans Bill.

"'When you're dead,' sez Marshy thoughtfully, 'we'll have a *post-mortem*, an' that'll settle the question.'

"'You're takin' a liberty,' sez Bill violently, 'an' if I had the use of me hands I'd belt your head off, you cheerful blighter.'

"As Marshy said, if only one of 'em would die, his theory would work out correct, but somehow nobody seemed anxious to prove his words. When Spud Murphy was took bad, Marshy haunted the hospital, enquirin' about Spud's temperature till the gentle hospital orderly said that if Marshy didn't push-off he'd catch him a swipe in the jaw. When Spud came out of hospital he went to look for Marshy.

"'I'm goin' to return his call,' he sez, 'an' if any of you chaps happen to want an afternoon's amusement you can come down to the cricket field an' see me diagnosin' Marshy's disease.'

"That put Marshy off detecting, an' it was a long time after the peaches in the orchard were ripe before the black wore out of his eye.

"But nothin' could keep him quiet for long. He was back at the old business, tracin' an' measurin' footsteps an' peerin' into other people's secrets again.

"He found out why Chancer Saul never had any letters from home owin' to his havin' nobody to write to him; he discovered where the quartermaster-sergeant bought his new piano an' where the money came from—out of the bank. He pried into the mystery of Nobby's box an' found a pair of my socks, an' a smack in the head from Nobby, who happened to come in at that minute, He shaddered Sergeant Toms an' his young lady an' found out there was a bull dog in the young lady's garden, an' wished he'd known it beforehand. In fact, Marshy went very strong.

"The Brinky affair wot I told you about nearly put Marshy out of business, but it was the case of young Lieutenant Forster that settled him for good an' all.

"As a rule, a chap in the army knows very little about his officer, except that he's got pots of money an' plays polo.

"He sees him on parade, he marches by his side on manoeuvres, an' sees him sittin' at a table handin' out the root-of-all-evil on pay days.

"He sees him sometimes at meals, when the officer happens to be on orderly duty, an' he hears him say 'any complaints?' an' sees him turn away before anybody can speak.

"What he does or sez; what the other officers think of him, whether he's a good chap or a bad chap, the soldier doesn't know. He guesses—but in nine cases out of ten he guesses wrong.

"This young Forster—Lieutenant Forster—was a fresh-coloured, cheerful kind of chap that we all liked. He played football an' could box, an' once I saw him ridin' out in his huntin' kit.

' Nobody knew exactly what happened, but when we was in Wynberg, the officers stopped talkin' to him. It happened suddenly. If they had to speak to him at all they spoke in a language that nobody understood, but which Marshy said was French, owin' to young Forster sayin' 'Wee wee.' You could see he was upset. He'd stammer an' stutter an' get confused, especially when Umfreville, who's a devil of a chap for French, spoke.

"Marshy said it was one of the mysteriousest things he'd ever had brought to his notice.

"'Anyone can tell what it means,' he sez. 'Young Forster's been an' done somethin' bad, an' the officers won't speak to him unless they can swear at him, an' that's why they talk in French.'

"So Marshy started to find out what Forster had been doin'. After two days pryin' he came to Nobby highly excited.

"'I've discovered it!' he sez.

"'I'll bet you have,' sez Nobby, admiringly.

"'I shaddered him last night,' sez Marshy. 'He went right through the village into the country. I shaddered him till we came to the woods near Constantia, an' in he goes an' me after. He started talkin' an' carryin' on to hisself—ravin' I call it, an' a feller of my experience could see that his conscience was bitin' him.'

"'I watched him for an hour, an' all the time he was talkin'—just as though someone was there. I looked an' looked, but I couldn't see anybody, an' I got as near as I could, but all I could hear was 'Wossy Lair, Wossy La Plume! Wossy Cray On, Dermont Pair.'

"'It was a sort of back slang, an' I couldn't understand it.'

"'My theory is,' sez Marshy, very impressive, 'that he's pinched something, an' he's got a pal a-hidin' in the wood.'

"Well, it turned out afterwards that young Forster was studyin' for some language examination—French it was—but bein' an easy goin' sort of young feller, an' much preferin' to spend his evenin's playin' bridge, he got a bit backward until the officers made up a plan only to speak to him in French.

"Billy Curtis, who's a waiter in the officer's mess, sez it was a bit of lark at dinner, because young Forster had to scratch up his French before he could get anything to eat. When he asked anybody to pass the mustard they pretended they didn't understand him till he asked for it in French. So if Marshy had started enquirin' in the proper quarters he'd have found out all he wanted to know in two ticks, but that wasn't Marshy's way.

"It wasn't the fact that he was makin' a silly ass of hisself that *kiboshed* Marshy, but something more serious an' unnatural.

"Marshy was crowded with the notion that Lieutenant Forster had a pal hidden in the woods.

"One day he had a talk with Nobby.

"'I've been shadderin' Forster," he sez, 'an' I'm goin' to search his quarters tonight.'

"Take my tip an' don't,' sez Nobby, who was a bit alarmed, 'an' if you do, don't say that you told me you was goin' to do it.'

"I think Nobby might have persuaded him to drop his fat-headed idea, only that afternoon there was a garrison call.

"Not far from Wynberg is a big convict settlement at a place called Constantia, an' we got the news that a feller named Magee had escaped. This here Magee was a well-known chap at the Cape—you must have read 'about him.

"He used to meet fellers who had just come out from England, smack 'em on the back, an' give 'em the hullo-old-feller-fancy-meetin'-you shake, an' the come-an'-have-a-drink pass, an' when they was fairly hypnotised he'd borrer a hundred pounds from 'em just to show his confidence in 'em. He got one or two doses of imprisonment, an' then he struck up against a bad judge who'd got theories about short sentences bein' no good for the risin' generation, an' this judge sent

209

him down for five years.

"Magee had done three months when he decided to leave. He left early one mornin', an' that afternoon there were two battalions of infantry picketin' the country on the lookout for Mr. Magee. Seven companies of ours was out, and Marshy, who happened to be in the company stayin' behind, thought the whole bloomin' thing was got up to give him the chance he wanted. He waited till it was dark, an' then he sneaked across to the officers' quarters. Lieutenant Forster had a bungalow at the far end of the lines. He shared it with another young officer, an' Marshy's luck bein' in, these two chaps was both on duty somewhere in the neighbourhood of Constantia.

"Marshy sneaked round the bungalow, tryin' the doors an' winders, an' at last he found a winder that was open. He waited till he was sure there was no one about, then he nipped through the winder an' found hisself in Lieutenant' Forster's bath-room. It was quite dark, an' Marshy didn't dare to strike a light, but after failin' over a pail an' bangin' his head against the wall, he reached the officer's bedroom. Marshy's great point is footprints an' secret drawers. He'd got an idea that all criminals write confessions an' leave 'em in secret drawers where nobody could find 'em, except detectives. First thing he did was to close the shutters an' pull across the curtains of the winders, then he started to search for damnin' evidence with a candle he'd brought with him

"There was a little desk in one corner of the room with lots of papers. Marshy read a few. Some of 'em began:

Dear sir, unless our account is paid in three days we shall be reluctantly compelled——

"Another commenced:

Dear sir, the enclosed account is long overdue, an' as we are makin' up our books for the half-year, we shall be glad——.

"But there was nothin' that Marshy could find that gave Mr. Forster away.

"He was just turnin' over a heap of letters when he heard a cough behind him, an' his heart went down into his boots.

"'Beg pardon, sir,' he stammered, an' turned round with his knees shakin'.

"The chap that stood behind him was a tall chap, nicely dressed in a yaller suit that didn't fit him, an' ornamented all over with big black arrers. Marshy gasped—but the feller only smiled an' started polishin' the barrel of a revolver he had in his hand on the sleeve of his coat.

"'Good-evenin',' he sez, as calm an' polite as possible, 'are you the servant of the officer who owns this bungalow?'

"'No, sir,' sez Marshy.

"'Don't say, sir,' sez the chap, 'I'm the escaped convict that your chaps are lookin' for.'

"'Oh, you are, are you?' sez Marshy, gettin' back a bit of his nerve.

"'Yes, I am, am I,' sez the chap.

"Marshy made up his mind—you can understand his feelin's at the prospec' of arrestin' an escaped convict.

"'Well,' sez Marshy, as bold as brass, 'I'll trouble you to come along with me.'

"The chap shook his head.

"'Not so,' he sez, 'but far otherwise. I have no partic'lar desire,' he sez, thoughtfully, 'of returning to Tokai. For one thing the work's too hard, an' for another thing, the food's not nice, an' the sleepin' accommodation is very horrid. I have decided to leave the country.'

"Marshy sez he swung his revolver around carelessly. "'The pistol,' sez the chap, 'belongs to the officer who owns this charmin' bungalow. So do the cartridges,' he sez. 'I thought I might be able to borrer some civilian clothes to get away in, but they're locked up, an' I can't break open the box without makin' too much noise.'

"Marshy was tryin' to think of a way of attracting the guard.

"'Of course,' sez the chap, very significantly, 'if I have to shoot you, that'll make a noise, but I've got to chance that.'

"'Certainly,' sez Marshy, feebly.

"'At the same time,' sez the convict, 'there won't be no necessity to shoot, because you're goin' to behave like a little gentleman.'

"'Certainly,' sez Marshy, rather weakly.

"'First of all,' the convict chap went on, 'I see you are dressed for walkin' out. Take off your clothes.'

"'Hold hard!' sez Marshy, 'let's argue this point—'

"'I'll argue with you as you undress,' sez the chap; 'look slippy.'

"Bit by bit he took Marshy's clothes from him.

"'Now your trousis,' sez the chap. 'Thanks,' he sez, as Marshy chucked them over.

"It didn't take the convict two minutes to get out of his things, an' in another minute he was dressed in Marshy's kit.

"'I'd make a fine soldier,' he sez, regretful. 'What a pity I didn't go into the army. Now, get into my things.'

"'Look here,' sez Marshy.

"'I'm lookin',' sez the convict; 'get on with it.'

"So pore old Marshy had to rig himself up like a convict.

"'Now, sit down it that chair,' sez the convict, 'and don't move whilst I tie you up.'

"With two or three straps from the officer's equipment he trussed old Marshy so that he couldn't move. Then he tied a towel round his mouth so that he couldn't yell.

"Then the convict chap lit one of the officer's cigars, an' stuck Marshy's walkin' stick under his arm.

"'Goodbye,' he sez, 'I'm sorry to take advantage of a feller burglar, but it had to be done.'

"'I'm not a burglar,' sez Marshy, very muffled. ' I'm a detective,' he sez.

"'A what?'

"'A detective,' sez pore ole Marshy. 'I was lookin' for somethin'.'

"'What you was lookin' for,' sez the convict, as he put the light out, 'was Trouble—an' you've found it. Goodnight.'"

17.—THE GHOST OF THE BROOK

If you add to the title of your romance (supposing that you are an author) the sub-title, "A true story," you may expect your readers to yawn in anticipation, for, as everybody knows, a true story is a dull story. The only "true story" I know that wasn't hopelessly dull, was the life and adventures of Louis de Rougevitch. This narrative was so exceptionally interesting that all shrewd people knew it was a lie. Truth is stranger than fiction, and infinitely duller.

Therefore, I place no sub-title to this adventure of Smithy's. I avoid explanation, save the explanation that is in courtesy due from writer to reader.

Simonstown is the most southerly town in Africa. South of Simonstown runs a rocky promontory, that ends at a rugged headland, which throughout the world is famous as the Cape of Good Hope. Locally, it is called Cape Point. Behind Simonstown itself rises a range of hills, and one towering above its fellows is known as Simonsberg.

Of Simonstown itself there is no need to speak. Its one straggling street that stretches from the railway station to the cemetery; its stretch of placid blue bay; its white warships, and trim dockyard; its tiny barracks perched on a shelf of hill.—I tell you of these, incidentally, and not because they are material to the story.

Smithy regards Simonstown from a different point of view. Smithy is practical, and utilitarian, and there is very little of the sentimental nonsense in Smithy's composition.

"I was at Simonstown before they started the new docks," he said, "an' naturally the beer wasn't half as good as it is now. In fact, Simonstown was a very dull place, so dull that Nobby up an' joined the Good Templars. That will show you how dull Simonstown was. Nobby wanted me to come along, too, but I'd got something else to do with my money. Nobby was a Good Templar for a week, after which he had a slight disagreement with a half-caste brother, whose name was Sams, an' the consequence of this was that some of Sams' black blood came out.

"Then Yatesey's sister sent him out a new spellin' game, an' we played that for a week. It was played with cards. You shuffled 'em an' dealt 'em, an' the feller who could make a word out of the cards in his hand won the money. It was a bit difficult, because when you put a word down the chap next to you could challenge you. Then you had to look in the dictionary an' see if it was spelt that way; an' if it wasn't you had to pay.

"'Molix,' sez Nobby, puttin' down the word.

"'What's "Molix"?' sez Spud, suspicious.

"'A "Molix,"' sez Nobby, thoughtful, 'is a little fish.'

"'I won't have "Molix" at any price,' sez Spud, so they looked in the dictionary an' found it wasn't there, an' Nobby paid.

"A little while after:

"'Domsin,' sez Nobby, putting down his cards very surefully, 'an' if you challenge that word, Spud, you'll lose your money, because I looked it up this mornin'.'

"But Spud challenged it, an' that wasn't there, either, so Nobby paid again.

"Next day, when they went to play, the dictionary—it belonged to Corporal Sims—was missin', but Nobby said he could remember most of the words in his head.

"Tiny White put down 'hair,' but Nobby said he couldn't pass it owin' to there bein' no 'h' in air. A little while after Nobby put down 'gromb,' an' when Spud challenged it, Nobby said that it meant 'fierce an' wild.'

"Nobby might have made the spellin' game pay, only the dictionary was discovered in the nick of time. They found it hidden under some shirts in Nobby's box.

"That bust up the spellin' game, an' me an' Nobby went in for fishin' with a line we borrered from Pug Wilson an' a lead we pinched from the quartermaster sergeant.

"The bait was our own.

"It was a nice easy life in Simonstown—no parades, eight nights in bed, (eight days between guards), an' nothin' to do but smoke an' fish.

"We'd arranged to go over Red Hill one day. We were goin' to take some grub an' a couple of bottles of beer, an' walk across country to the other side of the peninsular to see the place where the *Birkenhead* went down, an' had got our passes signed by the C.O., when somethin' altogether unexpected happened.

"As you know, there are two guards at Simonstown, the guard on the gate at the R.A. Barracks an' the guard on the *kloof* magazine. You've heard me talk of No. 2 Magazine at Anchester, an' the magazine guard at Peshawar. Well, they was absolutely nothin' to the *kloof* guard at Simonstown. It's away back from the town through 'The Brook,' an' right into the hills. It's a narrer, lonely ravine with a high waterfall, an' the chap on guard is away from light an' sound—except the sound of the baboons a-chatterin' on the hills, an' the splash of the water fallin'.

"It wasn't a cheerful place, but then you don't expect a magazine guard to be as lively as the Strand, an' though nobody liked the job, nobody shirked it.

"One night, it was the night before me an' Nobby went off for our excursion, we was sittin' outside the barracks talkin'.

"By rights we ought to have been in bed, for it was long after 'lights out,' but it was one of them glorious nights that you get in Africa, a bright moon making everythin' clear as day, an' the bay all glimmerin'. We was talkin' about how money flies (Nobby started it), when we heard the sentry on the gate:

"'Number one—an' all's well!' he yelled.

"We stopped talkin' an' waited for No. 2 at the *kloof* to answer.

"We waited an' waited, but there was no sound.

"'Who's on No. 2?' sez Nobby.

"'Ten till twelve—Why, it's Culley Carter,' sez Spud.

"We listened again, but heard nothin'.

"'He must have answered, an' we didn't hear him,' sez Nobby,' but just then we heard the main guard sentry—Happy Johnson it was—shout:

"'No. 1—an' all's well!' an' we knew that No. 2 hadn't spoken.

"Three times No. 1 called, an' three times there was no answer, an' then we heard Happy shout, 'Guard, turn out!'

"'Come along,' sez Nobby, jumpin' up, 'we'll cut along the back path to the magazine—old Culley ought to be warned the guard's comin' up.'

"We'd made our start, when the corporal of the main guard called again, an' in the clear night air you could hear him distinctly, although it was a quarter of a mile away.

"'No. 1—all's well?'

"He put it in a sort of questionin' tone—an' there came an answer:

"Land on the larboard bow, sir!'

"It wasn't the words that made our blood run cold; it was the voice.

"Harsh, an' cracked, an' almost screamin'.

"'That's not Culley,' whispered Nobby—an' we ran along the dark little path that leads to the magazine.

"There was half-a-dozen of us, but we came up to the railin's of the magazine almost abreast.

"As we reached it, we heard the tramp of the guard comin' through 'The Brook' below.

"'Culley!' called Nobby, but there was no answer.

"'Culley!' he shouted.

"We could hear the guard halt at the sound of our voices, and the corporal in charge challenged us in the darkness.

"'Halt! Who comes there?'

"'Friend,' sez Nobby. 'It's Clark, an' half-a-dozen of our chaps.'

"'What's wrong?' sez the corporal.

"'I don't know,' sez Nobby; 'we've come up to see.'

"The corporal opened the little wicket of the magazine with a key, an' he an' the guard went inside, an' we flocked in after him.

"We couldn't see anything of Culley for a bit, but after a while we found him.

"He was huddled up against the stonework of the magazine, insensible an' foamin' at the mouth.

"'A fit,' muttered the corporal.

"Nobby was lookin' at Culley's rifle.

"'Corporal,' he sez, suddenly, 'look at this!'

"The bolt of the rifle was open, an' a round of ammunition had been pushed into the chamber.

"'Old Culley was goin' to shoot somebody,' sez Nobby, 'an' that somebody was the chap who answered you.'

"The corporal turned quickly.

"'So you heard it, did you?—I thought it was some drunken sailor in "The Brook,"' (There's lots of low drinkin' shanties near 'The Brook.')

"'Couldn't have been a "mulloch," corporal,' sez Nobby, 'he wouldn't say "larboard"; he'd say "port!"'

"We got Culley down to the little hospital, an' a new sentry was posted at the *kloof*—Bill Mason, who's got nerves like brass—an' we all went back to barracks talkin' the matter over, an' wonderin' what had frightened old Culley.

"First thing we heard next mornin' was that Bill Mason had been found at five o'clock in the mornin' in a dead faint.

"I could have understood it if it had been anybody but Bill, but Bill ain't got any imagination at all. It took 'em nearly two hours to get Bill round, an' when they did he said he'd seen a ghost. He stuck to it, too, before the company officer, an' before the C.O. What's more, they managed to bring Culley out of his fit, an' Culley swore the same thing.

"'A gashley sight,' he sez, an' shuddered. He couldn't give any particulars, neither could Bill. All they could say was that they'd suddenly seen a most horrible face a-grinnin' at 'em between the railings of the magazine.

"The C.O. sent for the Chief of the Police.

"'Somebody has been trying to unnerve my men,' he sez, 'an' it will be a bad job for that somebody if he repeats his joke, because I've given orders to the sentry on the *kloof* to shoot at sight.'

"Instead of treatin' the thing as a joke this police officer was very serious.

"'It sounds like the "Ghost of the Brook,"' he sez.

"'Ghost!' sez the C.O.; 'stuff an' nonsense! Bosh!' an' a few other tactful remarks.

"'It isn't nonsense, colonel,' sez the police chap. 'The "Brook Ghost" is an old institution. I've been here twenty years, an' I've heard about that ghost from the first day I arrived here.'

"'Are you serious?' sez the colonel.

"'I am, indeed,' sez the police chap. 'I believe in him almost as much as the natives; he's been seen in every part of the peninsular; on lonely farms, at the outskirts of the town—why, there are at least three people in Simonstown Cemetery who have been scared there by the "Ghost of the Brook."'

"Porky Cook, who's a clerk in the orderly room, told us this, an' when the orderly-room sergeant came round askin' for volunteers for the *kloof* guard I was one of the first to get out of his way.

"'It's a double guard,' sez the orderly sergeant, 'an' although you can be "warned" for it, an' get cells for refusin', the colonel wants volunteers. You can choose your own pals for the double!'

"So Nobby up an' said that him an' me would take one relief, an' if it hadn't been for the sergeant bein' there I'd have clumped his head. But when I sat down to think of the matter seriously I was rather glad he volunteered, for I was a bit curious to see how it would turn out.

"After all, the *kloof's* a pretty place in the day time. We mounted an' nothin' happened till night. Nobby an' me was on second relief—the guard mounted at ten—which was from twelve to two an' six to eight. The fellers who were relieved at eight had nothin' to tell, except Boyle, a bit of an author, who said he saw a strange white light a-hoverin' over the hill.

"As it happened the warships was practisin' with their searchlights that night, so we knew what Boyle's strange, white light was.

"The men who came off at ten thought they'd heard peculiar noises.

"'Like what?' sez the corporal of the guard.

"'Like bones rattlin',' sez the chaps, solemn.

"'It was your knees knockin' together,' sez the corporal.

"We marched up through the Brook, an' over the little wooden bridge that leads to the magazine, an' the two men on guard were pretty glad to see us.

"'Anythin' to report?' sez the corporal.

"It was Spud Murphy an' Tiny White on guard. 'Nothin' much,' sez Spud. 'I thought I saw somethin' movin' in the *kloof*—somethin' comin' down the side of the rock.'

"'The waterfall, I expect,' said the corporal, who hadn't got to stay out all night an' could afford to be comic.

"The first half hour passed off quietly; it was terribly quiet, so quiet that the little waterfall sounded like a roar, an' the baboons talkin' just like human voices.

"We got 'All's well' from the main guard at one o'clock, an' returned it.

"Our voices were still echoin' through the *kloof* when I saw Nobby

217

bend forward as if he was listenin'.

"'Hush,' he whispers. 'Somebody's singin'.'

"'Somebody in the town,' I sez.

"'No—listen.'

"I listened, an' couldn't hear anythin', then, close at hand, I heard the voice—a broken, hoarse, old voice. You couldn't hear the words; it was a sort of croon.

"'There he is,' whispers Nobby.

"I could see nothin'—then my heart went up into my mouth, for suddenly, as if he'd come up out of the ground, I saw somethin' rise up not six paces from me.

"Dark as it was, I could see his face... I heard Nobby mutter somethin' an' he reeled back. Only for a minute—then up went his rifle.

"'*Bang!*'

"'Shoot, Smithy!' yelled Nobby, an' I shot at the place I'd seen the thing sink.

"I pressed close to the railings—I could see nothing.

"'Did you dekko the dial?' sez Nobby. I could feel him shakin', an' I nodded.

"The guard came up at a run, with their lanterns. We searched all about the magazine, but could find nothin'.

"'You've been dreamin',' sez the corporal. Then he jumped, for, from the darkness of the *kloof*, in the same cracked voice we heard:

"'*Rocks on the larboard bow, sir!*' came the hail, an' a sort of quiet chuckle that froze your blood.

"We didn't hear the ghost again that night; but when daylight came Nobby got permission to examine the ground where we'd seen the face. We found the marks of our bullets on a rock, but what he was so anxious to discover was footmarks an' there were none. We searched up an' down, an' went to the very foot of the waterfall, without strikin' on any clue.

"Nobby looks up at the face of the rock over which the water was peltin'.

"'Nothin' but a monkey could climb up there,' he sez. Then he made his first discovery. The ground was wet owin' to the spray of the fall, an' on a patch of sand he found a footmark. It was perfectly distinct.

"'A barefooted man,' sez Nobby thoughtfully, 'an' a big foot.'

"'A native,' I sez, but Nobby shook his head.

"'This mark is fairly fresh, an' there's been no natives near here

218

since daybreak,' he sez.

"By climbin' up the hill at the back of the magazine we got to the head of the waterfall, an' that's where Nobby made his big discovery, for it wasn't only that he found another footmark, but he suddenly dived down an' picked up a bit of paper, almost black it was an' greasy, an' when he tried to open it, it fell to pieces. He gathered 'em carefully together an' we got down the hill again.

"That mornin' Nobby saw the colonel, an' the colonel an' Nobby went down to Admiralty House, an' Nobby showed the admiral— Rawson it was, the best fightin' sailor livin'—the paper. Before twelve o'clock there was four hundred sailors an' soldiers searchin' the hills. They searched 'em till the sun went down, goin' carefully over every bit of ground.

"We was about four miles inland when the naval officer an' our officer decided to drop the search for the night, an' we was just formin' up to march back again, when Nobby broke away from the ranks an' ran to a heap of stone.

"'Here he is!' he shouted, an' started chuckin' the stones left an' right.

He'd only to move a dozen before we saw a big hole in the ground.

"He was strippin' off his coat to go in, when the man inside saved us the trouble . . . he climbed out, peering left an' right at the sailors. . . . Old! He must have been eighty. Dirty, with a long, dirty beard, an' dirty, grey hair, an' hands like the claws of a bird. He wore no clothes except a tattered old blanket, an' he blinked an' blinked in the light of the lanterns.

"By-an'-bye he spotted the naval officer an' staggered towards him.

"'Robson, sir,' he sez, in his cracked voice, 'I give myself up. I've lost my papers, but I'm Robson, A.B.'

"'Robson? My poor man, who is Robson?'

The old man chuckled.

"'I was at the wheel, sir,' he sez, 'me an' my mate. . . . I was at the wheel when she struck. . . . It was all my fault.'. . . He mumbled a bit, then he sez, 'They'll try me by court martial because I escaped. . .They was all drawn up in line, the sojers an' the marines an' the sailors, an' the skipper sez, "Stand fast, Birkenheads!"' '

"'My God!' said the naval officer, startin' back.

"'Out of Queenstown we sailed in January, '52,' the old man went

219

on, 'an' . . . I was at the wheel, but I got ashore an' hid. . . I've been hidin' ever since.'. . . He blinked at the officer.

"'Try me by court martial,' he muttered. . . .'I was at the wheel.'

"Nobby caught him as he fell."

18.—SMITHY ON HUMOUR

Sometimes I have the good fortune to meet Smithy in a philosophical frame of mind, and for my edification he will discourse learnedly and shrewdly on all manner of subjects ranging from the intimate talk of regimental affairs to the larger survey of matters of political and national interest. The other day I found him sniggering over the pictorial representation of the "Imps" adventures. I learned that the front page of *Ideas* is a source of constant joy to the Anchester Regiment. Hence, Smithy on Humour:

"It's a matter of disposition," said Smithy. "What'll make one feller laugh will reduce another chap to a mournful state of mind. There ain't any very sure way of making a chap laugh, but, gen'rally speakin', the easiest way is to tell a story about somebody gettin' hurt. There's nothin' quite so comic as a feller fallin' off a house, an' I've seen a yarn about a chap bein' run over by a steam roller send people into fits. It's the thought that it ain't you, but somebody else that's so comic. We had a chap in our regiment, by the name of Moggy, who could never see a joke. When all the other fellers would be rollin' about the door holdin' their sides, he'd be sittin' still with a puzzled look on his dial, sayin', 'An' what did the other man say?'

"Everybody tried to get a laugh out of Moggy, but nobody succeeded.

"Nobby tried his hand, an' told a yarn about a chap who asked another chap: 'If a herrin' an' a half cost three ha'pence what would twelve cost?' and the other chap said, 'One and sixpence.' 'No,' sez the first chap, 'they would cost a shillin', an' then explained it to him.

"'Oh,' sez the other chap. 'herrin's! I thought you said haddocks.'

"Everybody laughed except Moggy. He sat perfectly glum.

"'What difference did it make,' he sez, 'whether they was herrin's or haddocks?'

"That was the sort of feller Moggy was. Sometimes he would see the joke a long time after, an' in church, when the parson was in the middle of his sermon, Moggy started to laugh over a joke Nobby had told him a week before. He got seven days for improper conduct in church.

"'I'm very sorry, sir,' he sez, to the company officer, 'but I just happened to see a joke of Private Clark's. Why does a hen cross the road? To get to the other side. Whilst I was in church it struck me, sir, that perhaps there wasn't any other side, an' that made me laugh.'

"'Seven days,' sez the officer, 'an' perhaps the humour of my present remark will penetrate your thick head before the seven days is up.'

"Poor old Moggy was so upset that he wouldn't listen to any more of Nobby's jokes, an' one day, when Nobby caught his finger in the winder an' was dancin' about the room, Moggy sez, very solemn: 'If you expect me to laugh, you're jolly well mistook.'

"I might say that Moggy was an older lookin' man than most young soldiers, and although he said he was only twenty-one when he enlisted, he wouldn't let Nobby look at his teeth to make sure. I've always thought that Moggy had a bit of a history, but he was closer than an oyster, an' although me an' Nobby did our best to find out, an' even turned Marshy on to him, we never got anywhere near the truth.

"What annoyed Moggy so much was that whenever a bad crime, a murder or a burglary, got into the Sunday papers, Nobby used to put him through a cross-examination, such as 'Where were you on the night of the 14th?' an' 'Will you swear you did not know the deceased?'

"We found out the solution of Moggy's mystery in a very peculiar way.

"One night Nobby an' me was in town, an' met Moggy, lookin' worried and hurrying along the High-street. We stopped to talk to him, but he hurried on, an' we went on to the 'Phoenix' an' made up a bit about Moggy bein' chased by his wife an' three children. It was a bit of a joke, because when we put it about barracks every feller he met used to ask him how the missus was, and little Sid Carter spent a penny which might very well have gone in beer, on a baby's rattle.

"This joke made Moggy wilder than anything. He comes up to Nobby one day in the canteen, an' sez for two pins he'd put it across him. Nobby borrowed the two pins from the chap behind the bar.

"'If you think,' sez Mogg, very fierce, 'this tale about my wife an' three kids is a joke you're in the wrong box, *because the tale happens to be true, only it ain't three kids, it's five!*'

"After that Nobby said it was hopeless expectin' to get Moggy to see the comic side of life. It appears Moggy got married when he was young, an' not bein' able to get work he enlisted, an' every penny he got went to his missus, an' that when Nobby an' me had seen him

221

hurryin' he was goin' for the doctor for the fifth. Anybody who knows Nobby is well aware that there ain't a kinder heart breathin', an' in addition to bein' terribly upset at hurtin' Moggy's feelin's, he felt we ought to do somethin' for the pore old chap. Well, we got a sing-song up for him one pay night an' collected eighteen shillin's, an' Mogg thanked Nobby with tears in his eyes. This was just before we went to Gibraltar, an' the week before we sailed we raised another pound, an' little Fatty Golden, who's got a sister in the second-hand clothes line of business, wrote home an' got a bundle of things what his sister couldn't sell nohow, for pore Mrs. Moggy.

"But the change that came over the regiment gen'rally was the wonderful thing. Instead of treatin'' Mogg as they used to, they behaved like friends towards him in his sad affliction. It was 'Have a drink, Moggy, old feller,' an' 'Drink hearty, Mogg,' an' 'Don't you trouble about payin',' till Nobby began to think about gettin' married hisself.

"Once or twice in every three months there used to be a whip round for Moggy an' the missus, an' one Christmas time, when everybody was full of good spirits an' free beer, they collected as much as £2 17s. 3½d., a bad shillin', an' a Waterbury watch that wouldn't go, but which, as Nobby said (he gave it) had possibilities.

"I won't say that Moggy wasn't grateful, because that would be a lie. He was more grateful than lots of chaps would have been. He was always willin' to oblige, an' started gettin' a sense of humour. He laughed at Nobby's jokes once or twice, till Nobby got a bit huffy, an' told him not to laugh in the wrong place. After that Moggy would sit watchin' Nobby's face very intently, waitin' for the signal, so to speak.

"I remember one night Nobby was spinnin' a horrid lie about how him an' me an' Pug Wilson was nearly swallered by a rattlesnake in India. It was one of them serious tragic tales that Nobby liked to tell young recruits who didn't know enough to contradict him.

"'There was me,' sez Nobby, 'a-facin' him; his jaws was wide open, an' I could see him settin' his poison ready. I wasn't a bit afraid——

"'Ha, ha, ha!' sez Moggy.

"Nobby looks at him.

"'What the devil are you laughin' at?' he snaps.

"'Beg pardon, Nobby.' sez pore old Mogg; 'thought I saw you wink.'

"'There was me,' sez Nobby, goin' on, 'without a gun in me hand, an' the poisonous snake walkin' quietly towards me. I thought of me old home; of me mother——'

"'Ho, ho, ho!' roars Moggy, holdin' his sides, 'that's one of the comicalist things I've heard for a long time!'

"Nobby got up very wrathful.

"'If you can't behave yourself, like a gentleman,' he sez, 'hop it.'

"'I'm very sorry, Nobby,' sez Moggy, 'I was under the impression——'

"'Never mind what you was under,' sez Nobby, very wild, 'you come here interruptin' my story an' I'll knock your head off.'

"Moggy's intentions was good—even Nobby could see that—an' sometime after he went up to Moggy an' said that bygones should be bygones, an' invited him down to Mrs. Carey's 'do.'

"At that time, in Gibraltar, there was a lady named Mrs. Carey, who used to give a sort of party to soldiers. She hadn't got a 'home,' but used to hire a hall. She was a wonderful lady was Mrs. Carey, because she didn't think that soldiers was made to be prayed over, or snivelled over, an' she never used to ask 'em about their souls, like they do in the other soldiers' homes in Gibraltar, especially in one where they keep a nice clean-lookin' sailor to make inquiries of that sort.

"But Mrs. Carey used to treat a chap's soul as if it was his own private an' secret property, not as if it was a sort of cold in the head that you had to ask about every time you met a chap. Yet she did more good than a dozen soldiers' homes. She knew that a glass of beer never did any man harm, an' a pipe of 'bacca was as good as a meal to some chaps, an' when she tackled a feller it wasn't a case of 'Dear-brother-where-have-you-strayed?' but straight to the point. 'I hear you was seen on the Ramps last night in a wretched state of intoxication—I've a good mind to box your ears.'

"Fellers got to know' Mrs. Carey, an' they never tried to lie to her, or pretend they were sufferin' from giddiness when she saw 'em supported by the picquet. We had to have boxin' an' fencin', an' there was books an' papers to read, an' gen'rally, in the course of the evenin', somebody or other would sing a song.

"Moggy had never been to Mrs. Carey's. He never went anywhere unless somebody asked him to go. Nobby sez that Moggy enjoyed himself very much, especially with a young lady named Louisa. Mrs. Carey had always one or two friends to help her entertain. They was tradesmen's daughters and decent young fellers from the town. She wouldn't have anybody who thought they was a cut above a soldier, an' that's why Mrs. Carey's 'do's' was always such a success.

"The reason he enjoyed hisself with Miss Louisa was, said Moggy, she reminded him so much of what his eldest daughter would be when she grew up.

"'I've got quite a fatherly feelin' for that girl,' he sez to Nobby.

"'I dessay,' sez Nobby.

"'I've always been very fond of children,' sez Moggy.

"'So have I,' sez Nobby, 'of that age!'

"Mogg didn't want Nobby to take him down to Mrs. Carey's after that; he sort of drifted there natural, an' there was always one or two fellers there who'd stand him a cup of coffee for the sake of the little ones at home.

"He asked Nobby not to mention the fact that he was married to Mrs. Carey.

"'She's one of them generous kind of women who will want to give me money,' he sez: 'an' I want to keep me self respect an' not be a burden to anybody!'

"We respected old Moggy for that; we respected him so much that Bill Mason got up another subscription for him.

"Moggy got very good reports from home. 'The two pounds that we sent a little while back had bought a mangle,' he sez, 'an' the missus was gettin' quite a nice connection together. The children was keepin' well (he read a bit of the letter out to us), but little Ernest had had a lot of trouble with his teethin'. Young Sam had a bad cold, but was goin' on nicely. Imogene had fallen down an' cut her knee, but it was better. Clarence was gettin' on nicely at school with mathematics, an' could now say his multiplication table up to "four times four are forty-four." So no more at present, from your lovin' wife, Matilda.'

"What with these letters comin' in, an' the news from time to time about Ernest's teeth, we felt we was gettin' our money's worth, an' even Nobby suspended money-makin' operations, so as not to interfere with the support of Moggy's family. In a manner of speakin' we'd adopted him.

"'It's like what you read in story books,' sez Moggy, with tears in his eyes, 'about children bein' brought up by the regiments an' bein' the "Pets of the Battalion,"' he sez.

"'I wouldn't go so far as sayin' that,' sez Nobby, very cautious, 'but in a manner of speakin' they are very dear to us.'

"'Thank you, Nobby,' sez Mogg, gratefully, shakin' Nobby's hand, 'you've got a tender heart.'

"Moggy never could see a joke straight off.

"That same afternoon we saw Mrs. Carey driving in the Alameda an' saluted her. We was passin' on but she stopped the carriage an' beckoned to us.

"'Smith,' she sez, 'I hope you an' your friends are goin' to buy your comrade a nice weddin' present.'

"'Which comrade, ma'am!' sez Nobby, surprised.

"'Don't you know?' she sez. 'Why he's goin' to marry Louisa an' purchase his discharge, an' Louisa's brother is going to give him a position.'

"'What name did you say, ma'am?' sez Nobby, politely.

"'Mogg,' sez Mrs. Carey, an' Nobby sort of staggered.

"'Beg pardon?' he sez, faintly.

"'Mogg,' sez the lady, "a most careful, savin' young man. Now don't forget to give him something nice,' an' noddin' to us, she drove on.

"'Mogg?' sez Nobby, in a trance. 'give him a weddin' present?' he sez, dreamily. 'Yes, certainly—we'll give him a wreath.'

"Then he woke up.

"'Smithy,' he sez, fiercely, 'have we been supportin' Mogg's fam'ly for years or have we not?'

"'We have,' I sez.

"'Have we took what I might call a lovin' interest in Ernest's teethin' an' Imogene's knee or have we not?'

"'We have,' I sez.

"'Very well,' sez Nobby, firmly, 'then I ain't dreamin'—come on back to barracks.'

"We found Mogg polishing his boots.

"'Hullo, you bigaminous blighter,' sez Nobby, 'what's the game?'

"'Are you referrin' to my nuptials?' sez Mogg.

"'I am, you thief,' sez Nobby, 'what about that wife an' family of yourn?'

"'I ain't got no wife an' family,' sez Mogg, calmly.

"'What!' roars Nobby.

"'I never had one,' sez Mogg, breathin' on his boots to disinfect 'em, 'an' never thought of havin' 'em till you lumbered 'em on to me.'

"'Me?' sez Nobby.

"'Yes,' sez Mogg, 'you found 'em, you told the chaps about 'em; you invented 'em.'

"'But,' sez Nobby wrathfully, 'what about the money we've got together for you?'

"'That,' sez Mogg, carefully, 'will be used to the best advantage.'

"'You've robbed us,' sez Nobby.

"'Don't say that,' sez Mogg, pleadin'ly, 'or I shall think you've no sense of humour—I have,' he sez.

"'In fact.' he went on. 'I'm beginning to see the comical side of things more than ever I did. It's a great thing to have a sense of humour.'

"An' he shook his head, thoughtfully an' went on polishin' his boots."

19.—PIKEY'S LUCK

I associate Smithy with many Christmases. With a Christmas on the bleak wind-swept slopes of the little hill, whereon is perched the sinister bulk of No. 2 magazine; with a Christmas spent under the blazing sun where the Modder comes swirling to the Riet River; with a memorable Christmas in Anchester, and with a Christmas—another war-like Christmas—sitting patiently in a lonely blockhouse between De Aar and Nauwpoort. When I think of Christmas in the army, I think of garlanded rooms, of admirable and praiseworthy mottoes covering the walls, of centrepieces and floral designs carried out in bayonets and flags; of "Success to the regiment" over the door, and "Good Luck to the Officers" over the fireplace; of coal-boxes swathed in crinkled paper, and the bare walls of the barrack-room hidden behind a screen of greenery and holly.

"Christmas takes people in different ways," said Smithy, reflectively, "with some it's 'How are you, ole feller, come an' have a drink,' an' with others it's 'Don't you wish me a Merry Christmas or I'll give you a dig in the neck.'

"As a general rule, though, Christmas brings out all the best qualities in a chap; he can drink more an' eat more, an' lots of people who usually want to fight after their tenth gallon change their habits an' only want to cry. It's called seasonable greetin's. There's always lots of amusement, too, about Christmas in barracks. There's the gettin' ready, the decoratin', the paper-chain makin', an' the wonderin' whether 'Greasy' Sanders, the cook, will keep sober. An' there's generally a sing-song after dinner, an' a bit of a dance at night, an' for them who want to go out of barracks there's gen'rally a supply of civilian friends. Then there's always plenty to eat an' drink, an' cigars for them that want 'em, or are strong enough to smoke 'em—good cigars, too, that you couldn't buy under seven for a shillin', an' whisky, an' other

Christmas spirits.

"But, as I've remarked, different chaps have different ways, an' what's more than that, different Christmases perduce different feelin's.

"I remember one year when we was in Aldershot, when Christmas fell in proper Christmas card weather. Snow on the ground, an' holly in bloom, an' the old church bells a-ringin'. An' somehow all the chaps got taken up with the Christmas feelin' in the air, an' tried to act accordin'.

"'I feel proper good this mornin',' sez Nobby, when he got up. 'I feel at peace with me feller man. A Merry Christmas to you, Spud,' he sez, nicely.

"'The same to you, Nobby,' sez Spud Murphy.

"'Has any friend seen my blackin' brushes?' sez Nobby, lookin' under his cot.

"'I saw friend Taylor usin' 'em yesterday,' I sez.

"'Friend Taylor is welcome to anything I've got that I don't happen to want,' sez Nobby, 'but at this present moment I feel like bitin' friend Taylor's ear.'

"'In fact, the day started so pleasantly that I was a bit doubtful in my mind whether I didn't ought to get out of barracks before the row started.

'The whole regiment was shakin' hands an' invitin' one another home to meet the old people, an' Spud Murphy an' Nobby sang a duet about a kid that got lost in the snow, and had nowhere to go, no mother to help him, in the grave she lay low, lorst in the wide world was pore little Joe, or words to that effect.

"About seven o'clock the good-fellership began to get frayed around the edge an' baggy at the knees, an' when Nobby asked Spud for the tenth time to come an' spend a Sunday at home with his rich relations, Spud said 'No' very sharp.

"'Why not, ole comrade?' sez Nobby.

"'Because,' sez Spud, 'I'm very particular where I go.'

"Nobby was so took back that he hadn't anything to say—for a minute.

"'Christmas-time is Christmas-time.' sez Spud. 'but I've got to draw a line somewhere.'

"'This bein' what I might call a festive season,' sez Nobby, takin' his coat off, 'I'm goin' to celebrate the day by killin' the fatted calf. You,' he sez, 'bein' the calf.'

"The best pleasures of life," philosophised Smithy, "come in a manner of speakin' unexpected. There's nothin' worse than making preparations to amuse yourself; plannin' this an' that for weeks in advance, because when you've got everything fixed up, it's ten to one that it rains, or someone's forgot the corkscrew.

"Similarly, when a chap's lookin' forward to some 'do' or other with as much pleasure as a tramp looks forward to a cold bath, it's pretty sure to turn out the time of his life.

"There was a feller of ours called Pikey, who was chiefly remarkable for being a descendant of the original Jonah wot the fisherman used for whale-bait in the good old times.

"Everybody used to steer clear of Pikey because of his unluckiness. He was the sort of cove who got mumps two days before his furlough was due, an' had to go into hospital. If he was on guard there was sure to be a rough house; when he came aboard the ship had the worst voyage she'd ever had; an', takin' one thing with another, Pikey's name was trouble.

"Chaps wouldn't walk with him for fear of slates blowin' off the roof on to their heads, an' as sure as Pikey ever played football someone would be badly injured.

"If we met Pikey out in town we used to turn down a street quick, an' naturally this sort of thing got on Pikey's nerves. He challenged two or three chaps to fight, but nobody would take him on for fear of gettin' accidentally killed.

"Just before Christmas, 1900, the battalion was sent down from the Transvaal to hold the line between De Aar an' Norport. The colony was full of commandoes wanderin' from town to town, and British columns wanderin' after 'em.

"To prevent the Boers from losing themselves we'd put up a barbed wire fence for about three hundred miles along the line, an' armour-plated summer-houses at regular intervals. 'B' company held the 29th Section, an' me an' Nobby, Spud Murphy, Pug Wilson, Jonah Pikey, an' a dozen other fellers, beside a sergeant an' a corporal, was told off to No. 49 Blockhouse.

"It wasn't exactly a cheerful kind of prospect for Christmas. The scenery was mostly railway line an' bare plain, with some blue hills miles an' miles away in the distance; an' the weather was blazin' hot. In the daytime the blockhouse, bein' made of tin, was like an oven, an' in the night-time like a bloomin' refrigerator. We knew the kind of place we was going to.

"As soon as we found out Pikey was comin' with us, Nobby an' one or two other chaps handed in the names of their next-of-kin.

"'If anything happens to me,' sez Nobby, very gloomy, 'you can have my kit, Smithy. There's four pairs of socks, a new pair of boots, an' a brand new razor that I picked up at Modder River. Give my love to all at home, an' tell 'em I died like a soldier.'

"After we'd been posted we was busy for a couple of days makin' things ship-shape. We cleaned out the blockhouse (the Wigshires had been holdin' it before we come), an' Pug Wilson painted a board, 'Anchester Villa' to put up in front. Then we fixed up spring guns for brother Boer, an' dug two trenches full of broken glass for them to fall into, and put 'Welcome' in little white stones in front of each trench.

"Altogether, the first two days passed quicker than you'd think.

"Every day a visitin' picquet with an officer in charge used to come along to see how we got along, an' to take reports.

"Naturally, all the other blockhouses was very anxious to know what was happenin' at '49,' owin' to our havin' Pikey with us, an' when they found out, day by day, that nobody was shot or had sunstroke, they were a bit disappointed. On Christmas Eve the visitin' picquet brought us a bit of news.

"'Old Viljoen is comin' this way,' sez Jerry Jordan—he was one of the picquet—'an' it looks as if you chaps are goin' to have a merry Christmas.' He looks at Pikey an' shakes his head. 'I wouldn't be in "49" for a bloomin' pension,' he sez; 'not with old Pikey,' he sez.

"When the picquet had left, Nobby had a talk with me.

"'Smithy,' he sez, serious, 'here's three days passed an' old Pikey's done nothin'. He ain't shot anybody by accident, he ain't set fire to the blockhouse, he ain't mixed hisself up in one of them spring guns—I'm gettin' nervous.'

"'P'raps his luck's turned; everybody's luck turns at Christmas,' I sez, but Nobby shook his head.

"Christmas Day came up in a white blaze of hot sunshine. There was not a single thing you touched that didn't blister you. All the hills was a-quiverin', an' over the plains you could see extr'ordinary woods an' lakes made by the mirage.

"We'd got a bit of Christmas up, a bit of holly over the door, an' 'God Bless our Home,' done by Pug Wilson on a biscuit-box, an' a few paper chains to give the house a tone. An' they'd sent us along extra rations, a couple of fowls an' a bottle of beer a man. Nobby made a Christmas puddin' out of a receipt he found in a paper, an' it was very nice after the water was squeezed out of it.

"Nobby said there was nothin' in the receipt about tyin' it up in a cloth. As a matter of fact, it wasn't at all bad after we put it through a strainer.

"After dinner we had a sing-song. Nobby an' Spud sung their annual about pore little Joe out in the snow, nowhere to go, an' Sergeant Perkins recited, in a gentlemanly way, about a pauper refusin' his puddin' only last Christmas Day, an' Pug Wilson gave imitations of Irvin' in a way that was wonderfully life-like. Nobody had ever seen Irvin', so that made it all the more pleasant.

"Then Pikey gave an imitation of a clog-dance, an' we all drew back for fear somethin' would happen; that he'd kick up a stone an' blind somebody, or disturb a snake, or draw the enemy's fire. But nothin' came along to upset the harmony of the meetin'.

"In fact, when we paraded at sunset for guard, Nobby said it did look as if Pikey's luck had taken the first turnin' to the right. Guard mountin' at a blockhouse isn't like guard mountin' at home. For one thing, we dressed pretty well as we liked, an' the main consideration was to see that your rifle was oiled, an' your ammunition handy.

"An' it was different in this respect, that everybody's on guard punctually although only a certain number are told off for sentry duty. Pikey's relief was the easiest, ten till twelve an' four till six. Half the time of his second relief most of the chaps are awake, an' half the time of his first relief they haven't gone to sleep. We took no risks with Pikey.

"We'd expected to have a fairly busy night owin' to Commandant Viljoen bein' in the neighbourhood, and at eight o'clock that night a telephone message came through from headquarters to say that Viljoen had been turned northward by Henniker's Column, and we settled down for a quiet night.

"I'd just dozed off, when I woke suddenly to feel Nobby pressin' my hand. (Learnt by the British soldier in South Africa is this effective method of waking a man, press the hand and increase the pressure, and the sleeper will awake noiselessly.)

"'What's up?' I whispered.

"'Listen!' he murmured.

"I strained my ears an' then I heard *click-clock—click-clock* very faintly.

"'Firin','' sez Nobby, under his breath; 'an' the question is: What in——is Pikey doin' not to give the alarm.'

"I was reachin' out my hand to touch the sergeant when Nobby caught it.

"'For God's sake, wait,' he whispers, 'there's only two things that Pikey can be; dead's one, an' asleep's the other. Get outside as quietly as you can.'

"As silent as I could, I picked up my rifle an' bandolier, an' got outside. Nobby was with me in a second.

"There was no sign of Pikey, but there was a sign of somethin' else, for not two hundred yards away you could see a lot of shadders movin' across the *veldt*. There was no noise, for they were keepin' to the soft bed of a little dried-up river.

"'Pikey first,' sez Nobby, an' walked round to the other side of the blockhouse.

"There we found Pikey—Pikey the Jonah. On the flat of his back he lay a-sleepin' as calm an' as comfortable as if it was Sunday mornin' at home.

"'Get up, you worm!' hissed Nobby, an' Pikey opened his eyes an' said, "Merry Christmas."

"I couldn't see quite plain, because we only had starlight, but I fancy he opened his eyes, an' then grunted an' turned over an' went to sleep.

"Nobby took a kick at him that woke him up with a yell, an' just at that minute I raised my rifle an' fired at the shadows on the *veldt*.

"'Guard, turn out!' I shouted, an' I heard a scramble inside the blockhouse.

"Nobby an' I let fly together an' dropped down to cover, for the Boers are pretty nippy when it comes to *that* sort of thing. All through that Christmas night we lay tucked up against the sandbag entrenchment, firin' till the barrels of our rifles was scorchin' hot. The telephone wire had been cut, so we could get no news from headquarters.

"There was another blockhouse a mile an' a half away, an' firin' was goin' on there—it was their fire that Nobby had heard. I heard the sergeant say, 'It's Viljoen doublin' back,' an' I knew how serious it was, for we'd been warned an' threatened as to what would happen to us if we allowed Viljoen to get across the lines.

"'What I want to know,' sez the sergeant, between the firin', 'is how these chaps got so close to us without the sentry givin' an alarm.'

"'It's a dark night, sergeant,' sez Nobby.

"'Dark be damped,' sez the sergeant; 'all night's are dark, ain't they?'

"There wasn't much talk after this.

"The Boer Intelligence Department ought to have gold medals, for what they didn't know wasn't worth knowin'. They knew that '49' was weakly held, an' they turned all their fire on to us. If they could smash us up they could get across the line with their convoy, an' their fire was terrific.

"A chap of ours named Moley was the first to go down; shot through the lung, he went down all of a heap at my side. Then the sergeant was killed, an' fell without a word.

"Nobby closed up and took poor Moley's place.

"'If ever I get out of this,' he sez, 'I'll make Jonah sorry he ever gave up the whale business.'

"Corporal Thom was the next to go—he was lookin' over the trench with his night glasses an' Nobby pulled him down. He was a well-educated sort of youngster, an' he hadn't much experience.

"He shook Nobby off, an' rose again. He leant over the sandbags for a long time without movin', till Nobby said:

"'Corporal, come down out of that, for the Lord's sake,' and gave him a tug.

"Then he came down all of a heap, for he was stone dead, an' must have been shot the moment he went up.

"All the chaps were takin' the fire quite coolly; Spud Murphy was singin' a little Irish song to himself— his Irish blood always came out at times like this—an' Pug Wilson was sayin' what a good job it was it wasn't rainin'.

"Only Pikey lost his head. He was whimpering and moanin'.

"'I can't stand this much longer,' he sez.

"The bullets were patterin' against the blockhouse like hail.

"All this time we'd been holdin' the trench outside the blockhouse, but the fire got so hot that the other corporal, Higgs, ordered us to take shelter inside, an' we crept inside one by one so that our fire shouldn't die down.

"We'd hardly got inside before the Boers got a seven-pounder into action.

"The first shell went shriekin' overhead, an' the second went wide.

"But the third hit the roof an' carried part of it away.

"The fourth killed the corporal an' we was reduced to six men— reckonin' Pikey.

"Then I think Pikey must have gone off his head.

"'I'm a Jonah, a cursed Jonah!' he yelled, an' sprang from the little manhole where we'd crawled in.

"Before we could stop him he was through.

"Through the loopholes we saw him scramble down into the trench an' up on the other side, an' he stood there hesitating for a bit, as though he couldn't make up his mind what he was goin' to do.

"Then a most wonderful thing happened. For as he stood with not a bullet touching him, a dazzling white light fell on him, just as though he was on a stage an' a limelight had suddenly been turned on. Clear an' as plain as daylight he stood, for friend an' foe to look at.

"He realised his danger in a second, an' tried to run out of the circle of light, but it follered him an' follered him all along the edge of the bank as he stumbled an' ran.

"Then he stopped suddenly and faced the light, covering his eyes with his hands.

"That's how poor old Jonah Pikey died, an' that's how we found him when the armoured train came up to us.

"It was the searchlight from the train that was the death of Pikey.

"The light was intended to show us where to fire, an' to dazzle the enemy, an' it only shows how Pikey's bad luck held out to the last."

20.—THE BUGLERS

"When you are called to a murder," says Dr. Graham Grant, cold-bloodedly, "take with you paper and pencil, india-rubber, a tape measure, a lens, two microscopic slides, and a pair of old gloves." Thus runs the police-surgeon's emergency guide, but for my part, I could not imagine, were I the divisional surgeon of "H" Division, that I should do anything so methodical. Not nowadays. When I was a soldier and accepted sudden and violent death as part of the day's work, I might have acted with the cool promptitude that this brilliant police-surgeon suggests.

For all that is tragic in military affairs is intimately connected with the Royal Army Medical Corps.

I once knew a band corporal of the 5th Fusiliers who was going to marry the prettiest girl in Aldershot. He invited me to the wedding, and a couple of days before the ceremony, when he and I sat together in the little soldiers' club in North Camp, he took me into his confidence. We were chatting about football, I remember, when he broke off suddenly to tell me that he was the eldest son of the *Tsar*, and the bandmaster (to whom he had been sold as a boy) wars keeping him out of his inheritance.

I was politely interested. With a great display of secrecy he produced from a specially-constructed leathern sheath, which he had sown inside his trousers, a long amputating knife. I have no idea where he got it from. At the moment I was not curious, for we were almost alone. He informed me that he intended liberating himself from captivity that night. The band was to play outside the officers' mess, and during the second piece (it was to be *The Mikado*, I remember) he would expeditiously despatch the bandmaster to another, and, I trust, a better world.

I parted from him with some relief.

That night six of us descended upon him suddenly, and he gave us all the fight we wanted. But we strapped him to a stretcher, and got him into the padded cell, and on the day fixed for his wedding he died of G.P., which is an abbreviation for General Paralysis of the Insane.

"It stands to reason," said Smithy, "that there's more, what I might call scope for that sort of thing in the army than outside. Each feller is a little bit of life nipped off short. You don't know where his other life ended, or what it was, who his people were, or why he enlisted. When his relations come down to see him, you ain't surprised if they turn up in a motor-car, but you ain't surprised either if they turn up in drink an' have to be chucked out the gate.

"The tragicest thing I saw for a long time was when a chap named Stone was expectin' his rich aunt, what he'd stayed with when he was on furlough. A perfect lady she was. Had a greengrocer's shop, two servants, an' a musical-box—she gave him the musical box when he come away, an' he sold it to Corporal Toms for ten bob. We waited for days an' days to see her, an' Stoney was braggin' about how she had two houses of her own, an' money in the bank besides. She *did* turn up after a bit. Came down with two tec's, an' pinched Stoney for stealin' the musical box.

"I've seen other tragic things, such as Nobby bein' ordered by the C.O. to pay back money to chaps—money that he'd honestly earned, an' I've seen the real downright tragedy of war, an' cholera, an' other deadly diseases.

"But I've noticed that, however bad it is, there's always a light side to the worst of tragedies, an' there was one or two in the case of the drum-major's daughter.

"When I joined the regiment in—well, I won't gratify your curiosity by tellin' you when I joined—she was a leggy girl, who used to run about barracks with her hair a-flyin'. She was pretty even then.

A straight little nose, a pair of fine eyes, an' a firm, full mouth. Her hair was the colour of brown that had been washed in gold, an' hadn't quite lost its brownness, an' at the same time, hadn't got rid of its goldishness.

"I noticed her, as a chap notices kids, but the next time I noticed her, which was a few years later, she'd got to that stage where she wasn't a kid any longer, an' wasn't exactly a woman. Her father's name was Curton—Drum-Major Curton—an' her name was Cecila, an' her friends called her Cissy. I didn't have much to say to her. As you know, it is easier for a soldier to get into conversation with a princess than the daughter of a non-com. They don't want to know anything below the rank of colour-sergeant, but they much prefer the sergeant-major.

"Our sergeant-major at this time was a feller named Bensonberg. That ain't his real name, but if I called him Robinson, you'd probably get into trouble for libel.

"He was one of them dapper little chaps, all curled moustache, an' mincin' step, an' his quarters smelt like a perfumery factory after there's been a fire, an' all the scents have got mixed up. He was one of the youngest S.-M.'s in the service, an' he got his rank because, at the time the old sergeant-major died, he was the only colour-sergeant in the regiment who had a first-class certificate. He wasn't a popular feller by any means. Partly because he'd been a colour-sergeant of 'H,' he was tremendously down on 'B' company an' of all the chaps in 'B' he disliked Nobby Clark worst.

"Nobby used to give imitations of him that was so life-like that you could almost smell the O-dee-Cologne.

"Nobby was on fatigue once, cleanin' out the sergeant-major's quarters, polishin' the grate an' scrubbin' the stairs, an' he said it was the most ladylike quarters he'd ever been in. The sergeant-major was the sort of chap that some kind of women go mad over—the kind of women that are fond of dogs an' cats, an' any kind of pet they can tie up in blue ribbon, an' naturally when he put the dyin'-duck eye on Cissy he thought all the other entries would scratch, and it would be a walk-over.

"But there was a fellow in the regiment who was out for the second money, an' that feller was a corporal in the Drums by the name of Stanford. The finest bugler in the regiment he was, an' sometimes, when he took it into his head, he'd get up in the mornin's an' sound the 'Reveille,' an' the chaps would wake one another up to listen to him.

"He got to know Cissy in a curious way. She was a bit of a Tomboy as a kid, an' nothin' would satisfy her, but she must learn to play the bugle, an' it was Corporal Stanford who taught her down in the brickfield at Anchester.

"I don't know how long the lessons went on, but it appears that Stanford taught her other things besides the bugle, an' he learnt a few lessons from her. Her father was an' easy-goin', good-natured sort of chap, an' he liked Stanford. So there wasn't any obstacles put in the corporal's way.

"Then the sergeant-major came along, and the scene was changed, as the poem sez.

"The sergeant-major was good business, from a marryin' point of view, an' the drum-major made it very clear to Cissy that it was better to be Mrs. Sergeant-Major, an' live in the odour of Ess Bokay, than be Mrs. Corporal, an' live in the odour of soap suds.

"You'd have thought that Cissy would have jumped at the chance, but bless your heart you can never tell what a woman's going to do when there's a man in the business, an' it's perfectly impossible when there's two men.

"From what I heard afterwards she told the old man that she wouldn't marry the sergeant-major if he was the last man in the world. That it was corporal or nothin' for her. The drum-major was a very religious chap, so he hiked down his Bible an' proved to her that children that didn't obey their parents was in for a hot time, but she said that if it was no hotter than Poona an' the corporal was there, she didn't mind. The old man was terribly upset, an' sent for the corporal.

"'What have you been teachin' my girl,' he sez.

"'The "Last Post,"' sez Stanford, '"Officers' Call," "Fall In," "No Parade"——'

"'Never mind about that,' roars the drum-major, 'what have you been teachin' in the love-makin' line?'

"'The Reveille,' sez the corporal prompt. He was a smart feller with his tongue; almost as smart as Nobby, but not quite so glib.

"Try as he did, the drum-major couldn't get his girl to change her mind, an' when the sergeant-major started talkin' airily about the weddin' day—he took a lot for granted—the old man blurted out the truth.

"'What?' sez the sergeant-major, horror-struck. 'Won't have me?

Why, the girl's mad!'

"He wasn't as much upset as he was amused. He didn't think that any girl in her senses could refuse him. When he found out that Cissy had already fixed her mind on another chap he nearly had a fit.

"He was at Chunpore at the time, an' it was just before the rains.

"'I'll see this corporal,' he sez, in a rage, an' marches back to his quarters. He sent for Stanford, an' Stanford came.

"Me an' Nobby happened to be near the gate of the cantonment half an hour later, when up came Corporal Stanford in walkin'-out kit, lookin' a little white, but quite calm.

"'Nobby,' he sez, quiet, 'I've done in Smellin' Salts.'

"'Go on!' sez Nobby.

"'I have,' sez the corporal; 'he began talkin' unpleasantly about a lady friend of mine—no names mentioned—an' I laid him out. He ain't much hurt.'

"'I'm sorry,' sez Nobby.

"'I'm goin',' sez the corporal. 'If you should see the lady in question tell her I've gone. Tell her that I've got a friend in the town who'll hide me, an' that when she's ready, I'm ready.'

"With that he shook hands with us an' left.

"Ten minutes later, when the sergeant-major recovered his con-science an' picked hisself out of his cosy corner, there was the biggest row in barracks you ever heard. Where was Corporal Stanford? No-body had seen him go. Not the corporal who was on the gate (who was a pal of his), not Nobby, not me.

"They searched the barracks from end to end; they sent picquets through the bazaar an' native quarter, through the European quarter, an' through the town from end to end—but Corporal Stanford was gone.

"Cissy was frantic when Nobby an' me found an excuse to go over to the married quarters, an' the way he broke the news to her was the cleverest an' artfullest way you could imagine.

"We went over to ask for the drum-major, knowin' that at that particular moment he was listening to the S.-M.'s horrid tale of how Stanford had knocked him down when he wasn't lookin', an' jumped on his chest.

"Luckily the girl came to the door, an' not her mother.

"'I've got something to say to you,' sez Nobby, solemn.

"'Is it about Jack?' she sez, quick—her eyes was red with cryin'.

"'Who's Jack?' sez Nobby.

"'Corporal Stanford,' she sez.

"'Yes, it's about Jack,' sez Nobby, 'though I never knew his name was Jack,' sez Nobby. 'Most corporals is named Bill, an' sergeants Adolphus, an' colour-sergeants——'.

"'Yes, yes,' she sez, impatient. 'Tell me about Jack.'

"'Well, Jack's gorn,' sez Nobby; 'gorn forever,' he sez, very solemn.

"The girl went white.

"'For ever?' she faltered.

"'Perhaps,' sez Nobby, who always likes to work up a sensation, 'perhaps never to return.' When he'd got her nearly faintin', he delivered his message, an' we just managed to reach the barrack square in time to avoid the drum-major goin' home again.

"It appears from what I heard from the chaps in the 'drums' that Corporal Stanford was a savin' kind of feller, an' he'd put away close on a couple of hundred pounds in his service. It wasn't all savings, because he'd come into a little bit of money soon after he enlisted.

"'He'll be able to get out of India all right,' sez Nobby, 'but he won't go without the girl.'

"That's the idea the drum-major had, too, for he watched his daughter like a mouse, an' she hadn't a chance to send a note to the corporal, or receive one from him. One night me an' Nobby was returning from the canteen talkin' matters over, when suddenly Nobby stopped and laid his hand on my arm.

"Very clear, from the direction of the town, came a bugle call.

"Letters!' whispers Nobby. 'That's the post bugle—somebody is sayin' "I've sent you a letter"—an' I'll bet I know who that somebody is!' Nobody else seemed to hear the call, an' we waited. We waited ten minutes, then from the other side of the square came a sharp bugle call:

"'The "Standfast!"' sez Nobby, admiringly. 'That girl's got sense!'

"Then we heard the shout of the sergeant of the guard asking who in the name of various gentlemen an' places sounded the 'Standfast.'

"We could have told him, but we didn't. Nothin' occurred the next day or the next night. The picquets were called in from town, an' the general idea was that Corporal Stanford had cleared.

"But Nobby an' me knew better.

"I don't think Cissy could have ever got the letter the corporal said he was going to send her, because, just before the tattoo on the second night, when the drums was actually on the square, waiting to sound off the 'First Post,' somebody in the neighbourhood of the married quarters sounded

. . . the exact meaning of which is 'Come for orders.'

"Whilst everybody was in a state of confusion owing to this unexpected call, the bugle went again:

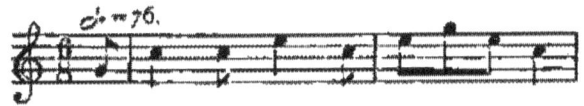

"'That's the officer's dinner call,' sez Nobby, wonderingly, an' we heard the far away bugle say 'All right,' as plain as plain, for Stanford could make a bugle talk.

"But we couldn't understand the 'Come for orders,' nor yet the 'Officers' mess' call. It puzzled Nobby considerable, an' I know he lay awake in bed thinkin' it out.

"As a matter of fact I found out the meaning first. The next night was guest night at the mess, when the officers invite their civilian pals to dinner.

"There's a private road to the officer's mess that's only opened on guest night. It's usually filled with carriages, because, as everybody knows, the Anchesters is one of the most popular regiments in the army. It was just after the dinner bugle had sounded, an' when the band was playing the first selection, that me an' Nobby, who had strolled round to the entrance of the private road, saw a carriage drive up, an' instead of turnin' into the carriage-way, draw up a little further along the main road. There was a man inside.

"We waited, knowin' it was Stanford, who was 'come for orders.'

"We hadn't long to wait, for bye-an'-bye a girl came flyin' down the drive, an' Stanford jumped out to meet her. He swung her into the *gharri*, an' off they drove like the wind, just as the old man an' the sergeant-major came pantin' up. . . .

"They got out of India all right, air I'm told she made him a splendid wife, an' that they settled down in Canada—so there's nothin' tragic in *that*. Where the tragedy part comes in was when we was all standin' lookin' in the direction the *gharri* took, out of the darkness came a bugle call, an insultin' bugle call, for it told the sergeant-major that the whole thing was the girl's own idea.

"'I called him, I called him,' sez the bugle.

"'I'll take my oath she did,' sez the drum-major, 'an' he'd have been a fool not to come.'"

21.—HONOUR

Of course, pickets are absurd, and, of course, the C.I.C., Aldershot, acted wisely in abolishing them. You may be sure that anything you do in the army that has never been done before will be hailed with delight, and acclaimed instantly as a much-needed reform.

"We are going to substitute hooks and eyes for buttons," says the War Office.

"Hooray!" says the public.

"Soldiers' trousers will be creased at the sides instead of back and front," says the War Office.

"Hooray!!" says the public.

"In future the army will wear mohair laces," says the War Office.

"Hooray, hooray!!" says the public, "this is real reform! Vive la (who ever happens to be in office at the time)!"

It's a fine thing to know that pickets are abolished and there is nobody left in Aldershot to run in the intoxicated soldier save and except about 500 military and regimental police, who will carry on as usual.

It is a splendid tribute to the commander-in-chief's faith in the rank and file—mostly file—that he withdraws the cold-footed and unemployed patrols, and leaves the young military gentlemen of Aldershot to their sense of honour and the "red cap."

This, I gather from the eulogies that have been showered upon the Aldershot authorities, is the general sentiment of the public, but personally I have no enthusiasm for the man who takes the chain off the dog and omits to unmuzzle him.

"There was an officer of ours," sez Smithy, "a young officer, who came to us from India, an' went on with us to the Cape. He wasn't a bad sort of feller, but he took a very serious view of things, especially morals. He was one of them fellers who thought the soldier wanted elevatin', an' he used to do his best to improve our minds. Started a 'botany ramble,' an' lots of fellers joined it. Nobby Clark was one. This was in India, an' it was pretty hot walkin'.

"'Here we have,' sez the officer, 'the *cannabis indica*, so called owin' to its petals bein' copratulated. It is mostly found in hot countries.'

"'It is hot, sir,' sez Nobby.

"'An' in dry soils,' sez the officer.

"'Like me, sir,' sez Nobby.

"He only went out once, did Nobby. When he found that there wasn't any free drinks attached he chucked it up, an' so did the other chaps. Nobby said it improved his thirst more than his mind, an' he couldn't afford it.

"This officer (his name was Holly) had an habit of putting chaps on their honour—that's what made me think about him. It was 'on your honour, did you borrow Private Murphy's blacking brushes?' an' 'on your honour, is this your shirt?' till the adjutant, who happened to overhear one of these honourable conversations, pulled him up sharp.

"'You'll wear out the honour of the "B" Company if you're not careful, Holly,' he sez.

"There was a bit of a dispute on about a razor that Fatty Green had lost.

"Fatty's number was burnt into it, but when he found it again on Nobby's shelf, it had been burnt out again, an' you couldn't tell which was a '9' an' which was a '4.' Nobby swore it was his: said he'd had it since the fourteenth of June.

"'Have you had this razor for a year, on your honour?' sez Holly, very solemn.

"'No, on me shelf, sir,' sez Nobby.

"'Are you prepared to swear upon your honour?'

"'I'm always prepared to swear, sir,' sez Nobby, very earnest; 'on my honour I am.'

"That's when the adjutant came in.

"Umfreville—that's the adjutant's name—was always ready to take a man's word, but he never used to go about the business the same way that Holly did.

"'Clark,' he sez, 'is that your razor?'

"'Yessir,' sez Nobby.

"'Has it always been your razor?'

"'No, sir,' sez Nobby.

"'Who did you borrow it from, an' forget to return it to?'

"'Private Green, sir, now you come to mention it.'

"'An' when did this razor accidentally fall on to the red hot poker and burn the numbers out?'

"'Last week, sir,' sez Nobby.

"'Very well,' sez the adjutant, 'you will be put under stoppages for a new razor for Private Green.'

"'Yessir,' sez Nobby. An' there the matter ends.

"If you try the word of honour dodge with the soldier, he thinks it's a new game, an' plays it to the best of his ability—but any two-handed game's a rottenly poor game when you hold all the two's an' three's an' four's in the pack, an' the other fellers got all the aces an' kings an' queens.

"Holly had all sorts of ideas for improvin' the soldier. He wanted to make 'em take a pride in theirselves an' that's one of the reasons he started a dog show. He tried a flower show first, an' Nobby got first prize for a beautiful rose tree in bloom, but he had to give it back because they found out afterwards he'd pinched the rose from the Botanical Gardens in Bombay an' stuck it in some earth with a few leaves round it to make it appear natural.

"The dog show was better, because everybody had a dog, although the regulations was against more than two or three to a regiment.

"Holly gave five pounds in prizes, an' the other officers put up a tenner between 'em.

"Holly wanted to divide the dogs into classes, thoroughbreds an' half-breds, but the adjutant, who knew more about soldiers dogs than Holly did, persuaded him to make it for one class only—No Breed.

"About this time, Nobby had a dog called 'Rags,' so called because, when he was layin' down asleep, he looked like a door mat that hadn't been shook for weeks.

"Nobby was very indignant when he found there was goin' to be no prizes for thoroughbreds, because, accordin' to Nobby, 'Rags' was one of the purest bred dogs that was ever born.

"'His father was a pure bred Scotch Terrier,' sez Nobby, 'an' his mother was a pure bred bull terrier, an' if that don't make him thorough-bred I don't know what does.'

"Spud Murphy entered a little fox terrier, called 'Spot'—a very uncommon name that Spud thought of hisself—an' he reckoned that he'd take first prize in the 'no class' division.

"For a week before the show all the fellers were busy gettin' their dogs clean an' fat. Nothin' was too good for 'em. 'Ginger' Carter fed his on hard boiled eggs till he could hardly stand. Nobby gave 'Rags' the best of everythin'. Once in the middle of dinner, 'Orderly Corporals' sounded, an' Corporal Hart, who was in charge of our room, had to get up 'an double as hard as he could to the orderly room. When he came back he looks round.

"'Where's my dinner?' he sez.

"'You finished it before you went, corporal,' sez Nobby, politely.

"'Did I?' sez the corporal, puzzled. 'That's very rum. I still feel hungry. I could have sworn I left two big slices of meat on my plate. I suppose none of these dashed dogs have been prowlin' about, have they?'

"'I couldn't tell you,' sez Nobby. 'All I know is that my dog's a vegetarian, an' never eats nothin' but fish.'

"Then some bloater paste disappeared off Spud Murphy's shelf. He'd put it aside for tea, an' when he went to look for it, it was gone.

"Spud was very wild, an' went in search of Nobby. He found him under the verander watchin' 'Rags,' an' 'Rags' was lickin' some brown stuff off his whiskers.

"'You've pinched my bloater paste,' sez Spud, very savage.

"Nobby was surprisingly mild.

"'Say not so,' he sez.

"'There it is!' sez Spud, wrathfully, 'he's chewin' the cud of it.'

"'That's not bloater paste,' sez Nobby, calm; 'that's brass polish that I'm givin' him—*to brighten him up!*'

"What worried Nobby most was a remark he heard the adjutant drop—the adjutant was to be the judge—about the colour of the dogs.

"'From what he said,' sez Nobby gloomily, 'he's goin' to judge how well a dog's looked after by his cleanness,' an' that put 'Rags' out of court.

"'Rags' was one of them dogs that couldn't keep clean if he tried. Me an' Nobby spent the best part of one night washin' him with a bar of carbolic soap an' dryin' him on Pug Wilson's woolly towel. The next mornin' 'Rags' wandered all through the cantonment lookin' for a puddle to roll in, an' found it.

"We washed him again, with another kind of soap (the corporal's box was locked that night) an' dried him on a sheet.

"He looked a perfect picture when we'd finished with him, an' even Spud, who came in late, admitted he looked fine.

"Spud grumbled a bit about his sheets bein' damp, but Nobby said it was in a good cause.

"'When we washed him he shook hisself,' sez Nobby, 'an' some of the water must have gone over your cot.'

"'It seems to me,' sez Spud, feelin' his sheets, 'as if somebody's been usin' 'em for towels.'

"'Sleep in blankets,' sez Nobby, 'it's healthier.'

"But all our trouble was for nothin', for next mornin' 'Rags' turned up with a smile an' fannin' hisself with his tail as black as a sweep's bride.

"'He's been down to the cavalry lines,' sez Nobby in despair.

"The dog show was only two days off, an' 'Rags' looked like a thousand to one chance, because the other dogs was in such good form, especially Spud's dog (what he used to rub over with pipeclay every mornin') an' Nobby saw that somethin' would have to be done. He thought an' thought an' thought, an' at last he sez:

"'I've got it!—*we'll dye him a colour that won't show the dirt!*'

"So me an' Nobby went into the bazaar an' saw a *baboo* chap, who now keeps a chemist's shop.

"'Dye?' he sez, 'what colour?'

"'Somethin' that won't show the dirt, Bobajee,' sez Nobby, 'somethin' blackish or brownish,'

"'What is the material for which dyeing is desired?' sez the *baboo*.

"'A dog skin,' sez Nobby, so the chemist chap got a powder out of one bottle an' a powder out of another bottle an' mixed 'em up.

"It cost us four *annas*, but, as Nobby pointed out, it was worth the money, for the first prize was worth twenty *rupees*.

"We didn't touch 'Rags' till the night before the show, an' then we caught him, an' gave him a good wash. It took us some time to catch him, for 'Rags' was gettin' a bit tired of the washin' game, an' as soon as he saw Nobby with a bit of rope he sort of pretended he was lookin' for a friend an' sneaked round the comer. We chased him for the best part of an hour, an' when Nobby got him he gave him a welt that made him pen-an'-ink most piercin'ly.

"'I'll learn you!' sez Nobby sternly. 'Whatcher mean by runnin' away from a friend that's tryin' to win you a prize, you ungrateful pie-dog?'

"We washed him most vigorous—poor 'Rags' shiverin' an' lookin' as if he wished he'd never been born.

"Then we dyed him. Nobby mixed the powders in hot water, an' we sponged 'Rags' over carefully an' tied him up to a little kennel which Nobby had made behind the cook-house.

"Next mornin' Nobby went to look at him, an' came back to breakfast very thoughtful. I didn't see 'Rags,' nor nobody else, because Nobby shut him up in the kennel for fear of his dirtyin' himself.

"'He ain't quite black yet,' sez Nobby, 'but I dersay he will be by the time the judgin' starts.'

"The dog show was held in the gymnasium, an' you never saw such a collection of 'sooners' an' 'may-be's' in your life. Each of 'em had a little ticket stuck on: Private Murphy's 'Spot' and Private Jordan's tiger spaniel 'Bill.'

"The most surprisin' exhibit was Nobby's. For we carried it in the kennel and stuck it up on the platform just as it was. Nobby had nailed two bars of wood across the front of the kennel, an' all you could see of poor old 'Rags' was a pair of miserable eyes an' the black tip of his nose.

"Nobby brought a card with him an' tacked it over the kennel:

Private Clark's
Greenland Lapdog,
"Ragski."

"'There's nothin' like a bit of swank,' sez Nobby, 'an' everybody knows that racehorses who are called "Prince of Empire" on the course are called "Jim" in the stable.'

"The fellers was a bit puzzled.

"'Is it "Rags?"' sez Spud Murphy, tryin' to peep inside.

"'Keep your dial away from the menagerie,' sez Nobby, 'you'll make him homesick.'

"'Is it "Rags?"' sez Spud.

"'No,' sez Nobby shortly, 'it's a new dog what's just arrived from me brother in Greenland.'

"Spud sniffed.

"'Me brother,' sez Nobby firmly, 'who's in the Greenland Mounted

Police—in the band,' he sez, 'sent me this dog yesterday.'

"'I don't believe it,' sez Spud. 'There ain't been a post in since Wednesday—how did it come?'

"'By telegraph,' sez Nobby.

"All the officers came, an' some of their wives, an' they enjoyed themselves immense.

"'What's this?' sez the adjutant.

"'A bull-retriever,' sez Fatty Green, prompt.

"'Has he got any points?' sez the adjutant, with his notebook in his hand, 'because if he has you'd better tell me what they are—I can't see any.'

"'He's a wonderful barker, sir,' sez Fatty.

"Other chaps had dogs that was wonderful eaters an' wonderful sleepers an' they all got marks. Spud looked like takin' the prize with 'Spot' for the tricks he did.

"He could sit up an' beg, an' shoulder a rifle, an' smoke a pipe, an' say 'Attention' quite plain. In addition to which he was a wonderful barker, a wonderful sleeper, an' a surprisin' eater.

"Then the judges moved on to Nobby's dog.

"'Hullo!' sez the adjutant, puttin' up his eyeglass, 'what's this?'

"'Greenland Poodle, sir,' sez Nobby.

"'Let me have a look at him,' sez the adjutant.

"'He's very shy, sir,' sez Nobby. 'He never comes out in the day-light—bein' a night dog.'

"'Nonsense,' sez the adjutant, 'take those bars away an' let him out.'

"Everybody gathered round to see Nobby's new dog.

"'I'd rather you judged him where he was, sir,' sez Nobby. 'He looks better in the dark, on my honour,' he sez to Holly.

"But the adjutant shook his head.

"'We'll see this bashful creature,' he sez, an' very reluctant Nobby pulled the bars away an' out steps 'Rags.'

"You could have heard a pin drop for a minute, an' then there was a yell that lifted the roof.

"'Why, Why!' gasps the adjutant, 'the *dashed dog's bright green!* '

"'Yessir,' sez Nobby, very agitated, 'that's why he's called a Green-land sheep dog, sir.'

"'On your honour,' sez Holly, very stern, 'is that the dog's natural colour? '

"'I won't say on me honour, sir,' sez Nobby, 'but *I'll say I hope I may dye if it ain't!*'"

22.—SACRIFICE

(This is also story Number 23 in 'Smithy' so has been taken out to avoid duplication for the reader).

23.—A SUPPRESSED BOOK

"Nobby Clark," said Private Smith in a tone of wondering admiration, "is a marvel. There used to be times when some of the things he did surprised me, but if Nobby come up to me today an' produced an elephant out of his trousers' pocket I should simply say 'Where did you pinch it?'

"Lots of people think Nobby ain't exactly honest, but that's a silly idea. Nobby wouldn't take anything of value from anybody.

"'It ain't the worth of the thing, Smithy,' he sez to me one day, 'Its the pleasure of gettin' it 'Nobby is what I'd call a mug-finder, an' when you have said that, you've said all that is to be said against him. His chief delight is to find a feller of a trustin' nature an' teach him to be careful in the future.

"There ain't a single game that Nobby ain't played. I remember once he filed a regimental razor into three parts, cut up a comb into three, fastened the bits of razors to the bits of combs, an' sold 'em for two bob each. He called 'em 'Clark's Safety Razor.'

"The rum thing about Nobby was that he never caught the real mugs. The silly chaps wasn't bright enough to jump at Nobby's ideas. It was always the fly fellers, who fancied themselves a bit, that got hurt when they run up against Nobby.

"When we was in Wynberg, after the war, Nobby got a bit sobered down by certain things that happened. For one thing, we lost too many good chaps to take a comic view of life, an' then there was a certain affair with a girl in Johannesburg. . . .

"Nobby didn't really start to buck up till Cully Park joined the company, from 'H'. We happened to be in the canteen one night when Bill Mason came in with his side arms—he stopped at the door to take 'em off—an' brought the news. He'd been C.O.'s orderly an' naturally he was what Nobby calls 'Oh Fay!' with all that had been happenin'. For one thing he'd took battalion orders round to the colour-sergeants, so when he told us that Cully Park was transferred to 'B' Company we knew it was true.

"Nobody exactly understood what Cully had been in civil life, though once, when 'H' Company was ordered to parade for identification, we guessed. But the lady who lost the watch couldn't pick him out, so the matter dropped.

"That sort of thing ain't calculated to make a man popular in the army. It stands to reason that amongst the fellers who enlist you get lots of chaps who go into the service for the same reason. Other fellers fly the country, but mainly they're detected very soon, an' the army's kept clear of the real bad classes.

"What made Cully rather unpopular in the Anchesters was his skill at cards. He was the luckiest feller in the world at that sort of game. It didn't matter what happened—Cully won, mainly because he sat an' sat till he did win, an' after he'd skinned the company regularly for weeks on end 'H' started a sort of anti-gamblin' league, the idea of which was 'We don't mind playin' "nap," but we don't play with Cully.'

"It's a surprisin' thing, but as soon as Cully was barred the chaps lost all interest in cards. The horrible fascination of seein' your money walk into Cully's corner of the table was gone, an' the game got so tame an' ladylike that 'H' Company took to playin' 'Coddam.'

"Gamblin' is one of the things that soldiers mustn't do in the army, an' there's a hundred others. But if a feller wants to enjoy life he's got to break dozens of regulations.

"Well, to get back to Cully.

"We found he'd been transferred to 'B' at his own request, because 'H' was gettin' a bit too slow. Nobby was rather thoughtful when he heard the news.

"'It's a serious thing for me, Smithy,' he sez. 'It's competition, that's what it is. We'll have to settle Cully.'

"You see, Nobby had got a big idea for bringin' out a book about the war, an' gettin' all the fellers to write somethin' about their experiences in it.

"The book was already started an' promised to be a big success.

"'Every chap who writes somethin' will buy half-a-dozen copies to send to his friends, explained Nobby. 'A chap will always spend money to see his name in print.'

"He'd made fine progress, when Cully came, an' he'd got a dozen experiences from various fellers, all ready for printin'.

"'How me and Browny pinched a pig at Bloemfontein, by Tiny White.'

"'A true story of my terrible adventures in the Transvaal, by Spud Murphy.'

"'A thrilling tale of how me and a feller of the Wessex got into trouble with the military police in Pretoria,' by Bill Mason.'

"An' things like that.

"'Our chaps won't have a penny piece by the time Cully's done with 'em,' sez Nobby, gloomily. 'It's a scandal.'

"So after what he said about Cully, callin' him a daylight robber an' a card-sharper, it was a little bit astonishin' to see what Nobby did. For when Cully strolled into the canteen one evenin', and sez, careless, "Who'll have a little game at "nap?" Nobby was the first feller to say 'I will.'

"It appears that Cully had arranged with Harry Young, 'B' Company's storeman, for the use of the little bungalow, where our stores (blankets, spare rifles, an' things) were kept. With blankets up to the winders., so that no light could show, a little party of six sat down to play 'nap.'

"The game started quietly, Nobby winnin' a little an' the other fellers winnin' in their turn. Then things got brisker, an' Nobby took two big 'kitties.' Cully didn't seem to mind, he was as affable as possible. Then Nobby got another 'nap' home, an' rose from the table.

"'What's up?' sez Cully.

"'I've got a bit of a headache,' sez Nobby, gatherin' in his winnin's.

"'It'll soon pass off,' sez Cully, shufflin' the cards. 'Sit down again an' have a few more hands.'

"'I'd rather not,' sez Nobby. 'You can't be too careful with a holler tooth——'

"'You said headache just now,' sez Cully.

"'Did I?' sez Nobby. 'I meant——'

"'What you meant was,' sez Cully, fiercely, "you're goin' to clear out with your winnin's.'

"Nobby shook his head as he made for the door.

"'You're unjust, Cully.' he sez, sadly.

"Next night Cully was on the watch, an' after Nobby had brought a fat 'nap' home an' got up sayin' the room was a bit too close, Cully got up too.

"'Look here,' he sez, nastily, 'you've just took six shillin's out of the crowd.'

"'Have I?' sez Nobby. 'I didn't count it, but I'll trust to your honesty.'

"'Before you go,' sez Cully, 'let me ask you a question, man to man: in two nights you've took over a pound out of us, are you goin' to give us a chance of winnin' it back?'

"'Man to man,' sez Nobby, earnestly, 'you shall have the chance tomorrer.'

"Next night Nobby turned up.

"'I've brought some smellin' salts,' sez Cully, 'in case Nobby's took bad, an' some carbolic acid for his holler tooth, an' a bit of corn plaster in case his feet hurt.'

"'Nobby smiled in an injured kind of way, an' the play started.

"Luck was against him for a bit, but by-an'-bye he landed a 'nap' hand, an' follered it with another.

"As he gathered the money in he coughed very loud.

"'What's up now?' sez Cully. 'Got consumption? '

"'No,' sez Nobby.

"'Do you feel faint or anything?' sez Cully.

"'No,' sez Nobby, coughing louder still.

"'I never felt better in me life.'

"'That's all right,' sez Cully, with a sort of relieved sigh.

"Just then came a gentle tap on the door, an' Harry Young's voice sez, 'Is Nobby there?'

"'Yes,' sez Nobby.

"'You're wanted at once by the colour-sergeant,' sez Harry. 'You'd better run.' Nobby got up with the air of a martyr, but Cully just glared at him.

"'It's a plant!' he sez, very wild. 'It's a plant between you an' Harry Young—that's why you coughed, you big-footed blighter, to let him know you was winnin'.'

"'I'll see you tomorrer,' sez Nobby, 'in the football field, an' you've got time between now an' then to prepare yourself for another life.'

"'I'll fight you now!' sez Cully, who was furious.

"'Not now,' sez Nobby, 'not with all this money about me,' he sez.

"When Cully cooled down he saw how silly the fightin' idea was, an' got out of it. But Nobby's habit of goin' away as soon as he won broke up the 'nap' party.

"First of all, Fatty Johnson follered Nobby's example. Took a 'kitty' of ten bob, an' went orf into a faint an' had to be assisted to his room. Then Spud Murphy, who'd been winnin' steadily one night, got somethin' the matter with his eyes an' couldn't see the cards properly, an' when a feller named Nathan sprained his wrist whilst he was rakin' in his winnin's, Cully said it was time to shut up shop.

"But he never forgave Nobby.

"When Nobby came to him an' asked him to write his experiences of the war, just to show there was no ill-feelin', Cully wrote about six pages entitled: 'A comical tale about Certain Parties who pretended they was ill, and the colonel hearing about it, sent them to hospital, where they caught enteric fever and died in horrible agony.'

"Nobby said the title bein' so long there was no necessity for the tale. He thought the story might spoil the title, so he cut the story out.

"Nobby got a printer feller in Wynberg to get the book out. It was to be called:

Gallant 'B,'
Or
How we Saved Great Britain an' Ireland.

"Nobby had it 'Great Britain' at first, but Spud Murphy, who's Irish, owin' to his name, wouldn't have anything to do with it unless the title was changed to 'and Ireland.' Nobby said Spud wasn't Irish at all, but that he took his name from the gentleman Spud's mother used to be housemaid to, but as Spud's two bob was as good as anybody else's he changed the title.

"That was the price the book was published at—two shillin's. It was honestly worth fourpence of anybody's money.

"Forty fellers wrote their experiences, an' Nobby reckoned on each chap buyin' three copies—one for his mother, one for his young lady, an' one for the other girl.

"Nobby brought me a copy round.

"'It's a bit thin for two bob,' I sez—it was about the size of Ideas, but not so interestin'. 'Do you think they'll pay two bob for it? '

"'I'm sure,' sez Nobby.

"An' it did seem as if he was right, because when we got to the canteen that night everybody came forward to ask when the book would be ready.

"'I want my copy to send home,' sez Cully.

"'Only one copy?' sez Nobby.

"'Half-a-dozen, if you like,' sez Cully.

"'That's how I like to hear you talk,' sez Nobby.

"'Of course,' sez Cully, "all the chaps who've written bits will get free copies.'

"'Eh?' sez Nobby.

"'Free copies,' sez Cully. 'That's what's always done—I asked a feller at the book-shop.'

"'Don't you go puttin' that notion about,' sez Nobby, very stern, 'the books are two bob each, there's no free list owin' to the great demand.'

"A sort of silence fell on the multitude.

"'What do we get for authorin'?' sez Spud.

"'You get,' sez Nobby, slowly, 'the credit; you get the satisfaction of hearin' your relations say: "I never thought our Bill could write like that," or words to that effect. You get the glory of seein' all the lies you've told in print; you get famous in a manner of speakin'. You get——'

"'Hold hard, Nobby,' sez Spud. 'What do you get?'

"'I get the satisfaction of knowin' I've done me duty,' sez Nobby, highly virtuous.

"'Don't you get any money out of it?' sez Cully.

"'All the money I get,' sez Nobby, 'goes to charity,'

"Battle of Belfast'I know,' sez Cully. 'I know all about charity—it begins at home,' he sez, '*your* home.'

"The next day the printer delivered the books—three hundred of 'em.

"He was a very nice young chap, this printer, an' was mightily struck on Nobby, an' when Nobby came to him with a long face an' told him that none of the chaps would buy the book owin' to Cully puttin' it about that the book was free to all who wrote in it, he was very sympathetic.

"Nobby tried hard to get the chaps to take copies, but Cully was here, there, an' everywhere, tellin' 'em that if they waited a bit they'd get it for nothin', an' then, suddenly, Nobby stopped tryin' to sell.

"He walked into the canteen one night with a light step an' a smile.

"'Hullo,' sez Spud, 'have you found a mug?'

"'Not till this very minute,' sez Nobby, pleasantly.

"'Have you found a buyer?'

"'No,' sez Nobby, rubbin' his hands, 'thank heavens, no!'

"At this all the chaps in the canteen pricked up their ears.

"'What are you thankin' heavens about,' sez Cully.

"But Nobby only shook his head.

"'There's been a slight error in printin' that book,' he sez. 'There's a certain thing in it that oughtn't to be in it—somethin' that'll cost me money.'

"'I know!' sez Cully, excitedly, 'you've libelled somebody,' but Nobby wouldn't say.

"'Look here, Nobby,' sez Cully. I'll buy a copy of that book.'

"'You couldn't buy a copy for a hundred pounds,' sez Nobby, prompt.

"By the next night half the battalion had been to Nobby, offerin' to buy a copy, but Nobby wouldn't part.

"It was put about that it was the colonel who was libelled, an' all the chaps who owed Nobby a grudge tried to get hold of a copy.

"Cully sent a feller named Sambo—owin' to his dark complexion—to Nobby, to get a copy.

"'I'll give you five bob for it,' sez Sambo, an' Nobby hesitated.

"'I trust you as a friend,' he sez, solemn. 'Will you take your dying oath that you won't show it to anybody?'

"'I will,' sez Sambo, eagerly, an' Nobby handed him a copy. He let Harry Jackson have a copy for three bob, an' Spud Murphy got one for 2s. 6d. Lots of other fellers came to him, an' after he'd made 'em swear by this an' that they'd keep the matter dark, he sold 'em copies.

"'I've only got a few,' he sez, 'most of 'em are destroyed.' Cully an' Sambo spent all one night lookin' for the libel.

"'I'll bet this is what it is,' sez Cully, readin' from Nobby's account of the Battle of Belfast:

General, Roberts ordered us to Advance.

"'He ought to have said "Lord Roberts,"' sez Cully. 'That's the libel.'

"After a bit he found another libellous sentence:

"'It was a dreadful sight. The Austretches prowled about the *veld* devouring our gallant men.'

"'It's libellous to say Ostritches eat humans,' sez Sambo.

"There never was a book read as that book was read. Chaps who got it worked away at it quietly, an' it wasn't till they was all baffled, an' started discussin' the matter with each other, that it came out that every other man in the regiment had a copy, what he'd bought from Nobby secretly. Cully tackled Nobby in the barrack-room one day.

"'About this book of yours,' he sez.

"But Nobby put his fingers to his lips.

"'Hush!' he sez, very mysterious.

"'Hush be blowed!' sez Cully, wrathfully, 'what I want to know is, what is there in the book that didn't ought to be in?'

253

"'Nothin'" sez Nobby, very calm, 'nothin'—now.'

"' Nothin'!' sez Cully, scandalised.

"'Not now,' sez Nobby, 'there was somethin' in it.'

"'When did you take it out?' sez Cully.

"'I didn't take it out, sez Nobby. 'You took it out.'

"'Me?'

"'You,' sez Nobby, very placid, 'you an' the other chaps who bought it. My money was in that book, Cully!' he sez, solemn. '*Invested in it, but it's out again—with profits,*' he sez."

24.—A Soldier and a Man

Sometimes, on cold dark mornings, when a carpet of snow lies on the ground, and white flakes come whirling through the air, I wake of a sudden, with the echo of a far-away bugle call in my ears. Long-drawn notes, sad and plaintive, come faintly from a distant guard-room, and I sit up in bed yawning, and reach up to the shelf above my head for my morning pipe....

But there is no shelf.... No muffled voice from the corporal's bed tells me, indelicately but tersely, to "show a leg." There is no pattering of bare feet upon a bare floor, or the clang and crash of closing bed cots; nor the sleepy grumbling of the men. Sometimes my hand mechanically gropes for my slippers—part of my unofficial kit—and missing them, I call upon Nobby Clark to return them instanter, or take the chance of a plug in the eye. But alas! the indignant denial of Nobby Clark comes not, nor is Smithy's protesting voice raised. Instead, comes a discreet knock upon my bedroom door and the voice of my hired servant, "Your tea, sir." Then I know that I have been dreaming, and that this is not Maidstone or Aldershot or Anchester; and no uniformed coat awaits me. "There's no parade to-ay"—no fatigue, no orderly man—nothing but the humdrum of civilian life.

Let me say this of the private soldier in all earnestness, before, for a while, I take farewell of Smithy and Nobby Clark:

He is the whitest and the best man on God Almighty's earth.

In my day I have achieved some little notoriety, accomplished things that have momentarily enlarged my hat size, but of all accomplishments of which I am proud this stands first: That I was a private soldier, and shared the fellowship and friendship of private soldiers.

If he has faults, they are the faults he shares in common with the rest of humanity—his virtues rank with the virtues of the Olympians.

"Soldiers," said Smithy reflectively, "are different to other people, an' I've never yet understood why. It's probably somethin' to do with the uniform. It's the authority an' the responsibility. I once knew a chap by the name of Grover who was the mildest, kindest-hearted fellow in the world till they went an' made a G.M.P.,(Garrison Military Police), of him, an' that changed his whole nature. Most ferocious he was, an' would have strangled a baby if it interfered with him in the execution of his duty.

"Then we had another feller who came from Poplar way, who used to think the world began at Hammersmith an' ended at Cannin' Town. But he wasn't in the regiment three months before he was the most geographical chap that ever was. What with hearin' fellers talkin' about India, and other fellers about Egypt, an' what with lookin' the places up on the map, he got to be the leadin' authority on the subject of Where-is-it? It was, 'When I was in Burmah in '98,' an' 'That reminds me of the time I was at Doolali an' got the "tap,"' although he'd never been out of England at that time.

"He would stand at the bar, an' dippin' his fingers into other people's beer, used to draw little wet maps on the counter to show the rout he took when he was marchin' through Africa to the relief of What's-his-name.

"'We started orf from Cape Gadget, as it might be here,' he sez, 'an' leavin' Lake Oogar on the left——'

"'You'll be leavin' part of your ear on the floor if you put your fingers in my beer again,' sez Nobby.

"'It's a map of me travels,' sez Day—that was the chap's name.

"'Then put in another little bit,' I sez, 'showin' the rout to the hospital from the canteen an' the rout to the cemetery from the hospital, an' a little tiny cross to show where they'll plant you, an' a bit of an epitaph:

> Here lies Private William Day,
> Who very sudden passed away,
> He messed about with Smithy's beer,
> An' that's the reason he is here.

"I don't doubt at all that it was the uniform that turned old Day into an explorer. It's the same way through all the ranks. A lance-stripe turns a decent soldier into a pryin' policeman, two stripes makes him take up fretwork an' other useless hobbies, three stripes makes him waltz an' go courtin', four stripes makes him fat, and so on.

"It is," said Smith, solemnly, "one of those extraordinary things that can't be explained—like coincidences.

"After the war, as I've told you about twenty times, we was stationed at Wynberg, an' very glad most of us was to get down to the loveliest part of Africa, where there were trees an' flowers, an' great grey mountains, an' the everlastin' scent of firs.

"The war made a big difference to Nobby, for reasons already stated. He was quieter an' gentler, an' didn't try his games on like he used to—except now an' again, just to see if his right hand had lost its cunnin'.

"He took to readin' books, an' generally got so ladylike that Spud Murphy took it into his head that he'd lost his dash, an' was quite saucy to Nobby.

"'The fact of it is,' sez Spud, 'Nobby's past his prime. It stands to reason that a chap can't always be fightin' fit, an' I think I'll go an' talk over a matter of five bob I lent him before the war.'

"To everybody's everlastin' surprise, Nobby remembered havin' borrowed it, an' returned it at once, an' Spud come back to the canteen quite hypnotised.

"'He's not only lost his dash,' sez Spud, 'but he' lost 'art, an' this is where I go an' remind him about certain statements he made about my face havin' been run over by a commissary wagon.'

"So over he went again, an' found Nobby readin' the life of a feller who started at the bottom of the tree, arrived in London with a half-crown, an' by careful attention to business, left the city owin' hundreds of pounds.

"By-an'-bye, back comes Spud, jubilant.

"'Nobby's withdrawn everything!' he sez, quite excited.

"I was astounded.

"'Did you pay him any money?' I sez.

"'No!' sez Spud, 'it was done spontaneous, in a manner of speakin'.'

"Now, the rum thing was that Nobby wasn't depressed or upset, or gloomy—he was just quiet.

"I didn't say much to him myself because I'd got an idea that I knew what was happenin', an' as things turned out I was right.

"'One day he sez to me: 'Smithy, I've had a letter from somebody who's sailin' for England tomorrow—she—she wants me to go down to the ship an' see her off.'

"I think I knew who that somebody was. There was a Dutch girl once, as pretty as a picture. . . .it was in Johannesburg, you remember, (Smithy's love affair), . . .an' she joined her brother's commando dressed as a boy an' was wounded. . . then she went down to the coast, an' disappeared out of our lives.

"'You're goin', I suppose?' I sez, but Nobby shook his head with a little smile.

"'No,' he sez, shortly, 'what's the good of me goin'? Who wants to see Private Clark in his red coat?'

"'Have you written to say you won't go?' I asked, an' he shook his head again.

"'I've never written to her,' he said, simply, an' then he went on—'Smithy, chaps like you an' me are fools. We're fools from the day we enlist to the day we get our "tickets." We fool away our time, an' we fool away our lives. If I'd given my time to a little study an' tried to make myself a better scholar, I could have written to her, but—but I'm ashamed to write. You know what my fist is, an' what my spellin' is? She only knows me as a man—please God, she'll never discover what a lout I am.'

"He drew a long breath.

"'There's a great big gulf betwixt her an' me. I know her people are rich, an' that she's a lady—an' I know what I am; a plain T.A., the son of plain people who never owned a hundred pounds between 'em.'

"He was silent for a while, an' I could think of nothin' to say, for what he'd told me was truth.

"'No,' sez Nobby, quietly. 'I'm off the map so far as she is concerned. I'm not such a conceited fool as to imagine anything else. We'll go into town to-morrow, Smithy, but we'll keep our distance.'

"It was from Signal Hill, next afternoon, that we watched the big white liner steer clear of the bay—watched her in silence, with Nobby's hungry eyes never leaving her as she put her nose to the north an' went out, dippin' her flag.

"'Goodbye,' I heard him whisper. 'Goodbye—God bless you, little girl—God bless you!'

"In silence we turned down the hill, an' Nobby's face was white. We were leavin' Capetown for India in a few weeks, an' knowin', as I did, how much Nobby was feelin' this affair of his, I hoped the excitement of preparin' for the 'Shiny' would help him to forget his trouble.

"'She's goin' to England,' sez Nobby, breakin' the silence as we reached Adderley-street. 'She's got some relations of her mother's there. She's goin' to live there an' asked me to call'—he smiled a little bitterly, an' I could see how hard he was hit.

"It was an unfortunate thing that we'd no sooner got back to barracks than Spud Murphy, who was gettin' very bold, come swaggerin' into the room, just as Nobby was hangin' up his belt.

"'Nobby,' sez Spud, 'I understand that there's a bit of a dispute regardin' a certain shirt wot you said I pinched. Now——'

"Nobby turned in a flash.

"'Are you lookin' for trouble, Spud?' he sez, quick.

"'If you've got any to give away,' sez Spud, easily, 'I shall be pleased to take it,'

"'Well, take it,' sez Nobby, an' landed him a smack in the jaw that didn't do him any good at all. But he was up again in a second, an' looks at Nobby very carefully.

"'I can take a hidin' with any man,' sez Spud, thoughtfully, 'if there's any occasion, or if 'there's a reasonable chance of gettin' a fair exchange of punishment. Nobby,' he sez, reproachful, 'you oughtn't to pretend that you've lost your dash—it ain't fair on the likes of me.'

"'Give him a dig in the eye,' sez a chap named Hooker, who was a great feller for pushin' other chaps into danger.

"'You try the experiment,' sez Spud, 'I'm busy.'

"There were lots of chaps who didn't believe that Nobby's dash had come back again, an' they fell into a great error. For Nobby went through a period of quiet savageness, an' two fellers of 'H' Company who came over one evenin' to pull his leg, was assisted back to their rooms by lovin' friends—they not having sufficient eyesight.

"As the time grew nearer for our departure for India he sobered down again, an' went back to his books, an' him an' me took long walks across the Cape Flats—but we never spoke about the thing that was uppermost in both our minds. Except once.

"'Goin' back to India,' sez Nobby, one day as we were returnin' to barracks after a long walk, 'is, in a way, the best thing. It means that we shall never meet, an' she won't be bothered with the thought that I'm anywhere around.'

"As we walked across the barrack square we heard cheerin' from all the bungalows. The fellers were yellin' their heads off.

"'Hullo!' sez Nobby, surprised, 'what's on? Somebody standin' the troops free beer?'

"We hadn't long to wait for any explanation, for as we passed 'G' we heard the chaps singin':

If I cross the briny
To go unto the "Shiney,"
To Quetta or to good old Chucajee;
Oh, who'll look after Biddy,
An' me mother, an' the kiddy?
Oh, Aldershot is good enough for me,
For me,
Aldershot is good enough for me!

"Nobby stopped dead, an' looked at me.

"'Go in, and find out,' he began, when along come Spud Murphy.

"'What ho!' he sez, singin':

I'm goin' back to the dear old land,
Far away over the sea,
Back to the scenes of me childhood—"

"'Stop bein' poetical,' sez Nobby, 'an' talk sense; what's the game?'

"'India's cancelled,' sez Spud, doin' a' little cellar-flap dance. 'We're for Aldershot.'

"An' so it was.

"At the last minute the War Office had decided to send a regiment home, an' they'd chosen the Anchesters. It was a joyful week we spent, an' everybody's spirits was sky-high. Nobby was a new man, an' on the boat he was the life an' soul of the ship—you heard how he carried on at Cadiz—an' in course of time we reached Southampton.

"I was the first to see the girl. She stood a little apart in her furs—there was a bite in the air—an' she looked a sweet picture—with her pale, young face an' her big, sad eyes.

"Then, in the confusion of disembarking, I missed her, an' was helpin' to get the regimental kit ashore, when the 'flag' came up to Nobby, who was with me, an' said a lady wanted to see him in the saloon. Nobby changed colour, but went without sayin' a word. He was gone a long time, an' when he came back he looked grave, but said nothin' to me.

"We marched into the Albuhera Barracks at the 'Shot that after-noon, an' was busy till night gettin' kit from stores. The regiment in the next barracks—the North Lancashires I think it was—cooked our dinner for us, an' invited us over to their canteen, but when me an' Nobby had finished our work, we got into our walking-out kit, an' went into town. It was Nobby's suggestion, We went down to South Camp, an' turned into the Church of England Soldiers' Club, an' got tea; then Nobby spoke up.

"'Smithy,' he said, goin' straight to the heart of the matter, 'her people want her to get married to a man with money.'

"'Well?' I sez.

"'She ain't rich, as I thought she was. In fact, except for a couple of hundred pounds she's got nothin'—I—I told her she ought to marry him.' He hung his head as he said this. 'I told her all about myself, that I wasn't anything worth considerin'; not because I'm a soldier, for I'm a better man, an' a prouder man now, than ever I was.'

"What did she say?' I asked.

"Nobby Clark shook his head.

"'There are some things I can't tell even you, Smithy,' he sez. 'I told her that I was a man who could never earn more than a couple of pounds a week—an' I told her why I didn't write to her.'

"'An' what did she say?' I asked. 'I want to know,' I sez, 'because everythin' depends on that.'

"He rose.

"'It's no good thinkin' about it,' he sez, very abrupt, an' that's all I could get out of him.

"We took our furlough together an' went to London.

"When Nobby said he thought we could afford to take lodgin's at Blackheath, I knew that the girl was livin' somewhere in the neighbourhood, an' that he wanted to be near her.

"She was livin' with an aunt, an' I saw her once drivin' in a carriage, an' in a roundabout fashion, I got to hear that the chap who wanted to marry her was an elderly feller, with pots of money. He hadn't got a nice reputation by all accounts, but he was madly in love with the girl, an' it was because Nobby, who was breakin' his heart over her, knew that the money would make her comfortable, that he was persuadin' her to marry him.

"Our furlough was nearly up, when Nobby told me he'd written her, an' was goin' to meet her an' asked me to come along with him. I think he asked me because he's got a very nice mind, an' didn't want the girl's reputation to suffer, through meetin' him alone.

"That mornin' I had the surprise of my life, for, as I was takin' a constitutional across the heath, who did I meet but the adjutant, Captain Umfreville. He looks at me in surprise.

"'Why, Smith!' he sez, 'what are you doin' in this part of the world?'

We talked for a little time, an' he offered me a cigar, an' told me his people lived close at hand. A nice gentleman is the adjutant.

"That afternoon Nobby an' me walked across the Heath, to the place the girl had chosen, an' there she was waitin' an' Nobby went toward her, whilst I stood round admirin' the scenery. They walked together, up an' down, an' even at the distance I stood I could see how upset Nobby was. I suppose they was talkin' for half-an-hour when I saw a man comin' across the heath toward 'em.

"A stoutish chap he was, walkin' very quick, an' puffin' an' blowin' like a grampus.

"He didn't wait till he got up to 'em before he started talkin.'

"'Hi! Marie! What the devil do you mean by this, miss?' he shouted.

"She turned towards him with a face like thunder, an' I walked forward, scentin' trouble.

"'I shall write to your brother,' sez the stout chap, furious, 'walkin' about in broad daylight with a common soldier? I'll——'

"'I think you forget yourself, Mr. Hoggin,' sez the girl, very dignified. 'You have no right to dictate to me as to what I shall do, or what I shall not do.'

"'No right!' he roars. 'What! aren't you practically engaged to me?'

"'No, sez the girl, 'I am not—nor shall I ever be. There is only one man in the world that I shall ever love,' an' she laid her hand on Clark's shoulder. I thought the stout man would have a fit. He spluttered an' stammered an' got purple in the face.

"'A soldier!' he almost screamed, a wretched shilling-a-day gutter child! You're mad! I'll report this man to his commanding officer—I'll write——'

"'You needn't do that,' sez a voice. I looked round, an' there was the adjutant.

"'I am Clark's company officer, if you have any particular complaint to make,' he sez, coolly.

"'Oh, you are, are you?' spluttered the stout teller, 'then let me ask you sir, if you allow blackguards of this kind——'

"'Private Clark is not a blackguard,' sez the adjutant.

"'He's a damned soldier,' swore the other.

"'So am I,' sez the adjutant.

"'He's had the impertinence to run after my *fiancée*—the stout man was absolutely beside himself with rage—'he's not in a position—he's an uneducated——'

"'That may be,' sez the adjutant, quietly, 'but he can improve himself; he can afford to wait, and so can the lady,' he smiled.

"'Do you mean to tell me,' sez the stout chap, gaspin', 'that you, an officer, can encourage a man of this class—'

"'I do,' sez Captain Umfreville, 'in two or three years Clark can make himself fit for a princess,' he sez.

"'Will you wait three years, Miss Vanhys?' he sez to the girl.

"'I will wait whilst I live,' she said, an' Nobby's arm went round her.

"'He's a private soldier!' roars the stout man, who couldn't get over the fact, an' you're standin' up for him!'

"'I know that,' sez the adjutant. 'In the army,' he sez, 'we make it a rule to stand by our comrades, an' I'm goin' to stand by Clark, an' help him to be worthy of a good woman's love.'

"'Do you call yourself a gentleman?' sneers the stout chap.

"'I call myself a man,' sez the adjutant."

Smithy and the Hun

1.—The Military Anarchist

"The worst of being a mug," said Private Smith, "is that you usually look it. That ain't my point of view, an' it's not original, bein' the idea of one of the grandest lawyers that ever went into the army. This chap's name was Grassy, and he joined our battalion owin' to some trouble he'd had with his girl.

"Offen and offen he's told me an' Nobby the story.

"'It was like this,' he sez. 'Me an' Miss So-an'-so was engaged, an' one night me an' her met at So-an'-so's. I happened to remark so-an'-so, and she up an' said so-an'-so, an' finished up by tellin' me that I was so-an'-so so-an'-so.

"'After them illuminatin' remarks of yourn,' sez Nobby admirin'ly, 'I can't see what else you could have done,' he sez. 'Naturally, after a lady has said so-an'-so to you, there's nothin' left to do but so-an'-so. What's your opinion, Smithy?'

"'So-an'-so,' I sez.

"Grassy never spoke out plain in his life. He was one of those fellers who was always scared of committin' himself, an' was always, so to speak, on his guard against givin' evidence against himself. One day on parade he made the drill instructor very wild.

"'When I say "Right turn," what do I mean?' sez the sergeant.

"'I shouldn't like to say,' sez Grassy—'not,' he sez, 'in the presence of witnesses!'

"That was his game—he was a born lawyer.

"'It's in me blood,' he told me an' Nobby one day in the canteen. 'I can no more help it than a cat can help likin' canaries. Me father was a nusher in a court, an', so to speak, I've imbibed the taste for lawyerin'.'

"'Is it hard to learn?' sez Nobby.

"Grassy shook his head.

"'It would be to you,' he sez, 'but it comes natural to me. It's like this,' he sez. 'Suppose Richard Doe owes five pound to John Roe, an' Richard Doe has give John Roe security for the said amount with a contingency an' Richard Roe can't pay on or about the appointed day, what does John Doe do?'

"'Is that lor?' sez Nobby, very impressed.

"'That's lor,' sez Grassy. 'Now I'll try you with another. A. promises B. a house on condition that C. pays B. what B. owes A.—do you foller me?'

"'No,' sez Nobby. 'But don't let that stop you.'

"When Grassy was pinched by the provost-sergeant for breakin' out of barracks an' brought before the colonel he got ten days' C.B.

"'Pardon me, sir,' sez Grassy; 'on a question of lor—I'd like to point out that the police-sergeant had his badge on the wrong arm, which, in a manner of speakin', invalidates the aforesaid conviction,' he sez.

"The colonel leans back in his chair, sort of weary.

"'Will you take my punishment or be tried by court-martial?' he sez.

"'On a point of lor,' sez Grassy, 'an' in view of the famous precedent of the King *v.* Cassidy, I'll be tried by court-martial, where,' he sez, 'the wells of justice, sir, will be untainted by the prejudice of caste.'

"So Grassy was tried by court-martial, consistin' of the adjutant, a young lieutenant who was scared of the adjutant and did what he was told, and a chap of the Rifle Brigade, who spent most of the time examinin' the probable starters an' jockeys what he'd got hid in the *Manual of Military Law*; an' the end of it was that Grassy got fourteen days' cells. He came out of cells a confirmed anarchist.

"One night he came into the canteen, flushed an' happy, as Mr. Garvis, the celebrated poet, sez, an' beckoned me an' Nobby aside.

"'Comrades,' he sez, highly mysterious, 'I've news to impart. We're goin' to abolish war.'

"'That's a very serious thing to do,' sez Nobby. "'What's to become of B Company?'

"'Us an' the Rochester branch,' sez Grassy, takin' no notice of Nobby's remark, 'have passed a resolution an' we're actin' with the Paris an' the Russian an' German branches. War,' sez Grassy, 'is a thing of the past. The moment it's declared me an' 40,000,000 others are goin' on strike. We're goin' to down tools,' he sez.

"'In that case,' sez Nobby, 'I'm sorry for you, Grassy, because it means you are goin' to sacrifice your jaw.'

"Grassy's best pal was a feller named Cheevie. It's difficult to describe Cheevie. He was one of those chaps who looked as though somebody had covered his face with glue and then dipped it in hair. If it was possible to unshave yourself you'd always look like Cheevie. He was a great feller on liberty an' freedom. His idea of liberty was that if a man didn't want to pay his debts hisself nobody had the right to make him. Him and Grassy used to talk by the hour about the Brotherhood of Man, an' how we'd all be a gran' family party if it wasn't for tyrants.

"'Do you know what my idea of a tyrant is?' sez Cheevie, very fierce.

"'Yes,' sez Nobby. 'He's any feller who makes you wash your neck.'

"But it was on the subject of war that Grassy and Cheevie was most talkative.

"'War,' sez Grassy—'horrid war! Raisin' your hydrant head an' squirtin' venom down the grooves of time!'

"'Oh, crool war!' sez Cheevie. 'Never again wilt thy mantle be drawn from the sheath of madness an' flown on the masthead of civilisation's pinnacle.'

"Then one day people began to talk about war with Germany. It came all of a sudden, an' the excitement amongst the peace-lovin' infantry was immense.

"'I don't believe there's goin' to be any war,' sez Grassy; 'but, anyway, at the first outbreak we've made our plans. We're sendin' out 1,000,000 four-page leaflets in English, French, German, Russian, Spanish, Italian, an' Irish,' he sez, 'work will immediately stop, factories will cease to fact, an' collieries will coll no more; but I don't think there'll be any war.'

"That night his pal Cheevie came up to see him in the canteen.

"'What will you do, comrade,' he sez, 'if this accursed war breaks out?'

"'There ain't goin' to be a war,' sez Grassy.

"'But suppose there is—you will lay down your arms?'

"'Naturally, comrade,' sez Grassy.

An' refuse to slay your brothers in Germany?' sez Cheevie.

"'Trust me,' sez Grassy. 'But there ain't goin' to be any war.'

"But one afternoon the news came to barracks. War was as good as certain, an' then the crownin' news of all that the reserves was to be called to the colours an' the Anchesters were warned for active service.

"It was one of them holy an' joyous moments when everybody shook han's with anybody. Provost-corporals shook han's with fellers they'd pinched in the town; even D Company was on speakin' terms with A Company, an' the quarter-master-sergeant was civil to the orderly man.

"Cheevie came into barracks in a state of great excitement. He met me on the square.

"'Where is Comrade Grassy?' he sez. 'Is he under arrest for holdin' them beautiful opinions? Is he in the han's of British military-ism for his true, patriotic action in layin' down his arms? Tell me the worst,' he sez, 'an' the world shall know.'

"'He's in the canteen,' I sez.

"'Ah!' sez Cheevie. 'He's thinkin' things out.'

"'No,' I sez. 'He's drinkin' things in.'

"I followed Cheevie to the canteen. There was ole Grassy, talkin' nineteen to the dozen.

"'Comrade,' sez Cheevie, seizin' him by the hand, 'the blow has fallen, the die is cast away; to your own self be true, as dear old Comrade Shakespeare sez, an' it follers you can't find fault with any other man.'

"'Halloa, Cheevie!' sez Grassy, very cold.

"'Comrade—say, comrade,' sez Cheevie, most earnest, 'what are you goin' to do?'

"'What am I goin' to do?' sez Grassy, amazed. 'Why, I'm goin' on active service,' he sez, very loud, 'accordin' to the lor.'

"'But, comrade,' sez Cheevie, very agitated, 'you ain't going to kill your brother German!'

"Grassy glared at him.

"'Don't you go castin' aspersions on my marksmanship,' he sez, very fierce, 'and don't you call me comrade, me man.'

"'What about your opinions?' sez Cheevie.

They're temp'ary suspended,' sez Grassy, 'under martial law,' he sez, an', turning to the fellers who was standin' round him, he sez: 'As I was saying when this low feller interrupted me, the best way to kill a German is to shoot him in the stomach——'"

2.—THE HEROICS OF PRIVATE PARKER

"I often wonder," said Private Smith, thoughtfully, "if Nosy will come back to what I might term 'the fold' in answer to one of them stirrin' appeals which the taxi-drivers are makin' to their feller-creatures.

"Fellers are joinin' the army now in a different spirit to what Nosy joined, and, anyway, Nosy's settled down.

"But havin', in a way, the dramatic instinct in his blood, he's just as likely to arrive unexpectedly.

"He was a fattish feller, by the name of Parker—hence the expression 'Nosy'—but in civil life he was called Mister Parker, owin' to his wearin' a watch an' chain an' sleeve-links.

"The first time I met him was at a 'do' given by the Anchester Young Men's Improvement Society. Me an' Nobby was invited, an' a lot more young gentlemen of B Company.

"I got fairly friendly with him, an', like a true friend, he began to lumber his troubles on to me. He was havin' a row with his girl over the question of her mother.

"'She's a bit too sarcastic for me,' he sez. 'The other day when I took a bunch of flowers up to Millicent she up an' asked me why I didn't buy her somethin' she could eat. I won't stand it,' sez Mister Parker; 'for two pins I'd—I'd join the army.'

"'What!' I sez.

"'I'd go for a soldier,' sez Mister Parker, very desperate; 'that'd bring Millicent to her senses.'

"'It would,' I sez; 'an' you.'

"I don't think he meant what he said at the time, but matters goin' from bad to worse, he got gloomier an' gloomier.

"'The old woman's sarcasticker than ever,' he sez, one night when I met him in the High Street. 'I hinted to her that if things didn't alter I'd go in for a red coat, an' she asked me what the army had done to deserve it.'

"'She's probably right,' I sez.

"'I've nearly made up my mind,' he sez, shakin' his head warnin'ly; 'it's either suicide or the army.'

"'Try 'em both,' I sez.

"Well, Mister Parker's love affair got worse an' worse, an' it ended up by Millicent walkin' out with another feller, an' the poor young feller—Mister Parker, I mean—got proper brokenhearted.

"An' the very next day, very pale and determined, down he came to barracks an' enlisted.

"Mister Parker's idea was that, havin' taken the step of joinin' the army, the worst was over, an' he was preparin' to sit down an' be comfortably miserable, but, unfortunately, there ain't any arrangements in the army for brooders.

"'A soldier's life an' a soldier's death is what I want,' sez Mister Parker, sittin' on his bed-cot; when in walked Corporal Jones.

"'Parker?' he sez.

"'That's me, me man,' sez Nosy, kindly.

"'Not so much "me man,"' sez the corporal, 'or I'll land you in the cage—you'll be for coal-fatigue.'

"'What's that?' sez Nosy.

"'Carryin' coal,' sez the corporal, 'to the married quarters.'

"'What's it like?' sez Nosy.

"'Very much like carryin' civilian coal,' sez the corporal, 'only it's a bit heavier.'

"What with scrubbin' floors and scrubbin' tables, and doin' other things too numerous an' disgustin' to mention, Nosy began to get an idea of soldierin' that he had never had before. He got into trouble for givin' lip to a sergeant, an' got extra drill for bein' too much of a gentleman to wash his neck on a cold mornin'.

"He hadn't seen Millicent since he enlisted, because, in those days, young recruits weren't served out with their swagger tunics for a month or so after they joined, but when that time came, an' he got his nice fine-cloth coat, he dressed up an' went down town.

"He saw her, and she saw him, an' went past him with her nose in the air, an' poor old Parker was terribly upset when he came back.

"'She must have mistook you for a scarlet-runner,' I sez.

"'No, it ain't that,' he sez, mournful; 'she despises me—I'll try her again.'

"So he did; stopped an' spoke to her, an' the only result was that her mother wrote to the C.O. an' said that if he didn't keep his drummer-boys from following her daughter she'd write to the papers.

"'Drummer-boys!' he sez; 'that shows her sarcastic tongue! Drummer-boys!'

"He was a great schemer, was Nosy Parker, an' he sat down to think of a good way to get the girl to see the kind of hero she was chuckin' away. After thinkin' for three days he struck an idea, an' came to me with it.

"'I'll rescue her,' he sez.

"'From what?' I sez; for now that Nosy's engagement was broken off I couldn't see what there was to be rescued from.

"'From ruffians,' sez Nosy. 'One dark night when she's goin' home from choir practice two fellers will spring out of a dark corner an' pinch her watch. Just as she is strugglin' an' at her last gasp, up comes a gallant young soldier. Who is it? By heavens, 'tis Private Parker! *Biff! biff! Smack! smack!* Down goes the two ruffians, an' the girl falls faintin' in me arms,' sez Nosy, very breathless.

"'Fine,' I sez; 'but suppose all the *biff! biff!* is done by the ruffians, an' you fall faintin' in her arms?'

"'That,' sez Nosy, 'I'm goin' to arrange for; in fact, it's what I've come to see you about. Will you be a ruffian?'

"'For how much?' I sez, cautious.

"'For five shillin's,' he sez.

"'I'll think about it,' sez I, an' went off to talk the matter over with Nobby.

"Money was very scarce, an' it was the longest month I'd ever lived, owin' to aforesaid.

"So we collected ten shillin's from Nosy, an' Nosy, who was a bit of a poet, wrote out the part. He wrote it out just as if it'd been a play. He used to write plays for the Anchester Young Men's Improvement Society till somebody stopped him. The play he wrote for us went like this:—

Scene—A lonely street, with nobody about except the moon. Enter Millicent, a fair young girl.

Millicent: Methought I heard the village clock proclaim the hour of half-past eleven. How weary I feel! Would that I had never quarrelled with Hector.

"'Wouldn't it sound better if she said "Nosy"?' I sez.

"'No, it wouldn't,' sez Nosy, short. 'Let's get on.'

Millicent: Oh! woe the day when a cruel mother tore me from his arms with her sarcastic tongue. But hold! I must away, for the hour waxes late.

(Enter two ruffians.)

Oh, heavens! who is this?

Ruffians: Woman! Stand! Deliver your watch and chain.

Millicent: Help!

Ruffians: Thy cries are vain. Hand over the stuff, or we will slit thy pretty throat.

Millicent: Help! Save me!

Ruffians (seizing her): There is no one here to help you.

(Enter Hector.)

Hector: Yes, I am. (*Biff! biff! biff!*).

"'Do you think you'll remember it?' sez Nosy, anxious.

"'The only thing I want to know,' sez Nobby, 'is this: do we hit you back?'

No,' sez Nosy.

"'Then I don't take no part in it,' sez Nobby. "But we persuaded him, an' when the night of the performance came round me an' Nobby went up to a little street where Nosy took us, an' waited.

"'She'll be comin' along in about ten minutes,' sez Nosy, all a twitter of excitement. 'I'll be waitin' round the corner. You'll know her by—anyway, I'll give you the tip.'

"Bimeby we got the office from Nosy, who was hidin' round the comer.

"'Here she comes,' he hissed, an' at the other end of the deserted street sure enough she appeared.

"When she got near us I steps up to her.

"'Beg pardon, miss,' I sez; 'have you got the time?'

"'Certainly,' she sez, sweet, an' pulls out her watch.

"'Quarter-past nine,' she sez; then she looks up.

"'You're in the Anchester Regiment, aren't you?'

"'Yes, miss,' I sez.

"'Do you know a young man named Parker?'

"'Know him very well, miss,' I sez.

"'How does he like the new life?' shesez.

"'He loves it,' I sez.

"'He's a very foolish boy,' she sez, with a sigh, 'an' he has made me very unhappy.'

"Just at that minute enter Hector. He came dashin' round the corner.

"'Ruffians,' he sez, 'unhand the lady!'

"He biff-biffed, but I wasn't takin' any.

"'Hold hard!' I sez.

"'Fall down,' he whispers, an' landed Nobby in the jaw.

"Nobby was so surprised that he hit back, an' down went Nosy.

"'Don't hurt him,' sez the poor girl, 'don't hurt him. Don't you know me, Hector?'

270

"'Ruffians,' sez Nosy, in a dazed kind of way, 'unhand the lady.'

"He was sittin' up rubbin' his head where Nobby hit him.

"'I am free,' sez the girl. 'Hector, be calm, dear—I am with you; nobody shall hurt you.'

"'Release her,' sez Nosy, wanderin' in his mind, 'or by heavens, my trusty bayonet shall find your foul hearts.'

"'The best thing you can do, miss——' sez Nobby, an' she snapped round at him.

"'The best thing you can do,' she flared, 'is to go away before I give you in charge. I never saw a more cowardly thing than to strike a boy when he wasn't looking.'

"'But, miss——' sez poor Nobby, flabbergasted.

"'Go!' she sez, very tragic; 'leave us.'

★★★★★★

"Nosy bought his discharge next week, an' before we left Anchester they were married. They didn't invite us to the weddin', so we didn't send 'em a wreath or anythin'. But me an' Nobby bought a card at the stationer's an' sent it to Millicent's mother. It was a nice little card, marked 'With Deepest Sympathy.'"

3.—At Mons

Private Smith came back from Soissons with no more than an earnest surgeon with the smallest spatula from the amputating case could make good.

They took off his little toe, which had been rather messed up by a ricocheting .311 Mauser bullet.

"Funny place to be shot," said Smithy philosophically. "Fellers have been askin' me how it happened, an' what with Nobby Clark sayin' I was standin' on me head shootin' Zeppelins, an' other chaps passin' remarks about the size of me feet, I'm looking forward to the tag—if you'll excuse the foreign expression—when I'm well enough to start conquerin' the world, beginnin' on Spud Murphy, of C Company.

"No, I shan't be decorated." Smithy smiled largely and mysteriously at the long window of the ward. "Decorations are a bit too common in the Anchester Regiment.

"When war was declared, an' all the Reservists who'd gone away years an' years before thankin' God that they'd never see the army again, started rollin' in, shakin' in their shoes for fear they didn't pass the doctor, Mr. Giddiner started his Sober Soldier League. Me an' Nobby, bein' broke at the time, joined it, for Anchester was a bit dull, what with the 'Globe an' Phoenix' an' 'The Stag's Head' an' all the best houses bein' out of bounds.

"The rough idea of the S.S.L. was that, whatever happened, a soldier should never leave the battlefield for a pub.

"'I can't understand,' sez Mr. Giddiner, 'why only you two gallant soldiers have joined. I thought this movement would have spread like wildfire through the army; you must help me to spread it!'

"'Trust me,' sez Nobby, very confidential; 'you give me all the tobacco an' flannel shirts an' things you want spread, an' I'll spread 'em.'

"But there was nothin' like that to spread—only Emblems of Purity which Mr. Giddiner had bought by the gross from a snide Brum traveller.

"'Disgustin', I call it,' sez Nobby, as we went back to barracks, 'wasting our time like that—not so much as a bloomin' cigarette picture!'

"But Nobby Clark," said Smithy impressively, "ain't the sort o' man to let anything go to waste.

"It was after Maubeuge an' Cateau an' Cambrai an' all them places o' interest on Trench's tour for Nature Lovin' Infantry that Nobby put it up to me.

"'The way the *Kaiser's* goin' on,' he sez, 'is simply sickenin'. I'm goin' to sell me Iron Cross of the Second Class and the Third Class—wot I got,' he sez, modest, 'for savin' life before Mons.'

"'Whose life?' asks Spud, very suspicious.

"'My life,' sez Nobby, an' took out o' his pocket a square- lookin' cross with a bit o' blue ribbon attached. 'There it is,' he sez, 'an' without the word o' a lie I picked it up on the battlefield: that cross,' sez Nobby, impressive, 'is one of the grandest army decorations in Germany. Zeppelin's got one, Von What's-his-name's got one, an' the *Kaiser's* got two—one for his uniform an' one to wear on his pyjamas.'

"'Let's have a dekko,' sez Spud—impressed; but Nobby shook his head an' slipped the medal into his pocket.

"'It's too sacred,' he sez.

"'Do you want to sell it?' sez Spud.

"Nobby hesitated.

"'It don't seem right,' he sez. 'After the war's over that cross will be worth pounds.'

"'I'll give you five for it,' sez Spud.

"'It's worth more than five pounds,' sez Nobby; 'but as you're a friend of mine——'

"'Shillin's—not pounds,' sez Spud, an' after a bit of hagglin' Nobby sold it for seven-an'-fourpence.

"'What's S.S.L. stand for?' asks Spud, examinin' the medal suspicious.

"'S.S.L.,' sez Nobby, very slow, 'S.S.L. is the motto of the German army—"*Swank Sauerkraut an' Laager*."'

"Well, things went on an' on. We got bucketed from hell to breakfast-time, takin' in Compeigny *en route*. Here there was a slight scrap which under normal circumstances would have been regarded as bein' slightly inferior to the Battle of Waterloo, but which under the new rules was put down as an affair of the ninth class. The Guards' Brigade and a cavalry division got home suddenly, an' came climbin' out of the pit o' war with guns stickin' in their hair an' a limber under each arm. We was on the left of the Guards' Brigade, shootin' what Nobby calls the misguided but barbarous mercenaries of culture, an' we were of the fight, but not in it.

"That night, when we bivouacked, Nobby produces another iron cross.

"'You couldn't have found that,' sez Spud nastily, 'because we ain't seen no Germans nearer than 600 yards.'

"Nobby nodded.

"'You're right,' he sez; 'but me own theory is that it dropped out of a Zeppelin. I bestow it upon you, Spud,' he sez, 'the Iron Cross of the first, second, third and dog-box class,' he sez. 'Down on your knees,' he sez, 'an' return thanks to me an' the *Kaiser* for this glorious day,' he sez. 'You can have it for a couple o' bob an' a packet o' *Stinkadoro Fransaze*.'

"By the time we got to Paris there was hardly a man in B Company who hadn't got one o' Nobby's Emblems of Purity.

"Then come the affair o' the third, when we stood shrapnel for three hours before we worked to the left, to find the place where He Didn't Want It, an' we got close in with the new bayonet, an' there was work for the Pomeranians.

"B Company came out of it sober, but happy, though there were gaps in the pay roll that makes me sick to think about. We were drawin' off that night when we passed a heap of German dead, an' on the top lay an officer, shot through the heart.

"'What's that?' sez Nobby, an' stooped.

"On his breast, near the collar of his grey tunic, was a little medal—a plain black cross.

"We looked at it, then Nobby looked at me.

"'That's the real Iron Cross,' he sez, very quiet, and, bendin' down, he tore it from its ribbon and thrust it deep under the dead man's tunic out of sight.

"'I wonder why you did that?' I sez a little later.

"'That's me culture,' sez Nobby.

4.—Smithy on News

Private Smithy moved his bandaged foot tenderly and cased himself up a little in the invalid chair.

"Another excitin' an' momentous week has passed," he said, "broken only by the low moan of anguish from *The Times* military correspondent, when he found that the command of the army had been handed back to young Jack French.

"Another week of patriotic endeavour an' valiant doin's. The bishop of Old Kent Road, writes:

> Let me enclose a letter I have written to the Archbishop of Canterbury about the war. For weeks I've seen other names appearin' in print an' have suffered the tortures of the at the thought that perhaps I'd never be able to hike meself into the limelight. An' here I am.—Yours truly,
>
> O. K. Roadimus.
>
> (Enclosure.)
>
> My Gracious,—This comes hoping to find you well, as it leaves us all at present. What do you think about askin' the soldiers to give up drink? I think it's a grand idea. I'm havin' special pledges printed, which will be served out with the ammunition an' collected by the ambulance. Drink is a curse. Especially on the battlefield. Look at the Germans!
> Your lovin' little brother in the bonds of holiness,
>
> O. K. Roadimus.'

"By the papers," continued Smithy, "I learn that the operations in the West continue; also in the East.

"The following official communiqué is published by the German headquarters staff:—

> On the right we continue to make progress in all directions with one trifling exception. There is some slight opposition to our advance which will be removed as soon as the Anglo-French Army is utterly annihilated.
> In the centre we have nothing to report, except that we are

advancing in all directions. We are leading the French to their doom.

On the left we are advancing in all directions with brief intervals of standing still.

The following news is published by authority:—

> London is still in the hands of the hostile Suffragettes an' the Bank of England, which stan's on the Thames Embankment, has been swept by the sea.
>
> Sir Keir Hardie has been made an honorary member of the House of Lords.
>
> An enthusiastic anti-war meetin' was broken up by the brutal police, both members of the audience bein' arrested.
>
> We have again made a successful attack on the *Iron Duke* and captured the crew whilst it was engaged in ironin' its trousers. This brings our list of prisoners up to three million an' six.'

"What is termed the German Lie Factory," continued Smithy, "is workin' shifts. Day an' night the magnificent buildin' is a scene of feverish activity. Its great, great chimneys belch smoke an' sparks an' the thunderin' engines revolve with masterly precision. On the other side of the street is the Iron Cross works. Outside great queues of men arc waitin' their turn to be served. There's von Hoppett, of the Intelligence Department, who got two Iron Crosses for agreein' with the *Kaiser* that it was a fine day; there's von Whoizitt, who got six for heroicly destroyin' a platoon of boy scouts. There's Admiral Salz-Sedletz, who wears Iron Crosses to fasten his braces on.

"Orders are pourin' in; never has iron been so cheap.

"But, despite—if I may be allowed to use the expression—despite, or in spite of the false gaiety of *Unter den Linden*, the *Kaiser* has his troubles.

"Twenty-six of his sons are lyin' dangerously wounded, and the empress is sittin' by their bedsides in Damsick, Poser, Berlin, Munich, Aches, Busseloff, Dresden, Humbug, an' other celebrated places.

"Twenty-eight have lost their legs, an' the *Kaiser* himself fell in a ditch and contracted congestion of the lung, as a result of which he is now commandin' the army in Eastern Prussia.

"The Serbian Army is now at Itchski—a bit of news which brings relief to thousands of throbbin' hearts that thought it was at Bobrinski

—an' the significance of the news that the Drina is still runnin' cannot fail to awake a responsive thrill in British bosoms."

Smithy scratched his nose thoughtfully.

"I've asked to be discharged from hospital," he said. "Me nerves are gettin' a bit fretted with the war in London—I sigh, so to speak, for the peace an' quiet of the River Aisne."

5.—ON THE LAWYER IN WAR

"What I like," said Smithy, "is the gallant way the brave lawyers of England have rallied to the colours. It's one of the grandest things we've seen in the war. Many a noble barrister has handed over his important cases at the local County Court an' flocked to the War Office to conduct the campaign.

"Gen'ral McKenna, one of the celebrated lawyers of the age, has put all the lights of London out.

"'In *re* Zeppelins,' he sez, that bein' the way lawyers talk. 'In *re* Zeppelins *v.* Another (me being the another), it is ordered that the action stand over to the Hilarious Term, both sides to pay costs!'

"Every night, surrounded by his gallant staff, the brave gen'ral rides round London lookin' for people who strike matches in the street to the common danger. He rules with an iron hand, his iron heel grinds opposition, his iron heart never quails as his iron eyes sweep the skies for signs of aeroplanes. Everything about him is iron—except his head, an' that's the same old lump o' stuff that floats.

"Lieutenant (temp'ry Colonel) Buckmaster. k.c., is holdin' the Press Bureau to the last nib against the enemy, that has caught more recruits than the finest bunch of lawyers that ever got into fat jobs for the askin'.

"Day by day the defender of Fort Inkpot issues his cheering report:—

On our left a heavy attack by *The Times* was beaten off with loss. The enemy opened a heavy fire with their famous Reppington rifles.

In the action the *Globe* brought its Naval Brigade into action. We lost one admiral.

On the right a mixed brigade delivered several damagin' sneers at our position, but they made no charge.

To sum up: our position is favourable but unhappy.

"The advantage of havin' lawyers in charge is that they take no risks. They never do anything that ain't in the book.

"Suppose the Germans come to England, an' Field-Marshal Haldane was in charge?

"'Me lud,' sez Colonel Buckmaster, 'the defendants have committed contempt of court by shellin' Buckin'ham Palace.'

"'Order out the heavy battery of Mandamuses,' sez the field-marshal firmly; 'deploy the 1st Royal Injunctions an' fight to the last man.'

"'Pardon, me lud,' sez Colonel Buckmaster, 'but in the case of Napoleon *versus* Wellin'ton it was laid down by Lord Chief Justice Nelson that Mandamuses shouldn't be brought into action until the Injunction had been thrown out of court.'

"The Field-Marshal looks grave.

"'Empanel a jury,' he sez. 'Bring me Chitty on Contracts an' the Army List—send McKenna to turn the lights out, an' give the enemy copies of my celebrated book, *Rot mit Uns*, to read whilst we get out a written judgment.'

"They're great believers in words," said the admiring Smithy. "They don't do anything till they're told. They had to be told to get bands to help recruitin', they had to be told that Zeppelins couldn't live in a ninety-mile-an-hour gale, they had to be told that the Germans had big guns. The only things they don't believe is they've no what I might term aptitude for conductin' war—an' that's the thing that everybody is tellin' 'em.

"In a sense I don't blame 'em," Smithy went on. "If you believed everything you was told it would be ridiculous goin' on with the war.

"Have you heard about the *Kaiser* bein' captured an' brought to England? Do you know that French an' Joffre are one an' the same person—'ence the expression 'French'! Do you know that the Gran' Duke What's-his-name of Russia an' the *Kaiser* are as thick as thieves? Are you aware that the King of the Belgians an' Colonel Seely are livin' at Harrogate? You haven't? Don't you go to your club?

"I've heard more things in the strictest confidence since the war started than I've heard for donkey's years.

"People are always comin' up to me most mysterious an' tellin' me what Kitchener told a friend of theirs.

"Confidence an' the Press Bureau are the two things you're allowed to abuse in these days.

"These are wonderful times," continued Smithy, shaking his head with melancholy pleasure. "Never before has what I might term the People got so into the ribs of the government that it can hear the great heart of the Cabinet throbbin' like a B.M.C. taxi.

"Secrets what in peace time would never get known are now handed out with the change. The newspaper boy in the street gives you your *Star* an' the latest gossip from York Cottage; the feller that cuts your hair can point out the very winder to the Tower where little Prince Looie was smothered by wicked Uncle Winston; an' even the 91st Royal Hoxton (Mike Cassidy's Own) use the time they're not drillin' between school-hours to hold councils of war an' discuss the marvellous way Douglas Haig has got on without influence.

"There was a feller in ours named Anthony Gerrard, who got well thought of by bein' mysterious. He never mentioned names—just like the War Office—preferrin' the use of the alphabet.

"Nobby used to say he got his name out of a telephone book, but Anthony Gerrard, Esq.—that's how he used to sign his name before he enlisted—said he scorned Nobby.

"'There's a certain Lord X.,' sez Tony one night in the canteen; 'I won't give you his name. But suppose I walked up to him an' offered him me hand—what do you suppose he'd do?'

"'Call the police?' sez Nobby.

"'No,' sez Tony, smilin' pityin'ly; 'he'd stagger back an' say: "Good heavens—is it J——"'

"'You bein' the Jay?' sez Nobby.

"'Me bein' J,' sez Tony.

"So long as a feller doesn't commit the error of givin' particulars, he can go on makin' impressions an' giving you the idea that he's in the brightest an' best class, an' that's what Tony did.

"It was a bit sickenin', because when Tony was around you couldn't talk about anybody.

"If somebody started 'They tell me that the Duke of Claremarket——' Tony would cough warnin'ly.

"'I'm here,' he'd say.

"Or suppose somebody started criticism' Balfour, Tony would stop it at once.

"'There's certain reasons,' he'd say, 'why I'd rather you didn't mention Mr. B. Certain family reasons,' an' naturally that would dry us up.

"Nobby was arguin' once about Napoleon Bonaparte. Not exactly arguin', but tellin' a feller that if he said so-and-so he was a liar. Nobby knows a lot about Napoleon, owin' to havin' read a book called *The Heroic Drummer Boy*, or *How England was Saved; A Tale of the Peninsular War.'*

"Nobby was in the act of tellin' the chaps how Napoleon used to go round pinchin' people's ears, an' anythin' else he could lay his hand on, when Tony, who was drinkin' solitary at the bar, an' listenin' with a very moody face, steps in.

"'Nobby,' he sez in a pained voice, 'don't think me foolish, but for certain reasons I'd rather you didn't mention N.B.'

"'For why?' sez Nobby.

"'I can't explain,' sez Tony, sorrorful; 'it would mean givin' away certain secrets that have been in the family for years. All that I'll say,' he sez, 'is this: Do you notice anythin' strange about me face?'

"'Yes,' sez Nobby.

"'I don't mean that,' sez Tony, hasty, 'but do you recall a certain resemblance to anybody you've heard about?'

"Nobby suggested a few people, but somehow didn't quite hit the idea.

"'You needn't be offensive,' sez Tony; 'amongst gentlemen there's no need to be rude an' personal. I asked you a civil question. Don't I remind you in some ways of N.B.?'

"'No,' sez Nobby.

"'Well,' sez Tony, drinkin' up his beer, 'we won't go into the question, but it's very painful for me to stand here an' listen to certain things said about certain people.' An' with that he walks out.

"It was about this time that Tony began to take up his family as a serious hobby. Previous to this, he'd only dropped hints at one time an' another, but now he began to work overtime on the job. He got gloomier an' gloomier; didn't talk much; used to sit in a corner of the canteen nursin' an unsociable pint o' beer, an' broodin'.

"It got to be the talk of the camp. Fellers from other regiments used to come over to our canteen to have a look at him. It got about that he was a German prince who'd been disappointed in love. Somebody told Tony this an' he denied it.

"'I don't mind admittin',' he sez, 'that I'm not a German prince. Not German,' he sez, 'at any rate.'

"In order to spare his feelin's, we had to wait until he'd left the canteen before we started an argument about any feller.

"If he happened to be present one of the chaps would go up to him an' say: 'Excuse me, Tony, have you any objection to us discussin' the *Kaiser*—or Richard Cure de Lions,' as the case might be.

"Sometimes Tony would say 'Yes,' but more often—especially the day we was arguin' about Moses an' the Bulrushes, an' how Moses got there—he said 'No,' he'd rather we didn't.

"Now, all this went on for months. We was shifted from Aldershot to Chatham, an' back again to Aldershot, and as far as me an' Nobby was concerned, we got a bit fed up with Tony an' his family pride.

"Nobby an' me went on leave to London, an' the night after we came back, we was sittin' in the library, so called because it's the only place you can get a cup of coffee, tellin' the other fullers all about our adventures, when in walks Tony, an' I could see the light of battle in his eye, to use a poetical expression.

"I was just in the middle of tellin' the fellers about a certain party me an' Nobby had seen—'The Marvellous Binko' he was called—when in rushed Tony, where a good many other fellers wouldn't have dared trod.

"'Pardon me,' he sez, 'the party you mentioned as I come in is on the stage, ain't he?'

"'He is,' I sez.

"'A short, stout party?' sez Tony, guessin' very' hard.

"'He is,' I sez.

"'Well,' sez Tony, 'all I can say is that when a member of a certain family disgraces hisself by goin' on the stage, it don't seem to me that it's a very friendly thing to chuck it in the teeth of another member of the same family.'

"'Meanin' you?' I sez.

"'Yes,' sez Tony, as bold as brass, 'if you're cad enough to make me confess it, yes!'

"'Is "The Marvellous Binko" a member of your family?' I sez.

"'I don't mind tellin' you in confidence that he's me half-brother,' sez Tony, 'an' all our family's very much upset about his goin' on the stage. I've done me best to persuade him not to,' sez Tony, despairin'ly. I've argued with him and talked to him. "Think o' the family," I sez, but he took no notice.'

"'Shouldn't think he would,' I sez, 'because the party me an' Nobby was talkin' about is *the Educated Chimpanzee at the Palace*. I tell you this,' I sez, 'in the strictest confidence!'"

6.—Von Kluck's Nephew, Ginger

"Talkin' as I was last week," said Smithy, "about people with relations reminds me of von Kluck's nephew, what we discovered in the course of a slight argument about Napoleon an' the *Kaiser*.

"The main difference between the *Kaiser* and Napoleon Bonaparte," said Smithy, "is that Napoleon is dead an' respected an' the *Kaiser* is alive.

"Other differences don't count. Everybody knows that Napoleon never 'made satisfactory progress'—he won. Everybody knows that Napoleon wasn't much of a speech maker, an' everybody knows that when he gave out the Iron Crosses of the period, so to speak, the fellers who got 'em had to earn 'em.

"When we was marchin' down to the Marne there was, as I say, a great argument—after we got our second wind—as to whether Napoleon was a better gen'ral than von Kluck.

"The only feller that stuck out for von Kluck was a red-haired chap named Ginger. Ginger had an aunt who ran away from home when she was a girl, an' disgraced the family by marrying a German by the name of Kluck, an' Ginger always spoke of von Kluck as 'Uncle Hector.'

"'It's my belief,' sez Nobby, 'that you're a spy, Ginger, an' you ought to be shot.'

"'That's no argument,' sez Ginger; 'an' if it comes to shootin', I can only hope that the firin' party will be rotten third-class shots like you.'

"'If,' sez Nobby, taking a long breath, 'if I wasn't on active service fightin' for me country,' he sez, 'I'd take them remarks of yours an' ram 'em down your throat with me entrenchin' tool.'

"'Don't lose your temper, Private Clark,' sez Ginger—he was a thin, tall feller, with a weary habit of speakin'. 'My Uncle Hector never loses his temper, an' that's why he's pushin' the British Army all over the shop. Now, Napoleon was always losin' his temper, an' spent all his life pinchin' corporals' ears, by all accounts. My Uncle Hector don't pinch ears.'

"'Your Uncle Hector,' sez Nobby, highly exasperated, 'would pinch the bones out of a kipper.'

"'If ever I'm took prisoner,' sez Ginger, musin'ly, 'I'll go straight up to the General an' say: "Hullo—how's Aunt Emma?" I'll bet he'll be surprised.'

"'If he ain't,' sez Nobby, 'he'll come out of this war alive.'

"Ginger had started by wonderin' if von Kluck was a distant relation, and sort of strengthened his the'ries, to such an extent that by the time we started comin' back he knew von Kluck better than he knew the holes in his shirt.

"'Often,' sez Ginger, 'he used to come an' see us down in Deptford. He'd pop over from Germany in his private clothes an' look in for Sunday dinner.'

"'What?' sez Nobby, incredulous, 'does he eat rabbit, too?'

"'My Uncle Hector would eat anything,' sez Ginger, enthusiastic; 'he's one of them hard Germans what you hear about that eats iron fi-lin's.' An' Ginger went on to describe how Uncle Hector would nurse the children an' take his mother out walkin' in Greenwich Park, an' pay for tea like a real gentleman.

"This went on for a long time—in fact, till we got half-way back to the Marne.

"There was a counter-attack made by the Germans. They came into action like a regiment of soldiers, with colours flyin' an' bands playin', an' after the attack had been boiled an' bottled the rumour went along the lines that von Kluck had been taken prisoner. Nobody knows how rumours like that get goin', but there it was, an' Ginger was all a-twitter with excitement. Our company was told off to take the prisoners back to the base—there was about 400 of 'em—an' to make matters more interestin', we was told that there was a German gen'ral amongst 'em who was not to be mentioned.

"'It's 'im,' whispers Ginger, agitated, 'Uncle Hector!'

"We got back to the base, an' all the way down Ginger was castin' his lamps over the crush. There was one feller who didn't walk amongst the prisoners. His uniform was different, an' he had cords an' lacin's all over his tunic.

"'That's him,' whispered Ginger to me; 'I'd know him anywhere—often I've sat on his knee——'

"'Shut your big mouth, Ginger,' sez the corporal of our section, very kindly; 'give the aviators a chance—you're upsettin' the aero-planes, you windy devil.'

"But just before we handed over our little lot Ginger had a chance. There was a German prisoner who spoke English, an' Ginger asked him, very mysterious:

"'Is there a feller named Kluck here?' he sez.

"'That's him,' sez the low Hun, and pointed to the distinguished-lookin' feller with the cords on his chest.

"I don't know what made Ginger do it, because nobody had bet him that he wouldn't, but he ups an' walks to the big chap an' holds out his hand.

"'Hullo, Uncle Hector,' he sez.

"The big feller louks at him, very surprised.

"'You're Kluck, ain't you?' sez Ginger, an' the big feller nods. 'Well,' sez Ginger, all of a tremble, 'I'm Fred,' he sez; 'don't you remember playing with me, Uncle Hector?'

"The big chap shook his head,

"'*Mit* you—no,' he sez, 'vor you—yis, perhaps. I am *der* big trommer of the Vorty-Eight Jaegers,' he sez."

7.—ON MEANING WELL

"Nothin',", said Private Smith, "succeeds in this world like knowin' what you want an' sendin' in somebody else to get it. Another grand way of gettin' on, especially in the lit'ry line, is to go out for things that nobody else wants an' pretendin' it's the only real goods in the market. Look at Bernard Shaw, the celebrated poet.

"There wasn't a day passed before the war but he wasn't tellin' unpleasant truths that nobody ever thought of tellin', because from *their* point of view they was lies.

"That's why I think we're wrong about Germany. They're tellin' the truth—from their point of view.

"When they burn down a cathedral they can prove that they're lendin' a helpin' hand to civilisation.

"'Hullo,' sez the *Kaiser*, 'what's this on the horizon?— Reims Cathedral or a picture palace?'"

"'That, your worshipful Magesty, amen,' sez von Kluck, 'is the cathedral.'

"'Shell it,' sez the *Kaiser*, 'in the name of *kultur*,' he sez, 'to encourage the poor bricklayers' labourers of France,' he sez. 'Hand me the unemployed returns of France which our head spy cut out of the *Daily Way*,' he sez.

"'Yes, Almighty-for-Ever-an'-Ever,' sez von Kluck, an' takin' a gilt-edged bit of the *Daily Way* out of his diamon'-covered satchel, he passes it to the *Kaiser*, an' the *Kaiser* has a dekko.

"'As I thought,' he sez, 'masons and bricklayers are unemployed— shell it,' he sez, 'in the name of humanity.'

"An' it was similar with Louvain.

"'What's the name of this place?' sez the *Kaiser*.

"'Holy sir,' sez von Kluck, 'the name at the railway station is Louvain.'

"'So!' sez the *Kaiser* bitterly, 'this is the place where all them old-fashioned authors is patronised,' he sez, 'whilst up-to-date fellers like Charles Garvice an' Hall Caine an' Edgar Wallace is starvin' on half salary—we will have a wave of progress,' he sez, 'a heat wave.'

"There was a feller of ours by the name of Gumbal—we used to call him Gumboil for short—who was always doin' things with a good object.

If you missed your blackin' brush an' searched his kit an' found it, he'd explain how he was doin' you a turn.

"'If it hadn't been for me,' he sez to Nobby very indignant, 'you'd have lost that pair of boots—I saw 'em kicking about an' took care of 'em.'

"'The nex' time you see 'em kickin' about,' sez Nobby very un-pleasant, 'you sit down quick, because my feet'll be inside 'em.'

"Gumboil's habit of explaining away things got him into trouble at Mons. At the height of the attack he had a feelin' that he'd like to go away to somewhere quiet an' lonely to think.

"'I've had the feelin' myself, so I don't blame him.

"He got up slowly an' was walkin' away in a dazed kind of manner when his officer called him.

"'Where are you goin'?'

"'Ammunition's run out, sir,' sez Gumboil prompt.

"It so happened that our section was runnin' short, an' the feller whose job it was to bring it up had been wounded.

"'You can't go yet,' sez the officer, 'the ground is swept by the enemy's fire.'

"'I don't mind, sir,' sez Gumboil.

"'Try it,' sez the officer, an' off Gumboil went, across a bit of ground where if he'd been any good to anybody he'd have been killed six times over before he got twenty yards. Bein' naturally awkward an' useless, he got to the ammunition wagon. They loaded him up, an', like a man in a dream, he walked back to the trenches an' distributed the ammunition.

"'You're a brave feller,' sez the officer admiringly, 'an' you can go again.'

"An' all that afternoon poor old Gumboil spent goin' backward an' forward across a bit of field that was so swept with maxim an' shrapnel an' Mauser bullets that you could hardly see across it.

"The next day, as we was edging past Mauberge, pore old Gumboil sez to me:

"'Smithy,' he sez, 'never explain away mistakes,' he sez, 'or you'll have to go on makin' the same mistake for ever. If the worst comes to the worst, say that you meant well.'

"To say that a chap 'means well' is to say that he's a fool. There's always more well-meanin' people in a country than them that don't mean well—the bad-meaners live in Park Lane an' drive home in gilt-edge motor- cars, an' the well-meaners go by Tube. You never hear tell of French or Joffre meanin' well, because they don't.

"Sometimes fellers will come a howler because their best is every-body else's worst.

"It was the time when the regiment was stationed at Borden Camp, an' we was tempor'ily under the command of a new colonel, who came from another regiment, an' had an idea that he'd only come to the Anchesters just in time to save 'em from being disbanded.

"It was Nobby who found out that the colonel was mad about botany. He discovered in a book called *Who's Which* that the colonel's recreation was botany an' geology, an' that his telephone number was 978416 Mayfly.

"So Nobby started his botany club. You had to pay tuppence a month to the committee, an' every week Nobby an' his club used to go out on a ramble with a book on botany an' a coke hammer.

"You wouldn't think a full-grown lieutenant-colonel would be taken in by that kind of guff, but he was, an' the members of the club got all the afternoon passes they required.

"The club used to march out of barracks very solemn an' stately with Nobby at the head—we didn't allow non-coms, to be mem-bers—an' when we got a good way from barracks Nobby used to deliver his address.

"'Today,' he sez, 'we'll study the habits of the famous Red Dande-Lion.'

"'I don't like the beer there, Nobby,' sez one botanist. 'Why not go on to the White Hart?'

"'Hear, hear,' sez the other students.

"'I'm the committee of this club,' sez Nobby sternly, 'an we'll go to the Red Lion. Besides, I've complained to the landlord, an he's having a special brew for us.'

"One day when we was comin' back to barracks we met the colo-nel.

"'Well, men,' he sez, 'I'm glad to see you returnin' from your healthy pursuits. What have you been after today?'

"'Dandelions, sir,' sez Nobby.

"'Ah! Excellent!' sez the colonel. 'And—what is the matter with Private Murphy?'

"'A touch of sunstroke, sir,' sez Nobby hastily; 'he was stoopin' to kiss a dandelion, an' the sun got him at the back of the neck—that's why he's singin', sir.'

"The colonel looks at Spud very suspicious.

"'He hasn't been drinkin', has he?' he sez.

"'Oh, no, sir,' sez Nobby, shocked; 'it's dandelions, sir—the smell of 'em gets into your head.'

"'That's a very interestin' discovery,' sez the colonel.

"He left us soon after, an' the next time Nobby went up to the adjutant with a club pass for signature the Adjutant tore it up.

"'If you want to drink,' he sez, 'go to the canteen; our dandelions are as good as the Red Dande-Lions, an' they're cheaper.'

"The Adjutant of the Anchesters was always a bad-meaner.

"Lots of people get the reputation of bein' well-meaners, because they do the right thing at the wrong time.

"Generals don't get up in a cinema theatre and criticise battle-films, an' acrobatic families on their way to the theatre don't find funny ways of crossin' the road. Similarly, it ain't good policy for officers to stick their noses into soldiers' business, except in regulation hours.

"For instance, there never was any good feelin' between us an' the Wigshires, owin' to a little trouble over the rotten way they kept kickin' the ball out of touch in the Army Cup semi-final of '93, when they was one goal up an' there was two minutes to play.

"This was followed by some slight unpleasantness at Aldershot, where one of the Wigs hit one of our chaps over the head with a bed- leg.

"We always had the good luck to be brigaded away from 'em, until three years ago, when we went on manoeuvres together, an' then, as luck would have it, we lay side by side in camp.

"The brigadier was one of them fellers who are always openin' soldiers' homes an' raisin' money for memorial tablets, an' he'd gone through life under the delusion that one regiment was as good as an-other, an' that the army was a great happy family where every soldier loved his comrade, an' two British regiments was alike as two army overcoats.

"Someone must have told him that there was bad blood between the Anchesters an' the Wigshires, an' he organised a Gran' Camp-fire

Concert for the two regiments, with the object of promoting brotherly feelin'.

"'I shall go,' sez Nobby; 'I ain't seen bloodshed for years.'

"It appears that there was a feller in the regiment who was known as the Rudyard Kiplin' of the Wigshires owin' to his habit of puttin' bits in the papers, an' before he went over into the Wigshire lines it leaked out that he was goin' to recite a poem called *The Brave Anchesters, an' how the Wigshires saved them at Klip Drift*."

"Now, everybody knows that at that historic battle the Wigs was only saved from decimation, annihilation, destruction, and other happenin's too numerous to mention by the gallant an' heroic action of B Company, Anchester Regiment—and especially of me an' Nobby Clark.

"'There's goin' to be trouble,' sez Nobby, when we got to the place where the concert was.

"A chap named Nosey, who was a sort of master of ceremonies, showed us the way to a seat near the fire.

"'I trust you men will enjoy yourselves,' he sez; 'me bein' the middle-weight champion of the Brigade, I was hopin' to entertain you with a boxin' exhibition, but there's nobody can stand up to me!'

"'We're bearin' the loss very well,' sez Nobby.

"'You've heard about me, I suppose?' sez Nosey.

"'I never read the police news, meself,' sez Nobby.

"'You're not tryin' to insult me, are you?' sez Nosey very fierce.

"'Not noticeably,' sez Nobby.

"The real trouble didn't start till Rudyard II started his poem. It began:

Oh, list, ye gallant Wigshires,
I will a tale relate,
About our glorious regiment,
That's very up to date.

"''Ear, 'ear,' sez Nobby, an' the feller went on about the bloomin' 'crush' till me an' the other fellers was nearly ill. Then came the wicked bit.

The shot an' shell is fallin';
We see the Boers attack.
By heaven, 'tis the Anchesters
That start a-fallin' back!'

"'On a point of order!' sez Nobby, risin', 'I should like to state, on behalf of me gallant comrades, that that statement is a lie.'

"'Order, order!' sez the Wigshires, very indignant, an' the poet proceeded:

> *They were too weak to vanquish*
> *The foemen at their front.*
> *It was the gallant Wigshires*
> *That bore the battle brunt.*

"'That's another lie,' sez Nobby loudly.

"He looked round quick. Somebody must have given the officers the tip not to come, for there was none present.

"'It's a lie,' sez Nobby again, an' Nosey stepped forward to do a bit of chuckin' out. . . .

"It took the 1st Royal Scots an' the 2nd West Kents the whole of that night to get us sorted out.

★★★★★★

"There was two whitewashed lines laid down between the two regiments," said Smithy, "just the same as you see on a tennis-court, an' the Army Act, King's Regulations, an' other deadly military instruments was used an' employed, so to speak, to prevent any further scenes of indescribable disorder.

"Any feller of the Wigshires or Anchesters who put his foot over his own frontier was liable to death or any less punishment as is in this Act mentioned. The papers had somethin' about 'disgraceful military riot,' but as me an' Nobby gave up readin' newspapers, owin' to none of their tips comin' off, it didn't worry us.

"But Nosey did.

"He gave himself out as the middle-weight champion of the brigade, an' offered to fight Nobby for the Honour of the Regiment an' five shillin's.

"'If I thought he had five shillin's,' said Nobby, 'I'd go into the enemy's country an' do great execution.'

"Receivin' no answer to his challenge, Nosey sent a spy into our camp by night, an' left an insultin' message pinned on to the flap of Nobby's tent.

"An' every day Nosey an' his pals would come down to their line an' shout things that'd make your flesh creep.

"We'd have gone over an' cleared 'em out, but the Adjutant got wind of the idea, an' paraded B Company.

"'There's a court-martial for any of you fellers that cross that line,' he sez.

"'Beg pardon, sir,' sez Nobby, 'but they're always throwin' notes over the line challengin' us to fight. What can we do?'

"'I'll speak to the Colonel of the Wigshires about it,' sez the Adjutant; 'but I don't mind you throwin' messages back, so long as they're civil.'

"That afternoon Nosey chucked over a letter:

Will you fite me? Yes or no? Will call for arnser at 6.

"Me an' Nobby spent all the afternoon writin' the answer.... No, it wasn't a long one, just the simple word 'Yes'; but it took us a long time, because Nobby an' me chiselled it on to a bit of pavin' stone, an' when Nosey called for his answer he got it—in the neck."

8.—The Persevering Soldier

"There's grand news from Germany in the paper this morning," said Private Smith.

> On the East we're makin' progress an' steadily fallin' back in order to deceive the enemy.
> On the South we're advancin' to the rear by short, sharp rushes.
> On the West we're holdin' our own and lots of loot belongin' to other people.
> To sum up, our position is distinctly favourable from a certain point of view, which isn't necessarily ours.

"Varyin' these with highly confident reports, such as, 'We are winnin' all along the line,' whenever they've got nothin' better to say, the Great General Staff—it sounds like a new omnibus company—manages to give a lot of happiness to people who, in the ordinary course of events, ain't very keen on fiction.

"Perseverance and cocksureness is all very well in its way, an' sometimes it succeeds. Sometimes it only looks as if it succeeds, as in the case of a feller of ours named Chooper. He was a very cocksure feller, an' there wasn't a single thing he wasn't certain about. He knew what kind of weather it was goin' to be; he knew who won the Boat Race in 1644; he knew who Tichborne was, an' why. He was a surprisin' feller. He was like a book of reference, full of printer's errors. He was cocksure about the army.

"When he enlisted he went down to the tailor's shop to be fitted for his uniform.

"'Halloa!' he sez, when they served him out with his uniform. 'Where's the stripes?'

"'What stripes?' sez the master tailor.

"'Them stripes that the chap wore who enlisted me,' sez Chooper.

"'You fathead!' sez the tailor. 'They was sergeant's stripes. You don't get them till you're promoted.'

"'Then all I can say,' sez the feller, very melancholy, 'is that if I'd known I wouldn't have joined. It's a swindle.'

"Bein' so certain, he was easy money for some fellers"—Smithy coughed—"because the only thing you had to do was to go contrary to his opinions and he'd bet you.

"He was a great feller for jumpin' at conclusions.

"'Commandin' officer's parade is postponed,' he sez one mornin', just before parade, an' the glad news spread.

"'Yes,' he sez, an' began unstrapping the equipment that had took him three hours to put together the day before. 'I saw the colonel talkin' to the adjutant, an' I heard him say that tomorrow would be a better day.'

"He'd got all his kit to pieces when the 'Quarter' bugle went; he was workin' like blazes to strap up his valise when the 'Fall in' went, and he got seven days for bein' absent from parade in consequence.

"Little things like that would have upset an ordinary man, but this feller wasn't put out in the slightest.

"I used to think that there wasn't anythin' in sanguineness, owin' to my experience with father and with this chap of ours; but I've changed my opinion a bit, because I've seen that bein' stone certain ain't such a bad game as it looks.

"We was stationed in Aldershot when I changed my opinion, owin' to certain things that happened to Chooper.

"Aldershot ain't the bad place that some people think it is. For one thing, there's a decent canal where chaps can go boatin', and it was on one of our trips up to Frimley that Chooper saw a girl on the towin'-path. He looked at her; she looked at him.

"'That girl wants to make me acquaintance,' sez Chooper.

"'A slight mistake,' I sez.

"'Didn't you see her smile?' he sez.

"'I saw her make a face,' I sez.

"'I'll come back here at the same time tomorrow,' sez Chooper.

'She'll be waitin' for me.'

"Now, the surprisin' thing was that when we rowed past the place the next day, there she was (a nice, pretty girl, too), standin' on the bank. She was one of those big, strong girls you see sometimes, and she could have eaten Chooper, who was a little feller.

"We'd have rowed on, but Chooper was steersman, so we pulled into the bank.

"'Good evening,' he sez, and she stared at him. 'I think you've seen me before,' sez Chooper.

"'I don't remember ever seein' a face like yours,' she sez, 'except in the comic papers.'

"This would have put end-of-message to anybody but this feller.

"'My name's Chooper,' he sez.

"'I'm sorry for you,' she sez kindly; 'but we've all got our burdens.'

"'Chooper,' he sez. 'We descended from the Dutch.'

"'It's very interesting,' sez the girl. 'When are you goin' to pick yourself up again?'

"'I see you're busy,' sez Chooper, who wasn't a bit put out. 'I'll call round tomorrow.'

"'Do,' she sez. 'Me dog hasn't had a square meal for a week.'

"Chooper was highly delighted when he came back to the boat again.

"'The only way to treat girls,' he sez, 'is to take things for granted.'

"The funny thing about the whole business was that he'd fallen in love with this girl, and, by all accounts, he met her the next day and the next. The first day he called at her house, and she dropped a bucket of water on his head. The next day he met her in the village, and she threatened to give him in charge. The next day he wrote to her, and got his letter back with all the spellin' mistakes underlined in red ink.

"'That girl's gettin' quite fond of me,' sez the sanguine feller.

"'You'll never know how fond she is,' I sez, 'till she gets the strangle-hold on you and rubs your face with a brick.'

"But somehow or another Chooper had got it well fixed into his head that this Miss Pink (that was her name) was most desp'ritly in love with him.

"One night he came into barracks very wet, havin', he said, been caught in a shower.

"'Come over to Frimley with me,' he sez next day. 'I'm goin' to call on me young lady.'

"'Do you want somebody to protect you?' I sez.

"'No,' he sez, very off-handed—'no; we've made up our little misunderstandin's an' we're as thick as anythin'.'

"So to Frimley I went, though I didn't believe a word he said.

"By luck we met Miss Pink just outside the village, and when she see us she stopped dead in her stride.

"'What!' she sez. 'You again, you little rat!'

"Chooper smiled.

"'She always goes on like that,' he sez to me. 'It's only her fun.'

"'Fun!' she sez, flarin' up. 'What did I do to you last night?'

"'You chucked me into the canal,' sez Chooper, very calm; 'but I got out again.'

"'I pulled you out,' she sez.

"'Let bygones be bygones,' he sez, pleadin'. 'Where shall we go tonight—Gertrude?'

"'How dare you!' she sez, very wild.

"And with that she gave him a smack on the head that knocked him sideways.

"'Love,' he sez, in a mazy way—'it's love that makes you do that!'

"This went on for a long time. I found out in the meantime that this Miss Pink was a hockey champion, a long-walk champion, a dumb-bell champion, and a few other things; so I gathered from the fact that Chooper continued courting her, and remained alive to tell the tale, that she needed him to practise on. I found out, too, that she'd a tidy bit of money of her own.

"One Sunday afternoon this sanguine feller asked me to go walkin'.

"'Not me,' I sez—'if it's courtin' you mean. She'll start on me next.'

"But he persuaded me and I went.

"This Miss Pink, Chooper told me, lived in a nice little house with a maiden aunt.

"'I haven't met aunt yet,' sez Chooper. 'I call her "aunt" because she's as good as mine; but in a way I'm sorry for her—Gertrude wants some living with.'

"There was no sign of Miss Pink in the village, but after Chooper had walked up and down outside her house whistlin' very loud for about five minutes, half a brick came over the wall, followed by a cabbage.

"'That's her,' sez Chooper, with a sad smile; 'it's a sort of code—a brick means "Wait round the corner," a cabbage means——'

"Just then a potato came over the wall—whoosh! It caught Chooper in the neck.

"'What's that mean?' I sez; but he hadn't time to invent anythin' before the big, high garden gate was flung open, and out ran Miss Pink, looking very wrathy.

"'Mr. Chooper!' she sez.

"'She knows me name!' sez Chooper, ecstatic.

"'Mr. Chooper, or Choppers, or whatever your funny name is,' she sez, most exasperated, 'are you goin' to leave me in peace?'

"'I'll recite her a bit of poetry I made up,' sez Chooper, and pulls a paper out of his pocket.

I cannot eat, I cannot think,
I love a lovely girl named Pink.

"'That's you,' sez Chooper.

She is the apple of my heart,
From her I'll never, never. . .

"The girl leant against the wall an' looked at him.

"'I suppose I'll have to marry him,' she sez, talkin' to herself. 'He's a queer-lookin' little fellow, but he might be handy about the house.'

★★★★★★

"In the course of time," said Smithy, "she married him. I didn't go to the weddin'—it wasn't safe—but I saw Chooper a few weeks afterwards.

"'You're a wonderful feller,' I said to him. 'Fancy perseverin' as you did with that girl! I suppose sanguineness is a gift?'

"He carefully stuck down the bit of sticking-plaster that was on his nose, and put another pin in the bandage that was on his wrist.

"'I ain't so sure it's a gift,' he sez, very slow and thoughtful. 'There's times when I think it's a bit of a vice.'"

9.—A DAY WITH THE CROWN PRINCE

"People," said Smithy, "talk about the hardships of soldierin', an' you'll find lots of misguided ole ladies sendin' Gen'ral French knee-caps an' wool mittens under the impression that he's havin' a bad time. There's some that pity the blokes in the trenches an' others that worry about the poor airmen, but the chap who sees what I might term the horrors of war is the O.C. Victories of the German Army.

"It's one of the hardest jobs in the world to get into the German Press Bureau. It requires a special trainin'. The officers are specially selected, an' have to pass an examination in military subjec's, as the Lie of the Land (Reconnaissance Department) an' Inventions (Engineerin' Department). Every feller has to serve three months in an English house-agent's office describin' Highly Desirable Properties situated in the heart of a Hunting Country (3 packs). Company's water, and Old-World Gardens, an' three months in an Income Tax Recovery Bureau. They then get on to the advanced course, where lyin' is done more scientifically—that is called the Diplomatic Service—an' they finish up with three months' prospectus writin'.

"They're then drafted to the German Press Bureau, with the rank of third-grade liar, an' gradually work up till they're in the same class as Miss Anna von Nias, that celebrated German lady.

"The work in war-time is very heavy. At 5 o'clock the reveille sounds, an' the first relief, springing out of bed, draw on their ink-proof pants, an' goose-step to the head factory.

"'Now, me lads,' sez the colonel, 'today is the *Kaiser's* Birthday, an' I expect you to surpass yourselves. Let's have our usual Monday conference.'

"The German lie conference is more serious.

"'There's been some fightin' at Ypres,' sez the head Bureau chap. 'We took three prisoners.'

"'What regiments do they belong to?' sez another.

"'The Wigshires, the Killarnies, and the 1st Tipperaries,' sez the head chap.

"'Let's say we've took three regiments prisoners,' suggests another feller. By the time the conference is through them three fellers have grown into a division with artillery.

"'What about us?' sez the second in command.

"'We'd better say that we have taken Calais, but had to leave it owin' to the absence of decent hotel accommodation,' sez the chief.

"'Anything about Russia?' sez the second.

"'We took ten lines of Russian trenches,' sez the chief, writin' rapidly, 'an' we're only waitin' for the enemy to dig another an' we'll take that—how many prisoners did we take?'

"'We took 108 in the first attack an' 131 in the next,' sez the second, 'an' they took 10,000 of ourn.'

"'We took 108,131,' writes the chief, 'an' we lost 5—now what about the sea?'

"'We had a bad biffing on Sunday,' sez the second, 'an' lost a battle-cruiser an' a light cruiser; we shall have to own up to one of 'em.'

"'What does the British Official account say?' sez another factory worker.

"'It sez that the admiral lost no opportunity and no time in comin' up to the raiders.'

"'Good,' sez the O.C. Victories, an' writes:—

The British suffered a severe reverse. They admit the loss of H.M.S. *No-Time* and H.M.S. *No-Opportunity*, two of their grandest Dreadnoughts, and the proof of their sinking is contained in the official message that both ships 'came up'—probably before sinkin' for the last time. This is the truth.

"It's a grand life," concluded Smithy; "in fact, I don't know anything finer. There's nothin' unpleasant to do, no hardship, no trouble—if you want a victory you pull out the drawer marked 'V' an' it's there.

"It's specially good when you can't get it in any other way.

"There's many things I'm glad I ain't," said Private Smith. "For instance, I shouldn't like to be a Belgian gun dog, and I shouldn't like to be the feller who has to explain away German victories; but, most of all, I shouldn't like to be the Crown Prince of Germany.

"We fellers that have stuck it in the trenches think we work an' suffer, but that young feller makes anythin' we do look like fish an' chips.

"'What's the day's programme, Hugo?' sez the crown prince, jumpin' out of bed in his bombproof pyjamas.

"'Exalted highness,' sez his valet, 'you're leadin' the Dead Head Hussars against the hated English.'

"'So I am,' sez the prince, drinkin' a gallon of lager out o' a priceless Sevres vase wot he picked up on the battlefield; 'bring me armoured train to the door; tell the princess I shall be late for dinner; an' send the proof of me new book, *Hints to Collectors; or, Hooks an' Crooks,* to the publisher; unchain me favourite Zeppelin; an' bring me another jar of beer—war is hell,' he sez.

"Up comes Mrs. Crown Prince with the children.

"'Kiss your father,' she sez; 'he's got a rotten job.'

"In a few seconds the crown prince, entirely surrounded by Zeppelins, Prussian Guards, an' Dead Head Hussars, are dashin' madly to the frontier, singin' 'Dutch lads after Ale.'

"When he's not singin' that he's changin' his clothes, an' when he ain't changin' his clothes he's doin' strategy with the chief of the staff.

"'My idea,' sez the crown prince, 'is to move on the enemy's left an' by a lightnin' dash across the front to seize his right, or *vice versa*. You,' he sez to his general, 'you go in front an' draw the fire an' I'll lead a charge o' the Dead Heads—at least,' he sez, 'I would lead 'em, only it don't seem fair to take the job out of better an' more worthy hands,' he sez. 'Anyway, I'll be waitin' for you when you come back.'

"An' the charge is made, an' as many of the Dead Heads as can be spared come back, an' the crown prince makes a speech, jumps on to his armoured train, an' dashes madly back to Potsdam.

"That night a mysterious stranger, wearin' a black velvet mask, is admitted to the hospital in Brussels.

"Is it the crown prince? Who can say?

"The next mornin' he starts off for Russia wearin' a fur-lined overcoat, a skunk muff an' a top-knot of caviare.

"His father says goodbye to him on the station.

"'Farewell, Willie,' he sez. 'Conquer or die,' he sez.

"'Come back on your shield,' he sez. 'There ought to be a lot of shield in these Polish castles—gold ones.'

"'Farewell,' sez the crown prince, drawin' his sword. 'Never will I return,' he sez, 'till me proud feet are wearin' a hole in the neck of the haughty Muscovite.'

"'Don't forget what I said about dyin',' sez the *Kaiser*.

"'Trust me, mein farder,' sez Willie in fluent German.

"So everybody sings 'Dutch lads after Ale,' and, surrounded by Zeppelins, Prussian Guard, an' Newspaper Cuttin's, the intrepid youth flies to the infernal snows of Upper Poland.

"The joyous news is flashed forth. It reaches the army.

"'Rejoice! The crown prince is hastenin' to join you.'

"The gen'ral staff turns pale. Von Hinkybug is observed to stagger.

"'Can't nothin' be done?' falters a fat general. 'Think of somethin', von Hinkybug—you're in charge of the strategy department.'

"'We might blow up the line,' sez Hinkybug thoughtful, 'or we might switch him on to the Warsaw branch.'

"But it is too late.

"The crown prince arrives, an', wipin' his feet on the prostrate figures o' the gen'ral staff, he tips the guard two Iron Crosses an' dashes madly into the Strategy House.

"'Bring up the 9th, 11th, 13th, an' 15th Corps,' he sez rapidly, 'deploy the cavalry, throw forward the artillery, an' let the battle begin.'

"'What a strategistical genius,' sez von Hinkybug, in such a low voice that he could be heard in the next block.

"The battle begins. It is watched with bated breath by the intrepid correspondents at Petrograd. The proceedin's are veiled in mystery. Drummond Fife, wires:

> I have just heard glorious news, I heard it from a friend in Moscow. He got it out of the papers. Ninety-six trains are on the way to Poland. They are empty trains. Why are they going to Poland? I can scarcely contain myself for joy. I can hardly digest me food. Oh, if the people of Petrograd knew what I know! Oh, if they did! Oh, if they could only read the Russian papers. Ninety-six empty trains! What does that news signify? I will tell you. It signifies four German Army Corps surrounded on two sides, battlin' desperately to get theirselves surrounded on three more sides. More tomorrow; but let me say this: *The Crown Prince is directin' operations and has already been wounded and killed.* The fate of Europe is hangin' in the balance. *Nitchevo.*'

> All day long the battle goes forward an' backward. The lunch score is:
> Germans: 40,000 prisoners, 230 guns.
> Russians: 50,000 prisoners, 235 guns.
> (Russia in play.)

"Surrounded as they are, the Germans move northward. Reinforcements are hurried from Berlin. Two train-loads of Iron Crosses are flung into the conflict. Hinkybug is made a field-marshal, the crown prince is made a full corporal, Cracow is in flames, an' Prezimizzle falls for the sixty- third time in history.

"In the evenin' the crown prince returns home wet an' weary, just as the family have finished supper.

"'Why, here's Will!' sez the *Kaiser.* 'Pull your wet boots off, lad, an' bring a chair up to the table—mother's put a bit of rabbit in the oven for you, an' you'll find a bottle of beer under the table. Well, what's the news?'

"'I got the enemy on the run,' sez the crown prince.

"'Did they catch you?' sez the Kaiser, anxious.

"Nobody can realise," said Smithy, "the strenuosity of the crown prince's life. Scarcely a day passes but some army corps put a card in the winder inscribed C.P. an' off he goes to deliver the goods.

"'He is the idol of Berlin. People weep to see him go out to war.

When he comes back they weep worse than ever. There is scarcely a dry eye in Unter den Linden as he passes on a wet day.

"Men swear by him; generals swear at him. There's some talk of gettin' up a testimonial to him an' raisin' the money for a wreath.

"His famous smile can be seen on every battlefield. Sometimes it's on one side of his mouth an' sometimes on the other.

"The Bavarians love him; the Austrians adore him; even the Russians follow him wherever he goes, an' the faster he goes, the faster they follow.

"To sum up, the crown prince is doin' two men's work, an' doin' it worse than six ordinary men.

"We're lookin' forward to seein' him," said Smithy. "We should like to call at his castle an' have a look round. It must be an interestin' place—the Lost Property Office of Europe, *I* call it."

10.—Nobby And The Lamb

"I'd like to meet Zepp'lin," reflected Smithy; "he must be the life an' soul of the German Staff just now.

"'I'm feelin' very depressed tonight, Willie,' sez the *Kaiser*, 'can't you suggest anything in the way of cheerin' me up?'

"'Come over to my dugout, Pa,' sez the crown prince, 'an' I'll show you a few articles I collected in France.'

"'I want somethin' comic,' sez the *Kaiser*.

"'I've had a new photo of myself taken nursin' a Belgian baby,' sez the crown prince.

"'That's an old idea,' sez the *Kaiser*. 'I'll tell you what we'll do—'phone up ole Zepp'lin an' ask him to come along an' tell us a comic story.'

"So up comes Zepp'lin, an' in a few minutes the whole German Gen'ral Staff is holdin' his sides whilst he tells the hum'rous tale about the Balloon that carried Bombs for Ballast.

"'That reminds me,' sez Admiral von Tirkfitz, 'about a great joke I had with Scarborough——'

"'Did I tell you,' sez another feller, 'how we treated the British wounded at Cologne? Your High Frightfulness ought to hear this story—it'll make you ill with laughter. . .'

"An' so the merry evenin' wears on, the Grand Duke of Wartbug givin' an amusin' anecdote of the grand bonfire he had in the East of France, an' how him an' another chap killed a ferocious baby in self-defence.

"All these yarns about Zepp'lins droppin' ballast an' only hitting back when they're attacked reminds me of an old story which you may have heard.

"When we was in South Africa, Lord Roberts gave an order that any regiment caught lootin' would be sent to the base, an' the soldier concerned would be hung. That was Bobs' little way. When he gave an order you remembered it every time you buttoned your collar.

"Nobody wanted to loot because the only lootable things we found was abandoned wagons an' empty farmhouses, an' even the most hardened looter thought twice before he picked up these little trifles an' sent 'em home.

"But later, when columns was wanderin' all over the country, an' when the supply wagons temp'rally failed to connect, the temptation to invite a stray fowl or two to dinner was more than most fellers could stand.

"'What I feel,' sez Nobby one day, comin' into camp with his tunic bulgin' with dead birds, 'is that it would be cruelty to dumb chickens to leave 'em on the *veldt* to starve.'

"'Many of 'em,' he sez, as he started pluckin' the feathers off, 'have lost all their relations; their parents have died of sorrer an' their children are bein' served as omelettes at the officers' mess.'

"On the march up from Bloemfontein we struck a very hungry patch. The bridges were down an' some of the wagons must have got stuck in the drifts, an' it was emergency rations an' biscuits for us—or nothin'.

"'Nobby,' sez Spud Murphy, who was company cook at the time, 'why don't you go wanderin' round an' see if you can find an orphan chicken who wants a good home?'

"'Talk sense,' sez Nobby, 'how can there be any chicken when Strathcona's Horse has been reconnoitrin' the ground?'

"None the less, he went on a foragin' expedition. He wandered almost to the outposts, an' every sentry he met he put a few inquiries to.

"'Have you seen anything of our regimental chicken?' he sez, so that nobody should think he was lootin'. An' then he explained that the chicken was a pet, an' marched ahead of the regiment. Nobby made up quite a pretty little story about that bird. How she laid an egg a day especially for the colonel, an' how the War Office was allowing her a medal for alarmin' the camp by crowin' when we was attacked.

"Nobby was explaining all this to a corporal of one of the advanced posts when he saw somethin' that made him gasp.

"'There she is!' he sez, an' ran to a little hollow.

"'That ain't a chicken,' sez the corporal, 'that's a lamb.'

"Nobby lifted up the little baa-baa an' put it under his arm.

"'When I said "chicken,"' he sez, 'I referred to our regimental lamb—his pet name bein' "hicken."'

"Nobby, overjoyed, carried the lamb back to a place where nobody could see him.

"'Lambie,' he sez, 'I hate doin' it, but "B" Company is hungry.'

"He'd just finished his work an' his bayonet was still in his hand, when he heard a jingle behind him.

"Lookin' out of the corner of his eye he saw to his sorrow Lord Roberts an' his gilded staff, an' even in that short look Nobby saw a very unpleasant expression on Bobs' face.

"But Nobby wasn't easily upset.

"He gave the dead lamb another jab with his bayonet.

"'Fly at me, will you?' he sez, very loud. 'Bite me after I've fed you on bird seed, will you? Take that, you f'rocious blighter!'

"Bobs didn't smile and he didn't frown: he just looked at Nobby.

"'We seem to have arrived in time to save your life, my man,' he sez, in that quiet voice of his."

11.—SMITHY AND THE MISSING ZEP'LINK

"These," said Private Smith, of the 1st Anchester Regt., "these are stirrin' times. Zep'lins goin' up in France an' lights goin' down in London, provide what Nobby Clark calls the infernal law of consternation.

"Day an' night them Zep'lin factories are workin'. Situated in the same street as the Iron Cross works—Germany's staple industry—this magnificent Zep'lin foundry is in full swing.

"Every hour a bran' new Zep'lin slides down the Zepple-shoot, an' is seized by painters an' marked in plain figures:—

This is a Zeplin.
It is *Verboten* to Spit on it.

"The output is ten thousan' a week. The sky is full of 'em, an' the shootin' stars *on root* to a place in the sun are obliged to go round the other way.

"They are comin' to London nex' week. That's why we've got a navy. Two millions of 'em will be circulatin' round London after ten lookin' for a pub that's still open. As soon as it is found a bomb will be dropped, all the lights will go out by magic, an' the landlord's licence will be seized. On the fallin' of the second bomb all German waiters will be interned in the basement of the *Evenin' News*; on the third bomb Mr. McKenna will deliver his famous lecture on the great war of 1911 an' why it didn't come off.

"Every precaution is bein' taken. Regent Street an' Piccadilly Circus are passin' the night heavily disguised as Brookwood Cemetery. Motor buses that used to kill people in broad daylight are now killin' 'em by night. Everythin' is bein' done to cheer up a people at war. Next to a heavy casualty list, a walk through London by night is more invigoratin' than *Fox's Book of Martyrs*.

"Taxi-cabs are burnin' cheerful blue lights in order to deceive the wanderin' airmen that they're chemists' shops.

"The most you're likely to see here in the way of trouble is one of Nobby Clark's Zep'links.

"When we was in the trenches on the Marne, an argument rose one mornin' as to which was the biggest airship in the world.

"Some said 'Zep'lins' an' some said 'Clement Bayrums'—or whatever you call 'em.

"'You're wrong,' sez Nobby; 'the biggest airship in the world is the Zep'link.'

"'You mean the Zep'lin,' sez Spud Murphy.

"'I mean the Zep'link,' sez Nobby, very firm, 'so called because it's a sort of link between a Zep'lin an' an aeroplane. It's a thousand feet long, made of aluminium, an' is blown up with a special kind of gas. It carries three howitzers, a Black Maria, an' a regiment of the Prussian Guard.'

"'Don't you try to come it over me,' sez Spud; 'there never was a bulloon that could carry all that weight.'

"Nobby shrugs his shoulders.

"'Wait an' see,' he sez very mysterious. 'If a Zep'link come along an' dropped half a ton of guncotton on your fat head, would you believe me then?'

"'Is it likely?' sez Spud.

"Nobody believed in that Zep'link—not even when Nobby told the troops that it could fly so high that it was out of sight most of the time.

"'That's why you don't see it,' sez Nobby; 'but all the time you're sittin' there eatin' bully beef an' concoctin' letters for your relations, the Zep'link is looking down on you.'

"The next day the troops got a bit more believin', an' by the end of three days, them that wasn't slaying the hateful Huns were crickin' their necks lookin' out for Zep'links.

"It was highly amusing to Nobby an' hardly a day passed but he didn't find some new point about the Zep'link that he hadn't thought of before.

"If I'd had, what I might term the inventive genius of Nobby Clark, I'd have been layin' concrete gun-beds all over Germany.

"'The Zep'link,' sez Nobby, 'is provided with magnifyin' glasses so that the chap in charge can read the names of the reg'ments he's attackin' on their cap badges. It's got a patent dart-throwin' machine that can wipe out a brigade at a time. It's got nine guns mounted on the top, an' carries fifty 200-lb. shells, and the whole contrivance goes by electricity.'

"'It oughtn't to be allowed,' sez Spud, very indignant, 'it's against the Hague what-d'ye-call-it.'

"'It's got one of them too,' sez Nobby. 'It's no good, Spud, you've got to stand it—anyway,' he sez, 'nobody is goin' to miss you when, so to speak, you're called hence by the Zep'link.'

"The adjutant come to hear of it, an' had a talk with Nobby.

"'Clark,' he sez, 'you're spreadin' alarm an' despondency amongst His Majesty's forces. The next time I hear about that fool Zep'link of yours, I'm goin' to give you a day's field punishment.'

"After that Nobby said no more, an' naturally havin' no time to gas, he had more time to think, an' he spent most of his time inventin' new parts to the Zep'link that he used to whisper in me ear when he was bivouacked for the night.

"Then he began to get serious, an' by the time we was entrenched on the north of the Aisne he wore that worried look which is usually only found in the face of the British soldier when he steps up to draw 14s. 8d. at the pay-table an' receives 9s. 7d.

"'What's the matter with you, Nobby?' I sez. 'You've only sung Tipperary three times since this mornin'—are you losin' your dash?'

"He looks round, an' he looks up.

"'Smithy,' he sez, very earnest, 'it ain't the Black Maria, an' it ain't the Prussian Guard,' he looks up again, searchin' the sky; 'it's this dam' Zep'link. Do you think there's anything in this yarn?'

"In my opinion," concluded Private Smith sagely, "it's the Zep'link that's expected in London."

"If I hadn't been a soldier in the British Army," said Smithy enthusiastically, "I'd like to be a sailor in the German Navy. Next to bein' an anarchist or the Sultan of Turkey, or bein' one of them bright an' happy fellers that walks about the grounds of Colney Hatch knightin' the keepers, bein' a German sailor is one of the finest professions in the world.

"'Beg pardon, sir,' sez A.B. Schmidt, 'I've just cut a baby's head off.'

"'For why?' sez his officer.

"'Not standin' up an' salutin' when the band played "Dutch lads after Ale,"' sez the A.B.

"'You are a hero-patriot splendid,' sez the officer. 'Which will you have—at once—an Iron Cross or a marble clock?'

"'Marble clock,' sez the A.B., 'or the money,' he sez.

"Look at the life they live! Dashin' madly down the Kiel Canal an' dashin' madly back again, rocked in the cradle of the lock or facin' the deadly bloaters of Yarmouth trawlers.

"When one of them poor fellers goes to sea, he never knows whether he'll be home to tea or whether the accursed war-party will keep him busy till supper-time. Often the ships go out of harbour and minutes pass before they return.

"The Mayor and Corporation of Williams Haven come down to see 'em off.

"'Farewell,' he sez, speakin' with emotion. 'Go forth an' conquer,' he sez, 'the deadly enemy is waitin' for you—the eyes of the Fatherland is on you—so is the eyes of the Uncleland. A strong fishin' fleet, many of 'em armed with dum-dum mackerel, is at our gates.'

"The diary of a naval officer swept up by a mine-sweeper tells the story:

1 o'clock.—We have left our dear fatherland—shall I ever forget it! How me heart beats. . . . We are now in deep water, and the ship is rollin'—but we are on our way! Travel brings out what is best in a man. Especially ocean travel.

4 o'clock.—I am wounded—terribly. I have been in my bunk for two hours. Is it a wound or have I been poisoned? I feel a curious sensation. Oh, these English, how I hate them!

8 o'clock.—We are off one of their deadly fortresses. It is called

Brighton. The whole front is full of forts. My captain points out Fort Metropole, Fort Royal York (where all the Big Guns go), Fort Royal, Fort Victoria. Men are pulling machine guns.... Hundreds of them, along the front. They are shaped like bath chairs, but (my captain tells me) they usually contain an explosive charge. We see through our glasses cavalry horses being exercised at Rottingdean. We hear that Wireless is there!! Will he ever win a race? Who knows?

8.15.—We are shelling Brighton, and the super-Dreadnought *Skylark* is throwing bricks at us. At last this is war!

8.50.—We have silenced Fort Royal York, where the English Cabinet Minister Preston lives.

8.55.—News has come that the police have been sent for. We are leaving—what a day!

9.0.—The greatest vessel of the English Fleet, *The Brighton Queen*, attacked us, but we escaped in the fog.'

"Sometimes it's one fortified place, an' sometimes it's another. Sometimes the German Fleet go scourin' the Kiel Canal looking for the English fleet, but the cowardly British are never there.

"An' every time the admiral goes out to look for the English an' don't find 'em, he gets an Iron Cross. It's worth it.

"'Once more you've saved the Fleet,' telegraphs the *Kaiser*. 'How can me an' God thank you! Am sendin' you (pay on delivery) a packet of Iron Crosses. Please give them to any of my gallant sailors who can find the missin' words in the following poem written by me:

The German Fleet the British knocks,
But when we meet he'll give us——

The Naval Correspondent of the *Berliner Catbag* writes:

At the end of four months' our Gran' Fleet is intact. Nothin' has happened to it. Let this be a lesson to every brave German. Spend your holidays at home, like our Navy does, an' keep the money in the country.

"There's one thing certain about the German Navy," concluded Smithy, "we shall never be able to give 'em as good a hidin' as they're givin' theirselves."

★★★★★★

"Nothin' depresses the German Navy worse than sinkin' a battle-cruiser an' a couple of Dreadnoughts.

"It doesn't depress Berlin, because Berlin don't know nothin' about the nerve strain of huntin' the British from the sea.

"'What's this?' sez the *Kaiser* to Von Tirkfitz, the celebrated man with the celebrated whiskers; 'what's this strange-lookin' biscuit tin with the dents?'

"'That, your Serene Godliness,' sez von Tirkfitz, 'is your cruiser-magnificent, *Dirtflinger.*'

"'I thought you said it wasn't damaged?' sez the *Kaiser.*

"'Not seriously damaged,' sez the admiral; 'we never reckon that a ship is seriously damaged so long as it floats.'

"'Praise be to *Allah!*' sez the *Kaiser;* 'an' what is that strange-lookin' article in dry dock?'

"'That, your Worshipful Highness,' sez the sdmiral, 'is our ever-grand and beautiful *Sedlitz,* what sank the *Lion, Tiger, Panther, Leopard,* an' *Pussy Cat.*'

"'*Bishmallah!*' sez the *Kaiser;* 'gather together as many of the crew as you've left, an' I'll say a few tender words of greetin'. After that, I'd like to have a few words with the head of the Frightfulness Department.'

"The conference is held behind closed doors. Sentries are posted at all the entrances, an' refreshments are passed through the winder at intervals.

"At the end of that time the new order is posted. It sez:

We warn all peaceful ships not to approach England durin' the next five years. We won't tell you what we're goin' to do, but it's goin' to be something awful!

"'That ought to do it,' sez the *Kaiser,* 'but we'll make things sure,' an' he issues another:

We warn the French Army not to support the British on or about February 10. We can't say what we're goin' to do, but you can reckon on somethin' very dirty.'

"'Somethin' ought to be done about Russia,' sez von Falkenbug; 'von Hinkybug is gettin' very wild with the way he hasn't been supported.'

"'I'll soon settle that,' sez the *Kaiser,* an' issues a real terror.

This is to give notice to the Russian Army that any attempt to advance along the Vistula will be met by very serious measures. We're doin' a certain thing in Poland that will spread terror and consternation throughout the world. Anybody who don't believe this will feel sick when it happens. Don't act the goat: be warned in time. This is for your own good.—

(Signed)   Wilhelm II.

P.S.—Don't say I didn't warn you.

"'An',' sez the *Kaiser*, 'it that don't upset the Gran' Duke Nicholas, I'm a square-headed Dutchman.'

"An' now the whole world sits down to watch the new way of makin' war take shape. All the neutral countries an' Roumania, all the b'ligerent countries an' Italy, all the pro-German countries, if any, sit with bated breath.

"The British Fleet goes over an' under the North Sea, the Russian Army goes in an' out the German trenches, the French Army goes up an' down the Vosgis, an' every minute we are expectin' to hear the worst. Will it happen?

"Opinion is divided. Some say yes, an' some say no. What will it be? Some think it will be a submarine Zeppelin, others say it may be a Flyin' Dreadnought with green funnels. Will it explode? Who knows?

"Things don't go as fast as the *Kaiser* would like. He calls another meetin' of the Frightfulness Lodge. The minutes of the last meetin' are read an' confirmed. Brother Wilhelm, Chief Fright (in the chair), moves a vote of confidence in the Chairman. Carried. Brother Wilhelm, junior (Vice-Fright), moves an address of welcome to the Hero of I.ongwys. Carried. Brother Hinkybug (Worshipful Bogey) moves a vote of thanks to the Conqueror of Warsaw. Carried. The Hymn of Hate is now sung by the lodge upstanding.

"It is proposed an' seconded that Scarborough shall in future be marked 'Fort Scarborough' on all German maps. Carried.

"'Worthy brethren,' sez the Chief Fright, 'I propose that we issue a new proclamation: the Secretary will now read same.'

"Brother Bestman-Golliwog (Frightful Scribe and Keeper of the Golden Lyre) reads:

The German nation gives notice that in future it will ignore the British Navy, an' will land 10,000,000 on the coast of Yorkshire. Any attempt on the part of the English railway companies to refuse to carry the army to London will be frightfully resented. Any attempt on the part of the British Navy to hamper our transports will be dealt with accordin' to law. This is our last warnin'. We don't want any more trouble; a nod's as good as a wink.   —Wilhelm.'

"I hear from time to time," said Smithy, "that our navy prevents Germans gettin' contraband. Copper's contraband because you make shells with it. Coal's contraband, an' lead's contraband. But I'm lookin' forward to the day when the government makes ink contraband—that'll finish the war."

13.—ON W.O. GENIUS

"There's no doubt," said Smithy thoughtfully, "that somewhere in the War Office there is what I might term the grandest mind that was ever heard tell about. It ain't an ordinary mind—it's just one big idea, an' the main idea is to help recruitin'.

"I don't know who the feller is so I'll call him Henry. He may be a gen'ral, he may be a colonel, he may be anything in the world, but I'll stake me boots an' cholera belt on his not bein' a private.

"Henry thinks of nothin' else, mornin', noon and night, but ideas for raisin' recruits.

"Often and often he puts his shirt on inside out, goes down the office in his bedsocks, owin' to his mind bein' too full of recruitin' to trouble about dressin' hisself properly.

"One day he has one idea, another day he has two. Sometimes he wakes up in the middle of the night, an' jumpin' out of bed writes furiously till daybreak. At other times he sleeps.

"He comes down to the Grand Military Recruitin' Room one day lookin' radiant an' happy.

"'I got a grand idea as I was washin' my neck,' he sez; 'let's put all the lights out an' shut all the pubs.'

"So they done it, but recruits didn't come any faster, owin' to their bein' required at home to sweep up the bits of Zeppelins that was expected to fall in the garden. So he blamed McKenna.

"Another day he came down to the office dancin' with joy.

"'What's the height standard for the infantry?' he sez.

"'Five-foot-four,' sez one of the experts.

"'Let's make it five-foot-six,' he sez, 'to encourage the people to grow.' That didn't bring 'em in so he blamed McKenna again.

"Then he discovered that pals who enlisted was allowed to serve together in the same regiment.

"'Stop that,' he sez, 'it keeps fellers out of the army who haven't got any friends.'

"Somehow that didn't increase the number of recruits.

"'McKenna again!' sez the public; 'dam' that feller, why doesn't he leave the army alone?'

"But what put the flagstaff on all Henry's ideas was the one he picked up when he was dinin' with Lady X——.

"Henry called the War Office Staff together in the middle of the night.

"'I've got a new one,' he sez, tremblin' with pride; 'let's put the soldiers' wives under police supervision. It will give the men confidence,' he sez, 'to know that their wives are bein' looked after. It will make our gallant fellers in the trenches fight better, it will bring recruits by the million.'

"The War Office knows a lot," said Smithy; "it knows that sentiment is nothin'. Fellers stand up in the House of Commons an' say 'K.' ain't got any sentiment at all (laughter).

"Sentiment is a rum thing; scraps of paper are sentiment, patriotism is sentiment; the feelin' that makes one regiment hold a line of trenches an' another give way is sentiment; sentiment is holdin' on to Ypres until hell freezes.

"Men aren't fightin' for one-an'-two a day—they're not chuckin' their lives away for a five-bob medal—they aren't sufferin' for anything that you can put on a cheque.

"If you cut out sentiment from soldierin' you're cuttin' out somethin' that contractors can't supply an' Woolwich Arsenal can't make.

"They ought to get rid of Henry an' give his sleepin' accommodation to a feller who has a Union Jack over his bed an' can't go to sleep till he has heard 'Rule Britannia' on the gramophone.

"He ought to have the wall of his room covered with pictures, pictures of them sentimental soldiers goin' down on the *Birkenhead*, pictures of sentimental Highlanders throwin' back the Russian cavalry at Balaklava, pictures of sentimental Captain Oates goin' out to die in the blizzard.

"Any fool can laugh at sentiment—you find civilians who laugh at God.

"The general who doesn't know the value of sentiment has had his military education neglected.

"My own view of the situation," said Smithy, "can be put in a few words. A civilian named Tennant said that 'K.' hadn't any sentiment. That's not true. 'K.' is a sentimentalist, and Tennant is a liar.

"As for Henry, with his grand ideas for gettin' recruits, I'd settle him in two jiffs.

"I'd hang him—for the duration of the war only."

14.—On Recruiting

"There was a feller of ours named Hokey, who had a brother—he's got him still, because Hokey's brother is one of those fellers who are pretty difficult to lose.

"When the war broke out young Hokey was a sailor on a P.O. boat, but naturally bein' a true-born Briton he told the head steward—that being the sailor department young Hokey was in—that as soon as he got to England he was goin' to enlist.

"'My country wants energetic an' fearless men,' sez young Hokey, 'an' I'll see that she gets me. Me for the cavalry—for if there's one thing I like more than another it's a good nag. I've got military blood in me veins, sir,' he says.

"'Go and put some naval blackin' on my boots,' sez the chief steward.

"When young Hokey got to England, he made up his mind to have a few days' rest, an' went to stay with a married sister—his sister, not anybody else's sister—down Deptford way.

"'I'm goin' to war,' he sez, 'it's me duty an', so to speak, me pleasure.'

"'Good for you, Horace,' sez his sister, an' when some of the neighbours came in to get Horace's opinion on the war, she told 'em.

"'He's going to enlist,' she sez, 'an' he's come all the way from abroad to do it.'

"'It's me military spirit,' sez young Hokey modestly.

"The mornin' after he'd arrived in England he went up to Town, an' the first thing he saw was a big poster which said:

RECRUITS WANTED AT ONCE.
FOR THE DURATION OF THE WAR ONLY.

"'That's me,' sez young Hokey, very pleased.

"On the back of his tram ticket was the words 'England needs you,' and young Hokey smiled. 'That's me too,' he sez.

"At Charin' Cross was a great big poster that said '100,000 men wanted at once—don't shirk.'

"'Who's shirkin'?' sez young Hokey, indignant.

"All that day wherever he went he was met by big pictures an' big placards callin' on him to 'Be a Man.' He saw it in the tube lift, an' he saw it on the newspaper placards. He couldn't turn his head without meetin' a picture of Lord Kitchener with the words, 'It's YOU I want!'

"When he got down into the bowels of the earth an' took his seat in a tube train there was another notice starin' him in the face.

WILLIN' MEN ARE HAPPY FIGHTERS.
DON'T WAIT TILL THE TRENCHES ARE DRY,
ENLIST NOW AND GET PATRIOTIC CHILBLAINS.

"'Oh, hell!' sez young Hokey, an' went home out of spirits.

"The next day he nipped down to Brighton. Walkin' along the front he met a *beau-chus* young girl who was wearin' a hundred pounds' worth of furs round her neck, an' was knitting a fourpenny ha'penny pair of mitts for the heroes of old England.

"'Excuse me,' she sez, lookin' him straight in the eye, 'England wants you.'

"'I dare say,' sez young Hokey.

"'Don't shirk,' sez the young lady.

"Young Hokey glares at her an' goes on.

"He came back to London, and went into a music-hall. The first turn was a lady who knelt on the stage an' stretched out her arms to young Hokey.

"'I don't want to lose you,' she sings, 'an' I think you ought to go, your king an' your country—bo-oth need you so. . .'

"Young Hokey went out an' tried another music-hall. He was happy whilst a chap was jugglin' cannon balls, but the next turn was a lady in short frocks who sang—

I don't want to lose you
But I think. . .

"Young Hokey went home.

"On his way to Deptford a fat old chap sittin' opposite in the railway carriage leans over an' sez:

"'Excuse me, sir—don't you think you ought to be with your friends in the trenches?'

"'I ain't got any friends in the trenches,' growls young Hokey.

"'We want every man in this war,' sez the old gent.

"'I ain't every man,' sez young Hokey.

"'Don't you love your country?' sez the old chap sternly.

"'No,' sez Hokey.

"'He's a German!' sez the old chap; 'I suspected it all along.'

"'That puts the lid on it,' sez young Hokey, an' the next mornin' before anybody was up he packs his traps an' goes down to the docks.

"'Hullo,' sez the chief steward, 'what do you want?'

"'I want to sign on for the next voyage,' sez young Hokey.

"'But I thought you was goin' to enlist?' sez the chief steward.

"'So I was,' sez young Hokey.

"'I thought you was going into the cavalry,' sez the chief steward. 'You told me you was lookin' forward to a nag.'

"'I was, sir,' sez young Hokey, 'but not the kind of nag I've been having lately.'"

15.—The Strategist

"We are confronted with a serious situation," Private Smith hastened to inform me when I entered the ward which has the honour of housing him till his toe heals. "The great heart of England is throbbing like mad, and there is doubt in every mind, suspicion in every brain.

"Are we doing as well as can be expected? Is the navy still knocking about? What's wrong with our strategy?

"England is goin' to be invaded. 'It's a perfec'ly absurd idea,' writes *The Times* military correspondent, 'but what am I to do? My plan for the German is this: come out an' fight the British Navy, an' whilst everybody's lookin' that way, send a quarter of million Germans across the sea an' land 'em somewhere. The best way of gettin' 'em to England is by ships. The duty of Englishmen is clear. Seize the nearest uniform an' get into it. Policemen's uniforms are easiest to seize. Havin' done this, all is plain sailin', for, as dear old Claude Snitch sez, do your best, if you can't do anything better.

"'In the meantime, the initiative is passin' from the War Office. The campaign is now in the hands of Winston Churchill an' the *Morning Post*. Why did Antwerp fall? Some people think it was because of the Germans, but the whole hijeous situation is now revealed. It was Winston. By sendin' ten thousand sailors to Antwerp he let it fall. Will France fall? It is a serious thought. It is an open secret that there is a British army there. Let us find out the feller that sent it an' replace him. If there is another reason for Antwerp fallin', it is because there was a Belgian army there too. Who was responsible for this? We seriously warn our readers that the conduct of the war is now in the hands of amateurs—*there isn't a single newspaper expert on the War Office staff!*'

"By the time I read the newspapers through," said Smithy, "an' have found the little paragraphs that all the big headlines are about, by the time I've read what the wounded soldier told the policeman an' what the policeman said to the reporter, I begin to rattle meself to death.

"We've got a strategist in our regiment called Gooley. Henry Arthur Hector Goole his proper name, an' if he hadn't been born in what I might term humble or Deptford circumstances, he'd have made a good general—cook-general.

"After the battle of Mons, when we was edgin' away from Mauberje, Gooley, me an' Nobby was in the same set of fours.

"'What I should have done if I'd been French,' says Gooley, 'is to strike straight into Germany, cut the communication cords, get round the rear of the enemy, an' then where would the *Kaiser* be?'

"'Ah!' sez Nobby, 'that's the question.'

"'What I should have done,' sez Gooley, 'would have been to send the Anchesters to make a flank attack on the left. I should then have sent the Belgian. . .' an' so on.

"'Where would the *Kaiser* be then?' sez Gooley again.

"So Nobby told him.

"'Never havin' a vulgar mind,' sez Gooley, 'I won't foller your argument. Take this place, for instance——'an' he waved his hand round the country.

"It was pretty to watch—especially the Wigshires bein' shelled as they moved along the slope of a hill. Never seen the 1st Wigshires movin' quick, have you? Well, if you'd seen 'em that day you'd have thought they was riflemen.

"'My idea,' sez Gooley, 'is this: we oughtn't to be retirin' at all. What we ought to do is to take up a position on that hill where the wood is, dig ourselves in, an' turn old von Gluck's left——'

"He'd hardly got the words out o' his mouth when the adjutant came gallopin' along the line.

"He stopped by the colonel, an' we, bein' in the leadin' fours, heard him.

"'Will you take your men to that hill on the right and cover the retirement of the 1st Division?' he sez.

"A minute later we had left the road an' was movin' on the hill. We got there at two o'clock, and at 2.1 the German guns got to hear about it. From 2 to 5 they shelled us, droppin' about 350 a minute.

"There we lay, crouched up close to the ground, firin' as an' when we could, but spendin' most of the time wonderin' if the family would go into mournin'.

"In the height o' the firing, Nobby crawled up to Gooley's side an' landed him a horrid kick.

"'Hullo, strategist,' hissed Nobby, 'how do you like it?'

"Poor old Gooley looked round, an' for a bit hadn't a word to say.

"'It's my mistake,' he sez; 'this ain't strategy, it's tactics.'

"And," concluded Smithy, "there's lots of newspaper fellers that's making the same mistake. Strategy is good, an' tactics is good, but using military strategy for party tactics is rotten."

★★★★★★

"Bein' a strategist ain't like bein' a poet—you have to be born to be a poet, you've got to be dead before you're a good strategist.

"Mokey was a good strategist, so was Napoleon, so was Wellin'ton—they're all passed to what Nobby calls the Great Behind. The *Kaiser's* a rotten strategist—he's alive. I'm hopin' the crown prince'll be a great strategist too, soon, but all the reports from the seat of war show that he's in good health.

"There are ten ways of winnin' battles. Nine of 'em is to have half as many troops again as the enemy, an' the other way is to have twice as many.

"Nowadays strategy don't count for much. Suppose the *Kaiser* was attackin' the British.

"'How many men have we got?' he sez.

"'Almighty Goodness,' sez his head general, 'we've got about half a million more than the enemy.'

"'Then I'll have to try some of my strategy,' sez the *Kaiser*.

"'Hold hard, your Imperial Hunship,' sez the head general. 'I'll wire for reinforcements.'

"If you was to have a competition in the German Army to find out what was the most popular thing in the world the figgers would be:

Sudden Death	9,753
Typhoid Fever	6,347
The British Navy	2
The *Kaiser's* Strategy	1

"That's, of course, if the *Kaiser* had a vote.

"I'm not sayin' that there's no strategy in Germany. There must be a lot. They got it through neutral countries, an' it was labelled 'cotton.' The only kind of strategy that's worth anything is bought by the ton in America an' shipped through Holland.

"There's another kind, as any one who reads the latest reports from

313

the front knows.

"A council of war is called, an' the *Kaiser* comes, lookin' pale an' haggard, wearing a mystic infectuous smile. His hair is white, an' he arrives chantin' a battle hymn.

"The crown prince comes in, his pockets bulgin' with strategy that he's picked up in the French chat-oos.

"The Kaiser takes his seat.

"'Where's the Sluis correspondent of the *Tyd*?' he sez.

"'Under the table, your Supreme Royalty,' sez General von Kluck.

"'Let the proceeding start,' sez the *Kaiser*. 'I have called you here to get your advice on the strategy of the war. I think we ought to crush the English an' annihilate the Russian. We will attack Warsaw an' Ypres, an' after that cross the English Channel an' sack London. I shall be glad to know what you think of my idea. Don't let anybody speak or there'll be trouble. I am German Mike, an' me word is law.— Anybody any questions to ask?—Carried unanimously. The meetin' is adjourned, an' me son Willie will now entertain you with a selection on his loot. Boy, bring me a Villa-Villa.'

"Sometimes the *Kaiser* gets a bigger idea than at other times. Take Scarborough, for instance.

"'There's a fortified fortress with forts called Scarborough,' he sez; 'it's heavily entrenched, an' is believed to be the headquarters of them ferocious boy scouts I've heard about.'

"'Go forth, Henry, *mein brutter*, an' reduce it to rags,' he sez, 'like my nerves,' he sez.

"'Is that good strategy, Holy Relation?' sez Henry.

"'It's safe,' sez the *Kaiser*.

"'But,' sez Henry, 'suppose one of them Dreadnoughts come up an' biff me?'

"'They wouldn't do anything so inhuman,' sez the *Kaiser*, 'but if they did I'd report the matter to me friend President Wilson, because,' he sez, 'if you an' your gallant comrades was sunk, America would lose good customers, an' if they lost good customers there would be a trade depression in America an' me friend Wilson would send one of his famous notes.'

"Strategy," Smithy went on, "is the art of deceivin' your enemy into believin' that he's deceivin' you. German strategy is the art of deceivin' yourself,

"The progress of Gen'ral von Hinkybug showed you what good strategy is. Hinkybug is a grand strategist. One of the first things he did when he was made a gen'ral was to get a telephone wire laid on to the *Kaiser.*

"'Give me Almighty No. 1 Potsdam,' sez Hinkybug. 'Is that your Serene Holiness? It is? I'm salutin' you—you can't see it, but it's true. The photographic correspondent of the *Damberg Tagblud* is takin' me picture. I just wanted to say that I am victorious all along the line. I thought you'd like to know—yes, all along the line. I could get a third-class ticket to Warsaw for a pfennig, only the trains ain't runnin'. Good *morgans, komrade! Hoch!*'

"The next day he rings him up again.

"'Is that you, Angel Face? It is; I beg to report that I am victorious all along the line. I've took Oomstockovo, Doomstockovo, and Pzmerz.'

"'Good for you, Hinky,' sez the *Kaiser,* 'cut yourself an Iron Cross.'

"'I've got one, your Magnificent Splendour,' sez von Hinkybug. 'Could I have a set of trousers stretchers?'

"'Yes,' sez the *Kaiser,* 'gold ones. *Hoch!*'

"'*Hoch!*' sez Hinkybug.

"Two days later von Hinkybug gets on to Almighty No. 1 and the *Kaiser's* voice answers him.

"'I'm victorious all along the line, your War Lordship,' he sez, 'everybody is in retreat—includin' the Austrians,' he sez.

"'Fine,' sez the *Kaiser,* 'what a strategist is lost in you, Hinkybug!'

"When he rings off the *Kaiser* calls up the exchange.

"'If that feller Hinkybug calls me up tomorrer,' he sez, 'tell him I'm spending New Year's Day in a Zeppelin,' an' to make sure he sends out a troop of *Uhlans* to cut all the telephone wires.'

"This war will be won by strategy," concluded Smithy, "the strategy of the Gen'ral Staff hidin' the fac's from Berlin an' the strategy of Berlin hangin' the Gen'ral Staff; but what's goin' to finish the business quicker than anything else is sendin' 500,000 of Kitchener's strategists to France in the spring armed with strategic rifles an' bayonets, an' strategi-in' theirselves all over the *Kaiser's* army."

16.—SMITHY SURVEYS THE LAND

Removed, as he is, for the moment from the immensely fascinating business of war, Private Smithy, who is, before all other things, a philosopher, devotes his attention nowadays to study of mankind in its relations to patriotism.

"Never," said Smithy, nursing his wounded foot and speaking with

315

that heavy enthusiasm which veils so many sentiments, "never in me life have I seen such patriotism as there is over this war.

"In Parliament Patriot Asquith shakes han's with Patriot Balfour, an' Patriot Bonar Law shakes han's with Patriot Lloyd George—who ain't been called a thief for so long that he'll forget what it feels like. An' Patriot Christabel Pankhurst shakes han's with the stomach-pump an' ties a Union Jack round the forcible feeder.

"Everywhere everybody's doin' their best for the dear ole Empire on the understandin' that the dear ole Empire will do its whack when the time comes round.

'I'm sixty-two,' writes one patriot to his favourite tuppenny paper, 'an' I'm as young now as ever I'm likely to be,' he sez. 'Can't some use be made of me? I can run, jump, swim, weed gardens, play hop-scotch, an' the organ. I have offered myself as a general, and yet,' he sez, 'nobody leaps at me: an' they talk about the shortage of officers!'

"Patriot young ladies are sellin' patriotic flags for patriotic objects. Patriot cabmen are defendin' the empire by flyin' the flags of all nations an' askin' their fares to join the army.

'I have given up eatin' German sausage,' writes Trueheart of Putney. 'Can't somethin' be done to stop German yeast risin' in our very midst?'

"All over the shop the same feelin' prevails: people are urgin' each other to enlist; young ladies who usually spend their lives stickin' feathers in their hats are now stickin' feathers in other people's coats. An' our wounded soldiers (God bless 'em!) we can't do enough for 'em! We're givin' 'em dressing jackets, hair-combs, hatpins, trousers stretchers, an' other medical comforts.

"Day by day the columns of the Press are filled with the narratives of our heroic defenders.

"Private Spud Murphy writes:

It was like hell in the trenches, an' when the shrapnel burst it was like hell, an' when it didn't burst it was like hell. Everything was hell, includin' the bully-beef.

"Corporal juggy Jones writes:

Nothing has reminded me so much of hell as that day before Paris.

316

"All the space that ain't devoted to hell is taken up with the pre-dictions of the military experts.

'The Germans,' writes Captain X, the military critic of the *Drapers' Herald*, 'now occupy the line Hier-Thair. Will they be pushed off? It is a great day for England. My idea is that if a million Russians could be landed on the line Hyer-Huppe or the line Loer-Doun, or the railway line, or even on a clothesline, the enemy would be awfully surprised. O if the country had only listened to my warnin' in 1904! O if they'd only read my book, *England and the War after Next* (a few copies of which may still be obtained by mentionin' my name and six shillin's in the same breath), we should have had a great army now! Thanks to my book, *Dreadnaughts or Draughts*, we *have* got a navy.'

"I am amazed," said Smithy soberly, "at the sacrifices the civilian population are makin'. They have even sacrificed all chance o' the soldier gettin' drunk after eleven.

"Everybody is doin' somethin' for the cause. Theatrical managers are keepin' their theatres open to employ the poor actors; the actors are workin' on half salaries for the benefit of the poor managers, lots o' businesses that have made a steady loss for the last ten years are givin' half their profits to the prince's fund. An' the women!—ah, the women are splendid!

"Girls are neglecting the house work to volunteer as Red Cross nurses: they have felt the call of England, and obeyed. They've got the uniform an' a pair of scissors, an' now all they want is a few patients to practise on. England, my England!

"The song writers are workin' overtime. There's one young fel-ler that's sounded the clarion note—it strikes a thrill through every heart.

What will I say, sonny; what will I say
When they ask "Did you carry a gun?
Did you march with the band to the arrogant land
And harass the horrible Hun?"
What can I say, sonny; what can I say?
I shall answer with pride, my dear chap,
I'm a poet all right, but poets don't fight—
They urge on the others to scrap.

"Every day *The Times* is filled with poetry. You know that it's poetry because the lines all begin with capital letters. It's poetry, though. It makes you choke—an' spit. Never in the history of the world was there such poetry; it may be many years before there is anything like it—with luck.

"An' we're goin' to capture German trade. Everybody's excited about it. There was a feller in here the other day—the sister will remember his name; he had whiskers—who could talk of nothin' else.

"'We're goin' to get the whole of the German commerce,' he sez, very enthusiastic. 'Take textiles,' he sez.

"'I'm takin' magnesia,' I sez.

"'I mean take textiles,' he sez, rapid. 'We imported or exported (I forget which) ninety millions—think o' that! What we've got to do,' he sez, 'is to smash the German Fleet, hang the *Kaiser*, get the trade, an' leave everything else to luck.'

"England," Smithy went on impressively, "never stood so firm. She's on the Right Side; the authors, after due consideration an' much heart-searchin', have written to say so. Them that haven't written wasn't asked. When the troops see that letter they'll go mad with joy. When the Wigshires, an' Anchesters, an' the Bloodshires learn that Mr. Jarvis, tire celebrated author of *Her Soulmate; or, Parted by a Cruel Stepmother*, has given his consent to the war, they won't be able to fight for laughin'. Everybody who is anybody has done somethin' for England. There ain't a patriot from Highgate to Norwood who hasn't sent at least two letters to the paper.

"Robert Scratchford, the celebrated Socialist, is writin' a page every week. What does he say?

The British boys are wonderful, they are unique, they are brilliant. They are in France, fighting; they are marchin', they are singin', perhaps they are dancin'. I went down to Aldershot last week. I was goin' by the 10.40, but I missed the train; I caught the 1.15. It was a nice railway carriage. I came back by the 5.40 and a soldier got in. He said that he'd been turned out of another railway carriage because they wouldn't let him smoke. The cowards! They wouldn't let him smoke in a non-smoker. "It was like hell—Mons," said the soldier, with a far-away look, in which horror, rage, hope, hunger, benevolence, an' pain struggled for supremacy, "an' they wouldn't let me smoke in a non- smoker. . . after Mons!

No, reader, I am not inventin' this story. Every bit is true, includin' the dots between the words.

Smithy lit a deplorable cigarette with tender care and breathed smoke through his nostrils.

"Out there"—he jerked his head France-ward, "we've got our troubles the same as Germany. There's a *Kaiser* in every regiment, I should say; anyway, there was one in the Anchesters. Slob his name is—Slob Jones, of B Company. That feller is (or was) one of the most celebrated speech-makers in the army.

"At cricket dinners, A.T.A., (Army Temperance Association), meetin's, Christmas Days, an' canteen *soirees* Slob would up an' speak his mind.

"He used to make speeches to recruits about their country, an' they used to make speeches to him about his face. He'd address meetin's in the back-field, on the ranges, on the line o' march, an' it was always about the dear ole land.

"Suppose a fatigue party was told off to weed the colonel's garden.

"'Go forth,' sez Slob, 'go forth an' fructify the earth; let one blade of grass show where two grew before. Show no mercy to the slugs; make your name as terrible to the worms as the name of Arthur Zerksees was to Arry Stottles.'

"A rare feller he was for diggin' up old-fashioned names, an' the way he used to talk about Juleus Cæsar ought to have made that celebrated officer turn in the grave.

"When we got to France, Slob was in his element. He used to address all the villages we stopped at.

"'Friends,' he sez, 'I bring you good tidin's,' he sez. 'The day has dawned an' the night has passed, an' the afternoon is comin', and so is tomorrow mornin'. Devote your attention to General French's contemptible little army, beginnin' on me,' he sez. 'I'm open to any attention that looks or smells like food,' he sez.

"Poor ole Slob!" reflected Smithy, shaking his head sadly. "He went out one afternoon on outpost duty and met a party of *Uhlans*. A chap of the 19th Hussars brought the news.

"'One of your chaps has been pinched,' he sez.

"'Who by?' sez Nobby Clark.

"'By the *Uhlans*,' sez the Hussar chap. 'I was lyin' doggo behind a hedge an' I see 'em go by. He was talkin' to them *Uhlans* somethin' awful about culture an' the sacred rights of man, an' they was listenin', sort of awestruck.'

"'That's bad,' sez Nobby, 'for Germany,' he sez. 'The *Kaiser's* bad enough an' Slob's bad enough, but with the *Kaiser* an' Slob in the same country Germany *will* be a rotten hole—it will be like hell,' he sez."

17.—Lieutenant X

"All the news from the front is favourable," said Private Smith, after a pause; "but I'm not so sure that it wouldn't be more favourable if the despatches was in the hands of a chap o' 'B' Company named Morses.

"Herbert Morses his name is, or was, an' next to Nobby Clark one of the finest despatch writers that ever drew the breath of life.

"Nobody ever knew what Morses did with his money; but that didn't worry 'em so much as tryin' to discover what he did with theirs.

"Morses was a great chap for borrowin' money. Sometimes he wanted it to send home to the old folks, sometimes he wanted to do a pal a turn, an' sometimes it was to save a soldier's widder from bein' turned out o' house and home by a cruel lan'lady.

"But one thing you could gamble on, he never wanted the money for himself, an' when chaps went to him for their bit o' stuff he was always mysterious an' dreamy.

"'I can't talk to you about it here,' he sez, 'not in public—I'll write to you.'

"'What's the good o' writin' to me when I'm sleepin' in the bed next to you?' sez the chap he owed it to, indignant. 'Four an' a tanner I let you have to save an ole pensioner from starvation.'

"'I'll write to you,' sez Morses; 'we'd better have it down in black an' white.'

"An' them letters o' his was wonderful. I lent him half-a-bar once, an' got literature to last me a month. It was all about the weather an' the state of England's Navy, an' the horrible economic condition of the East End, but nothin' about money.

"To read Morses' letter you'd have thought that there wasn't such things in the world as four half-crowns.

"Just about this time Nobby Clark was batman to a young officer of ours, whose name has been suppressed by the Press Bureau, an' whom I will call or term Lieutenant X.

"A nice young feller was Exy, full of life an' a desire for change—small change. Ten letters by every post, an' all that hadn't a ha'penny stamp on 'em was registered with the solicitor's name on the flap.

"One mornin', goin' through his correspondence, he sort of sat back an' groaned.

"'Clark,' he sez, 'I'm done for.'

"'Yes, sir,' sez Nobby, knowin' nothin' about it.

"'I'm done,' sez Lieutenant X., 'if I can't stave off this dam creditor I'm—my name is mud.'

"Nobby thought a bit.

"'Why not lure him down here an' get some of our chaps to set about him, sir?' sez Nobby; but Lieutenant X. shook his head.

"'It can't be done,' he sez, 'it's me uncle in the War Office.'

"It appears that Lieutenant X., in a lighthearted moment, had drawn a hundred from his rich uncle till Monday. He didn't say what Monday, but after about a hundred Mondays had come an' gone General G (that was his uncle) began to get worried an' sent Lieutenant X. a calendar with

Sunday's child is full of grace,
Monday's child has lost his place,

on it.

"And he follered this up with an insulting letter.

"'I've got to do somethin', Clark,' groans Lieutenant X. 'My uncle bein' at the War Office can hand me one.'

"'Write to him, sir,' sez Nobby.

"'What can I write?' sez Lieutenant X.

"'I'll think it out, sir,' sez Nobby.

"One day Nobby comes to me.

"'Smithy,' he sez, 'I've just lent Mossy two bob.'

"'Are you ill?' I sez.

"'Not critically,' sez Nobby, 'but the patriotic feller wants to subscribe to the Navy League an' I hadn't the heart to refuse him.'

"The very next day Nobby wrote to Mossy an' asked for his money back. It was a funny thing for him to do, for his way of collectin' debts is to get the feller alone an' chew his ear off.

"Morses wrote back thankin' Nobby for bein' such a gentleman as to write, an' tellin' him the latest news from Newmarket.

"Nobby wrote again next day, an' that same afternoon had eight pages about how the little birds fly home to their southern clime when the leaves begin to fall.

"He wrote reg'lar every day—sometimes it was all about drink an' the evils of bettin', an' sometimes it was about Home Rule—but it was never about the two bob he owed Nobby.

"An' every letter he wrote Nobby took to Lieutenant X., who done it up into proper English an' sent it off to his uncle at the War Office.

"One day Lieutenant X. was very happy.

"'Pack my kit, Clark,' he sez, 'I'm off to the War Office.'

"'Beg pardon, sir,' sez Nobby, 'I hope the general's acted fair to you.'

"'Yes, Clark,' sez Lieutenant X., 'he's forgiven the loan an' appointed me to the staff. He sez a man who can write pages about every subject under the sun except the subject he's supposed to be writin' about, is wasted in a regiment.'

"I often wonder," added Smithy thoughtfully, "if Lieutenant X. is at the front."

18.—THE LETTER-WRITER

"How's them war correspondents going on?" inquired Private Smith. "Are they still 'somewhere in the North of France,' or have they left Boulogne? I'm only askin' because I thought I saw a letter of Nobby Clark's in the paper this mornin' signed 'Sister Agnes.'

"This is a soldiers' war all right. Soldier bus-drivers, soldier engine-drivers, soldier mud-larks, an' soldier war correspondents. Before I 'stopped one,' (*i.e.* stopping a bullet, wounded), on the Aisne I often used to regret I hadn't any relations to write home to, givin' full particulars of me heroic deeds an' the terrible way I was killin' Germans. It's grand to see the way Tiny White an' Spud Murphy an' other gallant fellers of 'B' Company have been slaughterin' the foe, an' only them that know the true fac's realises how much they've got to thank Nobby Clark who, so to speak, was the originator of the idea for the most interestin' feature in the newspapers.

"I don't say that Nobby Clark foresaw the day when the public would be fed up with such items as:

On the Lyser there was an artillery duel.
At Alas we have made progress.
In the Allgonne there is nothin' to report.

"But what Nobby did know was that war correspondents wouldn't be allowed.

"It was when we was in billets on the Marne that Nobby sez one night suddenly:

"'I wonder where Hector is tonight?'

"'Who's Hector?' sez Spud Murphy.

"'Hector,' sez Nobby very deliberate, 'is me young brother.'

"It happened that Sergeant Hasty, the orderly-room sergeant, was billeted with us in the handsome an' commodious barn we was supposed to sleep in.

"Sergeant Hasty is—or was—one of them sharp-faced fellers who do sums in their heads, an' can tell you the date of the Great Fire of London without so much as lookin' at an almanac.

"'Clark,' he sez, 'accordin' to my memory, an' havin' seen all your papers, you haven't got any relations except an uncle.'

"Nobby didn't turn a hair.

"'Hector,' he sez again, 'is me brother, sergeant, an' if I haven't mentioned it, it's because of me family pride. Hector's got two shops of his own. . . .'

"'What sort of shops?' sez Spud.

"'Boot shops,' sez Nobby, 'where you sell boots. Naturally enough, bein' a master man an' highly respected, he don't want the neighbours to know that he has a brother servin' as a common soldier.'

"'That's what I call a snob,' sez the sergeant.

"'That's what other people call him,' sez Nobby, 'only I prefer to call him a bootmaker.'

"Never havin' heard of Nobby's brother I was a bit surprised until Nobby told me that he thought of writin' a letter to him givin' full particulars about the retreat from Mons.

"'The only difficulty is that I don't know his address,' sez Nobby, 'but I'm goin' to get over that in a highly novel way. I'm sendin' the letter to the editor of the *Daily Tribune*.'

"That was a bit hot, because it's a court-martial crime to write to the papers, but Nobby had arranged to get over that.

"'I'm sendin' a letter to the editor,' he sez, an' showed it to me when I was doin' my bit of trench diggin'.

Dear Sir,—The following letter composed by me is written for my brother, Hector Clark, Esq. Not knowing his address, will you publish same and pay my brother for same when he calls, as same belongs to him, only I haven't got his address? My brother will say, "Please give me the money for my brother's letters," and you will pay the same over. P.S.—My brother will be dressed as a soldier the same as me.—Yours truly, N. Clark.

"'There's a good many "sames" in that letter,' I sez, 'an' who *is* your brother, Nobby?'

"'Me an' him are the same,' sez Nobby Clark.

"Nobby was very proud of his grand idea, an' talked to a lot of people about it. All the troops agreed it was fine, except Spud Murphy.

"'It looks to me like daylight robbery an' fraud,' he sez.

"'That's a natural way for you to look at things,' sez Nobby, 'but all honest people will call it "stratagem of war," as the poet says.'

"It was soon after this that letters began arrivin' for the troops— the first mail we had had since we had been in the country—an' a reg'lar epidemic of letter-writin' set in.

"You couldn't walk up the village street where we was billeted without twenty fellers sayin':

"'What's another word for "terrible"? I've used it six times an' it's gettin' monotonous.'

"Sometimes it was 'terrible' an' sometimes it was 'heroic' an' sometimes it was 'undaunted.' but gen'rally it was somethin' about theirselves they was writin'.

"It was about this time when Nobby Clark an' Spud Murphy fell out over a question of money. It appears that Nobby had bought a pair of boots from Spud an' had borrowed ten shillin's on the top of it. Nobby had sworn to pay it back before the regiment left England, an' when he didn't he explained (on the boat comin' across) that his rich uncle had sent him a note sayin' that the money would be forwarded. Naturally, after the letters came, Spud hung round Nobby a lot.

"'It's no good your worryin' me,' sez Nobby. 'Me dear uncle's letter not havin' arrived I can't do anythin' for you.'

"'I don't believe you mean payin' me,' sez Spud.

"'The things you don't believe,' sez Nobby, 'would stock a library.'

"'I suppose you was hopin' I'd "stop one," sneers Spud. 'That's the sort of man you are.'

"'Don't you see I'm busy?' sez Nobby sternly. 'What d'ye mean by wurryin' me when I'm writin' to me dear brother?'

"But Spud wasn't to be put off. There was a rumour that we was goin' to march into Paris, an' he wanted to buy a few things to send home. He got so persistent that Nobby told him all about the letters he was writin' to the *Daily Tribune*.

"'I'll make lashin's of money,' he sez, 'an' all you've got to do is to be patient.'

"That sort of put Spud in a better temper, an' he said he'd wait.

"Them letters of Nobby was certainly worth money. You've probably seen 'em in print. There was one which began:

Midnight approaches an' nought can be heard but the sound of a sentry scratchin' his head as he peers fiercely into the night with one hand, an' grasps his rifle firmly with the other, singin' a low melody between his clenched teeth as his sleepin' comrades moan in their sleep thinkin' of home.

"Letter followed letter in quick succession. Nobby's description of the takin' of Mons, an' his description of the fight at Landrecics, an' Nobby's grand bit about the takin' of the guns at Compiegne are pretty well famous.

Dear Hector, how can I describe the events of the past week? Words fail me. I cannot describe them. They are indescribable. I will now tell you what happened.

"'They're mountin' up,' sez Nobby. 'That's four letters I've sent an' I'll bet you they won't pay less than a pound each.'

"Nobby described things he'd seen, an' things he'd heard about, but the most popular letters was them that told of things that nobody had ever heard tell of. It was Nobby who described how him an' another feller was carried off by Zeppelins an' rescued in mid-air by a French aeroplane. It was Nobby who saved the regiment by blowin' up a bridge an' swimmin' across the river carryin' a German prisoner in his teeth,

"When I was sent home I used to buy the *Daily Tribune* an' read about Nobby's deeds till I was dizzy.

We have received another vivid letter from Private C of the —chester Regt. (sez the paper), an' we doubt if any of our readers will be able to peruse the followin' story of a British soldier's gallant an' successful attempt to spike a 16-inch German howitzer without feelin' violently ill.

"I used to get letters from Nobby. He told me that the papers was payin' two pound for each letter, an' that Spud Murphy was worryin' him for money, an' what he was goin' to do to Spud, an' similar gossip.

325

"Then one day—about a month ago—I got a letter from the Union Jack Club in the Waterloo Road, an' to my surprise it was from Nobby!

"He had come over with an officer of ours who was carryin' despatches, an' was goin' to be in London for three days. I went up to see him—I'd got my sick furlough, an' could walk about quite nicely with a stick.

"'Smithy,' he sez, 'we'll go round to the *Daily Tribune* office, an' draw my money—at least my brother's money,' he sez, an' then he asked me if I'd seen Spud.

"'Is he home?' I sez.

"'Yes,' sez Nobby, 'rheumatism in the leg,' he sez. 'At least that's what he sez it is.'

"Curiously enough we met a chap of ours in the Strand who'd just seen Spud.

"Which way did he go?' sez Nobby interested, and the chap pointed to the Charing Cross end of the Strand.

"'He is the one fellow I don't want to meet,' sez Nobby cheerful. 'We'll go the other.'

"'The fact is,' sez Nobby, 'I owe Spud two pound odd—I tossed him double or quits, an' he won, an' on a joyous day like this, with me treasury chest flowin' with milk an' money, it'd be little less than a disaster to meet anybody I owed two pound to.'

"'Why don't you pay him?' I sez.

"Nobby looks at me pityin'ly.

"'Gettin' wounded has turned your brain, Smithy,' sez he.

"At the office of the *Daily Tribune* everybody was very decent, an' we was taken up in the lift to one of the editors.

"'So you're Private Clark's other brother, are you?' he sez, an' handed over four pounds. 'There was eight due to you,' he sez, 'but your younger brother called an' collected half.'

"'My younger brother!' sez Nobby faintly.

"'Yes,' sez the editor chap. 'He told me you'd be callin' for the rest in a day or two—here's his receipt.'

"He pulled out a bit of paper.

Received with deep thanks, £4—

"An' it was signed—

Spud Murphy Clark.

"Nobby came out of the newspaper office in a sort of dream, clutchin' the money in his right hook.

"'Smithy,' he sez in a holler voice, 'which way did that chap say Spud Murphy went?'

"So I told him, an' he called a taxi.

"'Drive toward Charin' Cross,' he sez to the driver, 'an' stop at the first ironmonger's you come to—I want to buy an axe.'"

19.—THE WEATHER PROPHET

"If you were to ask me," said Smithy, "who's got the quickest brain in the Anchester Regiment, I'd up an' say 'Nobby Clark.' Not because he's a pal of mine, not because him an' me has soldiered together in all parts of the world from Paris to Paardeburg, but because I've sort of stood outside meself an' watched him.

"Lots of people who don't know Nobby think he's unscrupulous. Spud Murphy thinks so, but then he don't know Nobby properly. Tiny White thinks so, but that is only because Tiny an' him fell out over weather prophetin'. The truth about Nobby is that he's a born prophet.

"Tiny always had a hobby of foretellin' the weather. It's easier than tippin' horses, because, so to speak, the field is half-way home before you give your Gran' Twelve o'Clock Final for the Big Race.

"He used to sit at the table with a sheet of paper, a pen and ink, an' an Old Moore's Almanac, an' give predictions that was highly impressive.

"'There's a depression approachin' these isles,' he sez one day, 'an' a hanti-cyclone workin' up from the Azoreys—takin' one thing with another, there ought to be rain in the north-west of Scotland tomorrer.'

"'What about the south-east of Ireland?' sez Nobby.

"'Fog,' sez Tiny prompt. 'Fog an' local thunderstorms.'

"Tiny's predictions never dealt with anywhere nearer than the north of Scotland, so we hardly ever knew for certain if they had come off. He used to tell us they had, but there was nothin' about it in the papers.

"Naturally, we didn't expect to read startlin' headlines like 'Rain at Strathbrassie,' 'Great excitement in Scotland,' every time Tiny struck a winner.

"Occasionally he'd go farther out, an' once he predicted a terrible storm in the Atlantic.

327

"'I'm glad I'm not on the sea tonight,' he sez; 'what with that low pressure comin' up from the Azoreys an' the high pressure revolvin' westward from Ireland, they won't half have a time crossin' the Atlantic.'

"We spent two days an' a lot of money buyin' the evenin' an' mornin' papers to see if anything had happened to the mail-boats. The only bit of news we had was that the crossin' had been very smooth, an' that the *Carmania* had sighted a dead whale.

"'Killed by the storm,' sez Tiny very solemn, 'higher up towards Greenland an' Iceland an' the North Pole,' he sez.

"'Why don't you do a bit o' weather predictin' nearer home?' sez Nobby. 'What's the use of wastin' your talents on the North Pole? Nobody cares if it snows there.'

"But Tiny wouldn't give any predictions nearer home—not unless he were obliged. They tried to get him to deliver a word or two about the weather on the day we played the West Kents in the third round of the Army Cup, but he wouldn't give it till within an hour of the match bein' played, an' even then he was wrong.

"I don't think Nobby took much interest in weather predictin' because, as far as me an' Nobby could see, there was no money in it.

"Tiny went away to the reserve an' was called up for the war. He used to be a very decent chap before what I might term the contaminatin' influence of civilian life got at him. He came back to the army wearin' spats—an' nothin' gives away a feller worse than spats.

"'Oh, yes,' he sez, very languid, 'I'm dreadfully keen on meteorology.'

"'What's her name?' sez Nobby.

"'Meteorology,' sez Tiny, 'the science,' he sez, 'of studyin' the weather. An' it's goin' to pay me,' he sez.

"Nobby was interested at once.

"It appears that before the Expeditionary Army went out, the government started a weather department to accompany the army in the field. It sounds a rum idea, but there is a lot of sense in it.

"Nobby explained it to me afterwards.

"Suppose the general is makin' arrangements for a big battle. He sends for the weather expert.

"'What sort of weather are we goin' to have?' sez the general.

"'Strong westerly breezes, mong general,' sez the weather sergeant.

"'Good!' sez the general. 'Then we'll attack the enemy from the east—they won't smell us comin'.'

"Tiny said that a friend of his in the weather department at Victoria Street had told him all about it. The New Weather Corps was to tell the aeroplanes how long they could stay up.

"'I've put in me name,' sez Tiny, 'an' I dare say I shall be transferred in a day or two. The pay is six shillin's a day——'

"'Say no more, Tiny,' sez Nobby, speakin' with great emotion; 'me an' you will transfer together.'

"'What do you know about the weather?' sez Tiny, very amazed.

"'I've been out in all kinds of it,' sez Nobby.

"The next mornin' Nobby paraded before the adjutant.

"'You want to join the Weather Brigade?' sez the adjutant, puzzled. 'An' what the devil is the Weather Brigade?'

"So Nobby up an' told him.

"'I've never heard of it,' sez the adjutant; 'somebody has been pullin' your leg—besides, you know nothin' about the weather.'

"'Sir,' sez Nobby, 'there ain't anythin' about the weather that I don't know.'

"'What sort of an evenin' are we goin' to have?' sez the adjutant.

"'Variable breezes,' sez Nobby, 'with slight rain in places; fine later; cooler.'

"An' all that Nobby predicted was true," said Smithy in a hushed voice, "just as he said it, it came off.

"The next day the adjutant sees Nobby goin' across the square and calls him.

"'Your weather prediction was good,' he sez. 'What newspaper did you read it in?'

"'Paper, sir?' sez Nobby surprised. 'I didn't know they had weather predictions in newspapers.'

"'What is the weather going to be like today?' sez the adjutant.

"'Cloudy, with local showers,' sez Nobby, 'and cooler.'

"'*Daily Telegraph*,' sez the adjutant.

"Nobby saluted.

"'Beg pardon, sir,' he sez, 'the *Telegraph* sez "warmer."'

"'Go away, Private Clark,' sez the adjutant, 'before I forget meself.'

"Now the rum thing was that, instead of bein' 'warmer,' as the paper said, it *was* cooler, and that's where Nobby Clark's reputation as a weather expert started to grow.

"An' it increased after we got to France, because, havin' no newspapers to go on, an' being obliged, so to speak, to depend on his own wonderful powers, the troops could see there was no hanky-panky, an' that Nobby was the genuine weather expert of the 1st Anchesters.

"Tiny White was nothin' to Nobby. Tiny was wild as anythin', but he had to take a second place.

"'What's the weather goin' to be like?' he sneers one mornin'—it was the day we en-motor-'bussed for X——.

"'Fine with thunderstorms,' sez Nobby, 'an' warmer in the evenin'.'

"'You're wrong,' sez Tiny. 'We shall have rain, and it will be cooler.'

"'*Noos verongs*,' sez Nobby.

"'What's that mean?' sez Tiny.

"'It's a French weather expression,' sez Nobby.

"Tiny was in D Company, an' me an' Nobby was in old historic B, an', as everybody knows, B Company and D Company of the Anchesters are on pretty bad terms.

"It was only natural that D should stand up for Tiny and B for Nobby, an' when we reached the advanced base it wasn't anythin' unusual to see the chaps of D Company diggin' little trenches round their tents to carry off the rain what Tiny said was comin', whilst B Company chaps was hangin' out their washin' to dry because Nobby had predicted 'variable breezes—warmer.'

"One mornin', when there wasn't a cloud in the sky, Tiny got out his prediction, 'Fine and pleasant for the next twenty-four hours,' and it rather looked as if Nobby would have to come into line, or else get himself severely tangled up.

"'Smithy,' he sez, 'I've got to do somethin'—the eyes of the battalion are on me.'

"An' that was a fact. Even the officers was beginnin' to believe in Nobby, and Major Anstruther of D used to bet the adjutant real money that his man beat Nobby Clark.

"Nobby sat down very serious, an' produced what I might term the most complete weather tip that's ever been issued. He wrote it down on a bit of paper, and Lance-Corporal Tingle of the orderly room made copies of it:

There's a heavy depression approachin' from the north, an' a big storm is expected with thunder and lightning. This is one of the biggest storms ever known. It will move in a southerly direction, and will carry everything before it. Warmer an' sultry.

Smithy paused and went on solemnly:

"Don't let anybody tell me that Nobby ain't a prophet. That same day our division was rushed to Mons, and by sunset that there depression from the north struck us—five army corps of it. It was the kind of storm I never want to see again, for it lasted till we was south of the Marne, an' the thunder hasn't stopped yet."

20.—THE INTERPRETER

"In this world," said Private Smith in his most philosophical frame of mind, "nothin' helps a man to overcome what I might term the difficulties of life so much as a good memory an' a knowledge of languages—ahem!"

Smithy and I met in the buffet at the Gare de Lyons. A wounded officer now convalescent was returning from Lyons, and Smithy was to meet him.

"Troops comin' out to France have, naturally enough, a desire to *mallum* the *bat*, (speak the language.)

"Lots of chaps gave it out, before the regiment left England, that what they didn't know about the French language might, so to speak, be safely left to the General Staff.

"Nobby Clark had a book sent to him by his brother—he bought it cheap in Farringdon Road—called *Easy Conversations Fransaze*, an' when it come out in orders that officers an' men acquainted with French should hand their names in to the orderly room, Nobby up an' proclaimed himself one of the finest French scholars of the age.

"The adjutant called Nobby out on parade.

"'I see you've put your name in as an interpreter, Clark?' he sez.

"'Yes, sir,' sez Nobby.

"'Do you speak French?' sez the adjutant.

"'We, we,' sez Nobby.

"'*Avec facilimong?*' sez the officer.

"'*Nong, nong, mong Capitong,*' sez Nobby.

"'I asked you if you spoke it with facility,' sez the adjutant.

"'*No, mong Capitong,*' sez Nobby, 'with a book.'

"'Not so much of the "*mong Capitong,*"' sez the officer.

"Anyway, they didn't take Nobby.

"Well, mobilisation began, an' Nobby, being bitten with the idea of walkin' about in an officer's uniform interpretin', hit on a plan.

"He had an uncle in London, an' every afternoon when he wasn't for duty Nobby went up to town to his uncle's, and, changing into civilian kit, went to Dr. Shlielsteimer's Celebrated School of Languages, an' took a couple of hours' lessons.

"'No good my goin' in uniform,' he told me, 'there's always a lot of girls at them places, an' I don't want to be, so to speak, conspicuous. Girls always run after me,' he sez modest.

"'So should I if I was a girl,' I sez.

"'Would you, Smithy?' he asks quite pleased. 'Why?'

"'Because,' I sez, 'if I was follerin' you about I shouldn't see your ugly mug,' I sez.

"Anyway for a couple of weeks he toiled an' moiled, an' he gave me a good deal of information about the pen of his aunt an' the books of his father's brother that I'd never had before.

"'I'm making good progress,' he sez very enthusiastic. 'The teacher is a feller named Meyerheim—he's a naturalised Austrian, an' he don't spare any pains.'

"Before the lessons was finished, Meyerheim had gone—had to leave sudden for Austria to see the aunt of his mother, takin' two pens, a pencil, an' the book of Thomas. At least, that's what Nobby said, an' as he told me first in French and then in English, I suppose he'd got all the facts.

"Anyway, Meyerheim was gone, an' Nobby took the last of his lessons from another chap.

"'Twelve bob it cost me, but it's worth every penny,' sez Nobby. 'I can talk French like—well, you wait till we get to France.'

"Well, we mobilised at Aldershot, an' off we hopped.

"I must admit that Nobby made himself understood remarkably well. When we got to Boulogne Nobby went up to the first French soldier he saw, an' sez, *'Polly voo Francay?'* an' the French soldier looked a bit staggered, but sez *'We, we.'* So there couldn't have been much wrong with his accent.

"And when it came to goin' round the shops buyin' things, nobody understood the language so well as Nobby. If he wanted two apples he'd hold up two fingers, an' say, *'Sieve voo play?'* An' when the lady told him how much it was, he'd give her a *franc* and count the change very careful.

"'How do you know how much she sez?' I asked him once.

"'I don't,' sez Nobby, 'until I've counted the change.'

"Lots o' people who didn't believe that Nobby could speak French at first altered their opinions. We used to be hard up for newspapers, the only ones comin' our way being the papers we got up from Paris, an' the troops used to bring 'em in an' sit round in a circle whilst Nobby translated 'em. Some of the papers was good, an' some was not so good. The one Nobby liked best was a paper called *La Vee Parisien*. A rare paper for war news that was, an' it gave pictures of patriotic French ladies who'd given all their clothes to the poor. Some people used to say that there was no war news in *La Vee Parisien*, but that only shows what a fat lot they knew about it.

"Nobby would turn the leaves over very solemn, turnin' his head away so that he couldn't see the pictures, an' by an' by he'd say:

"'Hullo—here's a bit.'

It is rumoured that another million German recruits are drillin' like mad.

"'What's "drillin' like mad" in French?' says Spud Murphy, the only suspicious feller in the whole battalion.

"'*Drillong au balmè,*' says Nobby, quick as lightnin', an' went on readin'.

"There he'd sit for hours translatin' the news. I don't suppose there's a paper in the world with the information of *La Vee Parisien*.

It is reported that the citizens of Hornsey are gettin' up a testimonial to that gallant hero, Private Spud Murphy, of 1st Anchesters, who is to be engraved on vellum an' bound.

"'Is that there?' asks Spud incredulously.

"'Do you doubt me word?' sez Nobby.

"'It's very likely,' sez Spud highly gratified. 'My family has lived in Hornsey for years, an' me father has driven the corporation water-cart since 1887—do they say what the testimonial is for?'

"'Yes,' sez Nobby, 'it's owin' to the decrease in crime since you was called up.'

"When the advance started an' we moved up to Mons to that celebrated battle, Nobby found lots of opportunity for speakin' the language. People brought us flowers an' grub, an' the way Nobby kept sayin' '*Mercy, mercy,*' was wonderful to hear. What's more, all these French ladies and gentlemen understood him. Two days before the battle we was billeted in the little town of X——. There was four of us chaps billeted in a labourer's cottage, an' the way those people put themselves out for us was wonderful. That night, after we'd had a reg'lar officers' mess dinner, Nobby was sent for. The adjutant was standin' in the middle of the street talkin' to a French soldier.

"'Clark,' sez the adjutant, 'you speak French, I understand.'

"'In a sense—yes, sir,' sez Nobby.

"'Well, you can look after this man—he's billeted in your house.'

"So Nobby pointed to the house with his thumb, an' the soldier understandin' the language, went along with him.

"It was a bit of a joke on the adjutant's part, for this chap spoke English. He'd come up from Charleroi, he said, an' had got cut off from his lot by a party of *Uhlans*.

"A nice affable feller he was, an' spoke as good English as me an' Nobby.

"'Do you speak French?' he sez to Nobby.

"'*Ung petty pair*,' sez Nobby, modest.

"'You'll pick it up,' sez the chap. 'I speak English because I was a waiter in London for years.'

"An' then he began to talk about the war an' how he'd left his old folks an' his wife in Amiens, an' how he hated the Germans.

"'When are you chaps movin' to Mons?' he sez, sudden.

"'Tomorrow,' sez Nobby.

"As a matter of fact, nobody knew when we was movin' or where, but Nobby is a sort of feller that never likes people to think that he don't know everything.

"'Where's your artillery now?' sez the French soldier.

"'Down the road,' sez Nobby, an' this French feller went on askin' all sorts of questions. He told us his name was De Boosong, or a name that sounded like that.

"Nobby went out soon after, an' me an' the other two chaps in the billet strolled out after a bit, talkin' about the troops an' where they was, an' how many big guns we had. We was lookin' at an ambulance waggon when up came Nobby, and behind him was the adjutant an' a file of the guard.

"'Take that man,' sez the adjutant, an' they seized the French soldier.

"'Your name is Meyerheim, an' you are a spy,' sez the adjutant.

"We made a rapid search of him an' found rough plans with the positions of all the troops from Boulogne to X—— marked in ink. Then we took him back to the cottage.

"The colonel came in, an' another officer, an' they tried him at the table where our supper had been laid.

"'You'll be shot at daybreak,' sez the colonel.

"The spy looked round at Nobby.

334

"'I remember you now,' he sez, 'you wore civilian clothes when you come to my class—ah, well!'—he shrugged his shoulders an' walked out between the guard.

"'How did you recognise him, Clark?' sez the adjutant.

"Nobby looked thoughtful at the ceilin'.

"'By his bad French accent, sir,' he sez.

21.—Nobby in Romantic Vein

"Nobby Clark wrote a poem of hate once," said Smithy, "an' as it happened before the war, an' was meant for a feller who'd gone away to join the 2nd Battalion in India owin' him money, it probably gave the German poet the idea which he's got all the credit for.

"Off an' on Nobby's been writin' poems for years an' gen'rally they've been successful.

"Often an' often me an' Nobby has had to come a long way round to camp instead of takin' a short cut through the Wigshires' lines, owin' to some little poem what Nobby writ about the Wigshire Regiment's way of playin' football.

"Nobby used to do verses at the front for some of the chaps. They was versus like:

Under the starry sky,
With the shells a burstin' nigh,
I think of you, my lass so true,
As in the mud I lie.

"Nobby has always been handy with his pen an' that's probably why he's always in trouble, for as the poet sez, 'the pen is flightier than the sword.'

"After the shockin' an' outrageous behaviour of the Germans who made me an' Nobby an' about 80,000 other fellers walk all the way from Mons to the Marne without givin' us time to change our boots, there follered a long time of trench work when we had plenty of opportunity for receivin' an' writin' letters. An' this wasn't all.

"Lots of people in England, anxious to do somethin' for the soldiers, were sendin' out mufflers, mittens, chocolate, an' cigarettes—which in addition to bein' highly appreciated was very useful.

"It was a bit of luck—what you received, I mean.

"Spud Murphy got *Pilgrim's Progress* an' a box of Turkish delight. Big Tony White, who had toothache all the way down, got a box of chocolate, but Nobby, who was born with a set of gold soup ladles in his mouth, got a couple of shirts which was both useful an' ornamental, bein' sky- blue in colour and hand-embroidered.

"But it was the note pinned to the shirts that appealed to Nobby who, as I say, was a born poet. This is what it said:

Whoever you are, whatever you be,
I've made these shirts with care for thee.
So, soldier, kindly write to me.
From Lady Gwendoline FitzMalling,
Knadsley Hall, Knadsley, Kent.
P.S.—Please send the answer enclosed in a letter to my servant
Mary Ann Gabbler at above address.'

"'I always thought I should get into society,' sez Nobby.

"'She wouldn't have written it if she knew the shirts was comin' to you,' said Spud Murphy. 'She thought they was goin' to officers—you can tell that by the decorations.'

"'Push off, kill-joy!' sez Nobby. 'Go back to your own bloomin' trench—you're bringin' us bad luck.'

"Certainly the decorations was very fine. When Nobby held up the shirt for the troops to see there was a lion an' a unicorn fightin' for a crown on the chest, a Belgian flag on one sleeve, an' a harp an' a crown on the other.

"'It's more like a drawin'-room carpet than a shirt,' sez Spud.

"'Don't display your ignorance before the young soldiers,' sez Nobby sternly. 'This is a shirt of honour—like you read about. It's the sort of shirt the Archbishop of Canterbury or the Lord Chief Justice wears.'

"'I've never seen one like it,' sez Spud.

"'Poor old Spud!' sez Nobby kindly. 'Havin' spent your life amongst low people who wear cotton shirts, it must be like heaven gettin' into close touch with real class.'

"'I'm goin' to answer that letter,' he sez to me later in the day—'I'll have to make up a real good one.'

"An' he did.

"It started:'Dear Lady Gwendoline, if you'll excuse the liberty,' and went on:

"'When I received your kind an' welcome letter I was rescuin' a number of comrades from death——'

("'That ain't true,' sez Nobby, 'but they like little realistic an' romantic bits.')

"'My thoughts often turn,' the letter went on, 'to Knadsley Hall, Knadsley, Kent, an' so do the shirts you so kindly sent, which I am wearin' now. How can a lonely soldier who has no friends thank you?'

("'That's romance, too,' sez Nobby.)

"'My history is a sad one,' Nobby wrote. 'Alone in the world—I shall never feel lonely now that I am wearin' your shirts—an orphan, an' my proud spirit crushed by a cruel stepfather. . . .'

"Nobby wrote one of the grandest letters that have ever been written, an' sent it off.

"'I don't suppose she'll write back,' sez Nobby; 'still there have been lots of romantic things happen in the world, an' perhaps. . . .'

"She wrote back all right. The letter was brought up to the fire trench one evenin' an' Nobby read it by candle-light. I saw him makin' happy faces as he read it, but it wasn't till the next mornin' that he showed it to me.

Dearest! I have not seen your face, but already I know you! Write to me, oh my heart! From Lady Gwendoline FitzMalling, Knadsley Hall, Knadsley, Kent.

"'This,' sez Nobby, speakin' with great emotion, 'is one of the most romantic, things that's ever happened.'

"It made a rare difference to Nobby, that letter. I never saw the answer he sent to it, but one day when we was in the reserve trenches he told me that he was as good as married.

"'Me an' Gwen will always be glad to see you, Smithy,' he sez. 'We'll send the dogcart down to the station for you, an' you can have your breakfast in bed. In the mornin' I'll be waitin' for you in the rosery, an' we'll have a pipe an' talk over old times.'

"'Yes, me lord,' I sez.

"'Say that again,' sez Nobby, an' I obliged him.

"'I suppose I shall be Lord Clark,' he sez thoughtful. 'Somehow, I always thought I should get on.'

"He had wonderful ideas, had Nobby. He couldn't make up his mind whether he'd breed pigs or horses. We had a long discussion about it one night.

"'I'd breed pigs,' sez Spud Murphy. 'They'll prevent you feelin' lonely.'

"'They'll also remind me of the low people I've had to associate with,' sez Nobby.

"'Don't you ever invite me down to your house,' sez Spud. 'I'm a Socialist.'

"'*Reste tronkill*,' sez Nobby in French.

"Another letter came from the lady—pages an' pages of it, an' Nobby got haughtier than ever.

"Spud Murphy saw the R.A.M.C. orderly at the collectin' station.

"'You might ask your bloke somethin' for us,' he sez. 'We've had a bet an' we want to decide whether Knadsley Hall is a lunatic asylum or a home for chronic drinkers.'

"Ordinarily Nobby would have resented this, but he only smiled superiorly.

"'Pore feller!' he sez; 'such lowness!'

"The R.A.M.C. chap asked his officer, an' the doctor surprised Spud by sayin' that Knadsley Hall was the home of the Earl of Knadsley, an' that Lady Gwendoline was his only daughter.

"'Me last hopes gone,' sez Spud bitterly.

"There wasn't a lot of time for confidences an' discussions after that. Von Kluck an' his friends got very busy, an' we spent most of our time countin' the shells that burst over our trench an' shootin' back the infantry attacks that follered.

"The story got out about Nobby an' his lady, an' the amount of attention our line created was truly astoundin'. Every time a shell burst over our trench, the chaps in the other trenches said: 'There goes the heir to Knadsley Hall,' or 'Another empty chair in the House of Lords.'

"Marchin' back through the darkness at night to our billets, fellers of other regiments would come to the side of the road an' ask: 'Is little Lord Fauntleroy still alive?' until Nobby began to know what it felt like to be famous.

"'I don't suppose her parents know anythin' about it yet,' sez Nobby one day. 'She's keepin' it dark—you can see that by the way she has her letters addressed to her servant.'

"Nobby gave me an idea how Gwen would break the news.

"The family would be sittin' at breakfast in the parlour one mornin' (accordin' to Nobby), an' Lady Gwen, very pale an' very tall, would get up, an' washin' her hands in the silver rose-bowl in the centre of the table, would say:

"'Papa—may I see you in the picture gallery?'

"An' the old lord would say: 'Certainly, child,' an' then she'd throw herself in his arms weepin' and confess the truth.

338

"'What!' sez the old lord, 'a private soldier—never!'

"'He is a hero, papa,' sobs Lady Gwen.

"'I'll have no heroes in my family,' sez the old lord. 'Go to your room in the north tower—you are no daughter of mine.'

"But by an' by he'd relent, an' the old bells of Knadsley Parish Church would ring out the glad tidin's.

"'An' then,' sez Nobby, 'I'll turn up one day with me eye in a sling, an' people will take the horses out of the carriage and draw me up to the Hall.'

"'The only bit I believe about that,' sez Spud, 'is that you'll turn up with your eye in a sling—but it will be after you've made your call.'

"There was lots of letters to an' fro, an' I didn't see 'em all. Just before Christmas Nobby had a grand idea.

"'I'll write direct to her,' he sez, 'a very gentlemanly letter that she can show to her people—it'll break the ice,' he sez.

"So one day when the battalion was restin' near Armentières, Nobby did up a fine letter:

Dear Friend (it went), weather-worn and scarred by war, water, an' worry, I take my pen in my hand to write to you. As I sit here in the trench writin' on a drum by the light of burstin' shells, me mind goes back to the two shirts which I am still wearin'. How can I thank you for your kindness an' how can I thank Mary Ann Gabbler for so kindly givin' you my letters? And how can I thank your dear father the earl for gettin' the home together, an' how can I thank your mother the earless for makin' me welcome as I'm sure she will, for she has a beautiful face accordin' to the papers. .

"There was a lot more like this.

"'I mention 'em all,' sez Nobby. 'You can't be too careful. Perhaps her servant knows some of the old earl's secrets an' will be able to put in a word for me.'

"Accordin' to Nobby, Mary Ann might be in a position to say to the earl: 'Either Mr. Clark marries Lady Gwen or I tell the story of the Red Room an' all that happened on the fatal night of August 22nd, 1876.'

"Nobby hadn't long to wait for an answer. It came one mornin' an' he was very silent. It was two days before he showed me. The letter was short an' written in a different hand to the letters he had been in the habit of receivin':

Lady Gwendoline FitzMalling presents her compliments to Private Clark and begs to inform him that she is wholly ignorant as to his references *re* shirts. She gathers that her maid Mary Ann Gabbler, who is a stupid and romantic girl, has been carrying on a correspondence with Private Clark in her (Lady Gwendoline's) name. Mary Ann Gabbler has in consequence been dismissed from her service, and her present address is Polcy Court, New Cut, whither Private Clark should address all future correspondence.

"Nobby was a bit cut up at first, but then he brightened.

"'These what I might term unequal marriages never turn out well,' he sez, 'an' if anybody asks you, Smithy, you might say that I've broke off my engagement—tell 'em me parents objected,' he sez."

Nobby or Smithy's Friend Nobby

DEDICATION

THE PHILISTINE

Of all the sins that do decide
The place you go to when you die,
The worst of all is wicked pride,
An' no one knows the reason why.
It bein' natural to drink
An' eat an' sleep. It's proper, too,
An' natural for me to think
That I'm a better man than you.

When that I lay me down to sleep
No doubt but what I pray,
For night 'as terrors which I keep
Out of my mind by day.
I have no daylight faith or fear,
Mine is a mid-day pride
But in the night a voice says,
"'Ere—Suppose you went an' died?

"Suppose your heart went wholly wrong,
Or stopped—as well it may
Suppose by night there came along
The Call of Judgment Day?
You, lying down in peace of mind,
Alive, and fairly well,
You would feel sick to wake and find
Your silly self in 'Ell!"

Therefore I say an humble prayer,
Which I will own to be

A slight attemp' to put things square
Between my God an' me
A slight attemp' to rectify
The sinful way I'm in,
An' with my penitence, to buy
Another day of sin.

When that I lay me down to rest,
I put my pride aside
An' pray for them that I like best,
An let the others slide.
An' often—when I keep awake—
I thank Him all I can
That He saw fit to take and make
Of me a soldier man!

That He took me an' set me down
Along with human men
Who live in barracks miles from town,
An' go to bed at ten,
Who sleep an' rise an' drink an' eat—
An' sometimes die likewise—
To certain bugle calls that meet
Occasions that arise.

An' I am thankful I have got
The strength of mind to see
It's wrong to sneer at them who've not
Advantages like me.
An' if I had the time to spare
I often would incline
To pray for them who cannot share
This sinful pride of mine.

Of all the sins that do decide
The place you go to when you die,
The worst of all is wicked pride,
An' no one knows the reason why.
It bein' natural to drink
An' eat an' sleep. It's proper, too,
An' natural for me to think
That I'm a better man than you.

1.—Nobby's Best Girl

Smithy sat on the canteen table swinging his legs, and all that was best, brightest, and most noble in the First Battalion of the Anchester Regiment sat round listening.

The glow of sunset lingered in the sky, but blue dusk sat on the eastern side of the barrack square; where, in the shade of the tall oaks— those oaks that had waved and rustled just as bravely when Clarendon of the 190th was preparing the regiment for the Peninsular Wars—the low-roofed married quarters twinkled with lights.

A bugle call interrupted the narrative of the *raconteur*; a sharp, angry, slurred call that sent two of the company at a jog trot to the guard-room.

But the interruption furnished at once a text and an illustration for Private Smith.

He addressed the audience generally, but mainly his remarks were directed toward the only civilian present.

"Bein' married is like bein' a defaulter," he explained, and was so struck with the sagacity of his reasoning chat he repeated it.

"When a soldier breaks out of barracks, or talks in the ranks, or does those things within this Act mentioned," Smithy was quoting the Army Act, "along comes an officer and sez, 'Private What's-your-name, you will be confined to barracks for seven days' an' the poor young feller has to do extra drill an' extra fatigues, an' answers his name regular every half-hour.

"It's very nice breakin' out of barracks," continued Smithy inconsequently, "an' so is courtin', but the end is the same. Up you come before some one or other, an' punishment is as sure as daylight. If a feller was to ask me which I'd prefer—to be married or to go to prison, I'd say 'prison' like a shot; because it's shorter an' not so crowded.'

Here Smithy paused to ruminate.

"You can never trust a woman," he continued bitterly. "A woman is like the bright green birds of paradise you buy in Petticoat Lane— all right till you've had 'em a day or two, and the natural-born sparrer begins to wear through. I'm not talkin' out of the back of my head, as you suggest, Tiny, but from my own blessed experience.

"When the Anchesters went to Dabbington there wasn't a nicer, smarter, or more friendly company on the face of the earth than 'B' Company. Nice respectable fellers they were, more like brothers than comrades. It was 'Lend us a pipe of shag, ole boy,' an' 'Certainly, ole feller,' an' 'Do you mind my borrowin' your best boots to go an' meet my girl in?' an' 'Let me clean 'em for you, ole chap,' till all the rest of the regiment used to come an' look through the winders of our barrack room to see us bein' polite to each other.

"It was the talk o' the battalion; they used to call us the Gentlemanly B's' till a chap from 'G' Company went an' spoilt it by callin' us the 'Pretty Pollies'.

"You don't know Dabbington, do you? It's a little garrison town with seventeen chapels, an' a market day. It wasn't exactly lively. Every year there was two select concerts an' a magic lantern lecture on 'My Visit to Rome' by the curate, but it wasn't exactly dull There was a sort of prejudice against soldiers in some quarters, an' in other quarters there was a feelin' that the soldier ought to be rescued from sin. A feller named Rogers, a young feller with spectacles, used to run a sort of Rescue Home, where the troops could be kept out of the nice, bright, sinful public-houses by bein' given a cup of coffee and last week's *Graphic* to read in a tin mission-hall. As a matter of fact, the public-houses in Dabbington wasn't so bright or lively, an' when young Mr. Rogers came round barracks an' began talkin' about the 'arty welcome, come-one, come-all, that was waitin' for us round the comer, Nobby Clark up an' sez 'We'll be round there tonight.'

"Young Mr. Rogers was highly delighted, an' said if we got there by seven-thirty, we'd be in time for the bright little half-hour service that the proceedin's started with.

"So me an' Nobby turns up soon after eight, an' there was Mr. Rogers waitin' to shake hands an' as pleased as Punch to see us, though a bit disappointed we hadn't come earlier.

"'What have you let us in for?' I sez to Nobby as we walked in after Mr. Rogers.

"'Close thy mouth,' sez Nobby, who always gets religious in a church. We was the only soldiers in the place, an' I felt a bit uncomfortable, but Nobby seemed to enjoy it. There was a lot of civilians present. Nice young ladies, an' young gentlemen in frock coats, an' they all got very friendly. One young gentleman with a very red face sez to Nobby: 'Brother, I extend the hand of friendship to you,' an' Nobby sez, 'Thank you, brother, the same to you.'

"'I suppose,' sez the young gentleman, 'you don't often see bright faces round you?'

"'Not so bright as yours,' sez Nobby, an' the young gentleman looked very 'ard at him.

"Then Mr. Rogers made a speech an' said he welcomed these two young military men, an' hoped they would be the advance guard—he believed that was the military term (applause) of the army element in Dabbington (applause).

"So then we played games. There was one game that two of the nicest young ladies knew, an' they offered to teach me an' Nobby. I picked it up at once; it was a silly sort of game, played on a lop-sided draught-board, an' one piece hopped over another piece. But Nobby couldn't seem to learn it at all, an' the two young ladies sat on each side of him, guiding his hand for half an hour, and even then he was still makin' mistakes. By an' by, Mr. Rogers came up to us an' asked Nobby if he could sing. Nobby said he'd got a cold, but he'd do his best, an' everybody started clappin'. One of the nice young ladies went to the piano an' Nobby leant over and hummed the tune to her for about ten minutes. It seemed to me that he kept on hummin' different tunes, but I might have been mistaken.

"I was a bit nervous, for old Nobby only knows three songs, 'Who Wouldn't be a Lodger?' 'All Through Going to Margate on a Sunday,' an' a sentimental song about a girl an' a soldier.

"I tell you I was a bit relieved when be said he couldn't sing without his music, an' promised to come another night.

"I asked Nobby how he'd enjoyed hisself as we was goin' home, an' he said First class, in an absent-minded way. I forgot to tell you that her name was Miss Elder—the girl who taught him to play 'Hoppit,' an' played the piano.

"Next day me an' Nobby went out of barracks an' strolled round town. When we came to a music shop Nobby sez, 'Hold hard, Smithy, let's go in an' buy a bit of music.'

"'What for?' I sez, amazed.

"'To sing,' sez Nobby.

"'Don't waste your money,' I sez, but Nobby went in, an' I followed. There was a young lady behind the counter; she wore spectacles, too, an' she sez in a voice about the size of an orange pip: 'What can I do for you?'

"'I want a song,' sez Nobby. 'A good religious song with easy words, for about fourpence.'

The young lady shook her head.

"'I'm afraid we haven't got anything at that price,' she sez. 'Nothing under one an' fourpence.'

"'Come away, Nobby,' sez I. ' Don't waste your money.' But Nobby wouldn't come.

"'You ain't got anything that's a bit soiled or second hand, I suppose?' he sez, and the girl said she didn't think she had, but she'd look.

"So she turned over a lot of music, an' every time she turned one over she said 'No' an' 'I'm afraid not,' an' 'I'm sorry, but I don't think—' in her little voice as big as an orange pip.

"By and by she stopped an' pulled out a sheet of music that was rather sunburnt about the edge.

"'You can have this for fourpence, if it'll suit,' she sez.

"'What's it called?' sez Nobby.

"So she said some name that I couldn't catch.

"'What's that?' sez Nobby, lookin' a bit disappointed.

"'*Ora pro nobis*,' sez the young lady. It's Latin.'

"Nobby shook his head. 'Give me one in English, please, miss. I haven't talked Latin for years.'

"'But the song's in English,' said the girl. There are only three words in Latin.'

"'How do you say 'em, miss?' asked Nobby, an' the young lady explained.

"'Thanks, I'll take the song,' sez Nobby, brightenin' up; so he paid his fourpence an' we walked back to barracks.

"We went over to the canteen an' found Fatty Morris, the chap that plays first cornet, an' asked his advice about learnin' the music, an' Fatty promised to run over it with Nobby the next day.

"So, sure enough next afternoon we all went down into the back field, me an' Nobby, an' Fatty, an' started.

"First of all Fatty run over the song by hisself, an Nobby practised the words a bit. By the time Fatty had got the song by heart an' had worked in two or three little trembly bits that wasn't in the music, all the chaps in barracks had strolled down to find out who was ill. Nobby pretended not to notice them, but they made him a bit nervous, an' when Fatty said he'd got the music all right, an' that Nobby could go ahead with the words, Nobby turned round to the crowd an' asked 'em what they wanted.

"'We've come to hear the music,' said Spud Murphy, who was one of the fellers. 'What are *you* goin' to do?'

"'I'm goin' to sing,' sez Nobby, very short, an' Spud pretended to stagger back, an' all the other chaps got ready to run.

"'Save the women an' children,' sez Spud, foldin' his arms. 'I'll be the last to leave the ship—to every man upon this earth death cometh

346

soon or late, an' how can man die better than—'

"'You close your face, Spud Murphy,' said Nobby, gettin' red. Nobody asked you to come here.'

"But Spud took no notice of what Nobby said, an' continued to act the goat, an' there would have been a rough house, only at that minute Corporal Boyle happened to stroll up, an' asked Spud if he was the funny man on duty, an' told him to give the soft-sighing breezes a chance of making theirselves heard. So Spud took the hint an' dried up, an' Nobby, who was gettin' redder an' redder, started to practise.

"Nobby's got a very nice, strong voice, but you could hear the cornet quite plain.

"In a couple o' days he'd got the song off by heart, an' on the last day of the practice every chap in barracks went down into the playin' field to hear him.

"Everybody was very curious to know where Nobby was going to sing, but we kept it dark.

"Spud Murphy started a rumour that it was to be in the Albert Hall—but we kept it dark.

"Then Spud Murphy an' a lot of other chaps—mostly of 'G' Company—'Dirty G,' we call 'em—said they'd foller us about till they found the place, an' for nearly a week me an' Nobby couldn't go out for a walk without twenty or thirty fellers walkin' behind in double rank. Wherever we went, they went. It got a bit monotonous, so I didn't blame Nobby when he slipped out of barracks once or twice without me an' went for a solitary ramble—so he said. Well, one night, off we went to the Soldiers' Rescue Home, an' the young ladies an' gentlemen were highly delighted to see us.

"'I'm much obliged to you,' sez Mr. Rogers, for bringin' your gallant comrades with you,' pointing to Spud Murphy an' about twenty fellers who were standin' at the door, lookin' rather uncomfortable.

"You see, they never suspected that Nobby was goin' to sing at a sort o' church, and they would probably have gone away, only young Mr. Rogers bagged 'em before they had a chance.

"So they all come in, walkin' on tip-toe an' speakin' in whispers; but one of the young ladies—not our one —went down an' talked to 'em an' showed 'em how to play Hoppit.'

"Then Nobby's turn came to sing, an' Miss Elder went to the piano. As a matter of fact, I began to get nervous myself, especially as I saw Spud an' the other fellers sittin' up with a grin. Nobby's voice is good enough, but there's a lot of it, an' what with singin' against a cornet an' singin' in the open air, I expected him to lift the roof off.

"But lo! an' behold! he sang as soft as soft can be, an' I could see that Spud an' the other fellers were disappointed. It was a song about a kid who died in the snow, an' it brought tears into your eyes to hear Nobby sing 'Horror!' in a quavery voice.

"After it was over everybody clapped, but I was lookin' at Spud.

"'Did you see that?' whispers Spud, when Nobby did a bow. 'Did you see that?' he sez, when Nobby closed the young lady's music. 'Did you see that?' he sez fiercely, when Nobby handed the young lady down from the platform. I must confess I was a bit puzzled to know where Nobby got his manners from. But we soon found out. This Miss Elder come along to us by an' by, an' she asked Spud how he liked the song. Spud was a bit put out by her speakin' to him, an' grinned an' twisted his moustache, an' said in a haw-haw voice that it wasn't loud enough.

"'Do you think so, Mr. Spud?' said the young lady, quite surprised. Why, I—'

"'His name's Murphy,' interrupted Nobby, who was lookin' rather agitated.

"'I'm sorry, Mr. Murphy; but do you really think so?' the young lady went on. 'Why, when he came—'

"Nobby was very rude, for he interrupted the young lady again.

"'Don't take any notice of what Spud—I mean Murphy—says, miss,' he said; but, somehow, Spud had got an idea, an' instead of takin' offence at what Nobby said, he went on talkin' to the young lady.

"'Yes, miss?' he sez, politely. 'You was sayin' that when Mr. Clark came—'

"And then it came out that Nobby had been goin' to Miss Elder's house to practise his songs in the evening.

"'He's goin' to join the choir,' sez Miss Elder.

"I looked at Nobby, very sad, for now I understood all about his 'solitary rambles.'

"'Joined the choir, has he?' sez Spud. 'Well, miss, I should like to join the choir too'; an' all the other fellers said they'd like to join—all except little Billy Morgan, who was a bit afraid of Nobby, an' didn't like the way be was glarin' at him.

"It's gospel truth," asserted Smith earnestly; "but before the end of the week half the bloomin' regiment applied to join the choir. You see, it came out that there was choir practice on Thursday and refreshments provided, and that all the nice young ladies in town were members. Fourteen men paraded at orderly room, and asked to be allowed to change their religion.

"'What religion do you want?' sez the colonel to young Jerry Jordan, an' Jerry said he didn't know exactly, but he thought it was the third chapel on the right as you went up the High Street.

"'Next door to the little tobacco shop,' all the other fellers chimed in.

"The adjutant, who was standin' by, didn't say a word till the colonel had gone, an then he sez, quiet—

"'What's the little game?' and all the fellers said, one after another, 'Nothing, sir.'

"'What's the attraction?' sez the adjutant. 'Free drinks?' An' all the fellers said, 'No, sir,' very indignant.

"'What is your present religion?' sez the adjutant to Jerry.

"'Follow the band, sir,' sez Jerry, meanin' Church of England.

"'And yours?'

"' Methodist, sir,' sez Private Cohen, a young feller from Whitechapel.

"'I'm goin' to find out all about it—fall out!' sez the adjutant. He found out soon enough, for in a week the regiment was singin' mad. 'F' Company was the bass company, because they wasn't so well fed as the others, an' consequently their voices was rumbly. 'A' Company was the tenor company, because they were mostly fat duty men, (soldiers with billets: officers' servants, etc.). As soon as ever parade was over, chaps used to get together an' start practisin', an' once, some fellers from 'H' got together under our windows at *reveille* an' sung, 'Awake, awake, put on your strength; put on your beautiful garments.' They got seven days C.B. for creatin' a disturbance in barracks.

"All this time Nobby was gettin' thicker an' thicker with Miss Elder. She introduced him to her father an' mother an' family, an' Nobby used to go there to tea on Sundays, an' carry the books home after the service. An' Nobby stopped goin' to the canteen, an' sounded his aitches, an' bought a nail-brush. An' when they had choir practice at Miss Elder's house, Nobby would stay behind to help wash up the cups with Miss Elder. Me an' Spud Murphy volunteered to stay behind once, but Nobby wouldn't hear of it. He asked me as a great favour not to queer his pitch, an' he told Spud in private that if he ever volunteered again, there'd be trouble.

"'I'm now a good Christian, leadin' the better life,' sez Nobby; 'but if I ever hear you talkin' about stayin' behind to wash up the cups, I'll knock bits off you, you putty-eyed blitherer.'

"So Spud was persuaded to stay away.

"The choir was a big success, although the young fellers at the chapel who resigned sooner than sit next to red-coats got very nasty, an' used to laugh when Nobby sang a solo (by request). I spoke to one of 'em about it, one night after chapel.

"'You look after your singin', my good man,' he sez, very haughty. It was the red-faced young gentleman who welcomed us to the Soldiers' Rescue Home, an' he'd been very cool to me an' Nobby. We was walkin' along a quiet street when I up an' spoke to him.

"'Look here!' he sez, very hot. 'Me an' several other young gentlemen have gone to a lot of trouble to rescue you fellers from sin, an' now you ain't satisfied with bein' rescued, but you must go an' monopolize our young lady friends, an' cold shoulder us out of the choir!' I didn't say anything for a while. 'Blessed feather-bed soldiers, I call you,' he said bitterly. 'Blessed namby-pamby soldiers. I call you!'

"'Me?' I sez.

"'Yes,' he sez, reckless. You, if you like.'

"I didn't like to hit him, because I was afraid he'd cry; but I proved that I was no Christian, an' he told me I ought to be ashamed to use such language on a Sunday night.

"Mind you," said Smithy impartially, "I'm not one to run down a soldier because he's a Christian. All these stories you hear about Christians havin' boots thrown at 'em because they say their prayers in the barrack-room is rot. It makes you uncomfortable to see a feller sayin' his prayers in public, an' it makes you feel uncomfortable to hear a feller blaspheme; but it's the same kind of uncomfortableness.

"I chucked up the choir myself, because they found out that I couldn't sing—only eat an' drink at the choir practice, an', to tell you the truth, I was a bit sore with Nobby. So what with hints from Miss Elder about my voice, an' hints from Nobby about my appetite, I gave up goin'. But one day along comes Nobby, seemin' very excited.

"'Come to choir practice tonight, Smithy,' he sez.

"'Thanks,' I sez, rather cold; 'but I've had my tea.'

"'Come along,' sez Nobby; 'there's goin' to be no end of a do tonight.'

"'Thank you, Private Clark,' I sez haughtily; 'but I haven't forgotten your remarks about the currant cake.'

"Anyway, he persuaded me. It seemed that Mrs. Elder was goin' to make some grand announcement to the choir, an' was givin' a sort o' stand-up supper to celebrate it, so I went along.

"Nobby was a bit excited an' a bit mysterious, but I didn't take much notice, an' then he started askin' if he told me something whether I'd keep it dark. So I said 'Yes.' So he said, 'Will you take your dying oath?' I said 'Yes.' So after he told me I was the greatest friend that he had, an' that he'd break my jaw if I ever breathed a syllable, he let out that he was in love. Laugh! I thought I'd break a blood vessel. Nobby got very fierce, an' after sayin' a lot of unnecessary things, he asked me if I thought I was a gentleman, so I said 'No.'

"He'd fallen in love with Miss Elder, an' was goin' to speak to her that night. This sobered me down a bit. 'She's much too good for you, Nobby,' I sez; 'she plays the piano, for one thing.'

"It was a mad sort of idea, but Nobby seemed struck with it. He hadn't said a word to her about it, but he was goin' to take advantage of the party.

"I must say that Mrs. Elder did the thing in style. Cake and thin bread an' butter, and jam. Mr. Elder belongs to the Chapel an' takes the plate round an' keeps a provision shop in the High Street. He was waitin' for us, smilin' and shakin' hands as friendly as possible. Mr. Rogers was there too, but he looked nervous.

"After we'd had a hymn or so, and finished off the grub, Mr. Elder said he'd got a few words to say to his dear young friends. He said there was a time for eatin' an' a time for sleepin', a time for buryin' an' a time for givin' in marriage. Nobby said, 'Hear, hear,' before he could stop hisself, an' then looked out of the window, pretendin' it wasn't him.

"'I have to announce the engagement of my dear daughter'— Nobby sat up straight, with his mouth open—'with our dear young friend and fellow-worker, Mr. Anthony Rogers.'

"I didn't look at Nobby till we got outside.

"We walked along for about a mile before he said a word.

"'That's a woman!' he sez bitterly. 'After what I've done, too! Sat in a bloomin' choir, an' all the time I never once missed sayin' "Amen"'"

"He didn't say anything more for a long time, but he seemed to be thinking a lot, and whenever I looked at him he managed to turn his head away. I didn't like to press him, but presently he sez in a queer kind of voice—

"'Washed the bloomin' cups, cut the cake, made the fire burn up, carried her books, an' sang anthems' he sez after a bit.

"We went into barracks together, an' turned down the road that leads to the canteen."

351

"Every man," said Smithy philosophically, "is really three men: There's the man as he is; an' the man as he thinks he is; an' the 'man as he wants *you* to think he is. We had a feller in our battalion by the name of Moss who was one of those chaps who are always making theirselves out to be worse than they are. He was most celebrated for what he was going to say to the colonel, whenever he got half a chance.

"'I'll say,' he sez, fierce as anything, 'I'll say, look here—'

"'That'll settle *him*,' sez Nobby; 'he's only got to look at you, Mossy, to wish he never did. If I was a doctor,' Nobby went on thoughtfully, 'you're the chap I'd employ to stand outside the shop to make people ill.'

"Mossy wasn't a very good lookin' chap, owin' to his beak. Nobby sez that when he was a baby, he must have been carried upside down, an' all the blood rushed to his nose. But what Moss was goin' to tell the colonel got to be a by-word in the battalion. He was going to give the colonel the biggest talking to *he* ever had.

"One day when we was all down in the back field watchin' the ridiculous attempts of 'H' Company to take 'B' Company's number down at football, the colonel came along with two or three other officers to see the disgustin' exhibition.

"We didn't want to see him just then, because it spoilt what I might call the flow of good fellership.

"Nobby was playin' centre forward for 'B,' an' we was encouragin' him with a few remarks like, 'Go it, Nobby—slosh him, Nobby—tread on him,' an' shoutin' 'foul' when the other feller hit back. It's a fine old English game, is Company football in the Anchesters—catch-as-catch-can. The colonel came just before half-time, an' whilst the interval was on, an' whilst 'H' was bindin' up their wounds an' the captain of 'H' team was givin' his fellers instructions how they was to trip Nobby up an' accidentally tread on his neck, the colonel strolled round the field, talkin' to some of the men. He spotted Moss and came over to him.

"'Ha, Moss,' he sez, in that sarcastic manner of his, 'have you been getting into trouble lately?'

"We all stood still with our hearts in our mouths waitin' to hear Mossy dress the colonel down.

"'No, sir,' sez Moss, as humble as can be.

"'Good,' sez the colonel; 'keeping away from the drink, eh?'

"'Oh, yes, sir,' sez Moss quite eager, 'oh, yes, sir; thank you kindly, sir. I'm a teetotaller, sir.'

"'Um,' sez the colonel, looking doubtful, 'any complaints to make?'

"'Oh, no, sir,' sez Moss, wrigglin' at the very idea; 'I shouldn't think of such a thing; nothin' further from my thoughts, sir.'

"I tell you, we was all struck of a heap to hear him.

"'Excellent,' sez the colonel, who's a fatherly old chap, except in action. 'I suppose you thought I treated you harshly when I fined you the other day?'

"'Oh, no, sir,' sez Moss, 'you did quite right, sir; I'm quite ashamed of myself, sir.'

"When the officers had strolled away, I looks at him.

"'Moss,' I sez sadly, 'you're a fine bloomin' Ajax, I *don't* think.'

"There's lots of fellers in the world like Moss—what Harry Boyd, the horse-racin' chap, calls 'future eventers.' They walk about dreamin' of what they'd have said if they'd thought of it, an' what they'd say if so-an'-so happened. But so-an'-so never does happen, that's the worst of it.

"Old Mossy was sayin' the other night—

"'If I ever come into a million of money, do you know what I'd do?'

"'Buy a new face,' sez Nobby, who's got what I might call a practical mind.

"'Takin' no notice of interruptions, that only shows the ignorance of your bringin' up,' sez Moss, 'I'll go on. If I had a million or so of money—come into it sudden, owing to an uncle that's gone to America dyin' an' leavin' it to me—'

"'Owin' to his bein' off his bloomin' napper,' sez Nobby.

"'I'd buy my discharge from the army,' sez Moss, takin' no notice of Nobby. 'I'd give every feller in barracks a hundred pounds; then I'd have me motorcar come an' fetch me; then I'd go up to the colonel an' I'd say—'

"'Yes, sir, please, sir; no, sir, please, sir,' sez Nobby very rapidly.

"'I'd say "Look here, old feller,"' sez Moss, '" you think you're a bit of a lad, I've no doubt, but let me tell you—"'

"'It'd be worth the money,' sez Nobby promptly, 'run along an' find your Uncle Moss, search him for the millions; then show him your face an' frighten him to death.'

"There was a chap of ours named Boyle; well connected he was.

He had a grocer's shop on his father's side an' a steam laundry on his mother's side, and from what Boyle said one of his cousins ran a tippin' business in Birmingham, patronized by the nobility an' gentry. Fellers who owned horses used to write to him to see if their horse had a chance, an' if Boyle's cousin said 'No,' why they scratched the horse. What makes me think of Boyle in talkin' about Mossy, they were both dreamers in a manner of speakin', the only difference was that Mossy used to dream about what he was goin' to do, and Boyle of what he *had* done. Lots of fellers called Boyle a liar, but Nobby sez you've got to make allowances, an' what Boyle was, was an author. Nobby sez that as soon as a feller believes his own lies, an' when he finds how easy one lie leads to another, he's an author, an' there's a lot in it.

"One night last winter, me an' Nobby and a lot of other chaps, was at the regimental coffee shop. Havin' no money, we could not go to the canteen.

"'Let's go down to the coffee shop,' sez Nobby, very disgusted; 'I've a good mind to give up the cussed drink altogether. It makes a man worse than the beast of the field,' he sez, so we all went down to the temperance place. The coffee shop ain't such a bad sort of show. There's a bagatelle board an' newspapers, an' you can always 'chalk-up' a cup of coffee an' a bun, if you're so inclined. The temperance chaps was quite surprised to see us. One of 'em—by the name of Adger— sez, 'What's up—got no money?' An' Nobby sez that we'd plenty of money, but we was seriously thinkin' of turnin' over a new leaf.

"'Drink don't pay,' sez Nobby, highly virtuous, an' walks up to the counter. 'Give us a cup of brown varnish till pay day, Bill.'

"Well, while we was all sittin' round the fire talkin' about the horrible state of the money market. an' wonderin' if we could borrow a couple of bob from Adger to send to Nobby's grandmother, what had the brokers in, the question of liars came up.

"I don't know how the argument rose, but I fancy it was over the question of Nobby's grandmother.

"'Wouldn't that be a lie?' sez a timid young chap of 'H.'

"'No,' sez Nobby very indignantly, 'that would be a piece of authoring.'

"Then he explained how Mossy was an author, an' Boyle was an author, an' nacherally the argument led up to money. In fact, all Nobby's arguments lead up to money. It's generally somebody else's money, but it's money, all the same.

"'What you two chaps ought to do,' sez Nobby to Boyle an' Moss, 'is to put your heads together an' perduce something thick. See what I mean? Mossy could put down the things what he'd do, if the other chap would let him, an' Boyle could put down some of the things what he sez he's done. You could put it into the paper an' make a lot of money out of it.'

"Accordin' to Boyle the things he'd done, an' been, before he joined the army would fill about twenty books as big as the Encyclo-what-d'ye-call-it. If he took a drop to drink an' a feller started singin' 'White Wings,' it used to remind him of the time when he was second mate of a lugger orf the coast of China; an' if a feller sung 'The Miner's Dream of Home,' he used to start cryin' because it called back the days when he was in California at the diamond mines, where he found a nugget of diamond as big as a baby's head. An' it didn't matter what you sung about or talked about, it always reminded Boyle of when *he* was there. I've seen him perfectly upset by seein' an advertisement in the paper for an engine-driver wanted for Central Africa, because of something it made him think about.

"'There was me, he sez, with tears in his eyes, 'as it might be here. There was me brother Frank—afterwards made a doctor by special licence—an' there was the King of the Central African Cannibals— old Oojy Moojy.'

"'Will you surrender?' sez the cannibal king.

"'Never,' I sez.

"'Very well, then,' sez the cannibal king. 'I admire your pluck, pale-face, but I've got to do my duty,' an' he shouts, '*Walloo, walloo, wal-loo!*' just like that, an' out jumps about a thousand savage cannibals all gnashin' their teeth by numbers.'

"The idea that Mossy and Boyle should write a book sort of caught on. Nobby said that the next day he'd go up an' see the young chap that runs the *Anchester Gazette*. Sure enough me an' Nobby went the next day, an' the young editor chap asked us into his office.

"He's a very nice chap with spectacles, an' he knows me and Nob-by.

"'Hullo,' he sez, 'what's your little game?'

"So Nobby told him about Boyle's an' Mossy's new book. He seemed to like the idea.

"'You tell the chap to come an' see me—the Boyle chap,' he sez; so me an' Nobby went back to barracks, highly pleased with ourselves. Nobby made Boyle put down on a piece of paper that whatever he got from the *Anchester Gazette* he was to share with us. Boyle saw the editor, an' when he come back to barracks Nobby asked how he'd got on.

"'Fine,' sez Boyle, as proud as a cat with two tails; I told him fifty yarns, an' he had a feller writin' it down in shorthand. He gave me a quid.'

"So we split up the money, an' gave the coffee shop a bye. We was walkin' down town—me an' Nobby—when who should we run up against but the editor. As a matter of fact, he was on the other side of the road; but he smokes a cigar that you couldn't mistake the smell of in a crowd.

"'Ah,' he sez, lookin' at Nobby very hard, 'you're the man I wanted to see.'

"'Oh!' sez Nobby.

"'Yes,' sez the editor, 'I wanted to thank you for sending Boyle to me—his stories are fine.'

"'Yes,' sez Nobby, very satisfied.

"'Especially that one about you,' sez the editor.

"The peaceful smile on Nobby's face sort of rolled off.

"'What one?' sez Nobby.

"'Why.' sez the editor, 'that one, where you and he were in Egypt, and you fell into the Nile an' Boyle rescued you.'

"'Oh, he did, did he?' sez Nobby.

"'Yes; and when you were ungrateful, lifted you by the seat of your trousers an' chucked you back again.'

"'Oh,' sez Nobby, very blank.

"'And a crocodile caught you by the leg an' you cried for help, and Boyle said, "sing to the crocodile an' make him sick." '

"'Excuse me,' sez Nobby, and turns an' walks off to barracks as fast as he could.

"We found Boyle, in the act of tellin' a story about an elephant he killed on the Mississippi.

"'Hold hard,' sez Nobby,' I've got a few words to say to you. What about that yarn you've been tellin' the editor chap about me an' the crocodile?'

"'Oh, that!' sez Boyle, in a light an' airy way, 'that's a row-mance.'

"'A author's a author,' sez Nobby, very stern, 'but when you start authoring about me, you're only a perishin' liar,' he sez."

3.—Private Clark's Will

"Nobby Clark went to hospital mainly on account of fruit bein' cheap," explained Private Smithy, of the 1st Anchester Regiment.

"Him an' another chap—a fellow named Beaky, of 'H,' went out into town one day, an' brought back two pound of apples fresh from the orchard.

"Nobby said he bought 'em, an' told the farmer chap who came into barracks an' said he could almost swear it was Nobby that he must have been mistaken.

"'To prove my words,' sez Nobby, very indignant, an' pullin' some money out of his pocket, 'here's tenpence. I went into town with one an' tuppence, an' that's all I've got left.'

"The farmer went away grumblin', an' said he'd shoot any more thievin' soldiers he found in his orchard, an' Nobby said if the farmer chap wasn't careful he'd make him prove his words.

"Nobby was 'ighly delighted with the apples, an' ate most of his share an' half Beaky's, an' the consequence was that next mornin' Nobby was carried orf to hospital, an' the Medical Staff chap said that Nobby hadn't got a boy's chance.

"All the chaps was very sorry to hear about it, especially the sergeant cook,, who's very sentimental, an' keeps funeral cards of all his relations stuck up in the cook-house.

"'I'm afraid,' sez the sergeant cook, shakin' his 'ead mournful, 'Nobby's goin' to leave us.' An' I tell you," said Smithy, in a hushed voice, "when I heard him say that, it gave me a bit of a turn, for our sergeant cook's very lucky at predictin' things of that sort.

"I got a message from the hospital that Nobby wanted to see me, so I goes up. an' there was poor old Nobby in a special ward by hisself, an' bein' treated so kindly by the Medical Staff chap that I knew it was serious.

"'Hullo, Smithy,' sez Nobby, an' very weak an' white he looked.

"'Hullo, Nob,' I sez, sadly, 'how goes it?'

"Nobby shook his 'ead with a sad smile. "'I'm afraid I'm booked, Smithy,' he sez.

"' Cheer up,' I sez; but Nobby took no notice, an' didn't speak for a bit.

"'Smithy,' he sez at last, bright'nin' up a bit, 'I think I'll make a will.'

"'What for?' I sez.

"'To leave somethin'.'

"'Don't worry about that,' I sez, tryin' to soothe him. 'You'll leave it, whether you make a will or not.'

"But Nobby wouldn't be put orf, so I got a pen an' a bit of paper an' wrote what Nobby said.

"'Put down that I'm a sound mind an' understandin'.'

"'Everybody knows that, Nobby,' I sez, to cheer him up.

"'Put down I leave all my kit to Private Murphy.'

"'What for?' I sez.

"'They won't fit you, anyway,' sez Nobby.

"'Put down I leave all my money to Smithy.'

"'How much have you got?' I sez.

"'It ain't what I've got,' sez Nobby, 'but what's owed to me.'

"It appears from what Nobby said that 'arf the regiment owed him money. Spud Murphy owned him one pound four an' tuppence, Pug Taylor owned him nine an' a penny, Tiny White owed him seven shillin's—in fact, all the money that was owed to Nobby took up two sheets of paper.

"I noticed, though," Smithy hastened to explain, "that the fellers who owed Nobby money were fellers he wasn't very friendly with.

"At last Nobby signed the will an' gave it to me.

"'Take it,' he sez, 'an' go out an' see if you can get 'old of any of the money these fellers owe to their pore dyin' comrade.' So I shook hands with Nobby an' went back to barracks.

"I put it about that Nobby'd made a will an' told the chaps I was goin' to read it to 'em in the canteen that night, an' there was a big gatherin', because Nobby's a very popular chap.

"I started readin' it, an', when I got to the bit where Nobby left all his kit to Spud Murphy, Spud got very sentimental, an' said Nobby was a honest, straightforward feller, who wouldn't 'urt a fly.'

"Then I got to the part where Nobby left all his money to me, an' all the chaps who knew Nobby hadn't got anything to leave come forward and said Nobby had done the right thing.

"Then I read a bit further, an' gave a list of the fellers who owed Nobby money, an' a sort of silence fell on the crowd, and Billy Mason, who's name wasn't on the list, stepped up, an' said, 'Friends an' comrades all: I hope the chaps who owe money to pore old Nobby will be men enough to pay their debts to our departed comrade'—which was a very nice speech.

"Spud was a bit dazed.

"'Nobby ain't departed yet,' he sez; 'read that little bit again, Smithy.' So I did.

"'One pound four an' tuppence,' sez Spud, agitated. 'I don't owe no one pound four an' tuppence, an' what's more, I ain't goin to pay.'

"All the fellers in the crowd who wasn't on the list shouted 'Shame!' an' Billy Mason, shuttin' his eyes, stepped forward, an' sez, 'Friends an' comrades all: I hope the chaps who owe money to pore old Nobby will come forward like men an' pay their debts to our gallant comrade who fills a soldiers grave.'

"'You shut up!' snapped Spud; 'you don't owe him anything, an' I keep on tellin' you he's not departed, an' he don't fill anything—except hisself with green apples. I ain't goin' to pay!'

"An' some of the other fellers on the list said the same.

"One or two of 'em, though, paid up like gentlemen, an' said they didn't remember borrowin' it, but they supposed it was all right.

"But Spud was wild, an' wilder still next day when it got all over barracks that he was tryin' to rob a dyin' comrade.

"He come to me an' said that before he paid he'd see pore Nobby—he didn't say 'pore Nobby'—to the other end of Hull, but I wouldn't argue with him.

"'You know your own conscience best,' I sez. 'I don't think I'd risk bein' haunted for the sake of a miserable one pound four an' tuppence; an' Spud got very wild, an' went over to the hospital an' asked if him an' Pug Taylor could see Nobby.

"They got permission, an found Nobby lookin' very bad.

"'Look here, Nobby,' sez Spud as soon as he got in the ward, 'what about this money?'

"'What money?' sez Nobby in a tiny, weak, squeaky kind of voice.

"'The money you say I owe you,' sez Spud.

"Nobby groaned.

"'What do you mean by sayin' I owe you money?' sez Spud, very wild.

"Nobby shook his head, very weary.

"'I'm surprised at you, Nobby,' sez Pug Taylor, sorrerful, 'saying I borrered nine shillin's to send to my pore old mother. I ain't got no relations.'

"But Nobby only groaned.

"'You must have been wanderin' in your head,' sez Pug.

"'No, I warn't,' sez Nobby, very quick. 'Don't try to get out of it that way. I was of sound mind an' understanding wasn't I, Smithy?'

"'Never more so,' I sez, prompt.

"'Fancy a man,' sez Spud, 'a man layin' on a bed of sickness, tellin' a lie like that! Where do you expect to go to, Nobby?'

"'Don't worry me, Spud,' sez Nobby; 'don't disturb my last day or so. Pay Smithy what you owe me, an' say no more about it,' an' then Nobby began to groan an' make faces. Spud picks up his cap an' glares at Nobby.

"'Don't you make no mistake, Nobby,' sez Spud; 'I ain't goin' to pay it, whether you 'aunt me or not.'

"'You've got a hard 'art,' sez Nobby, feebly; an' Spud came back to barracks wilder than ever.

"Next day I went up see Nobby.

"He was sittin' up in an armchair readin'.

"'Hullo, Smithy,' he sez, 'how much did you collect on the will?'

"'Seven an' fourpence ha'penny,' I sez.

"'Hold on to it,' sez Nobby; 'I shall be out of hospital tomorrow.'"

4.—On Advertising

"There was a bit in the paper the other day," said Private Smith, "about a regiment bein' bathed once week accordin' to regulations. I don't know whether it's true that it won't wash itself regular, but I do know this, that before our colonel went an' advertised the regiment by sayin' it didn't like soap an' water, he'd shoot hisself.

"There was a feller in ours once who used to dig up bits of Latin and French, an' he had one what said, 'Hot tongs, hot more,' *Autres temps, autres moeurs*, which meant that people are different nowadays to what they used to be.

"I've known the time when colonels used to go swaggerin' up to the War Office pretendin' their regiment was the only real regiment in the army, an' that all the others was likely at any minute to go all into a gallopin' decline as soon as they was asked to do hard work. But nowadays that's all changed. Most of the colonels are 'army reformers.'

"It's a sort of a game. The War Office calls all the colonels together an' sez—

"'Well, gentlemen, I suppose you know the army's rotten? If you don't you haven't been readin' the papers. Now, I want to know what you chaps have been doin' for your country.'

"Up speaks one gallant old feller—

"'I wrote an article for the *Friday Review* showin' how all the men are drawn from the criminal classes.'

"'Good,' says the War Office, 'I'll make you a general.'

"Then another hero speaks up—

"'I put a bit in the *Times*, about their not bein' as good as the German soldiers.'

"'Very good, indeed,' says the War Office. 'I'll put you in charge of the Intelligence Department—because you know a lot about Germans,' it sez.

"'I made a speech at a dog show,' sez another scarred warrior,' I said that British soldiers was naturally dirty, an' wouldn't take baths.'

"'Splendid!' sez the War Office. 'Will you have a V.C. or a pension?'

"'A pension,' sez the hero, quick, 'payable in advance.'

"To be a real army reformer," Smithy went on, "you've got to start out with the idea that things couldn't he any worse than they are, an' you can't see how they're goin' to be better. Then you'll please both sides, an' get a reputation for bein' a deep thinker. But the great thing is to keep your name in front of the public so that when a war *does* come along, the newspapers will say, 'We strongly recommend that the foolish an' old-fashioned generals now in the field be recalled, an' Major-General Gass-Hometer, the celebrated author of *Should Soldiers Be Disinfected?* be immediately placed in command.'

"It don't matter whether you're a fighter so long as you're a writer, an' it don't matter what you write, books or articles, or damnsilly orders, so long as it gets talked about.

"We had a feller in our battalion by the name of Hawkey—one of the nicest chaps you'd meet in a day's march. The only thing about Hawkey that was in any way wrong, was the fact that he was always livin' in a fret an' worry that he was wastin' his opportunities. He used to mark off the days that passed without anything happenin' to him with a big O.

"He was the chap that taught me about the newspapers.

"If you don't get your name into print you might as well be dead,' he sez, an' I must say he got *his* name in often enough.

"Once he was A Young Soldier Cured of Indigestion by Wilkins' Wafers, once he was A Fighting Soldier Cured of Nervousness by Nappers' Nervo. Another time there was a bit in the paper about him—how he always took a cup of Jeef Buice before goin' on guard. So what with bein' Made A New Man one week, an' being Saved from Death another week, Hawkey had a good time—in fact, he was the most celebrated man in the regiment for a while, an' every bloomin' post brought letters from old ladies askin' him if he could recommend anything for warts.

"Nobby Clark ain't what I might call a jealous feller as a rule, but Hawkey's success got him a bit on the raw, especially as Hawkey began to put on side an' start givin' medical advice on the strength of his cures. So when I saw Nobby thinkin', an' thinkin', very hard one day, I knew he had a scheme.

"He started readin' the newspapers which, as there wasn't any murders goin' on just about then, showed he was hatchin' something.

"Sure enough, about two weeks after, all the London papers came out with a lot of stuff about Nobby, with his photograph. How he suffered for years with Pains in the Head after Drinkin', an' Pains in the Legs after Marchin', an' Pains in the Arms after Carryin' Coal. An' how he always felt tired at night. an' never wanted to get up in the mornin's, but after takin' two bottles of Swink's Tonic he was a New Man.

"As soon as it got round barracks that Nobby was goin' to put himself up against Hawkey in the advertisin' line there was wild excitement. Most of the fellers backed Hawkey.

"'It stands to reason,' sez Spud Murphy, 'that Nobby ain't got harf a chance against Hawkey. Look how well Hawkey's name is known! He's been cured of fits an' cured of dyspepsia, an' cured of pains in the back for years an' years.'

"Hawkey opened the fight next week. There was a long account in the papers of how he was bald from his youth, havin' been born so, but, thanks to one bottle of Hair Jam his hair grew so fast now that it wanted cuttin' every two hours.

"Nobby wasn't a bit downhearted. His account came out in all the London and Manchester papers of how, years ago, he'd broken his neck in three places, but thanks to Malted Embrocation, he was now able to turn his head right round.

"Then Hawkey came out with a bit that started 'Years ago I was worn to a skeleton by fever and wounds. I was so thin that when the sergeant saw me sideways he reported me absent.' An' went on to tell about the benefit he got out of Fattem's Cod Liver Oil.

"Nobby soon replied to that. The papers had columns an' columns headed, 'Obesity in Barracks: Soldier who was about to be invalided out of the Service for Fatness cured by taking Smiler's Shadow Tablets!'

"Every new paper that came out had something about Nobby or Hawkey in it. Nobby's was the best because he showed so much what I might call originality He didn't stick to medicines like Hawkey did, but dodged about.

"Once he appeared in print like this—

Dear Sir, I send you one of your celebrated 7s. 6d. keyless gold watches, what I carried with me through the war. It kept good time, and was so regular in its habits that after a bit I got it to wind itself.—Yours truly,

Private Clark, 1st Anchester Regiment.

"Nobby bought the old watch from a feller for sixpence, and by return the Watch Company sent him a new one as a little present.

"Then Nobby wrote about fountain pens, an' boots, an' muscle developers, an' things of that sort, so naturally he got a bit ahead of old Hawkey, who couldn't get out of the medicine way of writin'.

"In fact it was Nobby that scored all along the line, and, what's more, after a little time, he got a jolly sight cleverer at Hawkey's own line of business than Hawkey was hisself—namely, in the patent medicine way.

"In my opinion, the best thing he ever done was how he broke down from brain work an' had to be carried to parade on a stretcher, but three go's of Little Champion Lung Polish re-ju-vern-ated him. That was only one of the long words he used—he was a long time makin' up that letter with the help of a dictionary—'reciprocated' was one, and 'rehabilitated' was another, an' 'revivify' was another. You see he opened the dictionary at 're' an' never got away from it.

"It was the last one Nobby did as a matter of fact.

"It was gettin' near the furlough season an' soon after this fine letter of Nobby's appeared, the Lung Polish people put it in the paper under the heading: 'A Modern Miracle: Soldier's Sad Story of Sickness and Suffering.' Nobby paraded at orderly room with a lot of other chaps for leave of absence.

"The adjutant saw 'em one by one, an' told 'em they could have their passes, or else they couldn't, as the case might be.

"When it came to Nobby's turn the adjutant sez—

"'Oh! Private Clark?'

"'Yes, sir,' sez Nobby.

"'What do you want?'

"'A furlough, please, sir,' sez Nobby.

"The adjutant looks at him in amazement.

"'A furlough?' he sez.

"'Yes, sir,' sez Nobby.

"'What!' sez the adjutant in astonishment; 'go on leave? In your sorry state?'

"'Haven't you got pains in your feet, an' pains in your head?' sez the adjutant.

"'Thanks to Lung Polish—' sez Nobby.

"'Won't you have horrid fits of nerves an' can't sleep at night?' sez the adjutant, who appeared to have been readin' the papers.

"'I used to,' sez Nobby, 'but thanks to Bright's Nerve Pills, I'm—'

"'An', sez the adjutant, 'am I right in believin' that you suffer from shortness of breath and palpitation?'

"'Years ago,' sez Nobby, very agitated, I used to, but, thanks to Bilker's Breath Beans, I am now a new—'

"The adjutant shook his head.

"'No,' he sez; 'I can't give a furlough. I can't let you loose on the world to spread all those diseases among innocent people. I want you here—under my eye,' he sez, so that if the worst comes to the worst we can bury you with military honours,' he sez."

5.—On Promotion

"Fellers who got on in the world," said Smithy sagely, "don't give themselves airs as a rule. It's the fellers that think they've got on. Me an' Nobby went to a 'do' in the town the other night. It was a lecture business with a magic lantern about Niagara Falls. The chap who gave the lecture was the head reporter on the *Wigshire Chronicle and Anchester County Gazette.*

"From what I could hear, he got a free pass to Canada on some ship or other. He was there two weeks, an' what he don't know about Canada now ain't worth knowin'. A young chap who sat next to me an' Nobby said he was a decent feller before he went, but since he's come back, his head's so big that he has had to have a bit let into his hat.

"I've known fellers who've got on to such an extent that they don't really know how much they owe. An' do they give themselves airs? Not a bit. It's 'Have a drink, Smithy,' an' 'Put it down to me, miss,' just as friendly as possible. An' it ain't always what a man becomes that makes him hefty-headed, it's what he dreams of becomin'. When a feller's had a good word from the colonel, an' walks about barracks seein' hisself with the sergeant-major's gold crown on his sleeve, he's a big sight more cocky than he is when the bloomin' warrant comes along.

"My experience is that a chap who's a private is a perfect little gentleman till some one gives him a stripe an makes him a lance-corporal. If he's got anything bad in him that's the time it comes out. Between the officer an' the man there ain't any middle-grades really. Non-commissioned officers I've never had no use for. They're mostly chaps who've polished up their school-board education to get out of the hard work that a Tommy has got to do.

"So when I see a nice, bright young feller suddenly give up playin' the goat, an' wearin' a worried, don't-come-near-me look, I know he's doomed for the stripe, and cut him off my visiting list, so to speak. But the most 'orrid thing that ever happened come about three weeks ago. On that very day I sez to Nobby—

"'Comin' down town tonight, Nob?'

"'No,' sez Nobby, quick and short.

"I looks at him for a bit, for there was something is his eye I didn't like.

"'Why not?' I sez.

"'Never mind why not,' he sez, as short as ever.

"'Got no money?' I sez.

"'Never Mind,' he sez.

"'Are you a prisoner or anything?' I sez anxiously

"'Never mind,' he sez.

"Then the 'orrid truth broke over me.

"'Nobby,' I gasps, 'Nobby, they ain't goin' to make corporal of you, are they?'

"'They are,' he sez and stalks away.

"I tell you, I was upset something awful. Me an' old Nobby have been pals for years, an I never thought it would come to this. Now I understood a lot. Why Nobby wouldn't join me and Swank Roberts when we went down town to clear out the *Peacock*. Why Nobby kept away from the canteen for hours at a time.

"It was all over barracks before long that Nobby was goin' to get promotion, an' fellers come from all parts to look at Nobby to see what a corporal looked like before he was born. Nobby took no notice, sittin' on his bed-cot pretending to read *Every Soldier's Guide to Promotion*, an' the fellers who come in one by one to ask him if it was true got a short answer.

"'I asked you a civil question,' sez Spud Murphy.

"'An' I've give you a civil answer,' snaps Nobby, still pretending to read his book.

"'You might call it civil,' sez Spud, 'but when I tell a chap to go to where you told me to go to, I don't reckon I'm bein' polite.'

"Nobby said nothing.

"'Is it true,' sez Spud, 'that you're going to be a corporal?'

"'It is,' sez Nobby. 'I've told you once.'

"'Well, all I can say,' sez Spud, very gloomy, is that the army's goin' to the dogs. What are they goin' to make you a corporal for—your good looks?'

"Nobby got wilder an' wilder, but said nothing.

"'Have they run short of soldiers?' sez Spud aggravatingly.

"Nobby got up quick, and Spud scooted.

"Pug Wilson come in some time after.

"'Hello, Nobby,' sez Pug sorrowfully, 'so they've caught you, have they?'

"'Whatcher mean?' sez Nobby, very fierce.

"'Ain't it true, then?' sez Pug anxiously, 'or has some one been tellin' lies about your being made corporal?'

"'Of course it's true,' sez Nobby.

"'Pore old Nobby,' sez Pug, wipin' his eyes, and walked sadly away.

"Nobby was very sore at the way chaps went on.

"'Look here, Smithy,' he sez, 'when I'm a corporal I'll teach these fellers to talk to their superior,' he sez.

"'A fat lot you'll do,' I sez. 'You'll be hitting somebody an' losing your stripe before you've had it a week.'

"Two mornings afterwards it came out in orders that our bold Nobby was to get the 'dog's leg,' (shape of the corporal's chevron), and the square wasn't big enough to hold Nobby as he walked across to the canteen.

"I met him halfway over.

"'Hello, Nobby,' I sez.

"'Corporal Clark, if you please,' sez Nobby, hoity-toitily.

"'Never mind your bloomin' title,' I sez, 'are you going to wet the stripe?'

"Nobby waved his hand in his grand way.

"'I don't drink with privates,' he sez, 'only with men of me own rank,' an' he turned into the corporals' room.

"When I got into the canteen I was so knocked over by Nobby's disgusting behaviour that I drank out of the first pot I could find.

"'Hold hard, Smithy,' sez Spud. 'That's my beer when you've done with it.'

"'Never mind about your beer,' I sez bitterly, 'I've lost a pal what's turned into a serpent.'

"We had a long talk about Nobby's promotion. It was a sort of meeting like Nobby used to have when he was respectable.

"'I can't understand Nobby taking the stripe,' sez Pug. 'Where's he going to get his money from—corporals ain't allowed to swindle nobody.'

"The end of our discussion was that corporal or no corporal, Nobby had to be taken down a peg or two.

"Next morning, there was Nobby on parade in the corporals' rank, a-twisting his moustache and frowning like anything.

He hadn't got many orders to give, but he managed to get in a few remarks, such as, 'Now then, Wilson, look to your front,' an' 'Stop talking there,' an' 'Don't scratch your nose in the ranks, Smithy,' till I felt like turning round and smacking him in the eye.

"When we got back to the barrack-room the fun began. We were all in before Nobby and waited. By and by in came his nibs, and Spud Murphy shouted, ''T'shun!' and we all stood to attention. Nobby got red, and frowned worse than ever.

"'None of your cheek,' he sez.

"'No, sir,' sez Spud, saluting.

"'Look here, Murphy,' sez Nobby, very hot, 'don't you come your funny games with me, or I'll give you a wipe—I mean I'll put you in the guard-room.

"'Yes, sir,' sez Spud, saluting again.

"'And don't you call me "sir," ' sez Nobby very fierce. 'Call me corporal, you putty-faced—I mean you disrespectful feller.'

"Just then Pug came up and saluted.

"Any orders, colonel,' he sez, saluting.

"Nobby was choking wild. You see, he was too much of a private to sneak, and he wasn't enough of a corporal to do the N.C.O. act.

We made his blooming life a misery for the next two days. If any of us met him when nobody was about, we used to salute him, Spud went down on his knees once an' tapped his head on the ground as Nobby passed.

"'Get up, you perishing recruit,' sez Nobby, 'or I'll put you in the guardroom.'

"But Spud still knelt, sayin', 'Hail, hail, great chief,' and things like that, till Nobby, looking round to see if anybody was in sight, took a fine drop kick at him.

"That rather upset the saluting business, but Vaney, who picked up a little bit of foreign language when he was on the motor-bus, started the '*Mong.*' It appears, from what Vaney sez—and its probably a lie—in the French Army, when a private talks to the colonel or the company officer, he sez '*Mong.*'

"Nobby told Vaney to do something one morning—Vaney's just been transferred to our company—and Vaney sez, '*Wee, wee, mong Colonel.*'

"'What's that?' sez Nobby quick, so Vaney repeated it.

"'I want none of your cheek,' sez Nobby.

"'That ain't cheek,' sez Vaney.

"'What is it, then?' sez Nobby, who didn't know more than the man in the moon.

"'It's French,' sez Vaney.

"'Well, don't do it,' sez Nobby sternly.

"The '*mong*' business was a great success. We *monged* Nobby till he nearly cried.

"'Smithy,' he sez to me one day, very solemn, 'if I have much more of this I shall do something pretty bad.'

"'Will you, *mong* Nobby?' I sez.

"'Yes, I will, *mong* fathead,' he snaps, and went away.

"I've always said about Nobby that he's got second-sight. He sez so hisself; in fact, when he was a little boy he had to wear spectacles for it. So when he said that something was going to happen, I knew it was coming true. It came about in an unexpected way.

"Me and Pug Wilson was down town one night. It was pay night, and Saturday night, too, and there was trouble in the blooming air. Just before we left barracks we had to call at the guardroom to get our passes. While we was there in came the provost corporal and said that Billy Mason was in town drinking like a fish. So the sergeant of the guard passed the word and got down the biggest pair of handcuffs he could find, and unlocked a cell door all ready for Billy. In the town we passed the picket, looking sad, and Pug said to me—

"'Smithy, I smell blood.' And I could smell it. too.

"It's a rum thing how affairs came about. Me and Pug passed a pleasant evening doing nothing, and we was coming back, talking about what a rotten place Anchester was, with the pubs closing at ten, when we heard the picket coming toward us at the double. As they went running past I saw that Nobby was in charge, and one of the chaps called out, 'Billy's got a rough house at the *Phoenix.*'

"So me and Pug went back to see the fun. There was a little crowd outside the public, and inside we could hear Billy's voice and broken glass.

"Nobby pushed through the crowd, and I went into the bar with the picket. Billy, with his tunic off, was at the other end of the bar-room with a chair in his hand.

"'Hello, Nobby,' he sez through his teeth, an' I could see he had one of his mad fits on.

"'Hello, Billy,' sez Nobby quietly; 'come out of this, old son.'

"'What are you going to do?'

"'Put you in the clink,' sez Nobby.

"'How many of you?' sez Billy, gettin' a grip of the chair.

"'Put that chair down, an I'll do it myself,' sez Nobby, who is a rare feller for meetin' trouble half-way.

"Then before he knew what was going to happen, Bill dropped the chair, and landing out caught Nobby a whack on the jaw that floored him, It's serious business to strike a corporal, an' when Billy saw what he'd done, it sobered him,

"As Nobby picked himself up, there was a stir at the doorway, and the provost sergeant pushed his way through.

"'Make that man a prisoner,' sez Nobby to the picket as quick as anything, and the picket closed round Billy, who was as quiet as a lamb.

"'Hello,' sez the police sergeant; 'what's this—did this man strike you, Corporal Clark?'

"'No,' sez Nobby.

"'What's that mark on your face?'

"'A birthmark,' sez Nobby, quick as lightning.

"When Billy came up at the orderly room he got ten days, an' the colonel said that if he's struck Nobby he'd have put him back for a court martial. But Nobby swore and swore that Billy didn't lift his hands. After Billy got his dose, Nobby went into the colonel's office

"At dinner-time, when we was all together in the canteen, talking about Nobby an' saying what a decent chap he was, in he walked.

"Spud was the first to do the handsome. He ups with his pot an' handed it over.

"'Here you are, corporal,' he sez 'drink hearty, an' let bygones be bygones.'

"Nobby took the pot.

"'Not so much of the corporal,' he sez, and then I saw his stripe had gone. 'I've given it up. private's good enough for me. I like a rank where, if a feller hits me, I can hit him back.'"

"Lots of fellows go home for Christmas, but lots more stay in barracks an' enjoy themselves," said Private Smith, who is spending a few days with me just now, "After all, going home for Christmas ain't much catch unless you've got a lot of pals with you. An uncle of mine asked me home two years ago. He said he'd come into a lot of money and wanted to do me well, but the feller the money belonged to found him out, and I only see poor Uncle Tim now on visiting days. He's in what Nobby calls the Civil Service.

"Give me barracks at Christmas time. There ain't a happier, light-hearteder lot of fellers than 'B' Company on Christmas Day, when everything's free, drinks included. Last year was the most excitin' Christmas we's ever had, more especially because of our pantomime what Nobby Clark got up, *The Babes in the Wood*, or *Princess Blue Bell*.

"It was all Nobby's idea, and he went an' saw the adjutant about it, and the adjutant gave permission. We rigged the library up just like a real, first-class London theatre, and you wouldn't have been able to tell the difference. Real limelight, a real band in front, and sawdust on the floor, and armchairs for the officers—it was fine.

"We thought of getting real young ladies to play the parts, but Nobby said that that was carrying the thing a bit too far, so we made Nobby play the part of the Fairy Queen, and Tiny White and Big Harvey was the two babes in the wood. Nobby got a feller named Ginger, who makes poetry, to help to write the pantomime. Ginger's the chap who wrote that bit about the wreck of the *Birkenhead*. I forget how it goes, but the first verse starts—

O, Comrades bold, come gather round,
And I will tell to thee,
A story of a gallant deed
Upon the briny sea.

"It's a fine poem, and I wonder somebody hasn't took it up an' put it in the papers. Well, from what Nobby sez, all pantomimes are writ in verse, and the way him and Ginger wrote that blooming panto was a marvel. The first scene was the 'Lower Regions.' Nobby sez all good pantomimes start in hell an' end nowhere.

"The Demon King was a chap named Jaggers, and he had to start—

O, comrades bold, come gather round

And listen to my awful sound.

"You see, Ginger can't write anything unless it starts 'O, *comrades bold,*' it's a sort of habit.

"Nobby had hard work making the chaps remember the bits they had to say. Spud Murphy was a sort of fairy godmother, and his bit went—

O, comrades bold, you see in me
A little fairy gay and free.

But Spud couldn't think what came after that, and Nobby used to get so wild that I thought he'd have a stroke.

"'Spud,' he sez, very solemn, 'if I've told you once I've told you six times that you've got to say to me—

I love you, little fairy queen,
You are the best I've ever seen.

"'And if I have to tell you again I'll give you a slosh in the neck.'

"What with one thing and another the rehearsals nearly killed Nobby. Two nights before Christmas the whole bloomin' show was upset by the Two Babes bein' put in the guard-room for fightin' a policeman in town. But the worst thing of all happened on Christmas Eve.

"Me an' Nobby had been havin' a last rehearsal, an' the play went fine. All except the demon king part. The chap who played that was a young feller named Jaggers, as I told you before. I could never quite make him out, He had a trick of lookin' the other way when you happened to be talking to him; he never looked you straight in the face. He was only a recruit in a manner of speakin', havin' been in the regiment a year, and bein' a quiet feller, with a bad temper—he got perfectly wild when he was upset—nobody said much to him. Nobby put him in the play because he looked like a demon king at times. That night, at rehearsal, Jaggers was very peculiar. He said lots of things that wasn't in the play, an' in parts he got very excited. I was quite astonished when Nobby didn't say anything to him, but just answered him as polite and patient as anything. By an' bye, I saw Nobby talkin' to him on the quiet, an' when he had finished Nobby came straight across to me.

"'Smithy,' he sez, as earnest as anything, 'cut across to the hospital an' tell the orderly on duty that something's wrong with Jaggers.'

"'What's the game?' I sez, for I know Nobby is a rare feller for

371

pulling your leg.

"'Here, wait a bit,' sez Nobby, an' wrote down something on a paper, 'give this to the chap in charge.'

"I could see that Nobby wasn't jokin', so I slipped off as fast as I could nip, an' got to the hospital just as the doctor was leavin' after his night visit.

"I handed the paper to the orderly.

"'What's that?' sez the officer, and the orderly handed it over. The doctor read it, an' I could see by the way he frowned that something was up.

"'Four orderlies and a stretcher,' he sez, sharp, 'an' bring along some stout straps—go back to the library, Smith.'

"I was as mystry-fied as could be, but when I got into the library I could see there was trouble.

"All the fellers were standin' in the middle of the room in their dresses—except Nobby, who bein' a sort of manager was only in his uniform. But what held me was Jaggers. He was standin' in front of Nobby, with a long knife in his hand an' his eyes were glaring something shockin'. Nobby was as cool as a cucumber, which is more than I should have been, for Jaggers, in his demon dress, was a gashly sight.

"He was shoutin' when I came in.

"'I know you!' he was sayin' to Nobby, 'you're the man who has been trying to ruin me!'

"'You're mistakin' me,' sez Nobby, very mildly for 'for my brother, who's very much like me.'

"'You Lie!' howls Jaggers, wavin' his knife about. 'You're the man, an' by—'

"Nobby was gradually edgin' round till he got Jaggers with his back to the door.

"If ever there was mad murder in a chap's face it was in Jaggers', and though I didn't like the knife a bit, I steps up to Nobby's side, an 'sez—

"'Hold hard, Jaggers ; you're makin' a bit of an error—'

"He turned on me like a devil.

"'You!' he sez, an' he tightened his grip on the knife 'you're the other villain—'

"Over his shoulders I saw the four men of the medical staff in the doorway, an' though I ain't no friend of the Poultice Wallahs, I blessed the sight of their little red crosses. They were on Jaggers in the minute, the knife was out of his hand, and he lay helpless on the door before you could count two, They can handle a man can the medical staff when it comes to a pinch, an' the way they strapped Jaggers to a stretcher was the neatest thing I've ever seen done.

"From what the doctor told Nobby, Jaggers was a natural born lunatic, an' how he got into the army nobody knows. But Jaggers goin' mad didn't upset the show. It takes more than a little thing like that to put Nobby out. It was what followed. For in half an hour, round came the orderly sergeants warning all sorts of chaps for guard. There had to be a double guard for Jaggers, who was marked 'dangerous.' About that time—we was stationed in a garrison town—the guard and piquets came pretty heavy on the men, an' as soon as I heard about the extra one, I knew where me and Nobby would spend our Christmas Day.

"Sure enough, we was for it. No. 2 Magazine, the most horrible bloomin' post in the garrison. A lonely stone buildin', on the top of a hill, miles away from everywhere, an' on the edge of the marsh.

"The only comfort was that it was a double guard, two men at a time, an' I knew that me an' Nobby would be together, It was snowin' a bit when we paraded on Christmas mornin'.

"'This is a nice happy Christmas, I *don't* think,' sez Nobby bitterly; 'an' me who was goin' to be a fairy queen.'

"Pug Wilson was paradin', too.

"'I'd sooner have your job than mine,' he sez, 'hospital guard over poor old Jaggers, an' him carryin' on something awful.'

"Spud Murphy was standin' at the gate as we marched out.

"'*A happy Christmas, Bluebell dear; it only comes but once a year,*' he sez, sayin' his lines with a grin.

"'When I get back,' sez Nobby, through his teeth. 'I'll take Spud by the neck, an' bash his fat head—'

"'Silence in the ranks,' sez the sergeant.

"It turned out to be a most perfectly rotten day. It snowed, an' snowed, an' snowed, an' the wind that came sweepin' round the magazine nearly cut you in two. Me an' Nobby was second relief, twelve till two and six till eight.

"We stood together in the afternoon, lookin' towards the barracks. They are about two miles away from the magazine, an' the guard-room's about a half a mile away.

"'To think,' sez Nobby, 'that me an' you are stuck here, doing sentry go, whilst a mud-faced Cockney plasterer like Spud Murphy is drinkin' free beer in barracks—why, it's enough to make a chap go cracked like poor old Jaggers.'

"That afternoon a feller who came up from barracks said Jaggers was better, but was still in the padded cell, an' nobody had gone in to him yet. It was a miserable day.

"When we was 'off' we sat in front of the guard room fire an' told yarns. Bill Hatchett told a yarn about a ghost in India, an' Nobby told a yarn about a chap who used to walk about barracks at Christmas time with his 'ead under his arm, an' another feller told a tale about a ghost *he* saw once.

"'When you've all finished tellin' lies,' I sez, 'you might wake me up, I'm goin' to snatch a sleep.'

'The corporal of the guard woke me an' Nobby just before twelve, an' I've never felt less inclined for guard. It was snowin' hard when we got outside, an' we stepped out smart to keep ourselves warm. It seemed a long walk to the magazine, but we got there at last, stumblin' along in the snow, with only the corporal's lantern to show us the path.

"The two chaps we relieved was Bill Hatchett an' Happy Johnson, an' they wasn't sorry to see us, I can tell you.

"'Any report?' sez the corporal.

"'No, corporal,' sez Happy, an' I thought by the light of the lantern he looked white, 'only me an' Bill heard some funny noises.'

"'Like what?' sez the corporal,

"'Like a man laughin',' sez Johnson.

"'You've been dreamin',' sez the corporal, 'quick march.'

"Me an' Nobby watched 'em disappearin' down the hill, the corporal's lamp a-waggin' till they reached the guardroom.

"'Cheerful blighter,' sez Nobby.

"Nothin' happened for a quarter of an hour. We heard the bells in the town strike quarter-past twelve, an' we marched round the magazine an' pulled up by the sentry box. We was talkin' quietly about fellers we knew, when suddenly Nobby sez—

"'What's that?'

"We listened. Then we heard something far away.

"'It's a bugle.' sez Nobby, in a whisper,

"Sure enough it was. As clear as a bell it came through the snow, an there wasn't any mistake about it.

"'It's the assembly,' sez Nobby.

"The assembly at half-past twelve on Christmas night means something extraordinary. They don't parade the garrison at midnight for nothing.

"'It can't be a fire?' sez Nobby, 'because we'd have heard the fire bugle?'

"He propped his rifle up against the magazine an' put both hands to his mouth an' shouted, 'Guard, turn out.'

"We shouted twice, an' then we heard another sound, a sound that made icy shivers run down our backs. It was somebody laughin' quietly, an' close at hand. I had my rifle at the charge in a second, and Nobby snatched up his.

"'Halt, who comes there?' he shouted.

Nobody answered for a second, then we heard the laugh again.

"'Halt, who comes there?' Nobby shouted again. 'Stand, or I'll fire!'

"I heard the bolt of his rifle snick open an' snap close again. Down below we could see the corporal's lantern winkin', an' by the way it jerked I could tell he was running.

"'Smithy,' whispers Nobby, there's somebody hidin' round the corner of the magazine—that "assembly" means something—halt!'

"We saw a movement by the wall, A figure crouching, it looked like, an' Nobby raised his rifle an' took aim.

"'Come out of that!' he called, 'or you're a dead man.'

"We waited then a voice said softly—

"'Nobby.'

"Nobby lowered his rifle.

"'Good God,' he whispered, 'it's poor old Jaggers—he's escaped. That's what the assembly was for.'

"'Nobby,' sez the voice again.

"'Yes,' sez Nobby softly.

"'I know my lines, Nobby,' sez the voice

Behold in me the Demon King,
I'm up to every single thing.

"The corporal an' the file of the guard was quite close now.

"'What's wrong?' shouted the corporal.

"'Show a light, corporal,' sez Nobby.

"When the light came, Jaggers was lyin' on the ground. He wore his demon king dress an' was perished with cold. Nobby knelt down an' lifted his head, an' Jaggers smiled.

"I took off my overcoat an' tucked it round him.

"'Nobby,' he sez softly, 'do I know my lines?'

"'No one better, old feller,' sez Nobby gently.

"Jaggers shut his eyes.

"'I heard a man say you were at No. 2, so I thought I'd come an' tell you I knew 'em,' he said.' I'm going to have a sleep now. I'll feel better when I wake up.'

"Poor old Jaggers never did wake up."

7.—Smithy—Ambassador

"There's a lot of fun in the army," said Smithy, "and there's a lot of blooming tragedy, too. In my service I've seen things that'd upset a sentimental cove like you something dreadful. Not the things you see on Christmas almanacs wot the grocer gives away, mind you. Not red soldiers dyin' on green battlefields an' dreamin' of blue mothers; but real, honest tragedies, with no hank whatever.

"I remember a young feller joining the battalion about ten years ago. A nice, quiet, pleasant-spoken feller, who you could tell with half an eye was a tip-topper. He was a clean soldier an' went about his work without talking, but me an' Nobby noticed something about him that we didn't altogether like. We got two posts a day at that time, and every morning an' night this chap used to waylay the postman an' ask if there was any letter for Private Morris, but none seemed to come.

"He waited an' waited, and it got quite a reg'lar thing to see Morris waiting patiently outside the barrack-room for the postman who brought no letter. One day Morris got up as usual. To our surprise instead of sayin' 'Not today,' as be usually did, the postman fished a letter out of his bag an' handed it to Morris, who stuffed it into his pocket an' walked away.

"Nobby an' me was fairly friendly with him, so after a bit we walked down to find Morris. Naturally we thought he was one of those fellers who get a bit of allowance from pa, and Nobby sez, 'The best thing we can do, Smithy, is to go down an' prevent this pore young chap from wastin' the money he's got from home.'

"We found Morris in the back field. He was lying down under a tree, an' his head was on his arm.

"'What cheer, Morris?' sez Nobby, an' was going on to say something about coming into money when we saw Morris' face. I tell you it gave us a turn, for it was as white as death, an' there was something in his eyes that made me shiver.

"I nudged Nobby an' started to walk away, for I could see that Morris was in trouble, but Nobby had seen something, too, and wasn't

376

going to be put off.

"'Hullo, Morris,' he sez, as cheerful as anything, 'somebody left you a fortune?' Morris didn't answer, but dropped his eyes on to the ground, and than I saw Nobby's game.

"He sort of sauntered up casually to where Morris lay, then, stooping quick as lightning, he jerked something from underneath his coat. Nobby was as cool as a blooming ice factory.

"'What's this?' he sez quite surprised. 'I'm blowed if it ain't a revolver, Smithy; where did you get it, Morris?'

"'Give it me!' sez Morris hoarsely.

"'Not me,' sez Nobby very calm. Infantry soldiers ain't supposed to have revolvers—especially infantry soldiers what have had letters from people that makes 'em look like dead men. Morris,' he sez, and Nobby was very earnest—for Nobby,'is it money or is it a girl because neither of 'em's worth—that.'

"Morris made no answer, but laid face downwards with his head on his arm.

"'Money,' sez Nobby, is hard to get hold of I admit, but girls is fairly plentiful; but gettin' money an' gettin' a girl is child's play compared with getting' a new blooming head once you've started blowing it off with a cheap pistol.'

"Morris groaned a little, an' turned over.

"'Leave me in peace, Clark,' he sez.

"'That's all right,' sez Nobby, cheerful;'it's leavin' you in pieces wot I'm worryin' about. I ain't going away from here, Morris, till you tell me an' Smithy all about it. And if me an' Smithy think it's bad enough to shoot yourself over, why, we'll go away an' leave you to it—we can't do fairer than that.'

"It was a long time before Morris would chuck his trouble off his chest, but bimeby he up an' made a clean breast of it. It was all about a girl, like Nobby said it would be. Morris didn't like telling us at first, but as soon as he began he told us everything, even to the girl's name and where she lived. It appears that Morris was in love with some girl who was in love with him, and they had a bit of a quarrel, so he had a row and went away and enlisted. From what I could make out the girl had a lot of money of her own, and Morris had about three an' tuppence with prospects—being a rising young feller in the painting line of business. An' her having money and him having none gave him the needle, especially when people said he was after the brass. So the end of it was be went away, leaving a letter, saying her money was between him and her, an' he never wanted to hear from her again, an' if she wrote to him she was to address the letter care of a bank in London. Well, the letter she sent was the one he got that morning. She said in very high-class language that if a chap allowed money to upset his love, he wasn't any chap for her, so farewell, an' never let me hear from you again. N.B.—My address is now 44 Elgin Gardens, S.W.

"Nobby was very indignant when Morris finished tellin' the tale.

"So that's what's makin' you shoot yourself, is it,' he sez, highly disgusted, 'because a girl with a bit of money wants to marry you?'

"'She doesn't want to marry me any more,' sez Morris very miserably.

"'If she's got any sense she don't,' sez Nobby, 'but if she's an ordinary kind of girl she'll want to marry you more than ever.'

"The end of it was that Nobby talked an' talked an' talked till Morris got ashamed of himself an' promised he wouldn't do any more monkey tricks. Me an' Nobby sold the revolver that night in town for eight-and-sixpence, an' had several drinks out of the money. 'What I can't understand,' sez Nobby, 'is what state of mind a feller gets into when he won't marry a girl with a bit of ready. Refuses to marry a girl because she's got money! Why, its blasphemous!'

"We had a long talk over the matter that night, an' next morning me an' Nobby paraded at the orderly room an' asked for special leave of absence to go to London.

"Going up in the train that afternoon we made up what we should say.

"'What's the name again, Smith?' sez Nobby.

"'Miss Dorothy Garratt,' I sez.

"'Very good,' sez Nobby, noddin' his head. 'Now, Smithy, you leave all the talking to me. I'll say to her, "Miss, are you aware that your *fiancé* is at present a soldier an' breakin' his bloomin' heart?" " "Good heavens, no!" she'll say. "It's a fact, miss," I'll say. "He's in the Anchester Regiment, what's just going out to war, an' it's six to four taken an' offered that he'll be killed—"'

"'Him being a reckless chap owin' to being in love,' I sez.

"'What you an' me are, Smithy,' sez Nobby, 'are ambassadors.'

"'What's that?' I sez.

"'A feller that sticks his nose into other people's trouble without bein' asked,' sez Nobby.

"Somehow, the nearer we got to the business the less me an' Nobby liked it. We sat over tea for a long time deciding what time we'd go,

378

and we kept putting it off, an' putting it off.

"It was about nine o'clock before we got to Elgin Gardens. No. 44 was a big, rich-looking house, and we stood outside for quite a long time.

"'I expect they've gone to bed,' sez Nobby ; 'it seems a shame to disturb 'em.'

"'Let's come tomorrow,' I sez; but Nobby sort of drew a long breath an' went up the steps an' knocked. I've always said about Nobby that you don't know what he *can't* do, an' the genteel way he rat-tatted on that door showed his education.

"We was both making up our minds to walk down the steps an' pretend that we'd knocked at the wrong house, when the door opened and there was a footman with a nice, white shirt-front.

"'We want to see Miss Dorothy Garratt,' sez Nobby as bold as brass.

"Bimeby the footman came back, an' sez the young lady would see us. He led the way upstairs—and the carpet on the stairs was soft an' crunchy, like snow—an' into a big room furnished better than any private bar I've seen.

"'Stand where you are, Smithy,' says Nobby; 'if you move you'll break something.'

"We waited about two minutes, when the door opened an' in came the prettiest girl you ever dreamt about.

"'You wish to see me about something,' she sez inquiringly.

"'Well, it's like this, miss,' sez Nobby, lookin' up at the ceiling, 'me an' Smithy thought we'd like to see you an' have a talk about a certain party. It's nothing to do with us, but he's a comrade of ours, so to speak an' we don't think it right.'

"The young lady looked puzzled.

"'I'm afraid—' she sez.

"'So are we,' sez Nobby quick, 'that's just what we are, we're afraid too. We're a respectable regiment, an' we don't want no horrible tragedies. What we want is a quiet, peaceful life, an' no bloomin' upsets—begging your pardon—an' the sooner you make him leave the regiment the better.'

"The girl looked more puzzled than ever.

"'I really don't know what you are talking about,' she sez.

"'Well,' sez Nobby, 'to put it plain an' above board, the chap's name is Morris.'

"'Morris,' she sez slowly. 'I'm afraid I don't know anybody of that name.'

"My heart went down into my boots, and so did Nobby's. I could see that by his dial. Poor old Nobby looked like a chap that's been dreamin' he's on furlough an' wakes up to find hisself in clink.

"'I'm afraid, miss,' he sez sorrowfully, 'we've made a slight error. We thought we was doin' a chap a good turn, but we've come to the wrong address. I'll bid you good evening, miss.'

"'Wait a moment,' she sez quick. Tell me about this Morris.'

"Nobby shook his head.

"'It's no good tellin' you, miss,' he sez, 'it would only make you feel miserable. He's a young chap of ours, who's only lately joined the army, an' he's in love with a girl, in consequence of which he was going to shoot hisself, only me an' Smithy stopped him.'

"'What is he like?' she sez, an' I could see her face had gone suddenly white. 'Is he tall?

"'Fairly,' see Nobby.

"'With blue eyes?' she sez quick.

"'I couldn't tell you about his eyes,' sez Nobby, but he's got a scar on one side of his head.'

"'Yes, yes,' she sez eager.

"'And he's a painter chap,' I sez.

"'A painter?' she gasps. 'Why, it's Jack, and he's enlisted, and he was going to shoot himself, and—'

"There was a lot more stuff like that. She asked about fifty questions in about ten seconds, an' she rung the bell an' ordered dinner for us.

"She was in a terrible state of mind, although Nobby told her it was no good thinkin' about going to Anchester that night.

"'Whatever you do, miss.' sez Nobby, 'don't you tell Morris tomorrow that me an' Smithy have seen you. Just write to him to meet you. There's a nice quiet hotel with a big garden where you can see him.'

"'How can I thank you, Mr Clark?' she sez, with tears in her eyes.

"'Don't mention It, miss,' sez Nobby, very agitated.

"She walked over to a desk, opened a drawer, an' took something out.

"'You must let me pay your expenses to London, she sez, an' she held out two banknotes to Nobby.'

"'Thank you, miss,' sez Nobby quietly, 'but our expenses ain't worth mentionin'. We're very much obliged, but we couldn't think of takin' money.'

"'I'm sorry,' she sez, flushing. 'I'm afraid I've hurt your feelings. Is there nothing I can do for you to show my gratitude?'

"Nobby shook his head.

"'Nothin', miss,' he sez. ' I've only one inclination just now—and so has Smithy.'

"'What is yours?' she sez.

"'A pint of Burton, thank you, miss,' sez Nobby.

"'Mine's the same,' I sez."

8.—HOGMANAY

"Nobby Clark was tellin' me a yarn the other day," said Private Smith, "about two blokes who got blown up in a quarry. One called Jack an' the other Bill. They used to hate the sight of each other, but they was put in beds next to one another, an' as Jack lost his nose an' Bill lost his ear in the explosion, they couldn't very well pass any unpleasant remarks between theirselves. Jack wasn't a bad-feelin' sort of chap, so on New Year's Day he ups an' sez—

"'An happy New Ye'r to you, Bill.'

"The other bloke got very wild.

"'An' a happy new nose to you,' he snarls, 'don't be so bloomin' personal.'

"What made Nobby tell me this was the nice kind sentiments that are goin' cheap just about now, where lots of fellers go round wishin' people they don't know, things they don't mean.

"Spud Murphy is one of the chaps who always gets sloppy about this time of the year, an' when he came up to Nobby a few days ago an' sez, 'A happy New Year', Nobby turns round an' sez, 'I don't want your good wishes. I've told you so about six years runnin', an' if I have to tell you again you'll get a dig in the eye!'

"New Year's Day," continued Smithy, "ain't nothing in the army unless you've got some pals in an Highland regiment. The 'Jocks' celebrate New Year's Day just the same as camels celebrate any day they happen to strike a river—they take in enough supplies to last 'em the rest of the year.

"There was a 'Jock' by the name of Ogilvie when we was quartered next to the 91st, who was a rare friend of mine an' Nobby's.

"He was one of them Scotsmen you never read about, freehanded an' liberal, an' he came from a little village called Glasgow—which is why he was called a Highlander.

"One Year's Eve he sez to me an' Nobby—

"'Come into our barracks for hogmanay.'

"'No thanks,' sez Nobby, 'I'm Church of England.'

"So Ogilvie explained it was nothin' to do with religion.

"'Is it something to drink?' sez Nobby, an' Ogilvie sez yes, so me an' Nobby said we'd be there.

"We turned up all right, and there was everything of the best, an' chaps was singin' an' chaps was dancin', an' one chap was playin' the bagpipes something awful.

"'I don't know why you call it hogmanay,' sez Nobby; 'it tastes like whisky—perhaps it's the Scotch way of spellin' it.'

"'It is,' sez Ogilvie.

"As I was for guard the next day I took a lot of water with my hogmanay, an' went away early. As I left, I heard Nobby tellin' a 'Jock'—

"'I'm a genuine Scotchman myself—having been born in Scotland—my father always wore kilts, an' me sister married a chap in the butterscotch line—'

"I didn't hear the rest of it. Nobby is what you might call 'adaptable.' Nobby got back to barracks about 3 a.m. I heard him, an' so did everybody else. He was singin' a song about a girl who was 'bonnie' an' lived in a 'bonnie' house in 'bonnie' Scotland, an' the way he'd got hold of the Scotch accent was simply marvellous.

"He was singin' another song about 'bonnie Highland Mary,' when the corporal of the room sez—

"'Now then, Mr. Blooming Clark, not so much "bonnie"; get to bed, or I'll be puttin' you where the pigs won't bite you.'

"Nobby must have got a lot of hogmanay into him, for he ups and sez—

"'Hoot, mon—dinna blether.'

"'What's he say?' sez the corporal.

"'Ye'll tak' the high road, an' I'll tak' the low,' sings Nobby.

"'Ye'll tak' the road to the guard-room,' sez the corporal, getting out of bed an' scrambling into his clothes, an' he orders me an' another chap to get out of bed an' escort Nobby to the clink.

"'What!' sez Nobby, lookin' reproachfully at me—'what! ma wee freen', ma brither Scot, ma bonnie Smithy—'

"'Shut up!' I sez, an' we led him over to the guardroom. He didn't say much, except that it was a 'braw munelicht nicht the nicht,' an' what *that* meant I don't know.

"The guard took his boots off an' put him in a cell, an', after he'd called the sergeant of the guard a 'low Southerner' or somethin' equally insultin', be went to sleep.

"When I took his breakfast across next mornin' he looked a bit silly.

"'Let this be a warnin' to you, Smithy,' he sez very solemn, 'don't take foreign drinks—beer's all right an' whisky's all right—but hogmanay is poison.'

"Now, everybody likes Nobby, an' the corporal of the room didn't want to jug him for drunk,' so he made it up with the sergeant of the guard that Nobby was to be 'crimed' for creatin' a disturbance in barracks after lights-out, and Nobby accepted the three days' C.B. with a thankful heart.

"The next day he said he was goin' to join the A.T.A. (Army Temperance Association), an' asked me if I'd join, too, so I said I would, an' we become members—section 'B' members, drink as much as you can carry, but don't make a beast of yourself—that's section B.'

(In justice to that admirable institution, I must explain that the membership is divided into two sections, A being for total abstainers, B for the moderate drinkers.)

"Our Sergeant-Major's cracked on drink," continued Smithy, "he can't see a bit of grease on a belt without thinkin' it's alco-what-is-it? Lots of chaps joined the A.T.A. to get a lance-stripe; me an' Nobby joined to start the New Year well.

"'Glad to see you, Private Smith; glad to see you, Private Clark,' sez the S.-M., shakin. hands with me an' Nobby as if we was human bein's.

"'Are you goin' to join?'

"'Thank you kindly, sir,' sez Nobby. ' I don't mind if I do.'

"'Shall it be section "A"?' sez the sergeant-major, smilin'.'

"'Make it "B," sir,' sez Nobby, 'an' we'll try to work back to "A" gradual.'

"So we puts our names down, an' after singin' a bit, an' hearin' two recruits recite 'Billy's Rose' an' 'The Last Shot,' we goes out.

"Just as we got up near the canteen, we heard some one say—

"'Here comes the new bun-thumpers; let's tempt 'em,' an' out comes Spud Murphy with harf a gallon.

"'What! me true blues!' sez Spud, offerin' the can, 'passin' by your old haunts without droppin' in? Take a swig, Nobby.'

"So Nobby took the harf gallon an' looked at it, serious.

"Then he sez, 'Away, tempter,' but held on to the beer.

"All the chaps the beer belonged to was larfin' like anything, an' saying, 'Go on, Nobby, break out—a little drop won't hurt you.'

But Nobby shook his 'ead, sorrerful.

"'I ain't got the face to,' he sez sadly, 'after me takin' the pledge an' all,' but he lifted the beer all the same, an' took a long sip. Then he handed the can to me an' whispers, 'Drink hearty, Smithy,' which I did.

"Then we handed the can back.

"Spud looks inside, and then looks at us.

"'You've drunk it all,' he sez, very fierce.

"'I know I have, Spud,' sez Nobby sorrerfully; 'I know I have—don't tempt me to drink any more.'

"'Don't worry yourself about that,' sez Spud hotly; what about the bloomin' pledge you've signed?'

"'That,' sez Nobby slowly, 'is what you might call a temp'ry pledge—and only applies to hogmanay. I'm goin' to keep off hogmanay for twelve months at least.'"

9.—On Finance

Private Smith was in a philosophical frame of mind.

"The world's a funny little place," be said sententiously. "As Nobby Clark was sayin' the other day, dear friends, wot you'd lost sight of and hoped was dead, are always croppin' up an' sayin', 'Hullo. Nobby, what about that two bob you borrowed in Bombay?'

"Nobby sez he read a sayin' about good people dying young, and that's true. Fellers you owe money to never die. If you read a bit in the paper about a feller runnin' to catch a train an' droppin' dead, or about a gentleman fallin' from the fourth floor when he's cleanin' the bedroom winders, you can bet nobody owes money to *him*.

"Antony Gerrard, esquire—him I told you about—sez, 'I neither borrow nor lend,' when Nobby tried to touch him the other day, so Nobby sez—

"'I don't want Scripture, Tony, I want a bob.'

"'If you take my advice—' says Antony.

"'I don't want advice, I want a bob till pay day,' sez Nobby, very patient.

"'Him that goes borrowin' goes sorrowin',' sez Antony.

"'I don't want advice, and I don't want poetry,' sez Nobby, still very patient, 'I want one blooming shillin' or twelve blooming pence.'

"The end of it was that Antony parted with eleven-pence an' two half-penny stamps.

"I know lots of people who spend money to make the time pass. But there ain't any quicker way than borrowin' a couple of bob till Wednesday. Why, you ain't got time to put the money in your pocket before Wednesday's come an' gorn!

"Nobby's the best borrower I know. Sometimes he pays back and sometimes he don't. He's very careless in money affairs, is Nobby; and when you see him cutting bits out of the paper about people who've suddenly lost their memory, you can be pretty sure that he owes a bit, an' is sort of making up an alibi.

"He owed a feller named Boysey—a red-headed chap —close on ten bob for months an' months.

"When Boysey came up to him on pay day to collect, Nobby's face got a worried look.

"'What about that ten bob?' sez Boysey.

"'What's my name?' sez Nobby, very bewildered.

"That staggered Boysey.

"'Why, Nobby Clark,' he sez.

"'Ha, ha!' sez Nobby faintly. 'Ha, ha! What a funny name!'

"Boysey got scared, and walked away quick, pretendin' he was in a hurry to get to the canteen before it shut.

"I met him comin' across the square, and he looked upset.

"'Pore old Nobby's gorn off his chump,' he sez excitedly, 'gorn clean off his bloomin' napper.'

"'What's up?' I sez.

"'Why, he don't know his own name,' sez Boysey, all of a tremble, 'and he's laughin' and ravin' like a lunatic.'

"When I got up to the room I found Nobby sitting on a bed trying to make up a limerick.

"'Hullo, balmy!' I sez.

"'Hullo, Smithy,' be sez. 'Where's Boysey?'

"'Gorn to get the key of the padded cell,' I sez. 'You're a nice feller, losing your memory.'

"'Smithy,' he sez, very earnest, 'it's the only thing I've got that's worth losing.'

"I've never discovered what Nobby does with his money. I asked him once, an' he told me he was supporting a widdered mother. Then I got to find out that he hadn't got a mother, and I told him so.

"Nobby wasn't a bit upset at being found out.

"'When I said "mother,"' he sez calmly, 'I meant my Uncle Bill, who's been a widdered mother to me.'

"The company officer asked him once—

"'What do you do with your money, Clark—I'm always hearing from people you owe money to?'

"'I'm savin' up, sir,' he sez.

"'But why don't you pay your debts?' sez the officer.

"'Nobby was very wild about this afterwards.

"'How can a chap save up if he's got to pay his debts?' he sez to me. 'Payin' your debts Is simply wastin' your money—why it's worse than drink!'

"From what Nobby said, it appeared he was saving up to go into business. Last Wednesday week the fellers were chaffin' Nobby about this.

"Nobby took no offence.

"'I'm going,' sez he, 'to open a high-class money-lender's.'

"We was so took back that none of us could speak.

"'A high-class *what*?' sez Spud.

"'Money-lender's,' sez Nobby, quite calm; 'people are getting so stingy in barracks that you can't borrow a bob when you want it without 'em coming to get it back again. So I'm going to lend money on a new plan. If you can't pay it back, go on owing it.

"The funny thing about Nobby's plan was that it was so simple. All that you had to do If you wanted money was to go and ask for it. It was so blooming simple that a good number of chaps who wanted money pretty badly, got suspicious.

"Boysey called a meetin' of Nobby's creditors.

"'It's like this,' sez Boysey. Nobby owes me ten bob, and he owes Pug Wilson four bob, and Antony two bob, and if he's got any money to lend, the first thing that he ought to do is to pay back the like of us. I vote that we all go to Nobby, one at a time, and borrow what we can, and when we've got the money stick to it.'

"All Nobby's creditors said that it was a good plan, and they tossed up odd man out to see who'd go first.

"Boysey won it, so up he went to Nobby.

"'Nobby,' sez he, ' I'd be greatly obliged if you'd lend me five bob.'

"'Certainly,' sez Nobby, pullin' out a bit of paper and a pencil.

"'What's this?' sez Boysey.

"'That's a paper what you've got to sign.' sez Nobby.

"'Whaffor?' sez Boysey, very indignant. 'I didn't ask you to sign an I.O.U. when I lent you ten bob.'

"'This is different,' sez Nobby, very serious, 'this ain't an I.O.U. it's a U.O.Me.'

"When Boysey signed his name Nobby collected a bob from him.

"'I've got to make a lot of inquiries,' sez Nobby, 'before I lend money.'

"Boysey didn't like parting, but he thought it was worth while.

"Spud Murphy wanted to borrow two shillin's till pay day, and when Nobby tried to corral a tanner for inquiries Spud sez Nobby was a swindler.

"But all this time Nobby was lendin' money to other fellers right enough. Fourpence for tuppence, an' sixpence for fourpence, an' it looked as though he'd got a good thing on. When fellers came who Nobby didn't trust he used to pull out his bit of paper an' make 'em sign, then get a shillin' out of 'em for inquiries.

"One day Nobby sez to me—

"'I'm doin' so well that I'm gettin' frightened. I made four an' tuppence last week profit. Everybody's paid back, an' nobody owes anything.'

"I think Nobby must have lost his head just about then, because he lent money to everybody.

"He came to me about a week after, lookin' 'orribly wild, an' the way be went on gnashing his teeth an' saying he'd kill old Boysey was as good as a play. Boysey hadn't paid back the five, and, what was worse, he'd put all the other fellers up to a wrinkle or two.

"'I'll show 'em,' sez Nobby, and that night him an' me went over to the canteen together to collect accounts.

"The first feller we saw was Spud Murphy.

"'Hullo, Spud,' sez Nobby, tryin' to be cheerful.

"'Where am I?' sez Spud.

"'You're in the canteen drinkin' another man's beer,' sez Nobby.

"'Who am I?' sez Spud, in a far-away voice.

"'Look here,' sez Nobby, very wrathy, 'don't you come them lost memory games on me, because I invented 'em—see? If you want to know who you are, I can tell you in twice. You're a bottle-nosed Houndsditch Irishman wot owes me two bob.'

"'I feel strange,' sez Spud in a wild way.

"'You'll feel stranger,' sez Nobby, chuckin' his cap on the ground 'you'll feel so strange that your mother won't know her darling child if you don't fork out that three bob.'

"'*Two* bob,' sez Spud, comin' round quick.

387

"'Three bob,' sez Nobby; 'two bob I lent you and a bob extra for the trouble in getting it back.'

"It was worth all the extra bobs Nobby could get, because all the chaps who owed money to Nobby got a fit or something as soon as Nobby got near him. Pug Wilson's memory was worse than Spud's, only Pug's way was more aggravatin' than Spud's.

"'What about that two bob you owe me?' sez Nobby, very pleasant.

"'What two bob?' sez Pug.

"'The two bob I lent you one night,' sez Nobby.

"'Was it rainin'?' sez Pug, looking very puzzled.

"'I didn't notice the weather,' sez Nobby, getting warm; 'I only noticed that I lent you two bob—two separate shillin's.'

"Pug was more puzzled than ever.

"'Did one have a hole in it?' he sez.

"'I didn't notice the hole,' sez Nobby shortly, 'I only noticed—'

"'Where was I?' sez Pug.

"'Here,' sez Nobby.

"'Was my back to the counter, or was I sitting down?' sez Pug, still puzzled.

"Nobby sort of drew a long breath.

"'Pug,' he sez kindly, 'if you ask me any more questions I'll put you down and tread on you. Pug, your life's worth two bob—pass it over.'

"By the time Nobby had collected twelve shillin's he was getting grey, and when Boysey came into the canteen I saw something was goin to happen. Nobby didn't see him come in, so I slipped over to Boysey.

"'Boysey,' I sez, quick, 'you owe five bob to Nobby. When he asks for it don't do the funny business or the lorst memory business—I'm advisin' you as a friend.'

"Just then Nobby saw him, and braced himself up; then he came over. Boysey didn't make his face blank or have a fit or anything. He waited till Nobby came up.

"'Five shillin's,' sez Nobby, very short, 'and look lively.'

"'Will you have it now,' sez Boysey, as bold as brass, or will you wait till quarter-day?'

"'I'll have it,' sez Nobby, chokin', 'whilst you're alive, Boysey. Don't worry me. Boysey, there's madness in me family. I've got a brother who killed a policeman an' another one who backs Captain Joe's naps. . .

"'That night Nobby said to me—

"'Smithy, let this be a warnin' to you. Never get hold of any money an' never lend it. The happiest feller is the feller that borrows. He's got nothin' to worry him—it's the feller that lends that's got all the worryin' to do—let's go down town and blue this cursed wealth.'"

10.—The Heroes

"Being a hero is not much catch nowadays," said Private Smith, gloomily.

"Not that I've ever gone in for that line of business except once. I've always thought it was bad for the eyesight. We had a feller in ours once who stopped a runaway cab in the High Street, and the Mayor and Corporation gave him a gold watch and chain. It quite altered the young feller. Before, he was the sort of chap who wasn't above coming back to barracks an hour or so after lights-out, as genial, kind-hearted and let's-have-another sort of man as you could wish to meet. But as soon as he got into the Hero class, he was changed. It was perfectly sickenin' to watch him. He'd start at half-past seven by pulling out his bright gold watch.

"'Hullo!' he says; 'I've got another two hours yet.' It was one of them watches with a hole in the case for you to see the time by. There wasn't any necessity to open it, but old Wilkie—that was his name— used to open the case every time and hold the watch close up to his eyes. Sometimes he wasn't sure it was going: then he used to hold it up to his ear for about three minutes, with all the chaps in the bar not daring to breathe while he heard if the 'tick-tick' was all right.

"Being a hero makes you short-sighted and hard of hearing, especially if you get a cheap rolled-gold American clock for being one. And every hour, regular, all through the evening, out would come his watch to see if it was time to get back to barracks.

"That's what fed me and Nobby up with the hero trade, and when the war started and heroes began to get as common as V.C.'s in a Highland regiment, we thought it was about time for Wilkie to forget all about the cab-horse performance.

"It was when the regiment was on the train going up to the front that Nobby told Wilkie what he thought.

"'Wilkie,' he sez, 'put away that cheap little ticker of yours and pay a little attention to your Uncle Nobby. Wilkie, the hero market is overcrowded. You're amongst the fourth-class shots in the hero squad, Wilkie. In a week or so this blooming battalion will be so full up with heroes that you won't be able to walk a yard without treading on one.

And they'll be real heroes, Wilkie, with their pictures in the papers, and if you start giving yourself airs about stopping that poor old cab-horse, wot wouldn't 'urt a fly, you'll be in much about the same position as a selling-plater in the Jockey Club Stakes.'

And sure enough what Nobby said came true. There was Hero Jordan, who brought up the ammunition wagon at Nelspruit; and Hero White, who carried 'Kinky' James out of the line of fire when be was wounded; and Hero Tarbut, the chap who saved the pom-pom—in fact the heroes in the regiment multiplied like rabbits.

"When the regiment got home again after the war we was all heroes. People we didn't know used to stop us in the street and shake hands with us, and uncles of mine I'd never heard of in my life sent me invitations to spend a week with 'em.

"You couldn't walk a yard without something being In the newspapers about it:—

'We hear that Mr. George Smith, our respected fellow-townsman, is entertaining his nephew, Private Smith, of the Anchester Regiment, who heroically fought at Ladysmith.'

"That was years and years ago, and the last time I went down to see Uncle George I got into the paper again:—

Isn't it time that the military authorities took steps to save Mudbury from the plague of soldiers? They seem to swarm in our streets, and our respected fellow-townsman, Mr. George Smith, has had an unpleasant experience. A drunken private, claiming to be Mr. Smith's nephew, called at his house and was very properly refused admittance. Whereupon he struck Mr. Smith in the chest and made off.'

"The hero business is played out now. The heroes are carrying coal and drinking beer like ordinary people, and as to old Wilkie—why, even he ain't one—and he was a civilian hero, too.

"I was speaking to Wilkie the other day about it.

"'I give up bein' a hero when the gold began to wear off the watch and leave little black patches,' sez Wilkie sadly.

"'What we want,' sez Nobby Clark, 'is a heroes' trade union.'

"'At so much a week?' says Spud Murphy unpleasantly, but Nobby took no notice.

"'We want all the heroes to join together and stick up for their rights,' he sez—Nobby was very great on societies and things of that sort. Well, the fellers were rather struck with the idea, but they was a bit suspicious of Nobby. But Nobby took his solemn oath, see-that-wet-see-that-dry- cut-my-throat-if-I-tell-a-lie, that he wasn't going to make a penny out of it, and it was agreed that a society should be formed for the Encouragement of Heroes.

"We had a meeting next night, and Nobby took the chair.

"'The first business is to get the heroes,' sez Nobby; 'now who's the first?'

"Nobody answered for a bit, but Wilkie coughed and looked round the room to show the fellows he was there.

"'Well,' sez Nobby, after a bit. ' I'll put myself down first.'

"'Wot have you done in the hero line?' demanded Spud loudly.

"Nobby eyed his steadily.

"'Friends and comrades all,' sez Nobby, shutting his eyes, like he always does when he makes a speech, 'I don't want to boast, but once on the line of march, when the regiment was on 'arf rations, I gave Pug Wilson my rations because he was hungry. Ain't that true, Smithy?'

"'It is so,' I sez, but it was because Nobby is what I call a dainty feeder an' very particular as to what be eats.

"So Nobby puts his name down.

"I next propose Smithy,' he sez, owing to his heroic conduct at Bloemfontein.'

"All the fellers were puzzling their heads trying to think what I'd done special at Bloemfontein, and I was a bit puzzled myself'.

"'When was that, Nobby?' I sez.

"'The night we pinched the chickens,' he sez calmly.

"'Here, hold hard,' sez Spud; 'there's nothing heroic about stealin' chickens.'

"'That,' sez Nobby, as calm as you please, 'depends on the chicken. These chickens were the fiercest chickens you ever saw.' So he put my name down.

"A lot of fellers had come to the meeting not hoping to get into the Heroes' Society, but when they saw how easy it was, and that there was nothing to pay, they started to hand in their names.

"Hoppy Sands joined because he once helped a policeman to take a drunken man to the station; Harry Gill came in because he was once bit by a dog.

"'I'll come in, Nobby,' sez Spud, who'd been hanging back a bit.

"'What have you ever done besides time?' sez Nobby.

"'Never mind what I've done,' sez Spud loudly; 'but if I'm not more of a hero than some of you fellers I'll eat my boots.'

"Nobby and Spud ain't very good friends, and Nobby got up and walked over to Spud.

"'Do I understand,' he sez, 'that you consider yourself a better hero than me?'

"'I do,' sez Spud.

"'For why?' sez Nobby quietly.

"'Because I could jolly well knock your fat head orf,' sez Spud, as fierce as anything.

"'The meeting is adjourned,' sez Spud, whilst me and this other hero go outside and see who is the best hero of the two.'

"It came out in the end that Nobby was a black eye and a tooth better hero than Spud, and it led to a lot of unpleasantness afterwards. What's more it *kiboshed* the society, because Spud found out that all the encouragement he got was from a lot of chaps who stood round and said, 'Go on, Nobby; give him the upper cut. Smash him, Nobby; oh, well hit, sir!' and things like that.

"Spud said that the Society for Encouraging Heroes only encouraged Nobby, and it was a bit too one-sided.

"The row went on for a couple of months. One night Nobby was coming back to barracks a little after twelve. He'd been over to see a gentleman who owns a rat-pit at Stokely, and he had missed his train and had to walk. He was taking a short-cut across some fields, and had just reached the big house that stands at the end of the town, a mile from the nearest house, when he heard an awful row. A girl came shrieking down the drive. Nobby could see she had her nightdress on and knew there was trouble.

"She was sobbing and shrieking, and Nobby caught her arm.

"'Here,' sez Nobby shaking her, 'what's the matter? What's biting ye?'

"He couldn't get anything out of her for a minute, and then a light through the trees told him what was the matter.

"'Fire!' shouts Nobby, and shook the girl.

"'Is there anybody in the house,' he roars, but the girl was nearly mad with fright.

"Nobby sez he gave her a smack on the head to pull her together.

"'Two children,' she wails, and clung on to Nobby. From what he could gather the master and misses were out at a ball and the other servants were away too. She babbled something about a 'soldier,' but Nobby didn't wait to hear. He was running up to the house. The front door was open, and the two top floors were ablaze, the flames coming out through the window.

"He took off his belt and ran into the house.

"The hall was full of smoke, but he stumbled along till he found the stairs, and went blundering up with his eyes shut. He got to the first floor, and could hear the fire roaring above. Up to the next flight Nobby ran knocking over the vases and things that the hall was decorated with.

"He didn't know where the kids were, but he guessed it was on the top floor, because being the most dangerous place for children, that's where all nurseries are.

"In the darkness he stumbled into a bathroom, and that was Nobby's salvation, for he had a minute to soak his tunic in water before be started to crawl up the next flight.

"He shouted at the top of his voice—

"'Is anybody there?'

"The smoke and the heat didn't upset Nobby so much as hearing a voice say, 'Yes,' for it was a voice Nobby knew.

"'Hullo, Spud,' he sez in astonishment, and then remembering he wasn't on good terms with him, 'Hullo, hero,' he sez.

"Spud's voice was choked with smoke.

"'Help get these kids downstairs,' he sez, 'you tuppenny-ha'penny chicken thief.

"Nobby had a reply on the top of his tongue, but the smoke got into his throat, so he groped about for one of the children.

"He found one little curly head, and lifted the child

"'Come on, Spud,' he sez, but he made no answer.

"'Spud!' called Nobby.

"He heard Spud's voice.

"'I'm done,' he sez weakly, 'get the kids out.'

"Nobby found the other child, and went floundering downstairs with the two. He got outside, and laid the children on the grass. He heard people running, and knew that the fire had been discovered; then turned back into the house again. It was harder this time to get upstairs, but he managed it. The top floor was like an oven; the smoke was worse than ever. He shut his eyes tight and went feeling about the landing. By and by he found Spud, who had fallen into a corner.

"'Spud!' he yells, but Spud didn't answer. He was too heavy to carry, but Nobby dragged him to the edge of the stairs and pushed him over, and Spud fell with a crash to the next landing.

"It woke Spud up, but before Nobby could get any sense into him he was unconscious again, so Nobby repeated the performance.

"Just then the firemen came in and got them both out.

"Neither Spud nor Nobby was any the worse for the experience the next morning when they paraded at the orderly room.

"Spud said he felt sore but Nobby said nothing.

"Talk about heroes! The paper was full of it. The colonel had Nobby and Spud up before him.

"'I am very proud of you men,' sez the colonel. 'I only regret that the regulations don't allow me to reward you,' he sez.

"'I've had my reward,' sez Nobby; 'I'd go through it all over again for the pleasure of chucking Spud Murphy downstairs!'"

11.—The Competitors

1

Not the least pleasant characteristic of Smithy is his touching confidence in my omnipotence.

Whenever he sees an article or story of mine in a paper or magazine, you may be sure that he addresses me as the "editor" of that particular production. Should by any chance a play or sketch with which I am remotely connected be in course of performance anywhere near Anchester, I know I shall receive peremptory demands for tickets, on the assumption that I own the theatre.

When Smithy called in at Kensington a few weeks ago and talked vaguely about journalism and the ethics thereof, and made rambling and inconclusive references to the probity of the Press, I asked him to come to the point, and, with an apologetic preamble, he came.

"I don't want you to give yourself away," began Smithy, alarmingly. "You've got to make your livin' as well as anybody else, an' it ain't for me to go pryin' into your business. But Spud Murphy said it's a swindle, an' Nobby said it ain't, an' lots of chaps take one side or the other, so I thought I'd come an' see you—you're the editor of *Ideas*, ain't you?

I destroyed Smithy's illusion with a word, and his face fell.

"I thought you was," he said reproachfully.

"Well, anyway, you'll know what I want to find out: are limericks swindles?"

I assured him that so far from that, limerick competitions were remarkably fair, and that the efforts of competitors received extraordinary careful scrutiny, and that the best lines won.

"But do the people get it, or does some pal of the editor's get it?" asked Smithy, with brutal directness.

"Why, you owl," I replied, "don't you realise that there are hundreds of disappointed people on the lookout for signs of favouritism, and that every winner's name and address is carefully verified and their family history inquired into by people who have got the same idea as you, and that—"

"That's all right," said Smithy easily; "that's what *I* say, an' Nobby Clark sez, but we thought we'd inquire first, because a tanner's a lot of money to chuck away.

He fished out from his pocket a paper, which he carefully unfolded, disclosing a newspaper coupon, which, borrowing the terminology of the second-hand bookseller, was "slightly soiled," and this, without preliminary and with due solemnity, he read—

There was an old man of Torbay
Who never had been to a play,
So to Faust he was led,
When he'd seen it he said,
. . . .

"Well?" said Smithy inquiringly, and I realised he wanted me to suggest a line.

"Work in something about 'the devil to pay,'" I suggested. . . .

Smithy told me the sequel last Wednesday.

"Nobby liked your line, the bit about the devil; so we got a line up, him an' me, an' sent it in.

"All that week we talked about that tanner. Nobby remembered about two hundred ways we might have spent it. Then when the week came round for the prize to be announced Nobby said we ought to forget all about it, an' then it 'ud come as a surprise. So we started tryin' to forget, an' the more we tried, the more we remembered.

"I kept quiet about it for two days, but I was thinkin' all the time what we would do if we got a fiver an' though Nobby said nothin' I could tell it was on his mind.

"On the second day he up, an' spoke.

"'Look here, Smithy,' he sez, 'it's no good of us reckonin' on that limerick; we'll suppose we've lost.'

"'Yes,' I sez.

"'Well, it's all over then,' sez Nobby, pretendin, 'an' we ain't got a prize or nothin'.'

"'That's right,' I sez, pretendin', too.

"'Limericks is swindles,' sez Nobby, very loud.

"'Daylight robbers,' I sez.

"'No more limericks for me,' sez Nobby. 'I've lost once—never again.'

"It got all over barracks that we'd lost, an' fellers who was waitin' to see if we won before they speculated themselves kept their money in their pocket an' said they knew limericks was swindles all along.

"That night, when me an' Nobby was in the canteen, the postman poked his head in the door an' shouts, 'Clark!'

"When Nobby went over to him he hands him a letter, an' Nobby looks at it an' turns pale.

"I looks at it, an' I went cold all over, for on the back flap of the envelope was printed the name of the paper, I looks at Nobby, an' he looks at me.

"'Let's feel that letter, Smithy.' So I gave it him

"'It don't feel very thick,' he sez, p'raps it's a consolation prize.'

"'Let's go up to the barrack-room,' sez Nobby. So up we went an' had a good look at the envelope. There it was right enough—

Private Clark,
B. Company,
1st Anchester Regiment.

"'Shall we open it?' I sez.

"'No,' sez Nobby, 'not yet; get your belt on, an' we'll go down town.'

"So we went out, an' walked down the High Street very solemn, Nobby with the letter in his inside pocket.

"We was walkin' along quite quickly, when suddenly Nobby grabbed me by the arm an' pointed. Over the road was Ruggle's paper shop, an outside was the placard of the limerick paper, and on it was—

OUR LIMERICK
ANCHESTER SOLDIER
WINS £125 4s

"I managed to drag Nobby into the *Phoenix Arms*.

"'My pal's had a bit of a shock,' I sez to the young lady behind the bar. 'Give me two penn'orth of brandy, miss.'

"'Beer,' sez Nobby, openin' his eyes for a second.

"I got him round after repeating the dose.

"'It's not us,' he sez, sad; 'it ain't thick enough, an' besides, it ain't registered, an' besides, it ain't us.'

"'Let's open it,' I sez, tremblin'.

"'You open it,' sez Nobby.

"'No, you,' I sez.

"Nobby took his penknife an' opened it careful.

"'I'll bet it ain't us,' he sez.

"'I'll bet it ain't us.' I sez.

"He opened the paper. There was a cheque, an' he read it. Then he sez in a far-away voice—

"'Kick me, Smithy—where it hurts,' he sez.

"So I kicked him.

"'Now stick that knife in me,' he sez, ' not too far, but just enough to make me jump.'

"So I did—an' he *did* jump.

"'Miss,' sez Nobby to the young lady, in his dreamy voice, 'would you be to kind as to tell me what I look like?'

"So she told him, an' that sort of woke Nobby up

"'Thank you,' he sez gruffly; then, 'Smithy, its *us!*'

"An' it was!

"'Here, Miss,' sez Nobby, excited, 'will you ask the gaffer to step this way?' and the landlord, who's a gentleman, though stout, comes along.

"'What's this?' sez Nobby, holdin' out the cheque. He kept hold of it tight, too.

"'This,' sez the bung, 'why, this is a cheque for £125 4s.' he sez.

"'Can you change it?' sez Nobby.

"The landlord looks at Nobby very suspicious.

"'No,' he sez, very short.

"'Will you give me a hundred quid for it?' sez Nobby. You can keep the rest.'

"'No,' sez the landlord again, an' then calls his potman an' whispers somethin' in his ear.

"'You needn't send for the police,' sez Nobby; it's a limerick wot me an' my pal Smithy's won,' he sez.

"We got out into the street.

"'Let's walk about all night,' sez Nobby, an' make up what well do.' Nobby hadn't had a furlough, no more had I, so next mornin' we paraded before the adjutant.

"When the adjutant sees me an' Nobby he sez—

"'Hello, you're the two fellers that won the limerick prize, aren't you?'

"'Yes,' sez me an' Nobby.

"'Well, what are you gain' to do with the money?' sez the adjutant.

"'Spend it,' sez Nobby.

"'Don't you think you'd better save it for a rainy day?' sez the adjutant.

"'No, sir!' sez Nobby, very firm. 'Smithy an' me are goin' up to London on urgent privit business,' he sez.

"'Were goin' to do it in—in a manner of speakin',' he sez.

"The adjutant looked a bit grave.

"'That's darn' foolish,' he sez.

"'Well, it's like this, sir,' sez Nobby, 'if we stay, in barracks we'll spend it anyway, an' get ourselves into trouble—to say nothin' of gettin' other chaps into trouble,' he sez, very earnest. 'So me an' Private Smith are goin' to London to see what it feels like bein' a millionaire—we shall never have another chance.'

"The adjutant shook his head, but he gave us seven days' leave.

"We got an empty carriage to ourselves, an' Nobby pulled out the money.

"'There's sixty-two for you, an' sixty-two for me,' he sez,' an' we'd better put the return halves of our tickets in our boots for safety—for we ain't likely to bring back much more than them!'"

2

"It's a wonderful thing," said Smithy, "how coming into money effec's some people. An uncle of mine lost his memory over a matter of two hundred pound. Couldn't remember people who'd done him kindnesses when he was hard up; couldn't remember money he'd borrowed orf my father an' couldn't pay back; couldn't call to mind hundreds of knowin' people who called on him to wish him luck. Another chap, whose gran'mother left him a row of houses out Walworth way, used to be a Socialist. Always wore a red tie, an' used hair-oil. Used to carry a banner in a percession, 'Death to the capitalists,' 'We demand more money an' less work,' and 'We demand the right to live.'

"Soon after he come into his houses, a pal came to see him.

"'Ain't seen you up at the club lately, Joe,' he sez.

"'No,' sez Joe shortly.

"'There was a fine argument the night,' sez the pal, 'between Jack Higgins, of Rotherhithe, an' Harry Wagg, of Poplar, on Moonicapel Lan'lordism.'

"'Oh,' sez Joe, very cold.

"'Yes,' sez the pal, 'an' we passed a resolution that nobody should pay rent.'

"'Oh,' sez Joe, very indignant, 'well, that's not my idea of true Socialism,' he sez. 'That's what I call robbery, an' you can tell the secretary to scratch my name orf the club books.'

"'But, Joe!' sez the pal.

"'I'm afraid I can't argue with you,' sez Joe, very firm. 'Me motor-car's at the door, an' I've got to go to a meetin' of property-owners to protest against the new drainage bye-law. Then I've got to go to me solicitor. Them new tenants of mine are complainin' about the roof leakin'. They're a dissatisfied, ungrateful lot,' he sez; 'why, it was only last week I had their backyards whitewashed!'

I must say about Nobby that, havin' sixty odd pounds in his pouch, didn't turn *his* head. All the way up to London we talked about what we'd do.

"'The great thing,' sez Nobby, 'is not to drink anything till quite late—you can't enjoy yourself if you've got a skinful.'

"The train pulled up outside London, an' people crowded into the carriage. There had been a race meetin', and all the chaps who got in was saying 'Did you ever see such ridin' in your life?' an' 'He ought to have won by the length of a street,' an' 'The jockey pulled his head orf,' an' 'I wish the White Prince had dropped dead,' an' similar light-hearted chatter.

Then one feller in a big box coat an' buttons as big as saucers took his coat down orf the rack an' folded it on his knees.

"'Gentlemen,' he sez, 'I've had a very good day, an' as I'm anxious to distribute me money for the good of the public, I will endeavour to show you a noo an' original game, invented by the Emp'ror of Germany, entitled, "Can you find the lady?" I have here in me hand three common or ordinary cards, the nine of di'monds, the six of clubs, an' the queen of spades.'

"So he juggles 'em all over the coat, and lays them face down.

' Now,' he sez ' I'll bet any sportsman a sov'reign he can't spot the lady.'

"Before I could stop him, Nobby had a quid in his hand.

"'Here you are,' he sez, an' picked out the queen.

"Anybody can pick out the queen the first time the chap does it, an' me an' Nobby used to make a lot of money at Aldershot Races spottin' the three-card chaps, an' havin' the first penn'orth, so to speak.

"The card chap paid over his quid. an' Nobby put it in his pocket.

"'Now,' sez the card chap, shufflin' the three cards again, 'I'll bet you five pound you can't spot the lady.'

"But Nobby didn't say anything.

"'I'll bet you five pound to three pound you can't spot the lady,' sez the man to Nobby, but Nobby was lookin' out of the winder an' whistlin' thoughtful.

"'Here—you!' sez the card chap, touchin' Nobby's knee, 'you're a sportsman, ain't you? You've won a quid of mine, now, I'll give you another chance.'

"'I never gamble,' sez Nobby, solemn.

"The card chap sort of choked in the throat.

"'You—you,' he gasps, 'why, you won a quid of mine just now.'

"'That wasn't gambling,' sez Nobby, that was a certainty.'

"'D'ye mean to say you ain't goin' to try your luck again?' sez the card chap, very fierce.

"'I do,' sez Nobby.

"'Then gimme back my quid,' sez the card chap, with his eyes bulgin' out.

"'I'll give you a push in the face,' sez Nobby, serious, ' if you ask me for money.'

"The card chap nearly had a fit.

"'Give the man his money,' sez one of his pals.

"But there never was a man in the world who could get money out of Nobby once he got his pay-hooks on it, an' they argued an' argued all the way to London, but Nobby sez nothin', except to pass a few remarks about the card chap's face.

"'I'll wait for you outside the station,' sez the cove.

"'As near the amblance,' sez Nobby, 'as you can get, an' you'd better bring your own doctor.'

"There was a quiet sort of feller satin' in the corner of the carriage, who kept quiet, an' after the card man found that Nobby was no go, he turned to the quiet man, an' offered to bet *him* that he couldn't find the lady. So the quiet man, bet an' lost, an' bet an' lost again, and that put the card chap in a better humour.

"'It's men like you,' he sez to Nobby, 'that ruin sport—blooming poverty-struck soldier!'

"'This gentleman is a sportsman,' sez the card feller, 'with a sportsman's 'art an' a sportsman's feelin's.'

"'I dessay,' sez Nobby, an' the quiet man grinned.

"When we got to the station, where we was gettin' out, we found the door locked.

"'Here,' sez one of the card chap's pals, 'who locked the door—it wasn't locked when we got in?'

"'I did,' sez the quiet man, an' he beckoned a couple of coppers on the station. An' lo an' behold! the station was full of 'em.

"'A little surprise for you gents,' sez the quiet man. 'There's a police officer in every carriage—I'm one myself—an' we're goin' to make a little haul tonight.'

"When me an' Nobby was watchin' the fellers bein' marched away, Nobby sez—

"'This comes of gamblin', Smithy—let this be a warnin' to you.'

"'What about limericks?' I sez.

"'That's not gamblin'—that's intellects.'

"We had a long argument whether we should go to a real tip-top hotel or whether we should stay at the club, (The Union Jack Club.)

"Nobby knew a high-class hotel in Stamford Street, where you can't get a bed under a shillin' a night, an' some of 'em's two shillin's, so we went there. Then we walked down the Waterloo Road an' bought some civilian clothes, an' had 'em brought back to the hotel. Nobby chose 'em. He's got a rare taste, has Nobby. Yaller boots an' yaller kid gloves, straw hats, an' a white weskit for him, an' a white weskit for me. We got cuffs an' 'dickies,' because Nobby said it was a pity to waste money on shirts.

"As we was comin' back, with a little boy carryin' the parcels be-hind, Nobby sez: 'Harf a tick,' an' dived into a second-hand jewel shop, where you can buy watches that nearly go, an' unredeemed pledges, an' that sort of thing. He come out again in a minute or so, an' we got back to the hotel.

"What with the salmon an' green tie that Nobby had bought, an' the weskit, I looked a treat, an' I must say that Nobby looked a perfec' gentleman.

"What worried me was the collar an' shirt front. I had to get a knife an' make holes for the studs, an' the way that dickey kept risin' up, first one side, an' then the other, was too cruel. I fastened it down with a pin, but that didn't make no difference. That only made it bulge up in front like a windersill.

"But when I saw Nobby, his collar sat on his neck as though he'd been born in it, as neat an' reglar an' even as possible.

"'How did you do it?' I sez,

401

"'It's a patent of me own,' sez Nobby, very proud. an' started pullin' on his yaller gloves.

"When we was ready to go out, Nobby sez—

"'Hold hard, Smithy, catch hold of this,' and he pulled out an eye-glass.

"'I've got two,' he sez, 'they've got little bits of wire to help you keep 'em in your eye.'

"'Which eye?' I sez.

"'Any eye,' sez Nobby, very calm, it all depends on what eye it fits.' It took me nearly an hour to get the bloomin' thing to stick, an' only then when I shut the eye it was in.

"We got two very fine *meerschaum* pipes for a shillin' each—you couldn't tell 'em from real ones—an' a couple of gold-mounted sticks for another two bob, an' we strolled into the Strand.

"There must have been something very takin' about our appearance, because everybody we met turned round an' looked at us.

"'How do we look?' sez Nobby.

"'Fine,' I sez, and I'm bound to admit that I fancied meself a bit.

"'If anybody asks you who you are,' sez Nobby 'you're Lord Smithy an' I'm Sir Nobby de Clark.'

"'Certainly,' I sez.

"We strolled up the Strand, an' saw lots of people waitin' outside a theatre.

"'Let's go in,' sez Nobby, so we joined the crowd.

"We had to wait a bit, an' nobody in the crowd took much notice of us, which annoyed Nobby. He can put on the hawhaw officer's voice very well, can Nobby, so he started.

"'Lord Smithy,' he sez, very loud.

"'Yes, Sir Nob,' I sez.

"'Awfully tejus waitin', ain't it?' he sez, very bored.

"A lot of the people looked round, an' that pleased Nobby.

"'I wish we'd brought our own private box,' sez Nobby.

"There was a chap with whiskers, who was readin' an evenin' newspaper, an' he looks up.

"'If you don't want to wait, don't let us keep you,' he sez, sarcastic.

"'What say?' sez Nobby.

"'I say, if you don't want to wait, don't let us keep you,' sez whisk-ers.

"'Who is this vulgar person?' sez Nobby.

"'Never mind about that,' sez the whisker-feller, who was one of those chaps who's always lookin' out for a row.

"'Smithy—I mean me lord,' sez Nobby, 'is this person with the creepers a friend of yours?'

"'No, Sir Nob,' I sez.

"'Then,' sez Nobby, very stern, 'all that I can say to him is, go home an' wash the cobwebs orf your face.'

"The evenin' might have passed off very pleasantly, for we got very nice seats, an' there was a young lady on each side of Nobby, an' he was gettin' on splendid. Then a young feller leant over from the back row an' tapped Nobby on the shoulder.

"'Do you mind changing seats? he sez.

"'What for? ' sez Nobby.

"'I want to sit by those young ladies,' sez the young feller.

"'So do I,' sez Nobby, 'an' I admire your nerve.'

"It appears that one was the young feller's financee, an' the other was his sister, an' the remarks that young chap passed when Nobby bought a big box of sweets between the acts for the financee, was somethin' shockin'.

"When the second act started, an' all the lights went down, Nobby got on splendider than ever. So much to that the young feller got up and touched Nobby again.

"'Are you goin' to give up that seat?' he sez, fierce, and very loud, an' everybody in the theatre sez: 'S-sh—turn him out—silence!'

"'Because,' sez the young feller, gettin' hold of Nobby's collar, 'if you don't, I shall chuck you out!'

"'Leave that collar alone,' sez Nobby, alarmed; 'it's new.'

"In a second the fatal thing was done, an' Nobby's 'dickey' was stickin' out of the top of his weskit.

"Nobby felt the disgrace horrible, an' after he'd hit the young chap once or twice an' a policeman an' a chucker-out had got Nobby outside by the pay-box, I managed to stick it in again for him.

"'It's not bein' chucked out that I mind so much,' sez Nobby, very bitter, but I've got no shirt on under that dickey.'

"'How did you fasten it down, then?' I sez.

"'With two bits of stamp paper,' sez Nobby.

3

"Bein' in London with nothin' to do except to spend money, is very much like bein' on duty linin' the road for a royal percession," said Smithy. "There's thousands of people behind you, pushin' and shovin'. and peekin' up their heads trying to get a peep, and there's you in the front rank, with nothin' to do but to see all the sights an' you're wishin' all the time that you was away carryin' coal or doin' somethin' equally intellectual. Doin' anything you've got to do is the worst thing in the world next to not doin' something you *want* to do.

"There used to be a chap in ours by the name of Hikey—so called because he was always givin' hisself airs—that used to play the flute like—like what-d'ye-call-him?—an' he used to be practisin' at that flute from mornin' to night. When other fellers was enjoyin' themselves at the wet-bar he used to be playin' 'The Last Rose of Summer' or 'Drink to me only with thine eyes.' He had a piece what he called the 'Moonlight Tomato' wot he used to play when he was on guard at the magazine, an' it got about that the post was 'aunted."

"He 'ad another bit called 'The hark that once tarara's 'alls,' an' what that meant I *don't* know, but it used to make you want to cry—especially if you'd took a little drink.

"Well, Hikey's playin' got round to the colonel's ears, and the old man took him, excused him all drills an' put him into the band

"'Let him practise as much as he likes,' sez the colonel to he bandmaster—so in a manner of speakin' Hikey's life ought to have been one gran' sweet song, as the sayin' is. But what did Hikey do? As soon as he found he hadn't got to practise in his spare time, but 'ad as much time to play his flute as he wanted, he started moanin' an' groanin', an' talked about desertin'! Said it was a dog's life, an' he wished he was dead, an' he hadn't joined the army to be a bloomin' minstrel boy.

"There was another feller by the name of 'Happy Johnson,' who used to spend all his time knittin' socks till he got married. One day there was an awful row at the married quarters, an' 'Happy' got hauled up in front of the C.O. for creatin' a disturbance because his sock wasn't darned.

"'Why didn't you darn 'em yourself?' sez the commandin' officer, who knew all about 'Happy.'

"'Wot did she marry me for, sir?' sez 'Happy.'

"'I don't know,' sez the colonel, 'wasn't quite right in her head, I should say.'

"When a man pays money to do hard work, it's an 'obby; but when he gets paid for it, it's jolly hard work.

"Me an' Nobby thought there wouldn't be anything nicer in the world than bargin' about London, with our pockets full of gold, an' havin' nothin' to do but spend it.

"'I'll bet,' sez Nobby, the second day when we was walkin' up the Strand, 'that if me an' you wanted to buy that cab we could.'

"So we went up to the cabby an' asked him what he wanted for the turn out.

"The cabby looked suspicious, an' told us not to act the goat, but Nobby was so jolly earnest about it, that the cabby told him.

"'There you are,' sez Nobby, an' we walked away leavin' the cab-man quite upset.

"After that we went into a shop an' asked the price of a di'mond tirara, because Nobby bet we could afford to buy it, if we wanted. Then we stood in front of a boot shop an' reckoned up that we could buy all the boots in the winder twice over. We got tired of this after a bit, because somehow we never saw anything we really did want to buy, except two framed texts in a little shop in the Charing Cross Road, an' they was only 4s. 6d. each.

"We tried havin' expensive dinners. We had one wot cost nearly half-a-dollar, an' then we had a bottle of wine—very high-class wine it was, too, with three labels—and that cost us another eighteenpence. We had a glass apiece, an' then a bottle of beer to take the taste away.

"'That's wine from the wood,' sez the waiter chap.

"'I know,' sez Nobby. 'I could taste the wood quite plain.'

"On the third day Nobby sez—

"'Smithy, how much do you think we've spent?'

"I knew how much I'd spent, an' told him.

"'Less than a bloomin' quid,' sez Nobby, very bitter. 'Smithy, we oughtn't have money, we don't know how to spend it.'

"That money got on our nerves. We tried hard to spend a parcel that day, we even rode in a taxicab, but the driver was struck honest or somethin', an' only charged the legal fare. We had a bit of grub in a Waterloo Road coffee shop, an' me an' Nobby was walkin' very gloomy towards the bridge when a little kid comes up an' sez—

"'Give me a ha'penny, guv'nor.'

"'What for?' sez Nobby, very fierce.

"'To get somethin' to eat,' sez the kid.

"'What do you want to eat for? ' sez Nobby, it'll only make you fat.'

"The kid was slinkin' away, when Nobby called him back.

"'Here's a tanner,' he sez, an' gave him sixpence.

"'Don't make a beast of yourself,' sez Nobby, an' the kid grabbed the sixpence an' started runnin' away, when a bright idea struck Nobby.

"'Here!' he sez, an' called the kid back again. This here little boy was a artful little chap wot thought Nobby was goin' to pinch the tanner back, but Nobby, who's got a wonderful way with wild animals, persuades him to come close.

"'Me an' my friend,' sez Nobby, 'will be back in five minutes, so you go an' tell all the little boys an' girls wot want a tanner to buy grub with to come here an' get it.'

"The little boy didn't believe Nobby, I could see that—but he nipped off, an' Nobby sez very solemn—

"'Would you like to do the Lord Hallin'ton act?' sez Nobby.

"Now I knew all about Lord Hallin'ton, because I'd read it in the papers. How he went round the poor parts of London givin' dinners to poor kids, so I sez—

"'Rather.'

"We went over to a bank an' we got nearly a hundred pounds in tanners.

"My word, it was heavy! Me an' Nobby was bulgin' all over an' weighed down.

"When we got back to where the kid left us there he was with a dozen other little kids.

"Nobby gave 'em a tanner each, an' made 'em swear see-that- wet-see-that-dry that they'd lay it out in grub.

"I don't know how the news got about, but by the time me and Nobby had walked into a side street there was about a hundred thousand kids round us.

"They was yellin' an' shoutin' an' strugglin' to get at us, an' a stout old gentleman forced his way to Nobby an' asked him what the game was. So Nobby told him, an' the old gent larfed like anything.

"'So that's the way a soldier spends his limerick money, is it?' he sez; 'well, go ahead, an' I'll try to keep these youngsters in order.'

"It wanted a bit of doin' an' I was afraid every minute that the p'lice would come up an' stop us. There was lots of loafers in the crowd, but Nobby landed one a dig in the eye, gave a few remarks to the others, and they left, but the tanners went like magic. It was a fine feelin' whilst it lasted, here was me and Nobby feedin' these kids—some of 'em come twice, but Nobby gave 'em a clump or two, an' that stopped *that*. At last every bloomin' tanner was gone (an' it took a bit of time to persuade 'em it *was* gone), an' Nobby sez—

"'I didn't think there were so many kids in the world.'

"The fat old gentleman larfed, an' asked me an' Nobby our names, then he shook hands an' went away.

"By the time we'd paid our bill at the hotel and got to the station we had about a quid each left.

"All the fellers in barracks were surprised to see us.

"'Hullo,' sez Spud Murphy, 'spent all your money already?'

"'Yes,' sez Nobby.

"'How?' sez Spud.

"'Drink an' riotchus livin',' sez Nobby.

"'Did you drink much?' sez Spud.

"'We haven't been sober for three days—have we, Smithy?'

"'No,' I sez.

"Spud looked at us very admirin', an' the chaps in the canteen gave us a bit of a reception.

"It was well known in barracks we was back, an' fellers come from all parts—even from the corporals' room—to know what we did with the money.

"So Nobby made up a most disgraceful tale, wot I won't insult you by repeatin', of our carryin's on, an' sat up in bed after lights-out tellin' how we went to parties with dukes an' earls, till the room corporal said if he didn't stop gassin' he'd put him inside.'

"Next mornin', when me an' Nobby was waitin. at the cook-house to draw the coffee, Nobby sez—

"'Smithy, are you sorry you spent that money?'

"'No,' I sez, an' I wasn't.

"'Do you ever want any more?'

"'No,' I sez.

"'Nor me, either,' sez Nobby, 'no more limericks for me.'

"When we got in to breakfast there was a letter waitin' for us. I opened it.

"'Dear sirs,' sez the letter, 'yesterday I had pleasure in witnessing your charity; as you were doing my work, permit me to recompense you.'

"It was signed 'Hallington.'

"'The little fat man!' sez Nobby, with a gasp. 'What's he sent?'

"I opened the cheque ; it was for a hundred pounds!

"'Smithy,' sez Nobby, shakin' his head, 'we'll never get rid of that money! Let's stick to it till flat racin' starts—then I know a way to make it go!'"

12.—Uncle Joe's Tract

"Nobby Clark," explained Private Smith, "has got an uncle who's fairly good. He keeps a ham and beef shop in Lewisham High Road, and naturally, being a bit well off, can afford to be eccentric.

"He's a very fine old chap," said Smithy warmly. "If he gets a side of bacon that's gone off, or a tub of butter a bit high, do you think he throws it away? Not he. He gives it to the pore."

Smithy glowed.

"He sends Nobby lots of letters of advice and tracks, and sometimes he slips in half a dollar in stamps. Nobby is always anxious to get his uncle's letters, but I've known him to have a slice of bad luck for six letters runnin'.

"One mornin' the postman brought a fat letter in. 'Private Clark,' he sez, and Nobby nipped along the barrack-room, but his face fell when he saw how fat the letter was.

"'It's a bit too heavy to be any good,' he sez very bitter, and weighin' the letter in his hand; 'if this is another Straight Talk to Enquirin' Sinners, Smithy, something will 'ave to be done.' He tore open the letter very careful an' took out a printed paper. 'Track.' he sez bitterly, 'a track about drinkin' an' quarrelin'.'

"Then be took out another paper.

"'Track,' he sez bitterer than ever, 'a track about smokin'.'

"Then he took out another paper.

"'Tra—' he stopped, 'no it ain't—here. Smithy, what's this?' Nobby was all of a tremble, an' so was I, for if it wasn't a fiver, a real white crinkly fiver, I've never seen one.

"Nobby was quite shook up an' so was I.

"'Smithy,' sez Nobby, his voice all broke, 'pick up them beautiful tracks that my dear Uncle Joe sent me.'

"'I can't, Nobby,' I sez, 'you chucked 'em on the fire.'

"'Did I—did I?' sez Nobby, horror-struck, 'did I throw away my dear uncle's tracks—did I burn them lovely words—oh, horror!'

"Then one of the fellers chipped in.

"'Spud Murphy's got the one about drink; 'e picked it out of the fireplace, Nobby,' he sez.

"Nobby stood lookin' at the banknote, crinklin' it an' looking at the watermark.

"'Spud Murphy's got no right to my dear uncle's track—but he's welcome to it. I only 'ope,' Nobby went on very solemn, 'that the words in that there track will do him good.'

"There was a letter along with the other goods, and Nobby read it.

"'My dear nephew,' read Nobby. 'This comes hopin' to find you—um—um—um. I am glad to hear you go regularly to—um—um, but am sorry to hear you are ashamed to go to the meetin's because you've got no money to put in the plate. . . . Can quite understand it. . . . I don't see why you should wait till I die before getting some of my money, so as a reward. . . I am sendin' you ten pounds.'

"'What,' I sez, an' Nobby read it again. 'Ten pound,' he sez, an' pulled the banknote out of his pocket to examine it. It was 'Five' right enough as plain as plain. 'I promise to pay,' etc.

"'Dear uncle's made a mistake,' sez Nobby, all trembly, or else the other five is comin' on.' He turned the envelope inside out, but there was nothin' in it.

"'Go on with the letter,' I sez.

"'. . . Ten pounds,' read Nobby slowly, but certain persons havin' said that you don't read my little tracks—' Nobby stopped and went white.

"'Go on,' I sez.

"'Certain persons havin' said you don't read my tracks nor my letters either, I—have—put—the—other—five—pound—'

"Nobby sort of collapsed on to the nearest bed-cot.

"'Where?' I sez.

"'Between the last two pages of the track on drink an' quarrelin',' he sez, in a holler voice.

"I tell you," said Smithy seriously, "it shook me an' Nobby up a bit, but bimeby Nobby pulls hisself together and jumps up. 'Smithy,' he sez, 'that low feller Spud has got my dear uncle's track wot he sent to me—I want to read that track; it'll do me more good than Spud. Where is he?'

"Then somebody said he'd seen Spud going over to the canteen, so me an' Nobby run as hard as we could to find him.

"Sure enough there he was, but our 'earts went down into our number nines when we saw him—he was sittin' by hisself drinking lemonade and looked very sad.

"'Cheer-o, Spud,' sez Nobby, in a chokin' voice. 'How goes it? What are you drinkin'?'

"Spud shook his head sorrerfully.

"'I've given up the cursed drink,' he sez, in a humble voice.

"'Since when?' sez Nobby, very loud. 'Since when, you low hypocrite?'

"Spud didn't take no offence. He only sighed.

"'Since reading your dear Uncle Joe's track,' he sez.

"'Spud,' sez Nobby, droppin' his voice an' shakin' Spud by the hand, 'Spud, you make me feel ashamed of meself. Perhaps I ought to give it up, too; perhaps them beautiful words might be the makin' of me; let's have a look at my uncle's track wot I lent you.'

"'Wot you chucked away,' sez Spud, very gentle.

"'Wot happened to slip out of my hand an' was picked up by a low thief who happened to be passin'',' sez Nobby, very ferocious, but managed to get hisself under control again; 'so, therefore, dear Spud, let me have a *dekko* at them lovely words.'

"'I haven't quite finished with it yet,' sez Spud, sippin' his lemonade and smacking his lips. This is the stuff to drink, Nobby. If I'd read your uncle's track earlier I might have been pounds in pocket.'

"I thought Nobby would have a fit. He got red in the face an' he gnashed his teeth.

"'Spud,' he sez, after a bit, 'Spud, old feller, are you goin' to see a comrade continue on what I might call the down grade without raisin' a hand to help him? And any way,' he went on, gettin' wilder and wilder, 'it's my bloomin' track; it was sent to me by my dear Uncle Joe, an' if you don't hand it over, I'll give you a wipe on the jaw.'

"All the fellers in the canteen began to gather round on the off chance of a fight.

"'Wot's up, Nobby?' sez Fatty Green, a very nice young feller with a curly head.

"'This perishing recruit's got a track of mine,' roars Nobby, pullin' off his coat, 'a beautiful track about drinkin' an' quarrellin', an' won't hand it over, so I'm goin' to knock his head off.'

"'Give the man his track,' sez Fatty, who was an off-an'-on teeto-taller, an' all the other fellers said the same.

"Things looked a bit rough-housish when suddenly the bugle sounded orf for 'orderly men,' an' Nobby staggered back.

"'That's me,' he sez, an' I felt sorry for him. In a manner of speakin' he was tore between love an' duty, as the song sez.

"'Smithy,' he whispers to me, 'I've got to go and draw the groceries; keep your eye on this blighter an' don't let him out of your sight.'

"When Nobby had gone I sez to Spud—

"'Spud, me lad—I want a few words with you.'

"''Ave 'em here,' sez Spud, sippin' his lemonade, but I took his arm an' walked him down to the back field, where there was nobody about.

"'Spud,' I sez kindly, hand over Nobby's uncle's track.'

"'For why?' sez Spud, looking round for someone to take his part.

"'If you ain't enough of a gentleman to understand that when a feller gets a private track from his uncle he don't want nobody else to read it, I can't explain,' I sez. Just then Nobby came runnin' back from the parade ground, 'avin' got another feller to draw the groceries.

"'Come on,' he sez, an' so we gave Spud a number two *jujitsu* push.

"'You hold his legs, Smithy,' sez Nobby, who was sittin' on Spud's head; 'now, you mouldy highway robber, where's that track?'

"'Lemme get up,' sez Spud, strugglin', but Nobby went carefully through his pockets.

"'Here it is,' he yells, an' pulls out the paper. Sure enough, snug between the last two leaves was the other fiver.

"'I'll report this,' sez Spud, when we let him up.

"'Do,' sez Nobby, very cheerful, 'do.'"

13. THE BAA-LAMB

The army is a queer place, and soldiers really do extraordinary things. Once there was a martinet colonel of the Anchester Regiment who was known at the War Office as a "strong man," and once or twice his portrait crept into the pages of illustrated papers. As a matter of fact, he was not a strong man at all, but a bullying, brow-beating, terrorising weakling, with a taste for whisky and bridge. Also he was a bad loser, and collected postage stamps. And if that description isn't enough to damn any man, I should like to know what is.

When the general came round on his annual inspection he remarked that there was a great deal of crime in the regiment, and the colonel spoke vaguely of discipline and the standard of recruiting, and after that the inspection was more "military" than ever.

The colonel used to live out of barracks, and one guest night he was driving to mess along a dark country road, and his horse took a tumble, and the colonel picked himself out of the road with a broken head and his features fairly well displaced. Then he discovered a fine wire stretched across the road, and knew that it constituted the regiment's vote of censure.

A few days later, as he was sitting at dinner, a heavy flint stone crashed through the window and all but brained him. So the colonel took the hint and went on half pay. During the war, the supply of "strong men" having run short, owing to the lamentable miscalculation which led them to match their strength against big, fat *kopjes*, the War Office sent for the colonel, and made him first a brigadier-general, then a local major-general. They gave him a brigade, which, to his—and its—intense annoyance, included the Anchester Regiment.

The general had many narrow escapes from death before he returned to England, "on account of ill-health," and he now lives near Farnborough, and spends his days explaining why the Boers cut him up at Veltfontein, capturing his two pompoms and decimal nine-nine-nine of his convoy. His friends call him "Mad Jack," and he rather likes the nickname, because there has grown about the title a legend of recklessness in danger which he does not object to at all. As a matter of fact, his madness took the form of losing his head on the slightest provocation and calling for help in a loud voice.

I am particularly concerned with this retired general, because he writes a great deal to the newspapers, nowadays, demanding that the Great General should be recalled from Babuland to "sweep the something stables of our rotten War Office, and reduce order from the chaos, etc."

Now this is not a bad wheeze at all. For once upon a time, before the Great General went to Babuland, an obscure captain of infantry wrote ecstatic letters to the newspapers of that delightful country, acclaiming the Great General as the greatest kind of Great General that ever was. And when the Great General arrived he sought out the obscure captain of infantry and made him a colonel on the staff, which everybody in Babuland knows, and talks about.

Now Smithy—Private Smith, as ever is—of the aforesaid Anchester Regiment, and I have had many earnest talks about the army and the War Office and Mr. Haldane; and when we have been in any kind of doubt we have summoned to our council Private Clark, whose other name is Nobby.

"The army *is* a queer place, and soldiers do funny things," said Smithy, shaking his head wisely. "You take the ordinary soldier an' start talkin' music-hall-soldier talk to him, an' likely as not he'll dot you one. A soldier hates bein' called a hero—when he's sober—an' fellers I know would go miles out of their way sooner than hear some fat-headed civilian talkin' about the dear old flag. Chaps mostly enlist because they're hard up, as everybody knows. Some chaps enlist because they have a row with their people.

"'When are you goin' to do some work, Bob?' sez the old man.

"'Next week,' sez Bob.

"'So you said this time last year,' sez the old man, an' if you think it's goin' to keep you through another flat racin' season, you're mistook.'

"With that Bob gets despondent.

"'I can't get no work,' he sez, very bitterly. 'I've been sittin' in front of the fire for the last week schemin' and thinkin' an' plannin', an' that's all the thanks I get!'

"'Why don't you go out and look for it,' sez the old man, at five in the mornin'—same as me?'

"'What!' sez Bob, very indignant, 'me go out in the mornin', riskin' double pneumatics, an' all! I'm ashamed of you father.'

"'I do it,' sez the old man.

"'You're older,' sez Bob, 'an' in a manner of speakin' 'ardened. I don't know what I'll do! I've a good mind to commit suicide!'

"'Why don't you go for a soldier?' sez the father, 'it's a nice lazy life—just suit you!'

"That sets the chap thinkin', an' before a week's past he's took the oath to serve His Majesty the King, 'is heirs, an' successors, an' the generals an' officers set over him, so help me, *etcetra*.

"His mother cries, an' sez he's disgraced the family, an' all his sisters start yappin', an' his little brother asks him to bring him home a sword or two, an' the old man breathes in a light-hearted way, an' sez that doin' nothing for seven years'll make a man of him.

"Pore feller! When he gets to the depot, an' is kicked out of bed at 5 a.m., an' made to clean hisself an' turn out on a square that ain't been properly warmed, he wakes up out of his trance.

"There's only two chaps I know that ever come into the army for glory, an' one was off his head an' the other was Conky Barlam. We used to call him 'Baa-Lamb,' owin' to his simple ways. He was, indeed, the simplest feller I've ever clapped eyes on. A perfec' child he was, an' always talkie about the 'dear ole regiment,' an' the 'glorious Anchesters,' an' was one of them chaps that's always energetic in doin' the wrong thing. Made up a song he did, an' the first verse went

The noblest regiment on this earth
That's always makin' stirs,
It is that corps of stirlin' worth
What's called the Anchesters.

"He used to volunteer for duty—would have gone on guard seven days a week if they'd let him—an' actually paraded before the colonel an' asked if he could see the reg'mental relics!

"We've got a lot—what with flags we've taken, an' stuff we've looted in various wars, an' the officers' mess is full of diamond-hilted swords an' gold saucepans, an' things that our illustrious officers have pinched from the hateful foe from time to time.

"The colonel was very pleased at Baa-Lamb's sauce, for the officers are as proud as Punch of the trophies, an' he actually took Baa-Lamb round an' showed him everything hisself!

"I was at the orderly room an' heard the colonel tell the adjutant.

"'By the way, Umfreville, that new recruit of "B" Company—Barlam's his name, I think—is a singularly intelligent feller. Took a tremendous interest—an intelligent interest—in the trophies—his father was a collector in a small way, an' the boy seems to have a fair idea of the value of our things.'

"'Yes, sir,' sez the adjutant, who don't hold with soldiers knowin' a 'fair knowledge' of anything, except marchin' an' shootin'.

"Old Baa-Lamb was fair cracked about the flags, an' the swords an' the relics gen'rally.

"'It made my heart swell,' he sez, 'to see them glorious trophies of many a stricken field,' he sez, 'where our noble officers have gone forth to victory or death,' he sez, 'or both. It makes my heart swell,' he sez, 'to see how them brave fellers have stormed palaces an' always,' he sez, 'gone straight to the place where the expensive loot was. It makes my heart swell—'

"'Dry up,' sez Nobby, or I'll make your eye swell!'

"'But think of them noble fellers,' sez Baa-Lamb, excited, 'amidst cannon roar an' flyin' shot—'

"'Get out!' sez Nobby, very disgusted.

"What pleased Baa-Lamb best was when he found a rhyme for 'di'mond-hilted sword,' an' wrote a little poem about it.

Our officers, they bravely led
The privates through the breach,
An' found the enemy had fled
Out of their lawful reach.
Ah! many a high an' stilted lord
That day exclaimed, 'Great Scot!
I've lost my di'mond-hilted sword

An' golden mustard pot!'

"You must understand that we sort of put up with Baa-Lamb because he was such a simple josser an' very kind-hearted. So when one mornin' me an' Nobby woke up an' found him missin' an' his bed not been slept in, we felt sorry for him, for the colonel's awfully down on chaps who overstay their leave, an' the night before old Baa-Lamb had gone out into town to meet his 'dear uncle' what had come down from London to see him.

"As a matter of fact, we didn't feel sorry very long, because it was soon all over barracks that Baa-Lamb had gone for good—an' so had the di'mond-hilted sword an' several other valuables wot he'd written poems about"

14. NOBBY'S DOUBLE

"You might say that soldiers have got most of the vices," said Private Smith, "because they're ordinary men. Most fellers have got a large whack of vice concealed about 'em, it don't matter what they are, I once knew a school-board officer who went round the country on his holiday as 'Old Bill Maggit of Bermondsey' what would fight anybody at twelve stone, an' I knew a quiet young feller who always put on a clean white shirt every Sunday, who's now doin' five years for robbery an' violence. We're all bad, but most of us are afraid of the police. When you find a chap who don't give two pennorth of sugar for the biggest copper that ever told a lie, you can bet he's going to be a criminal, because he don't possess the only thing what keep, people honest—and that's the fear of bein' found out.

"But whatever you say about soldiers, you can't say they bet. They play banker, an' nap, an' fives,' an' pontoon, (*vingt-et-un*-blackjack), an' lose fab'lous sums. But they don't bet, except very rarely. When they do happen to bet, it's a bad thing for the bookie. Close by Anchester there's a racin' stable, and from what me an' Nobby heard, there was a horse in that stable by the name of Mutton Pie what couldn't lose the Manchester Handicap.

"One of the stable lads was down at the canteen last Sunday an' said that Mutton Pie would be passin' the winnin' post when the other horses were scratchin' their heads an' wonderin' where he'd gone. Everybody in Anchester was on Mutton Pie, an' a lot of chaps in the regiment, too. Me an' Nobby was on to the extent of five bob each way.

"What made us fancy him so much was his intelligence. He was in a race once at Hurst Park; there was only four runners, an' every one of the others could beat him. So what did the noble horse do? Why, when he was at the startin' post he up an' kicks the favourite in the ribs. Then be kicked the jockey off the second favourite. That brought the field down to two, an' the other one would have won, only just before they got to the winnin' post Mutton Pie stretched his head round an' bit the other horse's ear off. So Mutton Pie won by a head an a bit of an ear he had in his mouth.

"'That's the horse for me,' sez Nobby, 'he'll win, if he ain't poisoned before the day.'

"The day before the race there was great excitement in barracks. That afternoon, when we were listening to a chap in 'H,' who was tellin' us that Mutton Pie hadn't got an earthly, an' that Jubilee was chucked into the race, the adjutant's orderly came in an' said that the adjutant wanted to see me.

"'Me?' I sez, astonished.

"'You,' sez the orderly, 'and look nippy.'

"So I doubled across to the orderly room.

"'Ah, Smith,' sez the adjutant, I want you to do something for me.'

"'Yes, sir,' I sez, wonderin' what was in the wind.

"'There's a boy joinin' the regiment, the son of the late Sergeant-Major Stevens.'

"'Yes, sir,' I sez.

"'The boy's got a stepfather, an anarchist or socialist, or something, who doesn't want the boy to join.'

"He waited a bit, an' I waited a bit.

"'Well,' he sez, carelessly, 'if you an' your friend Clark should run across this man—he's an awful brute from what I hear—I want you to treat him kindly.'

"'Yes, sir,' I sez, 'I will, sir.'

"'Don't hurt him,' he sez.

"'No, sir,' I sez.

"He looks hard at me.

"'Do you understand?' he sez, and winks just like that.

"'I wasn't long givin' Nobby the office. Afterwards we went up to the room to tea, an' we was half-way through when there was a knock at the door. Nobody knocks at a barrack-room door, so we knew it was a civilian.

"'Come in,' everybody shouted at once.

"The door opens, an' in walked the finest kind of blighter you've ever seen in your natural. He wore a big black hat an' a red necktie, with egg marks. His hair was long, an' his face was one of them oily faces that always shines. He looks round the room an' sniffs.

"'Do you want anybody?' sez Nobby, very polite.

"He sniffs again.

"'Or a handkerchief?' sez Nobby.

"The oily chap didn't take any notice of what Nobby said.

"'So this,' he sez, is a barrack-room. An' these are the licensed butchers what the likes of me pay taxes for.

"'The butcher's out just now,' sez Nobby, 'owin' to his havin' an appointment down town to meet a girl.'

"The oily chap looks at Nobby very scornful.

"'Come here, my man,' he sez haughtily.

"Nobby walks up to him.

"'Do you know who I am?' he sez.

"'Do I get a prize for guessin'?' sez Nobby.

"'I'm one of your masters,' sez the oily chap,

"'Go on,' sez Nobby.

"'I keeps you,' sez the chap.

"'Who keeps you?' sez Nobby.

"'The sweat of me brow,' sez the chap.

"Nobby looks at his oily dial.

"'Well you ought to be well off,' sez Nobby.

"The chap looked very fiercely at Nobby.

"'I'll have you understand,' he began, when in walked a kid.

"He was one of the nicest little kids you ever saw, with yallar hair an' eyes like china saucers.

"'Ha,' sez the oily chap, jumpin' forward an' catchin' the kid by the arm. 'You're the boy I'm lookin' for.'

"'Hold on,' I sez, what's the game?'

"The oily chap turned on me with a haughty look.

"'Don't interfere,' he sez, 'this boy's my son, an' was goin' to disgrace hisself by joinin' the army.'

"The boy was strugglin' to get his arm away.

"'Wait a bit,' sez Nobby, 'look after the door Smithy. Before we go any further, Face, I would like to ask you a civil question.'

"'What's that?' sez the oily chap.

"'It's this,' sez Nobby slowly. Would you prefer goin' out of this room by the door, or would you prefer to be chucked out of the winder—there's only two ways?"

"'What d'ye mean?' sez the oily chap, lookin' scared.

"'Years an' years ago,' sez Nobby, 'I was kidnapped by gipsies because of me good looks—did you make any remark?'

"'No' sez the oily chap.

"'It's a good job for you you didn't,' sez Nobby, 'the chap what kidnapped me had a face like yours, only not so bad, an I promised me Uncle Bill when be died, that if ever I met you I'd do you in.'

"'"Nobby," sez my Uncle Bill, "don't hurt the poor feller." "I won't, uncle,!" I sez. "Let his end be painless" "It shall, Uncle Bill," I sez. "Don't do it with an hammer, but just drop him gently out of a winder," sez my Uncle Bill, an' that's what I'm goin' to do,' sez Nobby.

"'You'll get into trouble for this threat, me man,' sez the oily chap, who was frightened to death.

"'I know I will,' sez Nobby sadly. 'A fortune-teller told me so. "You'll be charged with murder," she sez, "but you'll get off as soon as the jury has seen a photo of the feller you've killed."'

"I don't know how long this sort of thing would have gone on, but we heard a sword clinking in the passage outside, an' stood to attention as Captain Umfreville, the adjutant, came into the barrack-room He looked at the kid an' looked at the oily chap.

"'What's wrong?' he sez.

"'This—this scoundrel,' splutters the oily chap, pointin' to Nobby, 'has dared to threaten me! By heavens, sir, I'll have the law on you—'

"'Me?' sez Nobby, astonished. 'What for?'

"'Didn't you say—?

"'If I've opened me mouth,' sez Nobby in a shocked voice, 'except to pass the time of day, may I be blowed.'

"'What are you doing with that boy?' sez the adjutant.

"'My son,' sez the oily chap,

"'Your stepson,' sez the officer.

"'What's it to do with you?' sez the oily chap with a snort. 'Am I a free citizen to be talked to by a gilded nincompoop?'

"'I'm neither a nincompoop, nor am I particularly gilded,' sez the adjutant quietly, 'and if you cannot behave yourself, I will have you put outside. Again I ask you what your are doing with that boy?'

"'I'm taking him home,' sez the oily bird. I know the law as well as you, Mr. Blooming officer, and the law sez I can take him.'

"By the look in Umfreville's face I could see Greasy knew what he was talkin' about.

"'Very good,' sez the officer, 'you may take him.'

"'What, sir,' sez Nobby, 'are you goin' to allow a lobster like that—'

"'Be quiet, Clark,' sez the officer, ' you can take the boy, Mr.—'

"'Snieff,' sez the oily chap.

"'You may take the boy, Mr. Snieff, after I have made a few inquiries; in the meantime you may remain here if you wish.'

"'I'm not goin' to leave this den of iniquity till I leave with this young varmint,' sez Snieff.

"'Unless you can produce very excellent reasons why it should not be so, the boy will be sworn in tomorrow,' sez the captain.

"'Don't you worry,' sez Snieff, 'I'll produce reasons, an', what's more, I'll be there to see 'em enforced.' An' when the officer walked out of the room Snieff walked out behind him.

"We watched him strollin' about the square an' tried to lure him into the barrack-room, but it wasn't any go. After a bit he walked down into the field.

"'Smithy,' sez Nobby, 'how would you like twenty-one days' C.B.?'

"'About as much as I would like a kick in the back,' I sez.

"'I've got an idea,' sez Nobby.

"If I was a writin' chap like you, an' had to write a story about what happened to the oily chap in the back field (behind the Gymnasium where nobody could see), I think I'd start off like this: 'When the shades of night were fallin' fast, Smithy an' Nobby might have been seen carryin' a bundle, *viz.*, the oily chap.'

"We got him over the wall at the back an' on to the footpath. A little way along we found Pug Wilson an' Spud Murphy with a barrer.

"'I'm goin' to tie the sack up,' sez Nobby, an' if you make a sound I'll knock your bloomin' head off.'

"We got him through the town, by side streets, an' wheeled the barrer to the goods yard of the railway station.

"'It's all right,' Nobby sez. 'They're goin' to put an empty carriage on, an' I've found out which one it is.'

"We carried the oily chap along, over the rails, till we come to the carriage. It was a sort of horse-box, but there was a little compartment at the end for the stable-boy. We took Snieffy out of the sack an' tied his hands, an' shoved him through an openin' in the compartment into the horse-box itself. Then we got out an' strolled on to the platform. There was a lot of people waitin' to see Mutton Pie off to Manchester, and by and by they shunted another horse-box on to the train.

"'What's that for?' sez Nobby, to make sure.

"'It's an empty we're sendin' to Manchester,' sez a porter.

"Nobby kept an anxious eye on Snieff's box, an' when the whistle blew an' the train started to move somebody sez—

"'What's that scufflin' noise?'

"'It's only Mutton Pie,' sez Nobby.

"'But I heard a feller shoutin',' sez the chap.

"'Three cheers for Mutton Pie!' yells Nobby. 'Shout, Smithy,' he whispers, 'or they'll hear him.'

"So we all yelled together, an' the people on the platform joined in, as the train ran out of the station.

"'Where's the first stop?' sez Nobby.

"'Manchester,' sez the porter.

"'Good,' sez Nobby.

"'Have you backed Mutton Pie?' sez the porter

"'Well,' sez Nobby, 'I've done what you might call a double.'"

15.—The Fighting Anchesters

Once upon a time Smithy and Nobby Clark "put a bit in the papers" for their own immediate profit and glorification. The "bit" they put in was a gross libel, and the unfortunate editor had to apologise and pay £20 to a local hospital, but Smithy and Nobby got half a guinea for the "information," so that they were not greatly perturbed over the editor's downfall. But in a roundabout way the clonel of the 1st Anchesters came to hear of the part his two men had played, and acted accordingly. Since when both Nobby and Smithy have retired permanently from journalism.

I was reminded of this unpleasant episode by Smithy himself, who has recently been acting the part of mediator between Pug Wilson and Big Harvey. It would appear that the said Pug Wilson did wrongly and improperly describe the said Big Harvey as a "cellar-flapping gaol-bird," thereby bringing the said Big Harvey into ridicule and contempt; and, moreover, of his envy, hatred, and malice this said Pug Wilson used threatening and abusive language to the said Big Harvey, calculated thereby to cause a breach of the king's peace.

"I don't know what's coming over the army," said Smithy in despair. "There used to be a time when if a feller called another feller a liar, he had to go through it on the spot. To call a feller a thief was to ask for a plunk in the eye, and when one feller cast reflections on another feller's family it used to take six men an' a bugler to pry 'em apart.

"But they're improving the army nowadays. Were tryin' to get a superior class of young chaps who can write with both hands and do sums with his feet. Were gettin' men who call their girls 'young ladies,' and sound their h's, and when there's any kind of trouble going cheap these are the fellers that talk about reporting you to the company officer, or else takin' you into court to make you prove your words.

"There's two fellers in 'H' Company who are the limit. One of 'em calls himself Vane, and used to drive his own motorcar before he came down in the world. Nobby sez it was a motor-'bus, and that old Vane lost his job because his face frightened the horses, and the 'bus got the blame.

"The other feller's name's Antony Gerrard, Esquire (that's that he put on his attestation paper), and nobody knows what he was. We thought we'd found out once. But when it came to the pinch, the police couldn't recognise him, and although the lady said she was almost sure that that was the man who took her watch, Antony Gerrard, Esquire, got off.

"I've often been sorry that I'm not in 'H.' it's almost worth the disgrace of belonging to the worst shooting company in the battalion to hear these fellers talk to each other.

"All the room stands round and listens.

"'Well, Tony, dear boy,' sez Vaney, 'you and I are for guard tomorrow.'

"'Horrid grind,' sez Antony Gerrard, Esquire.

"'Beastly bore,' sez Vaney.

"'The whole system's rotten,' sez Antony Gerrard, Esquire, disgustedly. 'The economic wastage—'

"'*And* the undisputed shrinkage.' sez Vaney.

"'True, true,' sez Antony Gerrard, Esquire, musingly, 'all these factors count in the consideration of the vital principle.'

"Sometimes these two fellers fall out. 'Specially on pay nights. Vaney can't take much to drink. Two pints makes him cry, three pints makes him insultin', but fifty bloomin' pints wouldn't make him fight.

"Antony Gerrard, Esquire gets insultin' at the first pint, but bein' a very careful man, he keeps his mouth shut till he sees Vaney.

"The other night both of 'em was in the canteen, and Vaney had just finished his insultin' pint, when Antony Gerrard, Esquire, called him.

"'Vane,' he sez haughtily; 'Vane, you low hound, come here!'"

"Vane puts down puts down his pot with a terrible look in his eye, and walks across.

"'Did I hear you speak, you bounder-man?' he sez fiercely.

"'You did,' sez Antony Gerrard, Esquire; 'that is if your ears are as big as your mouth—motor-'bus driver.'

"Vaney pauses a bit an' then sez—

"'Gerrard, you are a low cad.'

"'Be careful what you're sayin', "bus-man," sez Antony Gerrard, Esquire.

"'You're a shockin' low cad—watch-snatcher,' sez Vaney, very pale.

"This brings Antony Gerrard, Esquire, to his feet.

"'Say that expression again,' he says, poking his face in Vaney's. 'Say it again and I will tear you limb from limb—hound.'

"'*You* would?'

"'I would.'

"'Try it.'

"'Say it again.'

"Vaney gets very pale, and so does Antony Gerrard, Esquire.

"'By heavens,' sez Antony Gerrard, Esquire, grindin' his teeth, 'I've killed better men than you, Vane, for less than what you've said.'

"'Kill me,' sez Vane, very faint; 'kill me, I dare you!'

"'You low, coarse sweep,' sez Antony Gerrard Esquire in a trembling voice.

"Nobby was sittin' close alongside when they was carryin' on this conversation. Nobby was tellin' a feller a yarn about a rich uncle who had a tailor's shop in Deptford, an' was warmin' up to it. This talk of Vaney's and Antony Gerrard, Esquire's, got on his nerves, so he looks up.

"'Touch me at your peril,' Vaney was sayin'.

"'Cad,' sez the other chap.

"Nobby chipped in—

"'If you two fellers don't shut up, I'll plug both of you so that you'll wish you was never born.'

"'Can't two gentlemen have a dispute without a third party intervenin'?' sez Vane haughtily.

"'No, they can't' sez Nobby, 'and if you call me a third party I'll smash you.'

"That's the argument that always settles *them* two. My experience is that fellers in this world ain't doubly gifted. If a chap can run he can't jump; if he can talk he can't fight, and *vicer verser*. Bill Mason is the worst talker in the battalion. Chaps who don't know him get a wrong impression.

"Vaney tried him once. Gave him a bit of cheek, and waited to see what he'd do. Bill didn't do anything, and didn't say anything, so Vaney went on.

"'What's that you call me?' sez Bill, after a bit.

"'A lout,' sez Vaney.

"'What's a lout?' sez Bill.

"'A lout,' sez Vaney, is a low, ignorant—'

"'All right,' sez Bill, 'I've got your meanin', and Vaney went down on the floor with a bang that shook two windows out of the room. But fellers like Bill Mason are gettin' scarcer and scarcer. Now and again we get a man into the regiment who's a bit of a surprise.

"Just after we came home from India, years an' years ago, a new recruit came from the depot. He was a nice quiet chap, who didn't say much to anybody. Drank his pint with the rest of us; made no friends, and took no liberties. He was a good clean soldier, and that's the sort of chap we like. Lots of fellers tried him on, but it was no catch, He'd got a way of turning things off with a joke. I think he must have been something decent before he joined the army, and Antony Gerrard, Esquire, said that anybody could see he was a gentleman.

"The new feller's name was Gordon—or that's what he called himself. Antony Gerrard, Esquire, tried to chum on to him.

"'By the way, old feller,' he sez one day, 'are you any relation to the Gordons of Loch Lomond?'

"Gordon looks at him with a quiet smile.

"'No, I'm not,' he sez, 'I'm a first cousin to the Gordon Highlanders.'

"That shut up Antony Gerrard, Esquire; he couldn't think of any repartee for ten minutes, an' then Gordon had gone.

"Nobby had toothache one day, and was a bit short in his temper, and somehow or other got foul of Gordon. Nobby has got a nasty tongue when so inclined, and what he said to Gordon meant fighting.

"Gordon was as quiet as anything.

"'I'll fight you, he said, 'but I'm not going to fight a man with jaw ache.'

"Nobby thought he was funking it, but as soon as Nobby's tooth stopped aching a day or two after, the pair went down into the back fields to settle the matter.

"Nobby came into the canteen, and I could tell by the look of his face that he'd fallen on something.

"'Hullo!' I sez, 'had your fight?'

"Nobby looked out of one eye an' nodded.

"'Yes,' he sez; then, after a bit, 'I'm sorry the toothache didn't last a little longer,' he sez mournfully.

"When Gordon came in he looked pleased with hisself, and that ruffled me, because I was fond of old Nobby.

"'Look here, Gordon,' I sez, in a bit of a huff, 'you needn't grin at what you've done to Nobby.'

"It was the only time I've known Gordon to get cross.

"'I'm not grinning, Smithy,' he sez. 'If you want to know why my mouth's this shape, ask your friend Nobby.'

"We all lived together in love and harmony for a long time after this. Sometimes fighting used to run through a regiment like measles through a bloomin' orphan school, but that time seems all gone past. We were gettin' down to Antony Gerrard, Esquire's class—we were 'orribly desperate talkers. That's what I said before. I don't suppose it's the fault of the army; the country's to blame.

"Nobody fights nowadays unless he's drunk. We was discussing it the other night in the canteen. The question rose over a question of tuppence wot Big Harvey said Pug Wilson owed him.

"One thing led to another, and Pug got a bit personal.

"'Well,' sez Nobby to Big Harvey, 'I wouldn't let a man say a thing like that about my nose if I was you, Big 'un.'

"'I'll make him prove his words,' sez Big Harvey.

"'Why not knock his bloomin' head orf?' suggested Nobby, who likes to see things settled one way or the other.

"'Not me,' said Big Harvey, 'I wouldn't bemean myself.'

"'Well,' sez Nobby, 'bemean him.'

"'Not me,' sez Big Harvey, who's big enough to eat Pug Wilson. 'I don't believe in hittin' a man wot ain't my size.'

"'Don't you worry,' sez Pug, 'there won't be so much of you by the time I've finished with you.'

"I don't know what else was said, because I only stayed an hour an' I didn't hear the end of it.

"Me and Nobby was going out of barracks that evening, as it was Saturday night. We got out into the High Street when Nobby told me what he thought about things in general.

"'The army ain't what it used to be, Smithy,' he sez, 'we're gettin' a bit too polite—there ain't none o' the old spirit left wot there used to be. Why, Happy Johnson told me the other day that he thought scrappin' was low an' vulgar, an' George Booth sez a man who strikes another feller is worse than the beasts of the field.'

"Poor old Nobby was quite downhearted about it. I had not noticed it so much myself till Nobby pointed it out.

"Nobby thought it was all owin' to the bad effect of Antony Gerrard, Esquire, and was for takin' him out of his bed one night an chuckin' him in the river.

"We got milder an' milder, an' louder an' louder, and when the regiment went down to Aldershot for the summer manoeuvres it got quite a scandal. They called us the 'Talking Hundred and Tenth,' an' said our motto was, 'All say an' no do.'

"We was brigaded with another regiment, the Royal Wigshire Light Infantry, the dirtiest regiment in the British Army, an' it got a bit too thick when these fellers started chipping up. As we went through their lines they used to shout 'Mama!' an' things like that.

"One of the Wigshires came over into our camp one night an' said he was the light-weight champion of the army, an' would give any feller a bob who could stand up to him for ten minutes.

"We had got into such a shocking state of peacefulness that nobody said a word, and the Wigshire chap went swaggerin' back to his lines larfin'.

"That night four of us was comin' back to camp.

"There was me and Nobby and Bill Mason and Gordon. We was takin' a short cut through the Wigshires' lines, when one of their chaps spied us an' a feller came up an' very politely asked us to go into their canteen an' have a drink.

"We all went in, an' I could see there was a bit of a lark on.

"'They've gone to get you your drink' sez the feller who asked us in, an' I could see him wink at his pals.

"'There's goin' to be a rough house,' I whispers to Nobby.

"'There is,' sez Nobby.

"A man came along with four cans.

"'Drink hearty,' he sez, with a grin.

"I looked in the can, an' saw it was milk.

"'It's only condensed milk,' he sez, still grinnin', 'but it's good enough.'

"None of our fellers so much as batted an eyelid.

"Nobby looked at the can, and when the laughin' died down, he sez—

"'Friends an' comrades all, I'm goin' to give you a toast.'

"Then I loosened my belt, for I knew that an Orangeman's bean-feast was a tea party compared with the little affair that was coming along.

"'Friends an' comrades,' sez Nobby, 'here's the health of the gallant Wigshires what run away at the Battle of Modderfontein an' left their officers to die.'

"He drank the milk with one eye on the men.

"There was a dead silence for a minute, then the whole crowd jumped at us with a yell.

"But they didn't meet the kind of fellers they expected. Nobby was out for blood, an' Bill Mason was hitting like a steam engine. I did my little bit, an' so did Gordon, who's got a lovely short-arm jab that's worse than lockjaw to the man he hits.

"But there was too many of 'em for us; they came rushin' into the canteen from every part of the camp.

"They drove us back to the counter an' started throwin' things. Then when the situation was gettin' pretty hot, I heard a yell outside, and in came the Anchesters, with belts an' billets of wood, an' anything they could lay their hands on. An', best of all, the first feller to chuck himself into the thick of the fight, yellin' like a lunatic, was Antony Gerrard, Esq., as ever was! The Wicks' didn't wait for a lickin'. They run like they did at Modder.

"Somebody shouted 'Get back to our lines!' an' then we heard the 'General Assembly' sound.

"Antony Gerrard, Esq., had got a whack on the head with a belt, an' was a bit dizzy, but me an' Nobby took an arm each, an' got him home.

"It got into the papers, 'Military Riot at Aldershot,' an' that sort of thing, but, as Nobby said, it was worth the scandal. It made a man of Antony Gerrard, Esq.; it was the first fight he was ever in, and he was so taken up with it that he's had a permanent black eye ever since."

16. Secret Signs

"You can find lots of ways of makin' money honestly besides workin' for it, especially if you read the newspapers," said Private Smith, who by the way has been taking part in "skeleton" manoeuvres, when pieces of paper stuck on a stick were supposed to represent impregnable positions, and three men and a drummer-boy stood for an army corps. Smithy is very pleased with himself for he has been representing in turn—

A brigade of infantry,

A quick-firing gun,

A convoy.

and the only occurrence that has clouded his joy was his unfortunate meeting (whilst he was pretending to be an infantry brigade) with the balloon section of the enemy (represented by Private "Swop" Taylor, of the Wessex Regiment).

The irate umpire who found the balloon section and the infantry brigade fast asleep by the side of a common lunch had first sworn, then threatened, then laughed, for he was an umpire with a sense of humour, and really ought not to have been an umpire at all.

"Some fellers," said Private Smith, "learn a lot from things that appear in newspapers.

"We used to have a chap in 'B' Company who was a rare one for finding out how many shillin's put end to end would reach from here to there, so to speak. 'Suppose you dug a hole straight down through the earth, where would you come out?' he sez.

"'The other end,' sez Nobby Clark, which was quite true.

"Well, this feller—name of Bertie—was full of information that nobody wanted to know, an' from what I've heard he got it all out of newspapers. The only feller who was interested was Nobby Clark, an' Nobby used to get Bertie to tell him things by the hour—such as the curious marriage customs of the South Sea Islands, how many pints of water there was in the North Sea or German Ocean, the number of left-handed people in Ireland, and that sort of thing.

"Bit by bit the thing sort of grew on Nobby, for he was always a bit interested in newspapers. You see, Nobby is one of those fellers who are always writin' for samples. If he sees an advertisement in the newspaper sayin' 'Send a postcard for a sample tin,' he ups an' borrows a postcard from some young chap who don't know him well enough to refuse, and before you know where you are, back comes the sample tin with a long letter showin' you how much of the cocoa turns into fat, how much into bone, *etcetera*.

"Nobby gets a big boxful of things, an' when he's short of cash he sells 'em off to the troops. Bottles of the stuff that the butcher shocks so, tins of cocoa, cards of pen nibs, bottles of nerve pills, stuff for making your hair grow, and any number of books about the Encyclo—what-d'ye-call-it?

There was one advertisement about a new language—what's the name of it again? Yes that's it. Esperanto. Accordin' to the book Nobby got, it was the sort of language everybody would talk if there wasn't any other language. Well, Nobby was very struck on it, and used to go about Esperanting. One day the orderly sergeant came in to tell Nobby he was for guard. '*Moodgy-koodgy*,' sez Nobby—it sounded like that, anyway—and Nobby was put into the guardroom for swearing at his superior officer.

"Nobby explained himself next day an' got let off with a caution.

"'No more bloomin' Esperanto for me,' sez Nobby ; 'I'm goin' to stick to fit cures an' bakin' powders,' he sez. 'Wot's the good of learnin' a language when there ain't no country to talk it in?'

"But somehow the Esper gave Nobby an idea, and a few days later he come to me an' borrows a shilling. I never mind lendin' money to Nobby, because he's very honest about money matters, and I know he'd pay me back if he had to steal it."

Smithy was silent for a moment, then—

"Have you ever heard tell of *Every Lover's Code and Sign Book*? No? Well, no more hadn't I; but Nobby saw the advertisement in a young lady's paper that he reads every week, so he wrote for a sample.

"The Code and Sign Company sent back a little handbill showin' how you can tell a young lady you love her by drawin' the first finger of the right hand down the side of your nose, an' certain other signs for 'We are observed,' an' 'Not tonight, but some other night,' an' 'Beware of the dark man.'

This pleased Nobby so much that he borrowed the money from me an' a stamp from another chap an' got the book, an' from the very first day he had that book Nobby made money out of it.

"It happens there was lots of chaps in barracks who knew girls by sight an' wanted to be introduced to 'em, but hadn't the nerve to walk up to 'em in a society way and say, 'Fine evenin', miss; what do you say to a stroll?'

"When Nobby explained that all the young ladies in town knew the book by heart, the chaps wanted to buy the book, but Nobby said that was a silly waste of money, an' he offered to teach the signs at the rate of six a penny.

"Nobby used to have a little class of a couple of dozen chaps down in the cricket field, and I used to collect the money whilst Nobby talked. Somehow, these meetin's turned into a sort of secret society. It was Nobby's idea, an' we had a pass-word, and Nobby was secretary and treasurer, an' we used to call each other 'brother.'

"There was one sign that Nobby was very particular about, an' that was the 'comrade-in-distress' sign. When you saw a feller rubbin' the back of his head very fierce it meant 'Lend me fourpence, an' I will pay you tomorrow.'

"Spud Murphy asked if that little bit was in the book, an' Nobby said yes, but when Spud asked to see the book Nobby said that was against the rules. Anyhow, if it was in the book it didn't seem to work, an' me an' Nobby wore a bald place in the backs of our heads one afternoon tryin' it.

"'Why didn't you answer my sign?' he said to Spud Murphy that night.

"'What sign. brother?' sez Spud, surprised.

"'The "comrade-in-distress" sign,' sez Nobby.

"'Good gracious!' sez Spud, or words to that effect, 'I thought that was the "I-have-loved-you-for-years" sign!'

"Nobby's idea in the secret society was that all the chaps was to club together an' pay tuppence a week, an' if any one of the brothers got into trouble the money was to go to bail him out, or buy him a weddin' gift or somethin' of that sort. Nobby was treasurer—I told you that before. Nobby drew up a list of the things you could draw compensation for. Struck by lightnin' was one; fallin' out of a balloon was another; bein' blown up on a motor-car was another. I can't remember the full list, but I know you could only get your money back if something happened that wasn't likely to happen once in a thousand years, and when Spud Murphy got fined by the colonel seven-and-sixpence for riotous conduct owing to his uncle coming down to see him and paying for the drink, Nobby said the fine couldn't be paid out of the society's funds.

"'For why' sez Spud.

"'Because,' sez Nobby, 'the rules say—

"'Wasn't it an accident?' sez Spud fiercely.

"'No,' sez Nobby, 'it was natural causes.'

"The secret society got into a bit of discredit soon after that owing to Happy Johnson, who's a very absentminded chap, meetin' the Colonel on High Street, and givin' him the 'let-us-part-friends' sign instead of the salute.

"When Happy came out of cells he said he'd been thinkin' things over, an' decided that the society wasn't all it was cracked up to be, an' he asked Nobby to call a meetin'. Nobby said certainly, so the brothers all met in the cricket field by the side of the river, and Happy moved that the society be broken up and that all the brothers get their money back.

"It was rather a slack time, toward the end of the month, and most of the brothers said 'Hear, hear.'

"Then Spud made a speech, and a feller in 'H' company made a speech, and a chap named Williams, who's got an uncle who was a guardian till they found him out, he made a speech, and everybody said the same thing, that the society was a rotten one and they wanted their money back.

"Nobby saw that something was goin' to happen, but for the life of him he couldn't think out a sign to give in reply to the rude remarks of his brethren. There he stood, as cool as a cucumber, listening to what they had to say.

"At the end of it all Nobby replied. I tell you," said Smithy enthusiastically, "Nobby looked fine. He wore a bit of blue ribbon round his neck to show he was the treasurer and secretary, although most of the fellers knew it, owing to Nobby drawing their tuppences every week.

"'Dear brothers,' sez Nobby sadly, 'the red-haired thief brother who has just spoke, an' the wall-eyed liar brother who spoke before, sez the secret society must be broke up. Well, it's broke up,' an' he sorrowfully took the blue ribbon from his neck and put it in his trousers pocket, an' commenced to walk away.

"''Ere!' sez Spud Murphy, 'what about the money?'

"'What money?' sez Nobby, surprised.

"'We want our tuppences back,' sez Spud. An' the other fellers said, 'Hear, hear.'

"Nobby thought a bit, then—

"'Give me the "want-my-money-back" sign' he set firmly.

That upset Spud.

"'Why—why,' he sez, bewildered, 'there ain't any such sign—you haven't taught it.'

"Nobby smiled sadly.

"'No, I know I haven't. I was goin' to teach you that sign next week; but the society's broke up, an' You'll never know that sign,' he sez, and walked away."

430

17. The Faith of Private Simpson

Dedicated to the Contributors to the Union Jack Club Fund

This story has the disadvantage of being a true story—
"disadvantage" because true stories are always dull. I vouch for
the truth, because I was with Private Simpson at the moment
of his passing. I remember the night as if it were yesterday. The
dark tent, and the flickering candle, and the straw on the floor
of the fluttering marquee. I remember it well, and I wish you
could have seen it—you who have contributed your money
towards justifying the faith of Private Simpson.—E. W.

"You quite understand," said Private Smith, of the 1st Anchester
Regiment, "that it took us a long time before we got the hang of this
here Union Jack Club.

"The army is full up of soldiers' institutes, and the places where
soldiers can get a Bright 'Arf Hour, an' one or two more or less don't
make much difference.

"But when me or Nobby get an invitation to a Bright 'Arf Hour
we always read the bill through to see if hymn books are provided, an'
if they are, we don't go—see?"

Smithy was in a hurry to explain.

"Don't think it's because me an' Nobby are down on religious
tea-fights an' bun struggles because they're religious, because you'll
be fallin' over yourself. I take my religion with the band on Sunday
mornin'—parade at 10.30 in church parade kit, an' march away, to
the admiration of the town. 'A' company bein' the first company on
parade, an' the first to march into church, we're nearer the pulpit, so, in
a manner of speakin', we get more religion than the other fellers.

"But the mistake that people make is that you can't do good work
without a hymn book, and that's where the 'soldiers' home' business
goes to pot.

★★★★★★

"Soldiers don't like bein' rescued all the time; they don't like bein'
saved from theirselves, an' that's why you find 'soldiers' clubs' never do
the same roarin' business as 'The Artillery Arms.' A lot of people run
away with the idea that he's a desperate character. They have special
meetin's for him, an' likely as not they get up a subscription an build
a home with a bagatelle board and an 'armonium to keep him out of
the nice, comfortable public houses.

"An' there's meetin' of the Young Soldiers Botanical Class on

Wednesdays, an a choir practice on Thursdays an the temperance section has a meetin' on Fridays, and there's an enjoyable Sankey singsong on Saturdays, an' coffee is provided at moderate prices.

"There was a chap of oure named Simpson—Snark Simpson of 'A'. He used to go in for politics; before he joined the army he was a waiter at the Deptford Liberal Club, and what he didn't know about Gladstone wasn't worth knowin'. He was aiways grousin' about things—about the army, an' the officers, and how it ought to be run. He was down on soldiers' clubs, because he'd got a funny idea that a feller could be good without singin' hymns. But mostly bis grumblin' took the form of sayin' 'What's the good?' Sometimes we called him 'What's-the-good Simpson,' an' it used to be quite a sayin' in 'A' Company, 'What's the good?'

★★★★★★

"When all the papers was full of the Dargai business, an' people at music-halls was singin' about the 'Gallant Gordons on the Dargai Heights,' old Simpson used to laugh an' sneer till me an' Nobby nearly hit him.

"'That's all right,' he sez, laughin', 'but what's the good of fellers chuckin' their lives away? People will forget all about it by Derby Day, an' if one of them gallant Highlanders goes into a private bar an' asks for a drink for a hero, the girl behind the counter will tell him that they keep a special bar for 'eroes—the bottle an' jug department.'

"'Well, old Simpson went on, an' went on, sneerin' an' grousin', an' said that if he ever had to choose between bein' a one-legged 'ero an' a two-legged shirker, he knew what he'd do.

"The war broke out, an' we was sent from Malta to the Orange Free State. We had one or two little fights, but nothin' to speak of.

"One mornin' Nobby sez to me, 'Smithy,' he sez, quits grave, 'there's goin' to be a big scrap to-day. I heard old Umfreville say so. I wish you'd keep your eye on Snarky Simpson. 1 don't want him to show up the company. As like as not he'll bolt.

"It started at daybreak an' went on till the afternoon. We got in a tight corner with four pom-poms playin' on the regiment. We sat tight for six hours, an' then advanced against the *kopje* where the Boers was. You'd hear fellers squeal like rabbits an' go spinnin' round an' drop, an' the regiment was absolutely white to a man—but we kept advancin'.

★★★★★★

"I kept my eye on Simpson, but he didn't look worse than any of the others. Then we charged—we charged a hill, an' we got halfway up when the Boers opened out on us. Ten men in my section wont down. Two of the officers dropped. Poor little Captain Grey... a horrible sight. The fire was worse than you can think of. The regiment stopped an' sort of hesitated—but Simpson didn't stop; I can see him now, with his bayonet fixed an' his khaki helmet on the back of his bead, stumblin' along over the loose stones. He didn't seem to realise be was advancin' alone, an' when he did, he stopped an' looked back. Then, above all the cracklin' an' tick-tockin' of the rifles, you could hear his voice: 'Come on, you blighters. What's the good...?'

"We laughed, yes, we actually laughed, an' then the company rushed forward, scramblin' over the rocks an' firin' steady at every chance. It was Nobby who caught hold of Simpson just as he was fallin'.

"'Hold up.' sez Nobby.

"'What's the good?' sez Simpson, talkin' like a man in his sleep; an' we laid him down.

"Then the grass on the bill caught fire, an' the medical staff worked like devils to get the wounded out before they was burned. Yes," said Smithy, seriously, "the old Linseed Lancers were heroes that day, an' I forgive them for all their sins. They came out black an' scorched, draggin' the wounded with 'em, but me an' Nobby brought old Simpson out. We got him down to the field hospital an' into the marquee. There was lots of chaps laid flat that day, an' it was nearly nine o'clock that night before the doctor could see old Simpson.

★★★★★★

"Me an' Nobby was sittin' with him when the doctor came. Nobby was was holdin' his hand, an'—an' I—"

I waited.

"I was readin' to him," said Smithy, quietly, 'a-readin' a bit of the Bible. The doctor looked at Simpson an' said gently :

"'You're badly hit, Simpson.'

"'Am I dyin'?' said Simpson.

"The doctor nodded his head, an' by an' by went away.

"Simpson lay for a long time an' said nothing; then after a bit he said:

"'Smithy, I know what's the good now,' be said.

"'What about?' I asked him.

"'About soldiers dyin' in action. Why,' he said, 'if chaps like me an' you didn't die, nobody would take any notice of them that live—don't you see, Smithy? Civilians'll think a lot more of soldiers because chaps like me. . . .' He stopped, but Nobby and me understood.

"At four o'clock in the mornin' he asked for a drink, an' then he said:

"'What's that?'

"It was firing—the pickets were engaged, an' there was a little fight going on: so we told him.

"He smiled a little.

"'Perhaps them chaps are wonderin' what's the good, too,' he said, an' shut his eyes. I think Nobby was cryin, because he was very fond of Simpson.

"When he opened his eyes again he said, 'The people at home will think a lot of us. . .' An' then I heard the regimental assembly go, an' knew the Anchesters was falling in.

"'We've got to leave you now, old feller,' sez Nobby. But Simpson took no notice, because he was dead."